WICKED AS SEDUCTION

SHAYLA BLACK

TREES & LAILA: PART ONE

WICKED & DEVOTED

SHAYLA BLACK

Steamy. Emotional. Forever.

WICKED AS SEDUCTION
Written by Shayla Black

This book is an original publication by Shayla Black.

Cover Design by: Rachel Connolly
Photographer: Wander Pedro Aguiar, WANDER AGUIAR :: PHOTOGRAPHY
Edited by: Amy Knupp of Blue Otter
Proofread by: Fedora Chen

ISBN: 978-1-936596-82-9

Books are magical…but writing is rarely easy. Authors sometimes need friends, and for Wicked as Seduction I had to call on a bunch fairy godmothers, because Trees and Laila took me on quite a ride that wasn't always in an enchanting pumpkin carriage.

Jenna Jacob – Thank you for listening, letting me ramble, reading aloud, talking me off the ledge, and just generally being there. I don't know what I'd do without you!

Rachel – As always, I can't tell you how much I love the amazingly hot cover. But thank you also for your insight, for questioning, for the laughs, the friendship, and for being invested in everything we produce as a team.

EK – I can't tell you how much I appreciate your quick opinions, your quick jokes, and your saucy brand of kindness. Books brought us together, but I love that you're my friend.

Lisa – Thanks for showing me how a newbie Wicked & Devoted reader comprehends this series via the beginning of this book. Your input was critical.

Stacey Kennedy – Your questions and insight were spot on, and it made the beginning so much more approachable for a Wicked & Devoted newbie. I owe you one!

ABOUT *WICKED AS SEDUCTION*

He'll protect her...even if he has to take her captive to save her.

Tech wiz and former elite soldier Forest "Trees" Scott had one mission: Rescue the woman being hunted by a vicious cartel and get her to safety. It should have been simple...but the minute he sees the wary beauty with haunted eyes, his desire for her complicates everything. So does her stubborn refusal to trust him. When Trees is forced to abduct her, she vows to hate him—even as he finds himself falling in love...

For six years, Laila Torres has known nothing but brutality at the hands of men, so when the massive stranger with the forbidding mien kidnaps her, she's frightened—and furious. But the giant's protective care shocks her. With every word, he proves steadfast. With every forbidden touch, he awakens the woman in her. Soon, she's facing the terrifying realization that he's also dangerously close to capturing her heart.

But their ruthless enemies are closing in, threatening everything Laila holds dear. When she's forced to make an unthinkable sacrifice, will she trust Trees and their love to save her?

CHAPTER

January 25, 11 p.m.
Orlando

"Stop worrying and enjoy yourself. Everything here is fine," Laila Torres said over the phone to her sister as she leaned over her sleeping nephew's crib to pat his rising-and-falling back. "Jorge fussed when I first set him down, but after a quick bedtime story and a kiss from his *tía,* he drifted off. How is the concert?"

"It is good. The next band will start in a few minutes, but maybe I should come home now?"

"No, you should not."

"Are you sure? I feel guilty, leaving you to babysit…"

"Why? I love to. Jorge is a joy. And mamás deserve a little time away for fun." Valeria had been single parenting since the boy's birth, and they had relocated to Florida three months ago with no sign of their dangerous past catching up to them. Surely, it was time to live. "Do not worry about me. Now that he is asleep, I will find something on TV and relax."

Valeria sighed. "Is the house locked? Every door? Every window? Is the alarm set?"

Laila shared her sister's anxiety. Despite the fact Valeria no longer had to worry about her late husband, Emilo, finding their location and trying to kill her for the sin of leaving him, the brutal thugs who had helped him run the vicious Tierra Caliente cartel were very much alive—and willing to carry out their boss's final wish. They were hardly the only concern. Rumor was that, following Emilo's surgical slaughter two weeks ago, his father, Geraldo, had decided Jorge must be brought back and raised to inherit the family narcotics empire.

If that was true and Geraldo succeeded, her beloved nephew would be taught to be all the things they'd run from—a drug lord. A killer. A rapist. She and Valeria would be unable to stop them from warping the little boy because they would be dead.

Laila preferred that fate for herself over the six dark years she'd spent in Emilo's lavish prison, but Jorge deserved a future that wasn't steeped in brutality and crime. "I have checked everything twice. All is well."

A squeak from the other side of the house rent the quiet. Laila froze. Since she, her sister, and Jorge had been forced to relocate here, she had catalogued every creak and groan the house made.

She had never heard this sound before.

The scrape of something—metal on glass?—followed.

Her heart banged with trepidation.

"Thank you," Valeria said. "You know I worry—"

"Shh. I hear something," she whispered. "I will call you back."

Laila didn't wait for her sister's reply before severing their connection and yanking the nightlight from the wall in Jorge's room, just in case. Darkness encroached, the monster she'd been living with for years. It ratcheted up her fear, clawing at her throat. Her heart thudded. Her palms turned sweaty. But for her nephew—for survival—she forced herself to tiptoe through the shadows and poke her head into the hallway.

When she listened again for the sound, she heard something far worse.

"You are certain they're here?" whispered one man from the living room, his accent like someone from her homeland.

They had been discovered again?

Laila sucked in a gasp. Fear seared her veins. Why was this happening? How had they found her family again? She had to get her nephew out of here.

"Of course they are," snapped a second man.

Victor Ramos. She would know his cruel voice anywhere. She'd heard it each of the countless times he'd growled taunts in her ear while pinning her under him and violating her.

Laila's fear turned to terror.

Why wouldn't Victor let her go?

Later. First, she had to get Jorge to safety. She wished she had kept the gun she wasn't supposed to have closer, rather than in her bedroom on the far side of the house, away from her curious, very mobile nephew. She would have to do without it and devise a plan in seconds or—

She couldn't think about the "or."

"What if the boy cries?" the first man asked.

"Shut him up until you secure him in the van. But do not harm him."

"And the women?"

"Expendable," Victor said. "Though I would like a last moment or two with Laila."

"You want to fuck her again," the first man said with a chuckle.

"Can you blame me? Her pussy is as sweet now as it was at fourteen."

Rage and shame burned, boiling into a familiar hate. Somehow, someway, Laila would make that man pay for everything he'd done.

She would forever be indebted to EM Security's sniper, Pierce Walker, for ending Emilo. In fact, she was grateful the team had rescued her from her brother-in-law's compound in Mexico last September. She'd hoped that was the beginning of a new life, especially after she had cooperated with the feds. Since then, the US government had seemingly done nothing to stop her late brother-in-law's narcotics operation. If they had, Victor Ramos wouldn't be creeping through her house now.

EM Security was seemingly no better. They had rescued Valeria nearly two years ago as part of another hostage extraction. Afterward, her sister had hired the private security team to get her into hiding. It had worked...for a while. But in the last four months, their location had fallen into enemy hands twice.

Who else could be to blame except them?

She was done trusting any self-serving alphabet-lettered organization. If she had to take down the rest of Emilo's nefarious cartel by herself for her family and her future, she would.

"I wouldn't know. You and Hector always hoarded her." The first man sounded bitter.

"If you help me find and subdue her, perhaps I will share." *Before he killed her*. That's what Victor meant. "Go search the west side of the house. I will look east."

The place wasn't large. It wouldn't take long. Time was ticking.

Laila eased Jorge's door shut and dialed emergency services while gathering some necessities and shoving them into Jorge's diaper bag. If she lived long enough for the police to arrive, hopefully they wouldn't question her immigration status.

"Nine-one-one. What's your emergency?"

Quickly, she whispered her dilemma to the dispatcher as she eased the bedroom window open. The burglar alarm didn't blare. Victor had somehow bypassed it.

She winced at the squeak of the pane sliding up the track. Hopefully, the indiscriminate racket of Victor's cohort searching the spare bedroom beside Jorge's masked the sound. But she couldn't get careless. She probably had under a minute before he burst into the room.

"I must hang up," she told the dispatcher. She needed both hands to get out of here alive.

"Help is on the way. Stay on the line—"

Laila ended the call.

As she tucked her phone into the back pocket of her shorts, a stranger burst into the room, a hulk of dark clothes and a flash of white teeth. Fresh fear razed her veins...but fury won out. She was done being a victim, nor would she let Jorge become like them.

"There you are," he said loudly enough to reveal he wasn't Victor but softly enough that her longtime tormentor wouldn't hear. Then he shut the door. "I've been looking for you."

Laila knew why, and she'd be damned before she let him force himself into her body.

She stood in front of Jorge's crib protectively. "Go away."

"Not possible. But I can make your death painless"—he dragged a fingertip down her bare arm—"with the right persuasion. Why don't you start by getting on your knees?"

Laila assessed her options. They were few and pitiful. He had her cornered. "No."

With a thunderous scowl, he seized her arm. His pupils dilated as if violence excited him. "So you like it rough? You want it to hurt?"

He didn't simply mean her murder.

She shuddered. "I do not want it at all."

"Then play nice." He reached for his zipper. "If you're extra good to me, maybe I can be persuaded to spare you."

"*Cabrón*," she snarled, fighting every instinct to retreat, but Jorge was the son she would never have. Leaving him unprotected wasn't an option.

Her assailant's eyes narrowed with violence and the promise of pain before he groped his way down her body and jerked her against the hard ridge of his penis. Savagely, he cupped her backside, snarling when he found her phone.

He tore it from her pocket. "Who did you last call?"

Laila spit in his face.

He wiped his cheek dry with his sleeve and shoved her against the wall with a glare that promised agony. She stumbled back into Jorge's diaper pail, its cold metal grazing her leg.

"Who?" He shook her. "The police?"

She pressed her lips together, refusing to answer.

"Bitch." The thug hurled her phone to the hardwood floor, shattering it beyond use. "You won't be calling anyone else."

Laila tried not to panic. Her link with the outside world was gone, but did it really matter? No one had ever fought for her. As always, she would fight for herself—and Jorge.

She pushed free and bent to the diaper pail, lifting it between them by its sleek chrome sides.

The criminal sent her an amused stare. "That won't shield you from me."

He was right; it wouldn't.

Instead, Laila swung it at his head.

The metal bin clocked him in the temple with a satisfying thud. He wobbled before crumpling to the floor, his phone clattering from his pocket and skittering to her feet.

She'd done it. No, she wouldn't feel remorse for hurting another human being. He would have raped and killed her if she hadn't fought back.

Now she had to get out before Victor finished on the other side of the house or got suspicious. The police were likely minutes away—if they were coming at all. In Mexico, Emilo and his goons had paid them all to look the other way. For all she knew, these assholes had already infected local law enforcement, too.

With trembling hands, Laila scooped up the stranger's phone, flashing the device across his face to unlock it. Quickly, she changed the passcode as nerves made each breath roar in her ears. She had to call her sister. Valeria must be frantic. But Laila couldn't let her sister run home—and straight into danger.

For now, she shoved the phone in her pocket, hoisted Jorge's diaper bag, along with some clean clothes she'd been folding before Valeria's call, onto her shoulder, and lifted her sleeping nephew from his crib. Thankfully, he didn't stir. Then she climbed the recliner in the corner and jumped out into the inky night.

Before she could shut the window behind her, the bedroom door crashed open. Her gaze connected with a familiar black stare, shooting fury and retribution.

Victor.

Clutching Jorge protectively, Laila ran.

Since arriving here after the breach of their safe house in St. Louis, she'd done one important thing to prepare for an emergency: learned the neighborhood and planned escape routes. She knew places to hide where Victor hopefully wouldn't find her.

As she dashed across the yard, her heart thudded painfully when he scrambled out the window in pursuit. Laila launched herself behind a pair of palms and through some overgrown oleanders. She crouched to hide, groping in the dark until she encountered the fence separating their house from the place next door.

Her first week here, she had discovered a gate buried behind climbing bougainvillea and clipped the fast-growing vine just enough to open it and slip free. The effort paid off now. Laila disappeared through the foliage, biting back a hiss when branches scratched her bare arms, then emerged into the neighbor's yard. The house sat dark since the single man who lived there worked nights.

She made her way to his shed, which he seemingly didn't lock, and breathed a short sigh of relief. Victor was undoubtedly wondering where and how she'd disappeared. It would take him a while—and a flashlight she would see coming—to figure it out.

Inside the dark, confined space, she watched through the tiny prefab structure's window for light or movement as she soothed a groggy Jorge with one hand and pulled her assailant's phone free with the other, quickly turning off location services. Then she rang her sister to reassure her.

No answer.

Laila tried to rationalize reasons Valeria wouldn't answer, other than Victor's brother, Hector, or another of Emilo's underlings somehow finding her. She couldn't imagine many.

Beating back panic, Laila dialed her sister again. After four rings, Valeria's voicemail kicked in.

With her heart racing, she cut the call and started to text—until she saw a flash of light eking from the gate she had just used to escape.

No time to warn Valeria. She had to put distance between her and Victor.

Jorge fussed, grunting, a furrow forming between his half-open eyes as he worked up a wail of displeasure.

"No. No..." Frantically, she used one hand to search the pockets of the diaper bag to find her nephew's pacifier while trying to placate him with the other.

If Victor got his hands on her, she was dead. And Valeria would never see her son again.

Anxiety choked Laila until she found the rubber nipple and worked it into Jorge's mouth. He took to it, sucking contentedly and settling back into her arms with a slumberous sigh.

Grateful, she let herself out of the shed and stole across the neighbor's patio through the shadows. On the far end, she let herself out the backyard on the side of the house, where she plastered herself against the fence, panting hard.

Thankfully, she didn't see any of Victor's other goons—yet. She needed to get out of the neighborhood, but Valeria had taken their one car to the concert. She knew none of her neighbors. The police still hadn't arrived. And she wouldn't get enough distance to escape Victor with a sleeping toddler in her arms.

She had to think.

Scanning the street, she spotted the house occupied by an older woman who walked her three dogs nearly every morning. Shortly after she and Valeria had been relocated here by the EM Security team, Laila had observed a gathering there. A wake, based on the fact everyone had worn black. The woman's husband had probably passed away since Laila had never seen a man there.

She had also noticed that the woman often left her keys in her car.

Taking one last glance around the empty cul-de-sac, she dashed to the small SUV, avoiding the streetlights, and said a prayer upward as she pulled the door handle. Unlocked. Thank God!

Since she had no car seat for Jorge, she clutched the sleeping toddler against her as she grabbed the keys from the middle console, then slid into the driver's seat and eased the door shut, hoping Victor hadn't heard.

Shaking, Laila shoved the key in the ignition and started the car, then looked in the rearview mirror. She gasped.

Victor stood at the end of the driveway, pointing a gun at the back windshield.

She was as good as dead.

January 26
EM Security Management
Lafayette, Louisiana

Forest Scott pushed back from his desk with a curse. Since driving seven hours, following the takedown of a crazy cult in the Texas Hill Country, he'd returned to the office and started analyzing the laptops of two fellow—suddenly former—operatives, looking for a miracle that would save his ass.

A sleep-deprived night later? Nothing.

At his elbow, his phone vibrated. He glanced at the display. If one of his bosses was calling at this hour, it wasn't good. "Edgington?"

"Yeah," Hunter confirmed. "Why are you at the office, Trees?"

What was the politically correct response for telling his superior that, contrary to popular belief, he wasn't the douchebag leaking the safe house location of their company's most vulnerable clients? "Checking out Cutter's and Josiah's machines before wiping them clean."

"At four a.m.?"

In other words, when we're not in the office to keep tabs on you.

"I figured there was no time to waste since you've already replaced Josiah with..." Fuck, he was so fried that he couldn't remember the small-town Texas deputy's name.

"Kane Preston," Hunter supplied.

"Right. He'll have a computer when he starts the job in a few hours."

But they both knew that making sure the new guy was set up with tech wasn't the reason Trees had foregone sleep.

Ever since Valeria Montilla's safe house in St. Louis had been breached last October and his fellow operative, Pierce Walker, had temporarily been taken captive by her late husband's cartel, he'd worried EM Security's owners—the Edgington brothers and Joaquin Muñoz—suspected he was selling info. His conversation with his best friend and fellow operative, Zyron Garrett, on their way back to Louisiana earlier had confirmed that. Trees had hoped that something on his former teammates' laptops would show that hackers, not a mole, were the root cause of their problem.

Nope.

Since both computers had been clean and the office network didn't appear to have been infiltrated, that meant someone on their team was cashing out company intel. As much as Trees hated to say it, his money was on Tessa Lawrence, the office's single-mom receptionist. But Zy had fallen too hard for the pretty blonde to believe her capable of betrayal. So until Trees could prove to the higher-ups that he wasn't the traitor, he was suspect number one.

We're going to figure out who's been selling our secrets. That's what he'd promised when Zy had asked him to help.

Their bosses had put his buddy between a rock and a hard place, ordering him to root out the identity of their turncoat, along with details about why and how Valeria's whereabouts had fallen into the wrong hands. He and Zy had been friends too long and nearly died together too many times for either of them to believe the other would sell out. But after a night with these computers, Trees was back to square one in finding a culprit. So despite his exhaustion, he kept searching. His ass was on the line.

"We have a developing situation," Hunter said. "You'll be leaving for Florida as soon as we get more information."

They were sending him on a mission? He'd just gotten back. Had they picked him because they were so short-staffed? No, they'd tapped him on the shoulder to get him out of town so they could perform a more in-depth investigation on him. Whatever. He had nothing to hide. Maybe the bosses would finally figure that out.

"What's up?

"Someone broke into Valeria Montilla's safe house last night. She was at a concert, but her sister and her son were there. She rushed home to find them gone. There were signs of a struggle. If Laila got out, she left in a hurry because her phone, wallet, and money were all still there. But that also might mean the cartel took her…"

Unfortunately, that was the most likely scenario. He had never met Laila, but he didn't see how Valeria's younger sister—a woman barely legal to order a beer—would be wily enough to escape professional thugs with a toddler. As unfortunate as that was, what he really wondered was why they were sending *him* to Florida if they thought he was guilty as hell.

"On our go, you and Kane need to get there. He'll bring Valeria back ASAP. Maybe now she'll finally grasp why choosing privacy over a round-the-clock guard is a fucking horrible idea." He sighed. "You find Laila and Jorge—whatever that takes—and bring them back in one piece. I doubt Montilla's organization has any interest in killing the boy, but Valeria's sister…"

The worry she wasn't long for this world hung heavy in Hunter's voice.

"She's nothing to them," Trees agreed.

"Except as a pawn they'll use to control Valeria, yeah. Apparently, it wouldn't be the first time."

Trees felt really fucking sorry for Laila. The cartel probably hadn't been kind to her. "I'm on it."

"Good. Be fast. Run clean. Report back often. And don't fuck up."

"Roger that."

Three beeps told Trees that Hunter was gone. It was a relief.

He rose and stretched. At six foot eight, he managed to touch the low, industrial ceiling. Longingly, he thought of the super-comfortable sofa in the conference room. Since he'd managed to wash everything in his duffel before leaving Texas, he could crash for a few hours, then change into clean clothes and bug out as soon as the bosses gave him the go-ahead. But running more tests on all the network software, just in case he'd missed something, was more critical—especially now that Valeria's location had been breached again, and the woman's sister and son were missing.

He had no concept of time passing until he heard the front door open a bit later and looked up to find Zy.

Trees rose from his chair. "Hey."

"Jesus..." His friend looked him up and down. "You're still wearing yesterday's clothes. Did you even go home last night?"

"No."

Zy grabbed some coffee, then sauntered back to his desk. "So...did you find anything? At all?"

Trees shook his head, then filled Zy in on all the ways he'd taken apart the info on the former operatives' computers.

"Did you check the network, too?"

"Only enough to ensure that we haven't been breached and don't have any detectable trojans or malware. But I haven't done any sort of deep dive through internal communications. I ran out of time." He sighed. "And now I'm out of steam, so I'm going to grab a few hours of sleep, and I'll be back to finish up. Hunter knows. He told me he's got a new assignment for me."

"Do you need me to take you home?"

"Nah. I'm good." He waved, then left the office, hopping into his Hummer, his eyes gritty like sandpaper.

Since the office would soon be too busy to Zen on the sofa and he was only going to get a few hours of shut-eye, Trees didn't waste time driving to his house forty miles outside of town. He loved the quiet, wide-open space there, but it wasn't convenient when he was in a rush. Thankfully, he knew people nearby.

Out in the dark parking lot, he dialed Madison. He'd met her because Zy had picked her up in a bar when he'd moved to Lafayette ten months ago, before falling for Tessa. Madison reminded him of a little sister—younger, a bit fragile, and uncertain of her place in the world. He tried to be kind; she didn't need more men using her. He put off a big brother vibe every chance he got...but sometimes she made that hard.

"Hi, Trees," she said after the second ring. He wasn't surprised she was already awake. "You back in town?"

"Yeah. It's been a long two weeks."

"It has. You want a home-cooked dinner tonight? I'd be happy to whip up something for you. Just bring the wine."

And there was the issue. She'd never come right out and said she was interested in him...but he suspected she took his attention for romantic interest. He didn't have the heart to tell her he'd made friends with her because Zy had done her wrong, and he wanted to make amends. Madison was nice. He liked her company. But he'd bet she had some notion he would be a pliant teddy bear of a boyfriend.

She was very wrong.

"Sorry. I can't." He crossed the lot and let himself into his vehicle. "I've already got a new assignment. I'm heading out of town this afternoon."

"That sucks. Any chance you'll be back this weekend?" she asked hopefully. "My dad got free lane passes at the bowling alley. It'd be fun if you joined us."

To meet her father? Even if he was home, Trees didn't think taking her up on the offer was a good idea.

"I don't know yet, but probably not. Um, I called for a favor." He hated asking, but time was ticking. Laila and her nephew were loose in the wind, and he needed to find them the minute he reached Florida.

"Sure. What is it?"

"Can I crash on your sofa for a few hours before I have to hit the airport? I pulled an all-nighter at the office, and I need some shut-eye before I fly out."

"Of course. Come on over. You can sleep in my bed. I'll read in the living room, and I'll be quiet as a mouse."

That sounded too cozy. "No need for that. You stay in bed. Just leave me a blanket on the sofa."

"O-okay. Sure," she said as he started the engine and backed out of the lot. "I'll make breakfast once you wake up."

A nice offer. Because she was a nice girl…or because she was interested in more than friendship? Trees wasn't sure, so he answered carefully. "I appreciate it, but don't trouble yourself. I have to be back in the office by eight."

"That soon?" She sounded disappointed.

"Unfortunately." He didn't want to hurt her. "We'll catch up as soon as I get back."

She murmured something that sounded vaguely like assent.

"Thanks, Madison."

As she hung up, Trees sighed. For her sake, he really hoped she found the right guy someday. But it would make his life easier, too.

After some sleep and a tango with his toothbrush, he returned to the office for a big cup of black coffee. He felt almost human again.

He hadn't been there ten minutes when all hell broke loose.

The front door crashed open, and Colonel Caleb Edgington, the organization's previous owner and team commander, charged in looking pale and frantic. A familiar hulking blond brute who looked ready to kill filed in beside him. What the hell was going on? Caleb had retired last year to spend time with his new wife, and Deke Trenton co-owned EM's sister organization, Oracle Security. He should be at Oracle's office across town, working his own missions.

"Where are my sons?" the colonel barked at Tessa.

"In the conference room. I can take you back—"

But Caleb was already striding in that direction with ground-eating steps, Deke, his big, bad son-in-law, on his heels.

Frowning, Trees followed, tension fisting his gut as the two men crashed hell-bent into the conference room.

"Colonel, sir?" Zy asked since he'd been holed up with the bosses for reasons Trees could only guess at.

"Dad?" Hunter queried Caleb as the two men paced into the corner room, frantic tension rolling off them.

Trees lingered in the hall, listening as the colonel got right to the point.

"Your sister..." He lost his battle with composure and dragged in a shuddering breath to gather himself.

The anxiety in the room notched up.

"What's wrong with Kimber?" Logan demanded.

"I received a threat recently. It wasn't specific, just a lipstick, a photo of the crew who originally smuggled Valeria Montilla from her husband's compound in Mexico, and a warning to hand her over before they took whoever the tube belonged to. I didn't know who—" Emotion stopped the colonel's words again. He paused, seemingly gathering the fortitude to continue.

Trees didn't blame the man for being distressed. Something bad had obviously happened to his only daughter.

Hunter turned expectantly to Deke.

Kimber's husband picked up where his father-in-law left off. "She's gone. She dropped the kids off at daycare, then made a trip to the grocery store...and didn't come home. A courier delivered this thirty minutes ago."

Everyone crowded around as he whipped out a picture of Kimber, her auburn hair tangled, her big eyes red rimmed, with a gag over her mouth, her hands tied behind her back, and a gun to her head.

Trees's heart stopped. *Oh, fuck.* A man like Caleb had probably made a lot of dangerous enemies over the decades. But falling into the crosshairs of a cartel... It was the worst development.

"We'll get her back." Hunter sounded determined—and pissed off. "We'll do whatever it takes—"

"You're fucking right we will," Deke spat. "I want my kitten home. Most of the Oracle team is at our office, strategizing. Any help you can spare..."

"You'll have it. We need to lock down the rest of the wives and kids."

"Fast," the colonel managed to choke out. "Before it's too late."

Then, barely holding it together, he ducked out.

The colonel was the most stoic man Trees knew. The worry and guilt that his line of work might cost his daughter her life had to be eating him alive.

Deke didn't look any less desperate. "Thanks for whatever you can do."

"Fuck that, she's our sister. We'll devote day and night to saving her."

Kimber's husband nodded his thanks, then he was gone, too.

After a terrible silence, Hunter dragged in a centering breath, forcing himself to find control. His younger brother, on the other hand, grabbed an empty coffee mug off the table and hurled it at the wall. It shattered on impact.

Joaquin Muñoz, the team's co-owner and their stepbrother, clutched Logan's shoulder. "We don't have time for this."

"I know. I fucking know," he shouted. "Goddamn son of a bitch!"

Hunter and Joaquin zipped out of the conference room, dashing past Trees and already strategizing ways to keep the rest of their family safe, he'd bet. Despite his harsh breaths, Logan seemingly dialed down his temper. Trees hurt for them.

"I'll come with you," Zy offered. "I'll devote all my energy—"

"No," Logan whirled on him. "This shit is centered around Valeria Montilla."

That was true. And nothing good had happened to the team since Caleb, the Edgington brothers, and another former operative had smuggled out the drug lord's pregnant wife under his nose almost two years ago. Apparently, it didn't matter that Emilo was now dead. Retribution was incoming.

"Since her safe house was breached last night, Trees and Kane are going to relocate her and her family *pronto*—and we'll be monitoring every step."

Then suddenly, Logan shut the door in his face and lowered his voice to a growl that only Zy could hear.

Less than two minutes later, it opened again. Logan tore out of the conference room, slamming the door behind him with Zy still inside.

"Take Kane and get your ass to Orlando today. I'm texting you Valeria Montilla's number. We gave her your digits, too. If she doesn't answer at first, keep trying. She won't take calls from unfamiliar numbers since she's been getting them all night. You and Kane will bring her to a location we'll disclose later. Her sister and the little boy, too…once you find them."

"Hunter already told me." More or less.

"Good. Don't fuck up."

After that warning and more door slamming at the front of the office, the place fell deadly silent.

Zy hauled ass out of the conference room. The rest of the team gravitated to the reception area, clearly shocked by the colonel's bombshell. Trees hung back. The truth was, none of them had seen this sudden, horrible development coming. But he should have. It would be a problem until they smoked out their goddamn mole.

Tessa rose from her chair behind the reception desk and grabbed Zy's arm. "Do you know anything beyond the fact Kimber has been taken?"

"No. No one does."

"I can't believe this is happening…" She wrung her hands.

"The bosses will do everything they can to find her."

"What if they can't?"

Her death would be terrifying, violent, and painful. But Trees didn't say that out loud. They all knew it.

"Don't think that way," Zy tried to reassure her. "The colonel, Hunter, Logan, and Joaquin are the very best at what they do. And I don't know Deke, but—"

"He's scary," Trees put in, in case there was any doubt.

"Then together, they'll leave no stone unturned to bring her back," Zy told Tessa. "Have faith."

"I'm trying."

Was Tessa's distress for Kimber real…or a well-rehearsed act? The women were supposedly friends…but EM indisputably had a mole. It wasn't any of the bosses. It wasn't Josiah or Cutter, the former operatives who had left to pursue new jobs and happily ever after with their new brides. It couldn't be Walker, since he'd both nearly died at the

Tierra Caliente cartel's hands and killed Emilo himself. It couldn't be Kane Preston since it was his first day on the job. It wasn't Zy. And Trees knew it wasn't him.

Tessa was the only person left who could possibly be guilty.

Trees drifted back to his desk and studied her. Once, he'd been convinced Tessa was as in love with Zy as he was with her. Now? She'd seemingly wrapped his buddy around her finger with her big tits and batting lashes over huge green eyes. How could Zy not see that Tessa might be playing him?

After launching another in-depth network scan, Trees headed to the back of the office for more coffee. Kane, the new guy, joined him, grabbing the java first.

"I've been here an hour, and shit's already real. Is it always this eventful?"

"No," he assured. "Hell of a first day, though."

Kane nodded. "You could say that..."

The guy seemed all right. Trees wasn't convinced he had the experience to fill the shoes of a former CIA agent and report up to a couple of former SEALs, but they had a mission to complete. Trees would perform to the best of his ability, regardless of Kane. From what he could tell, Valeria and her family had been through enough. She deserved some safety from the murderous cartel who kept hunting her. Her sister, too...if they hadn't already ended her.

Of course, their rescue lessened the likelihood that Kimber Trenton made it out of captivity alive.

Pierce Walker, their resident sniper, who preferred to be called One-Mile, approached, shaking his head. "Hell of a Monday morning."

"Yep." Trees poured himself a steaming black mug, then set the pot down for Walker, who snatched it up and dumped the last of the brew into his cup.

Zy approached then, muttering under his breath. "Those fuckers we work for left me in charge."

Someone had to be while the bosses devoted themselves to rescuing Kimber, but Zy was a rebel. Him being an authority figure was really ironic. Still, they trusted him. Besides, who else was there?

Kane was too new, Walker was crazy, and Trees…well, they thought he was guilty as fuck.

"Where are we with your trip to Florida?" Zy asked.

Clearly, the bosses hadn't told him much before they raced to their sister's aid.

"We don't know exactly where we're going yet," Trees said, then explained everything Hunter had relayed about Valeria's missing sister and son.

Zy nodded. "Logan said as much."

So they were on the same page. But something about this situation bothered the hell out of Trees. "If the cartel took Laila and Jorge, why would they have kidnapped Kimber this morning, demanding to know Valeria's location? They seemingly have hostages they can better use as leverage."

Zy shrugged. "Because they want to flush Valeria out fast and they're leaving no stone unturned?"

"Maybe." But Trees wasn't buying it. Maybe the woman and the toddler had somehow escaped…

"No one has heard from Laila?" Zy asked.

One-Mile shook his head. "She has my number. When I left Florida after relocating them, I made sure she knew how to contact me."

Without her phone, how could she?

"Unless you hear from her, we need to come up with a plan," Zy insisted. "If Laila managed to escape, every hour she and Jorge are floating out there without help or resources is another hour they're likely to be scooped up by Emilo Montilla's gang. Do we know who's running the show now that Walker put a bullet in his head?"

One-Mile shrugged. "I made a few friends while I spent a month in Mexico, trying to off the son of a bitch."

"And?" Zy prompted.

"I've heard that some underlings inside Emilo's compound are trying to seize power…but there's also gossip that his father intends to take over and oust anyone who gets in his way."

That made sense. Inside Tierra Caliente, Emilo had been a guppy. Geraldo was a shark.

Trees had a suspicion that the elder Montilla had given the splinter faction to his son in the hopes that he'd grow a set of *cajones* big enough to run the entire cartel someday. Now that his son was dead, Geraldo was too much of a narcotics king to turn over any part of his operation to Emilo's underlings.

Zy nodded. "Do we know where Valeria is holed up?"

"No," Trees answered. "I have a number to call. When we get to Orlando, we need to arrange a meet."

"And we're certain she still hasn't heard from her sister?"

"Yeah. She's had calls from an unfamiliar number, but she's been afraid to answer it. I'll tell her she should next time her phone rings."

Zy nodded. "Keep me posted."

The powwow was about to break up when a phone buzzed.

One-Mile pulled his mobile from his pocket. "Walker." A frantic, high-pitched voice on the other end had him frowning. "Wait. Wait! I don't speak Spanish." He pulled the phone from his ear and glared at the rest of them. "Who the fuck speaks Spanish?"

"Who is it?" Zy demanded.

"Laila."

Thank God. Hopefully, the woman had gotten free, and Valeria would have one less death to grieve.

"She's crying and too upset to speak English, so I can't understand a fucking word she's saying."

Trees was about to volunteer since he knew *un poquito* Spanish, but Kane beat him to the punch.

"I do. I'll talk to her." The new guy held out his hand.

"Thank fuck." Walker pressed the phone to his ear again. "I'm going to give you to another guy. He's one of us, so he'll help keep you safe." He slid the device into Kane's palm.

"Find out where she is," Zy murmured.

Kane raised the phone with a nod. "*Bueno*?"

The former small-town sheriff exchanged rapid-fire Spanish with the clearly distraught woman. Trees and the other operators watched, waiting impatiently until the new guy ended the call.

"Well?" Zy prompted.

"Laila escaped with one of her assailants' phones. She's got Valeria's son with her. They ran to a women's shelter. She didn't know where else to go."

That had been a resourceful move. The shelter's management wouldn't ask too many questions, and if cartel thugs showed up, the police would be called. "She needs to dump the phone."

"She turned off location services, but yeah, the longer she holds on to it the more of a liability it becomes. She's concerned that she'll be without any way to contact her sister once she trashes the device."

"Where did you two leave things? Did she tell you where to find her?"

"Not exactly. She wanted to know about Valeria. Laila was panicked because she's been calling her sister, who hasn't picked up."

That explained the unknown calls to Valeria's number.

"I assured her Valeria is fine and suggested she try calling her sister again. I also told her it wasn't a good idea for them to hook back up until we roll into town. I hope she listens." Kane shrugged. "By the end of the call, she seemed calmer…but she's still rattled. We need a plan. Let's put our heads together, gentlemen."

Chapter Two

Orlando

After nearly twenty hours, Laila would soon be reunited with her sister. But she didn't like how this was unfolding.

First, Pierce Walker wasn't involved. His friend, whom she'd spoken to on the phone, had come to Florida with a different operative to take them elsewhere. Both men were strangers. What assurance did she have that they were who they claimed to be? What did she know of their character?

Second, EM Security had relocated her to safe houses twice since they had helped her escape Emilo—and both had been breached. Obviously, they had a problem keeping their clients' locations a secret. Why should she believe relocating a third time would end any differently?

She needed a longer-term strategy. Valeria seemed happy to pay these men to hide them from their enemies. Her sister swore they were the best. Laila disagreed. True, they had freed her from captivity last September, but almost nothing had gone right since. She didn't trust them.

Then again, she trusted no man.

Beside her, Jorge played fitfully with a stuffed animal she had found in his diaper bag. He was bored. He was running out of diapers and food. There hadn't been even a bite to spare for her, and she refused to ask for charity. Night had fallen. Hiding in one place for so long made her nervous. Hector and Victor weren't stupid. They would guess—rightly—that she had not gone far with her nephew in tow. Undoubtedly, they were looking for her and Jorge. Valeria, too.

If she only had herself to worry about, Laila would have disappeared. But she wouldn't abandon her sister.

Glancing again at the phone she'd swiped from her attacker, Laila resisted texting Valeria. If her assailant logged in to his cloud account, he would see her messages. She didn't dare say anything that might give away her location or their plans.

Suddenly, the device in her hands rang. It was hardly the first time. Victor had called all night. She hadn't answered, but every time his name appeared, she'd fought panic. What calmed her was knowing that if he had any idea where to find her, he wouldn't waste time dialing.

Thankfully, the number on her display now was the one Walker had told her to expect.

"Hello?" she answered cautiously.

When the man on the other end asked if she was all right in Spanish, she recognized his voice. Walker's friend.

"You can speak English." She was calmer now.

"All right. I'm Kane Preston. I have your sister with me, along with fellow operative Forest Scott. He's called Trees. We're on our way to your location and we'll take you to safety."

Were they foolish enough to believe any place was secure from the violent Ramos brothers? From the ruthless Geraldo Montilla? "Where?"

"I'll explain when we arrive."

Laila opened her mouth to object.

"Jorge!" Her sister's wail filled her ear. "How is he? Is my son all right?"

Laila understood the worry, since she loved Jorge like her own. "Fine. You know I will protect him with my life."

Her sister sobbed in relief. "Thank you."

"I will always do anything I can to keep you two safe," she assured.

"You are so brave..." Valeria dissolved into tears.

Kane took the phone again. "Be ready to leave in ten minutes."

"The shelter?"

"The state. We're taking you far from Orlando."

Finally, a decision she agreed with. She had never felt safe in this city. Too many neighbors too close together. Too many unfamiliar, transient faces. Too many people seemingly stared, as if they knew she didn't belong.

"All right." Once she learned where Kane and Trees planned to settle them, she would decide if it made sense to remain. For too long, she had allowed her sister, and therefore EM Security, to decide. No more. She was captaining her own ship. No one else was making her choices. And if Valeria didn't agree, she would persuade her older sister to her way of thinking.

Seven minutes later, the same number rang back. "Yes?"

"We're here," Kane replied. "Exit the building into the alley. You'll find two vehicles. Bring the boy to the minivan. Then get in the RV."

She didn't like his authoritative demeanor. Walker had worked with her when, with the rest of EM Security's help, they had escaped Emilo and Mexico. Kane barked orders as if he knew the enemy better than her. *Arrogant man.*

"Why two vehicles?" Did he intend to separate her from her sister?

"I'll explain once you're outside."

In other words, trust me.

Laila scoffed. "I want to hear now."

Before she put her life and her nephew's well-being in the hands of strangers.

"Since we're blocking the alley, the shelter only gave us five minutes to collect you and get out."

That was likely true. The narrow lane had been used early this morning for delivery to the restaurant two doors down. A bank on the far end had received a visit from an armored car a few hours back. Besides, she couldn't continue risking everyone else at the shelter. They had problems of their own. That meant she either had to run away or comply. Since it was dark and cold, and she had no way to care for her nephew, she would follow Kane's edict—for now.

Was there any possibility he and Trees had planned it that way so they could lure her and her sister to their doom?

Kane sighed impatiently, and Laila's thoughts raced. She glanced around what had once been a bedroom in this old house. Now bunk beds lined three of the four walls—all full of women unfortunate enough to find themselves at the receiving end of some man's threat, including a sobbing woman with a bruised face and an infant. Laila's heart went out to her.

Then she caught sight of the paring knife a volunteer had brought the woman to cut her apple and some cheese. The blade still sat on the little cutting board…and the woman lay on the bed with her baby curled tightly against her.

"I will meet you outside." Laila hung up without waiting for Kane's reply, then lifted Jorge before hopping down from her bunk.

The diaper bag dangled from her shoulder, concealing her hand as she casually swiped the knife and tucked it against her side. She passed the same volunteer in the hall, probably on her way to retrieve the cutting board and utensil.

Definitely time to leave.

She wound her way to a sitting room, where a TV played the local news. Laila glanced at the broadcast, not surprised that a woman and her young nephew being attacked by two armed men was deemed too unimportant to mention.

As she reached the back door, another volunteer waited. "Will you be all right? The bed is yours for another night if you need it."

Valeria—and by extension, these men—knew where she was. The location was no longer safe. Since someone inside EM was leaking secrets, she worried Victor and Hector would soon come for her, guns blazing. She already felt guilty for the hours she'd stayed. "I will be fine. Give my bed to someone in need."

At the forty-something woman's understanding smile, Laila drew in a steadying breath and let herself out the door.

The Florida night was cool, with a hint of a breeze that quickly worked its way under her thin tank and chilled her exposed legs. Carefully, she tucked the stolen knife into the pocket of her shorts and avoided the hazy golden light illuminating the door, scanning the alley for her sister.

Instead, she found two men—strangers—each standing in front of a different vehicle, arms crossed, expressions somewhere between watchful and impatient. The one beside the minivan stood a bit over six feet with black hair, an olive complexion, broad shoulders, and a capable mien.

There was no sign of Valeria.

"Laila?" he asked, approaching slowly, hand outstretched. "I'm Kane Preston."

Walker's friend. Because Walker trusted him, she shook his hand. "Hello."

All the while, she side-eyed the other man—a mountain of muscle so tall and broad he made her heart stutter. If this man wanted to pin a woman down and force himself on her, she would have no chance at all of stopping him.

"That's Trees," Kane provided.

The big man stepped closer, holding out his hand to her. Instinctively, she retreated, cradling Jorge protectively. But it was a pointless gesture. If he intended to rip her nephew from her arms, she could do nothing.

To her surprise, he froze, then eased away, making no further move to come near her.

"He's safe. He's one of us," Kane assured.

She scowled. The men's blank expressions said that Walker's fellow warriors had no idea what she had endured at the hands of the Tierra Caliente cartel. Laila wasn't sure whether she preferred their ignorance or pity.

"Where is my sister?"

"In the van." Kane bobbed his head toward the nondescript gray vehicle behind him. "You two shouldn't be seen together."

Yes, there were eyes and ears everywhere…but Kane blocked the view of anyone who might spot them from the east side of the alley. Trees more than blocked the line of sight from the west. So why wouldn't they let Valeria out of the van for a few short moments? Was she even here?

"I insist on talking to her. I will not take another step until I do."

Kane cast a dark stare to Trees. He was a giant in his mid-thirties with short hair and a close-cropped beard, both in a warm brown. The seeming softness of his full mouth was offset by his massive hands. His intent stare made her shiver.

Trees nodded and pointed to the van. "Two minutes. Inside."

His deep voice rattled in his larynx with a hint of rasp, as if he hadn't used it in so long it had become rusty.

He intimidated her—more than any man ever had. Victor and Hector were thoughtless, vile, and cruel—but not physically frightening at a glance. This man could take them both apart simultaneously without breaking a sweat.

What could he do to you?

Laila refused to let them lead her to their van—with no escape routes—like a lamb to slaughter when she had no assurance her sister was inside. For all she knew, they had already ended Valeria and disposed of the body. "Then what?"

Kane cleared his throat, as if he realized she wasn't simply going to comply. "We'll get on the road. We think the best strategy is to minimize risk. Your intruders will be looking for two women and a toddler so—"

"We'll separate you and Valeria," Trees cut in, still taking her apart with those glittering eyes. "Kane will transport your sister and your nephew directly into hiding. You'll come with me."

Alone? Separated from her sister? With a man she could never escape? Away to an undisclosed location? For an undetermined amount of time? To be at his mercy?

Absolutely not.

Laila gripped her nephew tighter, glimpsed a speck of daylight on the west end of the alley, and started running as if her and Jorge's lives depended on it.

She feared they did.

Trees watched Laila take off with a sigh. *Son of a bitch.*

Kane muttered similar words. They exchanged a glance. Then the former deputy dashed to the minivan to preempt Valeria's escape. Trees darted after Laila, whose dark curls whipped wildly behind her. Since her legs were roughly half the length of his, this wouldn't take long.

As he ate up ground between them, he stared. She might be small, but she was a firecracker. Clearly, she didn't trust anyone—not that he blamed her. And as much as he hated to admit he'd noticed, her faded denim shorts flashed an enticing amount of juicy, round ass.

Not the time to ogle her, dude.

In less than a dozen steps, he was on her, wrapping one arm around her small waist to still her and the now-crying boy. With his free hand, he covered her mouth, cutting off the scream he knew was coming.

She thrashed like a feral cat, clawing and hissing, throwing her elbow and launching her knees wherever she thought she might land a blow. Still, he didn't release her—until she bit his finger hard enough to draw blood.

"Shit…" He shook the digit as she tried to lurch from his grip before grabbing her tighter. "Laila, stop."

She glared over her shoulder, hazel eyes shooting fire. "Stay away from my nephew. Let me go."

Her whole body trembled—lips, chin, hands. She was hauntingly beautiful—and absolutely terrified.

Time to try another tactic.

Trees released her and held up both hands. "I'm not going to hurt you. I'm only here to help."

"I have heard that before." She turned to him, scrambling back. "And I will not give you the chance to prove yourself a liar."

Her nephew began to cry, and she soothed the dark-eyed boy with soft, reassuring sounds. Her motherly instinct was strong. Clearly, she would protect Jorge at all costs. But she was running on adrenaline. It wouldn't last. She looked exhausted. When had she last slept? Or eaten?

Trees closed in slowly, hands still raised. "Let me help you, little one."

Laila turned even warier as he inched closer. If she was over five feet tall and more than a hundred pounds, it wasn't by much. Since his height alone must be imposing to her, he did his best to appear harmless.

Suddenly, she pulled a blade from her pocket, lunged on her tiptoes, and shoved the sharp edge against his neck. "You will not touch me again. You will not separate me from my sister. If you are capable of taking us to a new safe house and keeping us hidden—and I have my doubts—we will all go together. I will not budge until I see her."

Did she really think she could call the shots wielding a knife best suited for spreading butter? He'd been stabbed with far worse.

Trees stared impassively, considering the gentlest way to end her rebellion. "I already said you could have two minutes with your sister. Threatening me isn't necessary, Laila."

"Because I can trust you? Ha!" Her smile glinted like the blade at his throat. "I trust Walker. You are not him. I do not know where you have hidden my sister, but you will tell me now. And when I leave to find her, you will not stop me."

Trees seized her wrist. It didn't take much effort to shove the blade away, spin her around, and fold her arm behind her back, forcing the knife from her hand. As it clattered to the asphalt, he stepped on the blade and clasped his free hand around her throat. "Because I won't hurt you. You don't need to fight me."

She trembled, breaths harsh, as she clutched her nephew. He could practically feel her concocting ways to escape.

"Laila!" Valeria peeked out from the minivan where Kane stood sentry at the open door.

Gasping, Laila whipped her gaze around. "Are you all right?"

"Of course. Do not be afraid. These men are helping."

Laila looked unmoved. "We do not need them."

How did she figure that? Neither sister had been able to escape the Tierra Caliente compound without EM Security. In the harrowing hours since Emilo's dregs had broken into their Orlando house, Valeria had been more concerned with finding her son and her sister than protecting herself. It was a miracle she hadn't fallen into enemy hands. And how did Laila imagine she would get away on her own? Who did she think would save her if she was found?

"You called Walker," Trees reminded her. "You knew you needed help."

She struggled in his grip, holding the fussing boy even closer. "I knew he could help me find Valeria. And if mauling me is how you intend to 'help' me, I will do without. Let me see my sister."

Trees tried not to lose his patience. "We need you to cooperate."

"Please…" Valeria begged.

"We have less than two minutes to be gone," Trees reminded. "Time is ticking."

She tried to shrug him off, scowling when she failed. "After I see my sister, we will talk."

Trees had a feeling she'd already made up her mind, but he released her, hovering close in warning.

She darted for Valeria, who would have sprinted across the alley to meet her halfway if Kane hadn't stopped her.

The sisters reunited beside the van and threw their arms around each other, enfolding Jorge between them. Valeria sobbed as she peppered her son's head with kisses and thanked God. Laila clung to them both, stroking her sister's dark hair over and over, tears streaming in thanks that Valeria was alive and unharmed.

Their bond was deep, unmistakable, and moving.

Together, he and Kane closed around them, both to stop the sisters from fleeing and to block any prying eyes. Trees exchanged a glance with the other operative. In Kane's expression, he saw their shared knowledge that the women had only survived a difficult and cruel world because they had each other.

"Are you all right?" Laila murmured.

"Yes. How did you escape the house?" Valeria cradled her son, feverishly kissing his little head.

Laila explained her scuffle with the two intruders and her getaway through the neighbor's yard. She was both clever and resourceful—something Trees should probably keep in mind.

Valeria looked horrified. "Are you certain it was Victor?"

Hate burned in Laila's expression. "If anyone knows that bastard—"

"It is you." Valeria's pity told Trees that Victor had hurt Laila in the past. "How did you get away from him when he had a gun pointed at you and Jorge?"

Just what Trees wanted to know, but—

"Ladies, here and now isn't the time for this conversation. Talk later on the phone." Kane took the words out of his mouth as he nudged Valeria and Jorge toward the van.

Laila held fast. "You should have fled the area once you realized our house had been compromised. That was our agreement."

Valeria shook her head and swiped at her tears. "I could not leave you and Jorge to fend for yourselves."

"She refused to go anywhere without you," Kane confirmed.

"I would not leave you behind, either," Laila vowed. "Ever."

Trees had never had family willing to go to the mat for him. Not that they didn't love him; they simply hadn't had time. They'd been too busy surviving. His dad had worked constantly to feed the ten mouths in their house, and his mother had been continually overwhelmed by his seven younger siblings. As the oldest, if he'd had problems, he had been expected to handle them.

"It's time to go. We're too pinned in and vulnerable here. If the cartel finds you and fires their weapons..." Trees glanced meaningfully at Jorge.

Valeria clutched her son tighter. "You are right. We must leave."

"I am coming with you," Laila insisted.

Trees shook his head. "It's too risky."

She ignored him. "We were apart for nearly two years, *hermana*. No more."

"Just while we travel. Just for a short time. Once we reach our destination safely, we will be together as a family. No one will separate us again." Valeria squeezed her sister's hand. "Please..."

Laila scowled, then sighed in frustration. "Fine. *Only* while we travel." She turned and glared his way. "Tell me now. When will I see her again? Where?"

"I can't say for sure." There were too many variables, too many plans left to make.

"You cannot or you will not?" She pinned Valeria with a displeased stare. "You hear this nonsense, yes? How do you know this is not a trap?"

"It is not," her sister promised. "They will get us to safety. Trust them." When Laila huffed like pigs would fly first, Valeria tried again. "Trust *me*."

"You'll see her soon," Kane swore. "And you'll still be in the States. That's all we can say now."

"It will be fine," Valeria reassured her sister.

"Will it? They are strangers. Men. Twice they have relocated us. Both times, the cartel has discovered us. Think about it, Valeria. *They* must be the reason our location has been compromised."

As much as Trees hated Laila's mistrust, he understood it.

An older woman who probably ran the shelter emerged from the back door, standing just inside the dim light. "I'm sorry, but you must leave. We can't attract any negative attention when we have so many women in need here."

"Sorry. Of course." Trees nodded, then turned to the sisters. "Let's head out."

Valeria gripped her sister's hand and sent her a brave smile. "Go with him. We will talk soon."

Laila's expression made it clear she wasn't in favor of this plan. "You still have your phone, yes?"

"I do. What happened to yours? I assumed it was charging when Victor and his henchman broke in, but then I found it broken..."

"They smashed it."

"I'll get you a new one at our first stop," Trees promised. "Let's clear the alley."

Kane nodded and urged Valeria and her son into the van. "The longer we stand here, the less safe we are."

Valeria turned back to brush one last kiss on her sister's cheek. "Call me."

Laila held her sister tight and pressed her forehead to her nephew's for a long, silent moment. Then Valeria sat, and Kane slid the van door shut. Laila froze, worry and tears pooling in her eyes.

Her face told him she was wondering if she would ever see them alive again.

"Stay safe and in touch," Kane said to Trees as he hopped in the driver's seat, locked the vehicle, and pulled away, slowly rolling down the alley with his lights off until he turned onto the road and disappeared from sight.

The shelter manager nodded their way, casting Laila a regretful glance before disappearing inside, the snick of the lock loud in the otherwise empty alley.

Now they were alone. Trees saw the exact moment Laila realized that, too. Her breaths turned rough. Every line of her body went taut. She scanned the alley nervously. Resolution crossed her face.

Fuck, she was going to run again.

Laila slid the diaper bag she'd forgotten to give her sister off her shoulder and tossed it in his face.

Trees batted it away and cinched his hands around her waist. She was so damn small his fingertips nearly touched. Her ribs poked his palms. Unfortunately, he was also fucking aware of her pert tits spilling above the neckline of her soft khaki tank.

"Do not touch me," she hissed.

"Don't run." Trees lifted her off her feet.

Laila snarled, resisting him with more pounding fists and flailing feet. He understood. Even if her sister had been the boss's wife, life with a cartel had likely been brutal. She was in fight-or-flight mode. She didn't know him at all, and she had no reason to trust him. It would take time for her to learn that he would do anything to keep her safe.

His first order of business was to make sure she learned.

Trees banded his arms around her and carried her, kicking and writhing, to the nearby RV, bag in tow. She fought until he backed her against the side of the vehicle, pinning her in place with his body, and tangled his fingers around a fistful of her hair. With a growl, he forced her to look at him. "I know you don't trust me. But the way I see this, your choices are me or Victor. I'm the lesser of the two evils."

"I can survive on my own."

Maybe, but her sister wasn't willing to take that chance. Neither should she.

As he held tight, the smell of fear poured off of her. What the hell? Was she actually as afraid of him as she was of Ramos? "I've been paid to get you to safety and I'm going to do my job. Nothing will happen to you. Get in."

Thanks to his long wingspan, he could hold her immobile against the RV and still open the door. When he urged her toward the opening, she scratched and fought again, kicking and jabbing him while gripping the doorframe.

At the far end of the alley, a dark sedan breezed by...then backed up, paused, and turned down the winding lane, headlights blinding them. Sure, the driver might be lost. But he might also be hunting Laila and her family.

"Get the fuck inside." He shoved her through the door, then followed, locking it behind him as he tossed the diaper bag aside. "Stay down."

With one hand, he withdrew his SIG from his shoulder holster. With the other, he pushed her to the floor. He crouched beside her as a sleek black Mercedes pulled alongside them so slowly it set his teeth on edge. The tinted windows of the car made it impossible to see inside.

Whoever it was, they were looking for something. Or someone.

Beside him, Laila trembled. Horrible things had happened to her, and he'd dig into that later. All he could do now was assure her she was perfectly safe with him and try to earn her trust.

"Can you tell if that's him?" he asked.

She lifted huge, dilated eyes toward the windshield. "I-I am not sure."

But the terror in her expression said there was a good chance.

They were pinned in this fucking alley. He needed to maneuver the RV out of here and get on the road, but he didn't dare leave Laila to her own devices. He wouldn't put it past her to hurl herself out of a moving vehicle to get away from whoever was in that sedan —and him.

The black car crawled past the RV. He half expected the vehicle to stop, block them in, and come out with guns blazing. But finally, they cruised to the far end of the alley, then turned out of sight.

If that was Victor and his cohort, he and Laila had caught a break. Time to get the fuck out of Dodge.

"Stay here," he commanded, stepping around her to grab his duffel from the seat of the small eat-in table.

As he unzipped the bag, a crash on his right had him lurching around—just in time to see Laila shove frantically against the RV's door.

"Son of a bitch!" As he leapt for her, she twisted and tugged at the knob with shaking fingers, screeching at him with saucer-wide eyes.

He enveloped her against his chest and growled in her ear. "Are you crazy?"

"To want freedom? Put me down!"

"Someone is out there, hunting you. You get that, right?" Frustration crept into his voice. He'd slept maybe a handful of hours in the last few days. And just for shits and giggles, his stomach had decided to growl, too.

"I am the one who was nearly abducted last night. I got away from them without you. So why are you holding me against my will? And how does that make you different?"

In her head, he wasn't. She was fighting for her life.

"Because I'll never hurt you. I'm sorry I yelled. Quit panicking so we can get you out of this fucking tourist trap. It's great that you escaped last night. You did good. But I'm the professional here. I'm taking over. You're not making the demands, little one. Stop fighting me."

"Never." She squirmed as she spit rapid-fire Spanish at him. Trees only knew every third word, but it was enough to know that he was better off not understanding.

With a single lunge, he heaved her onto a seat in the little dining area, towering over and blocking her in with his body. He hoisted the duffel on the table and rifled through it, shoving what he needed into his pocket. Then he lifted Laila off the padded bench, stomped to the front of the RV, and dropped her into the passenger's seat. "Don't move."

Her eyes narrowed. "I will do as I please. You do not scare me."

"Bullshit. You're terrified. And I'm going to prove there's no reason to be—tomorrow. Tonight?" He fished the implement from his pocket, clutching the cold metal.

Then he clipped a handcuff around her wrist.

She gaped at the restraint before sending him an incredulous stare. "What are you—"

"Doing?" He anchored the other cuff to the sturdy door handle. "Making sure you can't escape."

Laila screeched a litany of curses in Spanish. Trees did his best to tune her out as he slid into the driver's seat, started the RV, and pulled away. When he eased onto the road, he glanced over. "Want to know where we're heading?"

The little spitfire merely continued cursing him. Too bad that didn't deter him from staring. Laila's dark curls tumbled past her flushed cheeks and smooth olive shoulders. She flashed bare midriff above her minuscule tank, and her legs… They might not be long since she was a short little thing, but they were smooth and firm—and too easy to imagine wrapped around his hips as he plowed into her soft, sweet body.

Dream on.

She was too much for him—too petite, too young, too wary, too beautiful. And too off-limits. He especially couldn't forget that.

A few months back, his former teammate, Cutter Bryant, had been bodyguarding TV star Shealyn West in LA. He hadn't merely stepped a toe over the client-bodyguard line. He'd stomped over it with unabashed glee, even being captured by paparazzi kissing the starlet into next year. The moment he'd been identified, all hell had broken loose. Hunter, Logan, and Joaquin had powwowed about firing him. They might have if Cutter hadn't quit to marry his starlet and move halfway across the country.

No, thanks. Trees wanted to keep his job. Not that Laila would have him anyway.

Now if he could just stop imagining kissing his way up her neck while sliding the thin strap down her shoulder and exposing the lacy bra he'd glimpsed under her tank…

Fuck, she was still cursing him, and he had a raging boner.

Not helpful.

Gritting his teeth, Trees stopped the RV at a stoplight. Streetlamps abounded, and neon signs gave off the kind of big-city illumination that ensured residents rarely saw the stars. When Laila turned to deliver another well-aimed curse, she caught sight of his erection tenting his jeans. Suddenly, her insult fell silent as she gaped at his overeager cock.

"Sorry," he muttered. Not that he could hide it. His shirt wasn't long enough to cover his reaction, and he didn't have a blanket handy to toss over his lap.

She scrambled back in her seat, against the passenger door. "Stay away from me."

The abject terror in her eyes made him wonder… Had she been not only confined by the Tierra Caliente cartel but violated?

"You have nothing to fear from me." He held up a hand to reassure her. "I won't touch you."

Laila huffed. "Your assurances mean nothing."

"I'm here to protect you. Give me time to earn your trust."

She didn't reply, just crossed her arms over her chest and turned away. Trees tried to stop noticing her plumped-up cleavage.

Words might never convince her of his sincerity. His actions would have to prove he meant what he said. Ogling her and sporting a hard-on definitely wouldn't put her at ease. He might be nearly thirty-five, but damn it, when he looked at her, his cock seemed to think he was a perpetually horny seventeen.

It would help if you stopped thinking about her naked.

Trees focused on the road and the vehicles around them. An uncomfortable silence fell. He wished he could think of something to set her at ease, but nothing came to mind.

Fifteen minutes later, they rolled up to a big-box store on the northern outskirts of Orlando. He parked between a big rig and a travel trailer, then killed the engine. "We need supplies, so this is how it's going to go. You'll come with me. You won't make eye contact with anyone. In fact"—he stooped his way back to his duffel and pulled out a ball cap—"you'll wear this. And you'll hold my hand every moment we're in public."

He'd give her a shirt to cover up with, too, if it wouldn't be so comically big it would attract even more attention.

Laila shook her head. "I will wait here."

"By yourself? Handcuffed to the door? Where you'll be vulnerable and unable to fight back if Victor and his right-hand thug find you?"

"Then uncuff me, and I will stay."

"No chance in hell. You'll be long gone when I come back. So you can either remain here—handcuffed—or come with me. Your choice."

"Stop backing me into a corner."

"I'm trying to keep you alive," he argued.

"Are you always this bossy?"

"Yep." *You have no idea…*

"I do not like you," she huffed.

"You don't know me. Are you staying here or coming with me?"

She heaved a frustrated sigh. "I will go."

"Good."

He let himself out the driver's side and scanned the parking lot for anyone or anything out of place. All he saw were singletons coming out in their work attire while juggling groceries, young parents with their kids carrying the makings of a school art project, and a few sad sacks clutching frozen dinners. Sure, he also caught a glimpse of the occasional tourist taking advantage of Florida's warmth and wearing shorts, despite the breezy January evening, but mostly they stood out —just like Laila would. But he couldn't let that stop them. They had to get in, get out, and get on the road before anyone found her.

Trees rounded the oversized vehicle and slowly opened the passenger door. Since she was cuffed to it, the move displaced her off the seat. When he caught her in his arms, she froze. Their gazes connected. She didn't breathe, didn't blink. He couldn't stop himself from noticing again how goddamn gorgeous she was. There was something so vulnerable about her that made him want to protect her, yet the strength—in her posture, her eyes, and her will—all told him not to let her size fool him.

"Put me down," she demanded in a breathy voice.

When she squirmed against him, he automatically caught her by grabbing palmfuls of her lush backside. The move crushed her breasts against his chest. As she slid down his unflagging dick, he found her pussy with the accuracy of a heat-seeking missile. Laila writhed against him, fighting for freedom.

She only aroused him more.

Fuck, he needed to set her down or he'd be tempted to take her up against the RV—without giving a shit how much attention they drew.

Letting out a rough breath, he dropped her to her feet. Yanking the ball cap from his back pocket, he gathered her curls in hand, their soft silk spilling over his fingers. Touching her this way felt impossibly intimate until he settled the hat on her head. Then he dug the cuff key from his pocket, careful to avoid any appearance he was playing pocket pool, and uncuffed her wrist, leaving the other end attached to the door.

"We're going in." He enveloped her small hand in his. "Don't let go of me and don't leave my side."

"Or?" Her voice was surprisingly unsteady.

Was there any chance she felt the pull between them, too?

Dream on, dude.

"I'll hunt you down and it won't be pleasant. But I don't want it to come to that. We're on the same side."

She rolled her eyes. "In a game where it is everyone for themselves?"

He gave up on her trusting him—for now—and shut the passenger door, locking the RV with the press of a button before pocketing the keys.

Wary and watchful, he made a mental note of supplies they needed for the next handful of days on the road as they headed for the automatic double doors.

"What are you looking for?"

"Trouble," he muttered as he snatched a cart. "Grab here." He pointed to the handle. When she complied with a frown, he gripped the far side, still clutching her other hand between them. "Follow my lead."

Laila was mercifully quiet as he grabbed the food and supplies necessary for the next few days, including her new burner phone and a purchase or two from the hardware section.

When he took her to the racks of women's clothing, she refused to even look. "No."

"You'll get cold."

"I will not freeze. It is Florida."

"We're leaving the state, remember?"

She pressed her lips together mulishly.

"Don't you want clothes that cover more?" He gestured toward her tits and the enticing poke of her hard nipples at the front of her nearly transparent tank.

Laila shook her head. "If I do not care what is covered, why should you? You promised that you will not touch me…"

But fuck, he wanted to.

And if she was afraid of being touched, why wouldn't she want clothes that covered her assets?

There was something going on with her…

For now, he tamped down his frustration. "Laila, if Victor sees you in these clothes, he'll know you on sight."

"I put an extra pair of shorts and a shirt in Jorge's diaper bag he has not seen. I will wear those instead."

"But that's one change. Are you going to wear that every day?"

She nodded resolutely.

Seriously? "What if we're on the road for a week? Or two? Maybe more?"

After all, Kane was taking Valeria straight into hiding. The bosses hadn't told him how long to keep Laila on the road and out of view, but given the fact they were wrapped up in Kimber's rescue, he didn't see his marching orders changing anytime soon.

"I will be fine."

End of conversation—as far as Laila was concerned. Whatever. They didn't have time to argue. Besides, this was Florida. Even in January, the store didn't sell sweats and parkas. He'd wait until they found more practical clothes. Right now, they needed to get on the road and put as much distance between her and Victor Ramos as possible.

Trees led her to the front of the store. The checkout lines were clogged, and he picked the shortest one, behind a sixty-something woman with a pair of teenage grandkids dressed in theme-park shirts, seemingly more interested in their phones than their surroundings, and braced himself for a wait. He scanned the nearby faces. The older woman sent them a kind smile.

Laila frowned, so Trees tried to act normal and smile in return. After all, she was seemingly someone's grandma. She'd done nothing wrong.

"Are you on your honeymoon?" the silver-haired woman asked.

Trees didn't sweat the question. Someone older and more likely to chitchat with strangers was nothing new in a state known for its snowbirds.

At his side, Laila slid him a distressed stare. Because she wasn't used to small talk? Or nice people in general? It couldn't be because the woman looked like a threat.

"It's so sweet to see lovebirds holding hands," she added. "So I assumed…"

"No," he finally answered. "It's not our honeymoon."

"Vacation? Romantic getaway? Babymoon?"

Thankfully, her questions gave him an idea. "We're seeing some of the country before our first baby comes."

"So your wife is pregnant?" The nosy stranger sounded excited.

"Not yet, but we're…trying." When Laila stiffened, Trees shuffled her behind him.

She dug her nails into his back.

"Best of luck to you both." The woman's smile widened. "Enjoy your trip."

"We will," he assured.

No one else seemed to care as the woman paid for her purchases, guided her phone-obsessed grandkids toward the door, and left with a wave.

Then the cashier started slinging his items across the scanner, and a teenage boy schlepped them into bags. Because Trees was a cautious bastard, he paid cash for everything, managing to wedge Laila between him and the counter for the brief moments he needed both hands.

Once their bags were in the cart, Trees gripped Laila's hand again and dragged her through the exit, into the brightly lit parking lot.

When they reached the RV, he cuffed her to the passenger door once more, carried the bags inside, then hopped down to return the cart to the corral.

Suddenly, Laila gasped, the sound so rife with terror he whirled to face the potential threat. The same black Mercedes from the alley—he remembered the plates—rolled slowly through the parking lot. They were looking for someone.

He'd bet that someone was Laila.

CHAPTER *Three*

"Fuck." Trees shoved the cart into another aisle, ducked into the lumbering vehicle, and started the engine.

Fear cascaded through Laila in a paralyzing drizzle as the sedan rolled past, two aisles in front of them. The car wasn't parking. No one emerged to shop. Like last time, the occupants seemed to be on the hunt.

If that was Victor, how had he found her again? Why couldn't she be free of men trying to control her life?

Without flipping on the RV's headlights, Trees pulled out of the parking spot before the sedan made its turn onto the nearest aisle. He hugged the shadowy edge of the parking lot before disappearing behind the big-box store. Laila kept watching out the windows until the sedan, still cruising at a careful pace, dropped from sight.

"Are you wearing anything they could be tracking?" Trees demanded as he steered the vehicle out of the parking lot and engaged the headlights.

"What do you mean?" She frowned as she watched him merge into traffic.

"Did he ever give you jewelry or clothing or—"

"Yes." Laila couldn't look at him. She hated to think about having once accepted Victor's and Hector's "kindness" so naively. "But I no longer have those things. I left Emilo's compound in nothing but a bath towel."

He frowned. "I heard that."

Laila didn't believe the concern or empathy or whatever that note in his voice was. "You were not part of the extraction team. Why?"

"I was sick." He grimaced, glancing in the rearview mirror. "I ate sushi from a truck stop and ended up in the hospital."

It seemed difficult to believe anyone sane would do something so foolish. "Neither was Kane Preston."

As Trees rolled through a yellow light and continued north, he checked behind him again, then seemed to relax. "This is his first day on the job. Are you wondering if we actually work for EM Security? Is that the problem? Call Walker now. He'll tell you."

"No. *Señor* Walker already made your association clear. Why is he not here?"

Pierce Walker had proven honorable, even in the worst of circumstances. He had never touched her beyond the ruse necessary for them both to escape. He hadn't even been erect when she had showered with him to make her "seduction" look believable for Emilo.

Trees? He had been visibly hard while looking at her fully clothed. In her experience, that was a terrifying sign of things to come.

Her supposed protector sent her a sour glare. "Other assignments. But we work for the same firm. We have the same priority to keep you safe. You need to trust me."

He sounded miffed that she didn't. Foolish man. If she had her way, she wouldn't be with him long enough to try.

"Hmm. Where are you planning to take me?"

"We need gas for this guzzler before we leave civilization, so I'll have to stop. Before I do, I'll put as much distance as possible between us and that Mercedes."

She would make her escape then. "All right."

"If Victor is in that car and you're not wearing anything he could track, how the hell does he keep finding you?"

Laila slid him a suspicious glance. "Perhaps they are tracking *you* somehow. With this enormous vehicle maybe? It sticks out."

"I'm thinking through that possibility, trying to come up with contingencies. But after we left the alley, they didn't follow us. I looked —more than once. Yet somehow they reached the store by the time we left."

"Is this not your area of expertise?"

"Yeah, but things aren't adding up. If they had an exact bead on you, why didn't they attack us in the alley?"

A valid question. "Because the area was too public? Because they did not want to confront you?"

Trees shook his head. "No one else was around, and they would have been happy to double-tap me in the head if it led to you. Drug runners aren't shy about murder."

Or any other crime. Laila knew that firsthand. "True."

"And if they had your exact location, how were we able to slip from the parking lot of the store just now without them realizing?"

Laila shrugged. Certainly, she'd been doing her best to avoid Emilo's men since her escape from the compound last September. She couldn't think of anything she'd done to compromise that.

Worry wrinkled Trees's brow, but she didn't make the mistake of thinking he cared. More than likely, he hated to be outsmarted. Most men did.

After another twenty minutes of silence, he pulled onto a side street, then rolled up to an older gas station. "I'm going to fill this up. It will take a bit. I won't be far."

Now was her chance. "I need to use the bathroom."

"There's one in the RV."

She glanced behind her. One of the closed doors hid a toilet? She had never seen a vehicle that also served as a small house. If she had time, she would explore it simply to assuage her curiosity. But his reply ripped away her excuse to disappear into the attached mini-mart and sneak out the back.

Time for another plan.

Laila held up her wrist, jingling the cuff against the rubbery door handle. "I cannot reach that far. You will have to uncuff me."

"Yeah." He reached into his pocket, then narrowed a glare at her. "No running. No tricks. No BS."

Or she would be sorry. The words hung unspoken. He was big and forbidding and strong as hell.

Though her sister seemed convinced he was one of the "good guys," he lived a life of violence. And he seemed to see straight through her.

"I can hardly run away when I am using the toilet." She glanced down at the sacks they had acquired at the store. "Maybe you could give me my new phone so I could call my sister? It would occupy me. I would use the one I took from Victor's thug, but—"

"You still have it?" He growled, lunging for her.

Laila resisted the urge to shrink back. Would he hit her now? Do something even worse? "Yes."

"You didn't ditch it last night?"

"No." Why would he think that? "I kept trying to reach my sister and—"

"Fuck." He banged his fist into the side of the vehicle. "Is it still on?"

"Yes. The battery is low, but—"

"Goddamn it. Give it to me."

And cut off her only source of communication? Her only way of calling for help?

"Now!" he snarled. "That's how they're tracking us. They're pinging the cell towers. Motherfuck."

"They can do that?"

"If they know the right people and drop enough cash, you bet."

Dios mío. If Trees was right, he was blameless—at least in this. *She* had foolishly given Victor the means to follow them.

Frantically, she tugged at the cuff. "Release me."

"Tell me where to find the phone."

"The diaper bag."

In a long-legged stride, he hurdled their purchases and swiped the toy-train covered tote from the floor, slamming it on the eat-in table and ripping into it. Moments later, he came up with the device. "What's the passcode?"

"What will you do?" Take it? Trash it? Punish her horribly for having it?

"Start by turning it to airplane mode so they can't track the fucking device anymore."

With an unsteady voice, she rattled off the four-digit code. Trees punched it in, and the screen brightened. His thumbs flew across the flat panel as he whizzed through the menus, then breathed an audible sigh of relief.

"Victor can no longer track the phone?"

"Every way he could digitally locate this device is off. But I'm going to trash it to be safe." Then he darkened the mobile and looked up. "You still need the bathroom?"

She didn't, but the urge to flee—before Victor showed up again—rode her even harder. Even if he couldn't trace his henchman's cell anymore, Trees was abnormally big and incredibly easy to spot. So was the RV he drove. She could blend in better on her own. Thankfully, the area was busy, and she'd seen more than one conceivable place to hide until she could devise a better plan. "Please."

He reached into his pocket and extracted a key that looked comically small between his large fingers, then came at her with a warning glare. "Don't make me chase you again."

Laila disregarded his implied threat. Now that Trees had stripped her ability to communicate, and Victor had likely seen her with him—twice—staying was too dangerous. She'd already considered the nightmarish possibilities of what Trees could do to her with his massive hands and his massive erection. He'd taken away her freedom, shoved her into this rolling motel room, and separated her from her sister for reasons that suited him. She would not allow him to force anything else on her.

"Of course not," she agreed. After all, she was incapable of making him do anything. If he chased her, it would be of his own accord.

His menacing expression spoke volumes about how much he didn't trust her, so she sent him her most innocent stare as he freed her wrist. When he stepped back, he positioned his big body between her and the door.

"Go on." He gestured to the bathroom.

As she tried to think of another means of escape, Laila made her way inside. Small sink, toilet, and a shower she couldn't imagine Trees wedging himself into. Above it, a thin rectangle of a window only a cat could slink through. But there must be other ways out of the RV. She refused to give up.

While she relieved her bladder and thought through the situation, the door to the RV opened and shut. She hurried through the rest of her ritual, then peeked out the bathroom door. He was gone. With a glance out the nearest window, she found him pumping gas and talking on the phone.

She prayed the distraction was enough.

Dropping to her knees, she crawled to the exit, lamenting the fact she couldn't risk prowling through the bags for her replacement phone, and eased the trailer door open. The wind howled. Trees had his mobile pressed to his ear, and the door was on the opposite side. If she was quiet, he wouldn't hear her escape.

The moment her feet hit the concrete, she eased the door closed, then darted to the edge of the parking lot before disappearing into the shadows blanketing the vacant lot next door. She was unfamiliar with this part of Orlando, but heading toward civilization and lights made sense. If she could find a place to lie low, she would flesh out a better plan.

Since Trees had been driving north, Laila circled back in the opposite direction, crossing the busy highway, then heading for a brightly lit hotel she had seen a few blocks ago.

Under the portico out front, she avoided eye contact with the valet, then walked inside as if she belonged there. She didn't dare stop to get her bearings, simply headed left, past a bar area, then through another set of double doors and into a center atrium not visible from the street.

She settled in a padded chair on a corner of the patio, away from children splashing in the hotel's pool under their parents' watchful eyes, and let out a deep breath. She couldn't stay here, but at least she had escaped. Now she had some breathing room.

Laila wished she knew where Kane was taking Valeria. But she would continue heading in the same general direction Trees had been until she could contact her sister. She prayed Valeria and Jorge remained safe.

Suddenly, there was a commotion in the lobby. Laila looked up, half expecting to see Trees snarling at a desk clerk as he searched the hotel. Instead, Victor and the thug who had attacked her last night rushed into the building, methodically scanning the space. Her heart stopped as they paused to speak to a hotel employee. The man pointed to the pool.

Fear gripped her throat, but she forced herself to stand slowly, head down, and slip behind a big, leafy bush along the perimeter.

When the two thugs spilled out onto the patio, they split up, Victor veering left. His determined lapdog headed her way.

Laila tried not to panic. Now what?

Behind the greenery, she inched along the wall, deeper in the shadows. When Victor's goon disappeared into an area marked EMPLOYEES ONLY, and Victor was nowhere to be seen, Laila sent up a silent prayer, ensured her dark curls were tucked under Trees's cap, then spotted a family heading into the attached restaurant. Trembling, she slinked from her hiding spot to merge behind the kids, trying to blend in.

A shout and the pounding of feet later told her that she'd been spotted.

Panic spiked.

With her heart racing, Laila ran blindly through the mostly empty restaurant, looking for an escape other than the empty parking lot behind the hotel. She stumbled into a hall and pushed into the ladies' room. But there was no lock on the door, and she wasn't naive enough to believe the gender orientation of the bathroom would keep Victor out. As desperate as it was, she hoped she wasn't in here alone. Another woman could act as a buffer. Victor would think twice about unleashing violence in front of witnesses, at least in the States. Maybe she could borrow the hotel guest's phone and call…

Who? Other than Walker, who would refer her back to Trees, she had no one on her side. Even Valeria couldn't help. And no matter how much the giant with the searing green eyes claimed he would protect her, she couldn't risk trusting him.

But fate wasn't on her side. The bathroom was empty.

Resisting the urge to cry, Laila threw herself into a stall and locked the flimsy door. Her panting sounded too loud in the still. As she crouched on the toilet, she squeezed her eyes shut and prayed she had lost Victor.

The world proved it had abandoned her again when the bathroom door squeaked open. "Laila. I know you're here, *chiquita.*"

She cringed every time he called her that. He only did when he was pissed and bad things were coming.

"I know because I saw you run across the street like a scared little girl and followed you."

Of all the terrible luck…

"The tall man can't help you anymore. Come willingly, and I will make your punishment bearable."

No, he wouldn't. She should have stayed in the middle of a busy area, around a lot of people, near security cameras. He would not have dared to drag her out of this hotel against her will with employees and protective families looking on. But all he had to do now was haul her out of the bathroom, down the isolated hall, then out the back door mere feet away. Even if there were cameras covering the door, Laila wasn't foolish enough to hope that anyone would care to look for her. And if Victor and his brother, Hector, had their way with her again—and again and again—they would make sure she could never get free.

"Not making this easy for me?" He tsked at her. "There are only so many stalls to hide in. Where else do you think you can go? There's no window, unlike your house. You can't steal a neighbor's car and nearly run me over to get away. It's just you and me. And no escape."

Tears stung her eyes and closed up her throat. He was right. But that also didn't mean she would just give in. He didn't know which stall she was locked in. She had the element of surprise.

Would you need it if you had stayed with Trees?

He would have protected her from Victor, yes. But who would have protected her from him?

"Time's up. I guess you want to do this the hard way. You know that suits me, *chiquita*."

She bit her lip to hold in a whimper, grabbed the sides of the stall, and braced to kick her way to freedom. And she prayed.

He smashed open the stall beside her and stepped in. The door clattering against the wall made her start. She managed to bite back a gasp, but fear gnawed her belly. Her heart beat so hard she felt jittery and faint. Every one of the twenty-two hours since she'd last eaten now haunted her. What if she didn't have the strength to fight off Victor?

As he spun and backtracked toward the front of the stall, Laila dragged in a deep but silent breath. The next ten seconds might determine if she lived or died.

The thought had barely buzzed through her brain when he grabbed her fingers, still clutching the top of the stall, then latched onto her arm and gave it a vicious yank. She fell off the toilet and stumbled face first into the metal wall. Trees's hat fell to the tile as Victor dangled her off the floor by her arm. She struggled to get her feet under her, fearing he would pull her shoulder from its socket.

Then abruptly, he let go. Her backside landed on the hard tile floor.

As she scrambled to stand, he appeared in the door of her stall, his dark expression straight from hell. She tried to retreat but had nowhere to go. He grabbed a fistful of her hair and used it to tug her against him, wrapping an arm around her body and pressing her close.

He was hard.

Victor sucked in a hissing breath as he rolled his erection against her. "You know I love it when you fight. Keep it up. It will only make your punishment sweeter."

He meant more painful. In the past, she would have lowered her head, promised to be good, and endured whatever he dished out, hoping she would live another day. Hector hadn't been quite as sadistic and had sometimes curbed his brother's darker impulses. But last year, Hector had moved to the States and taken an American wife. Laila felt sorry for the woman. Marriage to Hector must be like something out of a horror movie.

And what was being captive to Victor?

A terrifying level of hell—one she hated to endure again.

She hadn't fought back in years, not since that first awful time. She'd buried the horrifying night in the back of her brain and tried to forget…but she never had. She refused to let him take her again. She would rather die here than endure more of his torture.

He rubbed against her. "I missed you, *chiquita*."

No, he missed his morning blow jobs. He missed the demeaning way he'd fucked her in front of his friends just to prove he could. He missed being able to roll over in the middle of the night and use her at his whim. He cared nothing about her.

She stared back, stone-faced.

"Cat got your tongue? It doesn't matter. It's not your tongue I want now." Still gripping her hair, he spun her around to face the bathroom sink and forced her to bend over until her forehead smacked the counter. Then he shoved her shorts around her thighs and lowered his zipper.

Her fight instinct surged.

Laila kicked back blindly, ramming her foot into his knee. He cursed and released her, but his body still blocked the exit. She grabbed a palm full of liquid hand sanitizer from the nearby dispenser. The sterile stench of rubbing alcohol made her queasy.

When she turned back to Victor, he prowled toward her again, his glare promising retribution.

She flicked the clear liquid gel from her fingertips—right into his eyes.

He backed away with a curse. "Bitch!"

Laila sidestepped him, pulling up her shorts with one hand and reaching for the door with the other.

Before she could grab on, Victor seized her arm cruelly and flung her against the nearest bathroom stall, his eyes red like a demon as he curled his fist threateningly above her face.

She braced. It wouldn't be the first time he'd used her for a punching bag, but she swore it would be the last.

Then she realized she had a self-defense mechanism she'd never had in her brother-in-law's compound of horrors. And she smiled.

Right before she screamed.

Victor cursed and slapped a hand over her mouth, but she bit him and jerked away. He went for her throat then, gleefully squeezing tight to strangle her cry and cut off her air.

Her eyes bulged. Her lungs burned. Had she made a huge mistake in trying to enlist the hotel's guests or employees? Maybe no one had heard her. Or maybe no one cared that Victor might strangle her and leave her body here to rot. If that happened, would her sister ever know how she had died? Would Valeria ever be safe?

Laila kicked and scratched, but Victor dodged her, his face telling her that he was enjoying snuffing out her life one agonizing, suffocating second at a time.

Suddenly, the bathroom door slammed against the wall, and Victor was ripped away from her with an inhuman snarl.

Laila gasped in a burning draft of air as the sound of knuckles impacting bone filled her ears. A fist ramming into a face? Someone grunted. She blinked until her vision focused again.

And she saw Trees, holding Victor by the throat, against the bathroom wall, about five inches off the ground.

"Are you all right?" he barked her way.

Already the monster who had terrorized her for years had a swelling eye and wore a half-dazed expression.

Laila couldn't speak. Trees had come for her?

"Yes or no?" He looked her up and down as if trying to answer the question himself.

While she struggled to find her voice, Victor reached into his pocket and drew out a sharp, serrated blade.

She didn't stop to think about who she could trust, just pushed aside cold fear and screamed. "Trees!"

He jerked his gaze back to Victor just in time to leap away from the blade headed right for his ribs.

Trees banged her nemesis against the tiled wall again. On impact, his skull cracked in a horrifying thud. While he reeled, Trees plowed his fist into Victor's nose. Her assailant's eyes rolled to the back of his head.

When Trees let go and reached for her, Victor fell to the floor in an unconscious heap.

She looked up at her rescuer incredulously. "What are you doing here?"

"Did he hurt you?"

Laila stood mute. She'd never, ever seen anyone get the best of Victor. Not once. Not even Emilo. But this giant man who claimed to be her savior—albeit temporarily—had squashed him like a bug.

"Not much."

"Is that Victor?"

"Yes." Her voice sounded terrified, even to her own ears.

He scooped up the fallen knife and pocketed it, then settled Victor's unconscious form on the nearest toilet, cuffing his wrist to the flushing mechanism and shutting the stall door. "I'd love to kill the son of a bitch, but dead bodies raise too many questions. We need to go."

Now? Without calling the police? Then again, he probably wanted to avoid them. She certainly didn't want to stay in this city another minute. Nor did she want to answer an officer's probing questions. Maybe Trees didn't, either.

She just wanted as many miles between her and the Ramos brothers as she could get.

"C'mon. I'll get you out of here safely."

She hated to put her trust in this operative she barely knew, who had been at least partially responsible for the violation of their safe houses, who had taken her without her consent…but she had exhausted her options—and herself—tonight. If she wanted to avoid Victor and his wrath, she had to rely on Trees.

"Can you?" She wasn't sure. Trees had committed violence, so the hotel might have called the police. Or what if Victor's right hand was lying in wait to end them with a couple of bullets? Did they have any chance at all of leaving here?

"We're going to try." Trees took her hand. "Let's go."

Laila looked shaken and terrified, like she was holding herself together through sheer will. "All right."

It wouldn't be long before her adrenaline crash…

Trees wanted to scoop her up in his arms. He didn't dare risk spooking her. "That means you have to trust me, at least a little. Can you do that?"

She hesitated. "Yes."

He wasn't convinced, but he squeezed her hand, opened the bathroom door, and peeked down the hallway. It was blessedly empty. If they managed to get back to the RV undetected and unimpeded, he would deal with everything else.

Since the dinner hour had passed, the restaurant had mostly emptied out. A pair of octogenarians sat in a corner, sipping decaf. Near them, a family with little ones ate in silence, looking wiped out after a day in the parks.

At the end of the hall, Trees turned the corner and hugged the less illuminated wall, absorbing her against his body, all the way to the double doors. No one approached or challenged them. A few minutes earlier, he'd taken care of Victor's cohort in a service hallway, knocking the asshole unconscious. He freaking hoped there was some ice in the RV's freezer. His knuckles could use it.

Outside the hotel, they rounded the building and headed for the main road on foot.

"Did Victor hit you or…" If the scumbag had, Trees would be hard-pressed not to march back into that women's room and kill the motherfucker. As it was, the sight of the asshole's fist aimed at Laila's terrified face was burned into his retinas.

She didn't meet his stare. "He would have. So thank you. How did you find me?"

Trees gritted his teeth at the memory of filling the RV's tank and hopping inside again, only to find Laila gone. He'd been shocked by her brazen escape—and he shouldn't have been. She had fled her brother-in-law's compound without even a shirt on her back. He should have expected a woman willing to give up everything for freedom, even her dignity, to run. Given what he'd witnessed of Victor Ramos's treatment, he understood.

"When I realized you'd fled, I figured you would head for the road, maybe steal a car, and get out of this area."

"I do not know how."

Good to know. "Then I saw the Mercedes pull into the hotel. I followed, just in case they'd found you. Inside, I tailed Victor's little helper." Honestly, Trees still didn't know how the asshole hadn't seen him. "When I realized he had no idea where to find you, I punched the fuck out of him and kept looking. I was combing the restaurant when I heard you scream."

"How did you know it was me?"

He'd felt her cry all the way through his body. Deep in his chest. That would probably freak her out, so he simply shrugged. "I figured no one else had cause to scream."

The lights flashed then, signaling they could safely use the crosswalk. It was a far cry from his wild dash across the highway, in between cars and during rush hour to reach her.

As he guided her toward the curb, he scanned the traffic, scowling menacingly at a teenager who revved his engine and poked his head out the driver's window to get a good look at Laila's backside. The minute the little bastard caught sight of Trees's threatening expression, he piped down and rolled up his window, proving he had at least two brain cells to rub together.

Laila looked as if she might say more but didn't as they reached the RV, which still sat where he'd abandoned it, hogging two pumps at the gas station.

As they approached the door, she suddenly grabbed him and stumbled, as if her legs had stopped supporting her. There was her adrenaline crash. He'd barely gotten his hands around her shoulders when she doubled over and retched a thin stream of clear liquid. Fuck, she'd had nothing to throw up. She was dehydrated, starved, and exhausted.

Finally, she heaved a heavy sigh and went limp.

Trees lifted her in his arms. Laila protested, but he ignored her, carrying her inside and locking the door behind them. The fact she let him proved she had no more fight, at least not tonight.

He set her in the passenger's seat and crouched in front of her. "Are you all right, little one?"

"Fine." She turned away, as if embarrassed. "It has happened before."

Because Victor had terrified the hell out of her? That pissed him off. He managed to tamp down his anger—for now. She needed hydration, sustenance, and sleep. They could also use a less recognizable vehicle. But they needed to get on the road more, so waiting around until morning for the rental company to open wasn't an option.

Never taking his eyes off her, he dug through their grocery sacks, coming up with a bottle of water, a protein bar, and the burner phone he'd bought for her. He handed her the first two. "Slowly, okay?"

Laila looked at them longingly but shook her head. "I do not need that."

The hell she didn't. "Your body has to restore itself. When was the last time you ate?"

"I am not hungry or thirsty. I simply want to call my sister." She gestured to the phone still in its package.

She was full of shit, and he couldn't fathom why she would lie about something so obvious. Thankfully, BDSM had taught him how to deal with a stubborn female in his care. If she wouldn't take care of herself, he would do it for her.

Trees dropped his voice. "You want to talk to Valeria? Eat half that bar and drink half the water, and I'll give you five minutes with her. Eat and drink all of both, and you'll get ten."

If she exerted herself more than that, she was likely to keel over.

"Of course there's a price." Her smile was all cynical sneer. "What else do you want?"

What the hell else did she expect him to demand? "Nothing."

Suspiciously, she held out her hands. He gave her the bar and the plastic bottle, watching as she inspected both carefully as if she suspected he had tampered with them.

She shot him one last wary stare before she opened the bar and took a cautious bite. As she chewed, she opened the bottle and took a slow sip, swishing it around her mouth before finally swallowing.

"Why would I poison you when I'm trying to save you?" After everything she had endured in the last twenty-four hours, Trees wasn't surprised logic had taken a back seat to emotion.

Laila shot him a stare. It wasn't a warning. It wasn't even a rebuke. Instead, her face was carefully blank, as if she didn't want to give him anything, even her anger. Fuck.

"Keep eating and I'll get this phone up and running."

"I will eat more when the device is ready."

She didn't trust him at all—not even to uphold his end of the bargain. Hadn't he just saved her from being attacked and dragged back to hell?

How does she know you're not like those assholes?

She didn't. She was in a dark place, and she needed a safe space, along with guidance and boundaries that would benefit her. In short, she needed security. That's where he came in.

The question was, what would it take to shine light into the shadowy corners of her heart?

"All right." He ripped the phone from the plastic and had it set up to send and receive both calls and texts within three minutes. "Done. Your turn."

"How do I know it truly works?"

Trees sighed and dialed his own device. He pulled it from his pocket to show that it, in fact, rang. "There you go. Now eat."

She did so silently, but all hint of caution was gone. She scarfed down the protein bar even faster than she guzzled the water.

"Want more?"

She shook her head. "I want to talk to my sister."

He handed her the device.

With greedy hands, she grabbed it. "I need privacy."

Why? She and Valeria mostly spoke Spanish. He couldn't understand ninety-five percent of what she said, but after tonight, he wasn't ready to trust Laila. "Talk here or not at all."

Laila muttered something under her breath he'd bet was less than polite, but she settled back against the seat and dialed her sister.

Trees fired up the RV and glanced at the clock. "Ten minutes."

Then she needed to rest. Tomorrow, she and her sister could talk more. Laila wouldn't like the restriction, but she would learn he was a man of his word.

As Valeria answered the call, he headed the fuck out of Orlando, trying not to listen to the sisters' murmured conversation. Until tears began to spill down Laila's cheeks. Oh, her voice sounded upbeat, but she was fucking crying. He didn't know what the two of them were saying, but if Valeria was upsetting her, that was a big *hell no* for him.

He was shutting that shit down. "Two minutes."

She scowled at him, her golden-hazel eyes like a rainstorm. Then she continued talking as if he hadn't spoken at all.

And the tears kept flowing.

"Thirty seconds," he reminded a minute and a half later.

She sniffled. "I am talking to my sister, not someone dangerous."

Dangerous, no. Upsetting, obviously. "You're wasting time talking to me. Say goodbye."

She muttered what was probably another curse, then said good night to her sister and ended the call. Fury tightened her profile, but she merely set the phone aside, then folded her hands in her lap and stared out the windshield, patently refusing to look at him.

Something was going on in her head. He wished like hell she would confide in him. But that took trust, and trust took time.

Good thing he was patient.

"Why were you crying?"

"I miss my family."

Trees wasn't sure whether to believe her. "Did Valeria say something to upset you?"

"No."

Maybe that was true, but even if it wasn't, she would defend her sister. So he tried another tactic. "When was the last time you slept?"

"I am not tired."

This again? "You're exhausted, especially after your adrenaline crash."

She shook her head. "I am fine."

"And I am tired of your lies," he parroted. "We're on the same side, you know? I'm here for you."

She raised a brow at him. "Of course. Because you are paid."

"And because you need help. Let me help you."

Laila brushed aside his assurances as he veered onto a two-lane highway outside the city. "Where are we going?"

He didn't want to tell her he wasn't headed anywhere yet and might not be for weeks. Hearing the news they would be traveling together indefinitely would only freak her out again. "Off the beaten path. Victor and his goon will be after us again within the hour."

She looked alarmed. "The hotel will not call the police?"

Trees shook his head. "Based on security footage, they did nothing wrong. So as soon as they're conscious and free, the assholes will be on the road, looking for us. They've seen me with the RV twice. The vehicle and I are both hard to miss."

"True."

"And Victor knows now that we're traveling together, so we have to stay off the interstate and away from places where we might be spotted." Because if Ramos flashed cash, anyone who'd seen them would start talking.

"I understand." But she didn't look happy about it.

"So I need you to work with me here. The more you try to get away, the more time I spend chasing you. The less time we have to put distance between us and Victor."

She slanted him a glance. "Or you could just tell me where to find my sister. I can make my own way there."

"Nope. Valeria wants you protected. And after what I saw tonight, there's no way I'm letting you fend for yourself."

"But—"

"No, Laila."

He hadn't dropped his voice on purpose, but it had the desired effect. She lowered her gaze to her hands folded in her lap and pressed her lips together mutely.

Shoving aside the ramifications of her response—because if he didn't, he'd sport another erection that would freak her out—Trees focused on the road.

"Take a shower, brush your teeth, and go to bed." He knew from experience that washing away combat would help clear her head and relax her body. "Towels are in the cabinet, next to the sheets."

"No." Her refusal was instant but trembling.

She was afraid.

He tried not to take it personally. He didn't know what she'd endured, but her years with the cartel had damaged her. Tonight, he'd only scratched the surface of her mental scars. "You think I'm going to hurt you while you're vulnerable."

"What would stop you?"

The fact I'm not a dirtbag?

But she didn't know him. "I'll be driving. I can't touch you while I'm steering this thing, and there's no shoulder for me to pull over and do my worst to you. You're perfectly safe, I promise."

She seemed to consider his words, then she licked her lips and glanced over her shoulder, to the back of the motorhome. "Fine. I will sleep if I can lock the bedroom door."

He weighed her desire for solitude against the need for safety, but the back window was an exit. "Sorry. If you want more privacy, there's an extra sheet in the cabinet above the dining table. String it across the RV."

He would still hear if she tried to escape.

"I will not run again tonight."

Trees noticed she said nothing about tomorrow. "The door stays open."

Laila did not reply, simply pursed her lips together and turned toward the back.

He grabbed her wrist. "Just so we're clear, if you jump out the door while the RV is moving, either the fall or the area wildlife will kill you."

She yanked free, then tugged a string across the cabin meant to act as a temporary clothesline before she tossed a spare sheet over it, blocking his view.

Trees heard the bathroom door shut and the water running. He turned on the radio and stopped at the first station with decent reception so he didn't think about Laila naked. She didn't need to know that he hadn't felt an attraction to any woman like this in years—maybe ever.

The music sounded like it belonged at a dance party, all electronica and shit. He tried to get into it, but music these days just sucked, and his mind wasn't on tunes.

Finally, the shower cut off and he heard her rummaging around the back.

"If you need a T-shirt to sleep in, I have a spare," he called.

"I am fine."

Which meant she would either don her dirty clothes or the only clean change she had. Stubborn woman.

In the very back of the RV, the light flipped on. After some rustling, she climbed into the bed. He wished holding Laila would make her feel safer. She needed comfort and security. It sucked that, at least for now, staying away from her was more likely to put her at ease.

The bright lights in the bedroom cut off, plunging the back of the vehicle into darkness.

A whimper broke the quiet. After a squeak of the mattress and a huff of frustration, the overhead light in the bedroom lit up the back of the RV again. "Is there another light—something less bright—I can leave on while I sleep?"

She wanted a nightlight? "In the bedroom?"

"Please."

"You don't want to sleep in the dark?"

"No." Her voice shook.

Because she was afraid? After everything that had happened with Victor, maybe he shouldn't be surprised. "Leave the light in the bathroom on."

She sighed. Sheets rustled. Her footsteps padded toward the middle of the vehicle. Bright light flared through the white sheet before she headed back to bed.

"Better?"

"Yes."

"Good night, Laila," he called back.

She crawled between the sheets again. Ten minutes later, he hadn't heard a peep.

Now he could focus on his other problem, like the fact that when he'd stopped for gas and checked in with Kane, the new guy had let him know that, in the wake of Kimber's abduction, the Edgingtons were now using the safe house they had intended for Valeria and Laila for their own wives and kids. Trees understood that, absolutely. But where the hell should he be taking Laila once he got the green light to bring her in?

Since Zy was in charge, Trees grabbed his device and dialed his buddy, who thankfully picked up right away. "Hey, man."

Trees frowned. Zy sounded distracted. "Hey. I figured I'd check in with you."

"Yeah. Give me five?"

"You talking to me?" Trees asked.

"Sorry. Talking to Tessa," Zy replied. Then some rustling and some nighttime sounds told him that his buddy had stepped outside. "What's up?"

Shit, he'd been so wrapped up in his situation with Laila that he'd forgotten the bosses had removed the nonfraternization clause from everyone's employment contracts this morning, allowing Zy and Tess to finally be together—so Zy could investigate whether she was their mole. In his opinion, it was a stupid idea. Zy was way too into Tessa to do any part of the job thoroughly except the fucking. "Did you finally take her to bed?"

"If I had, why would I tell a nosy prick like you?"

"So that's a yes. Was it everything you thought it would be?"

"Let's put it this way: I have an appointment to look at engagement rings tomorrow."

Zy might be a rebel through and through, but he was rarely impulsive. "You're that sure?"

"One hundred percent."

Either Zy was convinced Tessa wasn't selling them out…or he loved her too much to see it. Either was a blind spot that could be dangerous. "Wow. Congratulations, man. That's awesome."

What else could he say when his best friend sounded so damn happy?

"Well, even if I buy a ring tomorrow, she's not going to say yes right then."

"A little gun-shy?" *Or a little guilty?*

"Yeah, that's what she says. And I get it."

Tessa had been through a lot with her ex, so it was possible. Likely, even. Trees just wasn't sure that was the reason for her reluctance to commit.

"But you didn't call to ask about us," Zy went on. "What's up? You and Kane get everything worked out with the sisters?"

"Finally." He sighed. "It was a fucking long, scary-ass day. But yeah, we're on the road now. And I need to talk to you." He spared Zy the gory details about the evening.

"What's up?"

"Kane and I connected with Valeria, and she got her son back. They left a few hours ago in a minivan. He plans to drive straight through. But since the safe house reserved for Valeria isn't available anymore, where do you want us to go? I'd ask one of the bosses, but with everything they have going on, I didn't want to come to them with more problems."

"Yeah." Zy sighed, seemingly as stumped as he was. "Let me…call Cutter. He's a local boy, and he and Shealyn are back from their honeymoon."

Good thought. Zy might not consider himself any sort of leader, but he was a damn capable one.

"Since her sister's wedding to Josiah got derailed by violence not long ago, they might be busy," Trees pointed out.

"Well, we're likely to have another situation like that on our hands if Cutter doesn't spare me five minutes."

"True. Yeah, call him, then let Kane know."

"What about you and Laila?"

"I rented an RV." He spilled to Zy about the cover story he'd developed on the fly at the store. "When the chatty woman started talking to us, Laila seemed terrified. She literally expects Emilo's henchmen to jump her at any moment." Not surprising since thugs had been on their tails for hours. "They messed her up."

"She feels safe with you, though. Right?"

"As safe as she feels with any man, but it's not much. She knows I'm a friend of Walker's. It helped. A little. He's apparently the good guy since he politely declined to rape her." As he'd heard the story, she'd offered herself to Walker for some escape scheme when he'd been captured and held in Emilo Montilla's compound. Since she was seemingly terrified of men, she'd obviously been desperate to escape.

"Jesus. So what's your plan?"

"We're going to make our way back slowly, be sure Valeria gets situated into whatever safe house you find for her. If it looks good, like no one is watching, then I'll take Laila there. If it gets hit…my plan B is to take her to my place." Though she would be furious at being separated from her sister.

"Well, it's secure enough."

"It should be, yeah. There's just one problem." Trees dropped his voice so she wouldn't hear. "Laila is so damn sexy I can barely keep my eyes—and everything else—off of her."

He felt like a shit for that. But he would never cross the line and come on to her. His desire wasn't her problem.

"Does she suspect?"

Thanks to the close quarters and lack of privacy they'd endured during their years of service, Zy had seen that he wasn't just tall but built big everywhere. "There are only so many ways to hide an erection like mine."

"Yeah. Do you need to speed up your trip?"

Because she was too afraid to be around him? That couldn't be a deciding factor. Her protection came first. "What happens if I do and Tierra Caliente figures out where Valeria is hiding? Laila will be collateral damage. After the hell I suspect she's been through, she deserves some fucking safety, man."

"Okay, let me see what I can toss together. You keep on keeping on, and I'll touch base with Kane soon."

Not a perfect answer, but the only one he was going to get now. Besides, in this big-ass vehicle, needing to avoid the interstate? It would take a day or two to reach Lafayette. "Great, buddy. Thanks."

"Talk to you tomorrow."

"Don't hang up." Trees had to give Zy some bad news.

"Something else going on?"

"Yeah..."

"Talk to me."

"Are you sitting?"

"No, and I don't have time now. What the fuck is happening?"

"When Laila escaped the house in Orlando, she couldn't get her phone. But she managed to knock out one of her assailants and—"

"How the hell did she do that? Because if you're attracted to her, I know she's a tiny thing."

"Fuck, I hate that I have a type," he grumbled. "Yeah, she is. And she knocked the son of a bitch out by surprising him with a loaded diaper pail to the face."

Zy chortled, as if he'd tried not to laugh but failed. "She sounds resourceful. Bet that guy thought it was a shitty fight."

"Yeah. Laila is...something," he whispered.

"Where is she now?"

"Sleeping in the back. Finally. That's why I wanted to call you. At our last stop, we pulled into a gas station." He explained how Laila got her assailant's mobile. "I browsed the phone while we were filling up. This guy was Tierra Caliente, and you won't like how they're communicating."

Zy groaned. "Don't say it."

"I don't want to, but I have to, man. They're using Abuzz."

Unluckily for Zy, his father—who was an absolute dick—owned and helmed the trendy social media app.

"Fuck."

"You have to call your dad." And break the news that criminals were using the platform designed for chat and interaction to coordinate illegal behavior…if Phillip Garrett didn't already know. And what were the odds of that?

But Zy would have to climb that mountain alone. Trees needed to focus on Laila.

The two caught up for a few more minutes, then Zy sighed. "Stay safe, check in, and keep your dick in your pants."

"The first two? No sweat. The last one? No promises," Trees joked lamely to lighten the mood.

They rang off, and Trees settled in with the road, determined to put as many miles between Victor Ramos and Laila as possible. He also kept his eyes on the other cars that came up behind him, leading west, because while the guy was an asshole, he wasn't stupid. By now, he had likely ditched the Mercedes and picked up something new, probably nondescript. And Trees didn't like the fact there wasn't a damn thing he could do about changing the RV's appearance.

Cruising the two-lane roads, he slowed through every pissant town, not wanting to attract attention. But at one in the morning, the road started swimming, and he was seeing double.

He found a little one-gas-station town and pulled behind a church to catnap. Did Laila realize this RV didn't have another bed that would fit him? Not that he'd let her sleep on the bunk over the front seats alone, given her habit of running…

With a sigh, he cut the engine, then headed to the back to check on her. Moonlight blended with a beam of light from the bathroom, lighting up her pale olive profile. She wore a skimpy pink tank top—no hint of a bra. It did little to contain her breasts. A strip of bare skin below her waist gave way to a pair of innocent white lace panties, which peeked above the sheet she'd thrust off in the Florida humidity. Her dark hair curled behind her, spread across the pillow. She was so still and silent, and Trees couldn't decide if she was deeply asleep—or faking it.

He wasn't taking a chance. And since he'd left his police-issue cuffs on Victor, he had to roll with the punches.

Rummaging through his duffel, he pulled out a pair of padded cuffs and headed back to the bedroom. Laila hadn't moved.

He wedged his way through the narrow walkway around the queen-size bed and knelt beside her. She was even more beautiful up close.

His gaze caressed her. His cock hardened. It would be stupid to linger.

After wrapping one cuff around the built-in nightstand drawer, he secured the other around her wrist, then he fixed the padlocks in the fastenings of each one.

He would answer her inevitable questions later, but for now at least, she wasn't going anywhere.

With an exhausted sigh, he let himself into the postage-stamp bathroom, hit the head, then did his best to wedge his big body into the shower. After bumping his knees and elbows on the enclosure at every turn, he gave up and toweled off.

As tired as he was, he almost dreaded lying beside Laila. Would he actually sleep or just lie there, hard for her?

His desire was damn inconvenient. Usually, he had no problem resisting. He was the guy everyone trusted with their sisters, girlfriends, and wives. Sure, he played at clubs and private parties now and then. He even dated some. But he rarely indulged in sex. Usually, he had to know someone for a while. Instinct had to tell him it was right. That they'd be good together.

Right now, his intuition must be all kinds of fucked up because it kept urging him to strip Laila down and bury himself as deep inside her as he could.

Not happening. He needed to get supine, close his eyes, and pray sleep came.

He tugged on a pair of clean basketball shorts, made sure the vehicle was locked up, set his SIG on the little nightstand, then got horizontal, putting his back to Laila. The damned light from the bathroom shined in his eyes.

But that wasn't what kept Trees awake. Now that he was beside her, he smelled her—a hint of the clean bar soap he'd stocked in the shower combined with some female musk that teased the fuck out of his senses. With every inhalation, he breathed her in. With a stretch of his long legs, he brushed her small feet and soft thighs. He could hear her, now whining softly in her sleep as if she was having a nightmare. Her chest rose and fell quicker with every breath she sawed in and out.

Her moans became cries. She thrashed, fighting an invisible enemy in her sleep.

She needed comfort.

Fuck.

"Shh." He rolled over to face her, then wrapped his arm around her small middle and dragged her body against his. "I'll keep you safe, little one. Rest."

Slowly, she stilled. Her brow smoothed. Her body relaxed.

His didn't. He'd splayed his palm across her abdomen. Under his thumb, he could feel the swell of her breast. Her lush ass wriggled against his steely cock. Finally, she sighed, falling back into a deep sleep.

He lay awake for interminable hours, enduring the next-level torture before finally drifting off. His last thought? How the hell would he resist Laila for days—or weeks—before they reached Lafayette and could go their separate ways?

Chapter Four

With morning light invading her lids, Laila opened her eyes and stifled a gasp. She didn't know where she was or what time it was. All she knew was that, for the first time in months, she was lying with a man's bare chest plastered to her back, his beefy arm constricting her middle, trapping her against his hair-roughened body.

She was in hell again.

Her first instinct was to fight. To kick. To scream. But she had learned the hard way that would either be futile or counterproductive. Instead, she lay frozen.

Inhale. Exhale. Don't panic. Devise a way to escape.

She glanced around the small bedroom. A window sat less than two feet from her face, taunting her with a view of a parking lot. Beyond that, the sun eked above winter-ravaged trees dotting an empty field. If she could close the distance between her and that wide-open space, she would be free. But she didn't dare make a move toward the door. Her tormentor was blocking her path.

As terrifying as it was that she couldn't remember being violated last night, she'd prefer to keep it that way.

Laila risked a glance over her shoulder, but she didn't find either Hector or Victor. Instead, Trees loomed behind her, taking up most of the bed and snoring softly. Memories fell into place. He had saved her from Victor and gotten her out of Orlando. He had let her shower alone. A glance down proved she was still clothed. A wriggle against his body told her he wore shorts. Maybe the man had merely slept beside her? Looked but not touched?

Then why is he in your bed if he didn't force his way into your body?

Maybe because he didn't trust her. Maybe because this was the only bed.

Or maybe because he wants to wake up with a proper screw.

Laila didn't know. But after last night, she had to at least consider the possibility she was unfairly painting Trees with Victor's brush. Even so, she had vowed never to be this close to any man again unless it was *her* choice.

Since Trees was asleep, now was the time to leave his bed. But last night had proved she shouldn't flee again until she had a plan. Without wheels, weapons, and money, she wouldn't get far. She had to think, concoct a solid plan to reach her family while keeping herself safe along the way. As soon as she did, she would be gone.

She refused to trust her fate to anyone else—especially a man she barely knew, who worked for an organization she didn't trust.

Slowly, she kicked the covers aside and stood—only to be stopped short by a cuff around her wrist tethering her to the nightstand. But it was nothing standard police-issue. With his line of work, Laila expected Trees to have those. Instead, the restriction around her wrist was made of soft, buttery leather that had been buckled in place and secured with a dangling silver padlock. Its match was attached to the nearby drawer handle.

Laila stared in horror, her heart hammering. She knew all too well what restraints like these were intended for. And Trees had used them to shackle her.

Panic rose. A scream stuck in her throat.

Suddenly, he flattened his big palm across her back. "Take a deep breath, Laila. There's no reason to be alarmed."

The hell there wasn't. "What do you want?"

"To go back to sleep."

"I am awake." And not willing to lie beside him again, especially if he was anything like Hector—partial to morning sex, the more against her will the better.

With a sigh, Trees rolled away and sat up. Somehow, the skin he'd been touching moments ago felt cold. Then he lifted his phone from the nightstand, glanced at the time, and stood. "All right. We should probably get on the road anyway."

That was it? He wasn't going to demand she spread herself open for him? Or use his superior size and strength to pull her back to the bed to relieve the tenting of his shorts?

"You need the bathroom?" he asked instead.

Yes. But she needed his cuffs gone more. "Please."

Nodding, he padded toward her. Too late she realized that, in order to release her, he had to come unnervingly close.

Laila swallowed as he rounded the bed, approaching her on enormous bare feet. His legs were harshly muscled trunks. His erection was large and obvious. His abdomen was muscled and corrugated like a man in peak physical shape. His chest, broad and hard and sprinkled with dark hair, was purely masculine. His shoulders—one covered in tribal ink—seemed impossibly wide, even for a man as enormous as him. The desire in his eyes as he took her in from head to toe was unmistakable.

Experience had taught her that showing weakness never resulted in mercy, so she stood her ground, refusing to flinch as he closed in, cutting off her only avenue of escape. Unless she wanted to scramble across the bed, of course. And what were the odds she could make it to the other side before he pinned her down and took advantage of her?

Her heart beat so wildly she could barely breathe, but she met his gaze straight on, painfully aware that she wore only a tank top he could probably see through and filmy white lace underwear. She did her best to ignore that and held up her wrist as much as the restraints allowed. "Get it off."

Trees took her arm in his grip, his touch surprisingly gentle, as he settled the key in the padlock. "It's not hurting you."

"A man only uses these to restrain someone for his sexual…urges," she spit at him like an accusation.

He paused as if mulling his response, then nodded. "But for me, that's never against a woman's will, Laila. Ever."

Mentally, she snorted. What other reason would a man have to manacle a woman he intended to have sex with? "Your urges are none of my concern. But if you are being paid to protect me, you should never restrain me."

After a minute flick of his wrist, he turned the key and extricated the padlock before unbuckling the cuff. Still, he didn't release her. "Since my other cuffs secured Victor to a toilet—the best place for him until he goes to hell—these are the only restraints I have. They aren't meant to alarm you, but I can't protect you if you keep running from me."

Since she couldn't conceive of a reason he would have brought them at all except to secure her to his bed, she disagreed but kept her thoughts to herself.

"And if you hadn't run, I wouldn't have used them on you at all."

So this was her fault? Of course. He was a man. He was never at fault for anything. "Let me pass. I want to get dressed."

For a long moment, Trees didn't move. Finally, he pressed his big back against the window and reached for the cuff still affixed to the nightstand. If she squeezed past him, every inch of her body would rub against his. And then what would happen? The possibilities terrified her, but he'd left her no choice.

Laila debated her approach. Turning her back to him would conceal her breasts, but her ass would brush the most rigid, male part of him, possibly exciting him more. Worse, she would be presenting him her vulnerable back, where she wouldn't see his attack coming.

Better to face him head on.

But Trees took up three-quarters of the space between the window and the bed. When she tried to step past him, his hard penis brushed against her belly. She gasped, instinctively trying to retreat.

She nearly fell back to the mattress.

Trees wound his arm around her middle, keeping her upright. The move pressed her body tight against his.

Heat poured off of him, chasing away the January chill while making gooseflesh erupt across her skin. But he was too big, too close. Too frightening.

"Let me go." Laila wriggled and writhed, but she only succeeded in making his erection stiffen and grow against her middle. It was all she could do not to scream.

"I'm trying. Stop moving. Fuck—" He grabbed her hips in a rough grip and used his brute strength to still her.

"Do not touch me!"

He worked his palms from her hips to her waist. "Take a deep breath, little one. Don't panic. I won't hurt you."

With every word, his voice went deeper. Softer—not more gentle but more velvety. She'd heard him use that tone before, and like last time, she felt strangely compelled to comply.

Her gaze flew to his. Their eyes met. His burned. He wanted her, and he wasn't trying to hide it. But everything else about his face was calm, almost reassuring.

Laila didn't understand.

Slowly, she went still.

"Yes," he praised, his voice lower and silkier than ever, as he locked his hands around her waist. "That's a good girl."

His words should have seemed patronizing, like someone crooning to a child, yet they soothed her. Some still-panicked part of her brain screamed that he was lulling her into cooperating before he forced her to the mattress and used her for his pleasure. But the thought had barely taken root when he lifted her around the corner of the bed, a foot away, then released her.

Laila gaped. That was it?

He met her gaze unblinkingly—a silent *yes*.

Maybe he wasn't awful. Maybe he wouldn't attack her.

Maybe…but she waited for her heart rate to return to normal. It didn't.

Why? She didn't want him to touch her again…but now that he wasn't, she was oddly aware of him.

Trees was the first to break their stare, turning his attention to the cuff around the drawer handle. He had giant hands, but they were both gentle and adept as he fitted the key in the padlock and unbuckled the cuff. When he turned, she was still watching him.

"Something you want to say, Laila?"

If you terrify me, why am I so curious?

She stifled the foolish thought. She was simply confused, not thinking straight. Of course she didn't want him coaxing her with that voice. Didn't want his hands on her. Didn't want him anywhere near her.

Yet some subversive part of her wondered why he felt different.

"Nothing," she muttered, then disappeared into the bathroom.

As she locked the flimsy door, she realized her hands were shaking. Her palms were sweating. Her heart was still racing.

After using the toilet, she washed her hands and looked at her reflection in the mirror above the basin. Her eyes looked wide, almost startled. Her cheeks were flushed. Her breaths still trembled in her chest. Why did Trees rattle her so much when he hadn't harmed her in any way?

After she emerged from the bathroom, she went straight for Jorge's diaper bag and retrieved the shorts she'd left there after her shower last night. Trees stood at the front of the vehicle, with his back to her, and rummaged through a plastic sack in his hands.

Below his thick neck, every part of him bulged and swelled when he moved—arms, shoulders, and back. Muscles even bracketed his strong spine as his shape narrowed from top to bottom in a V.

The longer she stared, the more her breath turned choppy. She swallowed a flutter in her belly she didn't understand.

As if he sensed her stare, he turned, his gaze sweeping her at once, making her feel almost naked. "Need something?"

His voice…she heard a note in it that she didn't know how to interpret. It invited her closer.

Laila couldn't explain how he was drawing her in or why she was tempted to accept. Because she wanted to study him? To figure him out? But that made no sense. She would never be interested in any man.

"What are you looking for?" she finally asked.

He pulled out some metal part on cardboard backing, wrapped in plastic, along with a small tool set. He tore into both, grabbing what he needed, then set the plastic bag on the table. "This stuff."

Items in hand, Trees faced the door and raised his arms. She found herself staring again at the ridges and ripples of his body.

Suddenly, he stopped, sighed, and faced her. "Just so there's no misunderstanding, I'm installing a lock on the door."

She frowned. "Does it not already have one?"

"Since you don't want me to use the leather cuffs on you again, this isn't to keep others out but to keep you in."

That filled her with panic. Even if he hadn't taken advantage of her this morning, he still intended to imprison her. "No."

"I can't have you running again, so I want to be crystal clear. I'm only trying to prevent you from fleeing and putting yourself in danger while my back is turned. I'm not locking you in because I intend to force myself on you."

So he claimed. Even if he meant that, he was still subjugating her and subverting her free will. "You will not cuff me to the car door or the nightstand again?"

"Nope."

"You promise you will not use the cuffs on me at all," she demanded, then nearly laughed at herself. He might be a less criminal man than Victor, but that didn't make his word worth more.

"I promise. I won't…unless you ask me to."

She scoffed. "I will never do that."

"I believe you." Regret crossed his face. "And that's a pity."

Laila frowned as she stumbled into her shorts, still staring at his broad back as he held up the part to the door with one hand, then sorted through the tools, now spread out across the table, with the other. There was no sense in asking him to explain, and she shouldn't care, but… "What do you mean?"

He turned to her with a sigh. "You know the cuffs are for sexual play. I can guess how Victor used them on you, but I would never do that."

"Then why have them at all?"

"I only engage in play that's consensual. If any woman says no, that means no. Hard stop."

Laila eyed him. "You want me to believe that, if any woman refused you, that you would leave her untouched?"

"Yes."

"Without violence?"

"Of course." He sounded as if that was obvious.

"Without anger?"

"I wouldn't be angry. Frustrated, maybe. But—"

"You would not force her?"

"Never."

He believed that—at least in his own mind. Laila wasn't convinced. "Then why restrain a woman to your bed at all?"

His eyes flared with heat again. "Some like it."

"Impossible." Surely he lied.

"Oh, they do."

And so did he. His face and the engorging of his erection again said so.

Why would a woman want to be manacled to a man's bed and held down while he did…whatever he pleased? "I do not believe you."

The buzzing of his phone interrupted whatever he'd been about to say. He scowled and pulled it from his pocket. "Zy. Talk to me."

There was a long pause, and she could hear another man's muffled voice.

Trees nodded before the other man even finished speaking. "Roger that." Then he flicked a glance her way. "I'll let Laila know." Another pause. "Fine. Yeah, I'll check in later. Thanks."

Then he hung up, and Laila was relieved to have a change of subject. "Do you have news about my family?"

He nodded. "They've arrived at their safe house after driving all night. Valeria and the boy are sleeping now. Your sister will call you later."

"Where are they?"

"Someplace safe."

Laila had heard that tripe before. Why wouldn't he tell her where EM Security had hidden her family, unless they intended to keep her and Valeria apart so they could use the separation to control her? After all, Emilo had been a master at that.

As soon as her sister had rested, she would call and verify Trees's claim—then make plans accordingly.

Trees turned his attention back to the lock he meant to install on the door, and she thought through the situation. What if he lied? What if he intended to use his restraints on her? What if she needed to escape?

She couldn't let him install that lock.

Trembling, Laila approached, touching her fingertips to solid concrete muscle over the surprisingly supple skin of his back. "You can stop. Installing that is not necessary."

"I think it is."

"What if I promised I would not escape?" And she meant that…at least for now.

"You'd be lying, and I'd be forced to cuff you again."

"No. After last night, I know Victor will not give up easily and that I am safer with you."

He hesitated. "I can't take that chance."

"Please. I would feel safer if I was not being kept prisoner. But if you lock me up against my will, I will always be afraid."

Trees hesitated, then sighed before he shoved everything back into the bag. "Son of a bitch. Fine. But I'm watching you. One more attempt to get free, and I won't hesitate to both lock you in and cuff you to whatever the fuck I need to, whenever the fuck I want to, until you realize that you have to stay. Are we clear?"

"Of course." What else could she say?

"All right." He shoved the bag away. "If I even suspect you're trying to escape me, I'm warning you now. I'll be all over you until you beg me for mercy. And I won't have any."

A day and a half later, Laila was still trying to understand Trees. Except the handful of hours he had driven to reach this campground in Nowhere, Alabama, he never took his stare off her. He watched her as she ate, as she paced the RV with nervous energy, as she talked on the phone to her sister. He stood guard outside the bathroom while she brushed her teeth or washed her face. He glared as she yawned and fought to keep her eyes open, then he ignored her protests that she wasn't tired and carried her to bed—cursing her stubbornness—eventually invading the uncomfortably small mattress and lying beside her to shield her with his big body.

A few times, he tried to initiate conversation, asking about her sister, Jorge, or her childhood. For what reason did he need to know those things? To use the information against her? He claimed he was curious, but why? Sometimes, she answered. Mostly, she ignored Trees, pretending she never noticed him at all—not that such a thing was possible.

But he hadn't touched her, despite the fact he clearly wanted to.

That confused Laila. They both knew she couldn't stop him. If he violated her, she could tell her sister, of course. But it would be too late. Then again, maybe Valeria would see that as a small price for her to pay to escape Victor and Hector Ramos for good. In some ways, she would be right.

Much to Laila's relief, Trees had also tucked away his soft leather cuffs, probably somewhere in his bag. She was grateful…but she couldn't forget his threat. If she "misbehaved," he would use them against her will. Would she even have to give him a reason? A couple of days ago, she would have said no. Today? He'd kept his promise so far. Maybe that meant something.

Maybe not.

"Hungry?" he asked from the front seat as he parked on an empty pad in the campground and cut the engine.

His idea of a meal seemed to be lots of eggs or chicken with a steady diet of broccoli and rice. She wasn't accustomed to eating so much or so often, even if the fresh, hot food that she hadn't had to cook was good. "No."

He glanced at his phone. "It's five o'clock. You haven't eaten since breakfast."

And he had—twice. Where did he put all that food?

She shrugged. "I am not hungry."

"Not eating isn't good for you." He pocketed the RV key and headed her way, looming above her while she sat at the dining table.

"Neither is eating too much. Why are we stopping here? When will you take me to my sister?"

"When we've made sure the safe house is actually safe."

"EM Security has yet to manage that feat. When did safety begin to matter?"

He sighed. "It always did, Laila."

"Then why did my brother-in-law and his men find all the houses your organization swore were safe?"

"We're working overtime to figure that out. Don't worry."

"Because I should simply trust you—a man I have known for two days?" She raised a brow. "What happens if I choose not to concern myself and the cartel finds me and my family again? Should I also not worry as they drag Valeria and me into the desert to make a quick end of us, then raise Jorge to be a criminal?"

Trees scowled. "Don't worry about it because, other than protecting you, figuring this out is my sole focus. I won't let anything happen."

He'd said such things before. Some foolish part of her wanted to believe him, but life had proven that no one would solve her problems but her. It seemed clear that someone in EM Security Management was selling their secrets to Emilo's men. Valeria didn't want to believe that, but Laila knew. Until that problem was addressed, they were all in danger.

"And you're changing the subject," he pointed out. "Skipping dinner isn't acceptable. Tell me what you want. I'll do my best to make it."

Victor and Hector had always expected her to cook for them before one or the other—or both—stripped her down and violated her. Trees had prepared his own meals when she had not been hungry. That had surprised her, but the fact he wasn't forcing her to do what Victor considered "women's work" shocked her far more.

"*Carne asada.*" That's what she wanted—not that she expected him to actually make it.

"I'll do my best. Why don't you take a shower?"

"I am fine."

"It's been nearly two days since you bathed." He dropped his voice to that low, silky tone she found difficult to disobey. "It wasn't a request."

"Will you force me?"

He scowled. "Have I truly forced you to do anything against your will?"

Not really. In that, he was light years better than Victor and Hector. But that didn't automatically make him a good guy. "What if I refuse?"

"I'll take your phone so you can't speak to your sister tonight."

Laila fumed. Trees wasn't forcing her in a physical sense, but he was coercing her to choose between her family and her sense of safety. That was no choice at all. Laila needed to hear that her sister and her nephew were well far more than she needed to protect herself.

"All right."

She made her way to Jorge's diaper bag, where she had stowed her other outfit she had washed by hand last night. Then she retreated to the bathroom, half expecting Trees would barge his way into the little room and take advantage of her while she was naked and vulnerable, despite supposedly being one of the "good guys"—if there was such a thing.

Laila rushed through her shower, but his intrusion never came. When she stepped out of the enclosure to towel off, the scent of grilling meat and spices filled her nose. She wriggled into her clothes, then wrapped a towel around her clean hair and whisked the bathroom door open. Trees hunched over the kitchen counter, chopping peppers as steak sizzled on the griddle pan he'd set over the gas burners.

He turned to her with a half grin. "Smell good?"

Delicious, but that wasn't what grabbed Laila's attention. She had not seen Trees smile before. It transformed the most forbidding lines of his hard face into something both beautiful and almost boyish.

Had she just found a man attractive?

"It does."

"I didn't have all the ingredients, and I didn't have a couple of hours to marinate the meat, but the recipe I found online called for a sauce I hope will give it some kick. We should be ready to eat in a few minutes." He reached into a nearby cabinet. "Why don't you have a seat?"

While he cooked?

She did. He said nothing for the next five minutes, simply focused on the meat hissing in the pan while he opened a can of refried beans and spiced it up with salsa.

It wasn't long before he moved the food onto a pair of plates, along with a lime he'd sliced, and turned back to her. "Wine?"

"Why?" The Ramos brothers had only given her alcohol to lower her resistance in bed.

"Isn't it supposed to be good with the meal?"

"You do not drink it yourself?"

"Not while I'm working, but there's no reason you can't."

Laila wouldn't make taking advantage of her easy. "I would rather not."

"Suit yourself." He shrugged. "Can you grab us some water?"

As he set the plates on the table, she retrieved two bottles from the refrigerator, then eased onto the bench again. She hadn't realized how hungry she'd been until he set the meal in front of her.

Quickly, she spread her napkin across her lap, then forked a tender bite into her mouth. Flavor burst on her taste buds. He'd managed to capture the perfect blend of citrus, smokiness, and spices. A moan slipped out before she could stop it.

"You like it?"

Laila opened the eyes she hadn't realized she'd closed to find Trees across the table where they inadvertently knocked knees, staring at her like her opinion mattered. "It is good."

The smile his face had hinted at mere moments ago became a full-blown grin. "I'm glad. Eat up." He lifted his own fork and dug in, biting into his first morsel with an appreciative nod. "You're right. It's decent."

It was better than that. As Laila dug into her plate, questions nagged her. "Why did you cook for me?"

He frowned. "We had to eat, right?"

"I mean why did you cook something I like? Why are you being nice?"

Trees looked even more confused. "We're on the same team, remember?"

"What team is that?"

"Team Save Laila," he said as if it was obvious, then he set his fork down. "Look, I can only imagine what happened to you in Emilo's compound. I'm sure it wasn't pretty. But I'm not Victor."

So far, no. But… "You are on my team simply because you are paid. I have no illusion that if he or his brother, Hector, paid you more, you would develop different allegiances."

He stilled, then leaned in, his eyes narrowing. "I wouldn't. This is my job, but I don't do it just for money. I have the size and skills to protect people. That's my goal. I have five younger sisters. If any of them experienced anything close to what you did, I would be on the rampage to fuck up some assholes and put them six feet under."

That sounded noble—unbelievably so. She had never met a man

who was more motivated by morals than money. But calling him a liar served no purpose, so she focused on the spiced steak.

Suddenly, he took her hand between his huge palms. She jerked her gaze to his, frozen by the heat of his touch.

"You don't believe me, and I understand why. But I swear I'm not the enemy."

That didn't automatically make him her ally, either. Slowly, he released her. She sensed his frustration.

"I know being here with me isn't what you wanted or imagined," he went on. "I'm a stranger, and it's uncomfortable. I'm pretty sure you're still looking for ways to give me the slip. But you need to stay close to me. We both know Victor won't give up looking for you."

"He will not." Victor's ego couldn't tolerate being bested by anyone, especially the woman he'd subjugated for years.

"There may come a time when your life depends on you trusting me to save you."

Perhaps...but doing that would never be easy.

The buzzing of her temporary mobile broke the tense silence between them. She hopped up from her seat, ignoring the strange flare of heat when her legs brushed his again, and plucked up her little device from the front seat.

"Are you well, *hermana*?" she asked her sister in Spanish.

"I am fine. But Jorge..." Valeria sounded both exhausted and teary. "He is burning up. He falls asleep but will not stay asleep. He is cranky and listless and keeps tugging at his ears."

Another ear infection. "How long has this been going on?"

"Twenty-four hours...but it is getting worse."

Which explained why Laila had barely heard from her.

"Remember the last time this happened?" Valeria wailed.

Laila couldn't forget. Late in the fall, his fever has spiked so high they had been forced to rush him to the ER. The possibility of that happening again ratcheted up her concern, but she had to calm her sister. "Do not assume it will be that severe again. What is his temperature?"

"I do not know. I forgot to ask for a thermometer. Zyron brought me liquid ibuprofen when I saw him this afternoon, but I am worried." She erupted into more tears.

"Take a deep breath. When you panic, Jorge senses your distress."

"I know. I am trying…" Valeria sobbed.

"Does he have any other symptoms?"

"He is congested, and he has a cough—just like last time."

Her answer worried Laila even more, but she kept that to herself. "He needs antibiotics."

"We have none. Even if I did, you know how he spits out medicine. He did it with his last dose of ibuprofen."

A big reason Jorge had needed to go to the hospital, so he could have medicine intravenously. "Keep trying."

"Of course. But what if I fail? What if his fever goes up again? Taking him to a doctor may give away our location." Valeria dissolved into tears again.

Laila couldn't leave her sister to handle this alone. "Where are you?"

"Lafayette, Louisiana. In an apartment."

How many hundreds of miles away was that? Why had EM Security taken Valeria so far from her? "Hang on. I will be there as quickly as I can."

She could help nurse Jorge and support her weary sister. Hopefully that would keep her nephew out of the hospital.

"Trees is bringing you here? Oh, thank goodness."

"He has not said when. If he is not going straight there, I will find you on my own."

"You cannot leave him!" Valeria screeched. "He is your bodyguard. He is keeping you safe from Emilo's men."

"While keeping me captive. How does that make him different?"

"Has he touched you against your will?"

"No, but if you'll recall, nothing happened when I first arrived at the compound. I was a naively trusting child then. I know better now."

"But I hired EM Security to—"

"I know why you hired them. And I realize you have faith in them. But I do not share your confidence."

"They rescued us both."

"Men who commit violence—whatever their reason—are still thugs. I neither want nor trust one to make my decisions, especially when he feels justified in doing it against my will."

"Is that really how you feel?" Valeria sounded shocked.

Laila didn't understand how her sister could see things so differently. "You are paying them money, and what have they done? Kept us apart while dictating when, how, and where we can go—over my objections, and despite the fact they have failed at keeping our location hidden more than once."

"But—"

"You never asked me how I thought we should handle the situation. There are ways other than trusting an organization with an obvious problem keeping secrets. If you want to continue trusting them, I cannot stop you. But I plan to stay safe in the way that best suits me."

Valeria sighed. "Stop being so stubborn. I am worried about Jorge, and now you are making me worry about you, too."

"No. Focus on our little man. I will be there as soon as possible, and I will be fine." Now that they had left Victor behind in Florida, and he had no device he could use to trace her, everything should be all right.

After a little more chatter, she ended the call and set the phone aside.

Time to make a plan.

"Laila?" Trees called, the steps from his big feet loud as he made his way toward her. "Everything all right?"

It would be soon. "Valeria needs me. I must reach her no later than tomorrow. You will take me, yes?"

"Not until I know it's safe, no."

"But Jorge is sick and—"

"In what way?"

"It seems he has an ear infection and—"

"His mother can take care of him."

"Valeria needs help and rest, and she is too distraught—"

"Laila, keeping you safe is my priority. Kane is with her twenty-four seven. He'll give your sister whatever help she needs."

"What does he know about children?"

Trees shrugged. "I don't know. But he's smart and capable. He'll figure it out. And you'll stay with me, safe and sound."

"So *you* have decided that I should abandon my sister when she and my nephew need me most?"

Trees scowled. "Don't twist my words, Laila. You need to let your sister handle her son—with Kane's help. If Jorge needs a doctor, he'll get the kid one. But there's nothing *you* can do, except put yourself at risk. I won't let that happen on my watch."

Laila stared up at Trees. The resolution on his face told her he wasn't playing around. As far as he was concerned, she wasn't going anywhere.

Too bad for him she had other ideas. Now she just had to figure out how to make them a reality.

Chapter *Five*

Five hours later, Trees pretended to read a news article on his phone while he watched Laila. Admittedly, that was his newest addiction. Everything about her was feminine yet fiery, both passionate and reserved. He was desperate to peel back her layers and understand her. Why? He'd never felt the impulse to do that with any other woman.

Not that it mattered. He terrified her. If he was drowning, she wouldn't throw him a lifeline—especially after their earlier argument. She was pissed he wouldn't abandon his marching orders to take her to Valeria. Maybe she'd understand…someday. But he wasn't counting on it.

Not for the first time, Laila stifled a yawn as she flipped through a fashion magazine he'd picked up for her after she'd eyed it in the big-box store. To his shock, she set it aside and stood, stretching her graceful arms above her head and arching her back. It was impossible not to see that she had great tits. He was a fucking heel for noticing, but why lie to himself and pretend he hadn't?

"I am tired," she announced. "I will go to bed."

He didn't have to coerce or even prompt her? That was a first. Usually, she fought sleep, even leaving lights on, he suspected because she feared being vulnerable in the dark. So why was she now volunteering? Was she finally starting to trust him?

"Go ahead. I'll be along soon." Once exhaustion had claimed her, he'd slink into bed and catch a few hours of sleep.

She shook her head. "I-I feel safer with you beside me."

Since when? "Let me check in with the office and make sure we're secure."

"But—"

"I'll only be a handful of steps and a few moments away. That will give you some privacy to get ready." He picked up his SIG and shoved it in his holster, covering the bulge with a baggy shirt. "You'll be fine, Laila. I promise."

And I'll see if you're up to something in the process.

He slipped on his shoes and headed outside. The January air was crisp, the wind cool and humid. But he couldn't complain. Tonight was probably a good twenty degrees warmer than his hometown in Fayetteville, West Virginia. Sometimes, he missed the hell out of the fog clinging to the mountains and the leaves changing spectacular colors to usher in fall. Not that this part of Alabama wasn't pretty with its moss-covered trees, white churches, and Southern charm. But it wasn't the same.

Vaguely, he wondered what the rest of his family was doing. Last he'd heard, his father's age and declining health had forced him to retire from coal mining. His oldest sister had taken a bunch of student loans and gone to college. She'd planned to move back home to teach but instead married a rich boy from Charleston and never looked back. His youngest had gotten pregnant in high school, failed to graduate, and stayed home to perpetuate the poverty that had marked his childhood. His brothers had apparently scattered to the wind.

It had been a few years since he'd talked to any of them. He'd walked away from that cramped, pale green clapboard house with its single bathroom, peeling paint, and a slew of memories, sure that leaving would lighten their load. Zy had become his brother after basic. Together they'd survived hostiles, war on foreign soil, and utter hell. He hadn't given his actual siblings much thought—until tonight. The way Laila gave and took strength from hers made him wonder if he'd given his family one less mouth to feed when he'd left nearly eighteen years ago…or abandoned them when they'd needed him most.

The vague sense of shame clung when his phone buzzed in his pocket and he answered. "What's up, Zy?"

"Long fucking day. How about you?" His buddy sounded tired.

"Not too bad." A total lie, but he didn't want to add to Zy's problems now. "But a few long fucking nights."

"What do you mean?"

"I'm driving this recreational tank from campground to campground, trying to take our sweet time returning to Lafayette."

"Yeah. Is the plan not working?"

"Oh, it is. We haven't been followed." At least not since they'd left Orlando. "I'm sure of that."

"So what's wrong?"

"Everything Laila has to wear is meant for Florida weather and seems two sizes too small. When I look at her, it's impossible not to see tits and ass and that wide fucking mouth. I stare at it all the time—I can't seem to stop—and my cock is like a divining rod that points only to her."

Maybe that was too honest. Sure, he'd given Zy a change of subject…but he needed to stop obsessing about Laila before he freaked her out, get himself under control, be a fucking professional, and get some damn sleep.

"You like her."

"Fuck yes, I do. She's…sweet." Well, the way she cared about her family was. "She's thoughtful. She's strong. She's the kind of woman I want to hold and protect while I'm aching to violate and defile her in every way known to man." He sighed. "And after one look, she was terrified of me."

"Can she hear you?"

"No. She's inside."

"What are you going to do?"

"What the hell can I do? I've got to keep driving her around in this hell on wheels until you tell me Valeria is safe enough in her new location and Laila can move in, no problem."

"You can head back to Lafayette," Zy said.

Thank God. His close confines—and his fixation—with Laila would finally end. Being with her sister would definitely make her happier, especially while Jorge was under the weather. As soon as he had a couple of hours of shut-eye, they would get on the road. "Where should I drop her?"

"The last time we talked, Valeria was convinced Laila will be in less danger if they don't share the same roof. And I can't really argue. Two women and a baby boy are a lot less common, so they're a lot more noticeable."

"I don't disagree." Trees wanted to, but he and Kane had shared a similar assessment in Florida. And the truth was, Emilo's goons were after Valeria. If the sisters were together, the cartel would be more likely to find them. Then Laila would be dead. She served no purpose for anyone in the organization, except the one Victor and Hector had forced on her. And Trees would be damned before he let her fall into their hands again.

Unfortunately, despite that truth and logic, Laila would never be happy apart from her family.

Your job is to protect her, not worry about her happiness, dude. Focus.

"Good. We just have to find Laila somewhere safe. Somewhere no one can get to her. Somewhere she'll be comfortable and have protection. Hey, I've got an idea."

Trees already knew what Zy had in mind. Hell, he'd once suggested it, but… "Don't say it."

"I have to. She's better off at your place."

He closed his eyes, envisioning Laila filling his personal space—and his thoughts—twenty-four seven. "Fuck."

"Look, I know it sucks. I know it's an imposition. But with the bosses consumed with trying to rescue Kimber, I'm the guy in charge, and my resources are limited. You've got a really secure place. She'll be safe there—at least until we can find another situation. And it's so big you'll hardly notice her."

Impossible. All he had to do to be aware of Laila was breathe. Even with the RV's wall separating them, he could practically feel her so close…yet so far. The urge to reassure her nearly compelled him into making promises about her safety he couldn't guarantee. The impulse was stupid. She would never take comfort from him, anyway. "Zy…"

"Who else can keep Laila safe? There's no one I trust more."

Put like that, there was no one else Trees wanted protecting her. What if another operative fucked up and she got dead?

"It's temporary," Zy promised. "She doesn't have to move in with you. Just…keep her until the bosses find Kimber and return to the office. Then they can figure out a permanent place for Laila. And hell, maybe that won't even be in Lafayette, so you'd never have to see her again."

Trees hated that idea, and he didn't examine why too closely. "I didn't say I didn't want to see her. I said I didn't want to live on top of her."

"I'm calling bullshit on that," Zy drawled.

"Back off. I'm trying to be a gentleman, but there's no fucking privacy here. Even the shower is so small it's impossible to jack off."

Zy laughed. "So you're having a…hard time?"

"Shut the fuck up. Do I need to remind you that you had a goddamn hard time with Tessa before the bosses finally took pity on you?"

Suddenly, his buddy sobered. "No. Not that it matters right now. She's barely speaking to me."

"What the fuck did you do, not lay her right?"

"The job called me out last night before I could touch her again. She seemed okay, though. Tired but not mad. This morning, she came into the office looking like she'd been sobbing. But nothing I've said persuaded her to open up. She claims she has a migraine…"

"Those suck."

"Yeah," Zy conceded. "But I don't believe her."

"Why would she lie?"

"I don't know."

"Hallie's not sick?" Trees asked of Tessa's baby daughter.

"Tessa would have said so. Whatever upset her, when I stopped by her place, she refused to let me stay. But my gut tells me she didn't really want me to go. So nothing makes sense."

Trees sighed. "I know you don't want to hear this, but…is there any chance she's guilty?"

"Of what?"

"C'mon, man. The bosses are convinced that either I'm their mole… or she is."

"They're wrong."

"Maybe. But you know I'm clean because you searched my shit."

"One room."

"Then go fucking search the whole place before I get home. You won't find anything, and you know it."

"Yeah. What's your point?"

"You haven't searched Tessa at all. Hell, you've flatly refused to even consider her a suspect."

"It just doesn't make sense. Tessa is no spy. She doesn't have the abilities or the connections or—"

"That you know of. But be logical." Trees went through the entire team, both current and former, then drew the only conclusion he could. "If it's none of us, that leaves Tessa, buddy."

"It can't be."

"Why not?" Trees asked, hoping Zy would stop thinking with his heart. If he didn't, he was going to get all kinds of hurt.

"Because this shit started when she was on maternity leave. She wasn't even around."

Valid point. "True, and I'm not saying she *is* the guilty one. I'm just not sure who else it could be. Let me ask you this: what happens if you don't figure out who EM's mole is?"

"She's fired."

Trees suspected she wouldn't be the only one on the unemployment line. "Look, when I get back, I'll sit down and perform a thorough, top-to-bottom scan of all the internal systems. I'll even come in on a weekend and scan every single person's computer so I'm not in anyone's way. But until then, you need to prove you can rule her out completely."

"How the fuck am I supposed to do that?"

Seriously? Zy had run more than one double-cross disinformation mission in the past.

Trees snorted. "Stop playing games with yourself, man. I know you love her—"

"I fucking bought her an engagement ring today."

Ouch. "Wouldn't you rather know now if you should give it to her?"

After a long pause, Zy answered. "When do you think you'll make it here?"

"I'm going to head in so I can get out of this rolling torture chamber by tomorrow night."

"I'll see you at your place then. And I'll try to have some answers."

"Before you go, did you talk to your dad yet?"

"Oh, yeah."

"Was he as warm as ever?" Trees drawled.

If he had stopped speaking to his family to be less of a burden, Zy had cut his from his life out of pure contempt.

"You know it. We exchanged insults for a few minutes. I'm the hotheaded, rebellious prick who blows up everything—figuratively and literally—wherever I go. I told him that was way better than being a sniveling shit who licked globalist ass for cash."

"So the usual?"

"Pretty much. But I did tell him about Tierra Caliente using Abuzz to coordinate their crimes. He said he'd 'investigate and take appropriate action.'"

"Why do I feel like that means he won't lift a fucking finger to stop it?" Trees cursed.

"You know my father so well."

"He's not hard to figure out… What else can we do?"

"I gave all the screenshots to Joaquin when I saw him earlier. Maybe something in them will help pinpoint where the cartel has Kimber stashed."

"Good call. Let me know if I can do anything."

"There is one more thing…" And Zy sounded reluctant to bring it up.

"Shoot. You know I'll do whatever you need."

"I…um, had a chat with Valeria when I stopped by earlier to drop off supplies to her at the new safe house."

"Is Jorge really sick? Laila is worried."

"Tell her not to be. We'll take care of it. But when I saw Valeria, she also had something else on her mind."

That tone told Trees he wasn't going to like it. "What?"

"She doesn't like the way you look at her sister."

She'd seen that in the alley? Trees winced. "Damn."

"Yep. And she wasn't shy about expressing her concern."

That he would touch her? Violate her? "I would never hurt Laila."

Even the thought made him sick.

"*I* know that because I know you," Zy pointed out. "But—"

"She doesn't know me." Trees sighed. "It's the same problem I have with Laila. She's really fucking wary." Except tonight. Which still didn't make sense to him.

"Valeria says her sister is fragile and desperate for safety. She claims that if you give it to Laila, she'll 'cling' to you."

Trees had to laugh. "Fragile? No. And she's the least clingy woman I've met. Like ever."

"I don't know, man." He heard the shrug in Zy's voice. "That's just what she said. So…be aware and be careful."

Laila grasping on to him wasn't even a possibility, much less a concern, so Trees didn't argue. "Sure."

After a few more minutes of shooting the shit, he hung up and headed inside. Hopefully, she would be asleep, so he could grab a quick shower and hit the bed. Maybe he would even be tired enough to sleep without erotic dreams of her plaguing him.

Through the door, he found the space silent. A few scattered lights around the campground peeked in, blending with the bathroom light Laila always left on, revealing the fact that she lay on the far side of the bed, cuddled beneath the quilts, her dark hair spilling over the white sheets and onto his pillow.

And just like that, he was hard again.

"Son of a bitch," he muttered as he stripped by the shower, knowing he'd find no relief in the tiny enclosure. At least he'd be clean.

After a quick rinse, he tossed on a fresh pair of basketball shorts, sans boxers, and made his way to the kitchen. He pulled open the fridge door, more to stall before lying next to Laila for another torturous night than because he was hungry.

On the top shelf in the middle was the half of Laila's dinner she hadn't finished, along with a small square of cheese and a banana, all wrapped up neat and tight. A bottle of water sat right beside it. Did she intend to eat that hodgepodge for breakfast?

Shaking his head, he shut the door and resolved to stop avoiding the inevitable.

The walk to the bed took all of five steps. Thankfully, when he eased onto the mattress, she didn't stir. Maybe she was getting more comfortable with him. Or at least beginning to believe he would never violate her against her will. Hell, maybe she really was starting to trust him.

He rolled to his side, away from her, and closed his eyes, willing sleep to come. That was the last thing he remembered.

Until he woke sometime later with Laila's mouth around his stiff, hungry cock.

Once Trees finished his long, low-voiced conversation outside the RV, Laila dashed to the bed, huddled under the blankets, and pretended to sleep. The door to the motorhome shut with a quiet click. His footsteps approached the little bedroom. Moments later, his gaze traveled over her. She repressed a shiver, but not because he scared her…at least not the way he used to.

What she felt tonight wasn't fear.

Understanding this unfamiliar feeling wasn't important. Reaching Valeria and Jorge was.

Finally, Trees turned away. When he started the shower and climbed inside, Laila scampered from the bed and stepped into her nearby shoes. As she crept through the vehicle, she found the bathroom door ajar and froze. Risking her escape was stupid. So was poking the bear. But before she could tell herself that, she was already staring.

The top of Trees's dark head, along with his elbows and his hair-roughened knees, stuck out from behind the shower curtain. What did the rest of him look like inside that steamy cubicle, all wet and naked? Was he as muscled and masculine everywhere as his shoulders and chest suggested?

Laila flashed hot at the questions and jerked away. What he looked like didn't matter, except when measuring the superior size and strength he would undoubtedly use to bend her to his will.

Quickly, she rifled through his duffel, but the cuffs she sought to bind him with, the ones with the dangling padlocks, were nowhere to be found. Ditto for the rest of the drawers and compartments in the motor home. That meant she had to scrap her easy Plan A. Plan B—running out the door now—it was.

But before she could grab her things and make a mad dash for freedom, the shower cut off.

Carajo! She wouldn't get far before Trees gave chase. In less than two minutes, he would realize she was gone. What were her odds of finding helpful strangers or a ride to Louisiana that quickly?

Zero.

That left only dreaded Plan C: seducing him into a good night's sleep.

Laila pressed a hand to her tightening belly, dragged in a shaky breath, and sneaked back to the bedroom. As she approached the bed, she trembled and prayed and told herself everything would be all right. She could handle what came next. It wasn't as if she'd never experienced sex or exchanged favors before. She simply had to gather her courage.

Don't think; just do it. It will be over soon…

Screwing her eyes shut tight, Laila dropped every stitch she wore, crawled into the bed, and closed her eyes, doing her best to dredge up gumption and calm.

The next few minutes passed in the blink of an eye before Trees emerged from the bathroom. He paused in the kitchen, and she held her breath, hoping like hell that he wouldn't notice anything amiss. When he shut the refrigerator door a moment later, she was sure she'd avoided raising suspicion. And when he settled onto the mattress beside her, turning away to give her the illusion of space and privacy, she waited, her lips pressed together to hold in a whimper as she stared through the window at the crisp, still night.

Soon, she would be out there—and on her way to Valeria and Jorge. All she had to do was make sure Trees slept soundly.

When she finally heard his soft snoring, she mentally counted to one hundred and tried to work up her fortitude. Then she did it again. Not that it helped. Trees would likely wake up before she finished the task ahead. He woke up anytime she so much as had to go to the bathroom in the middle of the night. And what would likely happen after that terrified her.

Once she reached one hundred a second time, Laila forced herself to stop stalling and eased the covers off her naked body, shivering in the winter air. Or was she trembling because she had figurative cold feet? After all, Trees hadn't given her permission to touch him. And he'd been nice...in a gruff sort of way. Definitely nicer than any of Emilo's lackeys and thugs.

But none of that mattered. Jorge and his health came first, so she shoved away the useless guilt. It wouldn't help her survive or bring her family back together. If Trees didn't like anything she did to him, he had the luxury of saying no and pushing her away—something she'd never had. She wouldn't force him.

But she'd bet he wouldn't turn her down.

Pushing the thought aside, she balanced on her knees and inched across the mattress to where he slept curled on his side, his back looking big and broad and impossibly strong.

Laila gulped. He could overpower her easily. In seconds. Without breathing hard or breaking a sweat.

But she had to push forward. Whatever he wanted from her, whatever it took to ensure he fell into a satisfied stupor, she would do it. Not fighting him would be hard. Pretending to enjoy his touch would be worse. But she didn't see another way.

Her heart rattled wildly against her chest as she reached under the blankets and slowly, slowly tugged the elastic of his shorts down, past his buttocks. He didn't jolt or wake or ask what the hell she was up to. Laila released the breath she hadn't realized she'd been holding.

Next, she pulled the blankets over his hip and his arm before laying her palm on top, then eased him onto his back. He hadn't slept more than a few hours a night since they'd left Florida. His fatigue should work to her advantage.

As he settled in the new position, his snoring stopped. Laila winced as she sat back and waited. Thankfully, it wasn't long before he resumed. Again, she counted to one hundred. Then, with her heart gonging like a drum, she eased the sheet down to his knees.

His snoring continued.

Still, she held her breath as she wriggled the elastic band of his shorts past his hips and settled it around his thighs. Mission accomplished. Thank God, he was still sleeping. She had an apology, albeit flimsy, in place in case he woke, but she needed the head between his legs to be doing his thinking by then.

Laila had tried to avoid looking at Trees *there*. His feet were huge and his thighs were nearly as big as her middle. God knew those massive hands of his could encircle her waist, and he picked her up as if she weighed nothing. So she expected his jumbo size to extend to the parts of him she hadn't seen.

But nothing had prepared her for what she saw now.

She gaped and froze, forgetting to breathe until her lungs burned. *Dios mío*. Flaccid, he was the size of most men erect.

How big would he be when all his blood rushed there and engorged him?

Laila bit her lip and pressed a shaking hand to her chest. If she managed to fit him in her mouth, how uncomfortable would it be?

It doesn't matter. Think of reaching your sister and your nephew.

Hopefully, all it would cost her was a few minutes of gagging, drooling, degrading discomfort. Then freedom would be hers.

Before she lost her nerve, Laila slowly wrapped her hand around Trees's warm, soft penis and began to stroke it.

His snoring stuttered as he swelled in her hand, growing, growing, growing until she could no longer curl her fingers completely around his steely girth.

Within seconds, he was at full—huge—staff, the massive head turning purple. He was definitely erect enough for her purposes, so she leaned in and opened her mouth. With her jaw straining, she wedged him between her lips and took him as deep as she could. When his crest hit the back of her throat, she hadn't even taken half of him on her tongue. How could she possibly shove all of him in her mouth?

Hector had liked it when she gagged. He'd taken particular delight in tying her hands behind her back and—

No. Now wasn't the time to think about that. She must focus on

Trees, on giving him pleasure. On stimulating him to climax so he slept through her escape.

Laila eased back, dragging her lips up his shaft, her hands following, before slipping down and sinking into a rhythm.

Impossibly, he got harder. And he moaned in his sleep, moving restlessly on the bed. Soon, his head twisted slowly from side to side, as if he was in sensual distress. His lids started jerking. What or who was he dreaming about? It didn't matter. She hoped he didn't wake until it was too late. If she was really lucky, he would never be aware she had sucked him off at all. He would simply fall into a deeper sleep and not open his eyes until morning. And she would be long gone.

But soon, her jaw protested. The discomfort forced her to lift up his shaft and focus on the head, licking and sucking the most sensitive spots. He moaned louder.

Once, she'd performed this act several times a day, especially if she wanted to eat. She was out of practice, yes. But this felt different. Of course, she'd never had a cock this large in her mouth. What made the experience truly unique was the fact Trees hadn't shoved her to her knees and yanked on her hair until her mouth opened with a gasp of pain, clearing the way for him to barge inside and fuck her face because her humiliation pleased him. He didn't try to choke or suffocate her. He didn't smell like sweat, desert, or another woman but like soap and man and the very trees from which he derived his name.

Suddenly he cupped her crown, urging her closer, before his fingers filtered through her hair. "Hmm…Laila."

She cut a startled stare to his face. But his eyes were still closed, his lids bobbing.

He was having an erotic dream? About her?

That didn't merely panic her. Oh, she felt the shaking anxiety. Her heart rate went jittery. But she also felt something warmer she couldn't explain. Maybe it had something to do with the sight of him spread out underneath her, all male and muscled and surprisingly nonthreatening.

He's asleep, you fool. As soon as he wakes up…

Laila didn't have to finish that thought. History told her what he would most likely do.

Time to redouble her efforts and make him climax quickly.

His free hand joined the first, this one sliding into her hair. He wrapped his fingers around her tresses and gave a gentle tug to pull her mouth off his penis. Then he nudged her back onto his erection with a tender suggestion from his fingers and moaned her name once more.

Another anxious glance at his face suggested he slept on. She could still get out undetected.

A terrified part of her wanted to defy his silent promptings and simply run away. But she'd learned to be pragmatic.

Laila gave in to the rhythm he set, closing her eyes, trying to separate her mind from her body and float away someplace else so she didn't have to be—yet again—giving a man pleasure at her own expense. Except…Trees's scent and gentle hands kept her in the here and now. The way he stroked her head. The way his moans sounded like praise. The way he rolled his hips under her, seemingly in thanks.

"Laila…" he whispered slow and soft.

Appreciation dripped from his sensual, sleepy groan. She wasn't eager to continue exactly, but for the first time, she didn't hate this act. A dangerous curiosity urged her on… She didn't feel like his victim but like a seductress working for her lover's pleasure.

That excited her. And it disturbed her, too.

Softly, she hummed. Victor had often demanded she do that because he liked the sensation. Trees also enjoyed it, if the low moan that suddenly tore from his throat was any indication.

Laila would have sworn it wasn't possible, but Trees got harder. His end must be near.

That realization was bittersweet. The fact she didn't loathe this act… It was a shock, a revelation. For the first time, she had some control over what happened between her and a man. She could exert her will, and he was merely along for the ride.

Oddly, it was…exciting.

She took more of him in her mouth, bobbing, sucking, swirling her tongue around him, experimenting to find what made him stiffen and moan. When his crest prodded the back of her throat, she paused. Victor and Hector had both demanded that she swallow on them.

Would that maneuver work on Trees? Would it be the thing that sent him into climax?

Laila dragged in a deep breath and worked her throat over him. He groaned again, this time louder, deeper. His hand tightened in her hair, and she braced for him to force her down onto his cock until she couldn't breathe. But he didn't. He merely urged her lower with a prod from his fingers and another lift of his hips. He was firm but not harsh. Urgent but not forceful.

She'd never experienced anything like this.

So she did it again.

Once more, a verbal growl of need tore from his throat. The subversive part of her was thrilled. Why? She was stimulating him in his sleep, against his will. If she enjoyed his reaction, did that make her any better than Victor and Hector?

Laila pushed the horrible question aside. She wasn't hurting Trees. And she wasn't taking him in her mouth for her own selfish pleasure. She would give him something he seemingly wanted. And in return, she would get something she needed. After all, everything came at a price. She'd learned that long ago. And she was merely paying up front for her freedom.

After she took another long draw on his steely staff, Trees's fingers tightened in her hair. To her shock, she didn't despise that, either, especially when his breaths turned choppy and his body went taut.

He was close.

Another deep plunge into her mouth while she worked him at the back of her throat ought to send him tumbling into ecstasy…then sleep.

But when she lowered herself onto his massive cock again and positioned him against her throat, he stiffened beneath her. And he called out her name. "Laila!"

She glanced up. His eyes were open and dilated—and fixed on her.

Chapter Six

Trees was awake. *Uh-oh.*

Laila froze. Anxiety seared her veins.

"What are you doing?" he asked through gritted teeth. Every muscle in his body shook and strained as he fought need.

Stop…or continue?

Her thoughts raced as breaths rushed in and out of her nose. Seconds ticked by. He tugged on her hair again, tight enough to take control. She was hyperaware of his touch, of the heaviness and masculine flavor of him on her tongue.

Laila didn't dare answer him truthfully. He would cuff her again. God knew what he'd do then. He might take advantage of her in ways that, despite the horror she'd endured, she had never experienced. Besides, she couldn't talk with her lips around him. She suspected he didn't want her to.

She closed her eyes and tried to lower her mouth on his length, but he held too tight for her to take in even another inch. So she wrapped her tongue around his shaft and slid up to bathe his engorged crest.

"Fuck…" He tossed his head back, his fingers tightening in her tresses. "Laila…"

"Let me give you pleasure," she murmured in her most seductive tone.

"I shouldn't."

"But you want this, yes?" She attempted to lower her lips on him again.

Trees stopped her, closing her mouth with a thumb beneath her chin. "More importantly, is this what *you* want?"

She nodded, giving him her softest, most suggestive doe eyes. Then she pursed her lips, which must be swollen after having him in her mouth. Men didn't usually need more encouragement.

His stare followed her gesture, but beyond his tight expression and choppy breaths, she couldn't gauge his reaction. That meant he was thinking.

That was bad.

Suddenly, Trees rolled her to her back and followed, hovering above her and pinning her down, thankfully without settling his weight on her. "Why? You've been terrified of me since we met."

"You have shown you will not hurt me." She arched her breasts at him enticingly. "I want to know what you feel like."

He searched her face. Then his gaze fell, fixating on her nipples. The buds felt hard. Tight. Blood scorched her veins and pooled where she began to ache. Because she feared him? Or for some other reason?

"It's not smart, Laila."

"I will feel safer with you..."

His eyes narrowed. "Will you? Really?"

Over the years she had learned ways to allay a man's suspicions. She sent flirtatious glances and fluttered her lashes. She licked her lips. She smiled invitingly. "Of course."

"I'm calling bullshit."

She tried not to panic. "Truly. You are not like any man I have known."

That was not a lie.

"Am I supposed to be happy you've decided I'm one step above a rapist?"

"Many more." She caressed up the rigid bulges of his biceps to his granite shoulders.

At least he had tried to be. It wasn't his fault she wasn't interested in his kindness since it surely came with strings.

"That doesn't mean you have to blow me, Laila."

"I want to make you feel good. You liked it, yes?"

He scoffed. "You know the answer."

"Then let me finish. Roll onto your back, close your eyes, and feel what I can do for you."

When she tried to wriggle out from under his body, Trees refused to budge. "No. I'm betting too many men in your past have used you like that. I won't."

Carajo, she must be more persuasive. Otherwise, he would likely roll away and fall into another fitful sleep. Or worse, leave the bed and wait to see what she was up to.

Laila pressed a seductive kiss to his steely shoulder. The unexpected softness of his inked skin over hard muscle made her horribly aware of his masculinity and power. "You are not like them. You seem…nice."

That wasn't a lie, either. In her brother-in-law's compound, Laila had known men with machismo, who had done unspeakably cruel things merely to prove they were "man enough" to be an asset to the cartel. But Trees seemed too sure of himself to bother with that.

"I'm trying, but you're making it difficult." He shook his head in the shadows. "Fuck it. I'm probably going to hell, anyway. If you really want this, we're doing it my way."

Her heart skittered. What did that mean?

"Do you hear me, Laila? Or we don't do this at all."

Just this once, she could give him what he sought. She could close her eyes, pretend she was elsewhere while he took whatever parts of her he desired. If he chose to fuck her, it might hurt since no man had penetrated her in months. But after he was done, the pain would subside. And intercourse shouldn't last long. She had sucked him close to orgasm. A little stimulation, a few pumps of his hips, a couple of grunts, and it would likely be over.

"All right." Her voice trembled.

Trees cupped her cheek. "I'll make you feel good, little one. I promise."

Impossible. Not that it mattered. But somehow his hushed vow made her dizzy and hot.

"Hurry." She managed to sound as if she was begging.

In a way she was. Her unexpected reaction to him aside, the later the hour grew, the less likely nearby campers would be awake to help her find a ride to Louisiana.

Trees shook his head. "I'm going to take my time with you. I don't think any man has ever savored you, and you deserve all the pleasure imaginable."

Then Trees did something no man had ever done. He lowered his head, laid his mouth over hers, and he kissed her.

Laila froze. Despite being a giant of a man, he brushed his lips over hers softly. Shock and heat flared inside her. He lingered, his warm breath on her face…then he was gone before she was ready for the kiss to end.

Trees cupped her face, skimming his thumb over her lips. "You okay?"

Why did he ask? Why did he care? "Yes."

"Good. I'm going to kiss you again. Breathe. Relax."

How, when her lips burned? When she was naked and acutely aware of the damp crush of his bare skin against hers?

"Laila, did you hear me?"

"Y-yes." She didn't trust herself to say more.

"Close your eyes," he instructed in that velvety voice that compelled her to comply. "Good. Now breathe in deep." When she did, he glided a gentle thumb over her cheek in silent approval. "Let it out."

As she exhaled, tension began to leave her body.

"Again," he prompted. "Do it slowly. Focus on my voice."

She did, feeling even more at ease. Then she blinked up at him. For approval, she realized the moment he smiled her way.

"Beautiful. Now I'm going to kiss you. And this time, I'm going to kiss you right."

He'd done it wrong before? Too bad. She'd liked it. His lips against hers had been…sweet.

As a girl, she'd known school friends who had crushes on boys. They had all giggled and whispered about their first kisses the summer she'd turned fourteen. She had been fascinated, even a little jealous, not to have captured any boy's notice. She'd been so curious to know what kissing felt like. Not long after that, she'd become horribly aware of men's desires, thanks to life in her brother-in-law's compound. Then she'd no longer cared that she had never been kissed.

But as with everything else, Trees seemed different.

"Is that all right?"

He was asking permission to touch her? Laila frowned. As if she could stop him.

Still, if real kissing—whatever that was—would excite him enough to demand a blow job, then her purpose would be served. She could escape afterward.

"Fine."

"I won't hurt you," he assured. "If anything I do scares or upsets you, just say *red*."

"You will stop touching me if I say that word?"

"Absolutely. Immediately."

He was lying. There was no way she could utter a simple word and he would cease taking his pleasure. That would be giving her all the power, all the choice. No man would ever do that. After all, what would be in it for him?

"Why?" she asked skeptically.

"Because we'll need to talk so I can understand what upset you."

So he could do it again? So he could do it harder? More painfully? More degradingly? Was that his game?

The tenderness in his eyes made her wonder if she was wrong. But her head—and her experience—said otherwise. Laila didn't dare show weakness. The word *red* could never cross her lips. "Okay. Kiss me."

As he settled his weight onto her, his stare never wavered, seemingly penetrating all the way down to her thoughts. Laila's breath caught. Her heart thudded. She felt shaky…and it wasn't fear. A nervous excitement she didn't understand made her tremble.

As he drew closer, Trees's approaching heat and his warm breath against her lips had her eyes sliding shut. Instantly, the dark made her feel too vulnerable. She squirmed, eyes flaring wide again.

"It's okay. I won't hurt you."

If he did, he wouldn't be the first. She would be fine once she reached Valeria and Jorge. But to get there, she had to give in and let Trees take over.

Laila closed her eyes again.

"Good girl." His mouth settled over hers, perching there as if gauging her reaction.

She held her breath. Tension gripped her. Would he stay here until her thundering heart beat out of her chest? Or attack her when her guard was down?

Trees did neither. He cupped her face and nudged her mouth open, drawing her bottom lip between his for a soft, shocking moment. Her skin sizzled as he sank deeper, stealing her thoughts, her breath, and her reluctance. She got lost in the dizzying sensation.

Before she realized it, she fell into his rhythm, opening beneath him to invite him inside.

Clearly, he knew what he was doing. She was panting when he pulled away to search her face.

"Laila?"

She couldn't look away. The moment felt terribly intimate. She was stunned to realize how much she liked his kiss. What was he doing to her? "Yes?"

The question was lost when he covered her lips again, this time urging them even wider. His tongue slipped inside and caressed hers. She recoiled against the new sensation, but he stayed patient and firm, cupping her nape and plunging in again. She couldn't avoid him, so she yielded, giving him free rein of her mouth until lightning—unlike anything she'd ever felt or imagined—flared through her veins.

The moment she moaned and surrendered, he wielded his power like a king. He ruled over her blossoming pleasure, using it ruthlessly to sweep through her mouth and take every inch, as if proclaiming that—at least in this moment—she was his to touch and please as he wished.

Dazed, she curled her arms around his neck as she tilted her head and yielded to him. He continued his siege, sweeping one hand down her rib cage, dipping in at her waist, before cupping her hip with a groan. "Laila…"

His whisper swept through her, blanketing her skin with goose bumps and tightening her belly with heat. If he was the king, why did he sound as if he worshipped her? It confused her, just like her desire for more of his touch.

"Want me to stop?"

Her body answered for her. "No."

After his slow smile, he didn't bother with words or a soft brush of lips. He seized her mouth again, thrusting in and overwhelming her. A fresh surge of desire left her feeling flushed and overheated as sensation spread through her body. Her nipples hardened to painful points.

The place between her legs began to ache. She felt a dangerous urge to open herself and welcome Trees inside her.

His other hand drifted down her body in a slow glide of fingertips that left her gasping. As he settled both on her thighs and spread them apart, she shuddered, her heart beating so rapidly she could hear the roar in her ears.

His hips sank between her parted legs. He nudged his erection against her sex.

Instantly, cold iced all the hot aches in her body. Every muscle tensed, preparing for the imminent, painful invasion of his massive penis.

You can endure this. Focus on Valeria and Jorge.

"Relax," Trees murmured as he glided his lips across her jaw and down her throat. "I won't do anything you're not ready for. Let me explore you, little one."

He proved again he was a man of his word when he skimmed her collarbones with his lips, then dropped lower with a soft drag of sweet, gumdrop kisses. Against her better judgment, Laila softened—until he approached her breasts.

She'd been groped, pinched, fondled, and squeezed against her will in the past more times than she could count. Hector had always called himself a "boob man" and had been seemingly fascinated with hers, often tweaking them until she cried.

But Trees proved himself different once more. He cradled one in his palm so gently she almost wondered if she'd imagined it. Then his thumb brushed over the distended tip. Laila gasped at the shocking new sensations skittering through her.

"You're so beautiful," he breathed against the hard crest. "I dreamed of you."

Though she'd known that on some level, she still trembled. "Why?"

"Everything about you makes me ache to touch you."

"And now you are."

"But I need to protect you, too."

"That is your job."

Softly, he shook his head as his lips caressed the side of her breast. "Not because I'm paid to, Laila. Because the man in me..."

He stopped himself from finishing that sentence. His silence unsettled her. What had he intended to say? That he felt sorry for her because she had been treated badly in the past? That he saw her as too weak to protect herself? "What?"

Trees stared, his gaze so piercing, so achingly personal, she felt penetrated without him even entering her. "Let's just say I don't want anything to happen to you for reasons that have nothing to do with EM Security."

What did that mean?

Before she could puzzle it out, Trees skimmed his lips up the side of her breast again, this time dangerously close to her throbbing nipple. Her thoughts evaporated. Against her will, she arched up, offering herself for his mouth.

Why? That usually brought teeth, biting. Pain. Had she lost her mind?

But Trees merely lapped at her hard bud with his soft tongue. His deep rumble of approval reignited her.

Laila met his stare, hot and dark and demanding. With their gazes fused, he enveloped her nipple in his mouth, closing his lips around the sensitive bud and sucking deep.

The pull jolted clear through her body. Her sex clenched. Her womb cramped. She whimpered as fire spread across her skin.

"Does that feel good?"

Lying never crossed her mind. "Yesss…"

The syllable had barely left her lips before he enveloped her tender bud again and sucked with a sensual pull that shook her to the core. Her other breast tightened with need. The tip—harder than ever—throbbed. She wanted his touch.

"Trees…" The plea slipped out. Before she realized it, she arched up in need.

"I'm here, little one. Just feel." He both soothed and aroused her by cupping her neglected breast, his thumb brushing the painfully taut tip.

A new wave of heat crashed over her. She hissed and grabbed his shoulders, her eyes sliding shut, her head falling back. She couldn't fight the urge to spread her legs even wider to him.

What was happening? What was he doing to her? Was she feeling the desire she'd seen in telenovelas and movies, the kind she'd always believed was fiction?

"That's it. That's my girl..." His voice, low and full of approval, filled her with an even more dangerous pleasure.

He sucked her aching nipple into his mouth once more while stroking the other. Laila hissed, unable to stop surrendering to the sensations. It was as if he controlled her body—and her mind. Despite being naked, she wished she could bare herself to him more. She ached to be closer, though he was already on top of her, pressed against her from shoulders to thighs. Laila settled for kissing his temple, wrapping her arms around him tightly, and lifting to him, desperate to erase what little space remained between them.

"I can't keep my mouth off of you. You're even sweeter than I thought." He devoured her with another hot sweep of his lips.

She savored the masculine flavor of his kiss as he gripped her hip with one hand and wrapped her hair in his fist with the other. Though his big body pressed her into the mattress, holding her exactly where he wanted her, she didn't feel trapped, just pleasured.

When he finally tore away, panting, he looked down her body, his eyes turning even darker. "I'm definitely going to hell."

His words had barely registered before he was on her breasts again—thumbing, rubbing, laving, inhaling. Her thoughts faded as he touched the desperate points, sucking them, nipping them until she moaned and melted.

His hands roamed the rest of her—torso, hips, thighs, backside—stroking, squeezing, and surveying as his mouth left her nipples, continuing down to her abdomen to explore her navel. He dragged his tongue over her skin and muttered growled words she couldn't hear over the roaring of her heart.

Soon he would mount her and push inside her. He probably wouldn't mean to hurt her. He might even care if he did. But he was a man; that wouldn't stop him.

Laila fought disappointment and told herself to be practical. Experiencing tingles and heady aches weren't the reason she was in bed with this man. Neither were goose bumps and racing blood.

She was in his bed to get him off so he would fall asleep, nothing more.

Spreading her legs wider, she lifted her hips to encourage him. Instead of impaling her, he continued down the bed, down her body, inching and kissing a little at a time until his mouth loomed over her *there*.

Laila blinked at him, wide-eyed, her heart suddenly zipping harder and faster than ever. He raised a brow, his blunt gaze scorching her. She held her breath.

Surely he wouldn't kiss her in that most forbidden place. Did men do that?

In the near dark, his eyes glowed hot with desire as he caressed her thighs, working his fingers under her knees and spreading her wider. "Laila? Honey…"

His deep-voiced entreaty made her whimper. Was he asking her permission?

"Do you want this?" He skimmed a pair of fingers over her swollen, shockingly slick flesh, igniting nerve endings she'd never known existed.

"Want what?" she panted.

"For me to taste you. Let me." His voice dropped another octave to a dark, compelling rumble as he raked a finger between her folds. Then he sucked the dripping digit into his mouth with a groan.

She shivered. Would he really do it? What would that feel like?

"If you wish." She worked to keep the whine out of her voice and not sound as if she was begging.

"Oh, I do. I'm going to make sure you love every minute of it." He lowered his head and dragged his tongue between her folds with a low groan, licking the most sensitive place between her legs as if she were a tasty treat.

Sensation stunned Laila. She shuddered and panted out a hard breath.

Dios mío! "What are you doing?"

Trees parted her wide with his thumbs and raked his tongue through her furrow with more gusto, nearly melting her into the mattress. "Enjoying the hell out of you. Does it hurt?"

He could ask that question with a straight face? "No."

"Good." Trees lapped at her again, then dragged her hard nubbin between his lips and sucked.

Blood and ache surged between her legs. Heat jolted through her body as her nipples stabbed the air. Laila struggled to breathe—and she no longer cared if he knew it.

"Are you uncomfortable?"

Only with the fact that his every touch thrilled her. "No."

"Glad to hear it." He flicked at her bud, tonguing the very tip before wrapping his lips around it and drawing it into the heat of his mouth again.

Her tingles didn't merely grow; they multiplied. Dizziness made her head float. Or was that her heavy breathing she couldn't seem to control? What was happening to her?

"Do you want me to stop?"

She should. But need crashed through her system and shut down her brain. It might be foolish and wrong, but she craved more.

"No. Please…"

With growled approval, he bent to her again. If he'd been taking her in one slow suckle at a time before, now he consumed her, opening his mouth over her sex as if to kiss her the way he'd seized her mouth. Sensations brimmed and roiled. She twisted and cried out, stunned and shocked and on fire. Something inside her was building.

He added to the sensations by working one of his big fingers inside her. It slid in with astonishing ease. No pain. No force necessary. She was wet—something she had never been in her life. His mouth wasn't the only cause.

"Trees…" Before she realized it, she'd moaned his name, plunged her fingers in his thick hair, and urged his face deeper onto her sex.

"Yes. That's it. God, you're sweet, little one. Fuck. Come on my tongue."

How? In her experience, orgasm was for men, but TV and films suggested otherwise. Maybe it was possible for her to cry out and gush with pleasure. The more he ate at her with his mouth, the more she felt that something inside her cresting.

If she climaxed, would she fall asleep afterward? Was that why he was heaping pleasure on her?

She couldn't let that happen. She had to reach her sister.

"No…" Laila meant her denial to be forceful.

"Yes. I want you to." The flat of his tongue stroked her sensitive bud again, swiping, flicking, teasing. He slipped another finger into her and twisted his hand to rub a spot that had her crying out for more. "Do it for me."

The rumbling timbre of his command sizzled through her, unbearably seductive. In that moment, she ached to comply.

"You can do it. Be my good girl. Come right here…" He stuck out his tongue, then marked the spot by manipulating her rigid bud back and forth, unrelentingly, unceasingly, his burning stare demanding everything from her.

She couldn't refuse.

Moments melted away with the sawing of her breath and the gonging of her heart. Under the onslaught of his tongue, it didn't matter why she was here, where she was going, or what she had planned. All she knew was the tension coiling and building in her body—gathering, swirling, tightening—and the man arousing it all.

"Yes!" She clutched the sheets and writhed, digging her heels into the mattress, unable to stop herself.

He groaned against her throbbing flesh and shoved another finger deep, sweeping the tips over a tingling spot high and inside her. Together with the vibrations from his mouth, he unleashed a firestorm of need. Where he penetrated her, Laila burned. The conflagration of pleasure threatened to roast her alive.

"Now." His command reached inside her and ripped away the last of her worries, questions, and restraint.

Her blood pooled and thickened. Her nipples puckered. Her legs went stiff. The tension between her thighs threatened to split her in two—and she didn't care anymore.

Her hips moved against him. She heard a whining sound in her ears, then realized that was her begging. The coming cataclysm was going to be dreadful and wonderful, and it might kill her.

Laila no longer cared.

Her heart banged against her chest as the churning sensations converged and melded. She thrashed and twisted, holding her breath, suspended in an impossible moment of rising pleasure-pain.

Then she exploded in a burning rush.

Laila grabbed his hair, her legs tightening around his shoulders, as she screamed in a voice high and dying with need. "Trees!"

Laila came like a woman discovering pleasure for the first time. Nothing turned Trees on more. She writhed and keened through an orgasm that jolted her whole body. He kept at her slick, swollen pussy, laving, licking, and heaping all the sensation on her he could, as if it was his biological imperative.

Because it was.

From the moment he'd set eyes on her, he'd ached to make her his. Might as well stop bullshitting himself. Sure, he'd fought the feeling because she was a client and supposed to be off-limits. And her fear of him had been palpable. None of that had stopped him from watching her every move. Listening to her every word. Guessing her every thought. Wanting her with every breath.

Once she'd touched him, resisting was impossible.

Now she dripped on his tongue, and the reality of having her under him, bucking for him while screaming his name in ecstasy, was way better than his fantasies.

Trees clutched her thighs and ate at her with unabashed zeal, dry humping the mattress like a teenager desperate for his first lay. Laila did that to him. She was beyond beautiful. She was everything.

Finally, her high-pitched shriek of excitement—one every person in a two-mile radius had likely heard—dwindled to soft moans, then the occasional cry. Whimpers followed before she twisted and tried to close her legs.

Too sensitive. Right.

Trees knew that in his head and tried to back off, but…she tasted so sweet and he craved more.

His brain had gotten the memo. His libido didn't give a shit. That part of him had zero intention of letting her go.

Sliding his way up Laila's body and taking her in his arms, he stared down at her flushed cheeks and parted lips, drinking in her panting breaths. She lifted her heavy lids and stared back. God, she took his breath away.

"Has that ever happened to you before?"

She looked away self-consciously. "A man putting his mouth on my… No."

Trees cupped her face and coaxed her stare back to him. "I meant orgasm. Ever had one?"

"No. Before you, I had never even been kissed."

Oh, Jesus. He'd been the first? How the fuck was that possible?

He scrubbed a hand down his face. Had he misunderstood her? "Laila, are you a virgin?"

She sent him a bitter laugh. "Not for many years."

How many? She couldn't be more than twenty-two. Fuck, he felt lecherous, wanting a woman who was more than a dozen years younger. But everything in his gut told him he could do more than keep her safe. He could make her happy, too. And damn if she didn't feel like his missing half.

Slow down, buddy. You barely know her.

Besides, what Laila had inadvertently divulged confirmed some ugly math. Never been kissed plus not a virgin, multiplied by orgasm deficit, divided by afraid of men equaled she'd been raped, probably by someone in Emilo Montilla's cartel. His money was on Hector and Victor Ramos.

Suddenly, Trees itched to go on a killing spree.

But Laila, looking defiant even as she tried to make herself seem small, needed him more.

"I'm sorry, little one. I'll never hurt you. Ever." He pressed a tender kiss to her forehead, drinking in her warmth and the hint of perspiration sheening her skin. "I meant what I said earlier."

She frowned in confusion.

"All you have to do is say *red,*" he reminded her. "I'll stop whatever I'm doing."

Her frown deepened. "Why?"

There were a lot of ways to interpret her question, but she didn't know or care about the Dominant code of conduct. She probably didn't believe that there were men who would never take pleasure in forcing a woman against her will.

He settled for the simplest answer. "I want you to feel safe with me. You should know that you have the ultimate power between us. If anything hurts, upsets, or scares you, tell me. There won't be any judgment, blame, coercion, or belittling. We'll stop. We'll talk. We'll work it out."

She traced a finger up his arm and licked her lips. "What if I want you to make me feel good again?"

Trees's heart jumped into his throat as he started to shimmy back down the bed. "I'm more than happy to. Spread your legs and—"

"That is not what I meant." She hesitated, biting her lip nervously. "Can you make me feel like that if you are inside me?"

Oh, hell yeah, he could. But short-term gratification—as much as he wanted it—wasn't the point. "Are you sure you're ready for that? I can be patient. I can love your body in a million other ways. We don't have to…"

"Fuck? I want to, if you can make me feel good again."

He fucking wanted it, too, but… "I can. I just don't want to rush you."

"Why wait?" She pressed kisses along his jaw, then drifted down his neck. "In a few minutes, you gave me more pleasure than I have ever known. I could be afraid of all that has happened to me, but if I let fear control me, they win."

Trees couldn't fault her logic. She hadn't mentioned any emotional attachment to him, but that didn't worry him yet. She had no idea he was already half in love with her. And after everything she had been through, did she even know what she was feeling, except the urge to be brave and accept her desires?

That was fine. He could work with it.

"Then we'll make sure they lose. What's the word to say if you need to stop me?"

"Red."

"Yep. Anything you know you don't like? Don't want?" *Anything guaranteed to fuck with your head?*

She bit her swollen lip, then brushed a stray strand of damp hair from her temple. "Do not hit me."

Trees swallowed back his anger to clarify. "Define hit. Spanking your butt?"

"As if I am a child?" She scowled, shaking her head as if she'd never heard of such a thing. "No. With your fist. To my face."

That was it. He was definitely going to kill some motherfuckers the second he got a chance. All she had to do was point them out, and he would end them—preferably with his bare hands so he could both feel it and ensure he inflicted maximum pain.

She recoiled. "If that request makes you angry—"

"No." Was she saying she'd let him hit her? "I'm not mad at you, little one." He forced his expression to soften and cupped her cheek. "I'm furious anyone would treat you with force and violence. But you have nothing to worry about from me. I only want to please you."

That wasn't totally true. He also wanted to protect her and avenge her. He wanted to love her, own her, and dominate her, too. God, she'd look beautiful in nothing but sheer lace and his collar. But he was getting *way* ahead of himself...

"Then I want you inside me now," she whispered.

Laila was unexpectedly blunt, and his aching cock didn't mind at all. "I'm happy to oblige."

Beneath him, she smiled and spread her legs.

Then something damn inconvenient occurred to him. "I don't have any condoms."

"The doctor in Florida tested me. I do not have any disease."

Her indignation was cute. "I don't, either. But you could get pregnant."

The image of her swelling and ripe with their baby made his desire claw at the door of its cage, determined to be set free. He didn't dare.

She shook her head. "My sister and I have had shots."

"For birth control?"

"Yes."

"Why?" If Laila was no longer being held hostage by her rapists and she had never taken a lover voluntarily, it didn't make sense.

"Valeria thought it was a good idea to maintain such things in case Emilo ever found us."

And they got dragged back to be abused again. *Fuck.*

"Your sister was thinking ahead."

"Yes." But now that they'd agreed to have sex and put the business end of the details to rest, she looked nervous again.

"Laila?"

She blinked. "I-I have never done this because I wanted to, only because a man demanded it."

And she didn't know how to act or what to do. He hurt like hell for her. She'd endured so much. Trees vowed to give her nothing but the utmost pleasure.

"We don't have to rush. I'll kiss you for a while and if you still want this and you feel ready—"

"No. I do not want to wait."

Because she had worked up the courage to have sex with him? Trees would like this loads better if she wanted it because she wanted him. But if he made her feel good, that would hopefully come. Maybe her feelings would, too.

He'd never expected to fall for a client, and the bosses were going to have his ass. But he didn't give a shit. Yeah, he might lose his job, but his sweet Laila had been through so much adversity, fighting for survival alone. She needed someone willing to fight for her, to take care of her, no matter what.

She needed him.

He cupped her face. "You're sure?"

"Yes." She surprised him by raising her head, slanting her lips under his, opening to him softly, and inviting him inside.

The kiss jolted him. Their connection kicked him. The rightness of it nearly bowled him over.

He didn't feel this way just because she was beautiful. He'd known beautiful women all over the world. It wasn't just because he ached to protect her. He'd protected the vulnerable for half his life. It was Laila herself. Her will was so strong, but her fragility underneath kindled every one of his protective instincts. Tonight, she had finally begun letting go of her wariness and suspicion and opening herself to him. He knew that because when he'd set his mouth on her, when she had been moments from orgasm, he'd felt her total and utter surrender.

Coaxing Laila, winning her trust slowly but inexorably... That fucking did something to him. So did knowing he'd been the first man to kiss her, the first man to make her come. Now he ached to give her first consensual sexual experience and make damn sure she enjoyed it enough to come back for seconds. For thirds. For more. Forever. So he would be the first—and last—man to win her heart.

Stop getting ahead of yourself, buddy...

Reluctantly, he ended the kiss. "Am I crushing you?"

"No."

"Would you feel more comfortable on top?"

"Of you?" She frowned. "I have never done that. How would that make me more comfortable?"

By Laila's own admission, she was no virgin, but in some ways she was sweetly naive. "Would you feel more if you were in control?"

Understanding dawned on her face, but she shrugged. "I do not know. What do you prefer?"

Obviously, she hadn't caught on to the fact he liked to be in charge, but he could pause that until Laila relaxed. "My goal is to give you what you need, little one. What would make you happy?"

"I have never met a man who asked questions before sex."

She'd also never been in bed with one who hadn't raped her. But they could talk in circles for hours. The truth was, Laila didn't know what she wanted in a lover because she'd never had one. He was accustomed to being in control, and it was his responsibility to give her what she needed. The anxiety plaguing her since he'd picked her up in Florida had only quieted when he'd inundated her with pleasure. So as far as he could tell, she needed more orgasms.

He was damn happy to provide them.

"Then I'll stop asking, but I expect you to tell me how everything I do to you feels. If you don't like it, I want to know. If you do, I want to hear you scream."

Laila nodded. "All right."

Not exactly a *yes, sir,* but someday he swore she would say those words to him.

But they were done talking for now. And the longer he stared, drinking her in, the more nervous she got. Time to dismantle her jitters so he could give her what she needed.

Trees took her mouth again, softly at first. She parted her lips, instantly yielding her mouth to him. She tasted like the spices from dinner and something addictively sweet. He chased her flavor, wanting more on his tongue as she wrapped hers around him, her legs around him, and gave herself over to him.

Their kiss went from exploratory to hot with a single beat of his heart. He slanted his lips over hers and delved deeper, gripping her hips to hold on as his desire rose hot and fast. Under him, she moaned. Then she began shifting restlessly beneath him—slowly at first. But with every sweep of his tongue and every caress of his hand, she shifted more, lifted, rolled, and arched in whimpered invitation.

Fuck, she was torching his self-control.

Thankfully, she seemed equally affected, clinging to him with needy fingers and locking them behind his neck as she gasped into their next kiss, spreading her legs wider for him. He tore away from her mouth long enough to see her dilated eyes, heavy lids, and flushed cheeks. She struggled for air, for understanding. For pleasure.

Trees didn't have to ask if she was aroused. He just hoped like fuck that penetrating Laila wouldn't cause her pain.

Tucking her knees into the crooks of his elbows, he prodded until his cock aligned against her slick, swollen flesh. "Are you ready, little one?"

Mentally? Physically, he knew she was.

"Yes," she breathed, her lids floating shut. Then she kissed her way across his jaw, pressing her lips to his ear. "I have never felt this way. Please…"

Why the hell would he ever resist that?

Slowly, he pushed forward, inching his way in. She closed around him like hot, tight silk. Her body gripped the head of his cock, twitching around him as if she sought to suck him deeper. Already she felt so epic his head began to spin.

He drove down another couple of inches. She tightened and gasped before breathing out in long, ragged pleasure while she squeezed him like a vise.

Holy shit.

He withdrew until the head of his cock barely kissed her opening, then he surged inside her, driving down until he met gentle resistance and he shuddered in a shocking flash of desire.

She was fucking going to burn him alive.

"Feel good, honey?"

Laila blinked up at him, soft, confused eyes framed by thick black lashes. She exhaled and all but melted against him. "Yes."

That fact surprised her. She didn't understand why she liked his touch. He'd bet her head tried to intrude on the instinctive pleasure her body was feeling, telling her to be afraid. Telling her to fight.

Trees wasn't letting that shit come between them. "Good. I won't do anything to your body that you don't love. Feel my touch, focus on my voice. Give in to the need."

She nodded, head bobbing slowly, as he packed another inch inside her so-tight pussy.

Again, Laila clenched. She dug her nails into his back. Her thighs tensed. But her expression—eyes sliding shut, mouth gaping open—was full of rapture.

He was already big and tall, but her reaction made him feel like a giant, like he was on top of the world.

Trees trailed kisses across her temple, to her ear where he nipped on her lobe. "You're so tight around me. It's heaven. I wanted you the moment I laid eyes on you, but this blows my fantasies away."

Her breathing picked up pace. "More."

In good time. "I don't want to go too fast. I don't want to hurt you."

She shook her head. "Please..."

With Laila begging, she was fucking impossible to resist. He wanted to be buried inside her, balls deep, now. Hell, he'd wanted that days ago. But she probably hadn't been touched in months, and there was no way he would plow inside her like an insensitive asshole when she was feeling pleasure for the first time in her life.

"In good time. I want this to be good for you."

Laila nodded but let out a whine of protest as she planted her feet on the mattress and lifted her hips, impaling herself with more of his inches.

"Jesus!" He dragged air in, starting to sweat as sensation tingled its way through his body and slammed down his spine.

She tossed her head back, body twisting, and gripped his shoulders. "More…"

He definitely had more to give Laila, lots more—inches, pleasure, and love.

Gripping her hips, he pulled back, again nearly withdrawing, then plunged forward with gritted teeth, a bellow of a groan, and a blindingly insistent urge to bury himself completely inside her—something he could rarely do with any woman, given his size.

Her back arched. She cried out, nails digging into him, as pure ecstasy softened her face.

It spurred him on, driving him to dangerous places. He needed to stop here. Give her the orgasms she'd asked for and play it safe. The risk of hurting her was too great.

But damn it if he wasn't dying to bury every inch he had inside her until she screamed from being packed so full. Then he'd take her over the edge with stroke after hard, driving stroke.

Telling himself to dial it the fuck down, he reached between them and dragged his thumb over her clit. It was slick and hard as stone. At his first brush, she gasped. Her body jolted. Her cunt clamped hard on him.

"You like that?"

She nodded. "What is happening?"

"Orgasm, little one. It's coming."

He could see it gathering inside her with the flush blooming across her chest, reddening her cheeks. Even her lips had gone full and red. Her nipples were like diamonds raking his chest. When she looked up at him again with a plea in her wide, glazed eyes, he felt her need in every cell of his body.

So, so close… He rubbed her clit again, starting a steady, demanding rhythm that matched his tempoed strokes.

She tensed, tossed her head back again, and cried out. "Trees…"

Yes. He was on fire for her, and it took everything he had not to shove deeper and bury himself to the hilt. But she was so close. No way he would risk that by hurting her, especially since submerging every inch in her sweltering clasp would set him off. He would come instead of ramping her up and pleasuring her again for the sheer joy of watching her unravel and knowing he'd done that to her.

"Ride it, honey. Feel the edge."

"It burns…" she gasped. "I feel blood rushing down, between…"

"Your legs?" He pumped her faster. "Filling your pussy like I am?"

"I cannot stop it."

"Just let it happen. Come for me."

She lifted her gaze to him, looking almost panicked. Her nails bit into his flesh as he pushed into her again, and her whole body went rigid. Pleasure flared across her face as she tightened on him, squeezing relentlessly. Then she wailed, her body thrashing, her hips rising, her legs curling around him as she pulled him in, closer, coaxing him deeper.

At her silent demand for more, Trees lost control, scooping her up in his grip, planting his knees on the mattress, and hurtling his way home—to the hilt—with one desperate stroke.

She took all of him, her orgasm seeming to rocket up to another level and sending her over an even higher cliff as she croaked out in agonized pleasure. "Trees!"

He roared into her over and over, pounding deep, until he lost everything—his restraint, his load, and his heart—pouring them all into her and never looking back.

His head swam and his vision went dark. The moment vibrated with the kind of ecstasy he'd never even fucking imagined.

What the hell had just happened?

Finally, he opened his eyes. His heart chugged like a runaway train. His breaths sawed in and out of his chest. He was still clutching her hips like his life depended on it, every inch of his cock shoved deep inside her.

Oh, fuck.

"Laila."

She blinked, looking shell-shocked and frozen. Oh, Jesus. Oh, fuck. What the hell had he done?

He'd lost control, and he deserved every curse she hurled at his head and every shred of fury she would most likely unload on him.

"Little one, I'm so sorry. I never meant to..."

Tears leaked from her eyes, trailing down her temples and disappearing into her hairline. They were like twin stabs to his heart.

Goddamn motherfucking son of a bitch.

Thirty minutes ago, he'd wanted to kill every man who had ever hurt her, but in the heat of pleasure, he'd buckled and wounded her, too. The fact he hadn't intended to didn't mean jack shit.

He wanted to touch her—softly, gently. Swear on a stack of Bibles that he would never cause her an ounce of pain again if she would just...what, trust him? Yeah, he'd fucked that up. He would be damn lucky if she ever spoke to him again. There was no way she would ever let him near her.

And he didn't blame her one bit.

Trees wiped her tears away with a gentle touch. When she flinched, it felt like she'd sliced his heart in half.

Slowly, praying like fuck he didn't hurt her more, he began to withdraw.

He was stunned when her arms and legs tightened around him as if she didn't want to let go.

"Honey?" He brushed a curl from her hot cheek. "What do you need? What can I do?"

She gaped. "What happened? I did not know..."

How deep he would plow her? How bad it would hurt? How much she would regret her decision to trust him? "What?"

"My body would respond in such a way. I have never felt anything like that. I..."

Wait? She wasn't hurt but shocked? "Didn't anticipate being able to climax with me inside you?"

"Yes. Earlier, when you..." Fresh red bloomed across her cheeks.

After what they'd just shared, she was embarrassed? "Licked your pussy?"

With downcast eyes, she nodded. "The pleasure I felt then did not surprise me. No man had ever done that to me, so had I nothing to compare it to. But when you fucked me—"

"I did more than fuck you, Laila." At least he'd meant to. "I was trying to show you"—*how I feel about you*—"that sex isn't about force but feeling good. Instead, I'm worried I hurt you more."

"I will be sore tomorrow."

That was a given. "I know. I'm sorry. So fucking sorry."

"It was not pain you made me feel." She sent him a crooked, coy smile.

"It wasn't?"

She shook her head, then stifled a heavy-lidded yawn. Trees tried to do the same. He was so damn tired after days without a full night's sleep, and the monster orgasm had nearly done him in.

"Don't do that," he scolded, unable to hold back his yawn.

Laila laughed, the sound so light and feminine, even full of joy. She liked him teasing her?

"Sorry. I will try—"

But it didn't work. She covered her mouth with her hand, but not before he saw her lips widen in another signal of exhaustion.

He laughed back. "So much for that."

She giggled in return.

The moment felt so sweet. Trees held her closer. He knew he needed to leave the softening clasp of her body and help her clean up so they could both have a good night's sleep, but he was reluctant to let her go. This playful moment aside, would she ever want or trust him enough again to let him love her?

Eventually, yes. He had to believe that. Something different had passed between them tonight—something he'd never felt. Their connection had been forged in passion, but it hadn't ended with their mutual climax. Usually, he showered a woman in aftercare. Once he knew she was sated and settled, he zipped up and beat feet. He never lingered.

Laila was different. He didn't want to leave—her body, their bed, this moment. Instead, he dipped his head to take her lips again. She met him with a soft, sweet kiss of her own.

Too soon, she pulled back. "Trees?"

"What is it, little one?"

"Did you enjoy sex with me?"

She was kidding, right? "Absolutely. That was…" Epic. Amazing. Earth-shattering. Angels had sung. His world had been rocked. "Great. Did you?"

Shyly, she nodded. "More than I thought possible. More than I ever have."

"I only ever want to keep you safe and make you feel good, Laila."

She gave him another encouraging smile. "Do you want me to be happy, too?"

Trees could think of very few people on this planet who weren't worthy of happiness, but Laila especially was. She'd been through hell, and she deserved a future that made up for all she'd endured.

He'd love to be the man to give that to her. He could picture them now, together on his property, hoping for the best future, preparing for the worst, and growing the next generation.

Really, you've got to slow down, buddy…

"Of course I do."

Her smile turned brighter, her pouty, built-for-sex lips curling up until her face filled with joy.

"Why would you think I wouldn't?" he went on.

"I-I did not know if…" She trailed off, biting her lip, reluctant to speak.

"What we did meant something to me?"

Laila took her time answering, but finally she nodded. "Yes."

He cupped her face. "You have no idea, little one."

She wasn't ready to hear what he was thinking or how he was feeling. If he freaked himself out with that shit, he would freak her out even more. And she'd suffered what he suspected was years of trauma. She didn't need anything more to deal with now. Besides, if there was even a chance she'd welcomed him into her body because she'd experienced anything like Stockholm Syndrome, he'd rather know that before he laid his heart at her feet.

"It meant a great deal to me, too. Thank you for showing me pleasure." She yawned again.

She was obviously tired—and no wonder. She slept fitfully most every night, and after a couple of climaxes… Sleep needed to be on the menu. He had to stop selfishly wanting to stay inside her forever and let her rest.

Slowly, reluctantly, Trees pulled from the snug clasp of her body and rose from the bed naked. He felt her stare on him as he stepped into the bathroom to grab a warm, wet towel.

When he returned, she watched him carefully, her stare both appreciative and anxious. Was she worried about his feelings for her? Or had she felt the crazy connection, too?

Trees turned those possibilities over in his head as he peeled the covers back from her body. Her naked beauty hit his consciousness one curvaceous inch at a time—her slender shoulders, her lush breasts, her tiny waist, her gently rounded hips, her sleek thighs, and her tiny feet. Damn if he didn't want to crawl back into bed and merge his body with hers again. His cock certainly stood up and saluted the idea.

Her drowsy, half-mast eyes reminded him that she was too tired.

"Spread your legs, little one."

Laila's stare turned cautious. Trees dialed back his disappointment. He was accustomed to subs, women who knew that he was patient and fair but firm as hell. If he gave an order, they followed, trusting that he had their best interests at heart.

But trust was exactly what he and Laila didn't share. Hopefully, tonight had helped to bridge some between them, but he was a realist. He wasn't expecting a woman who had probably been abused for years to trust him in a handful of days simply because he'd made her come.

For now, he met her stare with calm patience, letting her either ask him questions or work the situation out in her head.

Finally, her legs parted and she reached for the damp cloth. "I can do that."

He held it away from her. "I know you can, but I will. Lie back."

Again, she hesitated, and he sensed she wasn't comfortable. He nearly backed off, but he wanted her to learn that he would take care of her in all ways. He wanted her to realize that she could rely on him. And he needed her to understand that he had the drive and desire to care for her. That was part of his happiness.

After another stretch of silent seconds, she slowly complied.

"Good girl." He settled the warm cloth against her pussy and wiped her gently, lingering over her swollen opening. When he pulled the towel away, he glanced at it, wincing when he saw traces of blood.

He returned to the bathroom, cleaned himself, then slid into bed, where he found her watchful and silent. "I need the truth. Did I hurt you?"

Laila's dark brows furrowed. "There was some pain just before climax, but..."

"But?"

"That somehow added to my pleasure," she admitted almost as if she was afraid to. "I know that does not make sense, but—"

"It does." Perfect sense, and what it told him about her thrilled him all over again.

She could take every inch of his cock and be happy about it because she liked a little pain with her pleasure. Could she be any more fucking perfect?

Laila shrugged. "Are you going to sleep now?"

He'd rather stay up and talk to her, maybe make love again. But they needed rest, especially if he was going to drive this tank all day tomorrow to avoid highways and major towns to reach Lafayette.

Trees didn't want to think about what came next, after she realized she wouldn't be reunited with her sister. But one problem at a time. She would be better equipped to cope with the disappointment after a good night's sleep. Then he'd break it to her gently, help her understand the team's rationale.

"It's best if we do."

She nodded. "If you would sleep better, turn off the bathroom light. It must shine in your face."

"It doesn't bother me. I can sleep about anywhere. I want you to be comfortable. And I know you're afraid of the dark."

Laila sent him a sharp glance. "I did not say that."

"You didn't have to. It's obvious." And he was fucking dying to know why. Now probably wasn't the time to pry, but... "Do you want to talk about the reason?"

"No." Her answer was instant and emphatic.

"Okay. I won't push. But if you need the light…"

"I feel safe with you here."

That warmed him. Tonight had been good for them. Baby steps, but a start. Trees hoped like hell he could build her feelings into something as real and strong as his.

"We'll try it dark. If you get scared, tell me."

"You will turn on the light?"

"Or I'll hold you until you feel secure."

Laila closed her eyes. "Thank you for…everything."

What was the wistful note in her voice? "You're welcome. Sleep well."

She murmured something he couldn't understand, then rolled away.

Unsettled, he flipped off the bathroom light, then closed his eyes and hoped his screaming gut was wrong, that it was the jitters of new feelings putting him on edge.

Trees tried to stay awake to hear her deep, even breathing before he drifted off. But days without rest and the heavy, lazy drag of sexual gratification washed over him. He was asleep in under a minute.

He woke up sometime later to the sound of a click, like a latch slipping into place. He reached for his gun, then rolled over to find Laila, to protect her, only to discover her side of the bed empty.

She was fucking gone.

Chapter Seven

Laila's teeth chattered as she wrapped her arms around herself and darted along the edge of the campground, looking for lights that might indicate friendly people willing to help. She'd underestimated how cold it was outside and regretted not swiping one of Trees's flannel shirts from his bag when she had taken twenty dollars from his thick wad of cash. But her guilt had been too great to take anything more. Once she reached Louisiana and her family, she would return every penny.

For now, she shelved her remorse and scoured the area, knowing she wouldn't get far on foot, especially in flip-flops. But other than the campground's streetlamps, she saw no lights. Had everyone already gone to bed? She had no idea what time it was, except late.

Now what?

Every bone in her body screamed at her to go back to the RV and rest, back to Trees and the seeming safety she suspected he actually could give her.

But he wouldn't give her freedom or take her to her sister—two things she desperately wanted.

There must be someone awake in the campground. It wasn't full since it was a Wednesday night, but there were public facilities of some sort at the end of the lane. It was fully lit. Did that mean someone was using it? She didn't see anyone.

Then a door slammed behind her.

"Laila!"

Her heart stopped. Trees was already awake and after her? How? She'd left the RV three minutes ago.

Ducking behind a dumpster, she squeezed her eyes shut. Her mind raced. If she returned to him, she would be no closer to her family. If she ran from him, how far would she make it alone?

No, she couldn't be defeatist. She was resourceful. She was

resilient. She had once survived for ten days on a canteen of water and a bag of flour. She could reach Louisiana.

"Laila!" His voice sounded farther, as if he'd headed toward the entrance to the campground.

Following him wasn't an option. Nor was remaining here. There were too many lights; he would find her. That left trying to hide in the public facilities, where he would undoubtedly track her, or heading into the thick line of trees a few trailers away.

The forest it was.

She would hide there, wait until he gave up, see about keeping herself warm in a tree or with some leaves. Come morning, she would find civilization elsewhere. And help. She would be wrapped in her sister's embrace by tomorrow.

Peeking around the dumpster, she caught a glimpse of Trees's retreating back as he headed for the campground's office, now dark. She looked longingly at the RV. He had warmer clothes inside… But no, she had taken from him all she intended to. She had survived the last eighteen months in her brother-in-law's compound on her own. She would do the same here.

Sucking in a fortifying breath, she took off, darting toward the thick copse of trees less than fifty meters away. There was nothing between here and there to hide her, and the waxing moon was bright. But she made it, disappearing between a pair of tall trees and running headlong into the woods.

Branches overhead, mostly devoid of leaves, looked like jagged daggers against the moon. Laila shivered and circled around, trying to get her bearings, but the dense branches and the thick, rolling clouds soon swallowed up the moon.

Suddenly, the sky turned dark. Panic pressed in. She shivered, arms clasped around herself, in the pitch black.

A thousand terrible memories pelted her, threatening to unravel her.

Then she heard the howl of a coyote—too close for comfort. As if that one sang to the rest of its pack, others answered, even closer. More clouds drifted across the sky. The darkness turned blacker, thicker. Then she heard the crunch of leaves. A growl sounded nearby. The hair on the back of her neck stood up. She swallowed a scream.

Laila tried to penetrate the darkness to find a tree she could climb for temporary safety, but she could no longer even see her hand in front of her. Panic flowed like ice in her veins as she spun in a circle to find the direction the growl had come from. She heard it again, this time so near she let out an involuntary shriek.

Run. She could run. Out of the forest. Back to the campground. Hopefully, the people there would scare away the predatory pack.

But in the dark, surrounded by trees seemingly closing in, she no longer knew which direction she'd come from.

Another howl resounded, now right behind her. There was another growl on her left. Then she heard the stampede of animal feet in her direction.

With a cry, she dashed to the nearest tree and jumped to a low branch, trying to scramble up the rough-barked trunk. It scraped the skin off her knees and flayed a raw patch on her inner thighs, but the snarling below and the snap of sharp teeth blunted everything except her fear.

Laila could all but feel the coyotes nipping at her heels, hungry for their next meal as she hugged the trunk with all her might. Blood ran down her calves and rolled beneath her feet, warm in the bone-chilling cold, as she reached for the branch directly above.

It snapped off in her hands and sent her sliding down. Frantically, she clawed at the trunk, reaching blindly for another branch…and wishing like hell she could go back in time even fifteen minutes. Valeria had always said she was too headstrong and independent, that it would be the death of her.

Laila began to fear her sister was right.

If she failed to save herself, would Valeria ever know what had happened to her? Or would the coyotes consume her so completely that her body would never be identified?

No, she couldn't think that. She could endure bloody knees and raw fingertips. But she could not give up.

Suddenly, a gunshot rang out. She started and bit back a cry of fear. Who was out there? Why?

At her feet, a coyote yelped. Then two more shots rang out with deafening bangs. The other two animals scattered, fleeing quickly until she heard nothing but her own harsh breathing and runaway heartbeat. Was the shooter looking to kill her next?

"Laila!"

Trees. His footsteps closed in. Clutching the sharp, crumbling trunk in terror, she glanced over her shoulder. He came toward her with long, sure steps, holding a semiautomatic in one hand and a heavy-duty flashlight in the other.

"Laila! Can you see me? Follow the light."

"Trees." Her whimper cracked.

He jerked the flashlight her way, and the bright beam landed directly on her. "Son of a bitch!"

In seconds, he was beside her, wrapping his arm around her and lifting her into his embrace.

Laila couldn't remember ever being happier to see anyone in her life.

She scrambled to face him, throwing her arms around him and clinging to him as if her life depended on it. In truth, it had. If he hadn't come along and saved her from the coyotes, how much longer could she have dangled before her legs gave out and her fingers bled too much, and she fell to her doom?

He held her tight against him, as if he'd never let her go. "Are you all right? I saw blood..."

"None of them bit me. The tree... I was trying to get away."

His mouth flattened. "I know you were. Can you walk back?"

"I think so." Honestly, she wasn't sure. Adrenaline scorched through her veins as it drained out, and her legs felt like noodles. But she'd already shown weakness. She refused to crumble and fall now, especially after being so stupidly impulsive and impatient to escape.

With a clipped nod, he took her hand in his. She hissed at the contact of his skin against her raw abrasions. He released her immediately, giving her palm a once-over. Then he guided the light down her body, focusing on her legs.

"Fuck. Hold this." He thrust the flashlight in her hands. "Point it in front of us."

Before she could ask why, he bent and lifted her into his arms, against his broad chest.

She couldn't explain why, but when he held her close and searched her face with tight anger, she burst into tears.

Teeth grinding, Trees settled her closer, angling her face toward his shoulder as he stomped away from the coyote bleeding out on the leaf-riddled ground. It wasn't long before he broke through the trees and onto the campground. He headed straight for the RV and locked them in.

As soon as he set her down, he flipped on a light, surveyed her with a glance, and cursed.

He didn't have to speak another word to make her feel chastened.

"Trees..." But what could she say that wouldn't anger him more?

"Take off your shirt and shorts," he demanded.

Laila didn't ask why. Did he want to have sex with her now? Likely, and she didn't kid herself. This time he would punish her. There would be no toe-curling pleasure or explosions of bliss. He would use his body to punish her, and he would think she deserved it. She could only blame her own stubbornness and desperation.

She didn't fight him, merely peeled the shirt from her skin with a hiss of pain and lifted it over her head. Bark fell from the material onto the vinyl floor with scattered pings. But Trees wasn't even looking at her, much less like a man who intended to use or humiliate her. Instead, he pulled back the drape over the dining table and peered out as if he searched for trouble while she shimmied out of her denim shorts.

Laila shivered in the semi-dark, wrapping her arms around herself, terribly aware that she wore only her bra and a tiny pair of panties.

With a curse, he yanked the drape shut and tossed her one of his big T-shirts. "Put this on and don't say a word."

She did as she was told. His anger was too palpable to defy him.

The sudden knock made her gasp. She scampered to the shadows and listened as Trees yanked the door open.

"Howdy, we heard gunshots and saw you carrying someone here. Y'all okay?" said what sounded like an older man with a thick Southern accent.

"Fine. My wife went walking and stumbled into a pack of coyotes."

"They can be a problem around here. She didn't know?" A gray head appeared in the door, scanning the inside.

Laila shrank back, trying to disappear into the shadows of the bedroom.

"She's not from around here. Thankfully, she wasn't bitten, just got a few scratches when she fell. Probably needs some first aid, so if you'll excuse me…"

"My wife is a retired nurse. I can send her over—"

"Thank you, but we're fine. She just needs a few bandages and a good night's sleep."

"Are you sure?" The old man tried to look like an affable good ol' boy. "I think my wife would rest a whole lot easier if she got a look at your missus."

"My wife is very shy and would prefer privacy. But we appreciate the offer."

"How about in the morning?"

"We'll be gone early. Good night." Trees slammed the door.

Laila winced. Since he had done little to allay the man's suspicions, they would definitely have to flee well before sunrise.

But she stopped worrying about that when Trees stalked down the middle of the vehicle and headed straight for her like a man on a mission.

To punish her for running away?

When he reached the bedroom, she retreated to a corner and watched as he opened a closet and withdrew a black case. "Come here."

What would he do? How much would it hurt?

Laila had never been a coward, and she wasn't about to start now. But oddly, it wasn't his physical show of anger she feared. It was his tongue lashing.

Slowly, arms clutched in front of her, she made her way toward him.

"Shirt off. Lie down. Arms at your sides."

She shuddered but complied.

With an angry huff, Trees flipped on the bedside light. "Where does it hurt most?"

Everywhere, to be honest. She felt as if her entire body had been abraded by steel wool until she bled.

"M-my thighs."

Grimly, he nodded. "Stay here."

He stomped into the bathroom and flipped on the water. Minutes later, he returned with a warm, damp towel. Laila expected him to drag it across her raw, sensitive skin to teach her a lesson. Instead, he gently settled the cloth over her scrapes.

He wasn't punishing her but rendering first aid?

When she tensed at the sting, he cupped her shoulder. "I know, little one. But we've got to get you clean so infection doesn't set in."

He repeated the process twice more, pausing to pluck out pieces of bark and splinters meticulously before he cleaned the area. Then he opened the black case and rummaged through first aid supplies to apply antiseptic. It burned like hell, but she endured in lip-biting silence.

He repeated the process everywhere else on her body, his hands moving gently yet thoroughly. He followed that by giving her a couple of ibuprofen and a cup of water. Once she'd swallowed both dutifully, he sat and pulled her into his lap. "What the hell were you thinking?"

"I have to reach my sister. She needs me."

"We're heading to Louisiana in the morning."

Shock flared, followed by hope. "I did not know."

"You didn't ask."

True. She should have. "I am sorry if I caused you problems."

"Since I picked you up in that alley, you've caused nothing but problems. If I weren't so angry right now, I'd paddle your ass."

Laila reared back. "Because you want to humiliate me?"

"Because the stunt you pulled tonight deserves punishment. I suspect getting the hell scared out of you was a punishment all its own, but if that's what it takes for you to finally fucking grasp that we're on the same team…"

She looked away. "Thank you for saving me."

He took her chin in his strong grip and forced her stare to his. "I'm always going to save you."

"It is your job."

"It is. But after tonight, it's my responsibility. My right." Suddenly, he set her aside and stood, towering over her. "Or maybe I'm fucking kidding myself."

"I do not understand."

"Why did you seduce me earlier?"

Laila stared at him, not sure how to answer.

"It wasn't because you wanted me, was it? Or because you wanted to know what I feel like. It definitely wasn't because you would feel safer with me if we fucked. Was it?"

She bit her lip. If she admitted the truth, would he stop talking to her? Funny, in some ways she feared that more than him hitting her.

"Not going to 'fess up to the fact you wanted to make sure I was good and asleep so you could sneak out and run away again? Not going to look me in the eye and tell me that what we did in this bed earlier didn't mean a goddamn thing to you?"

If she told him it had, he wouldn't believe her now. Instead, she swallowed, curled her knees up to her chest, then wrapped her arms around them. "Sometimes, Victor or Hector would get too rough with me. I learned that when I gave them orgasms with my mouth, they would calm and go to sleep. I did not expect you to want more."

"Than your obligatory blow job?" Trees reared back. "No matter what I've said or done over the past few days, you're still determined to cast me in the role of villain."

What did he want from her? Everyone in Emilo's compound who had ever claimed he intended to help her had merely wanted pleasure. Once they had tumbled her a few times, they had been far less motivated to improve her situation or help her escape—and that's if Hector and Victor didn't find out someone had poached their "property." When they had, her "helper" hadn't lived long.

"I do not understand you," she said softly.

"It's fucking simple, Laila. I was hired to protect you until we could find another safe house closer to the team. You've done your best to defy and undermine me at every turn. And trick me. Can't forget that…"

She had responded to Trees with uncertainty and mistrust. But what else did she have to compare him to except criminals and rapists?

"Why did you have sex with me?" She turned the question on him. "You are angry with me for seducing you, but you could have said no. You did not because you wanted…what? Gratification? Easy pussy? The power of mounting and penetrating a woman smaller and weaker?"

Trees huffed out a bitter laugh. "No, I'm an idiot because I just wanted you. When I was inside you, I told you that I wanted you the moment I laid eyes on you. That wasn't a lie. I'm not interested in easy lays or cheap thrills. If I wanted a booty call, I could pick up the phone and have multiple choices. But I don't because I'm over sex that has zero meaning. And I'm the schmuck for hoping that what we did tonight meant anything to you except the means to an end."

A wave of shame overcame her. Usually, she didn't bother with guilt. It had no place in survival. When every breath, every morsel of food, and every bit of clothing was dependent on catering to monsters' whims, she had done her best to reserve all emotions for her family.

But Trees had slipped under her defenses. "I am sorry. It seems you are not like Victor, Hector, and their ilk."

And she meant that. More than once, she had apologized to one of Emilo's men without meaning it. How did she make Trees believe her now? His hand was inches from her. Perhaps if she reached for it, wrapped her fingers in his, and squeezed… But too much anger poured off of him. She doubted he would welcome her touch.

Laila kept her hands to herself.

"You're damned right I'm not." He knelt in front of her. "You can't fake orgasms like that."

Women did that? "I did not."

"You felt something with me," he growled.

She had. Something she didn't understand. Something that terrified her. Every other man lorded the power of violence and pain over her body. But Trees…he had the power of pleasure. He knew how to make her body melt, to make her thoughts float away like smoke, and how to make her entire being surrender to a blinding ecstasy she'd never thought possible. He had more power over her body than she did, and that terrified her.

Not for anything would she admit that.

"No reply, huh?" he challenged, then shook his head. "You know what? It doesn't matter. You're supposed to be a job, and I was wrong to take you up on your oral offer. For the rest of the trip, it will be strictly professional. And by tomorrow night, we'll be in Louisiana, and I'll do my best to make sure you're someone else's problem."

He turned away, slamming the bathroom door when it blocked his path, and rummaged through his duffel. Moments later, he turned back to her, padded cuffs in hand. "Give me your wrists."

She shrank back.

"I told you what would happen if you ran from me again."

He had, and she had believed him. But she hadn't had a choice. "Please…"

Laila hated the whine in her voice, the fear racing through her veins. It made her feel weak to beg for his mercy. After everything tonight, she didn't expect him to have any.

"Fuck me…" With a sigh, he marched back to the front of the RV, flipped on every light, dragged out his tools, and in a handful of minutes installed the lock he'd bought to secure the door from the inside. "There. No cuffs. But you're not going anywhere."

"I will not try."

"Trust is a two-way street, honey. So excuse me if I don't believe you. Go to sleep."

Trees turned away, utterly ignoring her as he doffed his boots, shirt, and jeans, then settled into the bed, turned out the lights, and rolled away.

Laila stayed awake, listening to his even, raspy breaths, drowning in regret and guilt. Sleep was a long time coming.

Trees couldn't remember a shittier night of sleep. Or a more tense day as he drove a circuitous route through parts of Alabama and Mississippi, avoiding highways and cities, before finally approaching Lafayette. When he had stopped for gas earlier, he'd called Zy and asked if there was anywhere besides his place to drop Laila off.

Of course there wasn't. He was stuck with a woman whose finger he'd mentally put a ring on, impregnated twice, and pledged his undying love to while she had merely fucked him to get away.

Good job reading the room, moron.

Worse, except when she was talking to Valeria about Jorge's worsening condition, she was too quiet. Not sulky but withdrawn. Remorseful? He didn't know. He didn't exactly make the effort to strike up a conversation. The stupid-ass part of him wanted to hold her, talk to her, resolve their strife. But he'd been too angry to handle last night well, and she was too damaged to believe anything he said.

They were a recipe for disaster. He needed to stop obsessing about her and move on.

A few miles from his place, he sent a text to Zy. `There in ten. Everything ready?`

`Yep`, Zy wrote back.

`Thank god. I need to be more than a foot away from this woman.`

It was late when he finally steered the lumbering RV down the dirt road to his house outside of town. The gate was open, the lights on, and the security relaxed. Zy stepped onto the front porch with a wave just before he pulled around the back of the house so no one could see the RV from the road. Then he cut the engine and heaved a huge sigh.

One trial down, a whole new tribulation about to begin. Laila would be staying here indefinitely.

As Trees stood and pocketed the keys, Zy jogged around his brick ranch house. Trees opened the RV door. Despite the chilly breeze, he stepped out happily and stretched. "Hey. So fucking glad that's over."

"I'm glad for you, man. Good to have you back."

It was good to be back, especially with his best friend, who would understand how rough it had been with Laila since he'd had problems of his own with Tessa. But when he looked at Zy, it was obvious something was wrong. "You look like shit."

"Well, stress, lack of sleep, and your girlfriend looking for the politest way possible to tell you to fuck off will do that."

Hadn't they just recently—finally—gotten together? And everything had already gone to hell? Trees hated to keep thinking the worst, but Tessa didn't seem like the kind of head case who would sabotage a new relationship with someone as awesome as Zy…unless she was guilty of something. Spying for the enemy, maybe? "No shit?"

Zy nodded. "It's been one of the worst weeks ever."

"Sorry, man." Trees clapped his arm, not sure what else to say. Badmouthing Tessa to Zy wouldn't make his friend see her as a suspect, so he bit his tongue.

Behind him, he sensed Laila and glanced over his shoulder to find her staring out the window over the dining table. She was a silhouette in the near dark. Her coffee-colored hair flowed past the satiny ribbon wrapped around her slender neck he hadn't seen her wear before. The tails of her choker and her abundant tresses floated down to her tits, barely covered by a pink tank. Half her damn midriff was bare. Beneath the tight, ought-to-be-illegal shorts, she flashed sleek legs. Yeah, he needed to fucking stop staring. His head and his heart both knew that. His cock wasn't on board with logic yet. It just wanted her.

"Did you bring everything I asked for?" he asked Zy.

"Yeah," Zy confirmed. "I had a little trouble. It took a couple of stores to find the right clothes, but it worked out."

Trees breathed a sigh of relief. "I owe you."

Behind him, he heard Laila's soft footfalls. Automatically, he held his hand out to her to assist her down. He told himself it was because of her injuries. But he was bullshitting himself and he knew it.

She laid her small fingers across his meaty ones and seemed to float down the steps, despite being barefoot. But she was gorgeous everywhere, even her dainty, polished toes as she scanned his property.

Trees knew exactly who she was searching for, and he wondered how long it would take her to realize her family wasn't here. He wasn't taking her to them, either. He'd put off that conversation because he knew fireworks would ensue. And yes, he knew it would blow up in his face.

"Hi, Laila." Zy stuck out his hand. "You may not remember me. I'm Zy."

She peered at him, then looked down at his hand, dragging in a breath—for courage?—and shook it. "Hello. Is Señor Walker coming?"

Trees leaned in, less than pleased. "She likes him."

"I trust him," Laila corrected.

And she still didn't trust him. That went both ways.

Then she brushed past them, curling her arms around her tiny middle to ward off the cool evening wind.

"See what I've been dealing with?" he grumbled as she headed toward the house, wincing as she tiptoed over dead branches and crisp fallen leaves with her bare feet.

"Are all her clothes that...brief?"

Trees rubbed at his eyes. "That's her modest outfit."

Zy's eyes bulged, then he shook his head. "Well, I brought her sweatpants and oversized T-shirts, just like you asked."

"Thank god. Maybe that will cool things off between us." Or at least help him stop wanting her so bad it nearly brought him to his knees every fucking time he looked at her.

"Sorry, buddy."

Trees groaned. "Can't you come stay with her for a few days? Maybe by then I can jack off enough to get some of the blood back to my brain."

"Nope. Whatever you do with your meat, keep that shit to yourself. But a word of advice? Don't fuck the client."

Too late.

"Technically, she isn't the client." Not that it would stop the bosses from firing him if they found out. He was already on thin ice.

"Valeria doesn't like the way you look at Laila," Zy reminded.

"Which is a really good reason for Kane and me to switch assignments. He can watch Laila, and I'll keep an eye on Valeria and her baby. Problem solved."

"No can do."

Because, according to the trio of cocksuckers they worked for, he was the mole. Of course they weren't going to let him anywhere near Valeria. If anything happened to her, their reputation would be toast and there would be hell to pay. He understood. He just didn't know how to prove that he wasn't guilty.

"What else do you need here?" his buddy asked, seemingly eager to change the subject.

"You in a hurry?"

"Not so much me, but I'm assuming the sooner you let her into your place, the sooner she can cover up everything tempting you."

"Good point." He headed for the house. "Anything new?"

Zy dodged the question. "Let's go inside."

That didn't sound good, and he needed to focus on business.

Trees opened the back door and let Laila in. "Come with me."

Zy hung back in the kitchen as Trees touched a hand to the small of her back and ushered her forward. Even that small touch had him sweating. Memories of her kisses, her touches, her body surrounding him as he impaled her deep just wouldn't be banished, no matter how hard he tried.

"Where are we?" She took in the shadowy house, gaze jerking all around. "This is not an apartment building, and we are not in Lafayette."

Couldn't say she wasn't observant...

"My place. We'll be staying here for a few days."

She whirled on him. "Why are you not taking me to my sister? You promised—"

"I said we were heading to Louisiana, and that's where we are."

"You deceived me."

"No, you assumed I was taking you to your sister." He hated using the bait-and-switch on her. She would see it as a betrayal. "We're still not sure that location is safe. So you're staying here until the bosses decide otherwise. I know you're disappointed, but it's not my decision. Take it up with Valeria. She signed off on this plan."

"But you had no problem lying to me." Laila jerked from his touch.

"I didn't enjoy it." Trees nudged her across the living room, down the hall, and into the guest room, then he flipped on the light. "You can put your things here. Shower if you want. Or go to bed. I'll be with Zy. And by the way, I've outfitted the house with the best security. No one is getting in—or out—without me knowing in a handful of seconds.

And even if you managed to make it off the property, I'm at least thirty miles from civilization in every direction. It will be forty-four degrees tonight. And if you thought the wildlife in Alabama was scary, it's a lot more deadly out here. Get comfortable. I'll be back."

Trees closed the door on her silent fuming, shutting her inside. He had the house alarm armed thirty seconds later, and he tried to relax… but he didn't dare. Laila wasn't done trying to reach her sister. He knew that as sure as he knew his own name.

He stomped back to the kitchen and plucked a bottle of beer from the fridge. "Thank you for picking these up for me. I need one."

Before he could open the bottle, Zy stopped him. "They're not cold."

Yeah, his pal probably hadn't been here long enough to fridge them.

"I don't even fucking care. That woman…" She was driving him to drink—literally.

"You can't imbibe on the job."

Why the hell did Zy have to be right?

"Fuck." Trees shoved the beer back in the fridge.

"Is she mouthy and difficult?"

"No." Well, not mouthy, anyway. "She barely speaks, and I swear sometimes I'd do just about anything to know what's running through her head. The problem is, I want to fuck her." And hold her while he promised to keep her safe and right her world. But she would have to trust him, and that wasn't happening anytime soon.

"Sorry," Zy said. If anyone understood wanting a woman he couldn't have, it was his buddy. Zy had lived through nearly a year of look-but-don't-touch torture with Tessa.

Trees shrugged. "I'll deal. What do you want to tell me?"

"Some friend of Walker's has temporarily joined the team to help with Kimber's recovery. Name's Matt. You probably won't see much of him. I met him. He seems okay."

"Even though he's a friend of Walker's?"

Zy nodded. "Trust me. I was as shocked as you."

"Why wouldn't I like that news? It's fine by me. Hell, whatever the bosses need to do to bring Kimber back…"

"Keep that in mind because what I say next might make you blow a gasket." Zy's apologetic glance told Trees this was going to suck. "They're thinking about using Laila as bait to help get Kimber back. Pretend to set up a hostage swap and—"

"No. Fuck no!" Were they crazy? Did they not grasp what Laila had been through? "Over my dead body. Absolutely not. End of conversation."

"It's not my favorite plan, either, but I think they're running out of options and getting desperate. Maybe they're thinking that Kimber is a wife and a mother with two small children who need her, and Laila is—"

"Expendable? That's fucking bullshit! She's a human being and she's"—he clenched his fists—"fragile."

"I know." Zy sounded sincerely sorry.

Trees was too pissed off to care. "You don't know! She's been bullied, abused, and raped since she was fourteen by the very people who want their hands on her now." At least he deeply suspected that's what had happened. "You'll have to kill me before I let anyone dangle her in front of a bunch of cutthroats. I'm dead fucking serious."

"Is there any chance such a plan will allow for the capture of those who wish to hurt my sister?"

Trees spun to the sound of Laila's voice and found her at the far end of the kitchen. When the hell had she sneaked up on them?

He cursed, doing his best to glare her into taking those words back. Her stubborn expression said she wasn't budging. *Son of a bitch*. Then he zipped around to Zy. His buddy understood that plan was a no-go for him and would bury that shit, right? Laila was his responsibility.

No, she was *his*.

But Zy gave him a regretful shrug since he was merely the acting boss and lacked real authority. "It's possible, but it's risky."

She scoffed. "Breathing around these people is risky—and certainly not a guarantee. My sister has endured too much, and she has her son to consider. I will do it."

Trees whirled, towering over her possessively with bared teeth. "You will not."

She stood unblinking and undaunted. "You cannot stop me. You brought me here safely, and for that I thank you. But I owe you nothing beyond my appreciation."

"I didn't ask you for anything. But I would consider it a personal fucking favor if you would please give a shit about your safety."

She cocked her head, and the sadness there nearly took him out at the knees. "Unfortunately, Emilo never gave us that choice. And I am certain his father, Geraldo, who is probably running his organization now that he is gone, will be even less interested in such things."

Unfortunately, from what Trees had heard, she wasn't wrong. "Fuck."

"If the Edgingtons or Muñoz ask me to help set a trap for Geraldo and his goons, I will say yes. My mind is made up."

Trees gripped her shoulders. "Laila, you'll be bait. Chum. Something my bosses will skewer on a hook and use to reel these bastards in. And if they lose you?" He shrugged. "Oh, well. Not their problem. Do you understand that?"

"Yes. But do you understand I will have no future if I refuse? No one in my family will."

With that, Laila turned away, then looked back at Zy. "I cannot pay you for the clothes on my bed. Please return them."

"It's not a problem," his buddy assured. "You left your house in a hurry and you weren't dressed for our winter."

"I will not accept your charity."

Then she was gone.

As soon as he heard her bedroom door shut, Trees lost his shit. "See what I mean? She's going to drive me crazy."

Zy shook his head, his face full of sympathy. "Take a breath. One day at a time, okay? You'll get through this."

Right now, it didn't feel that way, but arguing wouldn't change a thing. "Let's talk about something else. What's up with you and Tessa?"

"I don't want to bore you. I don't understand it enough to explain, anyway."

"She's pushing back?"

"She's pushing me away."

What the hell? "I would have sworn that woman loves you."

At least in her way. But maybe money had become more important to her than love.

"I thought so, too, but she's never said that in so many words. And now she's barely answering my texts. Something is…weird. Something is wrong."

"Well, that's definitely not right."

"I don't know. Maybe I pushed for too much too fast. I told her at Christmas that I love her. About three minutes after we got the all-clear to have more than a working relationship, I asked her to move in with me. She said she needs time to think. But it doesn't feel like she's thinking; it feels like she's just putting daylight between us."

"So what if you've moved fast this week? I don't think you rushing her is the issue. After all, you two have been eye-fucking and exclusive for months. You wanting to start a life with her didn't come out of left field. It's something else."

And Trees could only think of one thing. She was guilty.

"Yeah. I was at her place a little bit ago. She actually begged me to leave." Clearly, it was killing Zy because he was so in love. "And she's been lying to me. Sure, about little things like her headache. But still, lying."

"Any chance there's someone else?"

Zy pondered, then shook his head. "No. I think it's me."

"Or…she's guilty and she has something to hide."

"I don't see it."

"Because you don't want to. Keep pursuing her, man. You'll never be happy if you just walk away from her. But while you're doing that…look into her. Take her seriously as a suspect. Do your fucking job."

Zy sighed. "I don't have a choice. I guess that's priority one."

"Sorry, man. It's better to know than not."

"Roger that. You need anything else or are you two set?"

Wasn't that a good question? Honestly, Trees wasn't sure. But if Zy wasn't staying to spell him, then he might as well start dealing with Laila on his turf and figuring out what came next. He had a feeling they were in for a battle.

Chapter *Eight*

When Laila hung up with Valeria, tears streamed down her face. Jorge's condition had not improved. That worried her a great deal. So did her sister's exhaustion. If the boy wasn't better tomorrow, supposedly Kane would take them to a doctor. That was good news, but Laila hated not being there to tend to her nephew and support her sister. And she hated that, just like Trees had told her, Valeria refused to let her come there and help because she feared it wasn't safe. Arguing with her sister had done nothing to change her mind.

Trees had known that when he'd told her he would bring her to Louisiana. He had twisted his words to mislead her, then hidden her less than an hour from her family.

So close…yet so far away. It seemed cruel.

His deception hurt more because, despite plotting to seduce him, when she had given her body to Trees, he had somehow slipped under her skin. Because of the way he touched her. The way he had given her pleasure. The way he seemed to care.

For the first time, for a brief moment, she had felt treasured.

Now? He merely seemed terse and happy to put distance between them. She would oblige him. It was more important to focus on finding ways to help her family, especially ending the danger to her sister and Jorge. If that meant she had to offer herself as bait, she would.

Swiping the wetness from her face, she availed herself of the warm shower. The house was older but meticulously kept. The bathroom was entirely bright and white, except for the black penny floor tile.

Once she was clean, she dressed again in her dirty clothes and tiptoed out of her bedroom. The house was quiet. The motorcycle that had been in the front when they'd pulled up was absent. Zy must be gone.

She and Trees were alone.

Pressing her hand to her nervous stomach, she made her way

toward the only other light on in the house—the kitchen. He stood in front of the stove, heating something in a saucepan. It smelled good. Spicy. She was starved.

"You hungry?" he asked, pulling a can of green beans from his nearby pantry.

How had he known she was there? "I am fine."

He skewered her with a frown over his shoulder. "You're not. You haven't eaten in over twelve hours. And you're still wearing goddamn dirty clothes meant for Florida weather. Why, Laila? I'll take care of you if you let me."

"Nothing in life is free. Not the food you eat, not the clothes on your back, not the bed you sleep in. You have paid for all of those, yes?"

"Yes, but—"

"You did not expect anyone to give them to you for free. Because taking from others is wrong, and you are proud. So am I. Since I am without money, I only have one currency with which I could pay you. And when I left Mexico, I swore I would never whore myself out for my survival again."

He dropped the spoon in the pan, its clatter a loud clang in the kitchen. "You think I would make you fuck me for a meal? Or a shirt? Or a comfortable night's sleep?"

Laila hated to admit how she'd given herself to scum for years to survive, but she saw no other way to make him understand. "It is the way the world works."

"Not here. I'm choosing to give you things. You don't have to pay for them."

He was playing games with semantics. "That is the same thing."

"Why would you think that? I'm heating up soup and vegetables. I'm making enough for two, and I'm offering to give you some."

"In Emilo's compound, if I wanted to eat, I had to suck cock. If I wanted warmer clothes, I had to spread my legs. If I—"

"Are you listening to me? This is not Emilo's compound. I'm not asking you for anything in exchange for your meal."

"They did not ask. They simply forced."

"I would never do that, Laila." He looked furious. "Ever! So sit down and eat—"

"No."

He ground his teeth together, and Laila worried he would lift his arm across his body and backhand her. Or clench his fist and plow it into her belly. It wouldn't be the first time a man had done that. But even fearing pain, she stood her ground and put on her most defiant face.

"Why are you so stubborn?"

"Am I? Why is it, when a man wants to make his own way, he is proud? When a woman wants to do the same, she is stubborn?"

Finally, he heaved a frustrated sigh. "You ate food in the RV."

"My sister paid to get us out of Florida, including whatever I ate."

"She's paying for this, too."

"She is not. This came from your pantry."

"Be reasonable!"

"I am being realistic. I apologize if that upsets or offends you."

Trees raked a hand through his hair. "After everything, can't you extend me a little trust and believe that I'm offering you some food, no strings attached?"

"I would still feel the strings, like a puppet." When he glared at her, Laila sighed. She was going to have to get graphic with him. "The winter before I turned fifteen, Emilo had been keeping me in a bunker to punish my sister for not catering to his every whim. Valeria and my mother were allowed to see me for fifteen minutes a day. Those were the only fifteen minutes I wore clothes. As soon as they left, Victor and his brother Hector would strip me bare. It was merely humiliating at first, constantly being naked and fondled, passed from brother to brother, being forced to fuck one in front of the other. That was how I earned my meals. But as the winter went on, the bunker turned cold. I had no blankets, so I shivered every night and slept under the mattress for warmth. For Christmas, Hector offered me long pants, a new shirt, and warm socks. He told me it was a present, but that night I found out the cost of my present was anal penetration against my will. So perhaps you can see why I'm cynical."

Fury the likes of which she had never seen thundered across his face. Reflexively, she stepped back as Trees snapped off the stove and shoved the pan from its burner. He reached for her, wrapping his arms around her and bringing her close. "Little one… I'm so sorry. If I could kill them now, I would. I would strangle the worthless life from their bodies and gleefully watch them die. They deserve that and more for what they did to you as a child." He set her down and cupped her face. "But I would never, ever demand anything of you that you didn't want to give—no matter what. I gave you a safe word in bed: *red*. With that, you can stop me anytime. But I swear, I would give you the shirt off my back and my last morsel to keep you safe."

He probably meant that—at least in his mind. Likely, he saw himself as the noble savior come to rescue her from her wretched fate. And perhaps he was. After all, the rest of his team had saved her from Emilo's compound less than five months ago. She'd been wearing only a towel when the operation had gone down, and she'd been nervous everyone in the helicopter would expect her to fuck them in appreciation. Instead, an operative named Cutter had given her his shirt. Hunter Edgington had insisted she take a blanket he'd stowed in his bug-out bag. His younger brother, Logan, had given her his rations. None of them had so much as laid a finger on her or looked at her with anything more than pity.

Had she misjudged Trees because he hadn't been there and because she'd rarely been around good men? Perhaps…but did the nature of men ever really change?

"Thank you for those words."

"They aren't just words. I mean them." He nodded toward the stew. "Let's eat."

She shook her head. "I still have no way to pay you."

He heaved another frustrated sigh, as if he was struggling to hold his temper. "How about if you do the dishes? If you'll do that, I'll consider your meal paid."

His proposition surprised her. Laila turned his offer over in her head. "That is acceptable."

"Thank god." He settled the pan on the burner again and dumped the can of vegetables into a bowl, then shoved it in the microwave. Three minutes later, they were eating at his kitchen table in silence. And even if the stew had come out of a can, it tasted like heaven.

"How did you wind up in Emilo's compound? I know your sister married him, but…"

"Not by her own choice. My father married Valeria off to Emilo."

"Why?"

"Papá was a farmer with fallow land. We were dirt poor, and he wanted to be rich. He wanted to be important. Emilo sought to use my father's property to aid his growing drug empire. They came to an agreement, which included Emilo paying lots of cash to marry Valeria."

"So he sold her to that scumbag on purpose?" Trees looked shocked.

Laila hadn't been at all. "My father had been nothing his whole life, and now he could join his poor family to a wealthy one and gain influence. Others would look up to him. He could finally stop a life of toil and enjoy his days. Of course he did."

Trees scowled. "Did he know how dangerous Emilo was?"

"Everyone did."

"And he sold his daughter to that monster, anyway? How old was she?"

"Barely eighteen."

"Jesus… Then what happened?"

"Papá suddenly had money and he got a mistress. My mother was stunned and heartbroken, so when Valeria pleaded with us to come spend the summer with her, Mamá quickly said yes. We had no idea…" How their lives would change. That they would never see home again. God, how naive they had been. "Emilo quickly realized he could use me to control his headstrong wife's behavior. Mamá tried to protect me, so they separated us. As a last resort, I called my father to tell him I was afraid because I barely saw my mother and I did not like the way Emilo's men treated me." Her voice broke.

What had happened next had been nothing short of hell.

"What did he say?"

"That his life was much better without us. Mamá had grown old and unappealing. My sister and I were too spoiled."

Trees dropped his spoon in his stew. "He left you there, knowing you were being raped?"

"I did not tell him that exactly. I did not know the words for it. But he must have been aware." She had never been close to her father, but the sense of betrayal after he'd hung up had been absolute.

"So, for his own comfort, he left you to a bunch of drug thugs' nonexistent mercy?" He sounded stunned, horrified, and furious. "I'm adding him to my list of assholes who need killing."

"You are too late. When he got greedy a couple of years later, Emilo had him killed." She hesitated. "I have mixed feelings about that. Some would say he got what he deserved…"

He reached for her hand. "In my opinion, he did. But he was your father—your blood—even though he didn't fulfill the responsibility of a dad."

It was foolish to accept solace from Trees. It probably made her weak. But she needed comfort, and she soaked his in. "Exactly."

"What happened to your mother?"

"She got sick and developed pneumonia. Emilo refused her medical attention. I tried my best to help her, but…" Laila tried to swallow back tears—and failed miserably. "Then Valeria was rescued. I was happy for her, but…"

"You were alone." Trees squeezed her hand. "You've never had anyone to help you, and everyone you've ever loved has been taken away."

Finally, he understood. She didn't want to weep in front of him, but trying to hold back made her cry harder. "Yes."

Trees pulled her into his lap and gripped her chin until she met his gaze. "I'm here for you, little one. I know I'm not your sister. I know you want to see her, and I don't blame you. But it's not safe. Once it is, I'll take you to her myself. But until that day comes, I'm here and I won't let anything come between us. Do you hear me?"

She still didn't trust him completely, but he was all she had in the world right now. And he seemed determined to take care of her in a way only her sister had ever tried to. "I do."

He released her chin and kissed her forehead before he dragged her bowl across the table. "Good. Eat up."

Then he fed her patiently, one heaping bite at a time. Taking food from his hand was so intimate and oddly comforting. She followed the stew with a bottle of water. Once her bowl was empty and her stomach sated, her lids felt heavy. It took all her will not to lean against his reassuring strength, cuddle into his warmth, and drift off.

"You're tired. I'll do the dishes."

"No." She leapt to her feet. "We made an agreement. I will uphold my end of the bargain."

"You don't have to. I won't demand anything from you."

She almost believed him. "I will still do them, as I promised."

As she cleared the table and made her way to the sink, his phone dinged. He glanced at it with a curse, then shoved it in his pocket. "I have, um…a friend dropping by. Why don't you rest in your room? I'll finish this."

"I told you. Because it is my responsibility—"

"I need to talk to her alone."

Her. Laila's heart stuttered. A girlfriend? A lover? Everything inside her balked, and that fact stunned her. She should be happy if he gave another woman his attention and desire. She didn't want either.

Deep down, she feared that was a lie.

"Leave the dishes. I will finish them after she leaves." But what if she didn't tonight? The thought of this unnamed "friend" spending the night shot a hole in Laila's chest. "Or tomorrow."

"All right."

It was a good time to put distance between them and figure out why what this man did with another woman mattered. Why was she having feelings for him?

But her feet didn't want to move.

"Laila—" His phone beeped in warning, interrupting him. "Fuck." He punched in a code, then hit the screen a few times. Headlights flashed through the living room windows, which overlooked the front of the house. Then a little sedan came to a stop and a stylish brunette with a fresh balayage stepped out, wearing a trendy blue sweater and jeans that respectably covered every inch of her legs. Slim leather boots with chunky heels and a designer purse completed the look.

She was pretty, put together, and refined. Of course Trees wanted someone like her.

"I…will go."

Trees looked at her like he wanted to say something, but the woman knocked on the door, breaking the moment. "Thanks."

Every footfall felt heavy as she headed to the bedroom Trees had provided her and shut the door—mostly. She should not want to eavesdrop. It was nosy. It was rude. It was wrong.

But she couldn't help it.

Was this jealousy?

"Hi, Madison. Come in."

"Hi, big guy," the woman said with a sweet, soft Southern drawl.

Laila told herself not to, but she cracked her door a bit wider to peek at the two. Trees hugged the woman with familiarity, resting his chin on her head. She laid her cheek on his chest and closed her eyes with a smile.

Something ugly speared Laila. It very much felt like jealousy.

When had she started caring about Trees?

After he pulled away, Madison smiled up at him with obvious fondness. "I brought your key back."

She dropped it in his outstretched palm, and he pocketed it. "Thank you for looking after the house and the dog while I was gone. I owe you."

"You don't. I'm always happy to help. You know that, right?"

Was Madison flirting?

"You're a sweetheart. Did Barney behave himself?"

"He always does because he's a good boy. He scarfed up all his food in nothing flat every night and loved the scratches behind his ears."

Trees laughed, then opened the front door again. A big black dog with brown jowls and happy eyes barked at Madison before planting in front of her with a whine. "He likes you."

She shot Trees a teasing stare. "Barney always lets me know he's happy to see me. You…I have to guess about sometimes."

He forced a laugh. "Would you like a drink? You hungry?"

"No. I'm fine. I know you just got home, so I won't keep you." She petted the big dog, and he wagged his tail. "I just got off work anyway, and I need to stop off and check on Daddy."

"You sure I can't pay you for taking care of the house and the animal while I was gone?"

She cocked her head. "I wouldn't say no if you want to take me to dinner this weekend."

"I wish I could. I'm pretty sure I'll be working."

"Another weekend, then?"

Trees hesitated, then sighed. "Madison, you know you're a good friend, right? But I—"

Suddenly, the big black dog barked and turned in Laila's direction with a growl before darting straight for her. Laila gasped and tried to shut the door, but it was too late. The big dog crashed inside and took up a stance in front of her, ears peeled back with a growl.

She froze. What should she do to do to make sure a dog this size didn't decide she was a snack?

Trees was there in an instant. "Heel."

The dog sat, but he didn't look happy.

"Good boy." Trees petted the beast behind his ears. "You okay?"

"Fine."

Madison approached, giving her a discreet once-over.

Laila knew what the woman saw—a brown girl with an unruly mane of dark curls, wearing a dirty tank top and short-shorts that barely concealed the essentials. Trees's friend would probably think she was gutter trash. A nobody. She wasn't wrong.

Madison turned back to Trees. "I didn't realize you had company. I'm sorry." She faced Laila again, hand outstretched. "Hi. I'm Madison."

"Laila." She took the woman's hand cautiously.

"I'll leave now and let you two get back to your…evening." Madison flashed them a big smile.

Laila didn't believe it. Or maybe she only felt that way because she couldn't bring herself to smile back at the pretty flirt who batted her lashes at Trees.

"I'll walk you out," he offered, then turned to the dog. "Come."

The canine gave her another narrow-eyed stare before he headed out her bedroom door. Trees followed, then turned back to her, his gaze questioning.

Laila didn't know how to answer. How could she explain why she had been spying and eavesdropping when she didn't really understand herself?

"I'll be back," he said finally, then left.

From the cracked door, she watched Trees guide Madison with his big hand on the small of her narrow back. In the foyer, they disappeared from view. The front door opened and closed.

Laila raced to the window that overlooked the front of the house. She could just see them around the shrubs. Madison said something with a smile. Trees nodded solemnly. Then she rose on her tiptoes and threw her arms around his thick neck, planting a kiss on his cheek before hopping into her little car and driving off with a wave.

Suddenly, the front door slammed. Laila jolted as she heard Trees lock it.

He headed straight to her bedroom.

She held up her hands. "I am sorry. I did not mean to pry."

"Why did you? The fewer people who know you're here, the better. I don't want to put Madison in danger for knowing things she shouldn't. She didn't ask for that."

Madison hadn't, and Laila felt guilty for not realizing that her curiosity could put someone else in danger. "You are right."

She felt terrible. Madison's only sin was her "friendship" with the bodyguard who intrigued her more than she liked.

He sighed. "It's my fault, too. I didn't know she was coming over, and I should have explained why you needed to stay out of sight."

It would have helped, but ultimately, her inexplicable jealousy had been to blame. "She likes you."

"She's nice," he said neutrally.

"I mean she is interested in you as a man."

He hesitated. "Maybe, but I don't think she's into me specifically. I think she's looking for something."

"Love?"

"More than that, I suspect."

"She would warm your bed if you wanted." Laila hated to point that out, but surely he knew.

He merely shrugged.

"I understand. She already has." Laila wished she had never brought it up.

"No. We're just friends. Only friends. I don't know what she needs, but I know what she doesn't. Me. I could never make her happy."

So far, he seemed kinder than most men, so his assertion made no sense. "Why?"

"It's complicated. Why are you asking? Do you want me to fuck her?"

Laila gave a noncommittal shrug. "It is none of my concern."

He grabbed her shoulders. "But there's a reason you're asking."

"I merely pointed out the obvious. She wants you."

His eyes narrowed. "No. You want to know if I want her, too. And I don't. That's why I've never touched her. I never will."

"Despite the fact that she would say yes to you without hesitation?"

"I told you, I'm not interested."

It seemed Trees was actually telling the truth. Madison had given him subtle hints that she was quite willing to be more than his friend. Trees apparently had never taken her up on the offer. That amazed Laila.

Back in Mexico, Victor had often bragged about tumbling local women. One in particular, he laughed about every time they'd fucked. He claimed he had to close his eyes because she was so ugly, but her amazing tits made up for it. Victor's attitude was despicable, but she had expected nothing less from him. From either Ramos brother, really.

"I only want a genuine connection." Trees gripped her arms tighter.

And by his own admission, he felt something for her.

Laila felt something for him, too, though she wished she didn't.

"I would like to go to sleep."

Trees glanced over her head at the clock on the wall and cursed. "Yeah, it's getting late. You've got two choices tonight so I can make sure you don't escape: either I cuff you to your bed or you sleep in mine with me."

Laila reared back. "I will not run again."

At least not tonight.

"Sorry if I don't believe you. I know you'd rather be with your sister, just like I know you'll do nearly anything to get there. So pick. Are you staying here"—he nodded toward the comfortable queen bed—"or coming with me?"

"You will not cuff me to your bed?"

"No."

The thought of lying beside Trees, their skin brushing, their eyes meeting in the shadows… It was dangerous, but her heartbeat quickened. Would he touch her? Would he seduce her? If he did, would she say yes? If she got scared, would he truly stop everything with a single word?

Laila wasn't sure…but her curiosity was gnawing away at her good sense.

"I will sleep with you."

Trees couldn't have been more shocked when those words fell out of Laila's mouth.

"Not here alone?"

"Cuffed to the bed? No."

"If you're worried I'll come in here and take advantage of you while you're vulnerable, I won't."

She took a long moment answering. "I know."

When had she finally figured that out? "Good. Since I don't have any night lights, if you stayed in this room, you'd have the overhead light shining in your eyes."

"You have other lights in your room?"

"Yeah." The dim LEDs built into the crown molding cast a soft glow onto his ceiling. "It should be perfect for you."

"All right. I will go with you."

Probably for the best, but it was going to be a long night. "You need anything else before bed? A glass of water maybe?"

"To finish the dishes."

"There weren't many. They'll wait until morning. Can I talk you into sleeping in one of my T-shirts?"

She shook her head. "I cannot pay for it."

"Of course not." As much as he hated this shit, he understood. "How about if I let you do the laundry tomorrow to earn the shirt?"

Laila paused. "That is acceptable."

"Great." He took her hand and led her back through the living room.

It was so dark she tensed. For a moment, she clung to his hand, then had second thoughts and let go. Trees held in a curse as he whipped his phone from his pocket, letting the device illuminate the unfamiliar space around her.

Laila sighed with relief, even smiling when they reached his room and he flipped on a light. "Thank you."

He nodded. Bringing her to his bed was probably a really fucking bad idea. Even the thought of her beside him in one of his T-shirts, asleep and trusting, made his cock ridiculously hard. What the hell would happen when he actually lay beside her?

You had to give her the choice, dude. She would never trust you until you did.

True, but he really hadn't expected her to choose his bed—and him.

Worse, since realizing she'd been jealous of Madison, he wanted her ten times more.

And if he didn't think about something else, Trees feared he'd do something stupid, like touch Laila.

She glanced around the bedroom, her gaze skimming his bulky wooden dresser, the tall rattan king-size bed with its four posters and blue comforter, and the case full of books on the far side. The space was simple and comfortable, the way he liked it—original floors, striped burlap rug, reclaimed wood on the walls. What did she think? He couldn't tell. Her face gave nothing away.

Clearing his throat, he made a beeline for his dresser and pulled out a soft red shirt, then handed it to her. "You can change through that door. You need anything else?"

She took it with a shake of her head. "I will be back."

"Sure."

When she disappeared into his bathroom, he double-checked the house alarm. Set. He checked the windows. Locked. He glanced outside at Barney. Yep, on his sleeping bag in his doghouse. Everything was as it should be—except his fucking nerves. It made no sense. He'd been sleeping beside Laila every night in the RV, so this wasn't new.

But it was the first time she had *chosen* to sleep with him, and somehow that changed everything for him.

Or it proved he was being ridiculous and he needed to stop thinking with his dick.

Sighing, he grabbed something to wear from his dresser drawer, then shucked his jeans and donned nylon shorts for bed. As he yanked his shirt off, he heard the creak of the bathroom door and turned. His heart stopped. Laila looked fucking beautiful all the time, but in his faded red cotton tee that hung to her knees with her thick curls twisted on top of her head in a messy bun? She looked incredible. So feminine. So soft.

A thousand urges hit him at once—to hold her, to kiss her, to strip her, to sink inside her. But he also wanted to protect her, reassure her, promise her that all of the horrible things she had endured in the past —shit even worse than he'd suspected—would never befall her again.

He swallowed as he set his discarded clothes on his nearby rocking chair. Laila just wanted to sleep, and he'd better get his shit together. "Comfortable?"

Shyly, she nodded. "Very. Show me how you prefer to have your clothes laundered in the morning, and I will take care of the rest."

Because a freaking ratty-ass shirt couldn't be free. "Sure."

She bit her lip and wrung her hands. "You have a nice room. Cozy."

"Thanks. Here." He turned on the ambient lighting above his crown molding and turned off the overhead cans, plunging the room into a hazy dim. It felt soft and golden. Intimate.

Laila looked up, seeming to marvel at the muted illumination around her. "I have never seen anything like this."

No shit. If she'd only ever lived in a run-down farmhouse and a drug lord's bunker, there were a lot of things she hadn't seen or experienced. "It's nice when I'm getting ready for bed. Helps to prevent stubbing my toe in the dark."

"You have done that?"

"More times than I want to admit." He smiled to set her at ease.

"I am sure your toes appreciate the improvement." She gave him a ghost of a smile in return. "I left my clothes folded on your bathroom counter. I hope that is all right."

"Fine." He crossed the room to the bed, tossed off the checked decorative pillows, then folded back the heavy comforter. "I'll...um, give you the left side of the bed. You'll be closer to the bathroom, just in case." And he would be between her and every avenue of escape.

"Thank you." She padded past him slowly, her eyes all over him.

Because she was afraid he would put his hands on her? Or because she wanted him to? Trees couldn't answer that question as she climbed between his sheets and laid her head on his pillow, wrapping her arms around herself and curling into a ball.

"You cold?"

"I will be fine."

He glowered at her. "That isn't what I asked. Are you cold?"

She nodded.

"All you had to do was say so." Trees reached for the remote in his nightstand drawer and pressed the button. His electric fireplace snapped on, the hiss of blowing air soon distributing warmth through the room. He preferred to sleep cold since he put off heat like a furnace, but he would live with a little extra warmth tonight if it made Laila happy. "That should warm up the place quickly."

She sat up and gaped at the faux flames. "It looks like a real fire. I have never seen anything like that, either."

"It's nice ambiance with a little bit of warmth when I need it."

Laila nodded, then settled back onto her pillow with a contented sigh.

"Good night, little one."

She didn't say anything, simply curled up like a cat again and closed her eyes, long lashes brushing the tops of her cheeks.

He should stop staring, but he couldn't do it. He just wanted to drink in everything about her—the little baby curls around her hairline that framed her face, the hint of roses in her cheeks, the full lips that beckoned him whether she smiled or frowned, the delicate hands that clutched the blanket under her chin protectively.

In the real world, if he wasn't her bodyguard, she would never have looked twice at him. Trees knew he was a big brute without an ounce of polish. He was from "flyover" country. He hadn't finished college. Hell, he hadn't had running water most of his childhood. He lacked Zy's charisma, good looks, pedigree, and charm. Sure, he appealed to some women, but most were subs who wanted his gentle but firm discipline, not his handsome face or sparkling personality.

And Laila might be the most gorgeous woman he'd ever laid eyes on. Graceful. Sensual. Stunning. What the fuck did she see in him? Safety? Or was her seeming acceptance of the comfort of his bed another ruse?

Beside him, she shivered and scooted closer. Even from two feet away, he felt the chill of her feet.

"You want another blanket?" He had a quilt in the closet.

She gave him a drowsy-eyed glance. "No."

Then she inched closer.

Shit if that didn't make him harder.

With a sigh, he plucked his phone from his nightstand and checked in with one of his online prepper groups. Yeah, all his friends thought he was crazy, bracing now for the erosion of society into anarchy. When chaos ensued and there was no such thing as a supply chain anymore, he'd be set for years—and everyone else would be shit out of luck.

He tried to focus on the community chatter. Live below your means. Duh. Store water in collapsible containers. Double duh. Don't store all supplies on one place. So fucking obvious. No wonder he was way more aware of Laila stretching beside him before balling up again, this time even closer.

Her feet were seriously like ice.

"You're still cold." He set his phone aside.

She didn't answer, simply opened her eyes and met his stare.

Their connection zinged.

Jesus, how was he supposed to stop himself from touching her? But after everything she'd been through, he had to. He didn't want to give her any reason to think that she had to pay for the food she'd eaten or the shirt she wore in ways other than the ones they'd negotiated. On the other hand, he couldn't stand doing nothing while she shivered.

He sighed. "Turn over."

"What?"

"Lie on your other side."

"And put my back to you?" The way she said it sounded like a giant *hell no*.

"I won't hurt you, Laila. I won't touch you without your consent. Remember, if anything is ever too much, you can stop me with a word. But I'm simply trying to help you get comfortable so you fall asleep."

She hesitated before finally nodding and rolling onto her side, giving him her graceful nape and slender shoulders.

He hooked an arm around her middle and dragged her against his body, avoiding the ache of his cock. "Put your feet on me."

She stiffened but didn't move away. "I do not wish to make you uncomfortable."

"I'll be fine."

"All right." She wriggled closer and pressed her twenty-below feet against his thighs, then relaxed with a sigh. "Thank you."

"You're welcome."

Surely she felt him hard as fuck against the small of her back, but she wasn't freaking out. Did she trust him? Did she hope that if she didn't mention it, he wouldn't press her? Or did she not realize how fucking much she aroused him?

Slowly, her body lost its starch. She didn't fall asleep; he would have heard the change in her breathing. She was awake—and completely relaxed against him. He tried to close his eyes and get some sleep. Tomorrow would be another day of potential surprises and hell. He had to be prepared.

All he could feel was Laila's ass against his throbbing cock. All he could smell was the faint soap and feminine musk wafting from her soft skin.

Fuck, he should have grabbed a few minutes in the shower with his bath gel and his hand.

Five minutes turned into ten, then into twenty. Her breathing slowed and deepened, almost as if she'd dropped off…but not quite. To his surprise, she turned in his arms, facing him once more, and snuggled against him. Her head rested inches from his chest. He felt her every exhalation and shuddered at the thought of her breath bathing his skin.

Trees would have sworn it was impossible, but his cock stiffened even more, weeping in need for her.

But she was finally warmer. He could feel it in her toasty toes and the laxness of her muscles. He couldn't take that away from her just because his dick was nagging him like a toothache.

It was going to be an excruciating night, but Laila needed to sleep in peace.

He repeated that like a litany over and over, like a mental leash he used to jerk himself in line.

Until she sighed contentedly against him again. "Trees…"

Then she pressed her lips against his chest.

His whole body lit up. "What?"

Her lashes fluttered open, and she speared him with a soft, sultry glance. "Will you kiss me good-night?"

Was she serious? Was she crazy?

"I don't think that's a good idea."

Her full lips pursed into a pout. "Surely there is no harm in a kiss."

"Laila, I'm not going to want to stop there."

"I like kissing."

For Laila, that was a big admission.

"I like kissing, too. But if we're not careful, it will lead to more."

"It does not have to. Please." Her eyes slid shut and she lifted her face to him, offering him her pillowy lips.

He was a fucking goner.

With a groan, he rolled her to her back, wrapped his arms around her, and took her mouth in a desperate kiss, barging his way past her lips. Instead of pushing him away, her arms curled around his neck and she opened to him without hesitation. Then he thrust his tongue against hers, into the deepest recesses of her sweet, silken mouth.

God, she was heaven. She made his thoughts dissipate, his caution evaporate, and his desire roar.

Experimentally, he pulled back. To his surprise, she followed, moaning in protest as she lifted closer to renew the kiss.

Shit. Did she actually want this? Want him? Was this more than another escape attempt? Or was she merely trying to pay him for the roof over her head?

That jerked him out of the moment. "Why?"

Laila bit her lip. "Because you make me feel good."

"You want that now?"

"I need it. Without you, I would feel so alone."

Without her sister and her nephew—her lifelines? He could see that. He understood it. He just wasn't sure he one hundred percent believed it. "I'm here."

"Not as close as I want," she murmured, pulling him back down to her lips.

He didn't resist. What was the point? He could barely say no when she was reluctant, but when she was pleading in that husky, lost little voice…

Trees covered her mouth again, sinking deep and groaning as she met him halfway. His fingers tangled in her hair. She clung to his shoulders. Their hearts beat together, and he felt her breathing quicken. Passion surged, scorching his blood.

Fuck, how was he going to stop this?

She met his groan with a needy whimper, then broke their kiss, panting. "Touch me."

A livewire of want jolted him. Did she know she was flirting with trouble? "Laila…"

"Please."

Son of a bitch.

He slid a hand down to her thigh, carefully avoiding her abrasions, and lifted his fingers under the overlarge T-shirt, palming her hip. He made a shocking discovery.

Laila wasn't wearing underwear.

His raging heartbeat surged, thrashing against his chest as his fingertips continued their path up her body, dipping in with her waist, floating up her ribs, until he cradled her breast, thumbing his way over the rigid tip.

She arched to him, sighing into his kiss.

"More?" he asked.

"Yes. I want to feel the explosion you made me feel before."

She wanted to come. He was happy to oblige.

Impatiently, he worked at the big shirt covering her, sliding the cotton up her body until the hem settled against her collarbones. Then he dragged his lips down her neck, nipping at her ear until she shivered, before descending again, pressing kisses around the straining tip of her breast until she dug her nails into him with a protest that sounded like something between a huff and a groan.

He nosed his way up her nipple, then dragged his beard down over it. She gasped and began to writhe impatiently. He soaked up every moment of her sensual distress, loving the way she gave her body over to him second by second.

Finally, he closed his lips around the hard, rosy tip of one breast, pinching and twisting the other between his fingers. She responded with an anguished wail of need that torqued him up and urged him on. He abraded her nipple with his tongue, then followed with a soft bite of teeth before sucking it deep.

She grabbed him in a desperate grip. "Trees!"

"That's a good girl," he crooned. "Let me make you feel good."

"Yes. Yes…"

Whatever else she meant to say dissolved into wordless pleading as he switched from one breast to the other and repeated the delicate torture, stoking her desire and keeping satisfaction out of reach. He wanted her to not merely want him but to crave him like he craved her—a constant, clawing ache that would not be denied and would not go away.

Beneath him, her legs spread. Her hips lifted. Her lips skimmed his shoulder before she sucked at his neck, breathing hard against his skin, sending shudder after shudder down his spine.

Fuck, this was quickly becoming a runaway train that he didn't see ending without him inside her, thrusting every hard, aching inch deep until she begged him for more with unintelligible words, then cried out in bliss.

Trees wasn't thinking about anything else when he migrated a hand down her body, covered her pussy with his greedy palm, and shoved a pair of fingers inside her. Yep, wet—and not just a little. She was downright juicy, and the thought of her body softening and making way for his cock added another gallon of gas onto the raging fire between them.

With a mewl, she bit into his neck and gyrated herself against his hand, impaling herself on his fingers all the way to hilt. "Trees…"

"Need more, honey?" he murmured against her breast.

Frantically, she nodded, spreading her thighs even wider, wrapping one of her legs around his, then lifting to him feverishly.

How had this "good-night kiss" gotten so out of hand so quickly?

Does it matter? Are you really going to stop?

Fuck no. Hector and Victor Ramos had done nothing but crush her spirit before they'd abused her trust and her body. If he could show her real pleasure and make her realize she deserved it, hell yeah. This wasn't forever; he knew that. Why would she be happy in his three-bedroom ranch house in the middle of Nowhere, Louisiana? It was nothing fancy, and he wasn't anyone special. But he could make her feel good and help her build trust until she returned to life with her sister…and eventually paired off with the man she would marry. Whose children she would bear.

Some time with Laila was better than none, right?

In theory, but her leaving might rip out his heart.

Trees refused to worry about it now. He settled his thumb over her clit and thrust his way back into her mouth, making love to her lips like it might be the last time. Because it very well might. He wasn't taking anything for granted.

Beneath him, she tensed. She tossed her head back, breaking their kiss, breathing so hard he could see her chest rising and falling in the shadows, her diamond-hard nipples leading the way.

The sight of her, hot and wet for him, unhinged him. "What do you want?"

"More…" she whimpered.

The only way he could make that happen was to give her his cock. He shouldn't. She'd asked for a good-night kiss. But she'd also egged him on, offering herself up and begging him to partake.

No way could he say no to her.

"Fuck, Laila. All I do is want you…" He shoved his basketball shorts down to his hips, carefully climbed between her thighs, and gripped her as he desperately aligned his crest to her slick opening. "I burn and ache to have you."

"Why?"

"I don't know. I always have. It's impossible to stop." He took her wrists in his grip and settled them flat on the bed, pinning her until she was beautifully helpless beneath him. "Laila…"

He reared back and worked his cock into her a few inches at a time, drilling down, down, down into her sultry heat, so scorching and welcoming and wide open to him.

Finally, he bottomed out and tossed his head back with a feral roar of pleasure. "Laila!"

"Trees. Trees…" She tensed beneath him. "Red."

It took a long moment for that word to penetrate his haze of lust, but it finally stabbed its way into his consciousness. He stilled.

Gritting his teeth and dying inside, he speared her with a demanding stare. "Did you use your safe word?"

She nodded, breathing hard and choppy. "Yes."

Fuck. Gritting his teeth, every muscle in his body protesting, he withdrew from her and yanked up his shorts, then flung himself to the opposite side of the bed. "What's wrong? What happened? The scabs on your thighs hurt too much?"

Laila whipped the shirt down to cover her breasts, staring at him in wide-eyed shock. "You stopped."

"Of course. You safe worded."

She still looked confounded. "You told me one word would stop you, but…"

He understood now. She hadn't believed him, so she'd tested him.

Son of a bitch.

"I kept my word, Laila. If you need me to stop, I stop. I always will."

"You did." She still sounded shocked. "Thank you."

She softened, then inched across the bed toward him again. Every receptor in his body went off, and when she reached for him, wrapping her fingers around his shoulder and scooting even closer, his weeping cock ached to jump out of his shorts and burrow its way inside her again.

"I did not believe you."

"Clearly."

"I am sorry. You do not have to stop everything," she whispered, leaning closer. "I liked what we were doing."

Yeah, he'd liked it, too. But he needed to make a few things clear to her.

Trees pulled back, eluding her touch. "Your safe word? You're only supposed to use it if you're in physical pain or mental distress. You use it to stop me so I can understand how I've hurt you and we can discuss ways to ensure it doesn't happen again. It's not a tool to test me or a way to build your trust in me. If you have any doubt about a man, Laila, don't consent to let him between your legs."

She looked hurt. "I understand. You are right."

"You didn't know. Now you do. Don't use your safe word for anything other than its intended purpose again."

"I will not. Can we resume now?"

Having sex? In theory, yes. But she didn't get to yank his chain without suffering some consequences.

"Come with me." He grabbed her wrist and tugged her off the bed.

She trailed him to the bathroom. "What are you doing?"

He flipped on the jets in his big walk-in shower. "Shirt off."

Laila hesitated, her gaze searching. Yeah, she knew something was off and she was trying to read him. Trees didn't explain, simply waited for her to comply. Finally, she drew his huge shirt over her head and handed it to him.

He tossed it on the counter behind him without a word, then shucked his basketball shorts. He threw them on top of Laila's nightshirt. Her eyes bulged as she took him in from head to toe, her gaze lingering on his cock standing straight up between them.

Even her stare on him made his blood heat and his cock stiffen more. He was half a second from giving in to her. Goddamn it, she needed to understand that if she toyed with him, he would to do the same to her.

"Get in." He gestured.

"I-I do not need a shower."

"You don't want to get wet? Fine. Stand in that corner." He pointed to the very back of the massive stall. "You'll stay dry."

"Why?"

"Because I can't give you an opportunity to escape. And because you need to understand what's going to happen if you play with my feelings again. Go."

With her arms curled around her middle, she ducked past the rainfall head and tucked herself into the spot he'd indicated. It was a measure of progress that she complied, finally believing he would not beat or rape her. But he was too annoyed to be grateful.

Her eyes never left him as he followed her in and stood under the overhead spray, letting the warm water sluice down his body. He braced his hands against the dark tile wall and closed his eyes as the heat rolled down his back. He tried like hell to let go of his tension, of his need for her. All the while, he felt Laila's stare, both chastened and curious.

Fuck. That wasn't helping. He wasn't coming down from the erotic endorphin high of having her underneath him, her pussy around him, squeezing tight, as she begged him for more.

Might as well get this shit over with.

With a sigh, he reached for his shower gel and dumped a glop into his palm. "Did you really want to have sex?"

"Yes."

"Why?"

A long moment passed before she answered. "Because it feels different with you."

He didn't love being compared to her rapists, but she had no other comparison. He got that. "It's different with you, too. I wanted you, more than I should probably admit. More than I can remember wanting anyone."

Her shoulders slumped, and she looked away. "I am sorry."

"Honey, I understand you have trust issues. I know exactly why. I'm a patient man. I'll listen. I'll talk to you. I'll do my best to help you bury your fears. But I fucking won't let you misuse your safe word again. It's like crying wolf."

"I will not. I promise. If you will come back to bed, I will be available to you in any way you want."

He shook his head. "That ship sailed. I needed you to be honest and you weren't. Now neither of is getting what we want tonight. That orgasm you asked me for? Denied. You just get to watch. Don't look away."

He didn't explain more, simply lathered up the soap in his hands, faced her, braced his hand on the wall beside her head, and started stroking his cock with rough, unfinessed pulls.

Laila gasped, her eyes glued to his motions. "Y-You are…self-pleasuring."

It wasn't even a pleasure now, just a point he was making. "Yep. I don't masturbate much because I'd rather have a willing partner, but since you want to play games…"

"Trees—"

"The time for talking about it is over. Just watch me."

She did, her eyes never wavering as he tugged his way up his cock and jerked back down. He was making a point, punishing her by withholding his touch and her pleasure. He felt almost nothing but anger and regret…until he realized her rapt eyes were on him. Her mouth gaped. Her heart raced. He'd bet she had a wet pussy, too. One he couldn't have tonight, damn it.

Still, what began simply as discipline had turned into an unexpected thrill.

He continued stroking himself. His shoulder burned. His biceps protested. And Laila just watched, worrying her bottom lip between her teeth, her eyes unwavering, her cheeks flushing.

He needed more. He needed to be closer to her, to connect more with her.

Trees closed his eyes and tried to imagine that Laila hadn't safe worded out, that he was still inside her, still feeling her all around him, still one with her. It wasn't enough when he knew she was right in front of him.

"Look at me," he barked.

She dragged her gaze up to him. Their eyes met.

Zing.

His veins—and everything else—flooded with pleasure.

Her eyes darkened. Her nipples hardened. Their breaths mingled and merged. Neither blinked as they fell into the moment together.

Suddenly, he didn't care about anything except their now. He ramped up his strokes, losing himself in her eyes, groaning as the end edged closer.

In the silence broken only by their panting, she reached for him, touching his hip. Encouragement.

Her thumb slid across his skin, leaving a burning arc in its path. That nudged him even closer to orgasm. He could feel it brewing, hot and deep—a churning urge only she could fulfill.

"Laila…"

"Trees," she whispered back.

Then she cupped his balls and pressed a kiss to his shoulder, his neck, his jawline. "I cannot stop looking at you. You are so strong and so male. So beautiful."

Then she laid her cheek against his, and he could hear her aroused, uneven breaths in his ear. He jolted again, his desire ratcheting up.

Fuck it. If he was going to have to settle for coming by his own hand tonight, he was going to be as close to her as possible.

He yanked his bracing palm off the wall and gripped her chin, forcing her to meet his stare. They were mere inches apart, almost nose to nose. He buried the head of his cock against her stomach and rolled against her, his thumb working the rim of his sensitive crest over and over.

Need jacked him up. His blood boiled and pooled. His balls felt ready to explode.

"Laila." He couldn't say more. He was too far gone.

But she understood. "I am here. I am with you."

And she was—with her wide eyes, red cheeks, and soft touch.

That was all he needed.

The sensations surged, creating a choke point of tingles that finally burst open and gave way to a geyser of ecstasy. He cried out, a hoarse sound of rapture that wouldn't be denied. His semen coated her skin and drove him to a higher, gasping peak of bliss that seemed to go on forever.

Finally, the pinnacle broke and he tumbled into a heavy-limbed daze. His body felt momentarily sated, but he wasn't satisfied. Without being inside her, the orgasm had been hollow, like applying a Band-Aid when he needed a tourniquet.

Fuck, how far gone was he for this woman?

Trees jerked away. He needed some distance between them to sort out his thoughts. Quickly, he soaped and rinsed himself, then grabbed a towel and turned back to her. "Clean up. I'll get you a towel."

She blinked at him, almost pleading. "But I-I ache…"

A glance down showed him her slick, swollen pussy. He almost groaned—and gave in. But he was a Dom. He had to be fair but firm. "I know, but that's the consequences for using your safe word under false pretenses. Don't do it again."

"I will not, but…" Her fingers trailed across her thigh, then burrowed between her puffy folds. She began rubbing in circles.

He grabbed her wrist and stopped her. She howled out, her groan sounding pained.

At any other time, he would let Laila have pleasure. Hell, she deserved it all day, every day. By his hand, by her hand—it didn't matter. But tonight, he had to draw the line to ensure she didn't pull this shit again.

"No." He batted her hands away and washed her off, sending her a stern warning glare when she tried to circumvent him. Once she was clean, he led her out of the shower, dried her off, then shoved his big T-shirt back over her body. "Get in bed. Go to sleep."

"How am I supposed to do that?"

When every part of her ached. He understood. Despite his self-induced climax, he felt it keenly and wondered if he would ever stop wanting her.

"I will not sleep," she said in begging tones.

God, it was as if she knew how to push every single one of his buttons.

He jumped into his basketball shorts and dragged her back to the bed. "Well, honey, that makes two of us."

CHAPTER Nine

It was oh-dark-hundred when his phone vibrated on his nightstand. Groaning after a sleepless night of Laila resting fitfully beside him, Trees grabbed his phone. If Zy was calling at this hour, it must be bad.

"What's up? Talk to me."

"We've got a problem, buddy. A jogger came past the office about twenty minutes ago and found a trio of bodies in the EM parking lot. All men. All mutilated. Given everything going on right now, I doubt that's a coincidence."

Trees agreed. "The vics anyone we knew?"

"I don't think so. At least I've never seen any of these guys. We're waiting on IDs now, but the bosses called me here as soon as the police reached out to them. They all look to be Hispanic, late twenties to mid-thirties, tatted up and rough. But it's hard to tell actual identities when they had missing eyes or noses. It's gruesome shit. Someone is sending us a message."

Goddamn it. "But who? And why?"

Was it a warning from Kimber's kidnappers? If so, why kill three unnamed men when they had the leverage of their pretty hostage? They could drive home whatever point they were trying to make without killing her. A finger here, a toe there. Trees had seen it done to speed along the ransom process.

Was it retribution for Emilo's death by One-Mile Walker's bullet? If so, why not go directly after him? Why hack up three unknowns?

Or was another party with a different agenda jumping into this shit show? It was conceivable that more than one faction of the Tierra Caliente cartel wanted their hands on Valeria, not just Emilo's power-hungry father, Geraldo. Maybe someone else was throwing their hat in the ring to fill the power vacuum left after Emilo's death. Trees didn't have a fucking clue.

But he knew someone who might.

Trees turned to find Laila curled up into a ball, finally sleeping soundly.

"I don't know who or why." Zy sounded frustrated. "One-Mile is on his way here. We're going to pull the security footage and see if we can find anything helpful. The police have swarmed the place, too. Maybe they'll figure out something."

But Zy sounded like he had as much hope as Trees. Cartels didn't get to be powerful by allowing themselves to be tripped up by local law enforcement. And as good as the Lafayette PD might be, they were no match for this lawless group of drug-pushing thugs who ruled half of Mexico and beyond.

"What do you want me to do?"

"If I can get my hands on the crime scene photos, I'll send you the pictures. See if any of these faces look familiar to you. And make sure you've got Laila locked down."

"The bosses still want to use her as bait?"

"As of last night, they have no new leads on Kimber, so…yeah. I think that's still on the table. Sorry. I know how you feel about that."

Trees's gut tightened as he padded into the kitchen, started the coffeepot, and growled in Zy's ear. "What if that was Tessa? What if the bosses wanted to dangle the woman you love as a tempting little morsel in front of a bunch of brutal criminals in a game of winner takes all? You'd be out of your fucking mind."

"Are you in love with Laila?"

Sighing, Trees glanced back at his bedroom, seeing her wrapped up with her pillow. "I've never been in love, but if that's feeling like your head is upside down, your gut is in knots, and your heart has been through a blender, then there's a good chance."

"It's pretty much like that, buddy. Buckle up." Zy sounded grim.

"Things no better between you and Tessa?"

"Nope. And I don't expect them to get better."

But Zy still couldn't get over her. Trees feared his buddy was doomed for head-on impact with heartbreak, and there was nothing he could do to stop it except… "You gotta find out if she's guilty, man."

"I know. I know."

"Look, I know you don't want to, but if you investigate her and you can't find any evidence, then you can fight like hell for her without a shred of doubt." But if he uncovered her guilt—like Trees expected—Zy would crash hard. No matter what, his buddy would do the right thing. He always did because he had a core of honor. It was one reason they had adopted each other as brothers.

Zy sighed. "Yeah. I've avoided it because I don't want her to hate me if she finds out…but things can't get much worse."

"I'm sorry." The anguish in Zy's voice tore at Trees, too. "Really. But I'm here for you no matter what."

"Thanks. And I'll send over the pictures as soon as I get the police out of my hair and get the images."

"I'll be here."

"With Laila? That going any better?"

"No." Last night had been a hell he'd rather forget.

"Fuck." Zy laughed. "We sound pitiful."

"I think it's because we've become pitiful."

"Sadly, I think you're right. We've got to fix that."

"Amen," Trees seconded. "Never accept defeat."

"Ever. Talk to you later, buddy."

"Later," Trees said.

Then Zy was gone.

Trees wandered back into his bedroom and watched Laila turn, stretch, then cuddle up to his pillow. His gut kept telling him that the bodies in the EM Security parking lot had something to do with her. He had no fucking idea what, though. How could a woman who was barely five feet tall and had only been a legal adult for a few years be even slightly responsible for this kind of violence? Suddenly, he had a feeling that there were missing pieces to this cartel puzzle EM Security didn't know…and she might be able to fill in the blanks.

And after last night, wouldn't she love for him to interrogate her?

He sighed and started slamming back coffee. He had a bad feeling he was in for a fight.

Laila woke to the smell of frying bacon and country music echoing from the kitchen. She stretched, staring at the clock. Ten a.m.?

With a gasp, she bolted upright, then realized she wore nothing except Trees's enormous shirt.

The night came rushing back. It had taken hours for the ache between her legs to settle so she could finally drift off. But dreams had plagued her after that. Hot ones of her in Trees's arms, finishing what she had suddenly—and foolishly—stopped last night. Violent ones of her years in Emilo's compound. Terrible ones of her sister and her nephew in peril.

The last time she'd looked at the clock, it had been nearly four a.m. Exhaustion weighed on her. But she had duties to attend to—dishes to wash and laundry to do. She could not shirk those.

Rising, she tiptoed from Trees's bedroom and peeked at him in the kitchen, broad and shirtless and muscled, his big, bare feet hanging off the edge of the mat in front of the sink. Wincing, she tried to make her way undetected to her temporary bedroom. She probably looked horrible, and she felt even worse about last night. As soon as she brushed her teeth and changed her clothes, she would be more equipped to face him.

Laila had barely taken two steps before Trees turned. "Morning."

He didn't sound angry.

"Good morning," she said cautiously.

"Breakfast?"

"If you will allow me to do the dishes."

"Absolutely."

"Then I will eat."

"Then come on." He crooked his finger. "It's ready."

"I need five minutes."

"Food will be cold by then."

Was he suggesting she sit across the table from him and eat a civilized breakfast without underwear or a bra? "Start without me. I will join once I am dressed."

Trees dropped the fork he'd been turning bacon with on the stove and approached her. "You're wearing enough to eat. What's the real problem?"

"I have on nothing beneath your shirt."

"I know." A clandestine glance down told her that aroused him. "I've seen it all, little one. More than once. I've had my mouth on it, too. But I won't jump on you, and you can always stop me with a word. Last night should have proven that."

How could she explain this to him? "What you might do does not worry me. It is the memories... Eating this meal dressed in almost nothing will leave me feeling...exposed, like meals Victor and Hector forced me to endure."

His eyes narrowed. "Meaning?"

The memories were humiliating, and Laila hated to talk about them. But if she was going to be with Trees until her sister let go of the foolish notion that they were safer apart, she should help him understand. Thus far, he had seemed willing to listen and able to adapt.

"I will feel too vulnerable. The Ramos brothers took great delight in forcing me to various states of undress during meals."

"Did they fondle you while you ate?"

"Usually. Sometimes, they also made me suck one or both of them while my meal sat on the table, waiting for the moment I 'earned' it. It was not uncommon for Emilo and his lackeys to come in and out of the room while I performed these tasks. No matter how humiliated I felt, I was not allowed to stop."

"Bastards," he spat. "Did they ever make you service others?"

Humiliation stung. She couldn't meet his gaze. "Sometimes."

"Son of a bitch." Trees looked ready to lose his temper. It warmed her that he seemed incensed on her behalf. "Did Victor and Hector force you to fuck others, too?"

She squirmed, but what good did lying do? "When it amused or benefitted them."

He lifted her chin until she met his probing stare. "Emilo?"

Laila tried to hold back tears. She hated to show weakness—but it was futile. "Yes."

"They forced you to have sex with your own sister's husband?"

She nodded. "They watched."

Trees clenched his jaw as his hands curled into fists. Clearly, he was fighting to hold on to his temper. "I'm sorry, little one. Truly."

Laila felt desperate to change the subject. "I know you are angry about last night—"

"Not angry. Let's be clear. Disappointed. I gave you my word, and you chose to test me. I understand why, and that's the reason I'm not mad. But now you know I keep my promises."

Laila did. The lesson had been an unpleasant one, but she had never met a man willing to stop taking his own pleasure from a woman simply to make a point—until Trees. "I believe you."

He cupped her cheek. "Good. Then we're making progress. Now let's figure this out. Are you willing to eat with me, as you are right now, and believe that I'll respect your boundaries?"

"I worry about the memories..." They had been some of the most nightmarish of her life. What if they overwhelmed her and dragged her back to that dark place she knew too well?

Then again, the last few days with Trees...she hadn't felt so hopeless.

That realization shocked her. So did her certainty that her fears were from the past and in her head. She needed to move on.

"But I will try not to let them overwhelm me."

He brushed his thumb across her bottom lip, making it tingle, then he dropped a kiss to her forehead. "If they do, you know your safe word."

She frowned. "How will that help me?"

"I told you last night that saying *red* will also stop me from anything that brings you mental anguish. If you can't eat in front of me in nothing but that shirt, then say so. We'll discuss and come up with another plan."

Was it really that simple?

Trees sighed. "If you're ever going to trust me, you have to at least try."

He made a decent point, and not trusting him had always ended badly in the past—Victor, the coyotes, and last night's ache of desire that was still unsated. Maybe it was time to believe he wasn't like the others. "All right. I will try."

He guided her to the table, pulling out her chair.

"Can I help you bring the food to the table?"

Trees just shook his head. "Sit. I got it. You're doing the dishes, remember? Right now, I need to ask you some questions. There was a development overnight, and we're trying to understand it."

That sounded ominous. Slowly, Laila sat. "What?"

He ferried the bacon, a plate of eggs, and bowls of oatmeal to the table before sliding into the chair across from her. "Dig in. Let's get some food down you before we dive into that."

Laila didn't love putting off reality. Over the years, she'd learned that facing a situation was far more productive than burying her head in the sand. But she also suspected he put off the ugliness until she was fortified enough to face it.

Silently, he forked bacon and eggs onto her plate—way more than she could actually eat. But he only rolled his eyes at her protests, then passed her a bowl of oatmeal before adding a dash of milk and a sprinkle of brown sugar.

After he consumed even more food, watching her with an unflinching gaze as she ate, he finally pushed his plate aside. She did the same, stunned to realize that he'd kept her so engaged during their meal that she hadn't felt afraid or self-conscious for even a minute.

That spoke volumes about how much she was beginning to trust him.

Laila leaned across the table, propping her chin in her hand. "Shall I do the dishes now or—"

"Let's talk first. Help me understand the state of Tierra Caliente before EM extracted you."

"What do you mean?"

"Emilo ran the operation in the bunker. That was his fiefdom, right?"

She shook her head. "His responsibility was bigger. He ran that region of the country, along with some foreign export operations."

"He had help, didn't he?"

"Of course. Victor and Hector, his right and left hands, were always willing to lend their brain power—such as it was—and their muscle to enforce his rules as if they were laws. There were others, but they were bought and paid for. The Ramos brothers…they were intensely loyal to Emilo."

"And where were they when you were rescued from Emilo's compound? Still inside?"

She shook her head. "About a year ago, Hector moved to the US to spearhead another operation. I overheard that he married an American woman. But I do not know his wife's name or where they settled. Victor stayed behind to help keep operations and employees inside the compound in line."

Including her. If she'd thought life without Hector would be better, that she would have fewer degrading demands to adhere to, Victor had quickly dispelled that notion.

"You were gone from the bunker before Emilo was killed, right?"

"By several months. But I have no doubt the shock of his untimely demise staggered the cartel. And I am sure the infighting to assume his authority was almost instant."

Trees leaned in, all elbows. "So there were factions, right? Groups infighting for supremacy?"

"Yes."

"In any power vacuum, there always is." Trees nodded. "Tell me about those."

The situation inside the cartel had always been complicated. No one had ever explained the power structure to her, but merely by observing their behaviors and eavesdropping on their conversations, she knew who had likely been vying for power.

"Emilo ran his operation inside Tierra Caliente, of course. He had loyal enforcers—Hector and Victor. Whatever power they had only existed because Emilo made it so. Of course, Emilo's father, Geraldo, presided over the larger operations of the cartel, not just in the region but the organization as a whole. His word is law. He didn't often override his son's decisions on day-to-day operations. Emilo mostly had autonomy, but there were times...yes. Geraldo would step in and block Emilo from some plan or plot. The whispers said that Emilo was not good with understanding the way the political winds blew. He especially did not do well appeasing local politicians. Geraldo often had to care for such things himself, but he tolerated Emilo's spotty competence because that was his son and Emilo did a violently good job of eliminating competition. But after Emilo's death, Victor and Hector likely did their utmost to seize control of the compound and its operations. I doubt Geraldo would have tolerated that."

"So it's possible those two factions are at war?"

"I am sure they are."

Trees rubbed at his chin in thought. "Did Victor chase after you in Orlando because he didn't want to let you go? Or is it possible he had a more political reason for pursuing you?"

She gathered her knees to her chest. "Probably both. Victor never liked losing his 'toys,' but the Ramos brothers and Geraldo have been trying to get their hands on Jorge since his birth, I guess because he is the future of the cartel. The heir apparent."

"Whoever controls the boy controls the organization?"

Laila shrugged. "It sounds silly because Jorge is not yet two, but I can think of no other reason why both factions want Valeria—and thus, my nephew—so badly. If either side captured me, they would merely use me as a bargaining chip."

"To get their hands on Jorge. I get it." He frowned. "But it doesn't add up. The cartel is running without Jorge, and how does either side think a toddler will forward their business?"

"It puzzles me, too. Except, I suspect, they intend to groom him to take over one day."

Trees sighed like he was about to impart bad news. "Three men were murdered sometime overnight. Their killers dumped their bodies in the EM Security parking lot, almost like they intended to send us a message. But we don't understand. The victims' identities are unknown, but they were all Hispanic with lots of ink, between late-twenties and mid-thirties. That describe anyone in particular you can think of?"

Was he kidding? "Victor and Hector had those loyal to them and, thus, Emilo. But they always suspected Geraldo had his spies on the inside, telling him everything his son did. But they were all men. All pigs. Almost all fit that description."

With a frown, Trees leaned back in his chair. "Spies? If Geraldo didn't trust his son, why would he give Emilo responsibility for a chunk of his empire?"

"I cannot say. I only met the man a few times. Thankfully, he found me beneath his notice."

"Thankfully?"

"He terrified me. Emilo was violent and ruthless...but ultimately greedy and lazy. Sloppy. I do not think he would have ever been capable of running the whole Tierra Caliente cartel. I think his father tried to make it so by giving him the necessary experience, but it was beyond Emilo. Geraldo, however, is the perfect kingpin—shrewd, strategic, even diplomatic when need be. Of course, he is also ambitious and not afraid of violence. Victor described him as something of a chameleon, able to rub elbows with government dignitaries as easily as criminals. He knows exactly which moves to make, which people to pay off, and who he cannot trust."

"Good to know. Zy will send over some pictures of the dead bodies when he gets them together. Will you look at them for me?"

Laila wasn't sure if she could identify anyone, but she was willing to try. "Of course."

"Thanks. Why don't you shower and get dressed? Then you can do the dishes and start the laundry. I need to work on a few things."

With a nod, she stood. Trees's stare swept up and down her body. She flashed hot. Self-consciously, she tugged at his shirt, trying to drag it below her knees in a futile effort to feel less seen. But unlike the Ramos brothers, his stare wasn't a precursor to a sexual demand. Trees merely rose to his feet, withdrew his phone from his pocket, and headed to the corner of the house that contained his home office—the room beside hers.

After a shower, she realized she had nothing clean to wear until she finished laundry, so she donned Trees's overlarge red tee again, gathered all the dirty clothes, then started the washing machine. While the clothes agitated, she cleaned the kitchen.

That left her with nothing to do—a state she hated—so she made Trees's bed, then started tidying the rest of the house. As the weather warmed, he left his office. Together, they made lunch, then ate in relative silence. Afterward, he took her out back to better acquaint her with Barney. The big black dog still intimidated her, especially when he growled at her approach. But soon enough, he sniffed her outstretched hand, took a treat from her, and allowed her to pet him. Perhaps they would never be best friends, but she would settle for him not biting off her leg.

Back inside, afternoon shadows turned to evening. With that came thoughts of bedtime. Would Trees invite her to sleep there again? If he did, would they finish what she had so abruptly ended last night?

Laila wrestled with her mixed feelings as she tried to find interest in a telenovela. Eventually, the dramatics of the characters seemed too foolish to waste even another moment, and she drifted around the corner from her bedroom. The door to Trees's office was cracked enough to see the darkness inside, broken only by the glow of his computer monitors.

As she hovered in the doorway, his phone rang. He swiped it off the desk with a curse. "What's up, Muñoz? Any break on Kimber's case?"

Laila didn't mean to eavesdrop, but as she stepped back to give him privacy, his next words stopped her.

"No. Fuck no! Listen, let's cut the shit. Laila is safer here than anywhere else. Every inch of my land is monitored, and no one can set foot anywhere on it without me knowing. I'm armed to the teeth. I'm ready for any battle, even the fucking apocalypse. You know that; everyone on the team does. The only reason you and the Edgington brothers told Walker to come get Laila is because you think I'm fucking guilty of being your mole."

Shock froze her. Was it possible? Ever since their Orlando safe house had been breached, she had been wondering who inside their organization had leaked information to the wrong ears and exposed her family's location to Emilo. But Trees? In the past few days, she'd come to believe he was forthright. That he kept his word. That he was one of the good guys.

Isn't every man…until money is involved?

Was it possible he had sold out?

Would his own bosses think he was guilty if he hadn't?

She had to do something to protect herself. To protect Valeria and Jorge.

Thoughts racing, Laila tiptoed away from Trees and rushed to her bedroom, shutting the door with a barely audible click. She didn't want to believe Trees would betray her and her sister to men determined to kill them, then lie about it…but she hadn't managed to stay alive in a dangerous criminal underworld without being cautious—and using whatever connections she had.

She plucked up her burner phone and dialed one of the few numbers she knew by heart. On the second ring, she got an answer and exhaled with relief.

"Hello?" The voice was cautious—but thankfully familiar.

"Señor Walker, it is Laila Torres."

"You okay?"

He wasn't much for small talk, which suited her. "I need to ask you a question."

Walker would be bluntly honest. In Emilo's compound, their mutual desperation to escape had led them to team up. His three weeks in captivity had almost killed him. Her six years there had nearly destroyed her. She had found an outside line of communication to her sister to facilitate EM Security's arrival. One-Mile had hatched a plan to put them in the right place at the right time for their rescue. Together, they had succeeded. Then, when their first safe house in St. Louis had been breached, Walker had helped her and Valeria flee to Florida with perfect precision. He had never once made her doubt his loyalty or his intentions.

Should you really doubt Trees now?

She didn't want to. After all, EM Security's owners might be wrong. Or maybe there was a misunderstanding. It might even be an accident. Of course she wanted to find some way—any way—in which Trees wasn't guilty. But was that realistic? Was that her foolish heart talking? After all, she had only known the seemingly gentle giant a handful of days…but she had known the nature of men for years. Which should she really trust?

"Shoot. I've got a few minutes. I'm just waiting for my fiancée to finish talking to the florist. Our wedding is in two weeks."

He was getting married? Laila would have sworn the taciturn sniper wasn't the sort to take a wife, but he sounded downright happy.

She was thrilled for him, but she had to get answers while she could. "I am calling about Trees."

"Talk to me."

His cautious note set her on edge. "Why do your bosses want you to watch over me instead of him?"

"I'm sure they've got their reasons."

But his growl made her think he didn't disagree. "Is it because they believe that, in the past, he has leaked our whereabouts to Emilo?"

"Fuck," he spewed. "Where did you hear that?"

"It does not matter. What I want to know is if you think it is true."

He sighed. "Look, I don't want to throw a teammate under the bus. He seems like a good guy and all, but here's what I know. Last October, when we suddenly moved you to Florida, it was because we spotted Emilo in St. Louis, close to your house. We couldn't fucking figure out how he knew you and your family were even in the city. I worried we had a mole, and I worried it was Trees because he was with me when I got taken by Emilo's goons. Somehow, the lucky son of a bitch escaped. When I got free, I tested my theory that it was him by sending the exact address and the schematic of the St. Louis safe house to him via the office secretary. Within twenty-four hours, Emilo broke in through the back door with every intention of killing your sister. I don't know who else to blame."

"The secretary, perhaps?" Laila winced. She really wanted Trees to be innocent…and it was breaking her heart that the EM operative she trusted most was putting the nails in that coffin.

"I don't think Tessa has the know-how or the connections."

But Trees did. "I see. So he's guilty of selling you out?"

"I wish I didn't have to say it, but I'm afraid so."

Chapter Ten

"... The only reason you and the Edgington brothers want Walker to come get Laila now is because you think I'm fucking guilty of being your mole," Trees growled into the phone, wishing he could reach through and tear Muñoz a new asshole. Sure, he was pissed off that his own boss thought he was guilty and wouldn't man up and admit it. But he was way more hacked that the standoffish fucker had made the unilateral decision to take Laila away from him.

"We think she would be safer with him. And she trusts him. Last I heard, the same couldn't be said for you."

"Then you need an update. We've made progress. I've got her talking. I'm getting valuable information."

"Walker can get it, too. My mind is made up."

"Unmake it, goddamn it." He gripped the phone so tight he risked breaking it—and he didn't care. "How is Walker going to keep her safe?"

"He's one of the best fucking snipers in the world. We both know bodyguarding isn't your strength, and we have other jobs for you."

"Let's seriously cut the shit. If I was going to sell out Laila and her sister, I could have done that in Florida. Or anywhere along the road the last couple of days. Hell, I wouldn't have saved her when she fucking ran off in Orlando and was almost abducted by one of Emilo Montilla's thugs."

"What?" Joaquin sounded ready to blow a gasket.

Of course that was news. The bosses had been busy, and he hadn't broadcast all that shit to them. "Yeah. And if I was the kind of backstabber just here for the cash, I could sell her—and all of you—out right now. But I haven't. I won't. She. Is. Safe. Here. I would lay down my life to make sure of that."

In his ear, Joaquin sighed. "The circumstantial evidence is pretty damning."

"Ever think someone might be framing me?"

Muñoz didn't have an answer for that.

Trees barged into his silence. "Getting real? I know you three tasked Zy with proving I'm the mole."

"He fucking told you that?"

He had, but no way would Trees throw his buddy under the bus. "I could tell by the way he acted. You can't know someone as well as I know Zy and not realize his behavior was off. And I didn't have to guess too hard to figure it out. I can't prove to you that you're wrong, but you are."

"Maybe we are. Maybe we're not digging deep enough. But we can't unpack that right now. We have our hands full trying to figure out who's holding Kimber and where, so—"

"Which is another thing," Trees cut in. "Your little plan to dangle Laila as bait in some staged hostage exchange? No. That's not happening. You're going to get her killed—and Kimber, too. From what I've managed to coax from Laila, these aren't people you fuck with."

"You think we don't know that? We've been in that compound, One-Mile more than once. They left him with a long hospital stay and a broken jaw as souvenirs. You never even made it inside. So don't lecture us on how ruthless these sons of bitches are."

"They'll never fall for that old fucking trick you're trying to play."

"They might not. But we don't know unless we try." Joaquin sighed. "We're running out of options. Every hour that ticks down is another hour we wonder if and why Kimber's abductors would bother to leave her alive."

"A dead captive does them no good."

"That's what we're banking on, but they're running out of patience. We all feel it. Instead of playing defense, we need to go on the offensive and put an end to this."

"By offering up Laila, regardless of the risk to her? No."

"It's not your choice. She said yes."

Fuck, Trees wanted to punch Joaquin, mostly because he was running out of logic to fight back. And he didn't dare admit to his boss that he was falling for the woman whose body he had done far more to than guard. "Give me twenty-four hours more with her. She's beginning to trust me. With the information she has, she can likely help you locate Kimber and—"

"No, she can't."

"Do you know the players in this cartel drama? Everyone involved? The factions fighting each other and why? Who the power players are and who's likely to win? She does."

"Then I'll come get her and question her—"

"She was systematically and repeatedly raped for six years. Believe me when I tell you that winning her trust took time."

"You're telling me you managed to do it in four days?"

"Not one hundred percent, but I'm still four days ahead of you. Want to start the clock over? Will Kimber last that long?"

"That's where Walker comes in. She trusts him."

"And we're back to the fact that there's no place more secure to keep Laila than here."

Joaquin didn't answer right away, and Trees could all but hear him gnashing his teeth on the other end of the line. Finally, his boss cursed. "You have twenty-four hours. If we don't see some fucking progress by then, you'll turn her over to Walker, no questions asked. Agreed?"

Trees hesitated, his thoughts churning. He didn't want to agree to this shit. Who else would understand Laila's urge to barter for her necessities? Her fear of the dark? Her need for a firm but gentle hand? Not Walker.

But he also didn't have much choice.

"Fine. I'll get you usable information by tomorrow evening."

"If you don't, we'll be taking Laila off your hands."

Trees signed off with a grunt, then stabbed the button on his phone to end Joaquin's call. Why the fuck couldn't he convince his bosses that he wasn't a dirty sellout? Whatever. He didn't have time to rail about it. He needed to dig through Laila's thoughts and memories and come up with some theory about who kidnapped Kimber and why. What she'd spilled this morning told Trees a lot more than he'd known before—maybe even more than anyone else at EM knew. Had any of them asked either of the sisters questions?

Maybe they had, and Trees was just in the dark because they

thought he was the traitor. But if they hadn't…Laila and her knowledge might be the key to solving their problems.

Trees put his computer to sleep, then left the office in search of Laila. Dragging in a deep breath, he knocked on her slightly ajar door. It squeaked open. She spun to face him.

Her guarded expression told him instantly that something was wrong.

"Laila?" He entered the room slowly, gaze searching. "Little one?"

"I am fine." She refused to look at him.

"No, you're not. What happened?" He reached for her hand.

She recoiled.

Trees cursed. Something he'd done had freaked her out. The only thing that had happened between the last time they had talked and now and been Joaquin's phone call.

She'd overheard.

He tried to stay calm as he retreated to lean against the frame of her bedroom door. It was the perfect spot for two reasons: one, he had backed off, which hopefully would lower her anxiety. Two, she couldn't leave the room without going past him.

They were having this out now.

"Nothing." She didn't meet his stare. "I am tired."

He couldn't call bullshit. She'd been awake half of last night. He'd felt her restless and unsettled beside him. The dark circles bruising her eyes underscored that fact. "Want to nap?"

"Yes."

"Great. You know the rules. If you want to stay in this room alone, I'll need to cuff you."

Her big eyes widened. "I will not run."

"Yes, you will. You overheard me on the phone with my boss. You think I'm EM Security's mole."

"I-I do not know what you mean."

He eyeballed her. "You're a horrible liar. And if you'd think about this for more than two minutes, you'd realize I've done nothing but try to keep you safe since the moment I met you. But we need your help. We need information to try to rescue Kimber."

"What makes you think I can help?"

"Their ransom demand is Valeria's whereabouts."

Laila paled, then lurched for her phone.

Trees hauled across the room and grabbed her wrist before she could dial. "Your sister is perfectly safe. The Edgington brothers have no intention of trading your sister for theirs."

"You think I should simply believe you? Risk Valeria because you gave me hollow assurances?"

"I'm giving you logic. If they surrendered their client to get Kimber back, their reputations would be toast and their business would fold. Their livelihoods gone—forever. Besides, they're too smart to play this game the kidnappers' way. But they need help, information you have that no one else does. If we can uncover the identity of Kimber's kidnapper, we can take the fight to them. And we'll be better equipped to keep you and your family safe."

He watched Laila consider his words, just like he saw the moment she decided cooperating made sense. "What do you wish to know?"

Where the hell should he start? "Of the two factions fighting for control of Emilo's territory, you have any thoughts about which side is more likely to have taken Kimber?"

Laila paused, clearly considering. "When and how did the kidnapping occur?"

Trees relayed everything Caleb and Deke had told the office the day Kimber had disappeared, including the forewarning her father had received. "That's all I know."

"That tells me nothing. I am sure both sides are well aware of Colonel Edgington. Probably his daughter, too. I do not understand why they would threaten the man after he retired. Why not give the lipstick—and the warning—to one of your bosses? Or to her husband?"

A question Trees had wondered himself. "You can't think of a reason?"

Slowly, Laila shook her head. "The picture delivered with the lipstick is obviously of consequence. Retribution for stealing Valeria from them most likely. The cartel very much believes in revenge."

Trees didn't doubt that. "The men who participated on that mission were targeted. My bosses and the colonel. The other guy in the photo is an operative named Blaze Beckham. I've never met him. That name mean anything to you?"

"No."

Now that Trees thought about it… "The person with the closest connection to nearly everyone involved in Valeria's rescue is Kimber. She's the colonel's daughter, my bosses' sister…"

"Both Geraldo and Emilo's underlings are crafty enough to find the loved one important to all. That does not give me enough information to pinpoint who might be behind Kimber's abduction. It is perhaps more likely to be those loyal to Emilo since Hector is in the United States. Once here, he could move about freely and get close enough to take her. He is the kind of creeper who enjoys stalking a woman and pouncing when she least suspects it."

Then raping them in the most cruel, humiliating ways. Trees kept that thought to himself. "Do Geraldo and his thugs have trouble getting in and out of the country?"

"I do not know."

"I doubt it." The kind of money Geraldo had influenced people and opened doors. "So it's still possible either faction is responsible." Since that train of thought seemingly led to a dead end, Trees tried another. "Tell me what happened in the compound after Valeria was gone. You were left behind. Was Emilo upset or furious that she had escaped? Did he want her back? Or did he think it was good riddance?"

"He was furious. I have never seen him so angry. Honestly, that puzzled me because he barely noticed her. She was a possession to him, a thing mostly beneath his notice. He was neither kind nor faithful. He did not care about my sister. I assumed he would be happy to be rid of her. I hoped he would release me, too. After all, I would be one less bother. Instead, he gave Hector and Victor more tools to make certain I did not slip through their fingers. Then he took his anger out on me."

"He raped you more."

Laila hesitated, then nodded, her gaze skittering away.

He tipped her chin up until she met his stare again. "Listen to me. That isn't your fault. And that isn't your shame."

"I know you are right, but logic does not stop the feelings."

Her answer broke his heart, but when Trees made to gather her in his arms, she backed away. Because she was focused on helping Kimber? Or because she still thought he was the mole?

"Later, I realized that Valeria had been pregnant with Jorge when she escaped. Emilo probably realized it, too."

That made sense. The drug lord might not have wanted his wife, but he would want his son. "Did your sister know she was pregnant when she left?"

"That was the reason she fled. She knew her son would have no future except that of a criminal if she gave birth in that compound. So while EM Security was rescuing another captive, an influential doctor's daughter who had been abducted while providing medical assistance to poor villages, Valeria begged the team to take her with them."

"Why didn't they take you, too?"

"Nothing was planned, and everything happened too fast. That night I was pinned between Hector and Victor…"

When she trailed off, Trees fought down fury. Laila had suffered so much after Valeria's getaway. How could she have simply left her sister behind?

Isn't that what you did to your siblings? Didn't you see the opportunity to escape poverty and grab it with both hands?

Yep. And with a baby on the way, Valeria would have been even more motivated to escape.

Trees sighed. "So we're back to wondering why grown-ass drug dealers care that there's a toddler out there with Emilo's blood."

"It seems. If Emilo wanted his son back, I can think of no reason Hector and Victor are determined to grab Jorge except to fulfill the man's last wish."

"Then what would they do with the boy?" Trees scratched his head. "Jorge only has value for the Ramos brothers if he has value for Geraldo, too. A bargaining chip, if you will. After all, he is Geraldo's grandson."

"True. But he is even more valuable now that Emilo is dead. He was Geraldo's only son."

"Emilo's sister is gone, too. Clara tried to kill Walker's fiancée a couple of weeks ago to avenge her brother after One-Mile gunned him down. Walker and his buddies ended her."

"An eye for an eye," Laila murmured, then she frowned. "Was Clara the only one who pursued Walker for killing Emilo? No reprisal from Geraldo?"

"As far as I know, he didn't lift a finger." Trees followed her logic. "But why would Geraldo go to such lengths to get his hands on Jorge yet not avenge his son?"

Laila shrugged. "I can only guess his reasons. Geraldo's relationship with Emilo was complicated. Perhaps he had resigned himself to the fact that his son was ineffective and would never be fit to lead the cartel. He was not good at his tasks." Laila sighed in frustration. "I cannot think of the right word."

"Emilo was a fuckup."

"Yes."

"Would Geraldo want the fuckup's son?"

"Since Jorge is the only family he has left, likely so."

Slowly, Trees took that in. "Let's work off that theory. Both sides are looking for you or Valeria because they want Jorge—the Ramos brothers to use as a pawn and Geraldo because Jorge is the last of his blood, not to mention the heir of his nose-candy empire."

"Yes, but I still cannot say which side is more likely to have kidnapped Kimber."

He'd been afraid of that. "Maybe once we see the pictures of the bodies dumped in the EM Security parking lot, we'll get clarity."

"Maybe."

"Until then, let me convince you I'm not the mole who endangered you and your family."

She gave him a wary glance. "How?"

"I don't have any proof it wasn't me, but you know me, Laila."

"Do I?"

He sighed. "When have I not been a man of my word?"

"I find trust hard."

"Of course you do." And he knew why. Arguing about that did no good. Neither did spewing logic. He couldn't refute her feelings. He simply had to give her reasons to doubt those worries. "Tell me how I can convince you."

"There is nothing you can do."

He wouldn't accept that. "Listen to your gut. What is it telling you?"

"My gut has no facts. You were with Walker when he was taken in Mexico."

There was only one way she could know that, goddamn it. "You talked to him."

And Walker had thrown him under the bus. Of course, in Walker's shoes, Trees would probably think he was guilty as hell, too.

Laila stared stonily. "Yes. Is it true?"

Trees nodded. He had nothing to hide. "We went to Acapulco together on a mission. The afternoon we arrived, we stopped at a restaurant for an early dinner. In the parking lot afterward, we were surrounded by Emilo's thugs. Walker tossed me the keys and told me to get help. I drove away, only to pass out a mile or two up the road because our food had been drugged. The police found me in their parking lot twelve hours later."

She sent him a considering stare. "What about Emilo's break-in at the St. Louis house? Señor Walker sent you the address and the floor plan—"

"No. He sent it to our receptionist, Tessa, to send to me. Since I didn't give it to Emilo, she must have. There's no one else it could have been."

Laila looked skeptical. "Why would she do that?"

"Money, I guess. She's a single mother whose boyfriend ran out days before her daughter was born. Making ends meet has probably been tough. And before you ask how she would have made the connections necessary—"

"I would not. The cartel will make themselves known to anyone they find useful."

He hadn't considered it like that, but… "Exactly."

Trees was wracking his brain for another argument to convince Laila he'd never sell her out when she crossed her arms over her chest. "I would like to be alone. I need to think."

To decide if he was guilty? That put him on edge, but he didn't have any good reason to refuse—other than the thought of losing her scared the ever-loving shit out of him. "All right. The doors and windows are locked. The alarm is set. We should start dinner in an hour."

"I am not hungry. I will sleep here tonight. Alone."

"Cuffed? With the overhead light shining in your face?" Would she stay here under conditions she hated simply to avoid him?

Laila hesitated, then nodded. "Yes."

Trees lay in his solitary bed, eyes glued to the light filtering across the house from Laila's bedroom. He was hard as steel, but with her around that wasn't new. What was? Missing her. The big bed he'd always loved having to himself so his long arms and legs had spreading-out room felt too empty.

One night beside her, and she'd ruined him?

In his head, he replayed the moment he'd cuffed her to her bed for the night—her still wearing his T-shirt with a wary expression. She looked beautiful with her dark hair spilling across the white pillow, and he'd give anything to know if she was any closer to trusting him. But he had to be patient and let her work that out in her head.

Trees sighed and stared at the ceiling. Despite being exhausted, he suspected it would be a long night.

On his nightstand, his phone vibrated. The distraction was almost a relief until he scooped up the device and got a glimpse of the screen. Why the hell would Zy be calling him after midnight?

"Buddy?"

"My fucking life is over."

"That's dramatic," Trees returned tongue-in-cheek, mostly because Zy sounded half-sauced.

"Yep, but that's how it feels."

Trees frowned. "Are you drinking?"

"Absofuckinglutely." Zy sighed. "I don't know what the fuck to do. Tessa is our mole. Go on. You can say you told me so."

Trees bolted straight up in bed. "You sure? How did you figure it out?"

"Not two hours ago, I gave her a cover story, disinformation I hadn't spewed to anyone else. It didn't take long for the cartel's communications on Abuzz to light up like fireworks."

Fuck. That was bad. "I'm sorry."

"Yeah. Me, too. Especially since I just got off the phone with Hunter Edgington. He's pissed that I went rogue and decided to test her on my own. He feels stupid for being wrong, too. He was convinced it was you."

"No surprise there."

"You're off the hook with him, so there's that. But the other bosses need convincing. I've got six hours to give them proof it's Tessa before they move on it."

While Zy's heart was shattering? Damn… "You need help?"

"Yeah."

In that rough syllable, Trees heard his best friend's broken hopes for a future with Tessa and wished he could say something to make it better.

"Do you need me to come out there and get you?" He wasn't sure what he'd do with Laila, but if Zy needed him, he'd figure it out.

"No, I'm not trashed. I just need you to help me figure out how Tessa could have been the mole all along. She was on maternity leave during the first information leaks."

"You got it. I'll put on a pot of coffee and be waiting for you."

"Thanks." Zy hung up with a sigh that sounded more than tired. It was eat-a-bullet weary.

That worried the hell out of Trees.

With a curse, he rose and tossed on some sweatpants and a tee, then headed across the house to Laila. He half expected to see her curled on her side, tresses tumbling behind her, as they always did in sleep. Instead, she lay on her back, gaze glued to the ceiling.

"Laila?"

"What?" She jolted, then scrambled to pull the covers closer.

It wouldn't do any good to remind her that he'd already seen and touched all the parts she tried to hide. Even so, glimpsing the outline of her nipples through her shirt set his libido off again. Every time he fucking looked at her, he felt as if he hadn't had sex in decades, rather than being deep inside her mere days ago. "Zy is on his way over. It's work. I won't be getting to bed anytime soon, so if you want me to uncuff you…"

"Please."

He approached. The closer he came to her, the faster his heart raced, chugging like mad when he sat on the edge of the bed and took her hand in his. "If tonight works out the way I think, I can prove I'm not the mole who sold your whereabouts to the cartel."

Something brightened her eyes—hope?—before she blinked it away. "If you can prove it, I will listen."

Trees didn't blame her for being skeptical, but it frustrated him. "I wish you'd try to believe me regardless."

"Why do my feelings matter? You are my bodyguard. You are paid to keep me safe, nothing more."

Was she serious? "You think there's nothing else between us? Can you look me in the eye and tell me you don't feel a thing for me?"

Laila looked away. "Are you going to uncuff me?"

"Yeah." It wouldn't do any good to press the issue.

Seconds later, she was free. He left the room before he spilled more of his heart and headed to the kitchen. He flipped on the coffeepot before heading out front, shotgun in hand, to breathe in the crisp night air.

Twenty minutes later, Zy pulled up and stepped off his bike, gesturing to the firearm. "Is that your idea of a warm welcome? I can go if you're that adamant about sleep."

"Ha ha. Just being cautious, keeping out the riffraff, you know. But now that you're here, maybe I should shoot you just for the hell of it."

"Pass." Zy sighed. "Sorry. I'm all out of jokes."

Trees didn't doubt that. Frankly, he felt pretty much the same. "Yeah. You look like someone shit all over your life. I was just trying to lighten your mood."

"I appreciate that, but don't."

"All right. I'll zip it."

As his buddy hung his helmet on his handlebars, Trees opened the front door.

"Where's Laila?"

Since Zy had enough going on with the Tessa situation, Trees gave him a flippant answer. "In her room, waiting for me to fall asleep before she'll risk getting into bed and closing her eyes."

"She still doesn't trust you?"

"She doesn't trust anyone. I'm trying not to take it personally."

"Even if it's not a knock against you, that's got to be hard. You're the dude most people trust with whatever they value—vehicles, pets, girlfriends."

"Yeah." Wasn't irony a bitch? "She's not most people."

"Is she making noise about wanting to be with her sister?"

Trees stepped inside the house and locked the shotgun back in its case. "Some, but Valeria admitted to Laila she's the reason they're apart."

"At least she's not blaming you. Did she ever let you buy her warmer clothes?"

"Negative. No offense, buddy, but could we talk about your misery instead?" Besides, the clock to build the bosses a timeline of Tessa's guilt was ticking down.

"Why not? Everyone else is."

Together, they made their way to the kitchen, and Zy folded himself into a chair as Trees poured coffee and slid a mug across the table. "Sorry, man. Tell me what happened?"

Zy did, explaining that he'd fed Tessa his cover story. It had taken less than an hour for his disinformation to spread through their community on Abuzz. Trees suspected he'd heard the G-rated version of events because, even at a glance, it was obvious Zy hadn't managed to stay out of Tessa's bed. And that had fucked with Zy's head even more.

"This is killing you, and you still love her."

Zy frowned. "I try to tell myself I don't. That I'm in love with who I thought she was and I miss what it seemed we had. But I can't lie to myself. She double-crossed me, and she would only do that for some reason she thinks is necessary. And I can't make myself unlove her."

"I know." It was fucking sad. Trees had always suspected that when Zy fell, it would be real and lasting. He'd never imagined the reciprocation would be a lie.

"She's not capable of intentionally hurting people she cares about. Which says she could only do this because she doesn't really give a shit about me at all."

And that was killing Zy. "I don't believe that. I've watched her. I've seen the way she looks at you, and I think she loves you." At least as much as she would let herself. The attachment was there…but Trees suspected that Tessa loved money more. "Any chance she doesn't understand the ramifications of what she was doing?"

"No."

"Maybe she—"

"Whatever you're going to say, no. Don't try to make this better. You can't. So let's just get this shit done. The bosses want a timeline of the mole's activities, so…I guess we'll start at the beginning. Go through the backups. See what you can find in the electronic records on the EM servers."

"How long do you have?"

Zy glanced at his phone. "Another five hours, give or take ten minutes."

Trees scoffed. "The bosses don't want the fucking world or anything."

"They never do…"

"I've got a spare computer in the office. Would you grab it? I'll start capturing the data sets and pulling them down. Once I've got them, I'll show you what we're looking for, then you can search the records, too. This will go twice as fast if we both look."

"Sure. On it." Zy disappeared down the hall.

After a few minutes and a minor run-in with Laila, they settled back at the kitchen table.

"You ready to do this?" Trees tried to focus on the task at hand.

"As I'll ever be."

"I've got the data sets ready. We need to account for all the breaches in EM Security's information, times when the enemy seemed to know shit they shouldn't have, and see if we can trace it back to any communication from Tessa, identify who it was going to, and how she might have passed the information."

Zy nodded. "So what am I looking for?"

"Anything. Emails, website hits, log-ins to online locations that seem fishy. If I have to drill down to the keystroke level, I will. But let's see what we can establish without that since months of that info would take more than five hours to comb through."

"Sure."

"You take January through March. She was on maternity leave most of that time, so the majority of the emails and communications you'll be sifting through will belong to Aspen." Trees almost winced when he said the temp's name.

"Oh, god help us all. I'd forgotten about her."

"I'd like to..." Trees rolled his eyes. "I'll take April through August and see what kind of patterns emerge. Oh, and be sure to look at any cookies, plug-ins, or other programs she might have downloaded. I compiled a list of EM-approved software." He slid the paper on the table between them. "Anything else is something she would have downloaded without telling the bosses and worth looking at. If you have questions about what you find, holler. I'll figure it out."

"Thanks."

Obviously, he wasn't grateful at all. How could he be, actively working to gather evidence against the woman he loved?

Trees reached across the table to slap his shoulder in support. "You're welcome."

Then they both dived in. Trees worked faster since Zy's specialty wasn't tech but demolitions. Trees didn't pretend to be anything but functional when it came to blowing shit up.

"What is toy voyaging?" Zy asked suddenly. "Any idea?"

"No. What the hell?"

Zy looked it up, then just started shaking his head. "Who sends their toys with strangers so they can be photographed around the world? And why is that a thing?"

"Is it? Really?"

"It is for Aspen," Zy went on to explain. "Apparently, she got a kick out of that."

"Because that's not weird or anything," Trees quipped.

"Not at all. So here's a piece of software either she or Tessa downloaded on January thirty-first, exactly one year ago. The location suggests it was installed onto Tessa's machine. Was she in the office that day?"

Since Zy hadn't begun working for EM Security yet, he had no way of knowing, so Trees stepped in. "Let me bump that against a calendar I maintained. I told the colonel I wasn't a fan of letting the temp use Tessa's machine because we didn't know her, but we didn't have a spare at the time. So I kept track of who had control of it when." Trees flipped over to another document on his computer and scanned it with a frown. "That was one of Tessa's last days in the office before her maternity leave. She was supposed to have worked with Aspen the following Monday through Wednesday, as I recall. But she went into labor on Tuesday morning and didn't come back until the end of March."

"So Tessa probably downloaded this?"

"Most likely. What is it?"

Zy scowled as he scanned the code again. "Looks like some sort of spyware maybe."

"Let me see." Trees craned his head to study the screen—and he didn't like what he saw. "Fuck. This is some hand-coded shit that collects every keystroke, but it also enables stealth remote access from anywhere in the world."

Zy paled. "So whoever installed this could tap into Tessa's computer at will and could see every time she or Aspen hit a key? And they could access our servers without anyone being the wiser?"

As much as he hated to tell his buddy, Trees couldn't sugarcoat this. "Yep. I begged Aspen to let me scan that computer a couple of times. Every time, she said it crashed or she finger-flubbed whatever she'd been typing and ended up somewhere in the computer she shouldn't be, like a command prompt."

"Then Tessa couldn't have had anything to do with this. She's not a computer whiz, and she definitely doesn't know anything about writing code, especially something that involved."

"You think Aspen does?" Trees pointed out. At least Tessa was good at her job. The temp had been a wreck.

"Is it possible neither of them did this?"

"Possible? Anything is. Improbable? Yeah." And Trees felt really sorry for Zy. "Keep digging. See if you can find any traces of contact in March, around the time we went to Mexico and damn near got ambushed."

"Getting there. After that software is installed, there isn't much in the way of sent emails except to the bosses. It's like…Aspen didn't do that much."

"No, it's not 'like' that. She actually didn't do much. But no fishy communications around the time of our mission?"

Zy shrugged. "Not that I see."

"With remote access and keystroke recording, all anyone had to do was log in to our server themselves and they could mine almost anything."

"Do you think that spyware/remote-access garbage is still on Tessa's computer?"

Zy clearly hoped Tessa had been passing on information without even knowing it, and Trees had bad news for his buddy. "No. As soon as Aspen cleared the building, I restored the computer back to the factory settings, then carefully rebuilt Tessa's profile. I didn't trust Aspen not to have unwittingly screwed everything up."

"So the rogue software is gone? And we have no way of knowing who might have been accessing our systems and where the information was going?"

Trees winced. "When you put it that way, I should have looked to see what was on the computer before I wiped it, but I had no idea…"

"You couldn't have. You finding anything else?"

Yeah, and it wasn't good. "Let me finish. Then…we'll talk."

Zy stood and ambled to the coffeepot, brewing another. "Coffee?"

"Yeah. It's going to be a long night."

Zy glanced down the hall, where Laila's light was still on. "Should I encourage her to go to sleep?"

"You can try, but she won't."

With a grim press of his lips, Zy poured two cups of coffee and headed back to the table. Trees absently sipped the black brew and scribbled notes as he peered at the screen, working, working…until he came across something that made his heart stop.

When Trees looked up, Zy froze. "What?"

"There are footprints of communications from what looks like a Gmail account to an external mail host with its servers in Switzerland."

"Why is that important? Why does the server location matter?"

"Because the Swiss have some of the strictest tech privacy laws in the world. No one is getting their hands on that information. A lot of people use this kind of service. People who don't like their emails being scanned for keywords so that online retailers can market to them, for instance. People who don't love government intrusion into their personal life."

"So you have one of these email addresses?"

"Not this particular provider. This one is expensive. But I have one like it. It's also commonly used by people who have something to hide."

"Like criminals?"

As much as Trees hated to admit it… "Exactly. I'm not saying that anyone who has one of these is up to something nefarious, but I am saying that anyone up to something nefarious probably has one of these email addresses, rather than a simple freebie."

"Let me recap: Someone with Gmail sent messages to a party with a super-secure email address who might be a criminal?"

"Yes."

"And?"

"Because the information packet passed through our server, and I have some goodies residing there just in case, I can read the contents of the emails. But I can't prove who the Gmail address belongs to." But if they could prove it was Tessa's, then she was toast.

So was Zy's heart.

"Are the communications from this Gmail something to worry about?"

Trees hated to tell him the truth, but Zy needed to hear it. "August eighteenth. The Gmail account owner wrote a summation of the plan

Hunter outlined for Walker and me to spy in Mexico. The mission in which he was taken in the parking lot."

"Shit."

"Yep. Shit." That had definitely been the work of their mole. What chapped Trees's hide more was that the bosses would have come to him to investigate this sooner if they hadn't suspected him. "There's just one thing about this that's a little weird: the message was sent in the middle of the night."

Zy frowned. "Tessa takes her laptop home with her more often than not. She always said it was in case the bosses needed something during evening and weekends."

She was the receptionist. What were the odds of that? "Or maybe she does that in case a certain cartel needs answers day or night."

"How do we prove whether that message came from Tessa?"

"Without her computer, we don't."

Zy's frown became a scowl. "What about Walker's rescue mission in September? That went off without a hitch."

"The one I missed because of truck-stop sushi, where Laila had been freed. Right..." Trees searched the files for emails corresponding to those times. "No. Nothing."

"Were the bosses keeping the details of that rescue mission better under wraps? Or...wait. Wasn't that when she went to Tennessee because her father died?"

That sounded familiar. Trees clicked onto a calendar, then nodded. "You're right. She wasn't *around* to learn about the plan and pass it on."

He hated to say it, but he could *see* her step-by-step betrayal—just as easily as he could tell it crushed Zy.

"But she was back in plenty of time to rat out the location of Valeria's safe house in St. Louis."

Just to be sure, Trees cross-checked that timeframe, then nodded. "I just accessed the server's October backup. Sure enough, here's another communication from the Gmail account to the secure mail host, forwarding the email Walker sent me—via Tessa—with the location's floor plan. And like before, she sent the email in the middle of the night."

"She told the drug lord exactly where to find his estranged wife?" Somehow, Zy still seemed surprised by her duplicity.

He obviously didn't want to believe the woman he loved could be so guilty.

Trees hated it, but he had to keep bursting Zy's bubble. "Yep. All the way down to the location of her bedroom."

Zy's expression hardened over. "Anything else? Did she divulge the location of Valeria's safe house in Orlando, too? And who would she be talking to now that Emilo is dead?"

Valid question, one he'd like the answer to so he could explain to Laila. Maybe then she'd do more than try to trust him. "I can't tell." Trees clicked around, but no luck. "I don't see specific communications this month, but she might have realized someone was on to her and switched up her mode of talk. I won't know until I get my hands on her computer. You gotta get it for me, man. Now."

Zy nodded, looking like a man heading into a dangerous, bloody battle.

"I know this is going to fuck you up for a while. I hate that like hell for you, but without her computer, I can't prove what Tessa is up to or how she's doing it. And if I can't do that, more people may die." Trees looked down the hall, at the light from Laila's room shining this way. "People who deserve to finally live."

Zy nodded and stood, looking grimly resolute. "I'm on it."

Chapter Eleven

Trees sipped on another cup of joe and waited for Zy to return with Tessa.

Over the past couple of hours, his buddy had sneaked into the receptionist's house and prowled through her laptop to verify that the Gmail account they'd been looking for did, in fact, belong to her. Then Zy had cuffed the little turncoat to her car to bring her out to his place. In the meantime, Trees had asked Madison to hang out at Tessa's duplex in case her daughter, Hallie, woke in her crib. Thankfully, she'd agreed. Now he was just waiting for Zy and Tessa to roll up.

This was going to be ugly.

Since Laila had finally fallen asleep thirty minutes ago, cuffed once again to her bed, Trees paced the porch. Zy had ninety minutes before he had to call the bosses and present their timeline of Tessa's betrayal. Trees had already pieced some of it together, but to fill in all the blanks, Zy would need to question her. What his buddy really wanted was a pound of her flesh. Not that he blamed Zy. He'd like some revenge, too. Her greed or need for cash or whatever her excuse for going rogue had not only broken Zy's heart but nearly cost Laila and her family their lives more than once.

Finally, the pair pulled up, the little sedan's headlights bobbing down the gravel road leading to his ranch house. Trees jogged down to meet them and opened the passenger door, uncuffing Tessa's wrist before he tugged her out of the car. "Let's go."

With one hand, she clutched a blanket around her seemingly naked body and sent him an imploring stare. "Trees… Talk to him. Please. It's not what you think—"

"Shut up," Zy snapped, his command full of fury and heartache. "God, how fucking low are you willing to stoop? It's done. You're caught. We're over."

The pretty blonde shook her head. "But it's not—"

"I don't care!" Zy spewed the words, but he was clearly lying.

As he gripped Tessa and dragged her out back to the bunker, Trees scooped up her laptop, phone, and keys, then followed closely behind.

When they reached the opening, his buddy lifted the heavy metal lid to the underground shelter and gave Tessa a shove. "Get in."

She panicked, digging in her heels. "What are you going to do to me? What's—"

"A lot less than you deserve." Ignoring her screeches, he hauled her against him and descended into the shadowy lair.

"No! Don't. Stop, Zy! Please…"

With a heavy heart, Trees shut the door on them, then retreated to the kitchen, where he opened Tessa's laptop. Zy was counting on him to start assembling the timeline for their bosses.

The log-in screen flashed. Of course he could bypass it, but what the hell would he find? Would Zy be able to handle it?

Before he could start answering those questions, Zy emerged from the bunker again. Trees took one look at his pal's shell-shocked face in the back porch light and went running. If Zy had looked twisted in knots before, now he looked bent and broken.

Trees fought back the urge to throttle pretty, backstabbing Tessa. "She's destroying you."

"I don't know how to fucking stop it." Zy looked near tears.

Trees dropped a supportive hand to his friend's shoulder. "If you were able to do the forensic dive on her computer, I would interrogate her for you…"

But that wasn't possible. Trees had only basic interrogation skills. Zy knew the dirty ones, and he'd never had a problem doing what needed to be done. Then again, he'd never fallen for the enemy.

"I know."

"You're not up for this. We need to call someone else."

"There is no one, man. The bosses are wrapped up in saving Kimber. Kane has Valeria. One-Mile…"

Trees reared back. "You going to let that crazy son of a bitch near her?"

"Fuck no. Besides, I have to report something to the bosses in an hour. And if Tessa is at all involved in Kimber's kidnapping—"

"They'll call the police."

Zy nodded grimly. "I can't stop it."

"The universe owes you for this, man."

"I need a drink."

Instead of reminding him that he shouldn't imbibe on the job, Trees led his buddy into the kitchen, straight to the whiskey.

Zy knocked back three fingers with a tortured sigh. "Have you started going through her things yet?"

"No. I know I'm going to find more, and I hate to pile on right now."

"This is probably like ripping off a Band-Aid—better to do it all at once so the sting goes away faster."

"Maybe. I think what's killing you now—besides the fact she ripped out your heart—is the not knowing. Exactly what she did. Why she did it. Why she dragged you into it."

"There's a part of me that keeps insisting this isn't like her, that she would never hurt anyone—much less everyone—without a damn good reason."

"You mean other than money?" Trees raised a cynical brow.

"I know that's enough reason for most people, but..." Zy shook his head. "Or maybe she snowed me so fucking bad I was willing to believe everything, even her goodness."

"You have an instinct about her, and they aren't usually wrong. One of the things I've always admired about you is your people skills."

"You only think mine are good because yours suck ass."

"Mine do." They ribbed each other a little before Trees went on. "Straight up? You can get to the bottom of this faster than anyone. I said before that I think she loves you. And I still think it's true...in her way. Go use her own tools against her."

"What do you mean?"

"Emotion. Appeal to her good side. Get under her skin. Hell, peel off her clothes and fuck her brains out if that forces the truth from her. I can give you hard evidence, but only she can fill in the gaps and explain *why*."

Zy snorted. "If what we suspect is real, Tessa only has a passing relationship with the truth. Why should now be different?"

Trees paused and weighed the wisdom of venturing into territory he'd never charted with Zy. But desperate times and all that... "Did you ever ask yourself why I have handcuffs handy? You already asked once why I had rope in my nightstand drawer. You know I'm a control freak. Do the math."

Zy's expression told him the instant the truth hit. "You're a Dominant. Like the bosses."

Trees nodded. "Keeping it real, man. I think that's your instinct, too. But if you've never partaken, it's cool. Just...um, word of advice? When you want the truth from a sweet little thing like Tessa—"

"I think we've determined she's not sweet."

Trees shook his head. "Don't confuse her acts with the woman herself. She's gotten herself tangled up in this shit for reasons you and I may never fully understand. But your instincts are right. She's naturally sweet. A pleaser."

"Submissive?"

"Maybe. Probably. But you don't know if you don't try. So here's my advice: if you spank her and she comes up biting your head off, then probably not and you should stop immediately. But...if you try and she doesn't? If she melts? It just might make her pliable enough to be honest. Worth a shot, anyway."

"Hell, at this point, I'm willing to try anything."

Trees clapped him on the back. "You just might be surprised. And if I'm right, a bunch of my equipment is down there. You can thank me later."

Zy yanked his phone from his back pocket and settled it on the counter. "I know I'm running out of time. If the bosses call, stall them. But I don't want to be disturbed. I'm not coming out of that fucking bunker again until I have answers."

Trees gave his pal a last supportive clap on the back. As Zy descended again, he headed back into the kitchen with a sigh. He was fucking tired, and he needed another cup of coffee if he was going to outline Tessa's guilt and finish ripping out Zy's heart.

He poured a mug from the lukewarm pot and shoved it in the nuker. As it reheated, he made his way to Laila's room. The stupid, impulsive part of him wanted to wake her and insist he wasn't EM Security's mole and he'd never put her family in danger.

But it was pointless. So far, he had only circumstantial evidence, not proof. To fully trust him, Laila would need that. She deserved it.

When he reached the bedroom, he eased the door open. Like before, she lay on her side, burrowed under the blankets—except her wrist, attached to the bedpost. At some point, she had buried her face under a pillow to block out the bright lights overhead. She must be exhausted, and she looked uncomfortable.

Damn it.

Trees tried to stifle his guilt. Since Laila had run away one too many times, he was forced to cuff her to keep her here and safe.

The self-pep-talk was bullshit. Laila had been held against her will for years. Did the fact he was doing it for different reasons really matter? She was still a captive.

But what fucking choice did he have? It was dangerous out there, and if Victor Ramos or any of Emilo's men found her again, she'd never leave their captivity alive.

Cursing, he stomped to the office, grabbed a trio of items, then returned to deposit them on the dresser. Another errand across the house sent him into his hidden room under the master. He'd built it as a panic room...but he'd decked it out as a private dungeon. It hadn't been finished long enough for him to put it to good use, but he'd outfitted the place first class, eagerly waiting for the moment he found the right woman to bring here. The notion of using his new equipment on Laila messed with his head. He fantasized about bringing her here and putting her at his tender mercy for their mutual pleasure.

It's not happening, dude.

Trees grabbed what he'd come for, locked up, then dashed back to Laila. In three minutes, he had batteries in the electric candles Madison had given him for Christmas, their golden beams putting out soft ambient light.

Then he returned to Laila's side. She hadn't moved. Carefully, he unshackled her wrist and removed the cuff with the short chain, replacing it with one that stretched two feet.

Gently, he rolled Laila to her back, displacing the pillow from over her eyes. Trees didn't mean to stare, but every time he set eyes on her, she did something to him. Her curls were like a halo around her shoulders. Her graceful neck gave way to a firm jaw, a stubborn chin, and a pouty mouth that made him sweat. Her long lashes brushed her soft cheeks below delicately arched brows.

He'd had sex with her three days ago. Since then, he hadn't stopped thinking about her. Of course he wanted her underneath him again, but what he felt was more than sex. He wanted to protect her, help her, give her a better life. He wanted to be a better man so she would believe a good one existed.

Yeah, he was probably in love.

And if he wanted to prove he hadn't double-crossed her beyond any shadow of doubt, he needed to get to work. He also probably needed to stop hoping she would ever have real feelings for him. Every time he'd touched her, she had allowed it because she had an ulterior motive, not because she'd wanted him. He needed to remember that and keep his head screwed on straight.

Trees tore out of the room, flipping off the overhead light, leaving the soft glow of the candles to ward off the dark. Back in the kitchen, his coffee, still sitting in the microwave, had gone lukewarm again. He didn't give a shit at this point. It was caffeine. He needed to choke it down and be productive.

Snarling, he swallowed some of the black brew, wincing at its bitterness as he sat at Tessa's computer. Two minutes later, he was behind her log-in screen and prowling through her files…trying to focus on helping Zy and off of touching Laila.

He broke into Tessa's Gmail. Junk mail, correspondence from a sorority sister she hadn't answered, a bill reminder from the electric company. Then a few days ago, a slew of emails from someone with an obviously computer-assigned handle.

Trees opened it to find a video of Tessa's baby girl in a high chair eating chicken nuggets and a banana. Before he could figure out who had sent her the video and why, his phone dinged. Madison.

`Are you awake? Something's wrong!`

His gut tightened. `What?`

`Hallie isn't in her crib. She's gone!`

What the hell? Trees started to call Madison when he caught sight of the text attached to the video of Tessa's little girl. The words there made his blood run cold.

"Son of a bitch."

His heart pounding, he dashed off a reply to Madison. `On it. Stand by.`

But the rest of her emails didn't tell him much more, so he reached for Tessa's phone. He had a hunch... Sure enough, she'd downloaded the Abuzz application. She hadn't posted once, but she had DMs—all from the same shell account. Generic screen name, no picture, and no location listed. In other words, nothing to help him identify who it might belong to. But given the slew of messages this person and Tessa had exchanged over the last few days, the account was by no means inactive.

More images of Hallie were attached, along with messages confirming his fears.

He vaulted out of his chair, shoving the device into his back pocket, and ran hard for the bunker.

"Zy!" Trees banged on the metal lid.

Seconds later, his pal opened up. Trees jumped inside, only to find Tessa red-cheeked and barely covered in the quilt while Zy stood sweating, flushed, and emotionally wasted.

He scowled. "I guess you didn't spend your time with Tessa finding out what the fuck has been going on."

Zy cupped Tessa's shoulders and helped her to her feet, glaring back at him. "Can it."

No chance in hell, especially since Zy had no idea what Tessa was going through. Instead, he turned to her. "Why haven't you told him? Why haven't you told anyone?"

She reared back. "Y-you know?"

"Yeah, I do. And—"

"Know what?" Zy roared, looking back and forth between them. "Stop fucking talking circles around me and spill."

Trees waited for Tessa to say something. She'd obviously suffered, but if she would just give Zy the truth, he'd do anything—everything—to help her.

Tessa blinked away her tears. "The man who accosted me in the parking lot on Tuesday?"

"Yeah, I remember. I'm still trying to identify him."

"That night, he abducted Hallie. When I woke up Wednesday morning, she was…g-gone."

Zy froze as the implications sunk in. He scrubbed a hand down his shocked face. "Oh, god. Tessa…baby. You've been passing on information to save Hallie's life?"

Tessa broke down, tears flowing, her body wracked by sobs.

"Exactly," Trees answered when she couldn't.

Questions seemed to zip through Zy's head, probably the same ones he had. If one faction of Tierra Caliente had Kimber, the other must have Tessa's baby, but which had who? And why hadn't Tessa told the team the minute she'd realized Hallie was gone? And the bigger kicker? If the child had been gone a mere handful of days, who had engaged in the espionage that had fucked EM Security for nearly a year?

"Tell me what you know," Zy demanded.

"Not much since I didn't get to finish the forensic deep dive on her devices…" Trees explained Madison's texts and the kidnapper's communications.

"Tessa, I'm so fucking sorry." Zy lifted her grief-filled face to his. "Why didn't you tell me?"

"Because they threatened to kill Hallie if Tessa said a word to anyone," Trees supplied.

When he whipped Tessa's phone from his back pocket, he played the first video the abductor had sent for Zy, who seemingly watched in horror until the end. "You've been dealing with this, completely on your own, since Wednesday?"

"I couldn't risk her by telling anyone," Tessa choked.

"Oh, baby. If I'd known, I would have moved mountains to help you."

"They're watching me. They threatened… I didn't know the bosses think we have a mole, but I knew some things hadn't gone right. I'd overheard conversations that suggested information that shouldn't get out somehow had. I was too afraid of what would happen to my baby if I opened my mouth."

Zy tugged her stiff body close. Trees felt the device in his pocket vibrate and pulled it free. When he scanned the screen, he cursed. He hated to add to Tessa's trauma, but he didn't have the luxury of shielding her. Since her daughter was concerned, he doubted she'd want him to.

Trees nudged the phone in Tessa's direction. "I know this is tough…but you've got a new message." Then he turned to Zy with a pissed-off glare. "And I don't have to tell you what app they're using."

"Abuzz? Fuck." He sighed. "That cocksucker. I reamed him out once. He just never fucking listens."

"Who?" Tessa's hand shook as she took the phone and opened the app, looking terrified.

"Phillip Garrett," Trees helpfully supplied.

She frowned, clearly confused. "The billionaire who owns Abuzz?"

"Yeah." Zy sighed. "My dad."

Trees knew he hated to mention the connection, hated people thinking he'd been born with a silver spoon in his mouth. It didn't shock Trees that Tessa didn't know.

"Really?" Her eyes widened with hope. "He could help us track down or pinpoint the location of the kidnapper keeping Hallie."

Zy snorted. "The Tierra Caliente cartel has been using the app to communicate for months. I warned him once, and if it's still going on, they're paying him to look the other way. He won't help. Dear ol' Dad is more interested in making a buck than doing what's right."

"It's one reason they don't get along," Trees supplied.

"One of many."

Tessa looked stunned. "You grew up with a billionaire?"

Zy winced. "And the billion problems that go with that."

"You never told me." She sounded hurt.

Zy didn't respond to that. "The kidnapper sent a new message? What does he want now?"

Tessa's fingers trembled as she opened the DM and fresh tears fell down her cheeks. "Something I don't know how to give them."

"Let me see. Let me help you," Zy insisted. "You've been dealing with this by yourself for too long, and I can—"

"You can't," she screeched. "See for yourself."

When she shoved the phone into Zy's hands, Trees looked over his buddy's shoulder and scanned the message.

`Who is the mole leaking EM Security's information to outsiders? You have twenty-four hours to provide information and proof or Hallie will pay with her life.`

What the fuck? But the implications seemed clear. Whoever had kidnapped Hallie must not have been the same people paying the mole for information about EM Security missions—at least that seemed logical, but in a world of murderous thugs willing to sell deadly chemicals for cash, there probably was no such thing as loyalty. Anyone could be double-dealing.

"Can I see your phone again?"

Visibly shaken, Tessa passed it back.

Trees couldn't help but feel sorry for her. "If there's a way to solve this, we will."

Wordlessly, she nodded. But her terrified expression hurt.

Zy slung an arm around her, and Trees scrolled back through her Gmail. *Bingo!* The video of Hallie eating had come from a different address than the one the mole—someone other than Tessa?—had sent information about EM's missions and Valeria's whereabouts to.

Trees wasn't sure who the players were, but they needed to figure it out fast.

"Let's go inside. Tessa can get warm. We can dig more and gameplan."

The couple agreed. No wonder, since everyone was drained. Tessa wanted a hot shower, and Trees agreed to meet Madison halfway between his place and town to pick up some necessities for her.

After a quick grab of items on the side of the road, Trees squeezed Madison's shoulder in thanks. She gave him a tired smile and a kiss on the cheek.

"Go home and get some rest."

"Do you need more help?"

She was loyal and selfless…and she would make some man an amazing wife someday. Trees didn't know why he hadn't fallen for her. On paper, she was perfect.

One thing he did know? He considered her a friend, and he didn't want her any deeper in this. "We got it from here. Thanks for everything."

With a nod and a wave, she was gone. Trees headed back to his place, trying not to look at the clock and think about all the hours of sleep he was missing.

As he parked in back of his house, he received a text from Zy. `I have an idea. You going to be much longer?`

With a wry grin, he pocketed his phone and shouldered his way inside. "No, buddy. I won't be much longer at all." Then he turned to Tessa, holding out the overnight bag. "Madison said this should get you by for a day or so."

Tessa rose, gripping the blanket around her, and took the sack by the handles. "Thank you. And please thank her for me."

"She said she was happy to do it."

"I'll go change." Tessa headed to the bathroom.

"I'll catch Trees up on our theory," Zy called to her retreating back.

"Theory?" Trees asked once they were alone.

"We think we figured out who our mole is. Let's call the bosses, so I can explain this all at once."

They wandered to the kitchen together and sat. Zy dialed Hunter, who answered on the first ring. "You got something?"

"Yeah. You sitting?"

"Just a minute. Logan and Joaquin want to hear this, too."

Trees wasn't surprised they were all up in the middle of the night. Their lives had to be pressure cookers right now.

It wasn't long before Hunter spoke again. "We're all here."

"Tell us what the hell is going on," Logan demanded.

"Long story short?" Zy began. "Our mole is Tessa's ex-boyfriend. Here's our timeline. Last January, we think Aspen planted spyware on Tessa's laptop since she was using the machine while Tessa was on maternity leave."

Trees scowled. "How is that possible? She could barely find the button to turn the machine on?"

"The way I heard it, she wasn't good for much but answering phones," Joaquin drawled.

"It must have been an act." Zy leaned in. "At the time, Colonel Edgington hired Aspen to temp after Tessa's ex, Cash, recommended her."

"Yeah," Hunter confirmed. "I don't think Dad knew anyone else."

"That's how the mission last March, the one in which I was injured, went south," Zy explained. "Tessa returned a couple of weeks after that."

"I reformatted her computer then, which wiped out whatever spyware Aspen put on it," Trees added.

"Exactly. And every other mission went off without a hitch until August twentieth, when One-Mile was captured in Acapulco," Zy said. "It's no coincidence that Cash moved back in with Tessa to 'co-parent' Hallie on August ninth. Around that timeframe, emails started leaving Tessa's computer in the middle of the night, when Cash was supposedly gaming for work, a job that seems like a bullshit cover."

"Go on," Hunter prompted.

"The mission in September to rescue Walker turned out okay because Tessa was in Tennessee when her father died. She'd locked up her computer at the office, where Cash couldn't get to it. But Tessa was back and taking her computer home again when Emilo Montilla received the address and floor plan of Valeria's safe house in St. Louis at the end of October. I helped Tessa boot the asshole from her house for good in mid-November."

"That explanation makes sense, but there are holes," Logan pointed out.

"Exactly," Trees seconded. "Laila was nearly taken from what should have been a secure location in Orlando nearly a week ago. How do you explain that?"

"That's the one hole in our theory," Zy admitted. "I don't know how to account for it."

"Hang on. I think I might." Trees reached for Tessa's laptop, searched through the code on the back end, and found exactly what he was looking for. "The spyware is back. And this version is more advanced. It allows the user to search through our servers."

Hunter Edgington swore something long and ugly.

"Cash must have reinstalled it." Zy looked like he wanted to kill the motherfucker.

Trees wouldn't mind getting in on that. The asshole had fucked Laila's peace of mind for a buck.

"The little son of a bitch," Logan spit out.

There was just one problem... "If they had every keystroke and could break into our servers, why did they kidnap Hallie and make Tessa cough up information?"

"What?" the trio of bosses exploded at once.

"On Tuesday, Tessa was approached in the EM parking lot by a man we can't identify. He offered her money for information. She refused. She woke up the next morning, and her baby was gone. They've been using her to extract information from Tessa since."

"So I'm asking why, if they can read every word we've ever stored electronically?" Trees reiterated.

"Because, knowing we had a mole, we kept the locations of our current safe houses out of all digital communications," Logan said.

"So the cartel got desperate, I guess." Zy shrugged.

"But they've already kidnapped Kimber," Hunter pointed out. "So why take Hallie, too?"

"There are two different factions at work here." Trees explained everything Laila had told him.

Silence fell.

Hunter finally broke it. "That makes a shitload of sense."

"We've been wondering if Emilo's death splintered the organization. The fact it has sucks ass. Now we have to fight a two-pronged war. We've hired Walker's friend, Matt, temporarily to help us find Kimber. But we're still short two operatives."

"I know you're working day and night to bring your sister back," Zy said. "I have an idea on how to shut down Cash and the faction of the cartel that paid him while hopefully bringing Hallie home unharmed."

After a bit more conversation and some refining of the plan, they ended the call.

Zy stifled a yawn. Trees stretched, feeling exhaustion tug at him. The strategy continued, but both were feeling the lack of sleep.

Tessa returned, clean and dressed in fresh clothes, so they caught her up on the plan. She looked rattled. "Do you think that will work?"

Trees was as reluctant as Zy to tell her the truth. It was a long shot.

"It's the best plan we've got," Zy hedged.

Tessa nodded, but she appeared crestfallen. She could read between the lines. Trees hurt for her.

"We should all get some sleep. It's going to be a big day," he pointed out.

Zy nodded, but he looked Tessa's way, like they had unfinished business. After what the two of them had endured, Trees wasn't surprised.

"I'm going to grab some shut-eye since it's nearly five a.m.," he told them. "The futon in the office is available. 'Night."

"'Night," Zy returned, then he focused on Tessa.

Trees took that as his cue to give them some space. He let Barney in through the back door for a couple hours of warm slumber. As the big dog always did, he made himself at home on the living room sofa.

Shaking his head, Trees tuned out the murmurs of Zy and Tessa's argument and peeked at Laila. She hadn't moved a muscle since he'd last checked on her. He ached to pick her up and take her to bed with him, but she still thought he was EM's mole. He didn't love that she'd chosen to stay here alone, but he wouldn't ignore her wishes. But tomorrow, once the dust was settled, he'd be sitting her down and proving that he hadn't betrayed her.

Proving that he never would would take more time. Question was, would she even let him try?

Laila woke with a start and jackknifed up, letting loose a startled cry. It was pitch-black outside. The overhead lights were dark. When had Trees extinguished them? Why?

Then she caught sight of the trio of faintly beckoning lights from across the room, and her heart rate slowed. Candles. Had he brought them in here for her?

She raked her hair from her face—then realized the chain he'd used to affix her to the bed last night couldn't reach that far. A glance at her wrist, even in shadow, told her that he'd swapped out her cuff for a different one with a longer lead.

"Laila?"

Trees. She could barely make him out—big and shirtless in the doorway—but she felt his stare all over her as his deep voice wrapped around her, warming her even as she shivered. "Yes."

"You okay? I heard you cry out."

From across the house? "You did?"

"Yeah. I couldn't get comfortable in my bed, so I've been on the sofa with Barney. I had to bring him in since it was so cold." He ambled into the nearly dark room.

It sparked terrible memories, nightmares of past assaults where her only warning had been the sound of footsteps in the dark. She scrambled back against the headboard, breaths sawing nervously, as he approached.

He held up his hands as if to show he was nonthreatening. "Hey, it's okay. I'm only here to uncuff you."

Laila dragged in a breath and tried to relax, but his very large presence made her jumpy—and unbearably aware of him. She wanted to believe he'd only come to help, but the lesson that unscrupulous men had no compunction about taking what they wanted for their pleasure wasn't something she could simply unlearn. Granted, Trees had never done that. With her, he had been a man of his word…yet according to Walker, he'd probably sold her out.

But had he? Everything in her heart screamed he wouldn't.

Laila no longer knew if down was up or left was right. But she had to let him close, at least long enough for him to uncuff her. Nature was calling.

"All right." She held out her wrist.

Trees closed the distance between them and took her hand gently, then extracted the key from the pocket of his sweatpants and released her.

She held her free wrist against her chest, twisting and testing it as she stared. He looked tired. "Have you slept?"

Why did she care? Why should it matter?

He shrugged. "About two hours. There's a lot happening and"—he sighed—"I couldn't sleep without you."

His words warmed her. Despite her exhaustion, she'd also found it difficult to relax without his big body beside her. But that was foolish. He'd taken her captive, used her for sex when she'd foolishly invited him, and maybe even sold her out. Logic told her that she must stop thinking that him making some nice gestures meant he was a nice man.

Still, he'd brought her candles and swapped out her cuff. Why, unless he cared? Or was she sounding like someone with Stockholm Syndrome? Laila wasn't sure what to think anymore.

"Excuse me." She rose, escaping to the bathroom.

He said nothing, merely watched her until she closed the door between them. After she flushed and washed her hands, Laila crept back into the bedroom. Return to the bed, next to him…or stay five feet away where he could undress her with his eyes? But it was a silly question. It was too cold and she felt far too awkward to stand here half-naked.

Cautiously, she slid into the bed, tucking her legs under the covers and sitting against the headboard. "You barely slept. Go back to bed."

"I can't. It took most of the night, but I can prove I'm not the mole who put you and your family at risk."

She hadn't expected that. "How?"

"I have a paper trail. And this morning, we intend to catch the bastard."

A concern she didn't want to feel seized her. "Will it be dangerous?"

"I'm sure." He cupped her cheek. "Are you worried about me, little one?"

"No." But did being deceitful make her better than any of the people who had hurt her? "Well, some."

"What happens to you if something happens to me? I'm sure you're worried about that." He frowned. "You haven't figured out yet that I'm taking care of you. I'll keep doing it as long as you let me."

"You are paid—"

"Fuck that. This is personal. Maybe I wasn't clear last night. Whatever this is between you and me? It's not done. I feel it. I'm falling. And I don't think I'm the only one."

Her heart stopped. Was he saying he was in love with her? How could that both thrill and terrify her at once?

"Trees, I—"

"Look at me and tell me you don't feel something when we're this close. I know you're afraid, but the way you're looking at me…I'd swear you feel it, too. Your eyes say you want me to kiss you."

Some foolish part of her did. It was wrong. Getting closer to Trees would only complicate everything, but he was so comfortingly warm. She had once feared his size, but she knew how he used every part of himself to give pleasure. And she would be lying if she said she hadn't thought about the night he had kissed her over and over as he took her body.

"Trees…" Her objection came out breathy.

His eyes darkened. He leaned closer. She held her breath as her heart lurched, crashing against her ribs. Without thought, her lids slid shut. Her lips parted. She tried to resist, told herself to pull away. But when his mouth covered hers, the passion only he could make her feel robbed her thoughts and melted her resistance.

Trees grabbed her, folding her against the hot, hard ridges of his body. Laila whimpered into his kiss. Her arms found their way around his neck. Without conscious thought, she opened her lips to him. He surged inside, taking every inch she ceded, then demanded more with another branding kiss.

Her head swam. Tingles spread through her body. *Díos,* Trees could make her want him…whether she wanted to or not. He still hadn't proven he wasn't the enemy, yet it only took him moments to make her a slave to his touch. He had only to kiss her, and she wanted to turn over every part of herself to him—free will and all.

Laila tried to push him away, but his lips trailed down her neck, his beard sensitizing her skin, before he found her shoulder. The way he pressed his mouth to her skin felt like worship. And when his hand found its way under her hem, drifted up her waist, then settled her breast in his cradling palm, she gasped. Her thoughts spun away.

"Little one," he murmured so close to her ear. "I need you."

His words were a balm to their strain and strife. When he was touching her and whispering sweet words, she couldn't remember why she shouldn't let him. All she knew were his kisses, the build of pleasure, and the ache for the ecstasy her body had craved since the first orgasm he'd given her.

It was wrong. It was weak.

And she still wanted it.

His lips seized hers again. Instantly, she opened to him, like an addict seeking a fix, as he thumbed his way around the nipple straining for his touch. She moaned and pressed herself into his hand.

"Do you want more?" he asked against her lips.

Laila didn't want to admit that she did. He knew, right? He must. She slanted her mouth over his again in answer, nudging past his lips to the masculine spice inside that made her both hazy with desire yet sharp with need.

Trees edged away. "Answer me. I need the words."

Of course he was going to make her say it. It wasn't enough that he had inexplicable power over her body. Over her emotions. No, he wanted her to verbally bend her will to him as a show of trust. She couldn't do that before he produced proof that he wasn't the mole. Even then, was it really smart to give him so much dominion over her body? Should she really let him create and stir this need for his touch?

Laila tore away from him, panting hard. "Red."

Trees froze, then gritted his teeth. But he withdrew his hand, pulled away, and stood, putting distance between them.

Instantly, she felt cold.

"Why did you use your safe word?" he demanded. "How were you physically or mentally in pain?"

The way he asked that, it didn't sound as if being overwhelmed by her own fears counted.

He scowled. "Are you testing me again?"

"I was scared."

He sighed, and his voice softened. "I won't hurt you. I'll only ever make you feel good."

She knew that...but at what price, her soul? Every time he kissed her, he threatened to steal it. "Before anything, I must see your proof. Show me you did not endanger my family."

She should have demanded that all along.

His eyes narrowed. "Is that really why you stopped me?"

No, and he was too smart not to realize it.

Laila looked away. "I need to know."

"All right. I promised you proof. Come to the kitchen."

He was angry. No, that wasn't true. He hadn't raised his voice, accused, or threatened. He hadn't behaved as if he was furious. Like before, he was disappointed.

She was, too. She hated to lie. But the truth gave him too much power...

Wordlessly, she followed him to the kitchen to find laptops strewn across the table, along with several phones and pads of paper.

He tapped his finger on the trackpad of one computer. It came to life. "Your mole is our receptionist's ex-boyfriend. He was breaking into her laptop in the middle of the night and sending off our company secrets, probably for money."

Trees explained the scheme, backing up his theory with emails and dates that matched perfectly. Laila couldn't refute what he'd shown her. It was a huge relief to know Trees had not betrayed her. She almost felt guilty for entertaining the possibility, but it was easier to believe he was like the others than to hope the trust they had been forging was real.

"Thank you."

"You believe me?"

"Yes." *I'm sorry.*

He sighed in relief. "Thank fuck. Now I need coffee."

She felt horrible. Trees had given up sleep to prove his innocence to her, and she had pushed him away. Sure, she had more space and air now...but since he'd given it to her, she hadn't been able to truly breathe.

The things she felt for him were terrifying. For the first time, a man was far more than an adversary she should hate. She didn't know how to handle that.

"I'll get it." She bustled to the coffeemaker, poured out the old pot, then started a fresh one.

With a sigh, Trees sidled up behind her and leaned in, hands braced on the counter on either side of her, caging her in. She felt his hot breath on her neck, the warmth of his body against hers, which still ached from his touch. She trembled.

How could she be afraid of desire so sweet? But how could she surrender herself to something potent enough to enslave her?

Laila turned and stared into his solemn eyes. Against her, she felt his erection. Her body answered with a pang and a cramping of her womb.

"Talk to me, Laila…"

"I have nothing to say." Not until she'd worked these feelings out in her head. She wasn't making any sense.

"That's bullshit. What happened—"

"Will not happen again." It shouldn't, anyway. Trees was so dangerous to her peace of mind and her heart. Where he was concerned, she was weak…

She ducked under his arm to escape, then stopped short when she caught sight of Zy and a beautiful blonde watching them from the edge of the kitchen. Why were they here? When had they arrived?

"Hello," she said, horribly aware she was barely covered.

The pretty woman gave her a kind smile without any judgment at all. "Hi, Laila. I'm Tessa."

The receptionist whose ex-boyfriend had betrayed them? Laila shook her hand. "Nice to meet you. Excuse me."

She all but ran past Zy and the gorgeous blonde, dashing down the hallway for her clothes. As she left the room, she heard the murmurings of their conversation.

"What did you do?" Zy asked.

"Zip it." Trees sounded mad.

"Dude…"

"Don't 'dude' me. You're no saint, either."

What did Trees mean by that?

"Fine," Zy snapped back. "I need your help locating Tessa's ex. We have to find him ASAP."

Yes. And hopefully, they would make him pay for what he had done.

As Laila brushed her teeth and dressed, she tried to clear her head. But it was still filled with Trees and all the danger swirling around them. Hopefully, coffee would help.

When she returned to the kitchen, Trees, now fully dressed, turned to her with a groan. "This outfit again?"

She crossed her arms over her chest self-consciously, covering what she could of her pale pink tank and her Florida-appropriate shorts. "Nothing else is clean."

"I can bring you some things," Tessa offered.

"No, thank you."

"I already tried," Zy said.

"She's too proud," Trees groused.

Laila glared his way. "You know I refuse to owe anyone for anything."

Trees rubbed at his head as if it was aching. "Can't you consider some different clothes a favor, just this once?"

"I did not ask for this favor."

Trees sighed. "I'm asking you as a favor to me."

"No."

Trees shook his head. "You are a stubborn, stubborn woman."

"I have had to be."

To her surprise, Tessa laid a gentle hand on her shoulder. "How about as a favor to me, Laila? My baby is missing, time is running out, and Trees can help me. But he needs to concentrate."

Her child? Laila's heart froze. She worried about her family's safety, yes. But Tessa was dealing with her beloved little one actually being taken. "I am so sorry. I will help in any way I can."

Tessa looked relieved. "Would you be willing to put on a coat or wrap yourself in a blanket for a bit?"

She didn't think twice. "Of course."

"Thank god," Trees muttered as he grabbed her hand. "I'll find you something. Come with me."

Trees led her to his bedroom. It brought back memories of being in his bed, under his body. She glanced into his bathroom and couldn't get the steamy memory of him self-pleasuring out of her head.

He handed her a big green sweatshirt from one of his dresser drawers. "Here, put this on."

Laila pulled the garment over her head, not surprised it swallowed her from her neck to her knees.

Then he returned to the kitchen. She followed, rolling up the too-long sleeves as he sucked down a mug of black coffee, then got down to the business of locating Tessa's ex.

With no other way to help them, Laila started making breakfast.

As Trees was pounding away on his laptop, Zy's phone buzzed. He scowled. "Why is One-Mile calling me on a Saturday morning?"

Laila perked up. He was smart, shrewd, and seemingly honorable. Hopefully, he was calling to help.

Trees peered at his screen. "I hope all hell isn't breaking loose."

"Hey, Walker…" Zy answered.

Trees listened, then sidled close to murmur in her ear, "He's calling about the guy who took Tessa's daughter. The stranger threatened Tessa earlier this week."

Did Walker know something? Or had they found the little girl? But what about Tessa's traitorous ex-boyfriend?

"Does he know this guy's name? Or where to find him?" Zy paused. "Keep going." Another pause. "Yeah. And?" This lull was even longer. Then Zy motioned to Trees for a pen. Tessa lunged for one on the far side of the table, then Zy scribbled a name. JOHNSON. "Thanks. I'll run with it."

"The man from the parking lot is named Johnson?" Tessa demanded once the call ended.

"Apparently. One-Mile has been researching. He showed the guy's picture from our security footage around a police precinct this morning and got a hit. Someone arrested him a few months back for petty possession and remembered the belligerent SOB."

Hope lit Tessa's face. "That's great! If we can find him...he has Hallie and—"

"Not necessarily. But if not, we'll see what light he can shed as soon as I hunt him down. It would be fucking helpful if we had a first name."

Laila's heart went out to the woman.

"Where's his picture?" Trees asked, settling behind his computer again. "Along with a last name, I might be able to get something while the scan to find your ex-douche is working in the background, Tessa."

"Scan?" The other woman sounded confused.

"Yeah, it just takes a while to ping all the cell towers in the state."

"You can do that?"

Trees grimaced. "Well, I'm not supposed to, but..."

Tessa frowned. "How did you get Cash's number?"

He held up her phone. "I was doing a deep dive on this, so it wasn't hard to find."

"Look at Tuesday afternoon's security footage of the EM parking lot," Zy insisted.

"On it." With a few clicks, a new screen popped up. Video scrolled in rapid time across his monitor.

Laila turned back to the scrambled eggs before they burned and flipped the bacon in the frying pan.

"That's him," Tessa gasped. "The man who stopped me in the parking lot. The man who calls when he has a demand in exchange for Hallie's safety."

"And if she's not with him, he probably knows where she is," Zy surmised.

Trees nodded. "Now if I just had a fucking first name... He never mentioned it?"

Laila plated the eggs and forked bacon from the pan, then turned to deliver the food to the table. She glanced at the face on Trees's screen and nearly dropped everything. "Hector."

Tessa grabbed the plates from her numb hands. "Mr. Johnson's first name?"

"I do not know his name here, but in Mexico, in Emilo's compound, he was called Hector." The other hated Ramos brother. "He was greatly feared and fiercely loyal to my brother-in-law. He is not a man to cross."

Trees scowled and rose to take Laila in his grasp. "*That's* who hurt you?"

"Yes. Many times."

Trees's face turned molten with fury, then hardened with resolve. "He'll find out I'm not a man to cross, either. I'll make him pay."

Laila turned to him in horror. "You cannot."

"Oh, I absolutely can."

He pulled up a search engine unlike anything she'd ever seen and typed in HECTOR JOHNSON. Moments later, an address popped up. "Gotcha, you son of a bitch. He's in Lafayette."

Just as he said the words, another ding sounded. Trees flipped to that window, read a few lines of some long string of code, and the smile that stretched across his face was terrifying. "Gotcha, too. Should have known you assholes would stick together."

"What do you mean?" Tessa demanded.

"Hector and your ex? They're at the same address."

"Fuck," Zy cursed. "They're in this together."

To Laila, that made terrible sense.

"Cash helped take his own daughter from me?" Tessa sounded stunned to the core, and why wouldn't she?

"Let's go save Hallie and get the bastard," Zy suggested.

"Both of them," Trees growled. "I'm coming with you."

Zy scowled and sent a head bob her way. "You're supposed to stay here."

"One-Mile can come protect Laila for a few hours."

"You'd leave her with that crazy SOB?" Zy sounded horrified.

Which made no sense to Laila. Walker wasn't crazy at all.

"He didn't hurt her in Mexico when he had the chance," Trees pointed out.

Zy just shook his head. "Then I'll call him and tell him to get his ass out here."

"Tell him to hurry. We need him," Tessa implored.

But Walker wasn't available.

Trees cursed a blue streak. "I can't leave her here alone."

"I will not run," Laila promised. As much as she wanted to see her sister, knowing that Hector was nearby terrified her.

"I can't leave you unprotected," Trees corrected. "I'm not taking any chances."

Zy nodded grimly, and poor Tessa looked impatient. Of course she was; the terrified woman wanted her daughter back.

Suddenly, Trees took her hand. "Come with me."

Laila didn't have time to reply before he led her to his bedroom again, this time shutting the door.

"What are you doing?"

Trees's face tightened. "Promise me you won't freak out."

That set her on edge. "Those words scare me."

"You'll be fine, I promise. I'm not shutting you in the dark."

But he was shutting her up somewhere?

"I'm a man of my word, Laila. You should know that by now."

She did. It was her fears that made her belly flip and her breath feel short. But out there was a baby in Hector's brutal hands. She needed to get a hold of herself. "All right."

Laila watched, heart racing, as he opened his closet, shoved clothes aside, and punched in a four-digit code. She heard a click, then saw a rectangular section of the wall in the shadowy space separate, forming a door. Her eyes widened as Trees pushed it open.

"I built this as a panic room, a place to hole up if my place was ever invaded or there was large-scale civil disturbance. There's about a year's worth of preserved food and water here, along with meds, weapons and ammo, and some other necessities. Everything is packaged and stored along one wall."

Being prepared didn't sound wrong, so why did he look nervous? "Okay."

He reached in to flip on a light, illuminating a set of stairs. "The rest of the space... I fucking didn't want to have this conversation in a rush. I'm a Dominant. Do you know what that means?"

She'd heard of such things, but... "I do not understand."

"I was afraid of that. Look, this space doubles as a playroom. I'm in the process of moving equipment in here for... That's not important right now. It might look intimidating. It might scare or worry you. Just ignore it. We'll talk about it later." He nudged her toward the stairs.

Then she realized what he intended. "Are you leaving me here alone?"

He nodded. "I have to help Zy and Tessa. The clock is ticking for Hallie."

Of course it was. And it seemed the underground space had more than adequate lighting. That didn't alleviate her worry. "How will I get out if you are hurt or…"

Laila couldn't bring herself to finish that question. The only way Trees wouldn't come back for her was if he couldn't.

"I'll give you a way to communicate. Hang on." He rushed into his bedroom, then returned with a sleek silver tablet. As he handed it to her, he told her the passcode. "There are games, movies, TV shows, puzzles… The whole internet. If you get panicked or need help, you can call the police or Walker. Or me."

He was trying too hard to make sure she was okay when he had a bigger responsibility. She needed to swallow back her own fear. "Thank you. I will be fine."

But the thought of never seeing him again distressed her far more than she would have fathomed even days ago. More than she could process.

"So you're okay?"

"Yes. I am strong and resourceful. Rescue the baby, but be careful. Hector, like his brother, Victor, is more dangerous than you know."

"Yeah? So am I." Trees searched her face, then pulled her against him. He took her mouth in a rushed, passionate press of lips. It felt like a promise. Then he was gone, shutting the door behind him and leaving her alone in his most private space.

Chapter Twelve

Trees cursed as he locked the house behind him and headed for his Hummer. Zy was right behind him, Tessa gripping his hand, as they headed for her nondescript sedan.

Once he helped her into the car, Trees grabbed Zy's arm. "Have you thought about the implications of Cash and Hector being together?"

"Yeah. I didn't want to say anything in front of Tessa."

"Same. But if the intel from Laila is as solid as I think it is, then we've just narrowed some shit down."

"Exactly. If Hector and Cash have Hallie, it means they don't have Kimber."

"Right. Geraldo probably does." And he hated to say she likely wasn't even in the country, but that was reality.

"If that's true…the bosses are going to lose their shit."

Trees nodded. "If that was someone you loved, wouldn't you?"

"One hundred percent. But we shouldn't tell the bosses anything until we know we're right about Hector having Hallie."

"Agreed."

Zy looked reluctant to say what was on his mind. "Look, if Geraldo Montilla is holding Kimber hostage, the Edgingtons will be even more insistent about using Laila as bait."

Trees had already thought about that—and was also considering murdering the first one of them who suggested it again. "We'll deal with that later. Right now, Tessa looks ready to come out of her skin."

Zy glanced back at the receptionist. She was his woman, whether he still wanted to admit that or not. He was in deep. He was risking his life and his livelihood for her.

"Yeah. Let's go."

They pulled out, and Trees focused on the morning ahead. Rescuing Hallie had to come first, and if he had to leave Hector alive long enough to get the baby's whereabouts from the asshole, he would.

After that... Game on. If he could do anything to help end Laila's suffering, damn straight he would do it.

Mental violence filled the thirty minutes into town. Closer to the target, Trees dialed Zy's digits so they could solidify their plan.

Trees hated doing an op so blindly. Normally, he and Zy would case the place, get schematics, do hours of legwork, and plan for every possibility. *Then* they would go in, using whatever tactic made the most sense. This fly-by-the-seat-of-the-pants shit felt reckless, and he hated that the urgency of the situation didn't allow for strategy. Rushing was often a recipe for disaster.

Zy answered his call. "Talk to me, buddy."

"Why don't you cruise past the entrance? This is a mobile home park. A small one apparently. I'll call you as soon as I've gone in and scoped around. Hang tight."

"You got it." Zy overshot the entrance, pulling under a big tree to wait.

Trees turned into the neighborhood full of newish mobile homes and modest cars, searching for Hector's place. He found it—one of the twenty-something unremarkable residences in the community. It was still early, barely past eight. With any luck, he could catch Hector half-awake and unaware.

He cruised to the far side of the neighborhood, parked, then started trekking back to the target's location, dialing Zy again along the way.

"Whatcha got?" his buddy answered.

"Nothing visible from the street. House looks closed up, like maybe they're still asleep." He no sooner got the words out than he saw movement in the kitchen. "Wait. I spoke too soon. The front blinds just opened. I see someone in there. There's too much glare to a make out a face or an outline, but the place isn't empty. And there's a truck in the carport. I'm running the plate now."

"I don't want to know how you're doing that, buddy."

"You don't; it's illegal as fuck. Gimme a second. And what do you know? The truck is registered to Hector Johnson."

"So he's probably there."

Oh, yeah. And the son of a bitch probably wasn't braced for the fact vengeance was coming to his door. Anticipation zipped through Trees's veins.

"How do you want to play this?" Zy went on.

Normally, Zy would go in one side, Trees from the other. Together, they would flank the target so there was no escape. But they didn't know this place, and Zy had Tessa tagging along because she'd refused to stay home.

"I cased the perimeter of the mobile home park. It's enclosed inside a brick wall. The only way in or out is the entrance you're parked next to." Meaning Johnson couldn't sneak out the back.

"Excellent. That simplifies the situation."

"Yep. I should approach from the front. Neither Cash nor Hector knows me. I'll draw their attention while you slip around back."

"With Tessa."

Trees didn't like that at all. "I don't suppose she'd wait in the car."

Zy snorted. "Negative."

"Fuck."

"Yep." Zy's tone sounded almost apologetic. No doubt, he'd tried—and failed—to reason with her.

"Then put her behind you. Sneak in the back. See if you can find the baby while I keep whoever's inside occupied."

"You going to read their meter? Or sell them insurance?"

"I'll wing it. Something will come to me." It always did.

"You got everything you need?"

"Yep."

"Where should I roll in?"

Good question. They had to make sure Hector couldn't spot them. "The mobile home park is shaped like an *O*, so it's a curved street on each side, bisected by a long, straight drag of homes in the middle." Trees told Zy where to leave the sedan to best remain hidden. "From there, walk toward the left side of the park. Johnson is along that wall, in the middle. You should be able to pass yourselves off as a couple taking a morning walk."

"Roger that."

Once they hung up, Trees found himself approaching Hector's

place. His blood pressure surged. His lust for revenge roared as he knocked.

Open the door, motherfucker, so I can rip off your head and shit down your throat.

While he waited for someone to answer, he caught sight of Zy and Tessa turning into the development. They rolled to the far side of the community, then disappeared behind the row of mobile homes across the street.

He was getting fucking impatient before a short man with dark hair, a stained wifebeater, and a glower finally answered. "Yeah?"

Hector fucking Ramos. He looked enough like Victor that there couldn't be any mistake.

Trees gave him a shark's smile and forced himself to dial back his fury. "Hi there. I'm Scott from Pest-Away extermination services. I've been servicing some of your neighbors and they're really pleased with the results. So I came to talk to you about an amazing opportunity."

As Hector scowled at him, Zy and Tessa strolled by, hand in hand, heads bowed. Once out of Hector's view, the pair veered around the side of the house to wait for his signal.

Trees scanned the empty room over Hector's wide shoulder. The place was messy, but they didn't look braced for battle. Perfect.

"I'm not interested," Laila's tormenter groused.

"Your neighbors, Jessica and Bill, across the way"—he gestured vaguely as he gave Zy a barely perceptible nod to indicate this op was a go—"you know them, right?"

"No," Ramos grumbled.

"Oh, you should meet them. Nice folks. They started our service last month. Jessica swears nothing else worked before, but their roach problem is practically nil now, and she's seeing far fewer spiders."

"We don't have an insect problem."

"You do. You haven't been here long, right?"

"A couple weeks."

"Then trust me, you do."

Zy and Tessa appeared at the back of the mobile home, through the glass slider. He managed to work the lock free, then motioned Tessa inside, nudging her behind a big leather sofa on the left, where she shouldn't be visible if Johnson turned.

Trees rushed into a sales spiel to keep Hector distracted. "Did you know roaches will consume anything? Sweets, meat, and beer—for starters. They'll also eat book bindings, wallpaper glue, pet fur, dead skin, and soap. If that's not enough to unsettle you, they'll actually gnaw on your toenails and eyelashes in your sleep. They're tenacious little pests. Hey, they're over 350 million years old, so they even predate dinosaurs. But the worst thing about them is that they carry thirty-three kinds of bacteria, six different types of parasitic worms, and seven pathogens—that we know of. Having roaches in your house isn't simply a disgusting inconvenience. They can be dangerous, especially if you have asthma or allergies."

As he droned on, Zy eased the sliding door shut. It squeaked, forcing him to dive behind the sofa.

"What the hell was that?" Hector tried to turn around.

Trees grabbed the man's arm, as if this part of the pitch was urgent. "See? Insects. We're half swamp out here, so they're big. If you weren't used to that where you came from… Um, where was that?"

"I didn't say, and I'm not interested."

"I don't want you to regret passing up this deal. Have you asked the missus if she's seen any insects? I'll bet she has."

"No."

His short answer indicated that, just like Laila had heard, some woman had actually married this asshole. Was she around? She might be a kink in his plan, but so far he hadn't seen or heard anyone else…

Over Hector's shoulder, Zy leaned back and slid the door down the rest of the track without incident before settling behind the sofa with Tessa.

They were in now. Hopefully, they could find Cash and Hallie. They had to pray Tessa's baby was alive.

Trees tried to help them by focusing on Hector. "You know how women are these days. Trying to be all independent. My momma would shriek to high heavens every time she came across a spider in her kitchen, but my sisters—I've got three of them—they just whip off one of their ridiculous high heels and whap the spider out of existence. Your wife like that?"

"No. I said I'm not interested."

Over the sofa, he saw Zy mouth something to Tessa, who pointed to her ear, then to the right, toward the kitchen. Trees couldn't see much because a wall divided the two rooms, cutting off his sight lines, but he heard dishes clank.

A radio came on, which pumped out deejay chatter. Clearly someone was in there. The wife? Cash?

Since Zy and Tess were aware of the presence in the other room, Trees kept distracting Hector. "Listen, Mister… What did you say your name was?"

"I didn't."

As Zy crept across the open space so he could glimpse into the kitchen, Hector whipped his head around as if he'd caught movement in his peripheral vision. Zy quickly tucked himself behind a black recliner.

Trees grabbed the asshole's attention again. "Anyway, I'm up for a promotion. If I can sign up three people this morning, that would look real good to my boss. He knows I'm a go-getter, but he wants to see more hustle, so if you could help a guy out…"

The wail of a baby suddenly filled the air, seeming to come from the kitchen. Tessa's head snapped toward it, her profile telling him her heart was in her throat.

"Shut that damn baby up," Hector yelled. "Look, I said I'm not interested. I don't care about your promotion, your sisters, your knowledge of roaches, or your bullshit. Go the fuck away."

When he tried to slam the door, Trees flattened his palm against the sturdy fiberglass and shoved, wedging a foot onto the threshold so Hector couldn't shut him out. "C'mon, you don't mean that. We're getting to be friends here, I think. We're having a moment."

Zy better move this along. Trees doubted his cover would last another two minutes. If the baby in the kitchen was Hallie, Zy and Tessa needed to move now. Trees was more than happy to deal with Hector the Molester on his own terms.

"What the hell? The noise level around here…" A man emerged

from the right side of the trailer in a pair of boxer shorts, pulling a T-shirt over his head.

Cash. He presented a problem. Once the little weasel yanked the dirty tee down and finished rubbing his bleary eyes, he would be looking right at Tessa.

Damn it.

Zy poked his head above the chair, signaling to Trees with a finger across his neck.

Abort? Like hell.

Instead, he sent his widest smile to Cash. "You a friend of the family, sir? You've got to tell your pal here that he's missing an opportunity if he doesn't sign up for Pest-Away's platinum-level service."

"I don't fucking want it," Hector exploded. "Get your foot out of my house."

Trees just went on. "Here. Let me get you my card and..."

As he pretended to dig in his pocket, Cash lost interest in the sales pitch. Before he could stop the little douchebag, Tessa's ex turned toward the kitchen and spotted her.

Shit.

"Tessa, what the hell are you doing here? Get the fuck out." Cash dashed straight for her and grabbed her arm, tugging her toward the back door.

Zy pulled his Glock.

Fuck. There went the covert operation, plan A. Plan Fucked it was. Trees hoped he and Zy could find a way to end this well.

Hector, who had been watching Cash's drama with Tessa, turned back to him with a threatening scowl. But Trees was one step ahead, meeting him with the business end of a SIG, planting it against his forehead. "Hands up."

Hector complied, wide-eyed with shock.

"Just like that. Now step back, motherfucker. Nice and slow."

The asshole retreated to the middle of the living room. Trees kicked the door shut behind him, never taking his stare off Hector, while Zy emerged from the corner and aimed his barrel straight at her ex's face. "Let her go."

"Fuck you." Cash glowered.

"You don't want to give me a reason. I'm already half inclined to blow your worthless brains out."

Wisely, Cash stopped running his mouth and released Tessa.

"Now get your hands up," Zy insisted.

Muttering curses, Cash did.

"Tessa, in my back pocket are a couple of pairs of cuffs. Get them out. You"—Zy told Cash while she retrieved the handcuffs—"get to the middle of the room, by your buddy, Johnson. No. You can walk with your hands in the air."

Trees nudged Hector toward Cash until they bumped into one another. "Stand back-to-back. Now!"

Zy motioned Tessa to his side and took the cuffs from her. Then he handed her his gun. "If either one of them moves, aim in their general direction. This sucker is loaded with hollow points, so whoever you hit, we're talking maximum damage."

"O-okay." She nodded, looking resolute as she took the weapon and aimed it at the two scumbags.

"You're doing great," he told her in a low murmur. "I'm going to cuff them."

Then they could start asking questions. And find out if the baby in the next room was Hallie.

"No, you're not," said a woman appearing from the kitchen. "Let them go."

Motherfucking son of a bitch.

The woman was Aspen. She balanced Hallie on her bony hip—and pointed a Glock against her defenseless little head.

At the sight, Tessa looked ready to unravel. "Hallie, baby girl…"

The little one caught sight of her mommy and started wriggling and screaming, kicking and bowing her back.

"Stop it!" Aspen hissed, shaking the baby.

Tessa's expression turned murderous. Zy rushed in to de-escalate the situation, approaching the other woman slowly with his hands in the air. "All right. Let's not be hasty. You don't need the kid. You need information, right?"

Aspen scowled suspiciously. "Yeah."

"Okay, let's make a trade." Zy turned to glance past Cash and Hector, brow raised.

Trees met his friend's stare. What the fuck was Zy doing?

"What do you mean?" Aspen asked.

"Give Tessa her daughter. A baby doesn't belong in this situation, and I know you don't want to kill her."

The woman screwed up her face like he was an idiot. "I don't give a shit. She's just a whining, crying kid."

"But Hallie can't give you information. I can. I know everything you want to know. Every. Single. Thing. So let the baby go, and I'll come with you in her place."

Tessa gasped. "Zy!"

"It's okay, baby," Zy said to Tessa, laying a reassuring hand over his heart.

Zy intended to trade his life for Hallie's? Fuck no. Not if Trees had anything to say about it.

Tears rolled down Tessa's face like her heart was breaking. "Zy…"

"Shh."

"Why should I take that deal?" Aspen grabbed a squirming Hallie viciously and poked the side of her head with the barrel again, her finger dangerously close to the trigger.

Instinct kicked in, and Trees started game-planning. No one was dying here today—except the fuckers helping the cartel.

"Because it's a good deal," Zy argued. "You let Tessa, her daughter, and my associate"—he gestured to Trees—"go. I'll stay here with you three and tell you all the secrets EM has been keeping."

"Or your two cohorts could simply put down their weapons and I can take all of you prisoner while I extract the information I need from you," Aspen shot back. "If not, I'll off the baby. You've got ten seconds to decide."

"Hey!" Cash piped up. "This isn't what we talked about."

"Shut the fuck up, pipsqueak," Hector growled. "You don't get a say in this."

Aspen turned to Tessa. "Drop the gun. Or the kid loses her head."

She froze and turned to Zy with a panicked stare.

"Don't do it, baby."

"You better fucking do it," Aspen shouted. "Five seconds."

The situation was escalating too quickly. Trees braced for the worst. He could shoot Hector, no sweat. He could probably even nail Cash, too. But he wouldn't be able to shoot Aspen before she shot the baby.

That outcome wasn't acceptable.

"Now, bitch!" Aspen insisted. "Five, four, three…"

"No!" Cash stomped toward the woman. "That's my daughter, too."

"*Now* you care? You were the one who suggested kidnapping her."

He confronted Aspen, who gripped a screeching Hallie. "But you promised we'd give her back as soon as you got the information you wanted."

Was Cash really that naive?

"Are you living in dreamland?" EM's former temp rolled her eyes. "How the fuck did you think we were going to give back a baby?"

"Y-you *planned* to kill her all along?"

Aspen glared at Hector. "Bringing this idiot in was your worst idea ever."

"Hey, it got us information," he shot back.

Aspen scoffed. "But what a pain in the ass…"

Cash lunged in her face. "Answer me. You planned to kill my daughter?"

"Duh."

His face thundered over. "The hell you are."

Cash tried to pluck the baby from Aspen's grip, but the woman refused to let go. Hallie shrieked in fear.

When Hector tried to break free to help Aspen, Trees cocked his weapon. "Give me a reason, motherfucker. I would love to pull the trigger."

In fact, he almost hoped the bastard fought back. Trees didn't look forward to killing—but he'd make an exception for the man who had tormented and raped Laila for six fucking years.

Finally, Cash managed to pry the little girl from Aspen's grip, holding her tight against his chest. "Don't you dare touch her again."

"Or you'll do what?" Aspen pointed her gun at him. "Never mind. I'll just bury you both together."

Cash's eyes widened as if he finally grasped that Aspen wasn't fucking around. He set the baby on her feet and started backing away.

"Hallie!" Tessa called to her daughter, who went running, her little arms flailing.

A deafening gunshot filled the air, and Trees was half worried that Aspen had followed through on her threat to off the girl, but Hallie threw herself against Tessa's leg, seemingly unharmed. But Cash lay ominously still mere feet away. A hole in the middle of his forehead spilled blood all over the beige carpet.

"Tessa!" Zy gestured her to toss him the gun.

She did. He caught it as she scooped Hallie into her arms, clutching her daughter against her protectively.

"Go!" Zy pointed to the slider.

But when she reached for the back door, Aspen raised her gun. "You're not going anywhere, bitch!"

Another shot exploded, echoing in the room. Instead of seeing a hole in Tessa, Trees watched Aspen look down, seemingly shocked by the bullet Zy had put through her left shoulder and the blood spreading across her pale T-shirt.

"Honey!" Hector lurched for her.

"Stop!" Trees snarled, wrapping his finger around the trigger in warning.

The asshole ignored him, racing toward Aspen—leaving Trees little choice. He popped off a shot at Hector without a second thought. It hit him in the ass and sent him sprawling face-first into the carpet inches from Cash's lifeless body. The hit wouldn't kill him, but it would sure as fuck slow him down.

Aspen gasped in shock as she fell to her knees beside Hector. When she lifted her head again, she had murder in her eyes—and her gun trained on Tessa while she glared his way. "Drop it or she's as good as dead."

"Stop," Zy snapped, gun in hand as he barreled down on her.

"Always did think you were an asshole."

Hector reared up and grabbed Zy's ankle mid-stride, holding him back. Blood spread across the back of the bastard's pants. Hate poured from his eyes.

Zy nearly stumbled as he tried to pull free, but Hector refused to let go.

Aspen waved her gun erratically. "Stop. Or I'll kill all of you."

Was the crazy bitch not grasping the situation? Both she and Hector were shot, and Cash was dead. He and Zy were armed, uninjured, and ready to fight—to the death if needed.

"No, you won't," Trees corrected her.

Aspen turned her venomous gaze his way. "Before I kill you, I'll shoot your balls off for shooting my husband."

"Your husband is a rapist," Trees spat. "Let go, 'Johnson.'"

It was a fitting name for this tool.

Predictably, Hector didn't listen.

"Fuck you," the asshole growled, lurching up for his wife's gun.

"No. Fuck you." Trees aimed, stared down the barrel, and looked right at Hector. "This is for Laila."

Nothing felt better than pulling the trigger again, straight at Hector's head, and watching his shocked expression freeze.

The bastard went limp, deader than dead.

Trees roared in revenge, with relief.

But he didn't have time to celebrate before Aspen shot at Zy, plugging him in the arm. On his way down, his pal aimed and squeezed his trigger, hitting Aspen right between the eyes. Then Zy fell to the carpet, gun falling from his lax hand.

With a snarl, Trees kicked Hector's body to make sure he was dead, then did the same to Aspen, as Tessa dropped to her knees, holding Hallie against her, and applied pressure to his best friend's wound.

"Zy?" she sounded panicked.

He didn't answer. Fuck, had Aspen actually hit something vital?

Trying to fucking stay calm, Trees dialed 911 and crouched beside Tessa, nudging her aside to look at the gunshot. Flesh wound. It wouldn't be fatal, thank God. Had Zy fainted? If so, Trees would totally rib him about that later—as soon as he hugged the bastard.

"He's going to be okay," Trees promised Tessa. "You have your daughter back. It's over."

Tessa nodded, still looking terrified. He soothed her with a palm across her back.

But his thoughts turned to Laila. How would she react once he told her that Hector couldn't hurt her—or anyone—again?

After a grim chat with the police about the gruesome scene at the mobile home and a wait in the ER with Zy, who seemingly had a mild concussion from his head hitting the table on his way to the floor, Trees drove for home. Along the way, he called Hunter, Logan, and Joaquin and advised the bosses that Hallie was safe again with Tessa. On Zy's behalf, he also asked them why the fuck they had never once considered that their receptionist might be affected by the danger the team dealt with. Since the bosses admitted it had been an oversight, they agreed to provide her with a top-notch security system today.

That was the easy part of the conversation. The next part…Trees doubted would end well.

"Given what we found this morning, you understand that probably means Geraldo Montilla is keeping Kimber hostage?"

"Yeah," Hunter said solemnly. "If Cash was in cahoots with Hector Ramos, who was one of Emilo's boys, and they took Hallie for leverage, it stands to reason their enemy has Kimber."

"Except…here's what I don't get," Logan jumped in. "The note with the lipstick that Kimber's kidnappers gave Dad as a warning? It seemed almost bitter about the fact Valeria escaped her husband. Why would Geraldo Montilla give a shit? Pride? Machismo? He's probably full of those, but I don't buy that he'd take this kind of action merely because someone hurt his little feelings. And sure, Jorge is his grandson, but it's not as if ruthless drug lords are known for being family men. So why the hell does he want Valeria this bad?"

Trees hated to admit that Logan had a point. "We don't have another theory, except that Geraldo has no family left, other than the boy."

"As theories go, it's thin."

"Can you think of some other reason for Geraldo Montilla's behavior?" Trees challenged. "I mean, maybe Emilo's former goon squad splintered and started vying for power amongst themselves, rather than banding together to overthrow Geraldo, but…"

"That would be stupid and suicidal." Logan sighed. "Then again, people have been known to be both."

True, and Trees suddenly realized a way they might settle this point. "We haven't made any progress in identifying the three dead bodies left in our parking lot yesterday. Have the police?"

"No. Most were either missing fingers or had their prints burned off. It's going to take dental records. That takes time."

"Can you get me the pictures of the vics from the crime scene? I have a hunch." He didn't mention that Laila might know something. They would only find other ways to make her useful to their cause.

"A hunch?" Logan scoffed. "You mean a petite Latina you're trying to keep out of this. Is there something going on between you and Laila?"

"I'm just saying I can research this digitally." But he should have known they wouldn't buy his deflection.

"Uh-huh. I've heard you don't want her used as bait to draw out Kimber's kidnappers—"

"*Won't* have her used as bait," he snapped. "Let's be clear."

"Last I heard, she was open to the idea. And last time I checked, you don't own her. Do we need to remove her from your place?"

Trees didn't have any illusions; they would do it. And he'd be terrified for her safety every moment. "Goddamn it, you're going to get her killed. But I guess you think it's okay to sacrifice her for your sister. No one will miss Laila. She's not important or anything."

"That's not true, and we're not fucking amateurs," Hunter snarled. "We'll do everything in our power to keep her safe—"

"Everything in your power isn't a guarantee of her safety. You know what is? Leaving her at my place. I will protect her with my life, and—"

"Son of a bitch," Logan groused. "You're in love with her."

"My feelings—whatever they are—have nothing to do with my ability to protect her."

"Bullshit. You're compromised," Joaquin butted in.

"You're wrong," he snarled. "She finally feels safe for the first time in six years. You can't imagine what she's been through." Hell, even Trees couldn't because she hadn't trusted him with her deepest, darkest secrets. But he had no doubt what she'd endured had been brutal. "Yet you want to use her—put her at risk again—by dangling her like a tasty treat in front of the very kinds of people who once abused and raped her. But I'm the misguided one?"

There was a long pause. In the background, he heard a ringing phone and some mumbling. "We have to go. That's Matt. He has an update. We'll be in touch."

To try to take Laila from him. Fuck that.

Trees stabbed at his phone angrily and floored it out to his place as the sun began to set. There was rarely anyone on these bumpy country roads, and the Hummer could take the beating.

What mattered was Laila.

He shaved seven minutes off what should have been a twenty-minute drive and pulled up to his place with a slam on his brakes and a kick up of dust. Then he ran to the back door, opening it and disabling his security system just long enough to let himself in before he locked up and set the alarm again.

He'd been praying that Laila was all right. Had she felt safe in his secure, fire-resistant panic room? Or terrified because it doubled as a dungeon full of equipment she was likely to misunderstand?

Trees tore into his closet, punched in the code to his underground lair, then breathed a sigh of relief when the door popped open and Laila appeared at the bottom of the stairs.

"You are back." She sounded relieved.

She looked fucking beautiful, standing there in his overlarge sweatshirt, which made her look as if she wore nothing else except a pair of his too-big tube socks and a smile.

"Yeah." He sprinted down to her.

She met him halfway. "You are safe."

Laila had been worried about him? "Not a scratch. Zy has a flesh wound and a mild concussion. Tessa got her daughter back, and they're both fine."

"And Hector?"

"He's dead."

Laila gaped. "Are you sure?"

"I watched the coroner take him out in a body bag, along with his wife and Tessa's ex-boyfriend." He cupped her face. "Laila, I wasn't leaving until Hector was either behind bars or six feet under. I made damn sure he couldn't come after you again."

Her soft expression looked both stunned and grateful. "Thank you."

"I don't want you to thank me. I just want you to feel safe with me."

She didn't reply. Trees tried not to be disappointed. Though Laila hadn't told him that he made her feel secure, she hadn't said that he didn't.

"You hungry, little one?"

She shook her head. "I snacked on some of your prepackaged food. Is that all right?"

"Of course. Let's get you out of here."

Laila nodded, not balking when he took her hand and led her up the stairs. He shut the door to the dungeon behind him, helped her out of the closet, and moved his clothes to cover the keypad again.

"Trees?"

He turned to her in the shadowy room, lit by the last remnants of dusk. "Yeah?"

"Do you use the...implements in that room?"

Shit. Here came the interrogation. Of course she had questions. If she had ever seen equipment like his, it had been used for her torture, not her pleasure. She was likely afraid, and he had to tread carefully.

"I haven't yet."

"But you will?"

"Eventually." He took her shoulders gently. "Remember, everything I do is consensual. That's the reason I insist on a safe word. Ultimately, any woman I take to that room would have all the power. A word will stop me; you know that."

"Red."

"Exactly. I can only give as much pleasure as any woman trusts me to give. There are other safeguards I employ to ensure she doesn't feel as if she's performed any act against her will."

She frowned. "I believe you mean that."

But she didn't ask more questions, probably because she wasn't ready to hear the answers. And Trees wouldn't push her.

Besides, she wasn't staying with him forever. It didn't matter that he was in love with her. His sentiment wasn't reciprocated. What was the most he could say about her feelings? She didn't hate him. She didn't completely distrust him. That was progress, sure. But anything that would lead to a happy ever after? No. He lived in the real world. He had these stolen moments with her, nothing more.

When she left, it would fucking hurt because he'd probably never see her again.

"I do. Have you talked to your sister today?"

She nodded. "Jorge is improving. It is a relief."

"Glad to hear it. I'm going to grab a shower and some food. I'll probably watch a movie after that if you want to join me."

Laila didn't answer, just laid a soft hand on his arm. Tingles blasted through his body. "I have accused you of working against me, trying to hurt me, and betraying me. When I am wrong, I say so. I am sorry."

An apology? He'd never expected that. "You've been through hell, and I was a stranger. You've known me…what? Five days. I'm not surprised trust has been tough for you."

"You have not always been easy, but you have been fair. You not only protected me, you avenged me." She shook her head. "I know you did not kill Hector for me, but—"

"I did."

She sucked in a shocked breath.

"I told him I was pulling the trigger for you as I did it." He shrugged. "The truth is, he was reaching for his wife's gun so he could shoot me, which forced me to kill or be killed. But I have no remorse for putting a bullet in his brain. You might not have had justice any other way."

Laila's expression collapsed. He'd seen her cry tears of sadness, anger, and frustration. She'd shed tears in panic, relief, and satisfaction. But she'd never looked right at him and allowed herself to be utterly vulnerable. She was giving him trust she never had. That was even more evident when the first trembling tear rolled down her cheek and she didn't look away.

The sight wrecked him. He thumbed the hot drop away. "Honey…"

"Hector is one reason I fear the dark. A few weeks after I came to visit Valeria, she and Emilo had a fight. He told my sister to shut up or there would be repercussions. Valeria thought he meant against her." Laila gave a little shake of her head and looked away.

Trees tucked a finger under her chin. "You don't have to say more, little one."

"I want to. I have never told anyone."

And she'd chosen to pour herself out to him? "Not your sister? Or your mother?"

"I did not wish to make either of them feel guilty or risk themselves trying to protect me. But that night, Emilo locked me in an underground room with no windows. Two men came in as I slept and…" Laila couldn't finish her sentence.

He fucking wished he could go back in time and protect her. She had been a fourteen-year-old girl forced to endure the worst in men through no fault of her own. "Raped you?"

"They took turns holding me down while…" She pressed her lips together as another tear fell. "It happened again the next night. And the night after that… I-I did not even know who had violated me for days. Then one morning at breakfast, Victor came to sit on one side of me, Hector on the other. As soon as they spoke, I knew. I knew their voices. I knew their smells. I almost threw up, but I did not dare betray my reaction with my mamá watching."

"You worried what they would do to her if she retaliated?"

Laila nodded. "So I complied and became their whore."

Trees shelved a violent urge to go back in time and kill Hector all over again—with his bare hands. But Laila needed him now. "Don't ever use that word to describe yourself again. You didn't give yourself for a buck; you sacrificed yourself for your mother."

More tears fell down Laila's face. "It did not matter in the end. She still died. They refused her medical treatment when she needed it. I don't even know if or where she is buried."

Another stab in the heart. Trees wasn't sure if it was the right thing to do, but he brought her close, settling her head against his chest. "I'm so sorry, little one."

She sniffled and stepped away. "Tears are useless, and I should stop them."

"If they help you heal, then cry away. I'll hold you. I'll do whatever makes you feel safe."

"Thank you, but safety is an illusion."

It was a fucking sad statement, but he could see why she believed that. Every time she'd found some refuge—like the safe houses in which she had hidden after escaping her brother-in-law's compound—they had been repeatedly uncovered and invaded.

Trees shook his head. "Even if you don't think safety is real, I'll do everything I can to protect you."

"I believe you will try."

He couldn't help himself. He cradled her face and kissed her forehead. He'd love to do more to prove that she was safe with him, but in the moment, all he could give her was his word. "Always. I promise."

To his shock, she curled her fingers around his wrists and tilted her face under his. "Can I ask something of you?"

"Anything."

Her big hazel eyes turned imploring. "Take me to bed."

His heart seized up. She was asking him to get closer? She wanted to connect with him? Maybe, but she wasn't thinking about love. Did she even believe such a thing existed? "Laila, you don't owe me anything, especially not your body."

"I know. That is why I want you. For the first time, I will know what sex without hate, force, or desperation is like, where the only motive is pleasure. Will you show me?"

Jesus... He couldn't say no to that. But he didn't just want to give her a good time; he wanted to give her his love. "Are you sure, honey? You know I want you, right? How I feel about you isn't much of a secret. But—"

"I am sure." She rose on to her tiptoes and guided his face down to hers.

Trees groaned and covered her mouth with his own. Her pillowy lips parted, cushioning his entry. As she curled her hand around his neck, her tongue met his shyly. Her breasts pressed to his chest, and she exhaled with him, into him.

Desire gripped Trees, choking him with need. After making herself so emotionally vulnerable, she seemed ready to open herself sexually. It was far more than he'd ever expected.

He pulled back and thumbed her swollen lower lip, his heart jacked up on more than desire. "I'm going to make love to you, honey. I'm going to lavish every bit of pleasure I can on you. Tell me when you've had enough."

She nodded and reached for the hem of the sweatshirt.

He gripped her wrists. "Let me do that."

Obediently, Laila dropped her arms to her sides.

Trees tucked his fingers under the baggy fleece and slowly lifted it over her head. Underneath, she still wore the threadbare pink tank and the nearly illegal shorts that clung to her every curve and took his breath away.

He swallowed as he reached for her thin top, deliberately lifting it to give Laila a hundred opportunities to object. She said nothing, just affixed her darkening stare on him.

He swallowed as he shed the tank and tossed it to the floor. Next, he popped the button at her waistband. Her zipper followed, a sensuous scratch of noise in the quiet room. Then he peeled the shorts past her hips, eased them down her thighs, and let them drop to the hardwood floor. His breaths turned harsh.

In the winter chill, she shivered, nipples beading inside her plain cotton bra, but she made no move to cover herself. His gaze swept over her every petite curve and soft swell. Yeah, he wanted her. Of course. But not just because she was beautiful or his type. The way she was giving herself honestly made his desire surge. She had no hidden agenda to escape him, test him, or work him over. She simply wanted him.

"You okay?" He skimmed his knuckles over the swell of her breast. "You still want this?"

"Yes." She reached behind her back and unfastened her bra.

The tiny scrap of cotton fell between them. Suddenly, his view went from leaving little to the imagination to leaving nothing at all.

"Laila…" His stare swept down the heavy hang of her breasts and tight rosy-brown nipples, then scraped the valley of her waist, finally settling on the lush curve of her hip—interrupted by soft beige cotton.

It had to go. He needed her bare.

"You have seen me naked before."

"You get more beautiful every time I do."

"Pretty words are not necessary."

Trees braced his hands on her hips and brought her against his cock, which filled and throbbed for her. "I'm horrible with pretty words, but I'm really damn good with the truth. And that's what I'm telling you."

Then he didn't waste more time talking before he peeled away her underwear. He knelt as she stepped out of them, then tossed the little garment aside. That left him with a face full of her gorgeous pussy. The memory of her taste made him eager to get her on his bed, plant her on her back, and settle his shoulders between her legs again.

Later. Right now, he wanted to merge himself with her. She'd asked for pleasure, but he'd given her that once. He suspected Laila was aching for more, so he intended to tell her he loved her without saying a word.

Trees stood and lifted her against his body. Automatically, she wrapped her arms and legs around him, tilting her head for his kiss. She felt so fucking perfect in his arms as he closed the distance to the bed and laid her across the mattress. He followed her to the fluffy comforter, never breaking their kiss. She opened wider to him, her lips soft and sweet. Trees burrowed into her mouth, sweeping in to tell her silently how beautiful she was. How much he desired her. To promise her that, even after she left, she would always be in his heart.

Beneath him, she parted her thighs, trailing her hands down his back, then under his shirt. Her fingers on his spine made him shudder.

Laila slid the tee up his torso until it gathered around his chest. He had no patience for it—or anything else—coming between them, so he yanked it over his head, breaking their kiss only long enough to tear off the shirt. Then he swooped down to take her lips again, not giving a fuck where he tossed the garment.

Skin to skin, he pressed against her with a groan. Her breasts plastered against his chest so tightly he could feel her heart thundering.

Her fingertips gripped his shoulders, her nails pressing in as she broke away to trail her lips across his jaw and up his neck with rough little pants. "Trees…"

"There's no rush, little one. We have all night."

Tomorrow would be a different story. The bosses would likely be up in his business about Laila by morning. But goddamn it, between now and sunrise was theirs.

"I ache for all of you now, but I want it to last forever."

Holy shit. That was the closest she'd come to expressing feelings for him. Had he managed to steal into her heart more than she'd let on?

"I'll do everything I can to make tonight feel like a lifetime." He sealed that vow with a kiss, falling deeper into her mouth as he fell deeper under her spell.

Laila was wide open to him. She wrapped her arms around him and melted against him with a breathy sigh. He skimmed the curves of her torso, feeling his way down to her hips and anchoring her under him. She writhed against his hard-as-hell cock, tearing her lips free to skim them along his neck. God, she was everywhere—rosy-cheeked and breathing hard—pumping out a musk that teased his senses and told him she was aroused.

She nipped at his ear. He twitched and jerked as sensations ricocheted through his body. He growled. In return, she whimpered and offered her mouth to him again. Dizzy and impatient, he covered her lips and took control of their kiss, losing himself in her. He was in so deep he wasn't sure he'd ever find his way out.

He didn't fucking care.

Then he stopped thinking and his body took over, ripping at his jeans and toeing off his shoes. Fuck, he'd meant to make this gentle and unrushed, love Laila the way she deserved to be loved, the way she never had been. But she kept urging him on and destroying his restraint.

With a curse, he stood and shucked his pants. "If you need me to slow down, honey, tell me."

But a glance at her through the shadows told him her nipples were hard as stones. Her pussy was swollen and slick.

"No. I need all of you now."

They were on the same page—desperate to bond, to feel each other in a way they hadn't before.

"I need you, too."

But he had to stop himself from shoving every inch he had inside her, as he had their first time. It had been the tightest fucking fit of his life. She'd closed around him, clinging to him, clutching him every moment he'd been buried deep. And he hadn't gone easy on Laila, crashing into her stroke after stroke. This time, he needed to hold back, at least a little.

Trees repeated that objective in his head like a litany. And he was on board—until he lowered himself on top of her. He couldn't resist taking one of her breasts in his mouth and sucking at her like a starving man while working the other between his thumb and fingers.

Beneath him, she arched and cried out, threading her hands through his hair and wrapping herself around him even tighter. "Yes. More…"

He gave Laila what she begged for, sucking on her tender tips harder, nipping, laving, and tormenting until she went frenzied under him. Until he felt her nipples swell on his tongue.

"Trees…" She pressed kisses everywhere she could reach him, urging him on even more with her uneven breaths and mewls. "It feels so good."

He could do this to her all night. Hell, he could do this to her forever—if they had that long.

But they didn't.

Instead, he climbed up her body and took her face in his hands. "I want every part of you. I'm going to take you over and over tonight."

"Yes," she whimpered.

Then he tangled his hands in her hair, slanted his mouth over hers, and seized it again. Her lips clung to his. She opened to him, gave herself over to him with a shaky little breath.

The kiss seemed endless, as if they could love their entire lifetime in this single melding of mouths. He felt her, dazed and thrilled. He smelled her, female, musky, and mysterious. She aroused him in a way he'd never experienced. She touched him on a level no woman ever had.

Trees glided his hands down her body, pausing to worship her every dip and curve, before he reached her hips again and lifted her to his probing cock. When his seeking crest found her slick opening, he slid inside, delving down, down, down. Suddenly, she gasped and tensed. He stopped his forward press, settling into a slow, truncated rhythm that made him gnash his teeth and sweat. Everything inside him demanded he sink the rest of his aching length into her, as deep as he could, and imprint himself on her so she never forgot him.

He held back.

"Trees. Trees..." she panted, peppering kisses across his shoulders, his neck. "More. Please more."

Was she trying to undo him? "I don't want to hurt you."

She tossed her head back and forth. "Give me everything."

His heart hammered into his ribs. Desire soared. Thought went out the window. Instinct took over.

Even if he never said the words to her, she was his.

Fingers digging into her, he held her pinned to the mattress, bracing his knees against the bed, and groaned as he surged as deep into her as he could.

She cried out, her head falling back into his pillow. The look on her face, now bathed in moonlight, was pure ecstasy.

The trust she showed stunned him. The sexuality she gave back to him dazzled.

And something feral in him took over. Teeth bared, he pummeled inside her, eased out with back-twisting slowness, then fused them together again.

Her teeth sank into his shoulder. Her nails dug into his back. With every thrust, she keened, wrapping herself tighter around him and burrowing her way deeper into his heart.

His bed shook. The air around them seemed to stop. His body turned to fire. This couldn't last; he knew it. But he needed to see her pleasure—to feel it—before he gave in to the ecstasy threatening to undo him. Laila gripped him, undulating. She was so, so close...

"Come for me," he panted. "I need to feel you."

As if his words unleashed her pleasure, she tightened, her back bowing as she let out a hoarse cry that seemed to come from somewhere deep in her soul. She squeezed him tightly, milking him and totally surrendering to him.

Trees followed her over—a sheer cliff of ecstasy unlike anything he'd ever felt. There was no being gentle, no holding back. He poured himself into her, and when he was done, still panting and sweating, he knew on some level he couldn't put into words that she belonged to him. The other undeniable fact? He belonged to her, too. She was so deep in his heart he wasn't sure it would beat again without her.

Chapter Thirteen

Laila rested her head on Trees's bare shoulder, smiled, and sighed. She had only enough energy left to skim her palm across his naked chest, down the ridges of his abdomen, and back again. If his house caught on fire, she would just have to burn with it because he'd completely wrung her out.

And she loved it.

He caught her hand drifting down again and settled it over his penis. Despite the fact he'd taken her four times last night, he was erect again. Knowing he wanted her now flooded her veins with more drugging, addicting desire.

Yet more than hunger compelled her. They had chased pleasure for hours, as tightly tangled as two people could be. And she still wished she could spend all day giving herself over and over to Trees's demanding passion. But not merely for the orgasms. She loved being close to him—his scent, his strength, his compassion. Wrapped in his arms was the one place she felt as if safety might not be an illusion.

Closing her fingers around his shaft, she stroked him slowly. "Good morning."

Her voice sounded rough, husky. Like she'd been screaming for him half the night, mostly because she had.

He groaned. "Sun's not up yet. Until then, it's still night. And you're still mine."

Some part of her worried she would always be his—and it had nothing to do with her vagina. Instead, it was the organ in her chest that now beat and ached for him. That terrified her, but the truth was undeniable.

She had feelings for Trees.

"Yes," she breathed. "Yours."

As soon as the words were out, he rolled on top of her and pressed her into the mattress with his kiss. "You haven't had enough yet?"

Not even close. "No."

He grinned but didn't waste more time talking. She parted her lips and her legs, welcoming him. His tongue invaded her mouth as his hard inches made their way inside her again. Her nipples beaded so tight the painful sensation was a pleasure all its own. Her sex was hypersensitive. With every molasses-slow pull out, she tingled. With every deliberate stroke in, she ignited.

"You're not too sore?" He eased back, gritting his teeth in restraint.

"Not enough to say no." She lifted her hips, inviting him even deeper.

He didn't accept. "I don't want to hurt you."

"If you stay away from me, you will. Please..."

Trees cursed, then drove the rest of the way inside her with an agonized groan, holding nothing back. "I can't stay away from you."

Then he covered her lips with his again, cutting off all conversation. Talking with words wasn't important now. They were saying all they needed to with their bodies.

But what would happen next, once their passion was spent and reality could no longer be denied?

Laila didn't want to think about that. She wrapped her arms and legs around Trees and moved with him. Their bodies synched up—breaths, motions, heartbeats. They became one.

His strokes picked up pace. Everything inside her gathered and swelled. She couldn't breathe—and she didn't care. Nothing mattered more right now than being as close to this man as she possibly could.

But soon, pleasure began unraveling her and spinning her into a realm where he ruled her, body and soul. "Trees, please..."

"Laila." He gripped her face in his hands and stared to her soul with blazing eyes as he drilled down into her body. Every part of her surrendered to him as his lungs worked like a bellows, as his pounding strokes inside her quickened, as his erection thickened, as a growl escaped his throat, as he fisted her hair. "Come for me."

She couldn't stop herself. The ecstasy swirled and swelled in white-hot pleasure, overwhelming her. She gave herself over, opening her entire body, relinquishing every part of herself to him in an explosion of consuming, unabashed bliss.

Laila ached to give him more than pleasure in return, to prove that she trusted him, to tell him how unshackling that felt, and to convey how much she loved it.

His heart thundered against hers as he crashed into her over and over, his bed rattling and shaking. His body tensed, then he roared and flooded her womb, shuddering from head to toe. She clutched him against her with every shred of energy she had left, praying this moment would never end.

Laila had never felt closer to another human being in her life.

His expression was full of gravity, something solemn and steadfast she had never seen. Had he fallen in love with her?

She stared back, blinking and feeling tears burn her sleepless eyes. Trees brushed damp strands of her hair from her face. He said nothing. No words were necessary between them. Or maybe, like her, he simply didn't want to spoil the moment.

The outside world had no such compunction.

An alarm suddenly blared from his phone and echoed across the house from some unseen corner, spoiling their paradise.

He jackknifed up, cursing and scrambling for his phone, in full warrior mode. "Get dressed."

She sat up, clutching the sheet. "What is it?"

"The perimeter around my property has just been breached."

Her heart lodged in her throat. Had she been discovered again? "Is it Victor? If he learns that you killed Hector, he will come after you with a vengeance."

"He doesn't have to come after me. I'm looking for him. And I won't let him get away." Trees stared at his device, then sighed. "But it's not Victor. It's my goddamn bosses. Put some clothes on. This is going to get ugly."

Laila couldn't pretend she didn't know why. They had decided to use her as bait in a hostage exchange—her for their sister. It scared her, but if such a ploy ensured her family stayed alive, of course she would do it.

Trees hopped into his jeans and boots. He dragged on a tight black tee, slipped on a gun holster that crisscrossed his wide back, then grabbed a pair of semiautomatics from his nightstand. "Don't leave this room until I tell you."

"They came to talk to me."

He shot her a glance full of protective fury. "They'll have to come through me first."

Then he was gone.

Worry washed through her. She loved that Trees wanted to protect her…but he could not. She'd risk everything, even her life, to keep her sister and her nephew safe.

Laila heard beeping as Trees turned off the alarm, followed by the slam of the front door. Barney barked. As she scrambled into her bra and underwear, an engine rumbled up, then cut off. Car doors closed. Since she had nothing else to wear, she tossed on her tank and shorts. As she secured the final button, she caught sight of herself in the mirror above Trees's dresser and winced.

Her hair was tousled, her lips were swollen, her cheeks were still rosy from arousal, and her neck patchy and red with obvious whisker burns. She looked like a woman who'd had a lot of sex. And with every step, the friction of the flesh between her legs protested.

Still, if Trees wanted her again, she would say yes.

The front door opened, and she heard the timbre of deep voices as they entered the house. Taking a bracing breath, Laila let herself out of the bedroom and faced the men.

Predictably Trees looked furious that she hadn't stayed put. The other three—all big and dangerous, complete with steely demeanors—stared at her, taking her in from head to toe.

None of them said a word, but their disapproving gazes settled on Trees.

They knew what the two of them had been doing, and they were definitely not happy.

Finally, the oldest approached. He had blond hair, a sharp gaze, a chiseled jaw, and a whiplike mien. "Hi, Laila. You may not remember me. I was there during your extraction. I'm Hunter Edgington."

When he stuck out his hand, she took it reluctantly, trying to avoid Trees's disapproving gaze. "I remember. And I know why you have come."

"Straight to the point, huh? Then let's talk," said the one with dark hair and the same blue eyes gleaming in his hard face. "I'm Logan, Hunter's younger brother."

"Yes." She remembered.

"And I'm Joaquin Muñoz," said the big one at the end, who offered his hand next.

She heard a hint of an accent in his tone. *"Se habla Español?"*

A little smile tugged at his mouth. "Yeah, I speak Spanish, but it's not great."

Too bad. She would have liked to ask some questions of the man without Trees objecting, but like everything else, she would have to get her answers the hard way. "I understand."

"Laila, I told you to stay put until I came for you," Trees reminded. His voice sounded even, but she was too connected to him not to feel his worry. No, his panic.

He also knew why the trio had come.

"Would you like me to make everyone coffee?" she offered to avoid answering him directly.

Hunter shook his head. "It's not necessary."

"They won't be staying that long since they weren't invited," Trees snarled.

The older brother cleared his throat. "Laila, why don't you sit? We'd like to talk to you, show you some pictures, get your thoughts."

Logan pulled out a chair at the kitchen table for her.

As she crossed the room to them, Trees seized her arm. "Don't do this."

She glanced up, wishing she could comfort him with her touch. "I have to."

Then she sat. The other three did the same.

Trees stood at the head of the table, arms crossed over his wide chest, glaring at the men he worked for. "This is bullshit. You came onto my property uninvited and unannounced to take away any sense of safety I've managed to give Laila. You have no idea what she's been through and—"

"That's enough." Hunter spoke quietly but with such menace, Laila flinched.

"Fuck you. You're not risking her death to get your sister back."

"Right now, we just want to ask her a few questions. We've spoken to Valeria, but since Laila was in the Tierra Caliente compound a few months ago, her information is fresher."

"I will help however I can." She wanted them to know that. Not because she owed them. Her sister paid them handsomely with the money she had taken from her late husband before fleeing. She would help them because it helped her family. Then, as far as she was concerned, she would be happy never to see EM Security again.

With the exception of Trees.

But what came next for them, if anything, was unclear.

"We hoped you would say that." Logan whipped out a tablet from a backpack she hadn't noticed earlier. He turned it on and swiped a few times. "This picture and the next couple are the best we have of the three bodies dumped in our parking lot two days ago. We haven't been able to identify them. Neither have police. Your sister didn't recognize them. There's not a lot left to identify, so brace yourself."

They had no idea the kinds of things she had seen in Emilo Montilla's compound. Whatever they had to show her should not be any shock. "All right."

The younger Edgington brother glided the tablet across the table to her. "Have you seen these guys before? Can you shed any light about why their corpses might have been dumped near our office?"

The photos were brutal. Laila gasped aloud. Logan hadn't been kidding. There wasn't much left of the mutilated bodies to identify. She wanted to turn away, but she didn't have that luxury.

"I recognize some of the tattoos. Their names are Pedro, Miguel, and Juan. I do not know last names. They were all loyal to my brother-in-law. After his death, they probably served Emilo's nexts in command, Victor and Hector Ramos."

Hunter slanted a glance up at Trees. "Didn't you kill Hector yesterday?"

"Yes."

"And I have warned him that Victor will retaliate," Laila added.

Trees scowled. "He'll have to find me first."

Before she could argue that Victor was not merely persistent but vengeful, Logan cut in. "We'll get back to that. What else can you tell me about these bodies?"

Laila knew almost nothing else of the men, their backgrounds, or lives. It no longer mattered that Pedro had enjoyed watching one of the Ramos brothers forcing her to perform acts against her will, often masturbating to the sight. Or that Juan and Miguel had peeked in on her showers under the guise of "watching over her" all the time.

"Very little except the reason they may have been left in your parking lot. Geraldo Montilla surely knows you protect Valeria, Jorge, and me. He was telling both you and the Ramos brothers with one vicious act what will befall you and your loved ones if you do not comply."

Joaquin swore in Spanish, proving he grasped at least the dirty parts of the language.

Logan took the tablet back and tapped out a message. "We suspected that."

"He has your sister, does he not?"

"We're almost positive."

She sent him a sympathetic expression but didn't give voice to all the terrible atrocities Kimber was probably enduring right now. No good could come of it. Besides, they probably knew, too.

"Do you know Geraldo Montilla's hideouts?"

"No. I was beneath his notice. My sister visited at least one of his homes when Emilo was alive. Ask her where it was."

"We did. And we investigated it. Empty."

That did not surprise Laila. Men like Geraldo were shrewd enough to stay one step ahead of those eager to take them down.

"I know nothing more."

"All right. We'd like to talk to you a bit more about what comes next, but first we brought you something we thought might cheer you up. Trees, would you open the door?"

He glared. "What the fuck are you up to now?"

"Reminding Laila of the most important things in her life."

After a faint knock, Trees opened the door with a grumble and a glare over his shoulder at his bosses that promised violence. Then he stepped aside.

To her shock, her sister stood on the porch with her son anchored on her hip. Kane backed her up, wielding a gun and hovering over them with a watchful demeanor.

"Valeria! Jorge!" Laila leapt from her chair and went running.

"Lalita!" A smile broke across her sister's face.

"Tía!" Jorge lunged for her, arms outstretched.

She reached them both and wrapped her arms around them, eyes closed, breathing in her sister's petite strength and her nephew's baby smells. It felt so good to be with them, to be holding her family close once more.

"Are you well?" she asked Valeria, then turned to the precious boy beside her, tears streaming down her face. "And are you feeling better?"

"We are. Jorge started improving yesterday. He is sleeping and eating well again. We seem safe where we are, at least for now. What about you?" Valeria eyed Trees's stark, utilitarian home.

"Fine." What else could she say? Her feelings for her protector were a huge tangle she couldn't put into words. "It is very quiet here."

"Laila, I'm sure you and your sister want to have a little privacy so you can visit. Why don't y'all chat in your room?" Hunter gave her a benign smile.

She didn't believe it for a minute. Trees's bosses had brought her family here as a reminder of all she stood to lose. Those men wanted the women and children out of the room so they could talk—or threaten—Trees into relinquishing her to help them rescue Kimber. The fact they allowed Valeria and Jorge out of hiding to visit her said a lot about their desperation. Laila had no illusions why they had chosen her for this mission over Valeria. She was no one's widow or mother. She meant nothing to anyone.

Except her family…and maybe Trees.

"Of course." She led Valeria to the bedroom she hadn't used last night and shut the door.

Her sister raised a brow at the crisply made bed, then looked her up and down. "Do you know what you are doing with that man? He is big and dangerous. He can overpower you—"

"You do not need to be concerned." Laila frowned.

Valeria didn't look comforted. "The last time I saw you, you were terrified of that man. You have spoken very little about him since, except to say that he has not hurt you. And now you look… How can I say it?"

"Since you have never been one to hold back, I am sure you will tell me."

"You look like you spent all night having sex with him."

Laila's cheeks flared with heat. "If I had, why would it matter?"

"Caring about you and your welfare is not something I can simply stop, like a bad habit. Unless… Did you enjoy it?"

"If I did, will you judge me?"

Jorge got fussy, so Valeria set him down to roam and sighed. "I do not know everything that happened to you in my husband's compound, except that much of it was bad. For that, I am more sorry than you know. But you do not have to pay that man—or any other—with your body for safety again."

"I know. Trees made that very clear."

"You do not need to be his victim, either. He—"

"He is the best man I have ever known," she admitted. "So you can stop worrying. You do not know him, but I assure you he has done nothing that would make me feel violated or afraid. How are you doing with Kane Preston?"

Valeria accepted the subject change with a tight smile. "Fine. He is professional. I appreciate that he speaks Spanish. Unfortunately, he knows almost nothing about babies."

Jorge chose that moment to tug on one of the dresser drawers behind her. Laila raced to his side and distracted him with a quick game of peekaboo.

As her nephew giggled, she swept him into her arms and blew a raspberry on his cheek. "Well, if there is one man worth loving, it is Jorge. Isn't that right?"

"It is," her sister confirmed like a proud mother.

Laila kissed his forehead again, then settled her solemn gaze on her sister. "You know why they brought you here, yes?"

Valeria's eyes darkened. "Of course. I know their plan. We should discuss it."

"You cannot talk me out of helping them. If they need bait, I will volunteer. Victor Ramos is a problem for later, but he is alone now. He is weaker." At least Laila hoped so. "But we will never have peace until Emilo's father is dead or behind bars."

To her shock, her sister nodded. "I came to the same conclusion. I have spoken to Kane about this at length. I also had conversations with Joaquin. If we want a life beyond hiding, we all agree that something must be done. We can bear this now, while Jorge is very young. But someday, he must go to school. He will want friends. You and I will need to seek work. We have lives to live, and we cannot do that if we are constantly looking over our shoulder."

Since Valeria sometimes let her emotions overrule her logic, Laila was pleasantly surprised by her sister's pragmatism. "Exactly."

"When I first heard this plan, I volunteered. But after some debate, they convinced me that their version of the scheme works better. I'm sorry there are no better options."

Laila wondered what the debate had been, but she wouldn't risk asking questions that might change Valeria's mind. They both understood that her sister needed to stay with Jorge. "I know."

They passed the rest of the time making small talk, playing with Jorge, and simply enjoying these unexpected moments together. They hugged. They laughed. They teased one another, as sisters often did. If EM Security's plan went well, they could do this every day for the rest of their lives. Laila wouldn't go so far as to trust the trio of warriors who ran this business, but they knew who paid them. If anything happened to her… Well, since becoming a mother, Valeria had become both cautious and vicious. Her sister would avenge her.

But she truly counted on Trees. Somewhere over the past few days, she had learned to trust that he would never let anything happen to her.

Of course, he did not want her to risk herself at all.

Despite her bedroom door being closed, she heard raised voices. Trees's, for sure. Logan's followed. Then Joaquin entered the verbal fray with a growl. She couldn't hear the exact words, but she couldn't miss their tone. This wasn't a simple disagreement.

"Then fucking fire me," Trees roared. "I don't give a shit. But you aren't using Laila as bait, and that's final. Now get the hell off my property. And don't fucking come back."

The following night, a sharp pealing from both his alarm panel and his phone jolted Trees awake. He sat straight up in bed and grabbed his cell from his nightstand.

Fuck. Someone had opened a door or window around the house. Since he hadn't received any warning about the perimeter of his property being breached, that meant one thing.

Laila was trying to leave him.

That fucking hurt.

Trees vaulted out of bed and disengaged the alarm before hopping into sweatpants and steel-toed boots. Without bothering to lace up, he grabbed the Benelli by his bed—just in case—and a pair of cuffs from his nightstand, then pocketed the nearby flashlight.

Trees prowled across the house until he reached Laila's bedroom. He wasn't surprised to find the door closed.

After her sister and his bosses had departed yesterday morning, he and Laila had spent hours arguing. She insisted on being the decoy for Kimber's rescue. He swore he'd let that happen over his dead body. Apparently, he was the bad guy for not letting her put herself in harm's way, because she'd barely spoken to him since and insisted on sleeping in her room—alone. With the door locked.

She thought that would keep him from her? Ha.

Trees had her door open in a handful of seconds. Sure enough, her bed was empty. Her window was shut, but the air was chillier in here. She had obviously opened the window, set off the alarm, hopped out, and darted away.

Son of a bitch.

He doubled back through the house to the front door, plucked his jacket off the nearby hook, and shoved it on over his bare torso as he hauled ass onto the porch. Thank god he had a pair of thermal night-vision binoculars in his coat pocket.

Trees lifted them to his face and found Laila in seconds.

She was alone.

Sure, he was grateful someone hadn't tried to take her from him, but he was beyond pissed she was so willing to risk her life. Stubborn, stubborn woman. Stupidly brave, too. If she put herself in Geraldo Montilla's path, she might not get out alive. Surely she knew that. Why didn't she value her goddamn safety?

Because she valued her family more.

Trees refused to let her go on this suicide mission. There had to be another way.

Cursing, he bounded off the porch and ran after her. He'd catch up to her quickly for four reasons: First, she had nothing on her feet but flimsy flip-flops. Second, it was thirty-seven degrees, and she was covered only by her itty-bitty tank top and those damn short shorts. Third, since he was six foot eight, he had hella long legs, and her soft curves proved that, unlike him, she didn't run a few miles a day. Fourth—and most important—she might want to leave him badly enough to brave the elements at three o'clock in the morning, but he was far more determined to keep her under his roof.

Hell, he'd do almost anything to keep her in his bed. In his heart. In his life.

Time to drag Laila back, put his foot down, tell her exactly how things were going to be—as soon as he came up with another fucking plan.

She wouldn't budge otherwise.

It didn't take him long to catch her. He saw the flash of her sleek, naked legs in the moonlight, along with the puffs of her breaths in the cold.

Laila had no idea he even chased her until he was practically on top of her.

She whipped her gaze over her shoulder just as he hooked an arm around her waist and lifted her from the ground. He yanked her kicking, writhing form into his arms and against his body. Her flip-flops went flying.

"Let me go!"

"Nope." Despite her struggles, he managed to retrieve her shoes and shove them in his pocket.

The vixen did her best to wriggle free, even biting him. But, as his mother would have said, bless her heart. Every attempt Laila made to get free was both ineffectual and pointless.

"You cannot keep me against my will."

"Watch me," he said as he headed back toward his house. "I've already done it once."

"My sister and my nephew need me."

"To put yourself in danger? No, they don't."

"They are in danger."

"And you putting yourself in a drug lord's crosshairs isn't going to help. You're not going anywhere."

"I do not belong to you."

"I'm happy to fix that right now. Wanna get married?"

Laila gaped at him. "What?"

"You heard me."

"You have gone insane." She turned away and went stubbornly mute.

Actually, he'd been serious, but as proposals went…it hadn't exactly been romantic. Or practical. He got it. But the silent treatment? Fine. Two could play that game, and she'd figure out quick that he could get his point across without uttering another word.

Trees contained her wriggling form, bypassed the front door, then headed around to the back before flipping on his chipper shredder. It made a god-awful rumbling in the dead of the night. Thankfully, he didn't have any neighbors who might wake.

"No!" she screamed in terror, scratching and clawing, scrambling to get away from him as if her life depended on it.

What the hell? Did she think he intended to feed her into it?

"Calm down, honey. I'm not going to hurt you."

She looked at him with wary eyes. "Then what?"

He didn't bother to explain, simply plucked her flip-flops from his pocket and fed them into the machine, watching a pile of pink rubber emerge on the ground. Then he flipped it off. "Making sure you can't run."

"Are you crazy? Those are my only shoes!"

"Were. They're not shoes anymore. Let's go." He hoisted her farther up his body so her feet never touched the wintery ground, banding his arm around her tiny middle.

Gasping, Laila clung, wrapping her arms and legs around him to ensure she didn't fall. Being so close to her made him instantly hard. *No surprise there…*

Trees climbed the front porch, made his way inside, and set her on her feet. By the ambient security lights he'd installed last night to serve as nightlights for her, he watched anger and mutiny cross her beautiful face.

God, she had the power to steal his breath. He shouldn't be shocked since she'd already stolen his heart. It didn't matter that he hadn't touched her in what felt like forever. He hated the fact that, right now, she was hating him. Everything was a fucked-up tangle, but no one would risk her, even Laila. He intended to make damn sure of that.

"I needed those." She stomped her bare foot.

"Not if you were going to walk your pretty ass into danger."

Laila fumed—and tried to stifle it. She'd probably figured out that battling head on with him wasn't the way to get what she wanted. But she was clever. And she was desperate to save her family. She wouldn't give up.

Neither would he.

He took her by the arm, hauled her to the kitchen table, thrust her into the first chair, then wrapped his meaty hands around her shoulders. "What we have here is a failure to communicate."

"I understand your English. I simply have my own thoughts, and I disagree with you."

"I'm aware of that. I'm just making it incredibly clear that, whatever ridiculous scheme my bosses have cooked up, you're not getting involved. You're under my protection. As long as either faction of the cartel warring for control is after you, it's my responsibility to keep you alive. Since you don't seem to grasp that concept, we're going to make some changes around here until you do."

Without waiting for a response, he began patting her down. It was fucking hard not to notice her soft, lush breasts when he had to cup them. Impossible not to remember having them in his mouth or feeling them against his chest when he'd gripped her hips while riding her hard and fast. But now wasn't the time for this trip down memory lane —or his erection. He needed to find her phone.

Laila pushed at his hands and turned her body away protectively, but he finally felt his way from her chest to her ass and pulled the phone from her back pocket.

He saw three messages from her sister, which was no surprise. And one from Hunter Edgington—twenty minutes ago.

That motherfucking bastard.

"What were you planning exactly?"

Stubbornly, she pressed her lips together, crossed her arms over her chest in a way that made her tits look even more luscious, and jerked her stare out the window.

Damn it. How the fuck could he get her to talk? Turning her ass red and stripping the starch from her attitude sounded great. But he'd never tested her trust that way, and they were both too angry for a consensual spanking now, even if she needed it. Hell, did she even trust him to protect her anymore?

Undeterred by her silence, Trees waved her phone in front of her face until it unlocked, then he started prowling through the device.

"No!" She lunged out of her chair and reached for it.

Trees merely held it at eye level, kind of amused as he watched her jump for it. There were occasional benefits to being freakishly tall.

He found the message string he'd been looking for, scanned and scrolled, reading as he went—and lost his fucking temper. "You were running to the edge of my property to meet up with Hunter tonight? Where the fuck was he taking you?"

With a frustrated huff, she plopped in her seat again. Because she realized the jig was up? "It is none of your concern."

The hell it wasn't.

With a snarl, he flipped on the overhead light and headed to the coffeepot. If he was going to interrogate her, he needed some damn caffeine. Days and days—most without a full night's sleep—were catching up to him.

The instant he turned his back, she shoved out of her chair, legs scraping across the tile, and sprinted for the door. She'd barely reached it and pulled it open when he caught her around the waist again, lifted her, kicked the door shut, then carried her back to the kitchen. He pulled out the cuffs.

Her eyes widened. "What are you doing?"

He ignored her, managing to slap one cuff around her wrist before she started fighting like a hellcat. But she was too late. He'd already looped the chain around the rungs of the chair and grabbed her free hand.

"You cannot do this."

He clicked the second cuff into place. "I just did. Now we're going to talk. Want a blanket?"

He hoped like fuck she said yes because he was getting a full frontal of her under the kitchen lights, and it was impossible to miss her thick, beaded nipples.

Fuck, her body was his weakness.

"What will I owe you for it?"

This again? "Nothing. You're only borrowing it, not taking it."

She hesitated. "Fine. Then yes. Please."

He nodded as he grabbed a quilt from the corner of his bed. When he draped it over her, they both breathed a sigh of relief.

Then Trees turned the nearest chair backward and straddled it, resting his arms over the top. "Let's start over. Tell me why—exactly—you were meeting Edgington tonight. Have they figured out where Geraldo Montilla is holed up? Or contacted the person who sent the colonel the ransom note to set up this supposed hostage swap?"

Laila proved once again she was as strong-willed as she was beautiful when she looked away and refused to answer. He took her chin in his grip and forced her to look at him. As always, her soft hazel eyes undid him—not to mention that pouty, fuck-me mouth he remembered kissing feverishly in the dark.

"Or are they past that? Do they have a plan? A date? A location?"

Predictably, since he'd told all of his bosses to fuck off nearly forty-eight hours ago, they hadn't looped him in on their strategies to rescue Kimber from Geraldo Montilla—using Laila as bait.

Her white teeth bit into that pillowy lower lip, and Trees stifled a groan. She had no idea what she was doing to him, and he couldn't let on. She knew how to use his desire against him. He couldn't let it happen again.

Since she still stubbornly refused to say a word, he'd have to puzzle the answer out himself.

Laila glared at him and yanked her chin from his grasp. "Do not touch me."

He backed away. "Then answer me."

"I am going. And you cannot stop me."

That's what she thought. "I'm not going to let you put yourself in needless danger, Laila."

"But my sister and my nephew—"

"There's another way to neutralize this threat, and we'll find it."

She shook her head. "Geraldo is a dangerous man. He will keep coming. He will never stop until they kill her and take her son. He and all his men are animals. They will never give up."

"Then neither will I. I can be an animal, too. And I'll prove it."

That clearly worried her. "What will you do?"

"Tell me what's going on first. Have they come up with a plan?"

Laila pressed her lips together, saying nothing for a long moment. But she was thinking, so Trees let her. "I do not know."

"Seriously?" He laughed bitterly. "Who do you trust more, them or me?"

She didn't hesitate. "You."

Her answer poured relief through his system, but it also pissed him off. "When we met, you didn't trust them at all, but now you're willing to run off in the middle of the night to jump into danger for them when they don't even have a fucking plan?"

"They will have one. I was going to help. So was Valeria."

What the fuck? "Neither of you are trained operatives."

"Perhaps not, but we are the only ones who have met Geraldo Montilla. Together, we may be able to figure out where he is hiding and even identify any weaknesses he may have."

That was a fair point. He didn't know how useful her and her sister's information would be, but it was a tactic they hadn't tried before. And his bosses had never cut him in on their progress. Because they had their hands full? Because they'd believed he was their mole? Probably both.

Trees turned the situation over in his head. Bottom line? Everything needed to change.

He swiped through Laila's phone again and found Hunter's contact, then hit the button to call.

His boss answered quickly. "Where are you, Laila? I'm at the meet point, but I don't see you."

"She's in my kitchen and she's not going anywhere, asshole. Did you honestly think she could just sneak out my window and I wouldn't know?"

"Listen, I get that you want to protect her. I know damn well you've been fucking her, which is against the rules, and we'll be discussing that later. But goddamn it, she wants to save her sister and I want to save mine. Who the fuck are you to get in the middle of that?"

"Who the fuck are you to dangle Laila out as bait? Montilla wants Valeria, but you're holding back the queen and sending the pawn instead. It's bullshit, and I won't let you do it."

Hunter sighed raggedly. It was one of the few times Trees had heard the man be anything less than rock solid. "You're tying my hands and condemning my sister to a torturous death. I haven't slept in days. My dad… He's falling apart. He won't eat. He won't rest. The colonel isn't a young man anymore, and I'm goddamn worried about him. Deke is at the end of his rope, and the kids are crying themselves to sleep… I don't know how much longer this family can hold it together, especially since Deke got word last night that if we don't produce Valeria this week, my sister dies. We're desperate. We won't let anything happen to Laila. Hell, we'll never let Montilla even touch her. Please. Right now, we just want to talk to her."

Trees sighed. Edgington was in a shitty position. His whole family was, and the time to save Kimber was ticking down. It was his own protective instincts that had him snarling and fighting his bosses. The way they'd been snarling and fighting with him.

That wasn't getting the job done.

"Maybe you ought to try working with me, instead of going behind my back. Maybe collectively, we could come up with a better plan, one that doesn't require you to put Laila in danger."

Hunter paused. "Maybe you're right."

Damn straight, but Trees wouldn't give Hunter more shit now. It was counterproductive. But there would be a reckoning later, he was sure. "Go home and get some sleep. I'll interrogate Laila about what she knows. You do the same with Valeria. We'll circle back in a few hours and see what we've come up with."

"To be honest, you don't know what we know. Dad, Logan, Joaquin, Deke, and I have all been working on this for"— he choked— "God, it's been the longest fucking week of my life."

Forever in terms of keeping a hostage. He could only speculate that Geraldo hadn't killed Kimber yet because, if he did, he'd never see Valeria or her son again.

"So clue me in. But you don't know what I'm capable of, either."

Through the line, Trees heard Hunter start his car engine and pull away. "Fair enough. And I'm sorry we thought you were our mole. We should have just come to you."

"Yep. We could have worked together sooner."

"Once I'm home, I'll send you a zip file of everything we've collected so far. Unfortunately, it's not much. Some drug lords lead a really flashy life—parties, bars, whores, jet-setting. Geraldo Montilla… not so much."

"Still, he's got a weakness, a tell, a bad habit—something. We'll find it and exploit it."

"Yeah," Hunter sighed tiredly. "I'll call you in a few hours."

The line went dead.

Trees set Laila's phone aside. "You get all that?"

"I think so."

"If I uncuff you, will you stay put?"

"What will you do if I am able to think of anything helpful?"

"We'll plan around it, find some way to trap him so we end up sparing his life in exchange for Kimber. But we'll do it in some way that doesn't put you, your sister, or your nephew in danger. Can you agree to that?"

Laila looked reluctant to give up. She wanted to help her family and ensure their safety right now. He understood her urge to be actively involved. But he gave her a minute to think his proposal through.

"Yes."

He heaved a sigh of relief. "Good. Do you want to go back to bed for a while or—"

"No. I-I do not know how you and I will find that monster's weakness, but I want to start now."

Trees figured she'd say that. "All right. Tell me the first time you remember hearing about the man. The first time you met him. Any detail you can recall. Even the smallest, seemingly insignificant piece of information might be helpful."

She did. The memories of a fourteen-year-old girl about a man three times her age weren't particularly sharp. Or maybe that was because it had been nearly seven years ago. His facial hair, his style of dress, his entourage… Not really helpful. But they kept talking as Trees read through the files Hunter sent.

His boss was right; they didn't have much to work with. So he kept asking Laila questions—through sunrise, through breakfast, through the slow crawl of the sun up the kitchen window until somewhere in the afternoon when the sun began its descent through the living room window on the opposite side of the house. Together, they made a late lunch, touched base with her sister to talk through other memories. They netted almost nothing.

It was hard to find a clue when no one was even sure what the fuck they were looking for. But Trees didn't give up, despite feeling wiped out. Neither did Laila.

Finally, after a shower and some hot popcorn around ten that night, he tapped away on his keyboard, scouring search engines far more powerful than Google and coming up with a lot of scary chatter about Montilla's past violence, when Laila sighed. "The last time I remember Geraldo coming to visit Emilo was shortly after your team rescued my sister. He railed at his son for being so stupid and careless, then he asked me questions. But I knew nothing. Even I had been shocked to wake up the morning after Valeria's disappearance to find her gone. He barraged me with questions for hours, until he got frustrated and left. The last time I was with him, I looked out the window as he drove away in his flashy classic sports car. I remember thinking that I hoped never to see him again."

Trees's head popped up. "Classic sports car. Tell me everything you can remember about it."

She did.

His heart started revving. They might be getting somewhere... He tapped furiously on his keys, looking through bills of sale, pictures, auctions, and car shows before he finally found an image that brought it all together for him. A little more cross-checking later, and he pounded his fist on the table. "Motherfucking bingo. I got you, you son of a bitch."

"Are you sure?" Laila sounded afraid to hope.

"Oh, yeah." He reached for his phone and dialed Hunter. "Are you ready for some good news? Because I know exactly where Montilla is going to be in two days. All we need is a plan."

CHAPTER *Fourteen*

February 4

Trees stood by the front door at oh-dark-thirty in head-to-toe camo, a backpack hanging from his left shoulder, and frowned. "I should be back in twelve hours. Are you sure you don't want to spend the day in my panic room?"

Laila shook her head. "I will be fine."

Since Trees had drafted the plan to corner and grab Montilla with Hunter and the rest of his bosses, Deke and the colonel had blessed the scheme. Together, they'd put all the pieces in place. The mission required each and every available man, and everyone had a role. Time had been precisely accounted for to ensure Geraldo would have no escape.

Trees was locked and loaded and ready to go…but he worried about Laila.

"And you won't run?"

"No. Since you can save my sister and theirs without me, I have no reason to leave."

"By the time your head hits the pillow tonight, you and your family should be safe." Hopefully Kimber would be, too.

But Laila had been quiet, almost withdrawn, since they'd firmed up these plans. Why?

"I have an uneasy feeling."

She was worried. About him? Maybe that was a stretch. Since giving him the information about Montilla, she had kept to herself. Trees hadn't pushed or pried, but he'd love to know what the hell she was thinking. He'd also love to touch her again. That would have to wait until the danger passed. But then she would be leaving his house and his life—unless he gave her a reason to stay.

"All right. You have plenty of food here. Barney will keep you company. You know how to work the TV, and you've got internet. Call your sister all you want. I'll arm every alarm and turn on all the cameras in the house. If the house alarm trips, the police will come, but since I'm out in the country, they're about twenty minutes away. Do you want me to show you how to access the panic room, just in case?"

She shook her head. "It is not necessary."

Probably not. She had two possible threats. He and the team would have Geraldo Montilla in their sights. Victor Ramos had no idea where to find her. She should be safe. He just hated leaving anything to chance.

"All right."

"Will you call me when it is done?"

Her request probably had more to do with wanting to make sure that her family was out of danger than her worry for him, but hey, a guy could dream. "Sure."

"Thank you."

They stood face to face near the front door, staring at each other in the awkward silence. Finally, Trees couldn't take it anymore. He lifted Laila against him.

She gasped and wrapped her arms around his neck, blinking up at him. "What are you doing?"

"Telling you I love you, Laila. I know it's one-sided. I don't expect you to say anything. I just—" He stopped making an ass of himself by vomiting up his feelings and settled for what connected them. He swooped down and kissed her, a hard press of his lips on hers, trying desperately to memorize the feel of her while giving her something to think about in his absence. But if she was going to reject him, he didn't want to hear it, so he wrenched away, set her on her feet, and slammed out the door. A last look back at her through the living room window, stunned and red-cheeked, didn't give him a single clue about her reaction.

Did she love him, too? Even a little?

He alarmed the whole house from the app on his phone. Once it was secure, he turned the engine of his truck over and drove off, not looking back.

Before sunrise, he was at the hangar where the team planned to assemble. After a last-minute equipment check, they boarded the charter plane and took off. As the sun began to rise, they reviewed the plan collectively. In three hours, they would land at the private airstrip in Florida, less than thirty minutes from the event. By noon, Montilla would arrive for the private, high-dollar-stakes classic car race held annually. By then, Trees and the team would be in place.

Finding out the Tierra Caliente's leader would be there had been a lucky fucking break.

After he'd managed to jog Laila's memory about Montilla's love of classic cars, he'd scoured the internet for recent high-dollar sales. He'd found a 1962 Ferrari 250 GTO sold at auction for nearly fifty million dollars to an anonymous buyer. In Mexico. Because fewer than thirty of the classic cars were produced that model year, they now sold for record prices.

From there, Trees had worked backward, on the theory that someone who spent that much money on a car would want to show it off. Sure enough, he'd found a press release announcing that a professional driver by the name of Dantel Resendez had registered for the race in Florida, driving exactly the same rare vehicle. After that, he managed to dig up a picture of Resendez with Montilla, toasting in front of the red vintage sports car. Then he'd hacked the event organizer's files to find the VIPs attending this week's event. Montilla was on the list.

Bingo.

The Edgingtons, Deke, and Muñoz had come up with the tactical plan. It wasn't going to be easy. Montilla traveled with an entourage. But they had tried to account for every possibility and cover every angle. Now Trees could only hope they didn't encounter any unexpected curve balls.

"Hey," Zy approached him with a slap on the back. "How are you doing?"

Nervous as fuck to get back to Laila. Driving away from her this morning had been one of the hardest things he'd ever done. There was so much unspoken between them, and he was dying to know what she'd thought about his declaration of love. He was really fucking worried he'd put his foot in his mouth. "Good. Congrats to you and

Tessa on your engagement, man. I, um...heard it through the grapevine."

Zy pulled at the back of his neck. "Yeah, sorry I didn't call. We were...busy."

Trees bet they rarely got out of bed. After being artificially kept apart for nearly a year, then nearly splintered in two by Hector Ramos and his crew, they deserved happiness. "Hallie good?"

"Great. She's bounced back for the most part. The doctors don't think she'll remember much, and we'll get her some therapy when she gets older if she needs it."

"For sure. So, when's the big day?"

"We're working that out, but soon. Definitely soon. You'll be my best man, yeah?"

"Absofuckinglutely." Trees only hoped Zy got to perform the same service for him someday, but he wasn't optimistic.

"Great. Thanks. So...how goes it with Laila?"

Trees shrugged. He was hesitant to open this can of worms. "One step forward, two steps back. But—"

Suddenly, his phone blared. He knew that sound—and his heart stopped.

He yanked the device from his pocket, suddenly aware of the chatter around him falling silent and every eye on him. He swiped, opened the screen, and waited for the cameras to connect to his device. Thank god for Wi-Fi on the plane.

But it was the longest thirty seconds of his life.

Finally, he got visuals, and his heart seized up in his chest. Someone unauthorized was on his property.

He watched the sleek black truck with the plates obscured by a gray plastic cover rumble down the dirt road. Through the cloud of dust, he saw one driver in the cab, his face too hard to discern.

Zy looked over his shoulder, his face grave. "Who the hell is on your property?"

"I don't know."

His fingers shaking so hard he fumbled, he quickly dialed Laila. He had to warn her. One ring, two, three... Voicemail.

Trees fought for his next breath and tried like fuck to tamp down his panic. He called her again. No answer.

"Hey, everyone," Hunter shouted to the operatives on the plane, his voice grave. "Just got an update from the event organizer. The Ferrari pulled out of the race. Montilla is no longer on the VIP guest list."

Shit. So where was the bastard now? Was that who had driven onto his property? He and the team had been trying to surprise the drug lord and take him hostage...but had the wily old bastard played them instead?

The camera from his porch picked up the black truck rolling to a stop. The driver jumped out, pulled a ski mask over his face before Trees got a good luck at him, then fired a shot through the front window, shattering the glass. The house alarm started blaring.

Laila was alone with someone armed and ready to kill.

Fuck. Fuck. Fuck.

Switching his view to the inside cameras, he looked for any sign of Laila. There. She dashed from her bedroom, heading down the hall to the kitchen.

Trees's terrified heart threatened to pound out of his chest. Before he could figure out where Laila had fled, the intruder held up his middle finger to the living room camera, then shot it point-blank.

From the kitchen camera, he watched with surreal terror, like he was watching a horror movie, when the intruder stomped deeper into the house.

Suddenly, all the power went out. His redundant battery kicked on twenty seconds later. By the time the cameras reconnected, there was no sign of Laila, and the asshole stomped through his house, systematically shooting down every one of his cameras.

His screen turned black.

He was thirty thousand feet in the air and probably two hundred miles from home. If he didn't find some way to help Laila, she was as good as dead.

"No. No. No. No. No! Fuck! I have to get home—now!"

The End

Don't miss the epic conclusion of Trees & Laila's thrilling story!

WICKED AND FOREVER
Trees and Laila, Part Two
Wicked & Devoted, Book 6
By Shayla Black
(will be available in eBook, print, and audio)

Coming April 26, 2022!

Thank you for reading Wicked as Seduction! If you enjoyed this book, please review and/or recommend it to your reader friends. That means the world to me!

Want to know first about new releases, excerpts, covers, and freebies? Join my VIP newsletter!

If you missed One-Mile and Brea, catch up with the sexiest bad boy meets good girl story. Wicked as Sin kicks off the addictive, suspenseful Wicked & Devoted series!

WICKED AS SIN

One-Mile & Brea, Part One

Wicked & Devoted, Book 1

By Shayla Black

NOW AVAILABLE!

The good girl wants a favor? She'll pay in his bed.

Pierce "One-Mile" Walker has always kept his heart under wraps and his head behind his sniper's scope. Nothing about buttoned-up Brea Bell should appeal to him. But after a single glance at the pretty preacher's daughter, he doesn't care that his past is less than shiny, that he gets paid to end lives…or that she's his teammate's woman. He'll do whatever it takes to steal her heart.

Brea has always been a dutiful daughter and a good girl…until she meets the dangerous warrior. He's everything she shouldn't want, especially after her best friend introduces her to his fellow operative as his girlfriend—to protect her from Pierce. But he's a forbidden temptation she's finding impossible to resist.

Then fate strikes, forcing Brea to beg Pierce to help solve a crisis. But his skills come at a price. When her innocent flirtations run headlong into his obsession, they cross the line into a passion so fiery she can't say no. Soon, his past rears its head and a vendetta calls his name in a mission gone horribly wrong. Will he survive to fight his way back to the woman who claimed his soul?

SNEAK PREVIEW

Sunday, January 11
Sunset, Louisiana

Finally, he had her cornered. He intended to tear down every last damn obstacle between him and Brea Bell.

Right now.

For months, she'd succumbed to fears, buried her head in the sand, even lied. He'd tried to be understanding and patient. He'd made mistakes, but damn it, he'd put her first, given her space, been the good guy.

Fuck that. Now that he'd fought his way here, she would see the real him.

One-Mile Walker slammed the door of his Jeep and turned all his focus on the modest white cottage with its vintage blue door. As he marched up the long concrete driveway, his heart pounded. He had a nasty idea how Brea's father would respond when he explained why he'd come. The man would slam the door in his face; no maybe about that. After all, he was the bad boy from a broken home who had defiled Reverend Bell's perfect daughter with unholy glee.

But One-Mile refused to let Brea go again. He'd make her father listen…somehow. Since punching the guy in the face was out of the question, he'd have to quell his brute-force instinct to fight dirty and instead employ polish, tact, and charm—all the qualities he possessed zero of.

Fuck. This was going to be a shit show.

Still, One-Mile refused to give up. He'd known uphill battles his whole life. What was one more?

Through the house's front window, he spotted the soft doe eyes that had haunted him since last summer. Though Brea was talking to an elderly couple, the moment she saw him approach her porch, her pretty eyes went wide with shock.

Determination gripped One-Mile and squeezed his chest. By damned, she was going to listen, too.

He wasn't leaving without making her his.

As he mounted the first step toward her door, his cell phone rang. He would have ignored it if it hadn't been for two critical facts: His job often entailed saving the world as the people knew it, and this particular chime he only heard when one of the men he respected most in this fucked-up world needed him during the grimmest of emergencies.

Of all the lousy timing…

He yanked the device from his pocket. "Walker here. Colonel?"

"Yeah."

Colonel Caleb Edgington was a retired, highly decorated military officer and a tough son of a bitch. One thing he wasn't prone to was drama, so that single foreboding syllable told One-Mile that whatever had prompted this call was dire.

He didn't bother with small talk, even though it had been months since they'd spoken, and he wondered how the man was enjoying both his fifties and his new wife, but they'd catch up later. Now, they had no time to waste.

"What can I do for you?" Since he owed Caleb a million times over, whatever the man needed, One-Mile would make happen.

Caleb's sons might be his bosses these days…but as far as One-Mile was concerned, the jury was still out on that trio. Speaking of which, why wasn't Caleb calling those badasses?

One-Mile could only think of one answer. It was hardly comforting.

"Or should I just ask who I need to kill?"

A soft, feminine gasp sent his gaze jerking up to Brea, who now stood in the doorway, her rosy bow of a mouth gaping open in a perfect little *O*. She'd heard that. *Goddamn it to hell.* Yeah, she knew perfectly well what he was. But he'd managed to shock her repeatedly over the last six months.

"I'm not sure yet." Caleb sounded cautious in his ear. "I'm going to text you an address. Can you meet me there in fifteen minutes?"

For months, he'd been anticipating this exact moment with Brea. "Any chance it can wait an hour?"

"No. Every moment is critical."

Since Caleb would never say such things lightly, One-Mile didn't see that he had an option. "On my way."

He ended the call and pocketed the phone as he climbed onto the porch and gave Brea his full attention. He had so little time with her, but he'd damn sure get his point across before he went.

She stepped outside and shut the door behind her, swallowing nervously as she cast a furtive glance over her shoulder, through the big picture window. Was she hoping her father didn't see them?

"Pierce." Her whisper sounded closer to a hiss. "What are you doing here?"

He hated when anyone else used his given name, but Brea could call him whatever the hell she wanted as long as she let him in her life.

He peered down at her, considering how to answer. He'd had grand plans to lay his cards out on the table and do whatever he had to —talk, coax, hustle, schmooze—until she and her father came around to his way of thinking. Now he only had time to cut to the chase. "You know what I want, pretty girl. I'm here for you. And when I come back, I won't take no for an answer."

Don't forget to grab the gripping conclusion of this unforgettable couple…

WICKED EVER AFTER
One-Mile and Brea, Part Two
Wicked & Devoted, Book 2
By Shayla Black
NOW AVAILABLE!

The good girl is keeping a secret? He'll seduce it out of her until she begs to be his.

WICKED & DEVOTED WORLD

Thank you for joining me in the Wicked & Devoted world. If you didn't know, this cast of characters started in my Wicked Lovers world, continued into my Devoted Lovers series, and have collided here. During Zy and Tessa's journey, you've read about some other characters and you might be wondering if I've told their story. Or if I will tell their story in the future. Below is a guide in case you'd like to read more from this cast, listed in order of release:

WICKED LOVERS

Decadent

Deke Trenton (and Kimber Edgington)

The boss' innocent daughter. A forbidden favor he can't refuse...

Surrender to Me

Hunter Edgington (and Katalina Muñoz)

A secret fantasy. An uncontrollable obsession. A forever love?

Belong to Me

Logan Edgington (and Tara Jacobs)

He's got everything under control until he falls for his first love...again.

Wicked All the Way

Caleb Edgington (and Carlotta Muñoz Buckley)

Could their second chance be their first real love?

His to Take

Joaquin Muñoz (and Bailey Benson)

Giving in to her dark stranger might be the most delicious danger of all...

DEVOTED LOVERS

Devoted to Pleasure

Cutter Bryant (and Shealyn West)

A bodyguard should never fall for his client…but she's too tempting to refuse.

Devoted to Love

Josiah Grant (and Magnolia West)

He was sent to guard her body…but he's determined to steal her heart.

<u>WICKED & DEVOTED</u>

Wicked as Sin / Wicked Ever After – Pierce "One-Mile" Walker (and Brea Bell)

He's dangerous. She's off-limits. After one taste, nothing will stop him from making her his.

Wicked as Lies / Wicked and True – Chase "Zyron" Garrett (and Tessa Lawrence)

As the Wicked & Devoted world continues to collide and explode, you'll see more titles with other characters you know and love, so stay tuned for the conclusion of Trees and Laila's story, as well as duets about Kane, Matt, and others!

I have so much in store for you on this wild **Wicked & Devoted** ride!

Hugs and Happy Reading!

Shayla

ABOUT SHAYLA BLACK

LET'S GET TO KNOW EACH OTHER!

Shayla Black is the *New York Times* and *USA Today* bestselling author of more than eighty contemporary, erotic, paranormal, and historical romances. Her books have sold millions of copies and been published in a dozen languages.

As an only child, Shayla occupied herself by daydreaming, much to the chagrin of her teachers. In college, she found her love for reading and started pursuing a publishing career. Though she graduated with a degree in Marketing/Advertising and embarked on a stint in corporate America, her heart was with her stories and characters, so she left her pantyhose and power suits behind.

Shayla currently lives in North Texas with her wonderfully supportive husband, her daughter, and two spoiled tabbies. In her "free" time, she enjoys reality TV, gaming, and listening to an eclectic blend of music.

TELL ME MORE ABOUT YOU.

Connect with me via the links below. You can also become one of my Facebook Book Beauties and enjoy live, interactive #WineWednesday video chats full of fun, book chatter, and more! See you soon!

Website
VIP Reader Newsletter
Facebook Book Beauties Chat Group

facebook.com/ShaylaBlackAuthor
instagram.com/shaylablack
tiktok.com/@shayla_black
twitter.com/ShaylaBlackAuth
bookbub.com/authors/shayla-black
pinterest.com/shaylablacksb

OTHER BOOKS BY SHAYLA BLACK

CONTEMPORARY ROMANCE

WICKED & DEVOTED

Romantic Suspense

Wicked as Sin (One-Mile & Brea, part 1)

Wicked Ever After (One-Mile & Brea, part 2)

Wicked as Lies (Zyron & Tessa, part 1)

Wicked and True (Zyron & Tessa, part 2)

Wicked as Seduction (Trees & Laila, part 1)

Coming Soon:

Wicked and Forever (Trees & Laila, part 2) (April 26, 2022)

REED FAMILY RECKONING

Angsty, emotional contemporary romance

SIBLINGS

More Than Want You (Maxon & Keeley)

More Than Need You (Griff & Britta)

More Than Love You (Harlow & Noah)

BASTARDS

More Than Crave You (Evan & Nia)

More Than Tempt You (Bethany & Clint)

Coming Soon:

More Than Desire You (Xavian & ??) (November 1, 2022)

FRIENDS

More Than Dare You (Trace & Masey)

More Than Hate You (Sebastian & Sloan)

1001 DARK NIGHTS

More Than Pleasure You (Stephen & Skye)

More Than Protect You (Tanner & Amanda)

More Than Possess You (A Hope Series crossover) (Echo & Hayes)

FORBIDDEN CONFESSIONS (Sexy Shorts)

Sexy Bedtime Stories

FIRST TIME

Seducing the Innocent (Kayla & Oliver)

Seducing the Bride (Perrie & Hayden)

Seducing the Stranger (Calla & Quint)

Seducing the Enemy (Whitney & Jett)

PROTECTORS

Seduced by the Bodyguard (Sophie & Rand)

Seduced by the Spy (Vanessa & Rush)

Seduced by the Assassin (Havana & Ransom)

Seduced by the Mafia Boss (Kristi & Ridge)

FILTHY RICH BOSSES

Tempted by the Billionaire (Savannah & Chad)

Coming Soon:

Tempted by the Executive (January 24, 2023)

THE WICKED LOVERS (Complete Series)

Steamy Romantic Suspense

Wicked Ties (Morgan & Jack)

Decadent (Kimber & Deke)

Delicious (Alyssa & Luc)

Surrender to Me (Kata & Hunter)

Belong to Me (Tara & Logan)

Wicked to Love (Emberlin & Brandon)

Mine to Hold (Delaney & Tyler)

Wicked All the Way (Carlotta & Caleb)

Ours to Love (London, Javier, & Xander)

Wicked All Night (Rachel & Decker)

Forever Wicked (Gia & Jason)

Theirs to Cherish (Callie, Thorpe, & Sean)

His to Take (Bailey & Joaquin)

Pure Wicked (Bristol & Jesse)

Wicked for You (Mystery & Axel)

Falling in Deeper (Lily & Stone

Dirty Wicked (Sasha & Nick)

A Very Wicked Christmas (Morgan & Jack)

Holding on Tighter (Jolie & Heath)

THE DEVOTED LOVERS (COMPLETE SERIES)

Steamy Romantic Suspense

Devoted to Pleasure (Shealyn & Cutter)

Devoted to Wicked (Karis & Cage)

Devoted to Love (Magnolia & Josiah)

THE UNBROKEN SERIES

(co-authored with Jenna Jacob)

Raine Falling Saga (COMPLETE)

The Broken (Prequel)

The Betrayal

The Break

The Brink

The Bond

Heavenly Rising Saga

The Choice

The Chase

Coming Soon:

The Commitment (June 7, 2022)

THE PERFECT GENTLEMEN (COMPLETE SERIES)

(co-authored with Lexi Blake)

Steamy Romantic Suspense

Scandal Never Sleeps

Seduction in Session

Big Easy Temptation

Smoke and Sin

At the Pleasure of the President

MASTERS OF MÉNAGE (COMPLETE SERIES)

(co-authored with Lexi Blake)

Steamy Contemporary Romance

Their Virgin Captive

Their Virgin's Secret

Their Virgin Concubine

Their Virgin Princess

Their Virgin Hostage

Their Virgin Secretary

Their Virgin Mistress

STANDALONE TITLES

Naughty Little Secret

Watch Me

Dirty & Dangerous

Her Fantasy Men

A Perfect Match

THE HOPE SERIES (COMPLETE SERIES)

Steamy Contemporary Romance

Misadventures of a Backup Bride (Ella & Carson)

Misadventures with My Ex (Eryn & West)

More Than Possess You (Echo & Hayes) (A Reed Family Reckoning crossover)

SEXY CAPERS (COMPLETE SERIES)

Bound and Determined (Kerry & Rafael)

Strip Search (Nicola & Mark)

Arresting Desire (Lucia & Jon)

HISTORICAL ROMANCE

STANDALONES

The Lady and the Dragon

One Wicked Night

STRICTLY SERIES (COMPLETE DUET)

Victorian Historical Romance

Strictly Seduction (Madeline & Brock)

Strictly Forbidden (Kira & Gavin)

BROTHERS IN ARMS (COMPLETE TRILOGY)

Medieval Historical Romance

His Lady Bride (Gwenyth & Aric)

His Stolen Bride (Averyl & Drake)

His Rebel Bride (Maeve & Kieran)

BOXSETS/COLLECTIONS

More Than Promises (Reed Family Reckoning: Siblings)

Forbidden Confessions: First Time

Forbidden Confessions: Protectors

First Glance (A trio of series starters)

The Strictly Duet (Victorian historical romance)

NEW YORK TIMES BESTSELLING AUTHOR

SHAYLA BLACK

Steamy. Emotional. Forever.

BOOK BEAUTIES

Facebook Group

http://shayla.link/FBChat

Join me for live, interactive video chats every #WineWednesday. Be there for breaking Shayla news, fun, positive community.

VIP Readers

NEWSLETTER

at ShaylaBlack.com

Be among the first to get your greedy hands on Shayla Black news, juicy excerpts, cool VIP giveaways—and more!

Made in the USA
Las Vegas, NV
09 March 2022

Praise for *Entrenched*

"Riveting, brave, and transparent…The effects of trauma rule our lives until we take a chance, take charge and work through it. *Entrenched* will give you the courage to do just that."

—Marnie Grundman (TEDx Talk)

"Brave and insightful. *Entrenched* is an important addition to the literature of abuse and recovery. Blakemore documents the hard emotional journey survivors face as they confront – and overcome – obstacles to their healing. Among the many resources abuse victims can turn to, one of the most helpful is the personal narrative of someone who found the courage to face their demons – both external and internal – and the strength to change. Blakemore is that kind of writer: clear-eyed, perceptive, and willing to tell her truth no matter what."

—Sue William Silverman, author,
Because I Remember Terror, Father, I Remember You

"*Entrenched* echoes the message of resilience, determination, self-discovery, and hope. A must-read for survivors, advocates, and professionals."

—Cathy Brochu, AAS, BA, CHT, ADT,
Author, Speaker, Educator, and Consultant

"Blakemore writes with raw authenticity to bare her past and pave the way for others to seek healing."

—Tina Yeager, LMHC, award-winning author, speaker, podcast host, life coach, and founder of the Ten-Minute Turnaround Virtual Academy

---

"Emotionally evocative, courageous and spot on!"

—Paradise Kafri, Sexual Assault Advocate

"Vulnerable. Blakemore's willingness to share her story creates a space where survivors of childhood abuse/abandonment may relate and find comfort in knowing they are not alone."

—Debra Morrow, Executive Director of Middle Way House and Survivor

---

"*Entrenched* highlights the importance of facing the past and healing from trauma to live fully happy lives. Everyone will benefit from reading it."

—Kelly Mcinally, Sexual Assault Response Coordinator

"Well done. Blakemore's journey shows that we are our history, but hindsight can give us the clarity we need to move away from trauma..."

—Jan Biresch, Domestic Violence Literacy

"Blakemore's honesty about the decisions she regrets, and her willingness to be vulnerable for her readers, make *Entrenched* a compelling, powerful read."

—Rachel Anderson, Grove City Community Library

"Riveting. With sometimes painful and always poignant honesty, Linda describes her attempts to be "enough," her sometimes out-of-control behavior, and repeated relationship mistakes. Finally, when forced to face the emotional residue from childhood that ran her life, Linda talks about the freedom she has experienced after doing that hard work. I recommend this book to any woman with an abuse/abandonment history who strives desperately to be "enough" to deserve love. I also recommend this book to anyone who truly wants to understand the inner life of a woman with a similar history. Linda's story is compelling."

—Sharon Eakes, MA, BCC, Coach, Author, Educator, Retired Therapist, Pittsburgh, PA

"The emotional experiences we encounter as children shape and influence the decisions we make as adults, for better or worse. Linda Blakemore has courageously shared her personal journey in dealing with the aftermath of childhood sexual abuse. This well-written memoir will touch the heart of anyone who has had a similar experience in childhood and will offer much food for thought for all women. I highly recommend it."

—Anita LaLumere, PhD, Clinical and School Psychologist, Rosalyn Farms, PA

"Linda Blakemore's *Entrenched: A Memoir of Holding On and Letting Go* crossed my desk when I was doing somewhat of a 'deep dive' into trauma informed care and education. It was like a familiar train wreck I couldn't look away from. Each chapter kept me wanting more and I was captivated by the main character. Blakemore mentions her hope to use her book to help women and young women. I think this work will resonate with anyone."

—Katlyn White, Foster Care Coordinator, Cleveland, OH

"The great Toni Morrison said, 'The function of freedom is to free someone else.' In her vulnerable, honest, moving memoir, *Entrenched*, Linda Lee Blakemore dives deep into her own traumas of childhood sexual assault and abusive relationships to shine a light for others who may still be trapped. This courageous book offers a hand to anyone who's struggling to heal. It does what the best books do – it makes the world less lonely and, especially for adult survivors of trauma, it offers a way out of silence and isolation and confusion. This is a profoundly generous book."

—Lori Jakiela, author of
Belief Is Its Own Kind of Truth, Maybe, Pittsburgh, PA

"An amazingly relatable story. If you have been through trauma it will make you feel like you are...not alone. As a victim advocate I will definitely have my clients read this story because it will enrich their lives in so many positive ways and let them know it's okay to leave the ugly dirty past behind. It's a 10/10 on my book scale!!! Absolutely love it"

—Ariana Mancuso, Victim Advocate, Greater Boston

"*Entrenched* can help victims understand that they are not alone..., assist them as they work to overcome unhealthy relationships and self-abuse that often follows children's trauma/abuse, and help them find the courage to heal."

—Tina Morey, Sexual Assault Crime Victims
Services Specialist, Johnstown Town, NY

"The bravest women in the world are the ones who face their deepest fears, muster their courage, and write a memoir. Linda Lee Blakemore rips open her heart and exposes her pain to simply prove to other broken women that there is hope and a way out.

Entrenched: A Memoir of Holding On and Letting Go is a beautifully written, powerful story that will stay with me for a long time."

—Ann K. Howley, Author of *Confessions of a Do-Gooder Gone Bad*, Pittsburgh, PA

"We are told that one in five little girls is sexually abused. Many of them bury these memories so deeply they never come to terms with why as adults they think and act in self-destructive ways. In this raw and often emotional memoir that reads like a good novel, Linda Lee Blakemore frankly shares her personal journey from confusion and despair through discovering and surmounting her childhood pain, and finally to deep understanding and healing. Especially for people who also are dealing with childhood traumas, this intimate story of survival and growth is a must read."

—Roberta Grimes, afterlife expert and author of *The Fun of Dying, Liberating Jesus,* and other books, Austin, Texas

---

"In life, we all could go through many major traumas, such that we could bury ourselves under them and close ourselves up to many possibilities of life, but some, like Linda (Blakemore), will turn around and make a huge difference in others' lives through all the pain they've gone through and become committed to turning a liability into an asset in many others' lives. And I do appreciate that."

—Siamak Afshar, MA, CADC11 Transforming Life Treatment Center, Program Director, Yorba Linda, CA

"*Entrenched* kept me spellbound. Blakemore's sometimes out of control behavior demonstrates how our past can lure us toward unhealthy partners who, rather than help us work through unresolved psychological issues or fulfill what we did not receive as a child, use and discard us. Having myself lived with severe PTSD as a result of childhood incest, clergy sexual abuse & rape, like Linda, I have courageously faced, confronted & overcome. She and I have chosen to ask not "what's wrong with you?" but "what happened to you?" This book is a must read for every domestic violence sexual assault survivor, therapist & all who've remained complacent or silenced into shame and blame."

—BARBARA JOY HANSEN, International Award-Winning Author of *Listen to the Cry of the Child:The Deafening Silence of Sexual Abuse*, Milford Mass

---

"What differentiates Blakemore's story from others is her attention to underlying issues of her familiarity with and attraction to abuse and, even more importantly, the lasting impact of abandonment. Her story acknowledges and embraces a basic contradiction and psychological quandary...she came to see that 'staying with a man who left would keep her forever entrenched in the very thing she needed to move beyond.' Blakemore took the unusual approach of inviting her exes to read her drafts and provide their own stories of what had happened. Some declined. Others accepted, adding a focus on honesty and clarity that is evident through the trials and processes Blakemore endured to survive. *Entrenched* is more than a memoir about holding on and letting go. It's about considering the long- and short-term consequences of relationship choices. Women who live in, tolerate, or struggle with abusive situations will find Blakemore's descriptions thought-provoking, familiar, and revealing. Her story of life lessons holds hope for all who find themselves in her position—which is, sadly, likely to be an unexpectedly wide audience."

—D. DONOVAN, Senior Reviewer, Midwest Book Review

"In this powerful journey…*Entrenched* gives evidence of healing not only of oneself but of others who develop insight through sharing stories. Relating to incidences, understanding mistakes, accepting ourselves, and moving forward. We need to tell stories to understand our own struggle, and…to end isolation. I recommend this book not only to survivors of partner abuse, child sexual abuse, and people struggling with emotional relationships, but also to therapists…This book is for us all…. It is helpful and inspiring."

—NAHID FADUL, Consultation Liaison Psychiatrist. William Frederick award in the field of child sexual abuse 2016, Doha, Qatar

---

"The invisible climate of hidden fear, shame, and other emotions brought on by traumas forced onto our most vulnerable, often lead to a lifetime of silence for most. The enormous bravery shown by Blakemore…will empower others to understand and accept brokenness is not within them. Linda pours out her heart and soul in this revelation of life, igniting new charges of hope that a life filled with reciprocated authentic love for self, by others and for others is possible."

—DEBORAH DAVIS, Nurse Practitioner, Sexual Assault Nurse Examiner, Clinical Sexologist, Dallas, TX

"Breaking the silence, Blakemore takes every reader—and all who have shared a similar experience—on an empowering and courageous journey through the uncertainty and shame of child sexual abuse and intimate partner violence to a place of healing and happiness."

—CHYNA MCGARITY, Domestic Violence Survivor & Advocate – Purple Casket Campaign, Atlanta, Georgia

"*Entrenched: A Memoir of Holding On and Letting* Go kept me hanging on each page waiting to digest more and more. It is highly relatable to not just anyone who has experienced past trauma, but to what it means to experience difficult relationships and come out on the other side. Blakemore's story will move you and validate your own truths to relationships past. Her memoir is a powerfully vulnerable and important message to women that we are enough. I highly recommend this book to anyone on their healing journey."

—KATIE MCMAHON, Victim Advocate and Speech Language Pathologist, San Diego, California

---

"...Determination and Resilience...Blakemore offers a ray of hope to women...in this dark journey of infidelity and failed relationships and to all victims of childhood sexual abuse...This is a great piece and the author deserves commendations...I rate this book 4 out of 4 Stars."

—PIECE NKEM, Onlinebookclub.org

"As a 'learn from my bad decision/experiences' memoir *Entrenched* effectively displays the futility of constantly returning to a toxic relationship, and serves as a warning for those in the mindset to take it to focus on your own independence, security and wellbeing ahead of a relationship, and while in one. The book is very well-written and put together...it dealt with the more sensitive aspects of the narrative well. After such a heavy focus on the bad relationships, I would have liked to have ...heard more about the good marriage that followed, but as it is, this book focuses on a trying time in the author's life and ends with a happy ending and on a hope-filled note."

—LoveReading, UK

Entrenched

A MEMOIR OF HOLDING ON AND LETTING GO

LINDA LEE BLAKEMORE

PUBLISHED BY

LEONELLA PRESS

P. O. BOX 2033

CRANBERRY TOWNSHIP, PA 16066

Names have been changed and locations altered to protect those who appear in these pages. The author and Leonella Press shall have neither liability nor responsibility to any person or entity with respect to any loss or damage caused or alleged to be caused, directly or indirectly by the information contained in this book.

Printed in the United States of America

Library of Congress Control Number: 2021937355

Blakemore, Linda

Entrenched: A memoir of holding on and letting go. Linda Blakemore.—1st ed.

ISBN 978-1-7369947-0-2 Hardcover
ISBN 978-1-7369947-1-9 Softcover
ISBN 978-1-7369947-2-6 E-book

Book cover design and typesetting: Stewart A. Williams

To my children who endured my journey,
To my writing group who encouraged me every step of the way,
To my husband without whom this book never
would have been finished.

AUTHOR'S NOTE

What you are about to read is my true story. I understand that telling my story means telling the story of others, some who may not want their story told. For that reason, I have changed names and altered locations.

I also understand that my truth and my memory may differ from that of others, so I offered some who appear in these pages the opportunity to read part or all of what I have written. My second husband declined.

The conversations in this book are from memory. It would be impossible to recall all of them word for word, so I have retold them in a way that evokes the feeling and meaning of what was said. In all instances, the essence of the dialogue is accurate.

As for the trial, although some parts are condensed while others are paraphrased, the information, testimony, and court summation are all taken from actual transcripts.

I do not tell this story to hurt or expose anyone. I tell it in the hopes that what I have experienced, discovered, and overcome may help someone, even if only in some small way.

Lessons Cannot Be Taught
They Must Be Learned
The Past Cannot Be Dismissed
It Must Be Confronted

PART ONE

2010

I

I CAN'T HELP YOU

I HADN'T CRIED one drop. I had been too angry to feel sad. I don't know if I couldn't hold back any longer or if I just felt safe enough with Meredith, but the minute she motioned me into her office, tears streamed.

I sat in the armchair next to the empty loveseat. Meredith, in a crisp navy dress and perfectly sculpted bob, sat erect on her platform rocker. She opened a manila folder, flipped her tablet to a clean page, and clicked her pen.

"What's going on?" she asked.

"He's at it again." I pulled a tissue from the box on the side table next to me and dabbed at my eyes.

"How many times has he done this?"

"Five."

"Why is his behavior acceptable to you?"

I bowed my head. "It's not."

"What do you want?" she asked.

"I don't know, a miracle?" I forced a smile as my eyes rose to meet hers.

Meredith did not smile back. She stood, pulled her arms across her chest, and clutched my file. "I'm sorry, but I can't help you if you want him back."

Did my therapist just fire me? "What?"

"I cannot help you if you want him back."

Stunned, I rose and made my way out the door.

PART TWO

1992

2

THE DAY HE ENTERED MY LIFE

When I was a child, every Friday I arrived home from school to find my mother, cigarette pinched between two fingers, kneeling over a steaming bucket, the scent of bleach hanging in the air. A list of chores awaited my sisters and me. This was not a dust-vacuum-and-done kinda thing. No. My mother's "cleanliness is next to Godliness" was more of the *Mommy Dearest* variety. In addition to bathrooms and the kitchen, we scrubbed walls and windows, light fixtures and baseboards. Each week we did what others did once a year, if at all. So, although my mother would air dirty family issues to close friends, never would she air to anyone a dirty house. As an adult, I followed in her footsteps on both accounts.

That day in March 1992 wasn't a Friday, and the brand new, 3,200-square-foot brick provincial my first husband Tony and I had recently built wasn't dirty. But like my mother's home, it could never be too clean. When a burst of energy set me in motion on that chilly, rainy Wednesday, I grabbed the cleaning supplies and got to work doing what every devoted, repentant wife should do—clean. I scoured bathrooms, changed sheets, polished, and vacuumed myself out of each room. Then I washed, on my hands and knees, the ceramic tile floor all the way down the long entry hall and through the large, center-island kitchen. As I leaned back on my heels to take a breath, four soaking-wet kids plowed through the front door and promptly peeled off sopping backpacks and coats and shoes.

"Shit." I jumped to my feet realizing I had not returned the mat to the floor I had just washed. Then with a glance at the clock, I noticed the time. "It can't be 3:30 already. Can it?" I hurled the cleaning rag into the sink, tucked my snarled hair behind my ears, and grabbed a notepad and pen. "Shit," I repeated as I raced to the front door.

"Where are you going with my notebook?" Lizzi, thirteen and my oldest, asked.

"Meeting. I'm late." I grabbed my coat. "Watch your brothers. Do your homework. Don't make a mess."

"It's raining—" Lizzi was still talking when I closed the door behind me.

With a jacket tented over my head, I ran the short block to the newly constructed, vacant four-bedroom house around the corner where the Make-A-Wish planning meeting was already in progress. I knocked and without waiting for a response, stepped inside. To the right of the center hall entry, in the formal front room, a six-foot-tall boxcar of a man with broad shoulders and gleaming white hair stood in front of two rows of occupied folding chairs.

"Great. Linda's here." Jack motioned for me to take the only vacant seat on the far side of the room. "She's agreed to help us find and coordinate the volunteers we will need." Then he emphasized, "And we will need a lot."

As I made my way around the back of the room, I couldn't help but notice that everyone was clad in some form of business casual, a Franklin-type planner on his or her lap. Everyone, that is, except me. Normally I wouldn't have been able to think about anything other than how under-dressed and unprepared I was. But, that day, the only thing I could think about was Jack.

Prior to building new homes, Jack, like me, had been in real estate sales. Well, not exactly like me. He owned a successful company. I worked for someone at another. Although I had had a few transactions with Jack's agents over the years, prior to that day, he and I hadn't met. My first contact with him had come three days earlier when he called to welcome me to the team.

"I can't tell you how grateful I am to have your help." As soon as his mature tenor oozed through the phone, I tingled all over. "The next meeting is Wednesday. I hope you can come."

Now, seeing Jack in person triggered within me a just-as-visceral reaction. My body went from damp and chilly to warm and marshmallowy.

As I took my seat, Jack advanced the meeting. "Mary Beth, can you give us a marketing update?"

When the young woman, a local radio representative, stood, I opened my daughter's black-and-white composition notebook and clicked my pen. While the room full of professionals hummed with marketing strategies and event logistics, I took notes. But every second I could, albeit surreptitiously, I studied the face of the man who led the group.

Two thick lines creased his broad forehead. Around his deep green eyes, engraved in his slightly weathered skin, crow's feet darkened and exaggerated whenever he pulled a wide smile, which was often. His chiseled nose, which I would later learn had been broken twice playing football, turned up a bit when he spoke. Alone, each of his features was ordinary. Together they were in perfect scale. But it wasn't his looks, his voice, or even the way he commanded the group. There was something else. Something deep inside of me that drew me to this man with the intensity of an abandoned child starving not for food, but for his undivided attention.

I walked slowly home after that meeting, tugging at my ratty shirt. *I can't believe I dressed like this.* I shook my head. *Oh my God. What am I thinking? I can't believe I care.*

I'm not going to mess up my life—again.

3

RICHARD

THREE YEARS EARLIER, I had had an affair.

I met Richard the day my real estate mentor and best friend, Gail, met me after work at a local pub known for good food and generous drinks. I needed to unwind. She needed to find a way to save a crumbling sale.

"I told that woman the seller would fix whatever her client wanted fixed." Gail took a sip of her favorite adult beverage, Disaronno amaretto.

"Is the other agent being difficult or do you think the buyer has cold feet?"

"I don't know." She sighed.

Single and self-supporting, Gail was one month behind on her mortgage and a few short steps ahead of the IRS. Her financial mess had been brewing for years. Making matters worse, the abusive bum I introduced to her moved into her townhouse, quit his job, and filled his days with expensive pay-per-view events and unpaid gambling debts. When she finally threw him out, he left her with a throbbing bruise on her right arm, maxed-out credit cards, and a beat-up Sedan de Ville that shook when she drove it.

"I need this sale," she continued.

"I know you do." I nodded sympathetically, then took a sip of my cabernet.

Just then a tall, slender man, gray at the temples, appeared at our pub table in a far corner of the dimly lit room. We had chosen that spot because we wanted to be alone. He didn't care.

"Hello, ladies." Without asking, he snatched a stool from an adjacent occupied table and shoved the seat between us.

Gail rolled her eyes. He was gangly and nerdy and, well, just plain squirrely. Still, for some unknown reason, in an almost uncontrollable way, I was drawn to this older man—the way the child of an alcoholic might be drawn to a drinker.

"What's your name?" He leaned on one elbow, separating me from Gail.

My face flushed. "I'm Linda." Motioning toward Gail, I said, "That's…"

Without letting me finish, he pointed to my left hand. "You married?"

"As a matter of fact, I am. You?"

"Separated."

"Sorry to hear that," I said.

"I'm not." He snickered, then added, "And what do you do?"

"Gail and I sell real estate."

"What do you know, I'm looking for a house."

"Imagine that," Gail said as she shook her head and rolled her eyes.

❧

In the beginning, I showed Richard lots of houses. As the months passed, we spent more and more time together, less of it looking at homes. We talked for hours in his car, in restaurants and coffee shops, in the apartment he said he had rented. And we got to know one another, or should I say he got to know me. It's only in hindsight that I realize how little I knew about him. He introduced me to a few friends, but wouldn't discuss the status of his pending divorce or why he and his wife had separated. He told me about the financial services company he recently started, but changed the subject anytime I asked why he left a high-powered job with the Department of Banking and Securities just three years shy of an early pension. Rather than becoming suspicious, the more Richard withheld, the more I wanted to crack his shell and climb deep inside.

"Are you almost ready to be done with this charade?" Gail asked as we climbed into her car en route to a listing appointment.

The market was hot. Good homes were in short supply and Gail and I were up against two other, highly successful agents. If we wanted this listing, and we did, we needed to be on top of our game. But my head was anywhere but.

"Well—" My voice trailed off.

"Well, what?"

"He wants me to become his personal assistant." I buckled my seatbelt.

"And give up real estate?" Shaking her head, she started her car.

I couldn't keep the smile from filling my face. "And..."

"Here it comes." She took a breath. "And what?"

"He asked me to leave Tony."

"Please tell me you're not going to do that."

"Richard loves me."

She rolled the car to a stoplight and while clutching the steering wheel, twisted her body toward me. In a most emphatic voice, she said, “He’s married.”

“He’s separated.”

“He is not separated *and* he is the *last* thing you need.” By then she was almost shouting. It didn’t matter. Even the best advice of a best friend couldn’t stop me from making the worst decision I would ever make.

A few weeks later, at my request, Tony moved out of our house and I became Richard’s full-time assistant and fully committed lover. We spent every day at the office together and almost every other night in one another’s arms. We went to dinner, to the theater, on long walks under the stars. We giggled and planned our future. It was perfect. Or so I thought.

❧

One Friday, seven months after Tony had moved out, still beaming with the glow of new love, I rose from my desk when Richard walked through the office door. “Good morning,” I said in a singsong voice as I stepped toward him. “I missed you last night.”

Never taking his gaze from the pages he held in his hand, he brushed by me. “Morning.”

“Everything all right?”

“A lot on my mind,” he replied.

“Oh. Okay.” I followed him to his office and leaned against the jamb of his door. “Anything I can do?”

He hung his coat, took a seat behind his desk, and picked up the handset on his desk phone. “Yeah. Close the door.”

Dismissing his brusqueness to pressures at work, I did as he asked, then made my way to my desk, which sat in front of his office door.

That workweek ended with a closed-door meeting between Richard and Greg, one of the guys in our office. They had been discussing a proposal for a big contract they were trying to land.

When Richard's door opened behind me, I heard Greg say, "If it's okay, I'll get this to you first thing Monday."

"Monday is fine. Have a good weekend." Richard sounded cordial, not at all as curt as he had been toward me all week.

Greg took a step out of Richard's office, then turned back to our boss and said, "Oh and by the way, happy anniversary. Doing something special?"

"You know how it is," Richard replied and Greg nodded.

His anniversary. *Is that why he has been so distant?* My heart sank.

After I shut down my computer and grabbed my keys, I poked my head through Richard's door. "I'm heading out. Need anything before I go?"

"No," he said without looking up.

"You free to grab a bite later?"

"Not tonight." He gave me a cursory smile. "Things to do."

Things to do all right. Like an anniversary celebration with your wife!

❧

At home, after I had gotten the kids fed and settled in with the neighborhood sitter, I climbed into my car. It was a little past 7:30. I had no idea if Richard was going to celebrate with his wife. But I was going to find out. I headed straight for his favorite restaurant.

"Good evening, Madam. May I help you?" The maître d' looked at me from his podium.

"No, thanks." I pushed past the formal man in his formal attire. "Looking for someone."

The minute I rounded the corner from the entry hall, I saw him. Nestled in a booth on the far left side of the dining room, Richard held up a wine glass. He was toasting her, toasting their marriage, toasting them.

I couldn't get out of there fast enough. I hurried to my car and dialed his cell. He didn't answer. I didn't expect he would. But I wanted him to know that I knew where he was. I knew what he was doing. I called him over and over and over again. I left message after message. "What in the hell are you doing with her?" I said in one message.

"If you're divorcing her, you would not be celebrating your anniversary. You're nothing but a liar." I was in tears when I left that last message.

Then I called Gail.

"On my way," she said with no hesitation.

She found me in our regular coffee shop hangout, hunkered in a corner booth, sobbing. "You're right. He's married." I blew my nose.

"I know this is hard, but you have to accept it. If he hasn't left her by now, he isn't going to." Her voice was soft, but her words were firm.

Nodding in agreement, I cried harder.

"You need to get away from that jerk. Even if you don't want to go back to Tony (what she really meant was "if Tony won't take you back"), you need to get back into real estate."

"I can't."

"Yes, you can. Just quit. It's simple. You don't owe Richard anything."

"I have four kids to feed. Support isn't enough. I need a steady income."

"Then find another job. Whatever. Just get away from that asshole."

When I arrived home that evening, I was grateful to find the kids asleep. I paid the sitter, then poured myself a glass of wine. Before I could make my way to the family room or even begin to think about what I was going to do with the mess I had made of my life, I heard my front door open. I peered down the hall.

"Hello," Richard called softly as he walked toward me.

"What in the hell are you doing here?" Nothing would have pleased me more than to throw my wine, glass and all, in his face, but that would have left me one more mess to clean up. So I set down the goblet.

When he got close, he tried to put his arms around me. I backed away. "Don't you dare.

"I love you. I'm sorry. I had to."

"You did not *have* to do anything."

"I'm going to leave her."

"I don't believe you." I crossed my arms. "It's over between us."

"Don't do that," he begged.

"Why not?"

His eyes began to well. "I don't want to lose you."

"Then why are you still there?"

"We're having trouble with our daughter. You know that."

"You said it was only going to be for a few—"

"This is harder than I thought." He took a step toward me. "I need to get this right."

I backed away. "I don't know."

"It won't be forever."

He took another step, but this time I didn't move.

"I need a little more time."

"How much time?"

"Two months."

"I wish that were true." I shook my head.

"It is. I mean it. I love you." He put his arms around me and I felt myself soften. I wanted to believe him.

"Prove it." I looked up at him. "Stay with me *tonight*."

"Tomorrow. I promise." With that he left.

I should have ended the affair right then. I couldn't. I had become someone even I didn't understand—someone I hated. I didn't think about his wife or his kids any more than I thought about Tony or my children. I transformed all of them into cardboard cutouts, devoid of needs or feelings, lifeless figures I could walk past or step over without consideration. The only thing that mattered was Richard. When Richard needed time, I was patient. When he needed attention, I gave him sex. When he needed me to work more, I did that too. Anything to make him leave her. Anything to make him want me as much as I wanted him.

Each time one of his drop-dead dates came and went, I fell apart. One minute I screamed, "You said you were leaving her. You're nothing but a liar." But as soon as he'd turn to leave, I'd drop to my knees and beg, "Please don't go. I love you. I'll wait. I'll do whatever you want."

One day everything changed.

He was leaving her. This time he meant it. He would move in with me, spend weekends with his kids, pay child support. I refused to acknowledge the grimace on his face. I couldn't. Besides, it was settled. We hugged on it, kissed on it, made love on it. He would tell her Friday. Since my children would be with their father, we would have the weekend alone to celebrate.

He didn't come to work that Friday and I didn't hear from him at all on Friday night. I told myself they were ironing out the details. Fighting and crying. I knew what that was like. I'd gone through it with Tony. No need to worry. Right? When he didn't call me Saturday, I got nervous. Would he show up for our date that night? Then, out of the blue, as I stood in front of my living room window, all dressed and ready to go, watching and waiting and worrying, his car rounded the bend. He was right on time for our special date.

I didn't wait for him to come to the front door. I raced outside and got into his car. He took me to Angelo's, a restaurant we enjoyed often. As he drove, I was careful not to ask how it went with his wife the previous night; instead, I made small talk and I waited. At the restaurant, I sipped my wine and waited some more. Nothing. By the time our food arrived, I couldn't stand it one more second. I needed to know.

"Must have been hard, huh?"

Richard pushed pasta around on his plate, but said not a word.

"You talked to her. Right?" My voice was hopeful and upbeat.

More silence.

"You promised." I dropped my fork, appetite and hope gone.

That evening he didn't make another empty promise as he had before, and I didn't beg. We sat there, quietly, staring at our plates. Even the waitress seemed uncomfortable as she took away the barely eaten meals. As soon as she laid the check on the table, he pulled cash from his wallet, tucked it under his glass, and stood. I trailed him to the car.

In my driveway, he reached for the ignition.

"No need to turn it off." I climbed out. "You're not coming in." I slammed the passenger door.

He didn't listen to what I said. He turned off the car and followed me. I stepped inside and pushed the door closed in his face. Again he didn't care. He forced it opened and came into the house.

"What do you think you're doing?" I demanded.

He didn't answer and he didn't move from the entryway.

"Fine, then just stand there." I shook my head and marched upstairs. He followed me like we were some old married couple who had done it that way for years. Out to dinner, fight or not, up to bed. But that's not who we were. That's not what we did. Our pattern was dinner, sex, he would leave, I would cry. Somewhere in there I would beg him to stay and he would promise it would happen soon.

That night was different. I was different.

"I'm done." I nodded. Then I said, "I'm not doing this anymore." I got undressed and climbed into my side of the bed.

"You don't mean that," he said as he removed his clothes and slipped under the covers.

"What in the hell are you doing?"

He tried to kiss me.

"Get away from me." I pushed him.

"Come on. Let's make the best of what we've got."

"I'm not having sex with you."

"I love you," he insisted.

"This isn't love…it's…I don't know what the hell it is. But it isn't love."

"Come on," he coaxed.

"No."

It was the first time I had turned him down, and he didn't like it. He grabbed my arms and pulled them over my head.

"What are you doing?" I tried to pull my hands free. "Stop it."

He squeezed my wrists together in one of his large hands.

I pushed and I kicked. "Let me go."

He straddled me.

"Don't you dare," I cried and I fought.

He didn't care. He forced his knees between my legs.

"No," I wailed. But there was nothing I could do. He was on top of me, inside me, breathing hard, thrusting deep. Then he let off a deep, loud, long moan and went limp. Tears slipped from my eyes.

He rolled off, pulled on his pants, and grabbed his shirt. Without a word, he was gone.

Days passed before I found the courage to tell anyone. One day I couldn't stand it anymore. I opened up to a man at work, a man with whom I had no relationship. It was rumored that he, too, was having an affair. Maybe I thought he'd understand. Maybe I thought he'd comfort me. I don't know. Either way, telling him was the wrong thing to do.

"He'd never do that," he insisted. "You're just a scorned lover." As he walked away, he looked back over his shoulder and said, "Get over it."

He was right. I was scorned. I told no one after that. Not even Gail.

A single mother with four kids, I needed my job. With mouth shut and head down, I went to work. I avoided Richard. I avoided everyone.

❧

Weeks later, a young female co-worker appeared in front of my desk. She was the newest paramour of the married man to whom I had confided.

"What do you want?" I scowled at her.

"Going to the holiday party?" A smirk slithered across her face.

"No." I glared at her. "Not that it's any of your business."

"Shame." She folded her arms. "I'd love to see your face when Richard walks in with his new love."

"What in the hell are you talking about?"

"Surely you didn't think you were the only one." She snickered as she walked away.

Another woman? Another woman! After what he did to me! I filled with a blinding, thick black rage. I stormed into Richard's office and slapped a hand-written termination note that I don't remember writing on his desk. Then I hurried out of the building, shouting at the top of my voice, "Fuck you, asshole."

I sped home, planning to expose him for the bastard cheater that he was. I wanted to inflict the same pain he had, without remorse, heaved up and dumped on me. I grabbed the phone and dialed.

"Hello," his wife answered. "Hello?" After a moment she asked, "Is someone there?"

Except for keeping me embroiled in a love I never had but wasn't ready to give up, except for hurting an innocent woman I had already hurt, nothing good could come of any attacking words that would spill from my tongue. I hung up.

I felt worthless and discarded—an abandoned child. I fell apart. I blamed myself.

It took months, but I was grateful when Tony took me back.

4

THE MULLIGAN

By late March 1991, Tony and I had been back together a little over eight months. He was due home from another business trip. That evening, after our children were asleep, as I scoured and polished and shined, I reminded myself how lucky I was that Tony had taken me back.

The house was spotless, and a snack, covered in plastic, awaited Tony in the refrigerator. I slipped into pajamas and peered out the window, hoping to see his car. If his plane had landed on time, he'd be rounding the bend onto our street at any moment. But except for the streetlamp illuminating a soft rain and the trees swaying ever so slightly, the night remained dark and still.

Finally I headed to bed, nestled under the covers, propped my pillow, and grabbed my book. I must have dozed off. I never heard the rattle of the garage door, the hum of the microwave, or the crinkle of opening mail. When Tony entered the bedroom, I startled awake. Exhaustion filled his face. He had had a difficult three days, another challenging client, another rescued account. The company called on Tony to save them, just as I had called on him to save me.

"You must be beat." I laid my book on the night table.

He flashed a magazine in my direction. "There's an article in here about why women have affairs." He sat on the bed next to me, opened the magazine, and pushed through the pages. "Did I mistreat you?"

"Of course not." I sat up, caught off guard, but not completely surprised.

Anytime the pain of my infidelity boiled up inside of him like little volcanic eruptions, wherever we found ourselves—the family room, our bedroom, a crowded restaurant—I listened and I tried to find a way to fix the marriage I had shattered.

"Were you isolated or lonely or neglected while I was out working hard to support you?"

"Not at all." I lowered my head.

"Then why?"

I didn't understand what had drawn me to Richard, except that it was something I couldn't control. I knew better than to confess that to Tony. All I said was, "I'm sorry." I reached for his hand.

"You should be." He jerked his hand away. "I'm a good husband. You have a good life."

"You are. I do. It won't happen again. I promise."

"You're damn right." He shook his head. "It won't."

We sat quietly for a few minutes and then, cautiously, almost in a whisper, I said what I had been wanting to say for a long time. "Maybe we need a fresh start."

"What are you talking about?" He glared at me.

"A new house. New neighborhood. New beginning."

He pursed his lips and shook his head. "No."

"Gail told me about new homes being built around an eighteen-hole golf course."

"We can't afford that."

"That's the thing. With what we'll make on this house, I think we can. Plus, it's a semi-private course. Get a membership or pay and play."

He looked doubtful.

"You'll step out of our back door every night and be right on the course. On the green or on the tee. Play one hole. Play eighteen. Play every day."

"I don't know." He stared at the floor.

"Plus, it's minutes from the interstate. Your commute will be cut in half. That's more time to golf, to relax. More time for us to be together." Feeling hopeful, I lowered my voice to just above a whisper and said, "And once we're settled, I'll help. I'll go back to work. I promise."

His shoulders relaxed and he rotated toward me.

"We can put the past behind us. I know we can," I slipped my hand in his. "It'll be a new start—with no mistakes."

It took Tony a few months to agree, but after we drove through the neighborhood and he played the course, his resistance gave way. Together we selected a lot overlooking the ninth tee. I found a lender, coordinated construction, and made selections. It took six months for our beautiful four-bedroom, three-and-a-half-bath provincial to be built. The house was bigger than I expected, more than we should have spent. Tony was proud of our new home and excited to live in a golf course community. His happiness made me feel secure.

With boxes unpacked and kids settled in their new school, I submerged myself in the fast-growing subdivision and up-and-coming township. I volunteered in my youngest son's kindergarten room, became my daughter's middle school cheerleading coach, and started a card group in our neighborhood. Then I launched the new township public library, was elected president of the Community Action Task Force, and organized the first ever Community Day Celebration. When Jack called to invite me to participate in the Make-A-Wish Junior Pitch, Putt and Drive fundraiser, to be held on our neighborhood golf course, I said, "I'd love to."

The very move designed to give Tony and me a do-over, or as they say in golf, a mulligan, delivered me straight to Jack.

5

THE FUNDRAISER

JACK GLIDED ACROSS the paved parking lot, then stepped over the curb and onto the soft, grassy practice area of the semi-private golf course.

After six months of organizing, the 1992 Make-A-Wish summer fundraiser, a six-day event, was finally in full swing. Masses of children gathered. They formed single-file lines alive with excitement and nervous chatter about who would sink the longest putt, pitch closest to the pin, and manage that prize-winning drive. When he saw me, Jack raised his brow, tipped his head, and shot me a thumbs up. Then he worked his way toward the golf pro, Graham, who was intent on teaching a pigtailed blonde child the proper way to hold her club.

"Intertwine the baby finger on your right with the index finger on your left. Like this." After demonstrating, Graham handed the club to the little girl. "Now you try it."

"Graham," Jack called out as he approached. Graham's focus

shifted away from the child. Jack and he exchanged a firm handshake. "Thanks for all your hard work."

"My pleasure, sir."

"Where are the boys?" Graham knew Jack wasn't asking about children and he pointed across the crowded room. "Shane and Guy are over there."

As Jack moved toward the proud owners of the new golf course, a freckle-faced redhead tugged at my shirt. I looked down at the little boy.

"Where do I go now?" he asked.

"Aiden." His mother, who stood behind him, clutched his shoulder. The child took a half step back, bumping into her sculpted legs below her pleated, white tennis skirt.

I bent over to make myself eye level with the little guy. "See that man over there, the one wearing the red and white striped shirt?" He gave an exaggerated nod. "Take this to him." I tapped the scorecard he held tightly with both hands. "He'll get you started."

When the boy and his mother scurried off, my sights shifted back to Jack. He offered warm welcomes and genuine handshakes to every volunteer who had given up personal time to make each day of the fundraiser a success. He took time to chat and laugh with parents who brought participating children. He slapped the backs or ruffled the hair of every teen or child, thanking each for making Devon's Wish come true.

My time with Jack came later. That had become our ritual. Each night after tables were down and chairs folded, Jack and I met in the parking lot to count the take and figure out how much we still needed to accomplish the goal. Neither of us could accept failure – particularly of something as important as granting a wish to a dying boy. With one day left, the total was especially important.

Jack raised the hatch of his black Cherokee, reached inside, and spun the combinations of a hard-framed attaché, so beaten the black leather peeled at the corners, exposing its thick cardboard frame. I smiled at this commanding man, with his gold Rolex and crisp white handmade shirt, toting such a tattered case.

"What?" His face flushed. "I don't use it much."

"Looks pretty used to me."

Leaning back against his bumper, yellow tablet in hand, he tallied. I studied his face. Thick salt-and-pepper locks fell across his broad forehead, golden tan darkened in the creases around his smiling eyes. Large, strong hands would keep me safe.

He smiled. "We did it."

"With a day to spare?"

"Checked it twice." He raised his arm in a celebratory high-five. As soon as my palm met his, he entwined his meaty fingers with mine. Our eyes locked. My heart pounded inside my chest. He whispered, "I couldn't have done it without you."

A week later the presentation ceremony took place on a small, raised platform. Terri Callan, director of the local Make-A-Wish chapter, accepted the oversized cardboard check presented by Jack. Slightly off-center in front of the two of them, with parents on either side, the wish recipient, Devon, a local twelve-year-old, emaciated by the leukemia that would take his life in less than a year, sat frail in his oversized black wheelchair. Jack beamed at me nonstop as the photographer snapped the shot that would fill the local paper's front page. From my position amid the clapping crowd, I smiled back.

When the ceremony was over, Jack escorted Terri and her large cardboard check to her car. I figured I would never hear from him again.

I was wrong.

6

CARNIVAL NIGHT

TWO MONTHS AFTER the fundraiser, as I prepared dinner, my phone rang. I raced to the sink to rinse the egg-caked crumbs from my fingers.

"Hi." I said as I dried my hands, phone pinched between my ear and my shoulder. "I didn't expect…I mean…how are you?"

"I was wondering if you'd be interested in selling the townhomes I'm building," Jack asked.

"What? Really? Me?"

"Yes. Really." He chuckled. "You."

He wanted me. There was something about being wanted I couldn't refuse. I had even been known to jump at jobs I didn't want, simply because someone had picked me. But being wanted by Jack caused an eruption of feelings stronger than any I had ever felt. A gravitational undertow. A feeling not unlike that childhood night I will forever call "carnival night."

Carnival night, as I named it, occurred the summer following the seventh grade, days before my thirteenth birthday. I had always been on the fringes of friendships, somehow never a part of the crowd. That night I left the church festivities trailing behind three other girls also recently elected to the highly sought-after eighth grade cheerleading squad. Normally, I had to be home by ten, but this was the week-long, once-a-year event filled with nasally pipe music, squeaky carnival rides, the smell of funnel cakes in the air. Young couples holding hands, smiling girls clinging to stuffed animal prizes, sticky fingers dipping into bags of pink and blue cotton candy. The equivalent to the vacation my family never took. Each year on that special last night, Dad gave in, just a little, on his strictly enforced curfew.

Heading home that evening in front of me, Bobbi Jean, Amy, and Janice marched in synchronized motion, ponytails bouncing, flip-flops flapping, short shorts exaggerating gangly long legs. They giggled about how the school's basketball star, Tommy Morgan, would be even better next year. He liked Amy, but Amy liked Vinnie.

"What are you thinking?" Janice demanded.

Amy shrugged. "He's just another stupid jock. I prefer brainiacs."

They giggled.

We'd gone two short blocks from the festival. The girls in front of me chattered on about boys, the anticipation of next year's less-forgiving teachers, and the higher, more dangerous cheerleading mounts they wanted to attempt. Suddenly, seemingly out of nowhere, an old, beat-up sedan, splattered with gray and red primer, squealed a wide U-turn in the middle of the two-lane road. The car bounced up and over the curb, lurching to a stop right in front of us. It was full of boys, older boys. Five eager faces in all.

My friends continued on. I froze.

A teenager in the front passenger seat, with dirty-blond hair and a cigarette dangling from the corner of his mouth, cranked down his window and leaned out. As though he instinctively knew I was the weak straggler lagging behind the group, his intense sapphire stare locked on me. In a raspy voice that made him sound older and dangerous, he called to me, "Hey, beautiful."

I flushed with excitement.

"Wanna go for a ride?"

I didn't consider that I could be raped or murdered or left for dead in some roadside ditch. Nor did I remember my mother's unwavering orders that I was never to get in any car with any boy—ever. I thought only, *this handsome older boy wants me.* I stepped off the curb toward the dilapidated, revving sedan, my head bobbing like the plastic bulldog perched on the faded black dash. As I reached for the door, Bobbi Jean clutched my arm and yanked me back onto the sidewalk. "What are you doing? Are you crazy?"

❧

Jack had that same hypnotic draw on me. When he invited me to work for him, although my gut screamed, "No," without a second thought or a friend to stop me, without considering Tony or the possible consequence to my marriage, I said, "I'd love to."

7

GETTING INTO REAL ESTATE

NEWLY ENGAGED TO Tony, I was barely twenty when I came up with the wild idea to purchase an older duplex recently listed for sale. It was not far from my parents' home, where I still lived.

"A rental property." My father raised one brow and tipped his head. "You must have real estate running in your veins."

I didn't know about that, but I knew one thing, I did not want to rent. Plus, this was a win-win. Live in one apartment, rent out the other, cut our living expenses in half. Tony agreed.

Since Tony was in his last semester at Pitt, his part-time earnings didn't hold weight with the mortgage company. With a down payment from his parents and my full-time income as a secretary for a health insurance company, we wrote a contract on our first place.

As we approached the closing date, I noticed my name missing from the paperwork.

"We don't put the woman's name on the deed," the real estate agent explained.

What the hell? It was 1978, not the Stone Age. I wasn't having any of it. "If we're using my income, my name will be on the deed."

To the distress of all, my name was added and Tony and I closed on our first piece of real estate.

The next few months, in between jobs and school and wedding preparations, we worked hard renovating the tiny two-bedroom on the top floor for ourselves. We changed flooring, updated the bathroom, installed new appliances. And we hung lots and lots of wallpaper.

We planned to move in when we returned from our honeymoon. But by the time our wedding day arrived, we couldn't wait. We spent our first night as husband and wife in our new bed in our new home. Several months later, my younger sister, Shari, and her new husband moved in below us.

The following year Shari and I gave birth to little girls within months of one another. Tony's new full-time job didn't pay a lot, but it allowed me to be a stay-at-home mom, like my sister. She and I offered one another support. Since neither of us had a car, together we pushed our strollers to the corner market to get milk or bread or whatever we needed.

For a while it was great. But after the birth of my second daughter just twelve months later, the two-bedroom apartment became claustrophobic, and the trek up and down the stairs toting two babies became difficult. Tony and I began the search for a bigger place to live.

"We do not want to be in the city school district," I repeated over and over to the real estate agent who took us from house to house. But each home she suggested was in the city.

"Your budget is so limiting," she insisted.

After working with two more agents, neither of whom listened any better than the first, I stumbled across a Realtor who mentioned a darling, cozy Cape Cod in West View, a bedroom community just outside of Pittsburgh's city limits. She met us at the property. It had three small bedrooms, one quaint 1950s-style pink tile bath, and a level backyard. Bonus, it had a garage.

Even though it was the only house we saw with that agent, I announced, "This is it!" We wrote the deal.

My mother didn't agree. She crinkled her nose as she toured the home we would soon move into. "The kitchen is old. That rosebud wallpaper is awful, and the house is way too small."

A few years later, eighteen months after the birth of baby number three, and once again pregnant, my mother's assessment turned true.

"We're busting at the seams." I patted my growing belly as Flo and I chatted over coffee cake following one of our monthly Welcome Wagon gatherings. Flo was the only real estate agent in our group.

"Great," she said. "I'll come by and get it listed."

The house may have been tiny, but keeping it in "show condition" with three little ones and one on the way was no small feat. After a few showings, I developed a system. While the kids played, I cleaned. Then I strapped the children in the car and raced back inside to vacuum my way out. We occupied ourselves at the park or at McDonald's, depending on the weather, time of day, or the amount of change I could scrape together. Finally, after who knows how many showings and two very long months, Flo called. "We have an offer."

We sold our home to an investor. Because he had the cash to assume our FHA loan, he wouldn't need a mortgage. Great!

With the sale buttoned up, Tony and I started looking for our forever home. Every weekend we followed Flo from neighborhood to neighborhood. In the late stages of pregnancy, exhausted and cranky, I found something wrong with each house. Taxes were too high. The distance to the school too far. The driveway too steep. Once, when something about the exterior just didn't feel right, I refused to get out of the car. Flo was none too happy.

One day Tony and I drove neighborhoods by ourselves. Just as I was sure it was going to be another wasted day, we turned the corner and spotted a For Sale By Owner sign. Compared to where we had been living, the house was huge, the neighborhood prestigious, the half-acre lot flat as a tabletop.

Tony knocked at the front door and after a brief conversation, the gracious owners invited us into their meticulously maintained, four-bedroom, two-and-a-half-bath home with a two-car integral garage. It felt like a mansion to me. So clean. So perfect. The best part, a recent price reduction put this house within our range.

We signed the agreement and applied for a mortgage. We were on our way. Or so we thought.

A few days later Tony called in the middle of his workday, something he rarely did. I knew there was trouble.

"I just got off the phone with Countrywide Mortgage. Because our buyer is assuming our FHA mortgage, we could be held responsible if he defaults."

"What does that mean?"

"It means we have to qualify for both house payments."

"That can't be right. Surely Flo would have told us..."

"Flo *should* have told us," Tony snapped.

"I'll call her right now."

"You bought that house without me," Flo hissed. "You can solve your problem without me."

That evening, after the kids were asleep, Tony and I sat on the game room sofa. We had a house we couldn't buy and an iron clad sale we couldn't break.

"What are we going to do?" I twisted my hands in my lap.

"Papa made a call today," Tony said.

Tony's Italian immigrant father was the master tailor for an exclusive men's clothier in the city. He never lost his accent and never compromised his craftsmanship. Executives from near and far came to him for handmade suits and meticulous alterations, and, when available, a piece of his wife's delicious homemade lasagna. My father-in-law knew everyone. Having recently crafted a silk suit for a high-ranking official at Countrywide, Tony's father reached out on our behalf.

Tony continued. "Countrywide will do the deal if we pay them an additional $8,000 in penalty closing costs and a higher interest rate."

"How does that make any difference?"

"I have no idea, but they hold the money, and they make the rules."

To a young family about to have four children under six and an annual gross income of $35,000, that amount might as well have been a million dollars. We didn't have that kind of extra money lying around. We didn't have any.

"Do you think there's any equity in the apartment building?" Tony was reaching.

"I doubt it. We squeezed out every nickel when we refinanced it to buy this place."

There was only one way to make this work. Even though neither one of us wanted to do it, we had no choice.

"I'll ask my parents." Tony looked at the floor, shaking his head.

As soon as we moved into our new home, I announced, "If Flo can sell real estate, so can I." I took the required classes, passed the exam, and proudly waved my real estate license over my head. After joining the ranks of Hammel Quinlan, the neighborhood broker, I dove headlong into the sixty-hour, evening and weekend workweek of helping people buy and sell homes.

❧

Jack's path into real estate was different.

Eight years before I got my license, at a small table in a little diner, Jack sat across from a man who had quickly become his best friend. Frustrated with a stressful job that held his paycheck, his vacation, and his future hostage, Jack wanted to make a big change. He didn't want to leave TRM Systems to work for someone else. He wanted his own company—a real estate company. But no bank would lend him the money.

"What are they saying?" Victor had asked.

"I don't have enough personal capital and I don't have any real estate experience."

Both were true, although Jack's father had become a part-time Realtor in the influential suburb of Franklin Park, and Jack saw the potential of the emerging market.

"I can make a lot of money," Jack told Victor. "I know I can."

"No doubt," Victor concurred. "And it's a great time to get into this business."

Victor knew what he was talking about. Born into a real estate family, Victor's immigrant father had had the vision and foresight to plan and build, with his own two hands, brick by brick, an entire housing development and a shopping center north of Pittsburgh after World War II. The hospital Victor's father had proposed was later built by someone else in an adjacent neighborhood. By all accounts, such a comprehensive community plan was years ahead of its time.

Victor possessed the same insight his father had, and he had faith in his friend. "Phyllis and I talked about it last night," Victor said. "We'd like to loan you the money."

Jack never forgot what his friend had done, and he never missed a payment to the man who believed in him when no one else did.

By 1990, as Tony and I prepared to move into our fourth address in the golf course community of Long Iron, Jack had grown his real estate business to include four partners, six offices, and 149 agents. Still, they were nowhere near as large as other agencies. As Jack later explained it to me, he wanted to keep growing by adding a mortgage arm and a commercial division to enhance profitability and make the company more enticing to the corporate conglomerates beginning to infiltrate the area and buy up smaller companies. His partners weren't interested in growing or selling. Unable to strike a compromise, Jack sold out, accepted a non-compete agreement, and reached out again to his friend Victor.

This time the two friends joined forces in what would become Jack's first land development and residential new construction venture. Together they would build maintenance-free, one-level townhouses, a floor plan needed to meet the city's fast-growing empty nester population but difficult to deliver given the hilly terrain. Victor's design, a modification of a plan originally sketched by his father, satisfied both.

Jack and Victor worked together to find the land and change the zoning. Victor secured financing and then handed the reins to Jack. Jack engineered the site, installed the infrastructure (utilities, sewers, and roads), and managed the day-to-day construction. Erik, the site foreman, was brought on to coordinate the construction. I was hired to sell the townhouses Jack would build.

8

WORKING FOR JACK

In a black suit and buffed heels, I made my way up the three metal risers and through the front door of the construction trailer, our short-term office until the model home was complete. It was September 8, 1992, the first day of my new job. I hadn't worked for more than two and a half years—just long enough to forget Richard.

Jack greeted me with a broad smile. "Good morning."

"Morning." I blushed self-consciously in the presence of this handsome, successful older man.

He eyed me up and down. "Don't you look professional."

"Oh, this?" I brushed at my skirt. "A bit overdressed."

"Nah. You look great. Come on, let me give you the grand tour." Jack pointed to a room in the rear of the trailer. "Foreman is back there. You won't see him much. Has his own entrance and most of the time he'll be down at the site."

I nodded.

"You'll meet with customers here." He waved at a small table and four chairs. On the floor around the table, affixed to or leaning against one wall or another, were samples of carpet, flooring, cabinetry, faucets, and countertops. Jack nodded at a posterboard scale of the site pinned to the paneling on the opposite side of the trailer. With chest broad, he beamed. "We'll build sixty-six townhouses on these twenty-two acres."

"Sales?" I asked, pointing at two green dots.

"Yep," he grinned. "It's going to be a good project."

"Looks like it," I agreed, then gestured toward a closed door. "What's in there?"

He looked over his shoulder. "Oh that. Yeah. Bathroom. No plumbing." He laughed. "You'll need to make other arrangements."

"I can do that," I said.

"That brings us to the last stop on our high-end tour: the executive office suite." Jack took a few steps toward the front of the ten-foot-wide trailer. "Don't get too excited now, this is only temporary."

I smiled at the bright white Formica stretched atop three evenly spaced file cabinets. Two swivel chairs completed the side-by-side work areas.

"I split my time between my Ingomar office and here." He pointed to his side of the desktop, where papers and files were neatly arranged. "You'll be there." He motioned toward the right side, where a thick manila folder sat front and center. "Copies of floor plans and selections, bedtime reading." He laughed. "Should be self-explanatory, but if you have questions let me know."

"Will do."

"I'll leave you to it."

The minute he left, I dug in.

As soon as I mastered the floorplans, learned the options, and guided two customers through the selection process the old-fashioned, yellow-tablet way, I came up with an idea. A computerized method would make the process a lot easier.

Someone had given me database software, but I had yet to open the package and didn't have a clue how to use it. Truth is, I had barely made it through high school algebra. I wasn't sure I could figure it out. None of that mattered. Our process was inefficient and cumbersome. Plus, I wanted to impress Jack—make him look good in front of his partners. The weekend before I presented the idea, I peeled off the plastic, inserted the CD into my computer, and spent every waking moment learning and testing.

Finally, I was ready. After the construction foreman had left our Monday morning meeting, I brought up the subject. "What if we put all of our information into a database?"

"Sounds interesting," Jack said. "What can it do?"

"I think we'll be able to track client selections and final sales costs, generate work and vendor orders, maybe even run profitability reports."

"My partners are going to like that."

"Well, don't say anything yet. Please!" I felt my shoulders rise and my stomach tighten. The last thing I wanted to do was promise something I couldn't deliver. "I've never done this before."

"If anyone can do it, you can." Jack tipped his head, then added, "Pretty and smart."

I felt my face flush.

Over the next several days, at home and at work, I entered data and experimented. Sometimes it felt like a fight, but one at a time, formulas functioned and reports began to take shape. As the fourth day of being hunched over the computer rolled to an end, I sat up straight and stretched. I had been so engrossed in what I was doing I completely forgot Jack was still there. With his ankle propped on his opposite knee and his chair spun in my direction, his attention was fixed on me.

"How long have you been—" I started to ask, but the minute his rich green eyes locked on mine, I stopped speaking. I grew warm all over—and uncomfortable. I blinked. My eyes jumped to the wall clock. 5:45. "Oh no. I should go."

"So soon?"

"Kids have practice." I stood. "You know?"

"I know." He smiled. It was obvious. He knew he made me nervous, and that made me even more so.

I fumbled for my jacket, laptop, and keys. Then, as I opened the door, I glanced back at him. "See you tomorrow."

"I sure hope so," he whispered.

9

A GREAT TEAM

Jack didn't sell anyone anything. He offered solutions, met needs, and made friends. Although I was a pretty good salesperson myself, I had much to learn.

Our next prospect pulled in at 5:30.

"What's her name again?" Jack whispered as their BMW crunched ever so carefully across the gravel lot.

"Lori. Keith and Lori Jenkins," I said.

Jack stepped out of the trailer to greet them. He extended his hand in a warm hello. "Keith. Lori. We'll finish here." He pointed at the trailer. "Let's start down at the site." He motioned for them to climb into his Jeep. Keith took the front seat. Jack guided Lori into the seat behind him. I sat behind Keith with a view of Jack's profile.

As we drove the paved road, then with a bump the unpaved path, Jack explained the four phases of construction, three floor plans necessary to fit the changing topography, and the location of both cul-de-sacs. He detailed the land purchase, township meetings required to change zoning, site engineering, and installation of infrastructure. Then he talked of the financial strength he and his partner possessed.

"You won't have to worry about us going belly-up mid-development," he said with a smile.

Most buyers wouldn't think about that aspect of the business; some wouldn't feel it appropriate to ask. Since Keith was in the finance world, Jack knew Keith would want to know. Jack quelled the concern before Keith raised it.

Jack stopped just before the building where Keith and Lori would live. As we stepped out, he pointed to the adjacent land that lay below.

"That's the fifth green and the sixth tee of the Ironwood Golf Course. You golf, Keith?"

"Every chance he gets," Lori answered for her husband.

"I'll have to test your handicap one of these days," Jack said. Keith agreed. Jack extended his hand to Lori and noted a narrow gangplank stretched across the trenched foundation. "You okay with this?"

"I think so, not so sure about these heels though." She followed him up the bouncy board.

"Don't look down," Jack instructed.

"I can't seem to look anywhere else." She squeezed his hand.

"It'll be backfilled soon and you'll never know this was here."

"I sure hope so," she said.

After Lori was safely through the front door, Keith followed. I entered last. Jack glanced back. "You okay, Smiley?"

"Just fine."

I handed the couple copies of the floor plans, then took a half step back. Jack gave a room-by-room tour of the partitioned interior. He described the layout of the kitchen, the location of the first-floor laundry, the design of the first-floor master suite. When he reached the vaulted great room, he stopped. Looking out of the two-story windows at the rear of the property he said, "This will be *your* view from *your* deck." He pointed to the fifth green.

"A golf course view?" Mr. Jenkins smiled widely.

By the time they left the sales trailer, we had a signed contract.

"That's the last unit in building two." I grinned.

"Ahead of schedule." Jack handed me their $5,000 check. I took hold of it, but he didn't let go. He stood there, motionless, staring at me. This time I didn't flinch. Captivated, I stared back. I have no idea how long we were there, one foot apart, gripping that piece of paper, but every second felt passionate and exhilarating and terrifying.

In a burst of reality or maybe reason, I released the check and took a breath. "What time is it?"

"Time to increase prices and market building three." He laid the earnest money on top of their folder, "We can handle this tomorrow." Standing, he pulled his jacket from the back of his chair. "Let's grab dinner." Then Jack added, "To celebrate."

"I wish I could." Truth be told, I wanted to celebrate, to spend more time with him. But I couldn't. I shouldn't. "I have to get home." I pulled my purse onto my arm.

"Come on," he coaxed.

"I'm sorry. I can't…"

"It's just dinner."

"I know. But I really need to go."

He stepped in my path. "You better not..."

"I have to." I moved around him and opened the door.

Jack followed me outside. He stood on the stoop and watched as I got into my car and drove away.

❧

When I came up from the garage, I found Tony in the kitchen. He was loading the last of the dinner dishes into the dishwasher.

"I'm starving." I gave him a quick peck, then reached around him to grab a small piece of chicken from the plate on the counter.

"How was your day?" he asked.

"Sold another one."

"That's great."

"Can't wait to get out of these clothes," I said while chewing. "How was your day?" Without waiting for Tony to respond, I headed down the hall and up the stairs.

I was deep in my closet, wrestling my skirt onto a hanger, when my cell rang. It was Jack. "Hello? Everything all right?" I asked.

"I think you're one amazing woman."

I stopped what I was doing and stood perfectly still. I didn't know what to say. Jack was always smiling and happy, but I never expected that this handsome, successful man would feel that way—about me.

"I really enjoy working with you."

"You do?"

"Since I couldn't talk you into dinner tonight, will you do me the honor of lunch tomorrow?"

"The honor?" I repeated.

"You've been working so hard and doing a great job. I want to say thank you."

"Isn't that what I'm supposed to do?"

"Oh, and no blue jeans or cell phones. We're going somewhere special."

"Now I'm curious."

"I'll take that as a yes," he said. "See you tomorrow, Smiley." With that he hung up.

I never once considered the snake pit I had fallen into, headfirst, with Richard. That experience, right along with any life lesson I should have learned, had vanished from my head. Instead, with butterflies in my stomach and Jack's soft, deep voice in my head, I pressed my phone to my heart. *Somewhere special.* Everything about Jack made me feel special.

10

LUNCH

As soon as we crossed onto the Veterans Bridge, the city of Pittsburgh came into view. From the car window I studied the buildings that filled the skyline that stretched before us. My first job, right out of high school, was in the city. Since then, most of the squatty, dirty buildings—remnants of the old steel mill days—had been replaced, one by one, with five-star restaurants and impressive skyscrapers made of steel and limestone and glass.

"Where are we going?"

"You'll see," Jack said as he drove past several empty spots before rolling into a parking spot on the sixth level of the Smithfield Liberty Garage. Then he turned off the ignition and looked at me. "Have you ever been to the Chairman's Club?"

"No." I brushed at my skirt, thankful that I had chosen my best suit and shiny new wedges, rather than those old, comfortable pumps with the scuffed-up heels. "My grandmother dined there once. That was a long time ago."

"In those days women had their own entrance," he said. "In the door, up the steps, straight into the dining room or ballroom. They weren't allowed in any other part of the all men's club."

"Really?" I smiled at the thought of my mother's mother, decked in glitter and fur, gliding across the ballroom like she owned the place.

Jack stepped out of the car, walked around to my side of the vehicle, and opened my door.

We made our way across the parking lot and through a steel door that sat next to the dirty parking garage elevators. Considered a side entrance, the reception area had a door at each end, a desk with a mirror, a chair, and a phone. Jack picked up the receiver and, without dialing, spoke his name. The locked inner door buzzed and we stepped into the club. With his hand under my elbow, Jack guided me down the long, narrow hallway to a bank of elevators.

When we arrived on the first floor of the club, Jack held up one finger indicating I should wait. I did as he wanted, never taking my eyes from him. He approached the front desk of the business office and exchanged a twenty-dollar bill for four fives. He folded each bill narrowly enough to fit invisibly in his palm, then he slipped the money into his jacket pocket.

"Come on," he said when he returned to me. "I'll show you around."

He took me to a huge room off the main lobby with coffered ceilings. Rich antique furniture and oversized wingback chairs formed conversation areas throughout the room. One arrangement clustered around a massive stone fireplace; others, as Jack proudly pointed out, sat in front of the bulletproof windows.

"That's the president of National Bank and Trust." Jack nodded to the gentleman sipping coffee behind an opened newspaper.

He showed me the men's grill, the billiard room, and the founder's room, where lunch was in full swing. Then, he took my elbow again and we ascended the sweeping, double-wide staircase to the second floor. To one side of the expansive landing was the main ballroom. It was elegant, but not as striking as I expected. The room that stood out to me sat in front of the Marquis dining room.

"This is the library," Jack explained. In between floor-to-ceiling bookcases, rich red walls featured ornately framed canvases. I don't know if it was my love of red, my love of books, or something else, but that space captured my heart. I drew my hands to my chest. "It's so beautiful."

"Pre-dinner cocktails are served here," Jack said as the maître d' approached. Then Jack extended his hand to the well-dressed man, his thumb tucked against his palm. The men shook.

"Good afternoon, sir. Will you be joining us today?"

As soon as their hands released, the maître d' slipped into his pocket the bill Jack had so subtly passed. Seeing money exchanged like that was a first for me.

"Private room today, Carl," Jack answered.

"Yes, sir, right," Carl motioned to the man behind the bar, who picked up the phone and whispered into the receiver. "I'll send Joy right up." If Jack was trying to impress me with the benefits of privilege and power, it was working.

On the eleventh floor, a woman met us outside of a room, and unlocked the door. She pointed out the sitting area, the private bathroom, and the long, beautiful, dark wooden pedestal table. Although the décor details have faded with time, I do remember that the space maintained the same grandeur and elegance of all the rooms I'd toured that day. I also remember the fresh floral centerpiece. It wasn't in the center of the table, but rather in the center of the far end of the table where Jack and I would be dining. A place setting put Jack at the head, me to his left. As I approached the table, Joy pulled out my chair and when I sat, she laid my napkin across my lap. (Another first). Then she offered me a menu so large I needed both hands to hold it.

"Are the flowers to your liking, sir?" she asked while filling our water glasses.

"They're perfect. Thank you, Joy."

She took our beverage order and disappeared without another word, without a sound.

"You ordered flowers?" I asked.

"They're for you. Take them home." He paused. "If you'd like."

Even though this was perfectly legitimate and completely professional, I hadn't told Tony I was lunching with Jack today—especially not there. And there was no sense making up some story; Tony would see right through it. "Probably shouldn't." I shrugged.

"Right."

I opened my menu and perused the choices, but I noticed there were no prices. I looked on the front, then flipped to the back.

Jack smiled. "Only the host gets a menu with prices."

"Oh." A slight heat grew in my cheeks. I didn't know what to order without knowing how much anything cost.

"May I order for you?"

"Yes. Thank you." I laid the menu across my lap and allowed myself to relax.

When our waitstaff returned, Jack ordered crab hoelzel appetizers for each of us. I had never had it before and it may have been the best appetizer I had ever had. Then he explained the contents of the breadbasket, which included lahvosh, a thin, crispy, cracker-like bread made at the club. Another favorite. The rest of the meal was equally delicious, and our time together was unforgettable.

11

GIFTS

Over the next year, I grew more and more infatuated with Jack. I arrived to work early, stayed late, stopped by on my only day off. All the while I told myself, *this is not going to end well.* When common sense didn't prevail, I drew an absolute line. Work and home would not cross. At work I could flirt and have fun. Nothing more. At home, I'd be a faithful, married mother of four. But the minute I walked through my front door, as though he had been watching me, tracking me, my phone would ring. It was always him.

"Whatcha doing?" he'd ask.

"Nothing," I'd say, my protective guard falling away. Then, like a teenager with a crush, I'd throw myself across my queen-sized bed that I shared with my husband and talk to Jack, even though I should have been preparing dinner, helping with homework, or driving kids to or from one event or another.

Despite how dangerous my feelings were and despite the risks,

I embraced every hopeful, exciting moment. Just as I embraced every gift. Jack bought me topaz earnings while on a trip to Arizona with his wife; he gave me an engraved sterling silver tray he picked up while at lunch with friends at an antique café where everything, even the chair on which he sat, was for sale. He brought me bunches of brilliantly colored ginger and Bird of Paradise from every roadside vendor he passed. He'd tell me, "Their beauty reminded me of yours."

One day, several months after we had moved out of the trailer and into our sales office in the converted garage of the model home, Jack showed up with a very special gift. I was sitting at my L-shaped secretarial desk preparing a change order when he came through the door. Like a schoolboy he had his hands behind his back when he approached.

"Pick one," he said.

I stopped typing mid-word and spun toward him.

"Come on. Come on. Pick one," he repeated.

I tapped his right arm.

"Pick again," he laughed, rolling his eyes.

I tapped the other arm.

He brought his hand from behind his back. A silver toe ring perched on his over-sized baby finger. A tiny diamond chip glistened in the center. Jack fell to one knee in a proposal-like stance, took my foot in his hand, removed my high heel, and slipped the tiny ring around my toe.

Shocked and flattered and, well, plain terrified that someone might see us, I wanted to tell him to get up. Instead I only said, "It's beautiful."

"It is." He stood and took a step back with chest broad and smile wide.

Every time Jack gave me a gift, I imagined a duplicate in the car for his wife. Not this time. I had only met Jack's wife once. She had come on the job site a few weeks after I started.

"It's so nice to meet you," I extended my hand to her.

She barely touched my fingertips. She was about Jack's age, heavier than the photo he had on his desk. Bags under her brown eyes indicated exhaustion, maybe stress, more likely distress. Still, she was sophisticated and pretty. She had once been beautiful.

"I've heard about you." She eyed my size two petite suit up and down. "Overdressed for new construction, aren't we?"

"Oh, this." I brushed at my skirt. "It's nothing."

"I doubt that." She squinted at me as though I was some kind of an infiltrating terrorist. At that time, I had no idea that each night, whether they were lying in bed or dining with friends, Jack went on and on about how smart I was, how many townhouses I had sold, how eager I was to please.

Joan had circled that track with her husband before. First, he'd chatter on about whoever had caught his eye. Months later, he'd pack up and leave her and their home to be with his new love. One time he ran away with her best friend. Joan knew the rules of the race before I even realized the starter flag had been dropped.

As I studied the chip sparkling on my toe, I couldn't shake thoughts of her from my head. What would she have done if she had seen her husband kneeling on the floor embracing my naked foot? I wondered about Tony, too. It would have crushed them both. That was the last thing I wanted. Vowing to keep my emotions in check and my boss at bay, I pushed my foot into my shoe and returned to my typing.

12

RED GLOVES

With Thanksgiving over, my second Christmas working for Jack had arrived. It was December 22. Just as he had done the previous year, at the end of the day the model would be closed until after the New Year. I saw those twelve days away from him as a blessing and a needed break. Jack must have seen it differently.

In one last pursuit, he swiveled me around to face him, put one hand on each arm of my chair, and drew his face so close to mine our lips almost touched. I closed my eyes and breathed in his clean woody scent. I so wanted him to kiss me and had imagined a thousand times what it would feel like. But Jack once admitted he had so many conquests, he couldn't remember all of their names. I did *not* want to be some nameless, forgotten notch on that long belt of his.

I opened my eyes and with both hands, playfully slapped at his chest. "What do you think you're doing?"

We laughed, but it was not funny. The sexual tension was

growing harder for me to resist. Jack had something I needed. I craved everything about him—the way he made me feel, every deeply embedded emotion he unearthed. I wanted to ache for Tony the way I ached for Jack. But the more Jack filled my heart and my head, the less I had room for Tony.

Tony was kind and sensitive, a dedicated father, a loyal husband, and a great provider. If I asked for something, he'd do whatever it took to give it to me—even if it meant asking his parents not once, but twice, for large sums of money so I could have the home of my dreams. I was lucky to have such a good-hearted, hard-working, solid man. He loved me, but none of that mattered. Jack's flirtatiousness made me feel privileged. The secrecy assured me I was special. Fourteen years my senior, he satisfied something deep inside, beyond my understanding, out of my control.

No matter how strongly I felt about him, I had done a good job of fending off his not-so-innocent advances and keeping playful banter just that—playful. But the more I resisted, the more Jack pursued.

"I've made reservations for 1:00," Jack said.

"Oh, I don't know. I have errands to run and gifts to—"

"It's Christmas. We're going to have a nice holiday lunch. I won't take no for an answer," he insisted. "Carmichael's. In one hour."

I don't know if it was the snow falling or the Christmas music playing, but I gave in. I told myself I would keep it professional and get out of there quickly.

He sat in the far corner of the dining room, in an oversized booth facing the door. As soon as I made my way around the hostess station, our gazes met. He smiled. I walked through the crowded restaurant and slid into the dark leather bench across from him.

On the table sat two glasses of wine.

"I hope you don't mind," he said, gesturing to the drinks.

"Um, no. I mean not at all." I smiled. "I only drink red."

"I know." He raised his glass. "Merry Christmas, Smiley." Did he call me that because he made me smile or because I brought out the smile in him?

Our glasses pinged and I took a sip. "This is good." I watched the satin wick swirl up and around the inside of the crystal goblet. Then my gaze found his. He wore the proud smile of a man who had done well.

The waitress approached. "I see everyone has arrived. Are you ready to order?"

Jack glanced at me, "If it's okay with the lady, she'll have the Scallops Barsac."

I nodded. "Thank you." As the waitress shuffled away, I whispered, "How did you know?"

"You told me."

Is it possible that a man who couldn't remember where he'd left his hat or laid his notes wouldn't forget what I had said? "Do you remember everything I tell you?"

"I try." With that he handed me a professionally wrapped gift box.

"Oh no," I blushed. "I didn't—"

"Don't be silly." He patted the box. "Open it."

I untied the bow and, careful not to tear the paper, slowly slid my finger under the small piece of tape.

"Come on. Come on," he coaxed like an excited child.

"Okay." I flipped the narrow box and removed the lid. Nestled under white tissue was a pair of red leather gloves lined with mink. The softest leather I had ever felt. I touched them to my check. "Oh my God." I slipped them on. "They're beautiful." I stopped.

"Wait a minute. There's no way you could have known that red was my favorite color."

"You got me there." He raised his glass, again. "That was a guess."

With hands nestled inside the velvety gloves, I lifted my goblet to his, "Good guess."

"Great guess," he corrected and we giggled.

Being with Jack outside the office was comfortable. Too comfortable. I needed to get this train back on the tracks. "So, how are the changes to the new floor plan?"

"No. No. No," he said. "It's Christmas. We aren't going to talk about work. We are going to talk about you."

"About me? Oh boy, let me think." I looked away for a second, then looked back at Jack. "Okay, so I grew up in a blue-collar neighborhood in the city. My parents still live in the frame Craftsman I grew up in—"

"Not that." Jack stopped me in my tracks.

"What do you mean?" I asked, although I knew perfectly well what he meant.

"Tell me something about you—something no one else knows."

"Something no one else knows." I paused, then said, "Well, I guess no one knows I always wanted to write." I pinched my lips together nervously before I continued. "I dabble at it now and then when I have time. I even took a few writing classes in college. Bits of good writing in there, but I never had what it took." I shrugged. "One professor even told me I should give up the dream." I cleared my throat, then asked, "How about you?"

"Wanted to be a doctor."

"Really?"

"Wasn't smart enough."

"I doubt that."

"No, really. I tried. Each night I rewrote every class note I had taken that day and I studied as much as I could. I just couldn't do it. Funny thing is I was more disappointed for my parents than for me. Felt like I let them down." He shook his head, then added, "My second choice was to play major league baseball."

"No small dreams for you."

"After a successful college experience, I was invited by Mr. Lane, GM for the Pirates, to try out for the team."

"You were?"

"Told me I had the best swing he'd ever seen."

"He did?"

"Then he put his arm across my shoulder and said, "But, son, you just didn't hit enough pitches."

He laughed. I laughed. I felt myself melting. This strong, successful man had just exposed his hopes and fears, dreams and failures in such an open and vulnerable way.

When we reached my car, he took the keys from my hand. Knowing this could be a mistake even bigger and more painful than the one I had made with Richard, I stepped back. He moved closer. I found myself backed against my car.

He pulled me tight against his body. Snow gathered at our feet, but I didn't feel cold. I felt only him. Saw only him. Our lips almost touching, our breath steamy in the cold December air, he stared at me as though he could read my every dream, every hope, every fear. I wanted this older man to love me in a way no one ever had, in a way I desperately needed to be loved. In a way I thought only he could.

We stood there, in the middle of that busy parking lot, wrapped in one another's arms. I was scared, not of getting caught, but of how helpless I felt. Months of emotions had amassed into that one moment, erupting around me. In me. Overwhelmed by thoughts and desires I couldn't control, risks that were all too real, I looked down. He put his hand under my chin, tilted my head toward his, and kissed me. Even though what we were doing was forbidden and would hurt so many, I could no longer fight the need. I surrendered.

I had never been kissed like that. I wanted more.

13

CROSSING THE LINE

THE NEW YEAR began and I couldn't wait to get back to work. It seemed Jack felt the same. No matter when or how often I looked across the room, his gaze was locked on me, a gleaming smile across his long face. When I stood to make a copy or file a document, he followed me, spun me around, backed me against the wall, placed one large hand on either side of my face. Sometimes he closed his eyes, leaned in, breathed in my scent. Sometimes he stroked my hair or my face. Sometimes we just stood there, staring into one another's eyes. He didn't always kiss me. But when he did, each kiss had the same slow, purposeful build-up, the same hypnotic passion as the first. I don't know how our relationship managed to stay in the murky mess between a small mistake and one we could not undo, but it did. For that I was grateful. Either of us could say—to each other, to ourselves, to questioning spouses—"It was just a kiss; did not mean a thing."

❧

Then one day that spring we crossed the line.

"Hey Smiley," Jack called as he emerged from his office. "Besides paper and toner, what else do we need?"

"Can't think of a thing." I flashed a wide grin before returning to the file that lay open before me.

"Umm...What are you doing?" he asked.

"Umm...What does it look like I'm doing?" I smiled. "I'm working."

"That can wait." He extended his hand and helped me up. "Come with me."

"What about the model?"

"Lock it up. Put a note on the door."

A short ride later Jack pulled into a parking spot in the mostly empty shopping center. Before turning off the ignition he said, "We can get toner." He pointed toward the office supply store. "Or we can get a room." He pointed toward a hotel across the street. "What do you think?"

Since that first kiss months before, he'd asked me that question so many times I came to expect it. We can get lunch or we can get a room. We can look at flooring samples or we can sneak off to his Ingomar office. His pursuit flattered me—made me feel loved. But even though I needed him to want me more than I needed anything, I did not want to blow up my life again. So I always laughed and, albeit politely, I always firmly said, "No." Not that day. For some reason, that day I said, "Okay."

He knew what I meant, and I knew I had made a mistake. As I followed Jack across the blacktop, I thought of all the things I could say. Should say. *Just kidding. Don't think this is smart. Wish I could, but I can't.* What we were about to do could never be undone. It would change everything, even cost me my job or my marriage—or both. But just as Little Red Riding Hood followed the Big Bad Wolf to her demise, without a word I followed Jack.

I should have stayed back while he approached the check-in desk. I did not. The elderly clerk, a pinched-faced older gentleman, who had probably seen it all, did not even glance in my direction. As soon as he handed Jack the key, we made our way up the elevator and down a long hall. Jack unlocked the door, then pushed it open and motioned me inside. The opposite of the grandeur of the Chairman's Club, the sparsely furnished room, although clean, was in desperate need of an update. A fitting backdrop for such a fall from grace.

I sat erect on the armchair in the corner of the small room and I watched. Sitting on the edge of the bed, Jack drew one foot up and across his knee. As he untied his shoe, the lace knotted. Was this experienced man as nervous as I? Perhaps each of us realized this was a bad idea. Perhaps each wanted the other to stop it. Neither of us did.

After a few awkward hours, we drew to a close a most unfulfilling afternoon, for him as much as for me.

The next day, Friday, was my day off. Although I usually went into the office or stopped by on my day off, that day I did not. I focused on my home and my family, hoping that when I returned to work, somehow magically, it would be as though yesterday never happened.

On Saturday the model didn't open until 11:00. I did not arrive early, like I normally did. When I entered, it was dark and quiet. I hung my coat and peered around the corner to see if Jack was sitting in his office. He was not. I breathed relief. Then I noticed, on my desk, in a crystal vase, two dozen long-stemmed red roses, professionally arranged. I stepped around my chair and removed a tiny pink envelope from the bouquet. In Jack's handwriting the otherwise-blank card read, "Next Thursday."

I didn't see Jack at all that week. For that I was grateful, but I couldn't stop thinking about what he had planned for Thursday. Taking our relationship to the next level was the thing I most wanted; the thing I most feared.

❧

Thursday came. I climbed into my car, and as I made my way to the model office, my phone rang. I told myself not to answer. It rang again. I took a deep breath. Another ring. I would see him in a minute, no use delaying. "Hello," I said, my voice jittery.

"Marriott, room 918." Before I could protest or decline, Jack hung up.

I should have called him back and told him no. I should have done something—anything—to salvage whatever remained of our professional relationship and my dignity. I did not. Even though I wanted to end this before I ruined my life, I turned the car and headed for the highway.

The junior suite was adorned in gorgeous floral arrangements. At least seven different bouquets sat in vases all over the room. In the center of a small dining table, champagne chilled in an ice bucket. Strawberries dressed in dark and white chocolate tuxedos filled a sterling silver platter.

The man who could accept no defeat achieved success the second time. He filled the day with magic and love and passion. Any amount of logic or resistance or denial to which I might have clung vanished. For me, there was no going back.

14

BUSTED

A FEW MONTHS later, a client popped into the model. "I'm having a barbecue to close out the summer." Wade smiled as he handed each of us a postcard-sized invitation. "Hope you can come." When he turned to leave, he added, "Oh, and spouses are welcome."

Neither Jack nor I intended to bring a spouse, but for some reason I left the model that day with the invitation in hand. I took it into the house and laid it on the desk, where I promptly forgot about it.

The day of the party, Jack arrived first. About an hour and a half later, after closing up the model, I made my way across the street.

"You've done a great job," I told Wade as he guided me through his new townhome that we had recently built. Then, when we reached the kitchen, I handed him a bottle of wine. "From Jack and me."

"Be careful," he said as he accepted the gift. "Things aren't always what they seem."

Later, while everyone was laughing and talking and eating, Jack whispered to me, "Let's get out of here."

Surely, no one would notice we were gone. In separate cars I followed Jack to his Ingomar office. It just happened to have a comfy leather sofa. After we made passionate love, I went back to the party. As though I had just been out front, I walked around to the rear patio. Wade met me with a scowl. "Tony was just here looking for you."

"Shit!" I raced out of there and went straight home.

As soon as I saw Tony standing in the kitchen, I blurted out, "I was with a client."

"Don't bother. I stopped at the model and drove through the site." He turned and walked away.

Tony's trust was gone, things were strained, and I knew I was on notice. But we remained married—at least for the time being.

❧

There was no confrontation for Jack. That didn't mean Joan wasn't aware. After all, she'd been through it before. She knew the signs and did what she always had done. She immersed herself in work and activities, in family and in friends. The more she took care of herself, the more he complained to me.

"She's never home. She works all the time. She's never there for me."

How could she give up her support network or pull back on her job when her husband was about to leave her again? He had painted her into a losing corner. The very thing she needed to do to protect herself was the very thing he would use against her. The end was drawing near.

It was Jack's fiftieth birthday. A dinner celebration with his closest friends would be held at the Chairman's Club. I had no idea who planned it. But I knew one thing, he'd been looking forward to it for weeks.

"She better not mess this up," he declared one afternoon.

On the day of the party, Joan was late getting home from work. So busy on the phone negotiating a deal, she was delayed getting dressed. When they finally arrived, their friends had already enjoyed a round of drinks and a course of appetizers—without the host and hostess. Jack was furious.

The next day, in great detail, he told me that when they got home that night, he changed his clothes and got comfortable in his favorite worn leather chair, feet on the ottoman. He read the newspaper and waited for her to finish working. She didn't appear. He turned on the television and waited some more. Still no wife. Disgusted and disappointed, he clicked off the remote and went to bed.

"That's it," he said. "I've had enough." Then he spoke the words I had been longing to hear, "You're the one thing missing from my otherwise perfect life."

I wanted to race into Jack's arms that very minute. I'd like to think he wanted that, too. But his daughter's wedding was a year away. Since Jack had left his family four times before, once to be with her mother's best friend, Cheryl knew anything was possible. She put her father on notice. "Dad, promise me you won't get yourself in trouble before my wedding."

We had to wait.

15

A QUEEN OVERLOOKING HER CARNAGE

NINE MONTHS AFTER his birthday and four months before Cheryl's wedding, Jack pulled into the driveway, shifted into park and turned off the ignition.

I stared up at the oversized D pinned to the chimney of the stone home Jack shared with his wife.

"What are we doing here?"

Without an answer he departed the Jeep, disappeared around the tailgate, and appeared at my window.

"I can wait here," I offered as soon as he opened my car door. I loved all things houses: looking at them, designing them, decorating them. Nothing would have pleased me more than to see how Jack lived, but entering the house he shared with his wife was beyond the bounds, even for me.

He motioned for me to get out.

"No, really. I don't need to come in."

He took my hand, helped me out, led me up the concrete steps and along the uneven flagstone walk. Inside the front door, a living room sat to the right, dining room to the left. Even though the house had recently been updated, the décor somehow still matched the age of its owners. An expensive miss. I took silent pleasure in thinking that my home was more nicely decorated, as though that somehow made me better than his wife.

Like a child afraid of getting caught, I wiped my feet, then tiptoed behind him across the wooden floors. He guided me through the galley kitchen, the scent of bacon in the air. He pointed to the glass-enclosed sunroom where he enjoyed his morning coffee, then we made our way to a tiny television room in the rear of the house. The daily newspaper was strewn across the worn leather ottoman.

"This is the den," he announced. "Where I spend most of my time."

The stairs to the lower level creaked as we descended to the musty bottom. In the center of the semi-finished space, a billiard table sat mounded with clean, unfolded laundry. A busy woman's dumping ground. I wondered if she would be as mortified to know I saw that heap as I was to have seen it. Jack went around the corner and into the laundry room. "Here's the problem." He pointed to the water seeping in around the window in the aged foundation. "Remind me to tell Erik to get that fixed."

Gripping my hand, he led me back to the first floor, then up to the second. My heart pounded as I went where I should not go. At the top of the stairs, to the left, sat his daughter's room.

"That's where it was." He pointed to an empty corner where a pyramid of beer cans had once been erected. "Had a drinking party here while we were out of town. Pictures made the yearbook."

"Will they make it into the rehearsal dinner slide show?" I teased.

"No way her baby brother will miss that opportunity."

Next was a tiny room much too small for the stocky, six-foot, not-so-little brother. In between the two bedrooms sat the bathroom his daughter often locked her brother out of. "Boy, did they fight," Jack chuckled.

Jack led me to the end of the hall, floorboards creaking as we walked. The master had two tiny closets and a tight bath. The expansive bed featured a 1970s wraparound headboard with storage for the books she read while he slept (or so he said). *Outdated and not at all intimate,* I thought to myself as I stood there judging it, judging her.

Wanting to get out of there, I took a breath and a step toward the door. He grabbed my wrist and pulled me back. Holding up one finger, he instructed me to wait. Like an obedient child, without a word I stopped. He closed the bedroom door and returned to me. *Is he going to show me something?* With one hand on each of my shoulders, he guided me backwards—step by slow step—until I was against the bed. Then he knelt down and removed my shoes one at a time. My clothes next, then his. *Has he done this before?*

We made love in his bed, in their bed—in *her* bed. From the nightstand a picture of them stared at me—smiling, sun in her eyes, wind in her hair. The entire time we were in that bed, I couldn't take my eyes from that photo. I felt victorious. I felt sick.

16

HOLIDAY REGRETS

A LITTLE MORE than a year after Jack's fiftieth and a month after his daughter's wedding, it was finally time to execute our plans.

Tony moved out, taking the family room sectional and the master bedroom TV. Although the children didn't have a sofa to sit on or a father who lived with them, I was well on my way to everything I wanted.

In mid-September, Jack moved out of his stately stone home and into a tiny two-bedroom apartment in the twenty-four-unit building he owned. I wasn't with him the day he moved and I never went inside his apartment, so I had no idea if he even had furniture. I didn't care.

For the next three months we worked together every day. We ate together almost every night, either at my house or some out-of-the-way restaurant, never locally where we might be seen. Jack wasn't ready for full-on public disclosure, out of respect for our spouses. That was okay with me because most nights we slept together at my house. So, even though he hadn't yet removed his wedding ring, it never once occurred to me that he might consider going back—not even for Christmas or his twenty-ninth anniversary, which happened to be New Year's Eve.

But he did.

I had just gotten home from work one cold December afternoon when his call caught me off guard.

"I need some time," he said.

"What? Why?" I knew the answer, but hoped to reel him into a debate. Talk him through it; more honestly, talk him out of it.

He wasn't having any of it. "I'm sorry," he said.

"But my car is still in the shop." I don't know why I thought such a feeble ploy would make any difference, but it was all I could come up with. Besides, it was true.

"I'll send Erik over with the Jaguar. Keep it as long as you'd like." He hung up.

Later that evening, when I couldn't sit still and couldn't stop thinking about him (with her), I called the office phone. When the answering machine beeped, I begged, "Please reconsider. Please. I love you so much. You know you love me."

After five minutes, I called back. I deleted that message and recorded, "Don't forget all the reasons you left her in the first place. She was never there for you as I have been and always will be. I love you more than she does. I love you *better.* You know that."

A few minutes passed and I deleted that message and recorded, "I love you with all my heart. Even though I left Tony to be with you, even though I tore apart my family and hurt my children, I wish you happiness and love. If she's what you want, I'll stay out of your way."

As soon as I hung up, I called back and deleted that message, too.

I have no idea if Jack called the office to check messages in the moments after I had recorded but before I had deleted any of my heartfelt pleas. And I have no idea how much time he spent with her. I told myself not to think about that. I knew his daughter would be coming home for Christmas. His son was already home on college break. I also knew my estranged husband would have nothing to do with another reconciliation, holiday or not. No need to ask.

❧

As usual, my family's Christmas took place at my mom and dad's house on Christmas Eve. Men and children could be found in the game room playing pool or pinball. The women were seated around the dining room table, chatting and nibbling from paper plates piled high with chunks of American and cheddar, Ritz crackers, and any summer fruit my mother could find at the neighborhood grocery store. That year I did my best to nod and smile and avoid the cheerful "How are you?" and "What's going on?" questions I did not want to answer. And I did my best not to fall apart when Tony arrived to pick up our children.

On Christmas Day, as in years past, Tony and the kids gathered with his Italian-speaking family in his aunt's basement, clamoring loudly (almost yelling at one another) across stretched-together folding tables overflowing with his father's red wine. Freshly baked bread and the best homemade tortellini on the planet, a family tradition, filled the table. Across town, Jack's family would, as he had once described it to me, be toasting with Marquis flutes while opening expensive gifts in front of the big tree and blazing fire, a stuffed bird roasting in the oven.

My day progressed quite differently. Although I received countless invitations from family and friends who couldn't believe I'd be alone for the holiday—"how horrible"—I politely declined.

Instead, alone in the dark, I hunkered down on the family room floor in front of the television and, with Jimmy Stewart and my Swanson Turkey TV Dinner, cried my way through *It's a Wonderful Life.*

17

A NEW YEAR WITH NEW TURNS

I PROMISED MYSELF I would not quit my job with Jack until I had another. Truth is, I couldn't. So, when the new year began, I returned to work. While Erik, the construction foreman, was busy building, I was busy selling. Jack was conspicuously busy somewhere else. Perhaps he decided to work out of his other office. Perhaps he decided to whisk Joan off on some five-star honeymoon-type holiday. Either way no one knew where he was or when he would return. And if he was going to stay with her, it was just as well he stayed away from me.

But he did not. A few days after I returned to the office, out of the blue, without a call or a warning, as I sat at my desk preparing for an upcoming closing, he appeared.

"Good morning, Smiley." He strolled through the front door in his camel-colored Marlboro Man hat and matching coat. He laid his hat on the corner of my desk, took my hand, and pulled me to my feet.

I was stunned and excited and, if I'm being totally honest, hopeful. But the minute he tried to kiss me, reality struck. "Wait a minute!" I pressed my palms into his chest.

Before I could say another word, he touched his index finger to my lips and said, "It's over."

"What's over?"

"She and I."

"You and Joan?" Vagueness or ambiguity would not cut it for me.

"Yes. Joan and I."

"Separation or divorce?" I drilled deeper.

"Divorce."

"Are you sure, because I don't want to find myself—"

"I'm sure." Then he emphasized, "*I want you.*"

"Really?" I softened.

"Really. Come here." He slid his hand behind my head and gave me a long and passionate kiss.

I had no idea what sent him back to her or what happened between them over the holidays. It no longer mattered. He chose me.

"There is one thing," he said.

"Oh no." I felt myself deflate.

"Go away with me—to celebrate us."

Jack loved the high of the honeymoon stage. The reconciliation after the breakup. He was good at it, and I wasn't about to say no. I don't remember what trip came after that breakup (or was that a start-up?) but it may have been the time we went whale watching in Maui. We caught a glimpse of a magnificent creature cresting the surface. Afterward Jack and I took a small prop plane to Lanai, where we spent a few glorious days at a spectacular resort nestled in the rain forest atop the lush volcanic island. It was magical and luxurious and first class, and—as would always be the case with me—all forgiving.

We returned from that most-romantic vacation giddy in love and public. There would be no more hiding or sneaking or pretending. It was official. I was free to be at his side, no matter what. No one was going to take that from me.

❧

Weeks later, up against a tight deadline, we sat at the conference table with the architect and the construction foreman and discussed the changes I had been pestering Jack to make to the floorplan.

"Should we enlarge this closet and expand the second-floor rear dormer?" Erik, the construction foreman, asked, keenly aware the latter affected the roof trusses that should have been ordered weeks ago.

Jack rose from the table when his phone vibrated. "Excuse me, I need to take this."

"Everything all right?" I whispered.

He mouthed, "My brother."

Shortly before Cheryl's wedding, Jack's mother had been rushed to the hospital. Afraid he might not get there in time, Jack boarded the first available flight. Turns out his mother had caused that heart event herself. She stopped taking her medications. She said she didn't have the strength to attend the wedding. Although that may have been part of it, Jack assumed the bigger part was that she didn't want his father's drinking to embarrass the bride or ruin the day. After the wedding, Jack and his brother, Dave, moved their elderly parents from Jack's condo in Clearwater, Florida, to an apartment in Peachtree Corners, Georgia, where the elderly couple would live under the watchful eye of Dave and his wife, Judy, a knowledgeable and nurturing nurse.

After hanging up with his brother that February afternoon, nine months after the previous false alarm, Jack returned to the conference room door. "I've gotta go."

"What about the—"

"Do whatever you think is best." With that he was out the door.

18

A MOTHER LOST

This time the medical situation was serious and real. Jack's mother was fading fast.

At the hospital Jack joined his brother and his tearful father who, despite early dementia, clearly understood what was about to happen. Together the three men sat vigil, and when the time came, each said a private goodbye.

The next morning Jack phoned to tell me his mother had passed peacefully. "I'm calling the kids next. Can you call everyone else?"

"Of course." The first person I dialed was his best friend, Reed. After asking how Jack was holding up, Reed offered to call Joan.

"No, thank you. I can do it." I dialed Joan next.

At the time it felt like it was my place to call her. After all, I was now the woman on Jack's arm. Plus, Jack asked me to do it. I was careful to be soft and kind. But truth is, no matter how nice I tried to be or how entitled I may have felt, I never should have called her. I never should have called anyone. We were a brand-new couple and I had never met his mother. Plus, Jack had just spent Christmas with Joan. To top it all off, his soon-to-be ex wasn't his ex at all. She was *still* his wife. What in the hell was I thinking? So determined to show everyone I was the woman in his life, I lost all perspective and forgot all about common courtesy. I stomped on toes all over the place, and for that I would pay a steep price.

When Jack returned from Atlanta, he scheduled a service at Old Stone Methodist Church. Just days before the funeral, late one evening, as he sat alone in his office preparing the eulogy, he received a call from one of his children. I was at home when he showed up, white-faced, at my front door.

"If you go, Joan won't go. If Joan doesn't go, my kids won't go."

His children needed their mother to survive the loss of their most treasured grandmother, especially now, as they struggled to cope with their parents' impending divorce. I understood that. The fact that I had called Joan had only made matters worse. I knew that, too, but understanding didn't quiet my desire to be there. I wanted to go so badly I even considered slipping into the back of the church after the service began, sneaking out before it was over. I couldn't do that. He asked me not to go. I needed to respect his wishes. It was best for everyone else, even if it wasn't best for me.

While family and friends and those who worked with us gathered to pay respects and offer condolences to Jack, his children, and his soon-to-be ex, I sat at home alone. Again. Could the loss of a cherished mother who valued family and denounced divorce trigger enough grief—or guilt—to send the man of my dreams back to his wife?

I would soon find out.

In the brief moments between the service and the luncheon, Jack burst through my front door. "Linda, Linda? Where are you?"

I don't think I'd ever seen him so frantic. He hurried toward me, pulled me to my feet, wrapped his arms around me. "Life is short," he said. "I don't want to live one more minute without you. Please tell me you love me."

Could it really be that this handsome, strong man was every bit as afraid of losing me as I was of losing him? "Of course I love you—I love you more than anything."

He held me tight for a few minutes, then said, "I'm sorry. This day isn't done. I've got to go."

Flooded with a newfound confidence about our relationship, I watched as the man of my dreams climbed into his car and drove away.

19

MEMORIAL SERVICE

OLD STONE METHODIST was the church that Jack's parents had belonged to for many years. Jack and Joan had been active parishioners there as well. It was the church where Cheryl had recently married and Joan still sang in the choir. It was not the church where Jack and I worshipped. Still, when Jack suggested we remodel the barely used chapel in memory of his mother, even though we would be stomping all over Joan's sacred ground, I was all in. Jack was including me.

We made an appointment, drove to the church, and were met with the critical gaze of the decorating committee, most who worked, sang, and socialized with Joan. We received strict instructions (perhaps stricter than others might have received) on what we could and could not do. With the understanding that Jack would be allowed to hang a plaque to honor his mother, his only request, materials were ordered and demolition began.

For months—every day after work and on days off—we went

to the church. We tore out old carpeting, took down wallpaper, painted walls, and hung lighting and drapes. When Jack was there, I was there. I wanted this labor of love to be as much my gift to his late mother and her church as it was his.

I even contributed $500. Not a lot of money, but to a single mother who searched pockets and purses for spare change in the days before each paycheck, it was more than I should have spent. I was always doing that—giving more to the men in my life than I should have, financially and emotionally—making my children do without, leaving myself empty.

When the renovation was complete, Jack planned the memorial and headed to the church with a beautifully engraved plaque in hand.

"I thought it could hang to the left (or maybe he said to the right) of the chapel door," he explained to the reverend.

"I'm sorry. I don't know how this misunderstanding could have occurred," the reverend said. "We don't allow personal plaques."

"What?"

"Never have. Maybe you can hang it on the memorial garden wall." The garden was where Jack's mother had been interred.

Jack was crushed. With his commemoration in hand, he left. Plaque or no plaque, the chapel was set to be dedicated, the family was coming, and together we would honor and celebrate Grace's life.

❧

The weekend of the memorial service arrived.

On a warm fall day, seven months after his mother had died, Jack's brother, Dave, rented what everyone lovingly referred to as the church van. He and his wife, along with their two adult children and their spouses, made the trek in one vehicle. Jack put his brother and family up in the William Penn Hotel in downtown

Pittsburgh, where the likes of John F. Kennedy, Lawrence Welk, and Bob Hope had stayed. Jack's son, his daughter, and his daughter's husband came in from out of town and stayed, as they always did, with their mother. Joan was not invited. I never considered how it must have felt, staying with their mother who had known and loved Grace, while being required to memorialize their grandmother with me, someone who had never met the woman.

We gathered at the Grandview Saloon on Mount Washington to relax, overlook the city, and be together. As the family trickled in, it became clear that no one wanted to be together with me. No one spoke to me. When anyone sat near me, I saw only his or her back. It was the Dunigan family equivalent to being shunned. I did my best to hold strong; however, I spent a lot of that evening hiding in the restroom.

When Jack and I left that night, I didn't say a word about my ostracization. I knew how important this was for him, for all of them. This weekend was not about me. At least I was there.

The next evening, in a private room at the Chairman's Club, the family shared a meal. Beautiful floral arrangements adorned the long center of the table. I put a tiny wooden angel at each place setting. Everyone told stories of the woman they loved and missed. I sat quietly. No one acknowledged the angel keepsakes. No one acknowledged me.

Sunday, after the chapel dedication service, Jack's friend Reed and his wife welcomed all of us to their sprawling home for an afternoon picnic. It marked the end of the weekend. The food was delicious; the host and hostess were most gracious. Other than the two of them, even when I tried to engage someone in a conversation, again no one said a word to me. Even Jack, too busy co-hosting and sharing family stories, didn't seem to notice me. I ensconced myself in a chair far off in the corner of the large living room and tried to console myself that the weekend was almost over. As the afternoon progressed, I struggled to hold myself together.

"Great weekend, don't you think?" Jack said as we climbed in the car.

Tears slipped from my eyes.

He glanced back and forth between me and the narrow, unlit private road. "What's going on?"

"You didn't notice?"

"Notice what?"

"No one said a word to me the whole weekend."

"No one?"

I didn't want him to feel badly. After all, it wasn't his fault. At that moment it became clear that no matter what I did, I would most likely never be accepted by his family.

The next day, I didn't go to work. I suspect Jack didn't expect me to show up. He didn't call until around noon.

"I cancelled our tee time today," he said, referring to his plans to golf with his children. "And I brought both of my kids and my son-in-law into this office this morning. I reamed each of them a new asshole. I told them how disappointed I was at how they treated you. They had no right." He went on to say they apologized.

I hesitated for a long moment. "It's nice that you did that, and it means a lot that they apologized, but we both know they're never going to accept me. This relationship is going to be one continuous, ugly tug of war. I don't want to put myself through that or you either. It's just not worth it."

"It is worth it. You're worth it. This relationship is worth it. Besides, it's not going to be a fight. My kids know better. They understand how I feel, and they know exactly what I expect of them. The matter is resolved."

"I don't know."

"There's nothing to know. Get dressed. I'm coming to get you."

"No, you're not."

"Oh yes, I am. Even if you're still in your pajamas, you're coming," he insisted. "We'll grab a sandwich, then go for a drive. I want to show you some land."

"I'm not ready."

"Well, get ready, Smiley. Mrs. Dunigan's youngest son is on his way."

I couldn't help but giggle as I imagined him hurling me over his shoulder in my Victoria's Secret flannels. "Okay, okay. But I need thirty minutes."

"Thirty minutes it is."

❧

After lunch Jack took me to see a large parcel of tree-covered ground.

"What do you think?" he asked.

"It's beautiful," I said about the brilliant red, orange, and golden leaves that glistened in the afternoon sun.

"It is," he confirmed.

Jack wasn't talking about the foliage. He was referring to the potential of the undeveloped land that stretched before us. He understood the topography, knew where and how the streets would lay, and could tell you how many and what type of homes would best fit. When I looked at raw ground, I saw only trees and earth. But give me a footprint for any home, existing or to be built, and I could show you how to maximize the interior. We were a perfect fit.

20

NEW YORK CITY

Two and a half months later, as winter's chill filled the air, Jack parked in an alley behind an aging red brick home in a less-than-safe Pittsburgh neighborhood.

"What are we doing here?" I wrapped my old cloth coat tightly around me as I stepped out of the car.

"You'll see." Jack guided me down a flight of cracked concrete steps to a weathered basement door, then knocked twice as though it were a secret code.

One at a time I heard the first, second, third lock unlatch, and the heavy door squeaked open. A white-haired man with knobby fingers motioned us inside. As soon as we stepped into the cool concrete basement, we found ourselves surrounded by racks and racks of expensive pelts and coats and capes and wraps and hats. I had never seen so much fur. I thought nothing of the animals that once wore that skin or of their gruesome deaths. I thought only how having fur meant having wealth. Jack's estranged wife owned one. I saw her in a fur coat once, only for a moment. We passed each other on a downtown street. Tony and I were going to dinner; she and Jack were heading to a play. The full-length mink was gorgeous. In it she looked elegant and alluring.

"What a little thing," the man said to Jack in a strong German accent. Then he turned from us. As he disappeared into the sea of fur, he raised his hand above his head and called out, "Try on whatever you would like. I'll be back."

As I stood on a platform in front of a three-sided mirror, Jack slipped coat after weighty coat onto my shoulders. Some coats were the wrong color, others the wrong shape. Almost every one of them swallowed me. The old man knew his business. As soon as we finished telling him what we wanted to try, he unveiled the garment he had retrieved from the backroom.

"This one." He helped me into it. With his one hand cupping his opposite elbow, his index finger tapping his lips, he walked all the way around me. Then he said, "Almost perfect."

He was right. Other than being a little too big, it was the right color, the right pelt, the right cut for my body. Jack agreed. A few weeks later, we returned to pick up my perfectly altered, dress-length fur.

I slipped it on and before I had a chance to fasten it closed, Jack said, "Look inside. Look inside."

I opened the left-hand side of the coat. On the silk inner lining, in the most beautiful script, the furrier had embroidered my name—only my first name. Maybe Jack was going to change my last name? Maybe. Maybe. Maybe.

❧

As we pulled up to the curb, I couldn't ignore the small group of angry protesters marching back and forth in front of the St. Regis Hotel in New York City—the hotel where we would be staying. They carried signs and called out to no one in particular, "Wear your OWN SKIN" and "FUR IS DEATH" and "MURDERER." I wrapped my arms around my body and hugged the crystal fox fur that swaddled me.

When the taxi driver climbed out to retrieve our luggage from the trunk, Jack turned to me and said, "Be prepared. They might throw red paint on your coat."

"Paint?" As my heart pounded fast, I clenched my teeth. I had never been that close to a demonstration before, much less a demonstration in which I might be attacked. "What do we do?"

"Don't stop. Don't say a word. Keep your head down and hold on to me."

As Jack made his way around to my side of the taxi, I slumped down in my seat. He opened my door, took my hand, then hurried me past the protestors and into the hotel lobby. After we checked into our beautiful suite, we fell across the oversized bed giggling about how awful it would have been had if someone had thrown paint on my coat. How lucky we were.

"It's a sign," I said.

It was February 14, and our romantic weekend had begun. Over the next three days, the plan included dinner at the Metropolitan Club (with which the Chairman's Club had reciprocity), a Broadway show, dessert, coffee, and caricatures at the world-famous Sardi's. Whenever we could fit it in, we would shop Fifth Avenue, visit the garment district, and lunch at the Carnegie Deli. But not that night. It was Valentine's night.

Having unpacked, showered, and dressed for the evening, Jack hailed a taxi. "Tavern on the Green," he instructed the driver. Jack turned to me and said, "Wait 'til you see it all lit up."

Originally designed by Calvert Vaux as a sheep fold, the building was transformed into a restaurant by Robert Moses in 1934.

Nestled beautifully among the twinkling trees, it was an endless Christmas scene.

"We have reservations," Jack informed the maître d' as a member of the staff took my coat. The man shook Jack's hand, accepting the large bill concealed in his palm.

Wherever we went, Jack had folded money available anytime he reached into his pocket. Was it a part of dressing? Tie your tie, fold your money? Before Jack, I had never seen anyone do that. I found the notion of tipping so inconspicuously, so generously, both charming and powerful.

"This is a very special night," Jack reminded the man as we followed him to our table. "We do not plan to rush."

"Most definitely, sir," the man nodded.

Tucked in a corner, we giggled and toasted one another. We sipped expensive wine. And like a replay of the scene from *Flashdance,* all messy and sexual right there, right out in public, we hand-fed one another bites of buttery lobster and rare filet. Even though there was no way we could eat dessert given all the delicious food we hadn't finished, Jack ordered a plate of creamy French cheeses and sweet-ripened fruit along with my all-time favorite, crème brûlée. We nibbled at both; finished neither.

As we stood to leave, Jack asked, "You up for a carriage ride?"

"Of course!" I did not want this magical evening to end.

❧

We climbed high into the back of a big, red coach that brisk February night. The moon hung low and the stars shined bright. With no clouds to hold in the heat, the evening was crisp and cold. Really cold. Even though I was wrapped in fur, I shivered. Jack reached behind us and grabbed a blanket the driver had mentioned he kept on hand. As the horse clopped along, Jack snuggled me in the blanket and held me tight against him.

"I don't think this night could get any better." I gazed up at Jack.

"Maybe it can." He reached into his pocket and pulled out a tiny, black velvet box.

It had been four and a half years since I started working for Jack and a little less than two years since the finalization of each of our divorces. Was it really going to happen?

He opened the box. "Will you marry me?"

I burst into tears. "Oh my God! Really?"

"Yes, really."

Between kisses with my new fiancé I repeated, "Of course. Of course. Of course."

As soon as Jack slipped that gorgeous one and a quarter carat, pear-shaped diamond ring onto my finger, I stretched out my left hand, admiring the sparkle and shine. From that point on I was, as he teased, "very left-handed."

Jack had purchased that engagement ring about eighteen months prior on a western Caribbean cruise we took. While shopping in the market district of St. Thomas, we stepped into The Universal Jewelry Store, and Jack told me to pick any ring I wanted.

"Any?"

His cheeks grew pink. "Well, you know, not any."

The minute I laid eyes on the pear-shaped solitaire set among glistening baguettes, I fell in love. The center stone wasn't the largest in the case nor the most expensive, but it was the most beautiful ring I'd ever seen. As it sparkled under the store lights, I couldn't stop looking at it. After sizing the band to fit my finger and polishing the stones one last time, the jeweler packaged it up. Jack slipped that tiny, black velvet box deep into his pocket.

"Let's keep this between us. Okay?" he whispered as we left the store.

He was ready to buy the ring; not so ready to put it on my finger. I could live with that for the time being. But not telling anyone? For me that was nearly impossible. Unable to contain my excitement, I told my sister, Shari, the person to whom I told everything. Except for her, I kept my word to Jack and told no one else.

From that day forward any time we went out, especially if we had planned something special, I waited for him to propose. When he didn't, no matter how wonderful the evening may have been, it ended in disappointment. After a while, a part of me thought he might never ask. But he finally had. He asked me to marry him right there in that carriage in Central Park on Valentine's Day. My favorite holiday of all.

I wrapped my arms around my future husband's neck and gave him the longest, most passionate kiss ever. When the kiss ended, out of the corner of my eye, I caught a glimpse of the driver, a broad smile stretching across his long, thin face.

21

LIFE OF A SINGLE MOTHER

With my new fiancé spending almost every evening and practically every night at my house, it seemed there was more for me to do, less time for me to do it, and little time for my children. I couldn't figure out why—not that it mattered. It was what it was. Only one solution, go to bed later, start my day earlier.

If Jack wasn't there, I cleaned until I was too tired to clean anymore. When he was there, I went to bed with him. Sometimes I got up after he had fallen asleep to clean up, do laundry, or remove something from the freezer with the great hope that I might be able to prepare a home-cooked meal. Of course, whatever I did, I did it as quietly as possible. With so much to do at the house, I rarely brought work home. Instead, since my kids were adept at getting themselves up and out the door to school, when work piled to a point where I could no longer stand it, before anyone was awake, I rose, showered, and dressed. After I dried my hair in the basement bathroom, I made my way to the office.

That's what I had done that day when Jack came around my desk and gave me a kiss. "Good morning, Smiley. Getting an early start?"

"Trying to catch up."

"I see that." He looked at the stack of files, then studied my face. "You sure that's all it is? You look tired."

"Didn't sleep much. I don't know, lots to do." I shrugged.

"Well, take care of yourself." He took a few steps toward his office, then turned back to me. "Oh, don't forget, we have that fundraiser for the judge tonight."

"Okay." I wasn't as enthusiastic as I should have been, and I didn't look up at him when I spoke.

"You don't want me to go without you. Do you?"

"No. No. Of course not." I closed the folder I was working on and focused on him. Jack donated a lot of money to this cause and wanted to rub elbows and enjoy the festivities. I knew that. I also knew he didn't want to go alone. No matter how much I wanted to hunker down on the family room floor in front of the television with my kids and a bowl of Jiffy Pop, I needed to be at his side. "What time do you want to leave?"

"6:30," he said.

"I'll be ready. I promise."

An hour after Jack left for the day, as I was shutting down my computer, my phone rang. It was a little past 5:00.

"Hi, Linda. This is Vivian. I'm sorry to bother you, but I'm just not sure about that vanity we chose for the powder room. Maybe you're right. Maybe we should leave it a pedestal sink. After all, that's standard and we've spent so much money. I don't know what to do. What do you think?"

"Personally, I prefer the look of a pedestal, but it does lack the storage you said you wanted."

"So much to think about." She sighed. "How much time do we have to decide?"

"I'll be placing the cabinetry order early next week. Can you let me know by then?"

"Would you mind if we come by? Maybe tomorrow around 5:00? I'll feel so much better if we go over these decisions one more time. Just to be sure."

"No problem." I blocked off an hour in my calendar, hurried to the car, put the key in the ignition. The old Lincoln moaned and although it sounded like it wanted to start, it did not. "Come on." I pressed my forehead against the steering wheel and begged, "Please don't do this to me. Not now."

The alternator had been acting up, but I didn't have the money for the expensive fix. Truth is I didn't have any money. All I could do was cross my fingers and hope. Luckily, with another turn of the key, the engine kicked over and I was on my way. Leaving nothing to chance, I let the vehicle run while I raced into the house.

"Zach, two minutes," I called up the steps to my fourteen-year-old. He was my third-born child and my oldest son.

Zach didn't answer, but Alex, my youngest, greeted me. "Guess what, Mom?"

"What's up, kiddo?"

He followed me down the hall and through the kitchen. "Another science project."

"Great," I said sarcastically as my mind frantically considered what I could possibly pull together to wear that night.

"Counts for a full test grade," he emphasized with dread on his face.

"Okay, then. We'll give it all we've got." I dug through the washer looking for a particular black turtleneck I thought I might be able to pair with my red plaid skirt. "When is it due?"

"Monday. Teacher said just in case we need the weekend."

"Smart teacher," I replied, then I caught a glimpse of my sweater. "There it is." It lay on the top of the laundry basket with other items that still needed to be washed. *Should I fluff it and wear it anyway?*

"Mom, it's going to be hard." My twelve-year-old drew my attention back to him, listing every detail of the project. "We need to start tonight."

I stopped and turned toward him. "Alex, I've got to go out this evening, but we'll work on it tomorrow. I promise. In the meantime, make a list of what you need. If we don't have something, I'll grab it tomorrow on my way home from work. Okay?"

With that, I flipped a load from the washer into the dryer, scooped food into the dog's empty bowl, and rolled my eyes as I hurried past the pile of dirty dishes in the sink. Then I made my way back to the front entry.

"Come on, Zach," I called up to his closed bedroom door. "Don't want to be late for practice."

Zach came down the stairs and without a word went straight to the car. He wasn't happy that his parents were now divorced. Not happy about Jack. Less happy with me. Rightfully so. He had told me that he wanted to live with his dad. Terrified I'd lose my son and the child support I needed to keep all of us in our house, I couldn't let that happen. I told him no.

"Lizzi," I shouted up to my oldest, "I'm going to run Zach to practice and then pick up Tori."

She peeked out of her bedroom, her head wrapped in a towel.

"Will you take a look at that science project with your brother?

Please? I have no idea what it's about and Jack has this fundraiser thing tonight so as soon as I get back, I need to get ready."

"Well, don't shower."

"Why?"

"No hot water."

"What? This house is only five years old. Can't be the tank. I'll look at it tonight."

She shrugged, then asked, "What about dinner?"

"Oh, yeah, sorry. I forgot. I'll grab McDonald's."

With that, I left to accomplish too many tasks in too little time.

❧

By the time Jack arrived, the kids were in the family room—the room still without furniture—on the floor, eating McDonald's, watching television. Upstairs, I hurried myself out of my blue jeans and into the best fast, clean option I could find, my little black dress.

"Hey, guys." I heard Jack greet them. "Where's your mom?"

"Upstairs," Alex answered in between bites. "She just got home."

"She did, did she?" Jack called up to me, "You almost ready, Smiley?"

"Almost," I shouted as I fought to zip my little black dress. With no time to bathe, I hiked up my dress, rolled on deodorant, and spritzed some perfume. Then I pulled a brush through my hair and stepped in front of the mirror that hung on the back of my closet door. Far from perfect, but out of time, it would have to do. With matted red lipstick and glossy black heels, I hurried down the steps. At the bottom, freshly showered and perfectly appointed in a crisp navy blazer and creased camel-colored slacks, Jack waited. So handsome. So polished. So much better than me.

"What the heck have you been doing?" he joked as he gave me a peck on the cheek.

"Life of leisure," I replied, looking around at the messy house and sweet kids I did not want to leave.

"Let's go, Smiley." He slapped me on the butt. "We're gonna be late."

22

THE MEMORY

Four months after our engagement, Jack pulled into my driveway with a carload of his belongings. He would keep his apartment, but that was just a formality. He was moving in with me.

After he hung a few shirts and filled Tony's empty top dresser drawer with T-shirts and socks, we made our way to the family room. In order to make my home what I needed it to be—his, too—we got busy taking down some of my family photos, hanging ones he had brought. Halfway through, I took a step back. His pictures looked as though they had been there from the start.

Just then the front door opened. My kids were arriving home from a weekend with their father.

"What are you doing?" Lizzi, then seventeen, asked as all four children huddled together just inside the family room.

"Hanging Jack's pictures," I replied, oblivious to her angst.

"I don't want you to take those down," Tori, sixteen, pointed to our framed photos stacked on the floor.

"Me neither," Alex added.

"It's just a few," I said.

"I don't care how many," Zach chimed in. "Put them back up."

"Linda, maybe we should..." Jack began.

"No, Jack. It's your house now, too," I said in his defense.

"No, it's not," Zach declared.

"I don't want him to live here!" Tori added, and from the corner of my eyes I saw Jack pulling his fingers back and forth across his forehead. It's what he did when he was stressed.

"I don't care what you want," I snapped at my daughter.

"Linda, calm down," Jack insisted.

"Don't tell me to calm down."

Before Jack or I spoke another word, Alex wailed at the top of his lungs, "*I want my dad*!" The other children chimed in agreement and that was that. It became a full-out fight.

I should have stopped, sat with my children, been the mother they needed. I didn't. I became a child, in combat with my own children. Jack hated chaos. Couldn't handle fighting. As the battle raged, I watched him. He looked toward the door. He wanted out. I knew it. I could feel it in my gut, see it on his face. Then he did the very thing I feared most. He took a step—a step toward the exit. He was about to leave. I had given up everything for him—to be with him—and he was going to leave *me*! How could he? How dare he? Anger rushed over me. A surge of hot, thick, blinding, selfish, needy anger. I lost it.

"If you're going to leave, then get out." I threw my engagement ring at him. Then I pointed at my kids, "And take them with you."

The door slammed, everyone had left, the house grew still.

❧

I paced.

Around and around the dining room table.

With hands on my head, I yanked at fists full of my hair. "Oh my God. What have I done?"

Lap after lap.

And I sobbed.

"What kind of a mother throws her children out?"

I made another lap.

"You're a horrible person," I scolded myself. "A poor excuse for a mother—*the worst mother ever*! They'll never forgive you. None of them. Why should they? You don't deserve forgiveness. You don't deserve to live."

I circled one more time, my palms slapping at the sides of my throbbing head. "What's wrong with you?"

Jack had it all—money, success, looks, prestige. With grown children he had freedom. He could have any woman he wanted. I never felt good enough, even as I strived for perfection. Flawless, thin, successful, smiling, all while juggling house, job, kids, life, most of all Jack. Always Jack.

A rat on a wheel. Work seven days, race home. Feed the kids, chauffer to baseball, football, cheerleading, run through the grocery store—out of milk again—fuel the car, trash to the curb. Homework, laundry, straighten the house, empty the dishwasher, return that client call, note what I forgot to do before I left the office today, water the plants or are they dead? Did I let the dogs out? What time is it? Shower and dress for Jack. No beginning. No end. No rest. The life of a woman going mad.

And those bills. The 3,200-square-foot provincial built for Tony's income was too much for me. Even with generous child support, I had only seventeen dollars in my checking account until payday.

Jack wanted me to sell that house. I couldn't let it go. The kids lost their father because of me. Too busy making ends meet and chasing Jack, I couldn't take their home away from them, too. It was the only thing any of us could cling to in the surge of confusion and fear and uncertainty.

When he asked me to marry him, I flushed with relief. Maybe I was good enough. Maybe having him there meant having help. But with him came more rules, more needs, more expectations. No help. I worried more, hurried more, felt more pressure. Despite exhaustion, sleep eluded me. My childhood nightmare returned. At first occasionally, then every night.

A little girl is running down a rat-infested alley. On both sides brick buildings tower over her, one right after the next. No space in between. It's not just any little girl. It's me. A dilapidated streetlight illuminates a shadow ten times the size of an ordinary man. He's chasing me. He grows larger—closer. In the distance I see an opening. I race toward it. Into it. A courtyard. No doors. No windows. No way out. I turn. The shadow gets bigger. I step back. Another step. Against the wall. Trapped, I scream.

That nightmare should have been a clue. Maybe it was.

I stopped pacing, stood perfectly still, stared straight ahead. Then, the way the clouds parted and the moon suddenly appeared, there it was. Right in front of me. Like I was watching a movie. Like it was happening to someone else. But it wasn't someone else. It was me.

I let out a piercing scream and fell to my knees.

"Mom! Mom, are you all right?" Lizzi rushed to my side. She hadn't left with the others.

Did I tell her what I'd just remembered? I don't know. I can't recall much about what happened next except that she grabbed the phone and dialed my friend.

"Mom, were you and Jack seeing a therapist?" she asked. "Mom!"

she yelled. "Mom, Anna needs to know."

I nodded.

"Call her!" My seventeen-year-old waved the phone in front of me. "Anna wants you to call your therapist right now."

I took the receiver and dialed. "If this is an emergency, press zero." I pressed. I waited.

"Hello," Joyce answered. "Hello? Is someone there?"

I told her what I remembered.

"Call Pittsburgh Action Against Rape." She rattled off the phone number. "Call right now." She repeated the number.

23

PAAR

While my daughter stood over me, her face pinched with concern, I dialed.

I don't remember the name of the counselor I spoke with at PAAR, how long she and I were on the phone, or what she said to me. But the soft-spoken woman calmed me down and assured me I would make it through this. I didn't share her conviction. Like a picture under broken glass, everything I knew about myself was shattered. My childhood, my innocence, my future—*me*. As tears streamed across my cheeks, I wondered, *Can I survive this? Do I even want to?*

"Are you having thoughts of hurting yourself?" she probed.

I could buy a gun, swallow pills, sit inside the car running in the garage. But my kids. I had never been the mother I was sure other women so easily were. But suicide? That would leave four baby birds in an empty nest. No one to hug them when they were heartbroken, care for them when they were sick, remind them they could do the very thing they thought they could not do. And my daughter—in the next room. She stayed with me, worried about me. She would be the one to find me.

"No," I whispered. "Suicide is not an option."

"Are you sure?"

"Yes."

"Good," she said. "Let's get you an appointment."

"Will I see you?"

"I'm a phone counselor," she explained. "But all of our therapists are very well qualified."

"Okay."

"How about Thursday at 4:00?"

I agreed.

"And you'll call if you need us sooner?"

I answered yes.

"May I speak with your daughter again, please?"

I didn't hear what the woman said to Lizzi, but after they hung up, my daughter led me to my bed and gave me two Tylenol PM. I swallowed and lay back against my pillow. She pulled up the covers, left the water on the nightstand, and took the pill bottle with her when she left.

❧

In less than a week, I found myself walking toward the converted red brick church on 19th Street in Pittsburgh's South Side: The Pittsburgh Action Against Rape. Even when I say those words today, they unnerve me. I didn't belong there. I wasn't raped. But I was there, and shaking to the core, I prepared for the fight of my life.

I'm sure I approached the reception desk and checked in, although I don't remember doing that. I do remember being early, sitting on the edge of my seat in the tiny waiting room, dry mouthed, picking at the edges of my ragged cuticles. I wanted to jump up and run away from that place, from the thoughts in my head, from my new reality. I did not run. While flipping through a magazine, I focused on everything around me. Everything but me.

I watched a few workers move in and out of a room at the end of a short hallway. Each time the door opened, hammers and drills and the sound of men's voices filled the air. It reminded me of the fiancé, the children, and the life I had just thrown away.

At the creak of the front door, I looked up to see a confident thirty-something woman enter. In a tailored suit and shiny heels, she strode across the worn entryway. She knew where she was going. Did she work there or was she a client? She didn't look like anyone I could ever become. Her manicured finger pressed the elevator button. The steel door opened and a middle-aged matron, eyes red and puffy, stepped out. Gripping a wad of tissue in one hand, a thick, white, softcover book in the crook of her other arm, the woman padded quickly and quietly toward the exit. Her eyes were fixed on the floor. My gaze was fixed on her. She looked exactly like I felt.

A few minutes later the elevator dinged again. The single door opened and an earthy woman took a half step out. Leaning back against the automatic door, both arms wrapped around a manila folder, she smiled at the only person in the tiny waiting area—me.

"Linda?"

I nodded, rose, then followed her.

I don't remember her name. I call her Donna.

In a soft, kind voice Donna asked, "Can you tell me a little bit about what's going on with you?"

While looking at the floor, out the window, anywhere but at her, I told the therapist about the fitful day one week ago, about

Jack, about the relationship I destroyed. I told her about the job I no longer had, my precious children that I had sent away. And I cried with hurt and embarrassment and fear. I said nothing about the childhood memory. What someone had done to me long ago was not as important as what I had just done.

"It was your emergency," she reassured me. "Your cry for help."

Although I felt like I lost my mind and there was little (if any) justification for what I had done, hearing that others had done the same thing made me feel a little less alone, a lot less insane.

As our first one-hour session came to a close, Donna scribbled the title of a large white book on a small yellow sticky note. She held up her copy up so I would know what to look for. *The Courage to Heal, A Guide for Women Survivors of Child Sexual Abuse* by Ellen Bass and Laura Davis. That text would become my winding road to recovery.

I drove straight to the bookstore.

24

TELLING JACK

By my third session with Donna, I still could not bring myself to talk in depth about what had happened in my childhood. Before I could go back and fight past demons, I needed to stabilize the ship. There was only one way to do that.

"I'm going to tell Jack what happened that day." I wasn't sure how much I would be able to tell him, but surely I could explain why I reacted as I had. Surely, he would understand.

"I don't advise it." Donna shook her head adamantly.

Having him at my side would make surviving this possible. So, despite her warning, the minute I got home I called him.

He agreed to see me the next day.

❦

I stepped into his office, the office he and I had shared for the past four years. It was the middle of the afternoon. No one else was there. My desk was exactly as I left it. Three files stacked neatly in the right-hand corner, the files I had been working on, lay open in the center. That was a good sign. Right?

When he saw me, he stood.

"There's something I need to tell you," I said as I stepped hesitantly toward him. I had written it out. Rehearsed it. Every word exactly as I wanted to say it. I clung to that paper twisted and torn between my fingers.

He motioned and we sat at the small, round conference table.

"There's something I need to tell you," I repeated.

He waited, cross-armed and serious. He was a businessman in a business meeting.

"That day, after you left, I remembered." I lowered my eyes and my voice, "When I was a child…I was…" I swallowed tears. "I was sexually abused."

After a moment, he reached out and patted my forearm. "I am so sorry for you." His voice was soft and sincere.

I wiped a tear from my cheek, raised my head, and mustered all the courage I could. "Will you be there for me? Please?"

"Oh, Lin. I can be there—as your friend," he clarified.

I stood and gripped the back of the chair. "I have plenty of friends." I forced a smile. "What I really need is someone to love me through this."

"I'm sorry," he said. "I can't do that right now."

I nodded, then made my way out the door.

I managed to get out of Jack's office without falling apart, but the moment I climbed into the car, all of my frayed edges began to unravel. Everyone I knew was at work. I had no one to call. I could not go home. My daughter was there and I did not want to come apart in front of her—not again.

I clicked my seatbelt, put the key in the ignition, started the car. I drove. And I drove. I motored along without regard for where I was going or the thick, black, ominous clouds that lay ahead of me. And I cried. I cried harder with each passing mile.

After forty-five minutes of full-on sobbing and God knows what kind of driving, I was startled when the sky let loose with a flash and a crack, and a downpour of sheeting rain. The kind of rain you can't see through. As my wipers swished furiously, a tractor trailer blew by me, forcing water under my tires and onto my windshield. I gripped the steering wheel and tried to control the car. As though I had been jarred awake, I realized I had no idea where I was or how I had gotten there. I flushed with panic.

That's when I heard her words in my head. "Promise you'll call again if you need us." It was the voice of the phone counselor at PAAR. I don't know how I managed to navigate the car and my panic and the storm, but somehow, I grabbed the phone and dialed. When a woman answered I blurted through tears, "I don't know where I am."

She never asked my name or any other details. She simply said, "I'm here. It will be okay." Then she said, "Take a breath and tell me what you see."

"I don't know," I wailed. "I don't see anything."

"Do you see cars or trucks or buildings or trees?" Her soft voice calmed me and the rain slowed and the landscape took shape in front of me.

"I see a car. I think. Maybe...it's blue."

"Good. What else do you see?"

"A telephone pole and...I don't know...maybe some trees?"

"You're doing great."

"There's a shopping center," I said. "Up ahead."

She suggested that if I could safely do so, I should pull into the parking lot and stop the car.

I made a left at the light and drove into the first available slot, as far as possible from the store, the cars, and the people. I turned off the ignition, wiped my face, laid my head against the steering wheel.

I had been so sure Jack would be there for me. Of course he would. He loved me. For better or worse. He just needed to understand. But Donna was right. Telling him was the worst thing I could have done. The very thing I thought I needed to get through this—Jack's love and support—was *not* mine to have.

I had gone from my parents to Tony, from Tony to Jack, always someone there to take care of me. But this time, for the first time, the worst time, I was alone. I would have to find some way to do *this* by myself.

I took a breath, started the car, headed for home.

25

YELLOW PAGES

ASIDE FROM TWELVE years of Catholic education, my religious upbringing included my mother's example of fish-only Fridays, Lenten sacrifices, and confession before communion on whatever Sunday she chose to go to Mass. Although always faithful, my mother's oblations of reverence intensified following the traumas she had endured.

After two excruciating days, my two-year-old sister passed away from anaphylactic shock. I was ten days old. In 1957, people were either shock-therapy crazy or sane. My mother may have been wrought with grief but considered herself sane. While refusing her newborn—why hadn't God taken the infant she hadn't yet bonded with instead of the two-year-old she dearly loved?—my mother clung to her religion and the priest who offered her the only counseling she agreed to have. As years passed and pain faded and life grew busy, Mom slowly gravitated away from her church, but never from her God who reigned over Heaven and her lost little girl.

In 1989, as the need for an older, dangerous man (Richard) took hold of me and the debilitating effects of early onset Parkinson's took hold of my father, my mother reignited her staunch Catholic beliefs with an arduous pilgrimage up the treacherous slopes to the shrine at Medjugorje, Yugoslavia, a trek she took with Tony's mother, then my mother-in-law.

Even though I could never be as religious as my mother, I always adhered to her prescribed parental protocols, baptizing my children in frilly white outfits with godparents and cake, then sending them to strict Catholic school. The latter was as much my avoidance of shuttling them to and from weekend catechism as my gratitude for the discipline the school provided. But given that good people basically do good things and bad people do bad things with or without a scorecard, I gave little thought to the purpose of organized religion.

With the return of my repressed memories, there emerged the reality that some things are bigger than me—the loss of a child for one; abuse, another. Along with those bigger things came the need for a bigger, stronger God, or more accurately, for His bigger, stronger help.

Requiring assistance roused in me a daunting fear that He might have forgotten me as I had, for all those years, forgotten Him. It brought to mind the day one of my children questioned Santa. I replied, "If you don't believe in Santa, Santa might not believe in you." Although not the same, it felt the same to that child back then as it felt to me at that moment. Clinging to the hope that God never forgot anyone—despite the wrongs and hurt I had levied upon those I loved, as I lay alone in that big bed, tears streaming, I prayed to Him for strength and some small sign that I could make it through this.

So, when I wandered into the kitchen that pre-dawn morning,

a few days after my disclosure to Jack, to find the Yellow Pages laying open smack in the middle of the table, a large red circle around my gynecologist's name, I didn't know quite what to make of it. *Did I come down in the middle of the night and take the phone book out of the cabinet? Did I carry it to the table and flip it open to that very page?* I spent those sleepless nights pacing the dark house or tossing and turning in my cold bed. No matter how hard or long I racked my brain, I had no memory of having touched that phone book. I may never know how it made its way to the kitchen table, but I saw that event as a sign. Heeding the desperately needed Divine Intervention, the moment the clock struck 8:00 a.m., I dialed.

"Is this a routine exam, or are you having a problem?" the woman on the other end of the phone asked.

Was it because I told the receptionist that I had recently remembered childhood sexual abuse or was it some miracle of miracles that my gynecologist, always booked months in advance, suddenly had an opening? Of course I realize now why they made room for me, but back then I saw it as yet another sign.

The exam, always invasive and somewhat humiliating to me, was more so that day. Afterwards, as the doctor peeled off her purple latex gloves and tossed them into the metal bin, she concluded that my female parts were in good physical condition. She was less sure of my emotional well-being.

"Who is your primary care physician?" she asked with a seriousness that made me take heed. "Call him immediately," she instructed as she made a few notes in my file. "If he doesn't have an appointment today, I want you to go to the emergency room."

Keenly aware I was on the verge of falling apart, without question, I climbed behind the steering wheel, affixed my seatbelt, and dialed my PCP.

"Dr. Slagel said you'd be calling," the receptionist replied the moment I announced my name. "Can you come in now?"

I drove straight to his office.

Following a short stint in the always busy waiting area, where some folks distanced from coughing and sneezing, while others held onto one or another aching body part, the office door opened. A young lady in baggy blue scrubs announced my first name. I looked around to see if there was, perhaps, another person with my same name. There was not. To the stares of those who had been waiting before me, I got up and followed the nurse to the intake station.

"What brings you in today?" she casually asked while affixing the blood pressure cuff to my arm.

Did I have to describe to *everyone* the reason for my visit? I don't know exactly what I said, but without allowing her face to show a reaction, she replied, "I wish people would keep their hands to themselves." After taking the last of my vitals and jotting a few notes in my file, rather than sending me back to the crowded waiting room, she led me straight into an exam room.

"The doctor will be right with you." She left the room and closed the door behind her. I imagined her breathing a sigh of relief that I was no longer in her care.

Following a brief exam, I gave the doctor my promise to remain in therapy and he gave me a prescription for Prozac. "It could take up to six weeks to kick in," he cautioned. But within an hour of swallowing that first little pill I felt lighter; the world a little brighter. It was as though someone had removed the heavy blanket under which I had been living.

Feeling a bit stronger, I got back to the business of confronting my past.

26

GRANDMA'S HOUSE

Like his father before him, my grandfather couldn't handle the drink, but couldn't resist. Despite his brilliant engineering mind, his addiction stole from him and his family job after job. Around the age of eleven, using hard-earned paper route money, one route before school, another route after, my father put food on the table and managed to save enough to buy his little brother the only childhood bed Uncle Dean would have.

Expectations of my father never lessened. After my parents married, my uncle called upon my dad to help him open an auto body shop and provide ongoing business advice. He probably asked my father for money, too. My grandparents definitely did. They were often at our front door, hands extended begging for whatever they could get. They even dared to show up a few days after their granddaughter passed away asking to borrow some of the toddler's insurance money.

"Even if there was any money, which there was *not*," my mother recounted through gritted teeth, "I wouldn't have given them one red cent."

If my mother had any tolerance for my father's parents prior to that day, she had none after. I never did understand why, back in those early years, Shari and I were sent to stay with my paternal grandparents as often as we were. Maybe having us there kept Grandfather in line. I never once saw him drink any alcohol. Or maybe babysitting was a way to pay back some of the monies that would otherwise never have been paid. I didn't know. I didn't care. I loved going to Grandma's house.

During those lazy summer afternoons, she and I sat for hours on her half of the porch of the two-bedroom duplex that she and my grandfather rented. Despite fingers gnarled by arthritis, she taught me to braid by twisting yarn around the nails she pounded into the top of a large wooden spool. When time and money permitted, while Grandfather sat in the car, she took Shari and me on church scavenger hunts. They were a lot of fun, but while other children victoriously held up what they found, we rarely uncovered more than one or two of the listed items. Once Grandma let me ride an old brown horse around a small dirt track. I loved it so much she took me straight to the store to buy me my very own copy of *Black Beauty*. It became my favorite book of all.

Another time, after I was strapped into a Ferris wheel at a local fair, Grandma said she didn't want to ride and Shari was too little to ride alone. I shouldn't have ridden without her. As the big wheel began its slow, choppy ascent, I peered down over the handlebar of that swaying bright yellow bucket. I will never forget my baby sister's big, sad eyes staring up at me through the chain-link fence she gripped with both of her tiny hands.

I often wondered if Grandma had any inkling about what went on in that back bedroom my little sister and I shared with Uncle

Dean when we stayed over. The room was sparsely furnished with two twin beds and a small dresser pushed in between. The summer I remember most, Shari had just turned six. I had just made my first holy communion. I would soon turn eight.

Uncle Dean, about nineteen at the time, was handsome and mysterious. Here one day, he was gone the next. We never knew when he would show up or where he had come from. As an adult I learned that he had been in the military, but I don't ever recall seeing a military uniform anywhere in Grandma's house. Either way, anytime he showed up, he stayed only a few days and he always slept in the same room. Shari and me in one twin bed; he in the other.

From the start, Shari didn't want anything to do with him or his game. He didn't care. He sat on the bed, back against the wall, legs stretched, feet crossed at the ankle. Then he'd pat his thigh and call to her, "Don't you want to come over here and play?" No matter how many times he asked, Shari always said no. Then she would sink down in our shared bed, pull the blankets up to her nose, and pinch her little eyes closed tight.

He didn't need to ask me more than once. With his wavy, thick black hair, piercing grey eyes and Prince Charming charisma, I looked forward to every minute with him. He made me feel special. He made me feel loved. When he thought Shari was asleep, he'd whisper to me over and over again, "You're my favorite. You know that. Right?"

"I am?"

"Yes." Then he'd tap his long finger gently against my chest three times, once for each slowly spoken word, "You're. My. Favorite."

One day my uncle was finishing up a shower when I had to go to the bathroom. Bouncing cross-legged, I wriggled at the knob. "It's me," I cried out. "I gotta go."

"I'm getting out of the shower," he whispered sternly. "You *can NOT* come in."

"But it's *me*!" I mimicked his stern whisper right back at him.

"SSSSSSHHHHH!" he hissed.

I could not understand why I could see him naked in the bedroom, but not in the bathroom. And I had no idea that because of my relationship with him, everything about me had changed.

The day after I returned home from that summer visit at my grandmother's, I sat cross-legged on my mother's hope chest, looking out her bedroom window at the neighborhood kids playing in the street below.

"Why don't you go outside and play?" my mother encouraged.

Although I desperately wanted other kids to *want* to play with me, I didn't want to play with them. Not anymore. No longer a child, far from an adult, I wasn't like them. And I didn't want anyone to get too close. Someone might see my secret.

That summer came to an end and ready or not, the new school year began. One particular day, I walked home alone in the rain. The longer I walked, the more I got wet, the angrier I became. When I finally made it home, I pushed through the side door, kicked off my shoes, and threw my soaking wet jacket onto the floor. Water splatted everywhere.

My mother's sister, Rita, was sitting at the kitchen table enjoying coffee with my mom. Aunt Rita jumped from her seat and pointed at the sopping pile on the floor. "Pick up that coat."

With hands on my hips and a scowl on my face, I said, "You're not the boss of me."

"Who do you think you are?" Aunt Rita stepped toward me. "Your mother is not your maid. Now you pick that up."

"No!" I stomped my foot. "And you can't make me." I had

always been independent and defiant, but this was a new level, even for me.

"Then go to your room," she yelled, red faced. "And don't come out until you're ready to pick it up."

I rolled my eyes, let out a huff, and marched away. As I got to the bottom of the steps to the second floor, my little sister rounded the corner. With all my might, I pushed her to the ground. She landed with a thud and cried out for our mother.

"Big baby," I said, then I made my way up the stairs and slammed my bedroom door. I didn't come out at all that night, not even to sneak a snack. I'd show them. I didn't need their food.

When I came down the next morning all dressed and ready for school, my coat hung in the closet; my book bag and shoes waited for me by the door.

❧

In the middle of that third-grade school year my teacher called my mother to come to school. Mom arrived as all the other kids were leaving. I sat at my desk a few feet from the two most important women in my life.

Mrs. Dougherty whispered, "She's so smart. She knows the material. If I give her this quiz right now," she shook the pages she held in her hand, "she'll fly right through it. But sometimes she stares out the window leaving work incomplete and tests untouched. Is there something going on at home?"

My mother squinted at the professional woman who stood before her. Then, sounding annoyed, she said, "Everything at home is just fine, but thank you for asking." She turned to me and said, "Let's go."

I rose and took her hand. We made our way out of Mrs. Dougherty's classroom, to the other end of the long hallway and down two flights of concrete steps. As soon as the heavy steel door slammed behind us, Mom gave my arm a jerk and without looking at me or breaking her stride said, "Can you try to pay attention, *please*?"

Not another word was said about any of it that day or, for that matter, ever—at least not to me.

❧

Time passed and I grew and so did my lack of self-confidence. So much so I refused to try out for a sport, take a class, or come out to play whatever game the neighborhood children were playing if I wasn't absolutely sure I could master it. I thought I had to be perfect, just to be good enough. My hair had to be just right, my grades straight As and, with the newly posted call for eighth grade cheerleading tryouts, my splits had to be more sprawling than anyone else's.

I desperately wanted to be one of those girls cheering on the sidelines of the boys' basketball court. They were so pretty and popular, and they always got the smiles and attention of all the boys on the team. Having spent summers in my large side yard, turning cartwheels, doing front and back flips and sliding into full-on straddles, I knew I could do this. So even though I wore a walking cast on the lower half of my right leg (a green break to my ankle), every day I jumped and shouted and slid all the way down onto the linoleum kitchen floor. I practiced until my mother called out, "Please give it a rest." There was no resting for me.

As the big day approached, I couldn't sleep, couldn't concentrate, couldn't do anything but fret. If I failed at this, I wouldn't be good enough for anything. After school that day, a group of excited girls thundered down the steps and gathered in the cafeteria. At one end of the room, behind a long, white table sat one woman, a woman I had never before seen. Would she make the decision alone?

She stood, introduced herself, explained the process. "Each of you will perform two cheers individually, then I'll call girls up in groups of eight to see how you perform together." Before she sat, she motioned Sister Mary Martha over to her. While pointing at me, she whispered, "Tell her she cannot try out."

"Why?" Sister asked.

"She's wearing a cast."

"I will not. Tell her yourself."

Sister marched across the room in her thick-soled clodhoppers and with arms crossed, she took a seat at the end of the row. In stunned silence we waited. Thankfully the woman did not eliminate me. When my turn came, I stood proudly (and nervously) before her.

"You may begin," she directed in her less-than-welcoming voice.

With heart pounding, I gave it my all. When I finished, I took the required at-ease pose and waited. The woman looked at me, stunned. Unlike her reaction to the others, it took her a long second before she spoke. Finally, she said softly, "You can have a seat."

At the end of that stressful afternoon, I was one of the girls who made the eighth-grade cheerleading squad—broken ankle and all. I wasn't going to do anything to mess that up. All summer I arrived to practice early and stayed late. Since I was smaller and lighter than anyone on the squad, I was the one thrown in the air or lifted to the top of the pyramid. That was just fine by me. It was the first time I didn't hate myself for being the littlest!

❧

After eight years of Catholic education, many of my classmates longed for the freedom of the public system. I did not. As summer came to a close, Kimmy, a neighborhood girl, sat with me on the old, green glider on my front porch.

"I hear Missy and Carla are going to St. Catherine's Academy next year. It's an all-girls high school." She crinkled her face. "I'd never go there."

"Me neither," I replied.

"A lot of kids are going to Perry. You?" she asked.

"Another four years of nuns for me," I replied. "Dad says I have to."

Truth is, I hadn't even asked my dad. The thought of going to the public school terrified me. Large class sizes and rumors of chaos and freedom, none of that was for me. Neither was college. I didn't think I was smart enough. When the time came, I wouldn't be choosing Calculus or Physics. Typing, shorthand, and bookkeeping were perfect for me. But like all the girls heading into four more conservative years, college bound or not, I, too, wished the nuns would allow our skirts to be a little shorter, our blouses a little less blousy. The nuns did not and neither did my father.

My father also did not allow dating until I turned sixteen. I could have a boy walk me home, sit with me in my parents' game room, or take me to the pizza shop after a basketball game. But I could not get in a car with any boy until I turned sixteen. "Don't even ask," my dad often said.

When a junior invited me to go with him to his prom, I wasn't sure I'd be allowed. I raced home. "Mom, guess what?" I said as I burst through the door.

She spun toward me. "What on Earth?"

"He did it. Micky asked me to go to prom. Can I go? Please? Can I?"

"You'll have to ask your father."

That night, at the dinner table, Mom told Dad my exciting news. "Isn't that wonderful?" she said as she passed the potatoes. To my delight, even though I was only a sophomore and still two and a half months shy of the critical age of sixteen, Dad agreed.

As soon as Dad handed Mom the money, off we went shopping to a store filled with beautiful gowns both bridal and prom. In no time I found the perfect long and flowy baby blue dress. In the store and at home, I twirled like a princess on a ballroom floor, imagining a wonderful summer romance, maybe longer, with my handsome, older boyfriend.

That's not how it went.

I knew what a boy wanted. I knew as soon as he got it, he'd be gone. Although I was more than okay with steaming up the car windows with heavy kissing, for me, it ended there. I'm not sure if I gave Micky the wrong impression with all my flirtatiousness or if he just didn't like me, but two movie dates after prom, he called.

"Hello?" I answered excitedly, twisting the spiral phone cord between my fingers.

"I…umm…" he stuttered.

"What?

"I won't be calling anymore."

I didn't say a word.

"I'm sorry," he added before hanging up.

With no close friends to console me, I cried alone in my room for weeks.

No boyfriend, no self-worth. I'm not sure when or how I came to that conclusion, but there was no shaking the idea from my psyche. I spent the rest of the summer sulking.

27

TONY

Shortly after the start of my junior year, Tony noticed me watching him. He was standing at one end of a long, green table. Newly elected president of the senior class, his first order of business was to find a place where ping-pong tournaments could be held. An empty spot in the cafeteria met the requirement. During lunch and before and after school, kids lined up waiting their turn. As soon as Tony volleyed a game-winning serve, he laid down his paddle and tossed me a bashful smile. I flushed all over.

A few days later the phone rang. It was him. After we talked several times a week for a couple of weeks, he made it official. "Would you like to see a movie?"

I couldn't say yes fast enough. He was mature, responsible, popular, and headed for pre-med. Tony would never dump me, never cheat on me. Most attractive to me, he was eighteen months older. Beyond smitten—and terrified of losing him—I clutched onto my new love.

One day in the middle of one long week, after he failed to call two days in a row, the phone rang.

I began my inquisition. "I didn't see you today in the cafeteria."

"We had a student council meeting. Went longer than expected."

"Really? Is that why you didn't call last night either?"

"Yeah...I mean no. Last night I was studying for a calculus test."

I let out some kind of a huff and he redirected the conversation, "Mary Jo is having a party this weekend. Do you want to go with me or not?"

"I don't know...I guess."

When we got to the party, I gripped his hand. We made our way to the living room, where we said hello to Mary Jo's parents. Tony required we do that first, to be respectful. Then we headed to the game room, where he chatted with his friends. The seniors talked about the basketball team and student council meetings and teachers. They talked about college.

Like a dog on a lead, wherever he went I followed but didn't engage. I didn't want to be there. Living with the constant fear our relationship could, at any moment, come to an end, I didn't want to share the little bit of time I had with him. So, when the opportunity allowed, like a child, I tugged on his arm, "Can we go now?" Eventually he gave in and we snuck away to his car, kissing and talking, before he had to deliver me home.

Even though I clung to Tony with all my might, like Scarlet O'Hara at the barbeque, I craved the attention of every young man. Anytime a guy looked at me or flirted with me or paid me the least bit of attention, even if I had absolutely no interest in him, I couldn't resist. I batted my lashes and giggled right back.

More than half of the kids who attended grade school with me continued on to the affiliated Catholic high. Bobby Sue, from my eighth-grade cheerleader squad, was one of those girls. She had always been nice to me, even after she stopped me from getting into that car that awkward carnival night. Her best friend, Janice, also there that night, never spoke another word to me, except for the day she followed me into the high school bathroom.

"What do you want?" I stepped back as Janice stepped close.

With her beet red face inches from mine, Janice sneered at me through gritted teeth, "You better leave him alone."

I stuck out my chin and returned her squinted glare. "What are you talking about?"

"Ronny is *my* boyfriend."

"Well, *your* boyfriend approached *me*, and I'm not interested in him anyway."

"Keep your paws off." She poked her finger into my chest. "I'm not kidding." She turned and left.

Needing more male attention than other girls, I knew I was different. I just didn't understand why—not until that day, years later, when my memories returned.

28

WRITE BUT DO NOT SEND

In the first few months after my memories returned, although my daughter Lizzi occasionally visited her dad, she stayed with me. More than self-sufficient, her only requirement was to eyeball me each morning as confirmation that I was all right. For my daughter's sake as much as mine, even though I lacked my usual boundless energy, I dragged myself out of bed. I cleaned the house, tended to the dirty laundry, and paid the bills. With funds quickly dwindling, I needed to find a job. After the daily newspaper arrived, I combed through the employment ads, sent out my resume, and reached out to friends.

Beyond the household tasks remained my most important focus. A duty that in all of its pain and heartbreak would not be suppressed and could not be denied—the hard work of healing. In the early mornings before I got out of bed, in the late evenings before I closed my eyes, and any free moment I could manage in between, I dug in.

I plowed through a little less than one-third of the book recommended by the PAAR therapist, *The Courage to Heal.* I accepted what I had remembered, took stock of the carnage, and honored what I had done to survive. And I wrote. I wrote to the unprotected child within me, to the parents who didn't understand the little girl crying out for help, and to the ex-fiancé who couldn't be there for me. I wrote to my abuser. Letters, as the workbook instructed, were never to be mailed. But on one occasion, in the middle of one sleepless night, somewhere after the chapter on Anger and before I completed Disclosures and Confrontations, even though the book and my counselor emphatically declared I should never do it, I decided Uncle Dean was going to hear what I had to say.

I tossed the big fat softcover across the unmade bed. I ripped a few blank sheets from my blue-lined journal. And I began. I told him what I remembered. I detailed how he had ruined my life. I yelled out loud as I scribbled in an oversized, thick, black, messy, childlike scroll, "It's my turn. I'm going to tell the world what you did."

Shaking, I creased the pages, shoved them into a #10 envelope, scratched out his home address, and affixed a stamp. I don't recall grabbing the keys, getting into the car, or driving. But as the moon hung high in the warm summer night, dressed in my ratty pink Minnie Mouse nightshirt, I found myself standing barefoot in front of a big, blue curbside box. My left hand held down the hinged lever; my right hand clutched my retaliatory note.

I don't know whether it was fear or a sudden burst of reason, but I stopped, turned, and with letter in hand, climbed back into my car. At home, I mounted the white step stool in my closet and stashed the sealed threat in a shoebox along with all of the others I had written but never mailed.

As I slid between the bed covers, I could not deny it. I felt better, lighter, maybe even hopeful. I'll never know if feeling better was a function of passing time, hard work, therapy, medication, or some combination of all of them. It didn't matter. That night I slept as I had not slept in months.

❧

A few days later, not two minutes after I had hung up from a telephone job interview, a job I was really hoping to land, through the office window in the front of the house, I noticed Tony's vehicle. He rounded the cul-de-sac and rolled to a stop. I raced out the front door, down the steps, and into the street.

The other children were finally home.

I stood at the top of the driveway hugging them. "I'm so glad you're here. I've missed you so much." Tears filled my eyes as I told them I would somehow earn their forgiveness. Somehow.

Tori and I giggled about getting manicures as the boys talked of all the things they had done with their dad. Everyone agreed to a family dinner, a reunion celebration. As we made our way into the house, I saw my daughter Lizzi peering through the family room window. She never left, but I never took her for a manicure. Never celebrated her staying behind to worry and care for me. Never told her she had saved my life.

29

SELLING THE HOUSE

By the end of that summer my tiny emergency fund was gone.

I didn't want to sell the house, but I had no idea if the new sales job I was set to start in a few weeks—commission plus a small base—would pay enough to cover the bills. So I called a Realtor who was active in my neighborhood.

Since gossip in the real estate world traveled faster than debris in a Cat 5 hurricane, I didn't hold back. "You've probably heard that Jack and I are apart. I need to sell the house."

"I'm sorry," Isabelle said sincerely.

"Me, too." I swallowed. "Anyway, my license is in referral, so I can't list it."

"I'm happy to help," she replied.

She came by the next day and I gave her the tour.

"What happened here?" She pointed to the ceiling.

"Toilet leak. Plumbing is fixed. Painter is coming."

After looking through the house, she suggested a few more

things I might want to do, then added, "I'm taking my mother to the old country for ten days. Let's get it listed when I get back."

❧

Two days later Tony met me at the oral surgeon's office. Both daughters were having their wisdom teeth removed. He sat with me in the waiting room and helped me load the woozy teens into the car. Then he followed me home and helped me get the girls into the house. As soon as they were tucked into bed, with barely a goodbye, he was gone.

The girls threw up on and off that morning, and I ran up and down the stairs bringing them ice and dental rinse. Around noon, after I delivered a dose of pain medication to each of them, I went to the kitchen for a cup of coffee and a needed break. As soon as I sat, my phone rang.

"This is Wilma. I'm an agent in Isabelle's office. Isabelle mentioned you'd be selling your home soon."

"Possibly…."

"I have a client in town from Germany. I've shown him everything in your neighborhood. Nothing fits. I'd like to show him your house before he heads to the airport today."

"Oh…my…I…I don't know," I stuttered, "My girls had oral surgery this morning. They aren't feeling well and the house is a mess and—"

"He'll understand. We'll be there a little before four. That will give you a few hours." She hung up.

I could have called her back and told her no, but I didn't. I raced around the house. I straightened the kitchen, shoved boxes into closets, and removed the six-foot ladder standing in the middle of the dining room, under the freshly painted ceiling. Despite just having had surgery, the girls cleaned up their bedrooms and the Jack-and-Jill bathroom they shared as best they could. The boys tidied their room and their bathroom, then helped me straighten the rest of the house. Calling it a flurry would have been an understatement. It was all hands and nonstop until I piled the kids into the car just minutes before the buyer and his agent arrived.

While she was still inside my house with her client, Wilma, the buyer's agent, called me inquiring about price. Isabelle and I had discussed a range, but we hadn't buttoned anything down. A firm believer that if you've hooked a fish, be grateful—especially if your line wasn't even in the water—I gave her a number at the bottom of the scale. With the buyer's wife on the phone across the ocean, he accepted. Contracts were written. Everyone signed.

Before the kids could get used to the idea, the house that Tony and I built, furnished and decorated, the house designed to give him and me a do-over, was under contract. Even though the property had been awarded to me in the settlement two years prior, selling the house made the divorce very real and very final. The kids felt the sting, and so did I.

30

A NEW PLACE TO CALL HOME

"I NEED A place *soon*," I told the leasing agent who occasionally helped Jack find tenants. "I have four kids and three miniature poodles."

"That's a lot," Colleen said.

"I know."

"I've got one coming: three beds, two and a half baths, a game room. No garage."

After my breakdown, although Zach visited, he lived with his dad full time. Still, I needed a room for Tori, Alex, and most of all, even though she was heading off to college, Lizzi.

Lizzi had gotten accepted to other schools, but wanted to attend Clarion with her best friend. Her admission there was conditional. We set up an interview and off we went. The day I drove her there, so far away, while I prayed for her acceptance, my heart ached. I was not only about to lose my oldest daughter; I was about to lose the one who had been there in my darkest hour—my best friend.

I had no idea how to let her go.

"Three bedrooms won't do. Need four."

"Not going to happen," Colleen said. "This is all I've got. It's all anyone has."

I didn't know how to make that work, but I'd figure it out. I had to. The bigger problem was timing. "Any chance I can get in there the end of August?"

"Tenants don't vacate until Sunday at 5:00. Monday is Labor Day. Carpet cleaning Tuesday morning. I can get you in later that day."

"Tuesday?"

"Do you want to take a look?"

"I don't need to see it. I'll take it." I had no choice.

Isabelle wasn't back from her trip to Poland yet, so I left a message for Wilma, the buyer's agent.

"What's the problem?" she asked when she returned my call.

"I'm unable to get into my new place until September 2. Can we delay the closing a few days, please?"

"Not possible," she snapped.

"But I don't have anywhere to go."

"Ask your *boyfriend* for help."

"I don't have a boyfriend." I hung up.

❧

While furniture sat in the sweltering moving van, the kids stayed with their dad. I stayed with a friend. When moving-in day arrived, bodies were everywhere.

"Where do you want this dresser?"

"How about this bed?"

I had moved several times before and was always prepared and organized. Not this time. With boxes unmarked and everything everywhere, it was a mess. I was a mess.

"Where do you want this?" one of the guys asked at the end of that long hot day.

"I don't know." I pointed. "Put it over there."

As the movers stacked the last of the stuff along the dining room wall, I went upstairs to make the beds.

Lizzi followed. "Where am I going to sleep?"

In preparation for the smaller space, I'd purchased a trundle bed for Tori's room. "Since you'll be at college, I was thinking that when you're home maybe you could share with Tori or share with me or take my bed and I'll sleep on the..."

"Mom, I can't find my toothbrush," Alex interrupted. "And where are the towels? I need a shower."

"I'll be right there," I told Alex.

I wanted to tell Lizzi about the last option, maybe the best option. We could set up a bedroom for her in the game room. Her own space. We'd go shopping together, pick out whatever furniture she wanted. I'd have it ready when she returned. But she started to cry—then she turned and left. She went to her dad's.

I should have chased her, stopped her, found some way to make it right. Too emotional and more than exhausted, I thought it would be better to deal with it another day. Another day never came. The child who wouldn't leave me in my time of need always believed I left her.

31

JACK RETURNS

After I got us settled in our new place and Lizzi off to Clarion University, I got myself packed and ready to depart for new job training in Philadelphia. Practically all of my work experience had been in real estate, but the people skills and sales strategies I honed there would serve me well when peddling office equipment and supplies. Making the transition a little easier, I'd be learning my new trade alongside my best friend Gail. She, too, had recently turned in her lockbox key for a nine-to-five paycheck with benefits. Together we made the five-hour trek to the eastern side of the state, where we met folks from other cities with a wide range of experience. During the day we focused on mastering the innovative digital, multi-functional equipment each of us would return home to sell. In the evenings many of the attendees traveled into the city to enjoy the sights, dine together, and shop. We exchanged phone numbers, planned reunion weekend trips that would never happen, and had a great time.

When I allowed myself to think about it, I ached for Jack and the life I no longer had. It was going to take me a long time to get past that. But as I climbed into that hotel bed on that last night, anticipating my new home and my new job, I couldn't deny that for the first time in months, I was hopeful about the possibilities that lay before me.

❧

Gail pulled her car to a stop in front of my townhouse.

I shifted in the passenger seat to face her. "Thanks for driving. It was a good time."

"It was," she said. "See you Monday."

"With bells on!" I slid my suitcase from her rear passenger seat and waved goodbye. When I turned around, I found Jack sitting on the stoop outside my front door.

"What do you want?" I asked as I approached. "And how did you know when I'd be home?"

"Alex told me," Jack answered softly.

"Really?" I stuck the key in the lock.

"Can we talk?"

"About what?" I pushed the door open and reached for my suitcase, but Jack had already grabbed it.

"I've been seeing a therapist," he said as he followed me inside. "She told me to stay away." He bowed his head. "She said it would be best if you did this on your own—"

"Best for who?"

"I know." His face was sad, his voice sincere. "She was wrong." He took a breath. "It took me a long time to figure that out. I hope it wasn't too long."

Even though I was wounded and angry that he had abandoned me in my time of need, even though I was terrified he'd leave me again, I was desperate for his love and acceptance.

"This isn't going to be easy." I crossed my arms.

"I know."

"No, you do not know."

"You're right. I don't."

"You're going to have to be at my side—through good and bad. Sometimes you'll have to join me in therapy."

"I will."

Not wanting to appear anxious, I took a breath and acted like I had to consider the idea. "I suppose we can see how it goes."

He wrapped his arms around me. I should have resisted. I should have discussed it with the kids. I didn't. If Jack could love me, I was lovable.

❧

Weeks later, at a joint therapy session, Jack opened up. "I didn't understand. Who does that to a child?"

The therapist, Joyce, pinched her lips.

"And your reaction was so, I don't know, big. It scared me."

"It scared me, too." I went on to tell him about the "onset of my emergency" as the therapist at PAAR had called it.

"I guess I was afraid…" he said.

I nodded and looked down. "I'm still afraid." My eyes began to well.

"I didn't know if you could heal. And what if it comes up again?" I heard the worry in Jack's voice.

"Life has triggers," Joyce intervened. "Things come up when you least expect." Jack looked at her as she continued, "Over time the eruptions will occur less frequently, but they will always arrive with the same unearthing vengeance."

I repeated those words in my head: "*With the same unearthing vengeance.*"

"Can you handle that?" she asked Jack.

"I'll try," he said.

He said he'd try. I couldn't ask for more than that. My shoulders softened and I felt myself relax—just a little.

32

THE TRIGGER

JACK HANDED ME a Valentine's Day card. "Open it. Come on. Come on. Open it."

Inside, opposite the heartfelt verse, was a handwritten a note.

Will you go away with me on a romantic Valentine's Day weekend?

He had planned a trip to Waldon Country Inn and Stables, a five-star resort and spa.

I jumped into his arms. "Yes. Yes. Yes."

The weekend came and with the kids at their father's, I gathered a few last items while Jack loaded the car. As he stepped back into the house, my phone rang. To most it would have been nothing more than an obnoxious telemarketer. But to me that soft, raspy voice persuading, manipulating—the sound of his breath, hard against the receiver—was all too haunting to ignore.

"You know you want this. You know how good this is going to be. I won't take no for an answer. I'm not going to hang up until you agree."

It wasn't what the caller said, but how he said it. It was his voice—that piercing, whispering voice. Even though there was nothing outwardly threatening or sexual, almost instantly I became an unprotected seven-year-old in the arms of my abuser. As though it was happening all over again, I could feel him. I could see his Adam's apple moving up and down in his long, thin neck. I ran to my room and buried myself beneath the covers.

"Linda? Linda?" Jack sat on the side of the bed. "What's going on?" He rubbed my arm. "Did something happen?" Then he seemed to figure it out. "It's okay. It was just a phone call. You're safe. I won't let anyone hurt you." He sat quietly for a moment and then stood, clapped his hands twice, and said, "Let's go. We've got a great weekend planned."

I couldn't move.

"Come on. Don't do this."

After an unsuccessful hour, he left. I spent the next two days alone, in tears, in bed, under the protection of the blankets that somehow made the child inside me feel safe. Finally, the feeling passed and the memories returned to their place—in waiting.

33

FORGING AHEAD

Over the coming months, as I went about the hard work of healing, Jack had the difficult task of supporting me. At times it seemed it was harder on him than it was on me, but he hung in there. In fact, he did more than just hang in there. When he arrived home late one evening, I was seated on the sofa watching television. He approached me, took the remote from my hand, and clicked off the television. He told me where he had been.

"You went to PAAR?" I repeated, stunned. "Tonight?"

He nodded as he sat down next to me.

"I can't believe you would do that *for me*."

"I can't believe what I saw. Some of those women were so angry." He looked down. "One of them actually bought a gun. She was going to kill her abuser."

Understanding how that woman felt, I nodded. But I did not say a word.

I don't remember everything we discussed that night. And

given some of his comments, I wasn't quite sure if he understood, but I didn't care. He went to PAAR—*on his own.* I couldn't ask for more than that.

❧

By the time I approached the first anniversary at my new job, I had risen to the number two salesperson. With township meetings and engineering changes behind him, Jack was ready to launch his next residential development—just five walking minutes from my townhouse. By that time, Jack was practically living with me again. This time, while he awaited the delivery of his sales trailer, even his office was in my game room. As Jack had done before, he maintained his apartment, forty minutes away, but that didn't matter. He was always on the job site, at one of my children's activities, or at my townhouse. And our relationship was the best it had ever been. We laughed more, loved more, and trusted one another again.

One evening after dinner Jack said, "What do you think about a trip to Caneel Bay?

"I've never been. I'd love to go."

"Over Thanksgiving?"

Thanksgiving was one of two holidays we always celebrated at my mother's house. She wanted all of her children around the holiday table, but I'd poke a hole in my mother's wishes in a heartbeat to go away with Jack. "Yes. Yes." I smiled broadly.

"Maybe we could get married?" he casually added.

"What?" I slapped his shoulder. "Don't joke about *that.*"

"I'm serious." He pulled from his pocket the ring I had thrown at him. He slipped it on my finger.

His daughter's response to our first engagement hadn't surprised me.

"Why her?" She wailed through the phone. "She broke up our

family." Her sobbing and yelling came through loud and clear. "You can have anyone you want. I'm not kidding, Dad. Anyone—just not *her.*"

This time she said only, "You better not give her what is rightfully ours."

"She's right," Jack said as he hung up the phone. "We should have a prenup."

Even if his daughter hadn't insisted, I suspected Jack wanted one. Unlike his ex-wife who came from a wealthy and generous family, Jack had earned every penny he had by himself.

Jack's father couldn't keep a job. In a time when most women stayed home, his mother had to work. Despite her full-time schedule or the commute, dinner had to be on the table at exactly 6:00. Her husband insisted, and Jack's mother didn't mind. The sooner she got food into her inebriated husband, the sooner she could minimize his meanness that brewed from the drink.

When Jack was in middle school, his father landed a job selling building materials for expensive homes being constructed in the newly developing suburb of Franklin Park. "It's where the rich people live," Hank announced. Around that same time Jack's only, older brother began running with a rough inner-city crowd.

"It's time to go," Hank told his family. Then, with his own two hands and the help of his two sons, he built a three-bedroom, two-story, all-brick home in Franklin Park.

Not long after moving his family out of their inner-city rental, his father lost that sales job, possibly as the result of his drinking, or maybe because he stole from work to build that house for his family. In a neighborhood grounded in financial comfort, the loss of his job gave Hank more time and more reason to drink. The more he drank, the quicker he lost the next job and the next. The clerical salary his mother earned wasn't enough to provide for her family, satisfy her husband's insatiable thirst, and keep stride with the neighborhood's big corporate incomes. Jack went from being equal to his inner-city friends to being the new kid who couldn't compete in the haughty suburb.

During his eighth-grade summer, Jack's classmate and first love, Sally Pryce, took Jack to her country club for lunch. They sat at a big, round table, under a green-and-white-striped umbrella, at one end of the Olympic pool. Served by polite staff in starched white uniforms, Sally and Jack ate burgers bigger than any Jack had ever seen. Then Jack witnessed something amazing. Rather than paying for the food they enjoyed, Sally signed something called a chit.

"That's when I realized money was a source of privilege and power," Jack told me. Then he added, "At that moment, I became determined. Someday, I would have that lifestyle, too."

Working for every dime, Jack achieved for himself a thriving real estate business, a prestigious stone home atop a knoll in Franklin Park, a fancy car, respected and well-connected friends, a twenty-four-unit apartment building, a condo on the beach in Clearwater, and a membership to the exclusive Chairman's Club. Of course, it didn't hurt that his wife worked long and hard and remained one of the most successful real estate agents in the high-priced area.

When divorcing Joan, Jack undervalued the assets on his side of the ledger. When he handed his asset list to me, it came as no surprise that he embellished his income and weighted his worth. I didn't care about any of that.

"I'm happy to sign a prenup so long as it says what you bring into the marriage is yours, what I bring is mine. But the growth on the assets belongs to the couple. Anything we earn or acquire during the marriage is marital." I understood that to be law, so

I didn't think a prenuptial was necessary. But if he wanted it in writing, that was fine by me.

"That's fair," he agreed. "I'll have Marcus write it up." Marcus was a close personal friend of Jack's and a reputable, soft-spoken attorney.

❦

On a blustery October day six weeks before the wedding, I arrived home to find a manila envelope laying on my dining room table. Jack had left it there for me. I opened it, slid out the stapled document, and began to read.

"This isn't right." The words burst from my lips. The legal jargon was confusing and I could have been getting it all wrong, but the pages I held in my hand seemed to say what was his remained *his*. The growth on his assets would be *his*. Anything he bought during the marriage or earned during the marriage would be *his*. He could give away anything he wanted. He could purchase anything he wanted. I had no say and no right to any of it—*ever.*

Betrayal rushed through my veins. I didn't seek advice, think it through, or formulate a strategy. I did what I always did. I grabbed the phone and started yelling. "How could you?"

And "Why?"

And "How dare you. I won't sign this."

He listened without a word, and when I took a breath, he calmly said, "No prenup, no wedding."

For the second time, the engagement was off.

After I left for work the next morning, a moving van hauled Jack's belongings out of my ratty little three-bedroom rental. When I arrived home at the end of the day, there was a message on the house answering machine confirming the cancellation of our wedding.

Later that evening I sat on my side of my bed staring at the bulging, white-zippered bag that hung on the back on my bedroom door. In it was the dress I would not wear.

❧

Ten days later, I woke to pounding on my front door. It was 2:00 a.m. There was only one person it could be. I peered through the blinds. His Jeep sat out front. Determined to ignore him, I climbed under the covers, pressed the pillow over my ears.

As my phone rang and rang, Jack banged on the door while shouting up at my window, "Open this door. I mean it, Linda. Open this door."

Finally, I grabbed the phone. "Have you lost your mind? Someone will call the police."

"I don't care. Open this door or I'll break it down. I mean it."

He was drunk enough to do just that. With an outward huff but true inner delight, I padded down the stairs and unlocked the deadbolt.

He stepped inside and threw his arms around me. "I don't need a prenup. I need you."

That's all I needed to hear.

34

PRENUP #2

EVEN THOUGH I hated the idea of a prenuptial agreement, I hated even more having our marriage shadowed by the lack of a document Jack had to have. So I suggested we try again. "Find a compromise. Meet in the middle."

Jack's close friend Marcus, the attorney who created the first prenup, recommended an independent, resolution-based legal mind, Joel, who would draft a prenuptial we could both live with.

Coming from different locations that day, Jack and I met at Joel's downtown office.

"How ya doin'?" my future husband greeted me in a sing-song tone with a kiss and a smile.

Joel stepped into the waiting room. Jack stood, shook the hand of the award-winning lawyer, and followed him. I followed Jack. We sat.

"You'd like me to draft a prenup?" Joel asked.

"Yes," Jack said.

Joel gathered information about age, income, dependents, addresses, dates of previous marriages and divorces. Jack did most of the talking. Then Joel asked about assets. Jack handed him the same overvalued list he had included in our first prenup. I didn't need a list. I had a little over one hundred thousand dollars—the equity from the sale of my home—and a seven-year-old, high-mileage Lincoln Continental. That was it.

After making a few notes Joel looked up at us. "I think I have what I need." Then he turned to Jack and said, "Will you excuse us, please? We'll see you in the waiting room in a few minutes."

I didn't understand what was happening, but Jack must have. Without question, he got up and stepped out of the room, closing the door behind him.

Joel put down his pen and leaned back in his big, comfy swivel chair. "Are you sure you want to do this?"

"It's give and take." I shrugged. "Right?"

"What about the business?" he asked.

"What about it?"

"Do you want to give up your rights?"

My rights?

I worked at Jack's side every single day for five years. I helped him launch that business. I helped him build it. Together we were unstoppable. At least that's how it felt to me. I imagined we'd work together again one day, maybe after the wedding. For now, we worked apart. That was my doing. He never asked me to quit. I chose to walk away. I got another job. Besides, Jack and I weren't married. Didn't that make the business his?

"I don't know what rights I have. But I suppose if I have any, I'd like to keep them."

Joel stood. "Come on." He made his way around his desk. "Let's find Jack."

A few weeks later Jack and I sat in the very same chairs in the very same waiting room. Paperwork complete, we had come to sign. This time Joel called us back to his office one at a time. Jack first, then me.

When it was my turn, Joel handed me the bound document. I flipped to the signature page and grabbed a pen. Jack had already signed.

"Would you like me to review it with you first?"

If Joel recited any of the details contained in those pages, I never heard a word. I wanted it signed. I wanted it finished. I wanted to marry Jack.

In mid-November, before we left for the wedding, I received the invoice from Joel. I paid it from my Christmas fund—the only money I had.

35

FIRST HUNDRED DOLLAR BILL

My father brought home the first hundred-dollar bill I ever saw.

It was shortly after he opened his own auto repair business. Daddy waved those riches high over his head in a kind of celebratory man-dance. Daddy looked silly. Shari and I giggled behind cupped hands. Tears ran down Mom's face. Although I had only ever seen Mom cry when she was sad or spitting mad, this time she was happy. My little sister and I didn't understand the importance of that dyed green paper that fluttered wildly over Daddy's head, but it was about to change our lives.

My parents talked often about how hard things had been. I don't know if they wanted us to appreciate what we had or what they endured, but they told the story so many times Shari and I would put our hands over our ears and chant in unison, "You already told us that." They didn't care. They went on and on about how they arrived home from their honeymoon, unaware of Mom's wedding night conception, to a note telling Daddy he no longer had a job.

The next few years Daddy installed roofs, carried bricks, and did other demanding physical jobs that didn't last and didn't pay enough to support us. Mom took in laundry, but that made more work and little money. She gave that up to become a cashier. Since my parents shared one beat-up vehicle that Daddy took to various construction sites, Mom had to cart my sister and me by streetcar to her friend who watched us for free. Then she'd trolley to the grocery store, stand for her entire eight-hour shift ringing and bagging, until it was time to repeat the convoluted journey back home with tired, cranky kids.

We loved spending that summer at Aunt Rainie's house. She wasn't really our aunt, but Mom told us to call her that. She had two boys and one girl around the same ages as Shari and me. And she had a large, hilly side yard. It was thick with natural vegetation and the tallest trees. We built forts and played hide and seek and climbed trees for hours. A tiny creek ran through the side yard and Aunt Rainie repeatedly told us not to get wet, but we always did. She never got mad at us though. She'd just change our clothes and pack the wet ones in a brown paper bag for Mom to take home.

Mom's exhausting attempt to hold down a job ended the day she picked Shari and me up at Aunt Rainie's house so poison ivy-infested we required bed rest, ice packs, and medication! I told Mom that Aunt Rainie's kids had it too; I don't think that made my mother feel any better.

I was about seven when Daddy landed a full-time, well-paying position as an auto mechanic for Smithton Chrysler. From the time he was little, Dad could build or fix just about anything. I once saw him tear apart a dead radio. When he finished, despite a pile of left-over parts, music and news flowed with crystal clarity from that little brown box. But of all the things Dad could disassemble and put back together, he especially loved cars. This new job was the chance he'd been waiting for. It didn't take him long to get his state inspection license and a big promotion to head mechanic. It took Daddy even less time to realize he could make a lot more money working for himself.

"It's a risk I think we should take," he whispered to my mother as they sat in the living room after dinner one night. Typically, Mom had something to say about everything. That day all she could do was nod. It was a hesitant nod at that.

But Mom and Dad didn't need to worry. Almost instantly Dad's business showed a steady stream of income. There was plenty of money for new shoes, sometimes two pair when I couldn't make up my mind. (But that only happened when Dad took us shopping.) Shari and I no longer had to rummage through Mom's old purses looking for coins or return glass milk bottles for pennies to buy candy. Daddy was always in a good mood, whistling and smiling and twirling Mom around the living room. The heavy weight Mom had carried since the loss of her first child seemed to magically disappear, like morning fog under a summer sun. For a short while, Mom and Dad stopped fighting about almost everything, except Dad's parents who seemed to appear even more often, asking for even more money.

One night, a little more than a year after Daddy danced that first hundred-dollar bill across our green, thread-bare carpet, a very important question passed around the dinner table right along with the breaded pork chops and double-stuffed potatoes. Should we move into a new neighborhood and a bigger, fancier house? Or should we stay in the old inner-city frame insulbrick and build a huge addition to the two-bedroom, one-bath Craftsman-style home?

Growing up, Daddy had to work full-time to help support his mother and little brother, so he never graduated from high school. But in his freshman and sophomore year, he had become a championship swimmer. He sweetened the pot adding, "If we stay, we can have our own in-ground swimming pool, with a deep end and a diving board." He looked between Shari and me. "I'll teach you how to do cannonballs." Then, after a raised brow from Mom, he added with a chuckle, "After I teach you to swim." Shari and I giggled, as much at our own excitement as Daddy's delight.

Without thought for the declining neighborhood, Mom, who was terrified of change, immediately voted to stay in the same house and keep us in the same school near all of our—all of her—same friends. She emphasized the word *same* as though we'd be moving to Siberia and never see anyone we knew ever again. Shari and I quickly voted with Mom. Tracy was only about eighteen months at the time. Mom nodded at her highchair-bound little one until the curly-haired baby mimicked back, which Mom said counted as a vote.

It was unanimous. We were staying. Mom's pinched face, a combination of fear and anxiety, gave way to a rare and toothy grin. On that hot July night after doing the dishes, our required chore, Shari and I bounced from house to house in the non-air-conditioned neighborhood, boasting that we were getting a built-in, concrete swimming pool with a deep end and a diving board.

"My dad says you can come over and swim with us, but you have to call first. And one of your parents will have to come with you to make sure you don't drown."

The kids on the block asked hundreds of excited questions and, almost immediately, I felt the power of my newfound celebrity.

After that, Shari and I didn't go to Grandma's house anymore. I had no idea why. I didn't care. There was so much going on at home. With the help of his friends, Dad built a massive three-bedroom, two-full-bath addition, complete with a lower-level game room and kitchenette. By the end of August, we had a twenty-four-foot-long concrete swimming pool with, as he promised, a deep end and a diving board. From that point on, my sisters and I lived in one of the biggest houses in the neighborhood. Without so much as a penny in savings, we were totally dependent on Daddy to stay healthy enough to earn enough money each week. But as I watched my friends jump and swim and giggle and bob around in my swimming pool, my mother stirring up Kool-Aid or passing out popsicles she had split in half, I felt rich. I felt special. I had what other kids wished for.

It was a feeling I spent my entire adult life trying to recreate. To no avail—until Jack. And we were about to get married.

36

OUR WEDDING

To obtain a U.S. Virgin Island marriage license, we had to submit to the St. Thomas Courthouse, not less than eight working days prior to our arrival, a completed application, using our full names—no abbreviations. They also required court-certified copies of our divorce decrees, a letter to the court listing our arrival and departure dates, and the name of our officiant.

Jack took care of mailing all the required documentation, just as he took care of making the arrangements for our wedding and honeymoon. I was in charge of the folder containing the detailed itinerary and copies of our paperwork. My folder also contained a reference to Iris, the wedding coordinator.

As soon as we landed, Jack retrieved our luggage, then hailed the taxi that would take us to Red Hook, where we would board the ferry to St. John Island, a forty-minute water ride, the only way to Caneel Bay, a five-star Rockefeller resort. But first we had to pick up our official paperwork.

In less than ten minutes the taxi pulled up in front of the St. Thomas courthouse. Jack leaned over the high-back seat and handed our dark-eyed driver a large tip. "Wait here for us, please."

The man nodded, then, realizing what Jack had handed him, grinned widely, exposing a large gap between two over-sized front teeth.

I didn't expect the courthouse to be so stately. Clearly, they conducted more important business than merely issuing marriage licenses.

"Appropriate attire required. Where do you think you are?"

I spun my head to see a security guard refuse entry to a man wearing flip-flops. Thank goodness I had on my comfortable, yet appropriate, kitten heels.

Moving through the cordoned line was, I am sure, not at all as slow as it felt to me. Finally we made it to the large wooden desk where a beautiful woman, her face full, her hair pinched back into in a tight bun, looked sternly at us over her readers. Through the opening below the glass, Jack passed over our paperwork.

The clerk examined our documentation. After glancing back and forth several times between our faces and our passport photos, she returned our identification and the official marriage license we would deliver to our minister. "Congratulations," she said with a smile. As we turned, she called out in a most authoritative voice, "Next."

The taxi driver took us from the courthouse to Red Hook, where ferries departed for St. John on the hour. With ropes untied, the vessel began its journey. In addition to Jack and me, there was a handful of passengers aboard; however, no one else was staying at Caneel Bay. Crossing the wide channel, the open-air boat gently cut through the soft, frothy caps, filling the air with the smell of fish and the taste of sea salt.

Forty-five minutes later, as the boat inched into the dock, each passenger received a warm hand towel to clean away the spray. After I freshened up, a crew member guided me onto the dock. I giggled at the pickup-turned-taxi waiting for us. A bench seat lined each long side of the six-foot bed while a red striped canopy stretched tightly overhead. Jack took my hand as I climbed the homemade ladder. After luggage was safely stowed, he took a seat next to me and the truck began its bumpy ascent. We pulled into what appeared to be a small, empty cobblestone area, then rolled to a stop. The taxi driver helped us out, placing our luggage at our side. Then he drove away. I don't recall seeing a telephone or hearing anyone announce our arrival, but suddenly, out of nowhere, a golf cart appeared.

"No cars allowed on property," the driver explained as we made our way along the narrow path bordered by thick vegetation and the most gorgeous flowers I had ever seen. At the check-in area the driver said, "They'll take care of you from here." He placed our luggage at a designated spot, tipped his hat, and disappeared. After handing the clerk a credit card, Jack looked around for our bags.

"They've been taken care of, sir," the sweet young lady behind the desk whispered. Then she put her hand in the air and a young man appeared. While leading us to Cottage Seven, once the private home of Laurance Rockefeller, the man asked, "What brings ya to our beautiful island this beautiful day?"

"We're getting married." Jack squeezed my hand.

"Married, yo man! Congratulations to ya now." Then he unlocked the room, pushed open the door, and handed Jack the key. "I'll wait here, sir, while ya and ya lady make sure everytin is to ya likin."

Decorated in rich native influences, the room featured a large, dark wooden, four-poster bed draped in light bedding. Wispy sheers framed two walls of windows that afforded the most spectacular panoramic view of the Caribbean. A wraparound flagstone patio extended the living space and the breathtaking vistas. Inside, our luggage had been unpacked, our clothes hung, my toiletries neatly arranged on the bathroom vanity.

Due to a conflict with our reservation, we would have to move to a different guest suite—still in Cottage Seven—after just one night. One room nicer than the next, it didn't matter to us. We returned from dinner the next night to find our belongings again unpacked and meticulously placed in our new accommodation. A complimentary bottle of champagne and two flutes had been left by the resort. It was the night before our wedding. Jack popped the cork.

"To our last night single." I held up my glass.

"To the rest of our lives together." He pinged his flute against mine.

We didn't know that Del, the jewelry-making minister, needed to review with us a few last-minute wedding details. He called the front desk after we had checked out, but before the guest registry showed us in another room. He thought we left and almost cancelled our wedding. Iris saved the day.

Besides no phone or television, rooms did not have an alarm clock (and we didn't have cell phones). I'm not sure how or when Jack made the arrangements, but the morning of the wedding I was awakened to a gorgeous baritone softly singing "Good morning to you" just outside our door. When I opened my eyes, I saw my dress hanging on the back of the opened bathroom door. It was our wedding day.

I hadn't gone dress shopping with anyone. I already had had the big dress and packed church and four-hundred-person reception. None of that seemed appropriate the second time around. One day during my lunch hour, I zipped over to Saks Fifth Avenue, located the formal department, and pushed through racks in search of something that would complement the black dress slacks and white silk shirt Jack planned to wear. I tried on only one item. The dress was ivory and simple and elegant. It fit like it was made for me. Done.

The wedding coordinator arrived around 10:30. Ever so carefully she placed a ring of tiny, tightly woven, soft pink buds over the crown of my head. I looked at myself in the mirror. That's when it became real. Jack was about to get the exciting, young wife to complete his otherwise perfect life. I was about to get the older, wiser Prince Charming to make my fairy tale come true.

"Ready?" Iris asked.

Holding a brilliant Bird of Paradise bouquet, I followed Iris. Jack followed me. Settled in the rear of the golf cart, we giggled and waved to folks who applauded or gave a thumbs up, as Iris drove ever so slowly across the grounds. At Turtle Bay Point we took our places and waited. On cue, arm in arm, Jack and I stepped across the grassy aisle toward Minister Del, who performed our nuptials overlooking the crystal-clear Caribbean. After the ceremony, two native women standing off to the side offered bubbling champagne in crystal flutes. Those women were also the witnesses who signed our marriage license along with Del, the jewelry-making minister.

We were married. It was Thanksgiving Day. With the photographer snapping photos, we walked hand in hand through the white sand as frothy water lapped over our feet. I had more than I could ever want, more than I could ever need. I could never be thankful enough.

37

OUR FIRST HOME TOGETHER

WE ARRIVED HOME from our wedding to my tiny, dated, three-bedroom rental. With two teenagers and three dogs, I told Jack I needed a house. Truth is I wanted to replace the home I no longer had. Jack was past that stage in life. He didn't want to cut grass or repair roofs. So he built for us an 1,800-square-foot, maintenance-free townhouse in his newest development, Canterbury. The unit provided first-floor living for him and me, while the second floor had two bedrooms and a bathroom for my kids. Having evolved from changes we made at our Longview development, the floorplan was a sought-after design for which Jack had quickly became known.

Not long after we moved into our new home together, I learned that when you're married to a builder, your home is open to the public. In addition to showing the professionally decorated model, Jack always invited prospective buyers into our house to see where and how we lived. He wanted them to witness the benefits of our low-maintenance lifestyle. More than that, a builder willing to live in the neighborhood sent a strong message of integrity and quality. He would be right there should a problem arise.

We had been in our new townhouse about eighteen months and I was back in the business with my husband when a tall, thin, well-spoken teacher toured the model. As usual, Jack guided her through our house. She loved the size and upgrades we had made to our home and didn't want the higher cost or larger footprint of the new units we were building across the street.

"I'd like to buy yours," she said.

We signed the contract and Jack got to work on the new townhouse across the street that would be ours. Already under construction, it was ready for cabinetry, countertops, and flooring to be ordered. Working my previous job, I hadn't made any of those choices for the home we currently lived in; the decorator had done that. Although the home was beautiful, Jack knew it wasn't my style. Wanting this next house to be everything I desired, he said, "Make it yours."

"Really?"

"Anything you want."

At my request, he extended the footprint and redesigned the master bedroom and master bath with a see-through fireplace and a claw foot tub. He allowed me to reconfigure the cherry kitchen into a U shape with beautiful granite, and he added built-ins to my daughter's upstairs bedroom. In the end that townhouse was gorgeous—more than I hoped it would be. To this day it stands out as my favorite.

But Jack gave me more than five-star trips and brand-new homes. Being with him afforded me an opportunity I wouldn't otherwise have had—an opportunity to help my parents.

38

GIFT OF A NEW CONDO

AT THE PRIME income-earning age of forty-seven, my father ventured from doctor to doctor. No one could figure out why his brain, wanting to write a check or ratchet a bolt, was unable to make his hand perform the small motor task. It wasn't long before the gait of his walk began to shift. He did not swing left arm with right leg, right arm with left leg. Of course if you didn't know what to look for, you probably wouldn't have noticed any more than I did.

A friend of mine, married to a physician, was truly concerned. She asked her husband to look at my dad. He agreed. After sharing dinner with my parents and Tony and me in the dining room of our Cape Cod starter home, John escorted my father down the hall and into our bedroom. Although he did not label it, John recognized the culprit. He referred my father to a well-known neurologist. Dad took the first available appointment.

"Would you walk across the room for me?" the neurologist asked.

Dad did as the doctor instructed, then returned to his seat.

"You have Parkinson's disease, Joe."

"My grandfather had it," my dad replied. Or maybe he said it was his uncle. But whichever relative, that man was nowhere near as young as my dad.

"We don't often see it in patients as young as you," the doctor explained. "That's why it's been so difficult to diagnose."

As his disease progressed, my father's ability to perform fine motor functions diminished. Gross motor skill followed. Without a bathroom on the first floor, Dad had to climb the steep steps that did not have a handrail. Sometimes Dad managed fine; other times he fell all the way to the bottom, landing with a thud.

Years later, in the advanced stages, Dad suffered classic uncontrollable shaking and jerking. Tremors so furious at times they could wiggle him out of his chair and under the table in whatever restaurant my parents had gone to for a quiet meal. Once my father accompanied my mother to the liquor store to buy a bottle of Canadian Club for a small gathering my mother was hosting. The clerk refused to sell it to her claiming my father, shuffling and stumbling and clutching onto her, was drunk. He wasn't drunk. He didn't drink. The man couldn't even take a sip with the medication he was on. The clerk didn't care.

Shari and I didn't care what others thought. We cared about Dad's safety. We never knew from day to day how he would feel or when he would suffer the next fall.

In addition to the wrath of Parkinson's, my father's body was further taxed by the heart condition he inherited from both of his parents. Dad suffered three heart attacks, blocked arteries that required stents on several occasions, and a ruptured abdominal aortic aneurism that, despite a 90 percent chance of death, he somehow survived.

As my father's health declined, so did the neighborhood around him and the house he had totally renovated when I was a child. My parents couldn't afford to repair what needed to be fixed, particularly after Dad's unreliable body took from him his once thriving business. After a lengthy legal battle and many months without income, Dad won a small monthly stipend of Social Security disability. Not nearly enough. The proud couple who always paid their bills were forced into bankruptcy.

My mother's only work experience, punching at the round black keys of an old-fashioned cash register that no longer existed, offered little opportunity. Finally she and her best friend, who lived two doors up, both with ailing husbands and lacking funds, found jobs in the processing department of a downtown bank. Together they rode the bus to work and, when done, rode the bus home. New to that job market, neither had any idea they would be working under a taskmaster who demanded lengthy overtime despite limited transit schedules or the unattended sickly spouses who waited at home. Each night my mother returned home totally exhausted to a needy husband and a messy house.

❧

By the time Jack and I married, Shari and I were receiving monthly calls.

"The furnace isn't working."

"A pipe burst."

"Dad fell down the stairs, again."

It wasn't long before those calls started coming weekly. "Dad's had another heart event. Meet us at the hospital." Which, most of the time, was Allegheny General, the closest trauma center. Thank goodness the ambulance station sat at the bottom of the hill just below their house.

While Jack and I made the forty-minute anxiety-ridden trek

toward the ER, unsure what we'd find there, my concerns weren't only about my dad. Rather than wait for one of us to pick her up, my mother, shaking and crying, followed the ambulance in her less-than-reliable car.

Far on the other side of town, drinking expensive wine in my new, professionally decorated, maintenance-free home, with a sizable income and regularly scheduled full-body massages, I watched in horror as my parents struggled and suffered. I needed to do something.

I approached Jack. "I want to buy a townhouse in our neighborhood for my parents."

Without hesitation he said yes. He had done the same for his aging parents. When the cold winters made it too difficult for his frail mother to breathe, Jack sent his parents to live in his condo along the shores of the Gulf of Mexico in Clearwater, Florida. Jack's mother loved it there. She made friends and volunteered every day at the bird sanctuary. Jack made a difference in the length and quality of his parents' lives. He wanted to make that same kind of difference for my parents, too.

With the goal at hand, one evening after dinner Jack and I met my parents at their home. My father's mind was, for the most part, almost as sharp as it had always been. Still, while Dad hobbled around the dining room table, necessary to keep his leg muscles from painful cramping, we talked exclusively to my mother. Dad watched and listened; he never interrupted.

"Linda and I want to finish one of our townhouses for you." Jack emphasized the benefits of having everything on one level. "Linda will be just four doors away."

"Mom, you can pick out your cabinets, your countertops, the color of the paint on the walls, down to the last detail. I'll own it, but it will be your home. I mean that. And it will be brand new. If something does go wrong, you don't have to worry. Call me."

"That's so generous. Really." My mother adjusted in her seat. "But this is our home."

"Come on, Elsie." Jack looked at my mother. "A brand-new home with no steps for Joe. You know this is best for the two of you."

I saw the horror in my mother's face. I told myself, *She's scared. She doesn't understand how wonderful this is going to be. She'll see.*

With an anxious buyer wanting to purchase this last available unit, we needed an answer. Convinced we knew best, Jack and I pushed. Finally, a few weeks later, she surrendered. My sister called a Realtor she knew and in just a few days the For Sale sign perched proudly in the front lawn of my parents' home. My mother began forcing forty-one years of life into small cardboard boxes.

She was about to leave the home she had painstakingly designed, decorated, and scrubbed spotless. What to do with the baby grand piano that hadn't been tuned since I stopped playing around the age of, I don't know, ten? Who would take the barely-sat-on furniture in the "big living room," as she called it, where every year the oversized Christmas tree toppled out of its stand? She had to say goodbye to her prized, oversized blond dining room set where the overcooked turkey and all of its trimmings were joyously passed. And she had to walk away from the in-ground pool, for which she and my father had paid forty-seven dollars a month for nine years. It was the neighborhood home where family and friends gathered every summer to enjoy cannonball splashes, hamburgers on the grill and the heartwarming laughter of children and grandchildren. This was the home my father doubled in size with his own two hands. The home they planned to stay in forever.

My mother was parting with memories, giving up hosting her holidays, saying goodbye to traditions, and moving away from friends. She was leaving the only home she ever owned and moving into one she that would never be hers. If that wasn't enough, at sixty-four she was giving up her independence right along with whatever little money she and my father were about to get. For the purchase of the townhouse, I paid Jack $100,000, which I received when I sold my previous marital home. My parents added to it all of the proceeds from the sale of their house: $23,000. It was every nickel they had. Money I was too foolish to realize they needed.

Terrified of change, my mother embarked on the biggest, hardest change of all. She wasn't doing it because it was best for her or my father, even though in many ways it was. She wasn't doing it to protect assets should my father wind up in a nursing home. She was doing it because I made her. I had no idea that rather than giving them what they needed, I was taking what little my parents had.

As the movers muscled furniture out the door and onto the truck, my mother sat on her old green glider on the concrete front porch. She was sobbing so hard she could barely catch her breath.

She had every right to cry.

39

THE FAMILY PARTNERSHIP

SHORTLY AFTER MY parents settled into their new townhouse, Jack and I had our own moving day. A few minutes past noon I heard the door. From the center of my new kitchen, I peeked over a stack of unpacked boxes and saw Jack rushing toward me. In the driveway his car sat running, the driver's door opened wide.

"Forget something?" I unwrapped another glass.

Jack held out a stapled document. It was folded over to the signature page. "I need you to sign this." He handed me a pen.

"Sure. What is it?" He was always asking me to sign one document or another for the business or the bank, for the engineer or the township.

"This will protect the apartment building from the bank. You know—just in case."

A land deal required millions. The bank loaned 80 percent. We put up 20 percent by collateralizing our business and personal assets. In addition each of us had to sign a personal guarantee. If the deal went bad, the bank could take everything; nothing was off limits. Beyond that, they could hold us personally responsible for any unpaid debt. We heard about it all the time. This developer or that one went belly up. No matter how lucky or good, the risk was real. Protecting an asset, if possible, was paramount. Without reading, I scribbled my name.

❧

I don't remember how I discovered it or, for that matter, when. It probably had something to do with income tax or a slip of the tongue. When Jack drank too much of the silky scotch he so loved, he had trouble keeping secrets. No matter how it happened, one fateful day I learned those pages I had signed without reading created The Dunigan Family Partnership. Each of Jack's two children got 45 percent ownership of the twenty-four-unit apartment building. The remaining ten percent controlling interest belonged to Jack. Most likely that document wouldn't have saved the asset from the legal team at the bank, but it saved it from me.

I ripped into him. "How could you?"

"You're making too much out of this."

"How would you feel if I stole something from you?"

His face grew red. "I didn't steal anything from you."

"Undo it. I mean it. Right now."

"I will not." He rose from his chair, walked to the sink, poured his drink down the drain. Then he got into his car and drove away.

Jack couldn't live with the terms of our prenuptial, any more than he could live with the terms set forth by the bank. I couldn't live with the betrayal. After eighteen months of marriage and weeks of fighting, he moved out. I climbed into bed by myself. Again.

40

SITTING ON THE TOP STEP

When I was a child, my parents fought.

They were good at it. They fought in private. They fought right out in front of whomever they were with, wherever they found themselves, doing whatever they were doing. They didn't care. They fought over big things, like when my dad lent money to his parents, behind Mom's back, money my parents needed and his parents would never repay. They fought over little things like the decorated Christmas tree that toppled out of its stand breaking my mother's ornaments, or the name of that actress in that movie that neither of them could remember.

I don't know what my parents were fighting about one particular night, but they were going at it full tilt. The screaming was loud and the fighting was scary. The louder their voices got, the scarier it felt and the better I liked it.

I was sitting on the top step when Shari, white-faced, scurried out of our bedroom and plopped herself down next to me. She buried her little round face in my floral cotton nightgown. I was seven; she five. The screaming had woken her. Terrified her. Not me. I was drawn to it—the intensity and passion and excitement of it all—a fire I would rather be burned by than back away from. She needed me to hold her. I needed to be as close to the fighting as I could get.

Whatever our reasons, as our one-year-old baby sister slept unaware, nestled in her crib, Shari and I sat on that top riser of the steep, narrow staircase. Even though my little sister covered her ears, we both listened and we both heard.

"You're nothing but a low-life bastard from a worthless alcoholic family. They do nothing but take, take, take. Druggies. The whole bunch of them. Druggies," my mother wailed.

Anytime Mom said anything like that, the fights moved to the next level. I needed to be closer. I left Shari's side and tiptoed to the bottom. Engrossed in their full-scale onslaught, my parents never noticed me peeking around corner. Or maybe they saw me and didn't care.

"Bitch." Daddy didn't yell; he didn't threaten. He spoke just that one word. That's all it took.

"What did you just call me?" My mother, her face beet-red, thundered across the living room, grabbed his glass of icy Coca-Cola from the table beside his recliner and threw the cold, watery liquid into Daddy's face. He lunged for the tumbler. She raced out of the room, glass in hand. Game on.

Mom flew around the dining room table. Close behind, Dad swiped for the glass she held out in front of her. She tossed it from one hand to the other, out of his reach. When she dashed back into the living room, he tackled her onto the sofa. With one fluid motion, as she screamed and beat on his chest, as her legs kicked out wildly in all directions under him, Daddy pulled the glass from her hand and whaled the tumbler straight into the curved front of the black-and-white Magnavox. With a jolt and a zap, the picture tube shattered. That was the end of that. The room grew quiet, and for a second all movement stopped.

Daddy helped Mom to her feet. She dusted herself off and hissed at him, "Now look what you've done. I'm not cleaning that up."

That was my cue to get back to the top step, which I did in a hurry.

Mom stomped up the stairs and stepped past Shari and me, still huddled on the top riser. She went straight into her bedroom and packed a bag. On her way back down the stairs, she moved again around her two little girls. There was no mention of us being awake or out of bed or having heard their injuring words. She said only, "I'll be back for you later," like we were clothing or furniture to be dealt with at another time. As young as we were, we knew she wasn't going anywhere—at least not for long.

We were right. Just as she had done before, early the next morning she returned, timid and teary. Even though it was Mom who had started this fight, Dad apologized and asked her to come back home. I saw Dad as the strong one. Too strong. A bully. Truth is, he was neither the bully nor the instigator. He was the peacemaker. He mended fences and consoled my mother when she couldn't stop sobbing. He did it for her. He did it for us.

In the days that followed, behind closed doors, in a voice so soft she thought we couldn't hear, my mother whispered to her best friend how grateful she was to be home. She couldn't possibly support her children alone. But that wasn't the real issue. Dad knew then what my sister and I would come to understand later. Mom was afraid to be alone. She was afraid no one else would love her.

When Jack entered my life, my mother's panic became my own.

41

FIND YOUR OWN THERAPIST

Four days after our fight over the Dunigan Family Partnership and our first marital separation, Francesca, who preferred to be called Francie, marched across the street, homemade soup in hand. "You need to get out of this bed and eat something."

She was right. I was a mess. I pulled my pink bathrobe over the T-shirt and jeans I hadn't taken off in days and padded to the kitchen table. At her insistence I took a few sips of the best homemade chicken soup I had ever eaten. But even great soup couldn't rouse an appetite.

"I'll eat more later. I promise."

"You can't hole up in that bed forever, you know."

"I know."

"You need to get back to the business of living."

"I wish I knew how."

"Call that therapist you two were seeing. What was her name?"

I didn't answer.

"Anyway, maybe she can help."

Jack and I had been seeing Joyce, our therapist, since before we married. She advised us on how and when to go public and how and when to blend our families. Joyce was the therapist who told me to call the Pittsburgh Action Against Rape, and she helped us rebuild our relationship after. But she was also the therapist who told Jack I needed to do the healing on my own. After Francie left, albeit hesitantly, I dialed her.

"Hi Joyce, this is Linda."

"What can I do for you?" she asked.

"Jack left. I mean we're apart. I mean we're separated." I tripped over my tearful words. "I'm a mess. I'm sure you can tell." I forced a chuckle. "I really need to talk to someone. Do you have any openings?"

"I wish I could help you, but Jack is my client. If you two are no longer together, I cannot see you. I'm sorry. You'll need to find your own therapist."

42

FIXING WHAT HE BROKE

My birthday came two weeks into our first official marital separation. My children took me to dinner. It was wonderful having them all together and having them celebrate with me. What was not so wonderful was the sight and smell of food. I did not have an appetite. I took a few bites because I didn't want them to worry. But that was the most I could manage. The moment I arrived home that evening, as though the kids had somehow arranged it, Francie showed up with a candle stuck in a store-bought cupcake. I couldn't help but laugh.

Two days later I heard from Jack. "Can we talk?" he asked.

"About what?"

"About us?"

"There's no *us* to talk about."

"Give me a chance. Please. Tonight."

"I'm busy tonight," I insisted even though the only thing on my schedule was sulking alone.

"Tomorrow night?"

"I'm busy then, too."

"Cancel your plans."

"I will not."

"Then don't," he said. "I'll just follow you around wherever you go."

"Oh, for God's sake. Tomorrow night then."

When he knocked, I opened the door without a word. He trailed me to the family room. With a yellow tablet and a pen in hand, I sat on the sofa across from him. I was ready for whatever business discussion he wanted to have.

"I shouldn't have done what I did," he said.

"You're damn right. First you stole from me, then you lied to me, then you left me." I was seething.

"I didn't steal from you. I was protecting an asset."

"Protecting it from me."

"That was not my intention."

"I don't care. That's what you did."

"I was wrong."

"And it wasn't what you did. It's how you did it. I don't know if I can trust you again."

"I'll earn your trust."

"And I don't know how to be in a committed relationship with someone who doesn't stay."

"I won't leave you again."

"Yeah, right. Like I believe that. And you messed up my birthday." Tears slipped across my cheeks.

"I have your present right here." He patted the pocket of his jacket. "I was hoping I could take you to dinner for a proper celebration."

"I don't want to celebrate with you, and I don't want your gift."

He walked over to where I was sitting, took my hands, pulled me to my feet. With one hand under my chin, he tilted my head up to face him. "I love you, Linnie," he said softly. "I'm better when I'm with you. I'll make this up to you."

"What about leaving?"

"I won't leave you again."

"I don't know."

"I promise." He lowered his lips toward mine.

As soon as he looked at me, smiled at me, put his arms around me, I gave in. "You better not," I said as I closed my eyes and embraced his kiss.

43

CHANGING HIS WILL

For the next two years we worked hard. We sold townhouses faster than we could build them. We found more land and made more money than I'd ever seen. We jetted off on spontaneous romantic weekends, took vacations with Jack's brother, and visited Jack's friends. We bought a new BMW and lavished gifts on the children at Christmas. Then Jack rented, for just the two of us, a thirty-five-foot Power Catamaran. For two romantic weeks he captained us through the U.S. and British Virgin Islands. We dove off the side of the boat, swam among the turtles, picnicked in the sand. In the evenings, with the straps of my sandals between my teeth, I inched down the wobbly ladder toward my husband, waiting for me with open arms in the bobbing dingy. When I was safely aboard, he motored us ashore for food, music, and fun at Peter Island, Bitter End, and other world-famous resorts.

Anything I wanted, I could have, anything but the apartment building. Even though he promised he would put it back in my name, he never did. That left me always wondering what else he might do. Despite the insecurity, I resisted the urge to search his computer or dig through his desk. But if something was left on the computer screen or laid out on his desk for me to see it, I couldn't resist. As a therapist once said, "If you look you will find."

She was right.

Early one afternoon as the summer market was beginning to take a breath, almost two years to the day Jack last left, an appraiser tapped on the jamb of my door. "Hello," he called. "Anyone home?"

"Hi, Gene." I smiled at the always-pleasant man who stood before me. "How are you? How is Anita?"

"We're doing great. Thanks for asking. How about you?"

"Selling like crazy."

"I see that. Just finished…umm…" He glanced at the paper in his hand.

"Unit D, building three," I confirmed.

"Yes," he laughed. "Just need the PUD and I'll get out of your hair."

"Jack did it this morning. Let me get it." As soon as I approached my husband's desk, I saw it. Right there, in the center of his workspace, next to the Planned Unit Development form, as though it had been placed there for me to find, sat Jack's Last Will and Testament. It was all I could do not to grab it and read it, right then and there. I couldn't. But the minute Gene left, I raced back to Jack's office.

In addition to the prenuptial agreement, before we married Jack and I drafted reciprocal wills naming each other executor. Jack always believed he'd go first, but as I watched my girlfriend Daksha battle breast cancer at thirty-eight, I wasn't so sure. Our plan gave 50 percent to the biological children of the deceased,

50 percent to the surviving spouse. Apparently, he couldn't live with that arrangement either. In this new version of his will, upon his death his assets were to be distributed one-third to his daughter, one-third to his son, and one-third to me. I was no longer Executrix.

That evening as Jack kicked off his shoes, I launched into him. "First the apartment building. Now your will?" I followed him to the kitchen.

"What were you doing snooping around my desk?" He put ice into his glass.

"What were you doing changing your will?"

"I named Victor's son, Jay, my executor," he said as he poured himself a scotch.

"I see that. You also changed the distribution of your assets."

"Yep." He added a splash of water and rubbed the peel of an orange around the rim.

"Don't you want to take care of me? After all, you're the one who says I'm going to live a long time after you're gone."

"I think this is fair." He took a sip, then made his way to the family room.

"It's not what we agreed..."

"I'm not going to fight with you about this." He sat on the sofa and grabbed the remote.

"What in the hell does that mean?" I yelled. "This is wrong. It's not fair."

"I'm sorry you feel that way." He pulled his feet to the ottoman and turned on the TV.

From that point on, he left early each morning and returned late. Anytime we were together, at home or at the office, he was distant and secretive and angry. One evening a few weeks later, I raised the subject again. "It's not right." I fought tears.

"What's not right?" Shaking his head, he clicked off the television and looked at me.

"This thing with the apartment building and your will."

"I'm sorry you feel that way."

"Stop saying that to me!"

"What do you want me to say?"

"I want you to say you'll fix it."

"I'm not fixing anything." He drew a deep breath, then said, "I'm going to take ninety days to decide if I want a divorce."

"What?"

"I said I'm going to take ninety days to decide if I want a divorce."

"I heard you. What in the hell does that mean?"

"It means I'm leaving." He stood.

"What are you talking about? Leaving? When?"

"Leaving now."

I watched as he carried load after load to his car. His dress slacks, his blue jeans, his shirts. Finally, with gym bag in hand, he made his way to the front door. "I may need to come back to get a few more things."

I glared at him.

"I'll call you first."

It didn't matter that it was my birthday. It didn't matter that he promised he'd never leave me again. It didn't matter that I did not want him to go. The door closed and, for the second time since our wedding day, he was gone.

44

A DEAL HE COULDN'T LIVE WITH

Two weeks after Jack moved out for the second time, Francie slid into the booth across from me. "What in the world is wrong with that man?" She slipped on her readers and looked at the menu. "First the apartment building, now his will? And why is he always packing up and moving out around your birthday?"

"He probably didn't even think about my birthday."

"Obviously." She shook her head as the waitress approached our table.

"Something to drink, ladies?"

"Coffee and water," Francie answered.

"Same," I replied. When the waitress left to get our beverages, I continued. "This whole thing started with that apartment building. Wasn't even mine to begin with, but I can't get over it."

"Of course you can't. He breached your agreement."

"Why would he do that?"

"Struck a deal he couldn't live with."

"If he loves me wouldn't he want to provide for me after he's gone?

"Maybe it's time for *you* to take care of you," Francie said as the waitress returned with our drinks.

"Here you go, ladies. I'll be right back to take your order."

"It's not like any of us can count on Social Security." I stirred cream into my coffee.

"That's for sure." Francie took a sip of her hot brew.

"I don't know a thing about stocks or bonds."

"Then don't do stocks and bonds." She disappeared behind her menu. "Do what you know."

"The only thing I know is real estate."

"There you go. Find a way to use real estate to build your nest egg. And if he comes back…"

"He won't…

She lowered her menu and eyed me over her readers. "If he does, don't vary from your plan. And another thing, get your own job."

"But I love what I do…"

"Every time he leaves, you find yourself without a husband, without a therapist, without an income. Not a good place to be."

45

HIS MOTHER'S ENGAGEMENT RING

Weeks passed. He didn't call, didn't knock, didn't drive by the house. This separation wasn't going to be some short temper tantrum like the first. It very well could be *it.* After all, how many separated people reconcile twice? It was time to pick myself up and get a job.

I started with Ellen. After I sold her a townhouse, she and I had become fast friends. We both worked for small companies and we both found love in the married men with whom we worked. Jack had since left his wife to be with me. Due to financial constraints, Scott was still married to someone else. Ellen understood my predicament as others did not.

"Any chance you're hiring?" My voice cracked.

"Uh oh! What happened?"

I told her the story.

"Can you come in tomorrow? I'll set something up with Scott."

"Absolutely. What time?"

"How about 10:00?"

My father considered tardiness an intolerable sin. I learned to be always early. Not that day. Twenty minutes late, I hurried through the door of the second-floor suite. "I'm so sorry. A through road was closed and I had to turn all the way around." I shook the hand of the well-dressed man who stood before me. "I never do this. I mean it. It won't happen again."

At the conclusion of our interview, Scott slapped both hands on the table, then rose. "Ellen raves about you. Let's give this a go. How soon can you start?"

I arrived bright and early the next morning, ready to master their high-tech hybrid software, a task that for me did not come easy. But as soon as I knew enough to develop my sales pitch, I picked up the phone. I touted benefits and set up video demonstrations. When I landed an in-person appointment, Scott and I packed our bags and off we flew. I didn't particularly enjoy the phone work or the travel, but I liked my co-workers and appreciated the job.

In the evenings, that awful time of day when everyone else seemed to have something to do or someone to be with, I couldn't stop thinking about Jack. *Where is he? What's he doing? Who's he with?* When I couldn't quiet the voices in my head, I climbed into the car and drove to the apartment building he owned, where I believed he was living. When I found his car in the lot, I parked out front and watched. Lights turned on. Lights turned off. I tried to imagine which apartment might be his. When his car was not there, I drove off fretting about where he might be and with whom.

❧

Months later, as I was connecting with old friends and getting used to my new single life, Jack called to tell me he was going to his brother's house for Thanksgiving.

"I need my houndstooth jacket and black slacks. I'll be heading out around 4:30 or 5:00 a.m. I don't want to disturb you. Would you mind hanging them on the front door?" There was a pause, then he added, "Please?"

Before going to bed, ever so carefully, I placed Jack's clothes in a weatherproof suit bag. I zipped it up and hung it on the front door. Then I made sure the house was especially clean—not that it was ever dirty—and I turned on a lamp in the usually-dark living room. I got up around 3:30 a.m., showered and dressed, and heaved a big old bird into the oven. I have no idea why I decided to prepare a full-on turkey feast. The kids would be with their father, I wasn't hungry and…well…my soon-to-be-ex had no idea about any of it. Still I couldn't give up the hope that Jack would see me, forego his travel plans, and we would spend our fourth Thanksgiving-anniversary together. Around 8:00 a.m., when I hadn't seen or heard a thing, I opened the front door. His clothes were gone. I had no idea when he'd come to get them.

Thanksgiving passed, and after I spent another Christmas alone, New Year's loomed. I always believed I could predict my year based on the type of New Year's Eve I had had. Quiet New Year's Eve, quiet year. Fun—fun. And, well, lonely… I'm not sure how I concocted that notion, but it seemed to hold true, at least for me.

On a snowy evening, three days before the big ball drop, as I held onto a softcover book I had no interest in reading and stared at the empty corner where a Christmas tree had not been erected, there was a knock at the door. Jack stood on the other side.

"I miss you, Linnie." He brushed the snow from his shoulders, stepped inside, removed his hat. His face was gaunt and sad, not unlike mine.

"We can fix this," he said.

I shook my head. "I don't know." The thought of being with him scared me almost as much as the thought of being without him.

"Let me take you to Nemacolin for New Year's Eve."

"We'll never get reservations now."

"Already made."

"They are?"

"See!" He grinned widely. "You have to go."

"Oh, I do, do I?"

❦

That trip to the five-star resort was beyond my expectations. He showered me with massages, facials, pedicures, romantic walks, room service and, as was always the case when he was making amends, gifts. Each afternoon he arranged to have delivered to our room one beautifully wrapped present after the next: gorgeous silver-stemmed wine goblets; a marble cheese tray; coasters. If I admired it in one of the over-priced gift shops, it was mine. I had no idea that the biggest gift hadn't yet arrived.

In a grand ballroom on New Year's Eve, we sat at a round banquet table filled with fun and friendly strangers all dressed, as we were, in formal attire. On each table, an array of plastic hats and silly noisemakers were scattered around a beautiful floral centerpiece. Dinner was delicious. The band was amazing. And just as the emcee began the count to midnight, Jack got down on one knee, snapped open a tiny black velvet box, and revealed his mother's diamond engagement ring. Jack's brother and sister-in-law had been in possession of the ring; at Jack's request they relinquished the precious family heirloom so Jack could give it to me.

"Will you marry me?" Smiling, he held the delicate diamond between two meaty fingers.

Even though we weren't officially divorced from one another, I said, "Yes." As balloons fell from the ceiling and the band belted out "Auld Lang Syne," we kissed. Everyone at our table cheered.

I never met Jack's mother. Perhaps that was good. Even though Jack told me she and Joan were never close, his mother never would have approved of their divorce. She certainly would not have approved of me—the other woman. Still I wish I had had the chance to know this woman who held the respect and admiration of everyone she met. The woman whose ring I now proudly wore.

46

TAKING CARE OF MYSELF

We were back together not quite six months when one evening, while sitting across the dinner table, Jack hinted that he might need me back on the job site with him. Without consideration for the promise I made to myself or the thorny, co-mingled thickets into which I would again allow myself to be tangled, the next day I quit my job without so much as the courtesy of a lie. I said, "I won't be coming back."

Ellen never asked for an explanation.

When Francie found out, she clicked her tongue and shook her head.

"I'm not going to break the other half of my promise. I mean it."

She peered at me. "I hope not."

Even though I wanted Jack to want to take care of me, my friend was right. I needed to find a way to take care of myself. She was also right when she said, "Do what you know." The only thing I knew was real estate. Working exclusively in the new construction market, I was out of the loop when it came to resales. I called a trusted Realtor, Penny. "I'm thinking about buying a rental."

"Peacock Landing," she said without hesitation. "It's the only affordable game in town."

"Anything available?"

"A new listing just came on the market. I'll send it right over."

I had used the proceeds from the sale of my home in Long Iron, the only money I had, to purchase the townhouse for my parents. I called the bank to inquire about a line of credit. If approved the funds would become the source of my down payment. National Bank and Trust said yes. While they prepared the paperwork, I viewed the property.

The minute we stepped outside I said, "Write it up." With contracts signed, I secured a mortgage, and eight weeks later closed on the very first property I would own by myself.

"I did it!" I rejoiced over the phone.

"Always knew you could," Francie said.

Later that year, drawing on my line one more time, I purchased another. From that point on I saved every nickel. A little more than a year later, I scraped together enough for the down payment on a third. Counting my parents' home, I now owned four.

"I'd like to have five," I told Francie the next time we had lunch. "When they're paid off...in fifteen years," I chuckled at my own hopefulness, "each should generate around $500 a month net. Not a lot, but with that little pension from Tony and my Social Security, it just might be enough."

"Great plan," she nodded and sipped her coffee.

It was a good plan. Jack must have thought so, too. Although he already had a twenty-four-unit apartment building, the year I purchased my third townhouse, he bought two in the same neighborhood.

47

A NEW THERAPIST

In the years before Jack had met me, while Joan sang in the choir, Jack sat on the church's pastoral nominating committee. After considering several candidates, Old Stone Methodist invited Ted to preside over a worship service—an interview of sorts. At 5'9" he appeared passive and unassuming. But the minute he stepped behind the pulpit, he came alive. His Shakespearean oration exhilarated the conservative church with scripture and teaching and a most memorable tale. Without delay Old Stone extended an official Pastoral Call. Delighted that his candidate had been chosen, Jack couldn't wait to greet the out-of-towners when they rolled into town and personally guide them to their temporary lodging. Jack and Ted became fast friends.

Not long after Jack and I first began our love affair, I met Ted's wife, the woman who would come to understand and support me more than, well—almost anyone. Similar in age, at that time we both had young children at home. While I worked, she pursued her master's degree in clinical social work. Neither of us had time for friendships or hobbies, but despite life's restrictions, an unyielding allegiance quickly formed. Like me, Anna was younger than her well-seasoned second husband; and like me, she, too, had been victimized at the hands of an older man.

Anna grew up in a family where religion was precious and revered. It was not uncommon for her parents to be honored by their minister's frequent personal visits. It was also not uncommon for the man to be granted private access, behind closed doors, to the little girl in her little room.

Anna understood my struggles as few others could. Ever since the return of my memories, she remained my steadfast confidant. I, too, became hers. She called me one day after she saw a physician who reminded her so much of her childhood minister, she raced out of the exam room in tears. I phoned her when a series of obscene calls sent me into a tailspin.

"At first he was just breathing heavily into the phone. I kept asking, 'Who is this? Who is this?' He hung up. The second time, he listed the things he wanted to do to me—things he said I would enjoy." I shivered at the thought.

"How awful," Anna sighed.

"The awful part was his voice. There was something familiar about it. I don't know...like I'd heard it before."

"What did Jack say?"

"He told me to hang up, which, of course, I did. But what if this guy knows who I am? Shouldn't Jack be more upset?"

"Sounds like the two of you need to discuss this with a professional."

"Yes. But who? I'm not sure Joyce is the right therapist."

"I agree," Anna said. "After seeing her that one time, I didn't get the feeling she understood the issue." Anna was referring to the issue of child sexual abuse.

"Me neither," I concurred.

That evening when Jack and I sat down to dinner, as I passed the salad, he casually said, "I met with a new therapist this afternoon."

"What?"

"Her name is Meredith." He scooped greens onto his plate.

"I'm sorry?" I set the salad dressing down on the table.

"These calls are a big deal for you." He looked at me.

"Yes. They are."

"I didn't get it, Linnie." He reached over and squeezed my hand. "I didn't. Maybe this woman can help us get through this."

We met with Meredith a time or two over the matter of those calls. I don't remember what she said or how he and I reconciled the issue. But after speaking with her, I felt like someone finally got *me*, got *my past*, got *it*!

48

BRINGING HIM HOME

The next time we saw our new therapist it wasn't for me or about us.

"What brings you in today?" Meredith asked.

"My son. He went to Memphis around the time Linda and I went public," Jack said. "Moved in with Chandler, a high school buddy."

"What's going on?"

"I thought it was too much partying, not enough working. But I don't know, my gut told me there might be something more. I called Chandler's dad. He and I used to run in the same circle." Jack took a breath. "Turns out that Chandler is running drugs to support his habit."

"Is Brett involved?"

"Absolutely not." Jack was emphatic.

"Brett can *not* save his friend," Meredith said.

"No kidding. Rehab couldn't save him." Jack replied.

"This will take Brett down."

"Already happening. I flew down there two weeks ago." He cleared his throat. "All of his stuff, golf clubs, television, all of it in hock. I need to get him away from that kid."

"Yes, you do." Meredith nodded.

Jack turned to me. "I want him home. He can work with us in the business."

"Jack," Meredith began. "It makes sense to bring him back—"

"That's what I thought, too."

"But it is *not* a good idea for him to work for you. Not right away."

Jack looked stunned. "What do you mean?"

"He needs to work for someone else, outside your business, beyond your control, just for a year or so. Once he develops some skills and matures a bit, then you can bring him into your business."

It didn't matter what Meredith said, the minute we returned to the office Jack picked up the phone. "You're coming home."

"I don't know, Dad. I hate the cold weather. My life is here."

"That's no life. Start packing."

"I don't have a job up there."

"You don't have a job down there either. Besides, you don't need a job. You're coming to work for me."

❧

Two months later the moving van arrived and Brett made the road trip north. He didn't need to look for a place to live. In the divorce, Jack and Joan gave each of their children a mortgage-free townhouse. Before his son's arrival, Jack renovated Brett's unit top to bottom. He was all set.

Shortly after unpacking, Brett flew to the West Coast for a weekend with friends—a gift from Dad. The trip had something to do with a sporting event. I wasn't paying attention and it didn't really matter. When he reported for work, Jack called all of us around the conference room table. The young man who went south to escape his parents' painful divorce and the woman who caused it, found himself exactly where he did not want to be—across the table from her—me.

"Brett, as you know, Linda sells the units and Erik builds them. You'll handle clients after the sale."

Brett nodded.

"In addition to manufacturer guarantees, each customer receives a one-year builder warranty. If something needs to be addressed, you'll handle those post-closing calls."

He nodded again.

"Each client also gets a six-month walk-through so we can address nail pops and other non-emergency items."

"Make a list for Erik?" Brett asked.

"Yes. He'll schedule the service calls and pass along any items Linda needs to handle."

When Brett was attentive to the clients, it took a load off of Erik and me. When he blew off an appointment, felt the client was being unreasonable, or simply didn't follow through, my phone didn't stop ringing with complaints—like the one posed by Mr. James.

"Why bother sending him to look at this stuff if no one is going to fix it."

"I'm sorry, Mr. James. Tell me again what needs done."

"I'm not telling you anything. See for yourself—and where is that husband of yours with all of his promises?"

"Are you home now, Mr. James?"

"I am not. I've already taken one day off for this nonsense. I'm not taking another. I'll be home at 5:00."

"I'll see you then."

Working hard to address the issues and growing more frustrated, I did exactly what I should not have done. I hid the whole mess from Jack.

49

DOING WHAT COULDN'T BE DONE

Over the next year, while Jack spent evenings with his son, I enjoyed time alone to write. I had always written. As a child I could be found holed up in my room, lost in thoughts and words, a pad of paper on my lap. But the moment I unearthed my childhood trauma, writing took a serious and necessary turn. It helped me make sense of what happened. It helped me survive.

There's something about being a survivor. I was stronger, more resilient, more resourceful. If I survived *that* I could survive anything. I was who I was because of what I had endured. Truth is, I couldn't imagine myself any other way. It took the help of so many to get me through, and I wanted to give back.

Writing helped me understand and heal. Maybe my story could help someone else. Having barely passed two college writing courses, my ability may have been in question, but no one could deny my determination. I spent every spare second of eighteen months trying to draft a novel about a young survivor of sexual abuse. A story based loosely on my own, but not all that loosely. I read, took classes, attended workshops and weekend conferences. After one of those conferences, I joined a small, intense critique group, a serious band of female writers who met every Monday night. They helped me hone my craft.

Even though I managed to land an agent in California, a woman who edited and taught, I made little progress. Each month, along with a blank cassette, I mailed off to her one or two chapters. About a week or so later, I'd receive back the red-marked paper copy along with a cassette tape full of—let's just call her words unfiltered criticism. The day that envelope arrived was a day Jack dreaded.

"I don't know why you do this to yourself. I'm going to meet Brett for dinner. Maybe you'll be beyond this when I get back." He stalked off as I listened to her words and cried.

After months of tears, the agent suggested I try something different. Her idea was for me to write a memoir. She never called it that, but I understood.

"There's power in the truth," she declared.

I wasn't ready to bare my damaged soul to the world. My mother didn't know what my father's only brother had done. More than that, I didn't want to blow up my family or hurt my dad.

Then it happened. One day while volunteering at Children's Hospital (volunteering was another of the literary agent's suggestions), I learned about a ten-year-old who arrived at Child Advocacy for his forensic interview. I never saw the child, but his story was on the lips of every person who passed through the halls. Having been sexually abused for years, he lashed out, raping his five-year-old sister.

My stomach in knots, my mind could not rest. Prevention and intervention needed to destroy the walls of silence that lock victims in continued abuse. But how? I repeated the question all through the night and well into the next morning as I paced, cup after cup of hot coffee in hand.

Children were more likely to listen to friends than to any adult. My kids were no exception. That's when it hit me. Through their true stories and their amazing ability to survive, victimized children possessed the power to make a difference. There it was. I would write a book where children tell their true stories to help other children. A book of hope and healing. There wasn't another book out there like it, at least none that I could find. I couldn't get started fast enough.

Although I had a little desk upstairs, out of the way, I preferred the convenience of the kitchen table. Prepare dinner and write, do laundry and write, and when I could, work from home and write. Before long, the glass top was covered with paper, cassettes, pens, and various books about writing. Given that my husband couldn't tolerate clutter, and given that I'd been writing unsuccessfully for longer than our agreed-upon one-year time frame, it was no surprise that he did not share my enthusiasm for my newfound idea.

"You'll never finish it," he insisted one evening when he arrived home to find me at the messy table, buried in my thoughts.

Despite his lack of faith and the stress it roused between us, I forged ahead. I researched the information needed for the educational, intervention, and therapeutic chapters, and I wrote. Sometimes I worked so late into the night that the sun came up before I had gone to bed. When I wasn't writing, I networked with professionals to find the children willing to tell their true stories.

As I searched for one last story, I came across a newspaper article about a young lady. She had no idea her father had been photographing her in the shower and then selling the pictures on the internet. Her mother discovered evidence in his underwear drawer and immediately called her best friend, a police officer. Hope's story was essential to my book. I reached out to the detective handling the case. Like the therapists and agencies with whom I'd been working, he required I provide driver's license, Social Security number, and up-to-date child abuse clearances to prove I was the well-intentioned woman I said I was. I readily complied.

The detective contacted Hope's therapist. The therapist put us in touch. Hope agreed to participate, insisting I use her real name. I had all the stories I needed. In six months, as if it had written itself, the first full draft was done. Given my lack of credentials, I knew that if I hoped to sell this project to a publisher, I needed to confirm accuracy and demonstrate viability. I needed professional endorsements.

"Why would anyone endorse this?" my husband grumbled.

After mailing letters with sample chapters, I received responses from Pittsburgh Action Against Rape, Family Resources, and The Center for Victims of Violent Crime. Personal notes came from lawmakers and teachers, therapists, social workers, and medical professionals. One day I got a response even I didn't expect.

Jack and I had just stepped off a return flight from Charleston, South Carolina, when I answered the out-of-town call. It was the personal assistant to Jack Canfield, co-author of the *Chicken Soup for the Soul* series. "He'd be honored to endorse your project," the assistant said. "To what address should we mail it?" It was all I could do not to jump up and down right there in the middle of the crowded baggage claim area.

Even my disbelieving husband couldn't deny this one. "Way to go, kid." He gave me a smile and a wink and his signature high-five.

With endorsements in hand, I composed a book proposal and

clung to the hope that some publisher, somewhere, would find enough merit to bring this project to market. To my husband's shock and to my delight, a small publisher said yes.

While the book went through cover design, editing, and the required evaluation by six professionals in the field, I created my website, drafted my speech, sought out speaking engagements.

"Who's going to invite you to speak?" Jack shook his head. "And what in the world will you talk about?"

I had no idea if any group would want me to talk, but I knew what I would say. I would share what I had learned, discuss my book, and talk about the courageous children I met along the way.

In no time, I received my first invitation.

"You're going to Albany?" Jack sounded shocked. "Your book isn't even out yet. And what about work?"

"The conference isn't for months," I reminded him. "My work will be done before I go."

No one offered to pay me, of course, but I didn't care. I happily accepted invitation after invitation. Even though the conferences were months and months away, I promptly booked rooms and cars and flights.

50

SHOT HIMSELF AT 3:12

WHEN I WASN'T seeking additional speaking engagements or working on my speech, I sold out the next thirty-one-unit development. I made selections with each buyer, coordinated with those who needed mortgages, and resold two sales that fell apart. I suppose I should have expected things to slow down at some point, but not so abruptly.

That day, not a single person stopped by the model home: not a buyer, not a Realtor, not a subcontractor. No one called, not even my sister with whom I spoke every day. More than odd, it was eerie.

I spent the uninterrupted morning on a backlog of paperwork. After filing one last change order and a PUD questionnaire, I took a sip of cold coffee and took stock of my tidy desk and the empty bins that usually sat overflowing on the lateral file cabinet behind me.

Around noon I phoned an old friend. In high school he and

I had been inseparable, but we had only seen each other a few times since he'd moved to Florida many years earlier. I have no idea what made me think of him that day, but our unexpected calls had always been special. After saying hello and catching up, I said, "You'll never believe it. I'm going to be a published author."

"Always knew you'd be a celebrity." Then he reminded me about our senior-recognition assembly, one he had orchestrated and emceed. One at a time each senior proudly marched across the gymnasium to a surprise theme song chosen specifically for him or her. My friend assigned me the song "Brick House." I could have killed him. I hurried across the floor to cheers and giggles.

"That was your debut, Pebbles," he said, calling me by my high school nickname. "There's no telling how far you'll go." We chuckled and then he said, "Good luck with everything. I'll call ya soon. But right now, I really gotta get back to work."

After we hung up, the room grew still. With nothing to do, I dug through my desk. The top right-hand drawer was riddled with small slips of paper on which phone numbers without names or names without numbers had been scratched. I counted out $1.76 mostly in nickels and pennies, an old nail file, a wad of paperclips, a half stick of gum that had hardened at the opened edge, and a travel packet of aspirin. I kept the aspirin, pocketed the change, stuck the nail file in my purse, and threw the rest away. Then I polished the furniture in my office and, with rag and Pledge in hand, walked through the model.

Room to room I dusted, returned knick-knacks to their rightful places, and switched off lights. No sense having the place all lit up if no one was coming. I made my way back to my office, poured the last of the coffee, rinsed out the pot, and sat.

As the clock ticked past 3:12, I grew queasy. I grew light-headed and queasy, shaky and unsteady. More than that, even though I knew differently, I couldn't shake the unnerving feeling that I was not alone. I didn't feel a cold chill or hear a squeaky door. It was nothing like that. There was only silence. Stillness. Yet in all that nothingness there was something—an energy.

"Hello?" I called out. "Is anyone there?" The uncomfortable feeling grew. Not wanting to be alone, I dialed Francie. "Can you stay on the phone with me?

"Are you all right?" she asked.

"I don't feel...I don't know…something isn't right."

"Maybe it's your blood sugar," she said. "Did you eat today?"

"Yogurt."

"Is that all?"

"That's all I normally eat."

"Well, maybe you need to eat more today."

I tore at a package of peanut butter crackers and took a bite. While I crunched, Francie kept me busy with idle chatter about a trip she and Tim had just planned and some old friends she recently ran into. Little more than ten minutes went by and the feeling passed.

"Go home," she said.

❧

At home I turned on the news, uncorked a bottle of wine, started dinner, but I couldn't stop thinking about that odd feeling. What was it? I was about to find out. As soon as Jack and I sat down to eat, the phone rang.

"Linda. Linda!" my mother screamed. "You need to come over here *now*."

In bare feet, I raced to my parents' home, four doors away. Jack followed. When I stepped inside, I saw my father. Hunched at the kitchen table, his face in his folded arms, he was sobbing. I had never seen him cry, unless you count the tears in the corners of his eyes when he walked me down the aisle. I had never seen him like this.

"It's Uncle Dean," my mother blurted.

"What? What happened?"

"Today at 3:12. He called Aunt Dot, put a gun in his mouth, pulled the trigger." With that my mother turned back to my father.

I felt no relief at my uncle's self-inflicted demise. Although I had, until that moment, held out hope that he might one day face his own conscience about what he had done to me, any need for vengeance had passed years before when I privately forgave him. Instead, as I stood there watching my mother's futile attempts to comfort my father's inconsolable sobs, I felt only anger for the pain my uncle had levied upon my father. A depth of anger far beyond anything I had ever felt for myself.

51

MY MOTHER'S STORY

My father instinctively knew when I needed something. A few dollars when I was broke, a take-home bag when there was little in my fridge, a hug when I was sad. When my memories returned, he knew then, too.

I never told him what I had remembered, still he showed up on a day when I couldn't get out of bed. As he hugged me, I said something had happened when I was a child. I would not say what. I would not say who. I would not tell my mother. I didn't think she could handle it, given what she told me two weeks before my twelfth birthday.

Just as Friday had always been cleaning day, Monday was the day my mother did the laundry. All of the laundry in one day: clothes, towels, linens off every bed. When it was warm and dry, like that summer day, she hung the sheets outside.

From a metal eyehook twisted into the mortar on the back of our house, through a hole in a rusty pole and back again, a

V-shaped rope spanned the length of our rear patio. My mother wrestled a queen-sized fitted sheet from the basket and heaved it over the line. I took one end. She pulled at the other. We stretched the bleached white cotton wide across the old, weathered rope. I hated the rough feel of air-dried fabric against my skin, but I loved the crisp clean smell.

"Pin each end." Mom pointed to the wooden clips in the bottom of the wicker bushel.

After we hung the flat sheet and both pillowcases, Mother pushed a support pole into place to raise the sagging line to keep the clean linens off the ground. I loved to watch her work. She was serious and focused, even when it came to scrubbing and laundry. Truth is she was serious and focused about everything. There seemed to be little joy in my mother's life. On the few occasions when she did laugh, it was a deep-barreled, out-loud belly laugh, a culmination of built-up happiness that came pouring out all at once. Anytime she laughed like that, my sister and I would come running from wherever we were just to watch. There would be no laughing that day.

As the sheets blew in the breeze, I twirled between the fabric. Mom headed back toward the house to flip another load. Rather than stepping inside, she stopped, turned, and with eyes toward the ground, made her way back to me. She set the bushel on the picnic table, sidled onto the bench, and motioned for me to sit across from her.

I had always been my mother's confidant. As far back as I could remember, I was the one she talked to, cried to, yelled in front of when she and Dad fought or when my grandparents borrowed money they would never return. I wasn't sure what she needed to tell me that day. It seemed to come over her quickly. It seemed important.

"You are never to get into a car with any boy *ever.*" Her eyes fixed on mine. "Do you understand?" She emphasized each word.

Given that I challenged everything, I'm sure I asked her why. I don't remember doing that, but I'll never forget what she said next.

"When I was twelve, I went to the movies with my friend, Connie. Connie's older brother picked us up to take us home. There was another boy in the front seat so Connie and I climbed into the back. The boys took Connie home first, which I thought was odd. But I felt safe enough. After all it was my friend's big brother." My mother looked down and took a breath. Then she whispered so low I strained to hear. "Before they took me home, they stopped in an alley. They climbed in the back seat..." she hesitated. "Both of them." Tears formed.

"What did Grandma say?"

"I didn't tell your grandmother."

Even though I was not yet twelve, I knew that mental illness and sexual assault were sins to be hidden. Both a disgrace. My mother never spoke of it again. Except for writing this, neither did I.

52

DISCOVERED

I DON'T KNOW how they found me, and I never thought to ask. Out of the blue, a representative from *Seventeen* magazine called to see if I had a teacher-student story in my book. I did not. I told her about a gripping account of a young lady and her father and the internet.

"Thank you, but that isn't what we're looking for."

Two weeks later the magazine called back.

"Can you have your publisher overnight a copy of your book?"

I couldn't dial the phone fast enough. "You won't believe it. *Seventeen* magazine is considering doing a feature story about Hope," I cooed.

"That's exciting," my publisher said.

"Can you overnight a copy?"

"We can send a proof."

I gave him the address.

Hope was interviewed over the phone, and then we waited. A

few weeks later, we got the call. Her story would fill the center two pages of the November issue of *Seventeen* magazine.

Shortly after that, someone from the *Montel Williams Show* phoned. They wanted Hope and me to participate in the show. They also wanted another young lady from my book. The show's young producer called that girl. So did I. Still so traumatized from years of abuse, she couldn't bring herself to face her father or confront her ordeal, especially not on national television. I worried it might derail the show. It did not. Crews landed. Hope was filmed, due diligence was conducted, and video clips were pre-recorded. Again, we waited.

❧

"I just got off the phone with the producer of the *Montel Williams Show*." I stood at the door of Jack's office. "They're overnighting my ticket. Sounds like I fly out in two days."

"With all that waiting they don't give much notice." He seemed annoyed. Perhaps he thought the short window made it too difficult or too expensive for him to come. Perhaps he was waiting for me to extend an invitation. I didn't ask. He didn't offer.

Even though we flew out of the same city on the same day, Hope and her mother traveled on a different flight. We met in the hotel lobby.

"I'm so glad you're staying here, too," Hope's mother said. "I've never been to New York." Then she lowered her head and her voice. "This whole thing is a bit overwhelming."

"It's overwhelming for me, too," I said. "Would you like to take a taxi around the city this evening? Maybe we could see some sights and find a place to get a bite?"

"That would be great." Hope's mom smiled as we wheeled our luggage to the elevator.

The next morning, a little before 8:30, Hope and her mom

arrived in the hotel lobby. I was already there. Our limo driver dropped us off at a nondescript side door of a nondescript brick building. Inside, we followed a young lady down a long hall and into the professional hair and makeup area. Afterwards Hope and her mother were taken to one green room and I to another. Neither room had green walls. In addition to a comfortable sofa and chair, the room had a credenza with a variety of snacks. I can't speak for Hope or her mother, but I didn't eat or drink a thing. I was too nervous that I'd spill something down the front of my red sweater or mess up my perfectly applied lipstick.

Three shows filmed that day, all in front of a live audience. The monitor allowed me to watch if I wanted. I did not. I had no idea what Montel might ask, but as I waited, I rehearsed over and over what I wanted to say.

Finally, there was a knock at the door. A young lady requested the three of us to follow her. On stage, Hope was seated next to another child survivor. Hope's mother sat next to me in the audience, front row, center. When Montel Williams called on me, the expert, to speak, my brief presentation was fluid and seamless and professional, just as I had hoped. Everything was perfect. Everything but one thing—my husband was not there.

53

HOT OFF THE PRESS

Donned in my best suit, polished pumps, and the swagger of newfound confidence, I floated into Pizza Hut a little less than one year after I signed with the publisher, a few months after I filmed the *Montel Williams Show.*

"Look, look!" I waved my book in the air. "First copy."

"Good for you," Jack said.

"Can we go somewhere special and celebrate?" I asked.

"I'm going to have lunch with Brett and Erik," he said even though he hadn't yet ordered and lunched with them every day. "We can celebrate tomorrow."

I had done this alone. I would celebrate alone. I left Pizza Hut and drove to a fancy restaurant with starched white tablecloths and miniature floral centerpieces, my book prominently displayed on the corner of my table for one.

"What are you reading?" the waitress asked as ice and water plopped into my glass from the side of her frosty metal pitcher.

"My book. First copy. Got it from the publisher today."

"You wrote this?" she asked.

"I did."

"May I?" She set the pitcher down on the table.

"Sure."

She picked up my book, flipped it over, read the back cover, "Wow. That's awesome." She held it up and spun around. "Look. Look," she announced to all the tables around me. "A celebrity. She wrote this book."

❧

When the time came to travel and speak, I shipped boxes of books ahead of me if I flew or carried them along with me in rented cars. Sometimes I traveled miles without cell service, always without navigation (GPS wasn't readily available yet). I trekked alone across barren country roads and up and over desolate, snow-covered mountaintops, where, at times, not an animal or a person, or even a streetlamp, could be found. I motored in the early mornings before anyone was awake and late at night after most were asleep. Much of the time I drove with the interior light shining down as my eyes jockeyed between the broken yellow line and the hand-written directions crumpled between my fingers and the steering wheel. Sometimes I headed home in between engagements. Other times I went from one stop to the next.

I made my way to cities like Albany and Birmingham and Phoenix and Lake Charles, speaking and selling signed copies of my book before and after I took the podium. Along the way I met extraordinary professionals, in the trenches every day, witnessing horrific crimes. These remarkable people never wavered in their fight to keep children safe and there they stood, gripping my hand, thanking me.

54

RETURNING HOME

Finally home after months of traveling, I reached for my red skirt, black sweater, kitten heels. Those clothes may not have suited the new construction job site, but they suited the new me. I had bared my damaged soul to the world, made a contribution to help others, listed myself as a writer on my tax form. (I'm not sure that last one was necessary, but it sure felt good.) Although I returned to the same life, I was not the same person. I was ready to take on whatever the world might throw at me next.

When my friend Jennifer met me for lunch, she said, "You look like a writer."

I wasn't sure exactly what a writer looked like or how many writers she knew, but I liked the sound of it. And when I walked into the office that first day back, my husband noticed, too.

"Wow." He pulled himself erect in his chair. "You look...*great*."

I loved his reaction and I loved him. As I looked across that big desk at the strong, handsome, silver-haired man smiling back at me, I couldn't deny how much I had missed him. I should have invited him to the taping of the *Montel Williams Show.* The hurt between us was as much my fault as his. It was time to fix things. If I could write a book, get endorsements, find a publisher, have an article about my book in *Seventeen* magazine, and appear on a national television show, I could fix this marriage.

"I've got it," I told Francie. "I'll make Jack's upcoming sixtieth birthday everything his fiftieth was not.

"I hope that works." She shook her head and pinched her lips.

I knew the band I wanted to hire. They had played at Cheryl's wedding. Jack loved them so much that for two years in a row on New Year's Eve, we paid an astronomical ticket price and fought crazy crowds just to dance to their tunes.

"They're booked," the agent told me. "Would you consider another band?"

"Let me think about it."

I didn't have to fret long. Two days later the booking agent called to tell me the wedding had been cancelled and my date had opened up. I charged it to my credit card on the spot. Thank goodness the club had an available room.

I spent hours choosing the menu, tablecloths, centerpieces, and invitations. With a floor plan in hand, I placed tables and food stations, locations of the bars, and the all-important dance floor. In addition to hiring a photographer, I'd place disposable cameras on each table, and afterwards Francie and Tim would amass a keepsake album for Jack.

When it was time to send out invitations, I gathered most of the addresses from our wedding list. I had to sneak a few from Jack's computer. RSVPs went to Francie as the surprise event drew near.

When Jack walked into the Founders Room that Saturday night, he was truly surprised. Smiling ear to ear, he shook hands and gave hugs to each of the guests and family members who filled the room. About an hour into the evening, while I was on the opposite side of the room answering a question about the cake, Jack stepped onto the dance floor.

He cleared his throat and tapped the microphone. "Good evening." Heads turned toward the guest of honor. "I'm a little overwhelmed and I don't know what to say..." Being speechless wasn't at all like him, and the crowd tittered and giggled. "So...umm... thank all of you for coming. I'm humbled and grateful to have all of you with me this evening to celebrate my sixtieth birthday."

He extended his hand and said, "Cheryl, will you come up here, please?" He put his arm around his daughter and choked up. "I'd like to share with you the best birthday gift any father could ever get." Jack looked at his daughter. "Cheryl just told me she is going to have another baby." While the room clapped, Jack took a handkerchief from his pocket and dabbed at his eyes.

Throughout the night, Jack stayed busy chatting with guests, and I kept busy making sure every detail was perfect. He and I hadn't eaten together, visited friends together, or danced one single dance together. When the band announced the final song, hoping to end this special night with a special moment, I made my way across the room toward my husband. Before I reached him, he located his daughter and took her by the hand. He led her onto the dance floor. Alone, I stood on the sidelines and watched.

⚜

Jack was up and out early on Monday morning, as he had been in the weeks before his party. The minute I arrived at the office he called to me from behind his desk, "Hey Linnie, can I see you for a minute?"

I danced into the room expecting thanks and praise. That's not what I got.

"The club sent this over." He handed me a piece of paper.

"What is it?"

"The invoice."

"For what?" I looked down at the statement I held in my hand.

"For the party."

"Invoices don't come out for another week."

"I had them send an advance copy."

"You couldn't wait?"

He didn't answer.

I walked to my desk, wrote a personal check for the full amount, and handed it to Jack.

55

A SCORE SETTLED

"I NEVER EXPECTED my husband to pay for any part of his party. I never expected him to demand payment in advance." Meredith listened as I poured out my heart in a private therapy session.

"Maybe his feelings have more to do with him than you."

I considered her statement. "What do you mean?"

"Did he ever re-title the family partnership jointly?"

I shook my head.

"If he doesn't keep his promises, why would he expect you would keep yours?"

"Hadn't thought of that. Doesn't matter. I paid for the party and the family partnership is what it is. I can't make him give it back to me."

"No, but you can take care of yourself."

"I'm doing that," I said. "The book is one way and I've bought four rentals so far. That's a lot less than what Jack has, but I hope to buy one more. Problem is I spent so much on my half of our last family vacation, traveling for the book, and Jack's party that… well…"

"What do you plan to do?"

"Wait and save." I shrugged. "What else can I do?"

"Have you considered asking Jack for some financial help to buy the place?"

I felt myself backing up at the thought.

"Might make you feel better about the apartment building."

I looked at her.

"Might make him feel better, too."

At our next joint session, Meredith posed the idea, and with little visible resistance, Jack agreed.

A few weeks later, so excited to tell Jack and Meredith the news, I started talking the minute she greeted us in the waiting room. "I found it. A three-bedroom townhouse." I followed her into her office. "It's exactly what I wanted."

"That didn't take long." Meredith looked at Jack.

"So few of them have two and a half baths. Penny showed it to me this morning. It won't last. It's priced right."

"How much will you need?" Meredith asked.

"About thirty-four thousand."

Stunned, Jack repeated, "Thirty-four thousand dollars? Will you get some of the money from your line?"

I shook my head. "I wish, but National Bank and Trust won't extend it. Not a nickel."

The room fell silent.

"Jack, do you understand why this is important to Linda?"

"Yeah. She's still pissed about the apartment building."

"She's trying to build her own retirement and her own independence with her own properties."

He didn't say a word. He didn't have to. I knew he was thinking: *How does using my money make her independent?*

I interrupted any thoughts he might be having. "I know you think this is a good idea. You bought two townhouses in that development, too."

He didn't respond.

"Come on. I work just as hard as you do, but you make a lot more money. Now you have twenty-six units. I'm just trying to get five."

Meredith brought the matter to a head. "Jack, it doesn't sound like this can wait. If Linda is going to buy this property, she needs your help."

"I suppose," he grumbled.

A week later, even though I woke early, Jack was already gone. As I fixed my coffee, I noticed on the kitchen counter a check for the exact amount. *Did Jack write this?* His signature was almost illegible.

56

TERMINATE THE PRENUP

I HADN'T SPOKEN to Joel since Jack and I last separated two years earlier, so I was surprised to see my attorney's name on my caller ID. It was three months after Jack's birthday party.

"I need to see you in my office," Joel said the moment I answered.

"Is everything okay?"

"Can you be here tomorrow at 1:00?"

"Yes. Yes, of course."

"Do not tell anyone you're coming. Do not agree to anything. Do not sign anything." He hung up.

I was making dinner when Jack arrived home that evening.

"How was your day?" I asked as I always did.

"Good, talked to Tanya at Union." Union was our business bank.

I set out plates, napkins and silverware. "How are things?"

"On track." He went into the bedroom to kick off his shoes.

"Dinner's almost ready," I called in to Jack. "Would you like some wine?"

"I think I'll fix a scotch." He emerged from the bedroom, fixed his drink, joined me at the table.

"Will you be at the office tomorrow?" I asked casually.

"I need to take a look at another piece of land. Why?"

"Nothing really. I need to head out around lunchtime."

"Okay."

That was the end of that. I had planned to tell him I was meeting an old friend for lunch. But he never asked, and I never said another word about it. Maybe he already knew.

❧

Joel was waiting for me when I arrived. He escorted me back to his office and closed the door.

"Yesterday Jack called to ask me to prepare a termination of the prenuptial."

"I'm sorry?"

"I told him I couldn't do that for him. I represent you."

"You represent me?"

"You paid me."

I remembered taking the money from the Christmas fund. "Oh, yes. I guess I did."

"No one ever wants to terminate a prenuptial without good reason," Joel said. "So, I reviewed it." He flipped through the pages and then stopped, pointing at a paragraph. "The prenup gave you 50 percent of Dunigan Enterprises."

"Half the company?"

Joel leaned back in his big leather swivel chair and folded his hands in his lap. "I strongly advise you keep the prenup intact."

I nodded.

"And be careful." He raised a brow. "Don't agree to anything unless you talk to me first. And don't sign anything."

I was my own worst enemy. I had signed the prenuptial without reading it. I had signed the Dunigan Family Partnership without reading it. I had signed lots of things I should have read first.

"Looks like I'm going to need you again," I said as I stood.

"I hope not. But if you do, I'm here."

❧

The next day Jack called me to the conference room. "Sit down."

"I'll get a tablet—"

"No need."

I sat. "What's up?"

"I've decided to give Brett half the business."

"Half?"

"Yes, half."

The reason for the dissolution was now clear. Without the prenup Jack would have given Brett my half. I stood and gripped the back of my chair. "You can give him your half if you want to." With that I left.

57

BLAKE

Another month went by. I pulled into the construction site at 9:00 a.m., like I did every day. After I placed the MODEL flag in the pole and stood the OPEN sign at the end of the driveway, I noticed a teal Ford F-150 parked on the street a few doors away. I had not seen that vehicle previously. Just beyond the truck stood a man who was Hollywood handsome. He had a chiseled frame, undeniable in his tight jersey tee. As I stared, he tucked a wide, flat pencil behind his ear. He had to be a new subcontractor. Although I usually participated in the hiring process or was at least aware when someone new started, given the tension between Jack and me, the nonexistent communication, I had no idea who this person was.

"I see you met Blake," Erik said as he approached.

"Not officially." I smiled. Blake smiled back.

"Electrician." Erik disappeared into the model.

My mother's mother, a striking Sicilian with olive skin, a gleaming smile, and thick black hair, was feisty, confident, and always dressed to the nines. My mother often told me I was like her. I could only hope. I once saw a photo of her, something you'd expect in a Rita Hayworth movie. Sitting with her sculpted legs stretched across the bow of a boat, she had my grandfather's sailor's cap cocked on her perfectly coiffed head. According to family stories, my grandfather, a talented musician, was unfaithful; she, a formidable homemaker, unforgiving. After my grandfather's early death from an aggressive form of leukemia, my grandmother was never without the company of a good-looking, overly generous man. She knew about men and she always had advice.

One day, while visiting, she said, "Don't tell me nothing's wrong. I can see it in your face."

"Jack wants to give my half of the business to his son."

"And?"

"I said no."

"Good," my grandmother said, with a firm nod of her head.

"You know him. When he wants something, he'll do whatever it takes to get it."

"Too bad. If he wants to leave, let him go." She flapped her left hand in the air, then spoke her famous words: "Men are like streetcars. Another will be along in ten minutes."

As I watched Blake pull wire that day, I thought, *maybe my grandmother is right!*

58

SELLING OUR HOUSE

Francie had invited a recently widowed friend to her house for dinner.

After touring Francie and Tim's townhouse, four doors up from ours, her friend said, "This would be perfect for me. I need to get out of that house. Is anything for sale in here?"

Canterbury, the development where Francie and Tim and Jack and I lived, had been completed for over two years. Nothing was for sale. Pendleton Place, the development we were currently building, was already sold out.

"They're starting a new plan in Butler County. Might be another six or seven months but that would give you time to get your house sold," Francie told her friend, a woman with whom she had worked. A woman with whom Jack's mother had worked.

"The timeframe works fine, but I don't want to move out that far," she said. "My life is here."

"Well, those Dunigans are always on the move," Francie said.

"Let me see if they have any plans to sell anytime soon."

When Francie approached us with the woman's story, Jack turned to me. "What do you think?"

I shrugged. "Fine with me."

Francie set up a time for her friend to tour our home. In addition to warming up introductions by talking about his mother and the working years the two women had shared, Jack gave his usual soft, but effective sales pitch. He walked her through our house, pointing out features and upgrades. Then he emphasized, "This wasn't a spec. We custom built this home for ourselves. Quality, craftsmanship, spared no expense. Loaded with extras." He pointed out the see-through fireplace, the clawfoot tub, and the huge addition to the master bedroom. "No other unit is this large."

Francie's friend was excited to purchase our home. We agreed on a price and a closing to occur a few weeks after I purchased my new rental.

59

GOING SEPARATE WAYS

"HOW ARE THINGS?" Meredith asked as we sat.

"I closed on my property and renovations are almost done. Nothing big, of course. I updated the powder room, added a few lights. The painter is scheduled to start this afternoon."

Meredith looked at Jack. "Is that where the two of you plan to live?"

"That's where Linda will go," Jack answered flatly.

"What about you?" Meredith asked him.

"I'm going to take ninety days to decide if I want a divorce."

It was not a surprise that he, once again, used that threat. If the distance between us had been obvious when he gave me, under protest, the money to buy my most recent rental, it became undeniable when I refused to give his son my half of the business.

❧

The box truck backed into the driveway. Ramps were put into position, and dollies wheeled out. I opened the front door.

"Good morning," Russ said as he entered the house. "Where would you like us to start?" Russ stood about 5'10" tall and weighed, I'd bet, not a pound over 160, but he was as strong as an ox. His father had been a mover before him, and Russ learned his trade well.

"Did you get the model home furniture out of storage?" I asked. "That furniture will be going with me."

"Already on the truck."

"You're on it." I laughed, and he smiled back. "Okay then, all of these go." I pointed to rows of boxes and items lined against the long living room wall. "The wardrobes in the master go as well, and so do the boxes in Alex's room." I started to walk away, then turned back to look at Russ. "If it's not packed, it doesn't go. Doesn't look like Jack is coming with me."

"Okey dokey," Russ replied as he piled boxes onto his dolly.

Russ had moved me out of my house in Long Iron and into the townhouse when Jack and I separated. He moved Jack and me from my rental into our first home across the street. Then he moved us from that unit to this one. He also moved my parents. His reputation was without question; nothing was ever lost or stolen or broken. Whether the change of address was a happy occasion or, like this one, a breakup, anytime Russ moved anyone, he never said a word, never told a soul.

I spent that weekend setting up my new home. By Sunday evening I was exhausted, but beds were made, boxes unpacked, and pictures hung. Even better, the painter who moved at a glacial pace was, finally, out of the way. The townhouse looked darling and it felt like home.

The minute I slumped onto the sofa and grabbed the remote, there was a knock at the door.

It was my new next-door neighbor, Rhonda. "Hi Linda," she

said as she peered inside. "The house looks darling. Wow, you got a lot done. You must have been working hard."

I took a breath and exhaled. "I have."

"Wayne and I don't want you to be alone on your birthday. Come on over. Wayne is putting burgers on the grill."

They learned about my birthday the day before when a gift for me accidentally arrived at their front door. That's also how we met.

"That's so sweet," I replied. "But honestly, I'm exhausted. Can we do it another time?"

"Of course."

She left and I made my way to the kitchen, poured a glass of wine, returned to my resting spot on the couch. As soon as I propped a pillow behind my back and pulled my aching feet onto the coffee table, the doorbell rang.

Now what? I dragged myself back to the front door. Jack stood on my covered porch, an envelope in his hand.

"What do you want?"

"I don't want you to be alone on your birthday."

"Is that right?"

He nodded as he gave me the greeting card, then added, "Can I buy you dinner?"

"No."

I shut the door, bolted the latch, closed the blinds. I returned to the sofa and picked up my wine. Even if the house went up in smoke, I was not getting up again.

60

NATIONAL BANK AND TRUST

I WAS SEATED at my desk when the phone rang. It was one week after I had moved into my townhouse and one week before the closing on the home Jack and I still owned.

"Mrs. Dunigan, this is Tom McNamara from National Bank and Trust. I'm working on the payoff for the sale of your home next week. It appears there's an $80,000 line of credit that was inadvertently placed against your marital home at 618 Canterbury Lane instead of against the home you own individually at 624 Canterbury."

"I'm sorry?"

"I believe your parents live in that property.

"How do you know who lives there?"

"According to our records, this line was issued to you personally so you could purchase two of your rental properties."

"How do you know what I used that money for?"

"As I said, the line was inadvertently placed against your marital home."

"Inadvertently?"

"Yes, ma'am. It appears this was our mistake. Your husband asked me to discuss with you the steps we need to take to get that line moved..."

"Why am I hearing this from you and not my husband?"

"I umm…I don't know."

"Well, I do. This conversation is over." I hung up the phone.

When Jack returned to the office, he got right to the topic at hand. "Did you talk to Tom at National?"

"Yep."

"You need to get this lien removed."

"No." I spun toward him. "I do not."

"Then we can't sell the property."

"Fine. Then we won't sell the property. I'll move back in. You can give it to me as part of the divorce settlement. Up to you. Let me know what you decide." I turned back to my work.

A week later the closing took place as scheduled, and the line of credit was paid off.

61

SKIRTS AND SPIKES

No matter how well I dressed after I returned from speaking and selling my book, as soon as Jack and I were officially separated, I ramped it up. I'm sure Jack thought I was doing it for him, but it was all for Blake. I found excuses to visit the townhouses where Blake pulled rough wire or hung final fixtures. I discovered his favorite hangouts by asking his counterpart on the job site. Over the next two months, each time my single friend Nora and I ran into him *accidentally*, I flirted.

When I flirted, most guys launched into avid pursuit. Not Blake. He winked and engaged in playful banter. If I saw him at a local pub, he bought me a drink and made sure I arrived safely to my car. But he never called, and he never asked me out. That made me want him even more.

One Friday night in late October, a group of friends and I went to a trendy downtown night club. As soon as I arrived, I remembered how much I hated the bar scene. Drinks were expensive, the music was too loud, and everyone, including me, was trying to be someone each of us was not. By midnight, I couldn't stand it anymore. There wasn't anyone I was interested in, most of my friends had gone home, and even though I told Blake where I would be, he hadn't showed.

I was searching for my remaining friend to tell her goodbye when, suddenly, I saw Blake glide around the front of the bar. He headed straight toward me. I don't know if it's possible for a heart to skip a beat, but at that very moment mine did.

"Can we get out of here?" he asked.

"My place?" I suggested.

"Nah. Jack might drive by."

"You think he'd do that?"

"Never know."

We left my car in a downtown lot and found a twenty-four-hour coffee shop in the Strip District a few miles away. It wasn't a fancy place with exotic blends; it was like Blake, simple and clean with good bones and great brew. As we shared a slice of the best apple pie he said he had ever eaten, he told me that he hesitated to ask me out, not because he wasn't interested, but because he knew he would fall in love with me. He also said he was afraid he would lose his job. Despite his fears, we started dating one another secretly.

❧

We'd been dating for four wonderful, under-the-radar months when Blake showed up at my front door one Friday evening. I expected we'd order a pizza and settle into a movie. I dressed accordingly. He had a different idea. Sporting a plaid button-down and pressed khakis, Blake smelled of the cologne I had given him. In his arms were two T-bones, two oversized baking potatoes, and a bottle of red wine.

"Look at you. Should I change?" I asked.

"You're perfect just the way you are." After giving me a peck, he followed me to the kitchen.

Spuds in the oven, he opened the wine. I set the table with fine china and two tapers. It seemed this was an impromptu celebration and, tired as I was, I wanted to enjoy every minute. He stepped outside to grill the beef while I boiled some veggies I dug out of the freezer. When Blake returned with perfectly seared steaks, I lit the candles and he poured the cabernet.

"To us," he said.

"To us." I raised my glass to meet his. Then I added, "How about we toast to you?"

He laughed. "What are you talking about?"

"You know what I'm talking about. Your birthday is next week. How would you like to celebrate?"

"I don't know." He blushed. "Can I think about it?"

"Absolutely." With that, we toasted again and enjoyed our meal.

After dinner Blake stood. "Let me help you clean this up."

"You don't have to do that."

"Really?" He gathered dishes and made his way to the kitchen.

"What do you think of my new dishwasher?" I asked as he rinsed and loaded the machine. "What a mess."

"Sorry you had to go through that."

"Leaking all over the floor not once, but twice."

"You didn't know."

"Three attempts to fix it cost me more than the new dishwasher itself. In the end I paid for the thing twice," I grumbled.

Drying off his hands Blake turned around and leaned back against the sink. "Maybe we could make this dishwasher ours?"

I closed the refrigerator door and faced him. "What did you say?"

"Maybe we could make this dishwasher *ours*?" he repeated more slowly, pulling me against his well-toned body.

I looked at him. I didn't know what to say. He wasn't talking about money. He was talking about cohabitation. I liked him a lot. I felt safe with him, and secure. But I wasn't anywhere near ready to commit to him or to anyone. I didn't even know who I was or what I needed. More than that, even though I wanted to be, I wasn't over Jack. Not yet.

"I'm sorry." He released his embrace. "I didn't mean to—"

"No. No." I shook my head as I took a step back. "You just caught me off guard. That's all."

After we watched a movie, Blake stayed the night. I lay next to him staring at the ceiling. With Blake I wouldn't have five-star trips or a professionally decorated new home. And I definitely wouldn't have the financial comfort I had with Jack. None of that mattered. Blake loved me. He'd never go behind my back and he'd never leave me. A relationship with him was worth an honest chance, but I still worked with Jack, *for* Jack, every day. I wanted to listen to my attorney and stay at my job until after we divorced, or at least until after we came to a settlement. Maybe it was time to rethink that strategy. I would call Joel on Monday.

I rolled over, snuggled against Blake's warm body, and fell fast asleep.

62

CAUGHT IN THE MIDDLE

JACK BURST INTO my office, leaned on my desk with both hands, and glared at me. "What in the hell is going on between you and Blake?"

"That's none of your business. You left me, *remember*?"

His face inches from mine, his nostrils flared. "Are you sleeping with him or not?"

"What do you care? You don't want me. Are you now saying no one else can have me?"

"Are you or aren't you?" He slammed his fist against my desk so hard my pencil cup jumped up and tipped over. "Answer me!"

"Once," I blurted as I stood. As soon as the word was off of my tongue, I knew I had made a mistake.

"Damn you." Jack stormed out of my office and through the front door. From my window I saw him rip into Blake; then I watched Blake climb into his truck and drive away.

When Jack returned, I screamed, "What in the hell did you do?"

"Only what I should have done," he replied.

"You fired him?"

Jack didn't respond.

"That's it." I packed up my desk. "I've had enough."

"What are you doing?" he demanded.

"What I *should* have done—months ago." I grabbed the small box of whatever personal items I had thrown together, took my laptop, and left.

The minute I got home, I called Blake. He didn't answer. I waited a few hours then tried again. This time when I heard the beep, I said the only thing I could think to say, "I'm sorry." I did not call him again after that.

Two days later he called me back. I couldn't get to the phone fast enough. "I'm so sorry. Are you all right? I feel awful."

"What are you going to do?" he asked.

"I don't know. What do you mean?"

"Of course you don't know. You're not over him."

"It's going to take time."

"Doesn't matter how much time. He can give you a life I can't. You'll never leave him."

"No, no, no." I tried to talk as he hung up.

I called him back. I wanted him to know it wasn't about the money, but he didn't answer. The person I did *not* want to talk to—Jack—would not stop calling. I didn't answer any of his calls. He filled up my inbox. I didn't listen, but I didn't delete the messages, either. That way he couldn't leave more.

❧

About a week later, as I emerged from my kitchen with a plate of re-heated lo mein, I saw Jack's SUV circle the cul-de-sac. Alex, living at home during his freshman year of college, had just come downstairs from studying. He looked at me. "Do you know Jack has been driving past the house for, like, the last three days?"

"Yep."

"Okay then," he laughed. "How long is it gonna be this time?"

"What are you talking about?" I tried to match the levity in my son's voice.

"Each time you guys break up, we bet."

"Who?"

"Us kids."

"You bet?"

"Yeah." He laughed again. "We bet on how long before the two of you get back together."

The color slipped from my face.

"You're not mad, are you?"

"No." I forced a smile. "No. It's just that...I don't know." I plopped down next to my son on the sofa, set my plate on the coffee table, and grabbed the remote. "Can we watch something mindless? The last thing I need is some Valentine's Day Hallmark heartbreaker. I've got enough rattling around in my pea brain."

"Sure, Mom." Alex stretched his arm across the back of my shoulders and gave me a sideways squeeze. "Whatever you want."

❧

Days later as I sat at the dining room table, coffee in hand, ready to launch into another job search, I heard an odd sound. I opened the door and found Jack standing there, a sheet of paper under his arm, a long piece of tape between his fingers.

"What are you doing?"

"Since you won't answer my calls, I thought I'd tape this note to your door."

"Tape away. What do you want?"

"I was mad. I screwed up," Jack explained.

"Damn right you screwed up."

"Will you at least talk to me?"

"Not until you give Blake his job back."

"I will," he said.

"We'll see." I closed the front door and bolted the latch.

By the end of the following day, I had a voicemail from Jack. "I apologized."

Doubtful.

"I offered Blake his job back."

Possible.

"Blake said no."

That I believed.

63

BLENDING FORCES AND FINANCES

IT TOOK WEEKS for me to work up the courage to reach out again to Ellen. It took her and Scott a few weeks to agree to hire me, again. I hadn't been working there long when Jack called.

In a frantic voice he said, "I need to meet with you tomorrow at noon at our office."

"You mean at your office."

"I mean *our* office."

"I don't work for you anymore, remember?

"It's important."

"Are you in danger or in the hospital?"

"No, but—"

"Then it's not that important." I hung up.

He called back.

"I'm working. What do you want?"

"It is important and someone is sick. I'm not kidding."

"Oh, for God's sake. What's going on?"

"I'll explain tomorrow…noon…our office." With that he hung up.

❧

"Rachel's bad." Jack started talking the minute I stepped into his conference room. "Cancer has spread to her brain."

"I'm sorry to hear that," I said as I sat.

Rachel wasn't just a leasing agent. From the time Jack bought his twenty-four-unit apartment building near the airport, and only for that property, Rachel was his property manager. She found and screened tenants, coordinated repairs, paid all of the bills including the mortgage, and generated the quarterly income and expense reports Jack needed. She lived west of the city and knew that market. She did a great job.

"Her sisters have been covering for her, well…trying to cover," he continued.

"Sounds like you've got a problem. Why am I here?"

"Eight vacant."

I looked at him, stunned. "Twenty-five percent?"

"That's nothing. You should see the place. Carpets are torn, walls are filthy, apartments are trashed. I'm getting calls every day about unpaid sewage and water bills. I have no idea if rents are even being collected."

"Is the mortgage paid?"

"I don't know. I can't get anyone to call me back or give me the year-end statement I need to do our taxes." He shook his head. "This is *our* biggest asset."

Did I hear that right? Did this monocratic man use the word "our" when referring to his apartment building?

He reached across the small round table and squeezed my hand. "I can't do this without you."

"You've always needed me."

"I know. I was stupid."

"Yes, you were."

He pinched his lips, then added, "I need us together."

"Together? How?"

"Husband and wife."

"Oh…I don't know." I pushed back from the table and pulled my hands down to my lap.

"I mean it—shared responsibilities, shared decisions, joint assets."

"Nothing done unilaterally?"

"Nothing."

"Joint assets?"

"Even the apartment building."

"I'll believe it when I see it."

❧

As soon as Marcus completed the new wills, deeds, and corporate documents, we met at Jack's office to sign. It was official. I would sell the new construction and salvage the apartment building. He would run the building and land development business. Our assets would be joint and all decisions would be made together. It was the change I had been asking for; the change our marriage needed.

"One more thing," Jack added as I got up to leave.

"Here we go." I rolled my eyes.

"Move in with me."

"Live in the model? I don't know. What about the dogs?"

"You mean Piss, Poop, and Bark?" Jack joked.

I tilted my head and pinched my lips.

"Yes. The dogs, too," he laughed.

In my new role as property manager, I listed my townhouse for rent and Russ hauled Alex and my personal belongings into the

4,500-square-foot, professionally decorated model in Burlington Heights. Jack and I were together in a way we had never been together before.

64

BUSINESS IS SHIFTING

I STOOD IN front of the living room window, looking across the paved street at the barren lot where, a little more than a year ago, the construction trailer had sat. Jack came up beside me. It had never before taken us this long to sell five units.

"Hard to believe it's been more than a year since I moved in here with you."

"How long have we been doing this?" he asked.

"Building or relationship?"

"Building."

"Fourteen years."

"We've had a good ride," he said. "Haven't we?"

"Had?"

"Things are changing."

Pittsburgh real estate had always been more stable than other markets around the country, with a steady 3 to 5 percent increase and few decreases. But we knew we'd feel the pinch if the markets were heading for a downturn. New construction was always the first to go, last to recover.

"Did we go too big, too expensive, too fast?" I asked.

"Probably. But there's something more going on here."

"Sales are a lot harder to come by," I added.

Jack shook his head. "Gotta be on top of our game."

"Speaking of that, I've got that dentist appointment Friday, but a Realtor is bringing someone by. Can you cover for me?" I asked.

"Brett will do it," Jack said.

Selling new construction was different than selling existing homes. A client had no way to access the property, no way to know what came standard, what we charged for an upgrade. They also wouldn't know which units were available or when we could deliver them. Add to that, we had our own sales agreement and our own sales process. One of us always had to be there. That someone had always been me.

Friday afternoon around 3:30, as I pushed through the double glass doors, relieved that my dental work was both minor and over, my phone rang.

"No one's here," the Realtor blurted into the phone, anger in his voice.

"What?"

"The place is locked up tighter than a jail cell."

"Are you kidding me?" I took a breath. "I'm sorry, I was at the dentist. Someone was supposed to cover. I can be there by four—"

"We've already waited thirty minutes. My client doesn't want to wait any longer."

"Can we reschedule?"

"We'll see," he said, which meant no.

A few days later, I approached Jack. "Can we talk? Privately please?"

He nodded and I closed his office door. "This isn't easy for me..."

"Just say it."

"It's about Brett."

"What about him?" Jack's voice was protective, maybe even defensive.

"Ever since he blew off that appointment on Friday, apparently to go golfing, I've been trying to find some way to tell you this."

"Tell me what?"

"Sometimes Erik and I...have to...cover for Brett." It was true, but as soon as those words left my lips, I wished I hadn't said them.

Jack's face washed white. "You'd never cover for my son. *Never.*"

"I would and I did."

❧

Another month passed and I secured sales on the last two units in Building One, but each sale was a struggle. We were feeling the effects of the national slowing trend. Jack was growing more concerned about the money we owed to the bank, and he was nervous about how far behind we were on projected sales. We were in breach and the bank could call our note at any time.

Jack did what he always did when he needed advice. He turned to Victor. After a meeting with his best friend, a builder and developer who was also behind on sales, Jack called me into his office.

"Capital wants to buy out the rest of our developed lots."

"But they're a tract builder."

"They want to build their first-floor master bedroom design."

"Has it come to that?"

He hesitated a long moment, then looked at me. "We don't have a choice."

"Will you still be the developer?"

"Yes. They want me to develop the rest of the lots here. Then

I'll start looking for more land to develop for Capital and other builders." His voice was hesitant, nervous. Developing meant more risk, more expenses, less profit.

"What about Brett and Erik?"

He shook his head. "That's going to be hard."

"Maybe Meredith can help?"

❧

Meredith said, "Give Brett and Erik as much notice as possible. Whatever you do, stand together. Tell them together. You both own this company. You are a *team*."

Later that week Jack took Erik and Brett to lunch alone, as he often did. He told them without me. I have no idea what he said. But when Brett and Erik returned to the office, neither of them looked at me or said a word to me.

65

THE FLOOD

It was not a fire, although smoke alarms blared.

It was February 2007. The weather had been a freeze-and-thaw nightmare for several days. Temperatures dipped as low as 12°F below zero, then suddenly climbed to an unexpected high of 40°F, sending thawed water through a broken sprinkler pipe in the attic above my son's bedroom. Jack had been at his office. I was at the apartment building all day. Alex was away at college. With no one home, water pumped at 120 pounds of pressure per minute for over six hours.

I showed up shortly after Jack. I had never seen anything like it. Water shot across the loft and through the banister splashing down onto the hardwood floor. Light fixtures, wall switches, electrical outlets, ductwork all became outlets through which water poured. Puddles formed on countertops and beds. Ceilings caved. Drywall buckled and then, almost in slow motion, crumbled and peeled off the walls.

I stepped inside the house. "Good God. What happened?"

After Jack shut off the main and dismissed the firemen who were kind enough to pump most of the water out of the basement, he climbed into his chair behind his desk in our home office, the only room somehow untouched by the water. He cradled his head in his hands and rocked back and forth. Usually, he was the one to step up and take charge in a crisis. His military training had taught him well. But he didn't call a restoration team. He didn't try to sop up water or raise the furniture. He did not tell me everything would be all right. This time it would have to be me. Fearful to turn on my computer, I grabbed the Yellow Pages and began calling restoration companies.

"A water break—a big one." I may have been yelling, but Jack never told me to lower my voice or calm down, as he usually did.

"I'm sorry, ma'am," the answering service said. "We're unable to take on any more work at this time."

"But this is huge. The entire house, all three floors…" I was hoping the magnitude might sway her.

"The best I can do is to give them your message in the morning."

"By then everything will be ruined."

"I'm sorry," she repeated calmly, unfazed, as though she had heard those words from every caller.

I dialed number after number, but everyone was on another job rescuing someone else. Finally, just as I was about to give up, a man answered.

"The last twelve hours have been unbelievable, if you know what I mean." He sounded tired. "One job after another. But doesn't sound like you can wait till morning."

"We cannot. Please," I begged.

"Hold on while I see what I can do." He put his hand over the receiver and called out, "Hey, Buck, you up for another one?"

"Tonight?" Buck called back, his voice less than enthusiastic, "I guess."

"Call Uncle Chet and Len. You better call George, too."

He returned to me. "We'll be there in an hour."

"Thank you. Thank you so much." I fought tears of relief that help would soon arrive.

As he was about to hang up, I heard him shout, "Get the blowers and the dehumidifiers from the shed. All of 'em. And get the movin' straps. This is a big one."

It took six men to carry each waterlogged mattress and box spring to the garage. They pulled up sopping carpets and pads. They stuffed sodden custom-made bedding, draperies, blankets, and pillows, like useless rags, into oversized garbage bags. By 2:00 a.m. large furniture was up on blocks, smaller pieces were either standing on top of countertops or upside down on top of larger items, and for the first time since we arrived home that day, mixed with exhaustion, we both gave a sigh of relief. The crew left for the night. We salvaged a few personal items in the dark and found a hotel.

66

REBUILDING

The house would be uninhabitable for months.

I sought out a furnished rental, for which our insurance company agreed to reimburse us, and Jack put together his plan for the restoration.

"I don't care if you prefer someone else run the job," I overheard Jack on the phone with the adjuster. "I am a general contractor. I'm not hiring one. I've built over one hundred and eighty of these units. It's what I do every day. No one knows this house better than I do. I built it once, I'll build it again."

Even though Jack didn't personally install the fire suppression system or the insulation that slipped away from the high-pressure pipe allowing it to freeze, somehow he felt that this was his fault—his failure. He needed to build a second time what had not been built right the first. We had so much going on with the renovation at the apartment building and the shift in business, maybe it would have been better if someone else took the reins.

There were so many times when I opened my mouth and wished I hadn't. This was one time I didn't say a word and wished I had.

Jack wore the stress of that remodel around his neck like a millstone, too heavy to carry, impossible to remove. I saw firsthand, as if in slow motion, how a home that had been loved, like a favorite pair of torn jeans or worn slippers, impossible to walk away from—was even harder to rebuild. Walking away was not an option. We had to rebuild, even if it took every ounce of patience and fortitude and faith we had. At times it did.

"What do you mean Travelers wants us to sand and refinish the hardwood floors? Come on, Louise. They were under water, for God's sake! They need to be replaced."

"What do you mean you thought I was getting the paint? You're the damn painter, Craig."

"What do you mean you don't know if he'll be back? He just went to pick up a blade for his saw."

Despite adjusters who denied repairs, workers who didn't do what they said they would, and subcontractors who left and never returned, with each passing day we saw tiny bits of progress.

67

THE CALL

WE RARELY COOKED in the tiny two-bedroom townhouse where we'd been holed up since the flood displaced us eight weeks prior. That night, like most nights, we enjoyed a sandwich out. It was Thursday, April 5, Holy Thursday, four days before Easter.

As Jack pulled into the driveway, his phone rang. "Hey Victor. How ya doing?" My husband chimed in his sing-song happy voice. "I didn't expect you'd be back from Florida so soon."

"Coming home Thursday," I could hear Victor speak in a most serious tone. "I need to tell you something. Can you talk?"

"Sure." Jack pulled his index finger to his lips instructing me to be quiet. "What's up?"

"You're going to read about it in the newspaper. I wanted you to hear it first from me."

"Read what, Victor? Are you okay? What's going on?"

"I've been charged with possession of child pornography."

The blood drained from my husband's face. "Has to be a mistake."

"Happened a year ago," Victor explained.

A year ago and Victor never said a word to my husband?

"I'm here for you." Jack's voice shook. "Whatever you need."

The men planned to meet when Victor returned, then Jack hung up and got out of the car. I followed my husband through the garage and up the basement stairs. Although each step was physically painful for him, he didn't say a word. He needed a new knee. Doctors told him to wait, or maybe Jack wanted to wait. Maybe Jack didn't think he had the luxury of a new knee with everything that was going on. Unable to get comfortable, he barely slept. Unable to sleep, he got no relief.

The fact that our temporary lodging forced him down two full flights each day, from the bedroom to the living area, from the living area to the driveway to retrieve his newspaper or get into his car, didn't help. The fact that our beautiful townhouse was being rebuilt by subcontractors who didn't show or didn't do what they had been hired to do didn't help. And now, my husband's best friend was in dire trouble.

Even though it was early, Jack went straight to bed. Tossing and turning, he didn't seem to sleep at all. At one point I woke to find him lying on his back, staring at the ceiling. He had so much on his mind, but nothing was more important than his friend.

Victor was quiet, church going, law abiding. As far as I knew, he had never been in trouble, not even a traffic ticket. He was not impulsive or irrational, impetuous or reckless. He was the voice of reason, the man to whom everyone, especially Jack, went for counsel and help. Victor had been there when the banks wouldn't loan Jack the money to start his real estate business. He was there when Jack left real estate sales for building and development. He was there through every one of Jack's messy separations and his divorce. Victor was always there—the baluster in the turbulence of life—offering advice and money and moral support no matter what. Even though Victor hadn't asked and even though Jack didn't say it out loud, I knew my husband needed to find some way to fix this.

The next morning, Good Friday, Jack got up, showered, and dressed. As he did every morning, he kissed me on the forehead before he left the house. It was life as usual—with my husband on a mission. Giving him space to do what he needed to do, I pressed forward with our plans for an Easter Sunday gathering with our children.

We didn't have space in our small dining room for a big family dinner, so everyone agreed to stop by, all at the same time, for a bite of dessert. A perfect solution. While Jack was gone, I readied the house.

On Saturday I shopped. From the grocery store I picked up plates and napkins, soda and mixers. From the liquor store, I grabbed an extra bottle of wine. From the bakery, I purchased the sweet buttercream bunny cake I had ordered. The cake was so cute with its pink flower nose, mini-marshmallow cottontail, and oversized lashes strung from the thinnest black licorice.

Preparing for our children that Easter Sunday afternoon, Jack and I found ourselves together in the kitchen, bumping into one another, as we gathered plates and set out glasses. Avoiding what my husband was not ready to discuss—his friend—I turned my attention to something we could, at least partially, control—our home.

"The washer and dryer are coming tomorrow," I reminded him with a glow. "We'll be moving back home before you know it." I returned to my task. "I hope Craig is there today painting that laundry room, like he said he would."

Craig always had a phone in his hand when he should have

been holding a paintbrush. Or worse, he was often out somewhere solving some family emergency when he should have been at work. It was no surprise that he found himself so far behind, or as Jack put it, "always up against it." And it was no surprise that to catch up, he often had to work one holiday or another. It was selfish, expecting someone to work on Easter Sunday for my benefit. But I didn't want anything to delay our move, especially not now.

"Do you think we should call Craig?" I laid out the forks and the napkins. "I mean just to make sure?"

"Say what you mean," Jack snapped. "You want *me* to call him."

"No…no, that's not—"

Jack's face flushed beet red and he let out a roar, the likes of which I had never heard come out of anyone. Then, without warning, he grabbed the sweet little bunny cake from the box and threw it across the room. It hit the floor with a splat, sending icing and chunks of vanilla cake everywhere.

"What's wrong with you?" I screeched as I fell to my knees trying to press the little bunny back together.

Without another word Jack turned and left the house. I had no idea where he went that night or most of the nights that followed. But I knew one thing, the shock had passed and the magnitude of his friend's dilemma had punched my husband smack in the gut. From that day forward, nothing, for either of us, nothing would be the same.

68

WRITING LETTERS

"START PACKING," JACK said.

"But the house isn't finished."

"It will be," he declared.

I could see it in his eyes. He needed to be out of that rental and back into our home so he could focus on the task of saving his friend.

"Get it done," he ordered every subcontractor he spoke with on the phone, saw at the house, or ran into unexpectedly at Home Depot. And everyone knew he meant what he said.

❧

A few weeks later, subcontractors stepped out of the way as delivery men hauled in new furniture and Russ's team carted items from our storage unit and our little rental. Each man heaved his side of the awkward loads past freshly painted walls. They moved around standing ladders and opened paint cans and light fixtures still in boxes waiting to be hung. All the while the cleaning crew did their best to make themselves efficient yet scarce, scurrying out of a room every time someone interrupted them.

Jack showed up three quarters of the way through the activities, and while glaring at Craig, promptly announced to every subcontractor still working in the house, "You have until the end of this week to get this house finished." Then he turned toward me and softly said, "Whenever you get a minute."

"Sure." I nodded as he went up the stairs to the home office.

"Lamps, ma'am," a burly man holding one in each of his meaty hands asked.

"Master bedroom." I pointed to the back of the house. Then I made my way up the steps to the office and Jack.

"Absolutely, Jay. Doing everything we can. I'll keep you posted." Jack hung up with Victor's son and turned his attention toward me. "How's it going down there?"

"It's all good," I smiled. "How's it going up here?"

"We're asking everyone to write a letter—a character reference with a plea for house arrest in lieu of prison."

"Are letters admissible?"

"The judge has agreed to review them."

"That's good, right?"

"It's a long shot. But Victor could get four years. We've got to do everything we can."

"Four years?" Hope's father had taken hundreds of inappropriate photos of her and sold them on the internet. He only got something like nine months.

"Victor is wealthy and well-known." Jack answered the question I did not ask. "They're going to make an example out of him."

"Doesn't seem right."

"It's what they're going to do. The more letters, the better." Jack put down his pen and looked squarely at me. "It would mean a lot to me if you would write one." He knew it was a huge request and added, "Will you think about it, please?"

"Ma'am?" one of the men called up to me.

I nodded to my husband as I closed the door behind me. "Coming."

At the bottom of the stairs, the man pointed to a small decorative piece he clutched in his hand and the stack of unmarked boxes behind him. "What about these?"

"Just leave them." I made my way to the kitchen. "I'll figure it out later." I needed a break, a cup of coffee, a second to think about the letter Jack had just asked me to write.

Victor had always been kind to me. When most of Jack's friends were hoping Jack would rekindle with Joan, Victor made me feel comfortable. He seemed to know, more than anyone, how much I loved Jack. He did good work in the community, too. If he wasn't hosting a fundraiser, he was providing support to his church or the food bank, or organizations like Boys and Girls Clubs, Make-A-Wish, and Girls Hope.

But the most amazing thing was the way he took care of his dying wife. He could have hired someone to care for her, or at least hired someone to help. But he did it himself. He prepared her meals, bathed and dressed her, made sure she had every one of her medications precisely on time. He carried her up and down the stairs to the car and took her to every medical appointment. He sat bedside at every hospitalization and comforted her before each of the endless tests and multiple surgeries she was forced to endure. He cleaned the house, paid the bills, learned to do the laundry. He even slept on the floor next to her hospital bed in the family room, just to be sure he could hear her faint calls in the middle of the night. In the end, when a medical mistake took her life, he refused to sue.

But I also knew the consequences of sexual abuse, the hard work of healing children devastated by these crimes. Would I be turning my back on them if I did this for my husband? For Victor?

"I don't know what to do," I told my therapist friend, Anna.

"Touching and non-touching behaviors are different," she reminded me.

She was right. If Victor was guilty, he hadn't directly hurt a child. Still, when those tapes were made a child had, in fact, been hurt.

Anna didn't need to think about whether she would write a letter. When her minister husband, Ted, brought up the subject, she stopped him cold. "Don't even ask." Of course, the man of God wrote a compassionate plea. So did many others. Letters poured in to the court—131 in all.

In the end I wrote one of those letters. I wrote it because I wasn't sure if Victor had done it. Most of all, I wrote it because my husband had asked me to.

69

THE PRECIPITATING EVENT

While subcontractors worked on the final stages of our renovation, I moved items to their rightful spot and discovered things that had been misplaced or thought lost. "Oh, look at this," and "I'd forgotten about that." When someone asked how I was doing, I replied, "Great! It's an opportunity to redecorate." Nothing could have been more honest. I took my time picking out new bedding and draperies, choosing coordinating paint colors, and selecting accent walls I wished I had accented the first time.

My husband didn't share my enthusiasm. Pulled between his business and his friend, the restoration was more than a nuisance or a distraction, it was a thorn—a huge thorn. I added to the problem. Jack told me, more than once, the time it took me to make each of those final selections delayed completion. When I had finally made my last decision, the accent color for the rear wall of our master bedroom closet, I couldn't wait to tell him. Craig could finish and get out of Jack's hair. Surely that would make my husband happy, or at least give him one less thing to worry about.

As soon as I heard the garage door, I hurried to greet my husband with the good news. But the minute he stepped inside, I stopped. His expression was flat, his face colorless.

"Are you okay?"

"No."

I watched as my husband moved from the bedroom to the kitchen to the family room and back again. Pacing was my thing, not Jack's.

I walked toward him. "I didn't cook. I'm sorry. Maybe we can order in?"

"I'm not hungry." Also not like my husband. He sat on the sofa and grabbed the remote. Rather than turning on the television, he stared past me at the black screen.

"Did something happen?"

His eyes met mine. "What do you *really* think?"

"About what?" I made my way around the coffee table and sat next to him, hoping he was not referring to Victor.

"Do you think he did it?" Jack pulled each word, slowly.

Victor lived alone in the four-bedroom house where he and his wife had raised their kids. A lot of people had been in and out in the months before she died. A lot of people after. The CDs were discovered after her funeral. I guess it was possible that someone else could have done it. But who? Who would have watched, downloaded, and saved six CDs from Victor's computer? Who would have stuffed them up inside the suspended ceiling of his basement?

"Did someone say something?" I asked.

"No one said a word. I want to know what *you* think."

"I don't know."

"I want the truth," he insisted.

I couldn't answer as Jack's wife or as a friend of the accused. I could only answer as a survivor. Black or white. Right or wrong. As much as I wished for some gray area between touching and non-touching crimes, for me there was none. I did not want to have this conversation, but we were having it.

"If you really want to know…" I stopped mid-sentence and looked at my husband.

"Yes, I really want to know."

I took a breath and said, "Yes, I think he did it."

"Why, Linnie? Why in the hell would he do something like that?"

"I don't know." Then I added, "If you study the profile of a pedophile—"

Jack's puckered face turned blistering red. He jumped up. "Did you just call Victor a pedophile?"

"That's not—"

While glaring at me through gritted teeth, he said, "He is *not* a pedophile." Then he grabbed his keys and stormed out of the house, slamming the door so hard the living room windows shook.

From that point on, except for his worn clothes in the laundry basket, it seemed Jack was never there. Nothing moved on his side of the bathroom vanity. Not a single piece of paper shifted on his desk. I had no idea if the bills were being paid or his work was getting done. I did not ask. He left each morning before I woke, returned each night after I was asleep. Sometimes I felt the mattress move as he got into or out of our bed. Other than that, we didn't share a meal or speak a word to one another.

70

MEREDITH'S OFFICE

In a session with Meredith in the days shortly after we first learned of Victor's charges, Jack and I agreed that either of us could see her privately. We also agreed that we would see her together on the first Thursday of every month.

I had no idea whether Jack had seen Meredith alone. I had. And given the chilly state of our relationship following that fight we had over Victor some three weeks before, I had no idea if Jack would show for our next joint appointment.

It was the first Thursday in June. I arrived early. With hands on a magazine and eyes on the clock, I waited. Twenty long minutes passed and, finally, three minutes before one, Jack walked through the door.

"Hello," he said as he took a seat across from me.

My eyes rose to meet his. "Hello."

"I'm sorry this is hard," he added.

I hated it when he said that to me, but he was right. The rift between us had been hard, especially given the subject matter. I nodded at my husband as the office door opened and our marriage counselor appeared.

Jack stood. Without a word or a glance in my direction, he followed Meredith. I followed him. As usual, he settled into the loveseat. I found comfort clinging to the arms of the overstuffed chair to his right. A dark wooden side table holding a lamp and a boutique-size tissue box separated us. Meredith opened her manila folder, flipped her tablet to a clean page, clicked her pen. Jack handed her eighty dollars in crisp twenties and Meredith began.

"Jack, has anything changed for you since our individual session a few days ago?"

"No," he replied.

"Is there something you want to tell Linda?"

Sitting with one leg crossed over the other, he looked at me. "I want a divorce."

I repeated his words in my head, *I want a divorce.* I knew he'd leave. After all, that's what he did. He left his first wife five times in the last ten years of their marriage. This would be the fourth time he left me. When he got to this point there was no sense begging or pleading or throwing myself at his feet. I'd done all that. Nothing worked. So I did the only thing I could do. I folded my arms and squeezed out the word, "Fine."

"I'd like things to move quickly," he continued.

In the past he had always asked for ninety days to decide if he wanted a divorce. Not this time.

Meredith turned to me. "Linda, I mentioned to Jack I'd be happy to assist the two of you in mediation. That would support the emotional side of the process that's often neglected, help things move along, and hopefully, prevent the attorneys from getting the bulk of your assets."

"Fine," I replied, but my mind whirled. *Mediation...already?*

Meredith glanced up from her calendar. "How about noon, two weeks from today?"

Jack nodded and for the third time I said, "Fine." But none of it was fine. It was anything but fine. "Why, Jack?"

"This marriage is too hard," he said.

Our marriage had been hard, blending families and finances, my childhood issues, his unrelenting needs. If that wasn't enough, four months ago life dumped on us more than even Jack or I could have imagined. The flood in our home had been stressful enough. By the time we learned about the charges against Victor, it felt like we couldn't handle one more thing.

"These aren't marital problems, Jack. They've come at us from the outside."

Jack shifted in his seat but didn't speak.

"Except for that one big blowup over Victor, we were doing okay. Weren't we?"

He didn't respond.

"Come on. We've overcome so much. Giving up now won't fix anything."

He didn't move.

I turned toward Meredith. I trusted her. Of all the therapists I'd seen, she was the only one who understood my childhood history. She was also the therapist who'd helped Jack understand the situation a little when a series of obscene phone calls sent me into a tailspin. I even felt like she had my back, ethically of course. She'd never do anything she shouldn't, and she'd never tell me anything Jack told her. He'd have to do that.

"Can you tell Linda what's going on for you?" Meredith asked.

With his eyes on the floor, Jack spoke in a soft voice, "I need to get away from your sexual abuse issues."

"What? What did he say? *What did you say?*"

He looked at Meredith as though begging intervention. She shook her head and made a few notes but said not a word.

"I need to get away from your abuse issues," he repeated a little louder.

"You bastard!" I clapped my hand over my lips to keep from saying anything else.

Like my mother, I can be emotional, overly emotional. I know that more than anyone—say nothing of my reaction when you add the issue of child sexual abuse. I didn't want to blow up our relationship again as I had when my childhood memories returned. That's why in the past eight weeks, since we learned of Victor's charges, I stuffed my feelings and shut my mouth. I did anything—everything—my husband asked of me. I only shared my feeling once. Only when Jack insisted.

"Why are you doing this?" I held back tears. "I was a good wife, wasn't I?"

"You were."

"I didn't balk when you started spending every night and every weekend with Victor."

"You didn't."

"I didn't make you choose."

"You didn't."

"When you asked, didn't I write a letter requesting a lesser sentence?"

"One of the best they received."

I looked to Meredith. "Me, a survivor, a child advocate, asking the judge for leniency. What more could I have done?" Then it hit me. "Wait a minute. When we had that fight, you said I called Victor a pedophile. Is that what this is about?"

"He is *not* a pedophile," Jack snapped.

"Jack," Meredith intervened. "Some people make the mistake of misdirecting their anger, many times toward the person who's closest to them. Is it possible that might be happening here?"

He folded his arms. "I doubt it."

"Okay then," Meredith glanced at the clock, then back at Jack. "Have you thought about timing, living arrangements, finances?"

It was all moving so fast. I couldn't get my head around any of it, and Meredith was drilling down into divorce details. What the hell?

"I'll continue to pay the bills as I have been doing and give Linda copies of all written checks."

Damn right you'll pay the bills. Divorce is going to cost a lot more than that.

"What about living arrangements?" she asked.

"Victor has offered me his spare bedroom."

There it was. I felt sick. Some men move in with another woman. My husband was moving in with a man who had just been charged with possession of child pornography.

"When?" Meredith asked.

"I don't know." Jack shrugged. "In a day or..."

I jumped up. "I want you out *now*."

"But I have meetings this afternoon."

"After work then." I pulled my purse to my shoulder and headed for the door.

71

THE STAIRWELL

EVEN THOUGH IT was only one flight down to the ground floor, given Jack's bad knee, I knew he'd take the elevator. So I slipped into the concrete stairwell. The door slammed behind me and after the cold echo faded, it was silent. Vacant. I leaned back against the wall, trembling with hurt and anger, as much at myself as at Jack. Each time he moved out friends and family cautioned, "Don't take him back, he'll just do it again." They were right.

Even a fortuneteller had wagged a warning finger. Ten years ago, a few weeks before we had gotten engaged, Jack took me to New Orleans to see the city, enjoy the NFL Experience and, his personal favorite, attend the Super Bowl. The Steelers lost the NFC championship after we'd made our reservations, so our home team wouldn't be playing. But that didn't keep us from wanting to go. In fact, we couldn't wait to check into the quaint bed and breakfast in the heart of the French Quarter. We weren't disappointed. Dressed in rich, dark antiques, the room was beautiful. To our delight we woke each morning to the smell of warm, homemade, buttery croissants and a row of doves lined along the balcony cooing for crumbs.

As we hoped, K-Paul's was fabulous. Chef Prudhomme, massive in his wheelchair, glided around his restaurant soaking in the accolades of his delicious creations, signing cookbooks, taking photos. I wasn't about to miss an opportunity like that. Without hesitation, like a tiny bird, I perched upon his wide lap, erect, and giggling. Afterwards with autographed cookbook snug in my arms, Jack and I walked the uneven cobblestone streets of the vibrant city. We discussed jazz, about which he knew some and I knew nothing, and the infamous Preservation Hall, where we would end our evening.

We hadn't gotten far when, up ahead, I noticed a fortuneteller. She stood in front of a huge pair of beautiful black wrought iron gates guarding an old stone church. I couldn't take my gaze from her. Almost hypnotically and without a word, I made my way toward her. Jack, who typically dictated everything from where we stayed, to where we ate, to what we did, didn't say a word. As though he knew there was no swaying me, he quietly followed.

When I approached, the woman motioned me inside her tent. I sat across from her. Jack took a seat to my left, out of the way. I extended my hands into her opened palms. Her eyes were deep and black, her hands warm and firm.

"There's something you need to know," she began.

I had never met a real mystic, if she was one. But she looked exactly as I imagined one might look. Dressed in a multicolored, layered, long skirt, she had a multitude of beads around her neck, rings on every finger. The scarf on her head tied on its side, allowing the long ends of her thick black curls to bounce when she moved.

"Do not marry this man," she warned, her gaze piercing me.

I didn't want to believe her, although the distress in her whisper left me with a shiver.

She was right. There was no fairy tale here. Just pain and heartbreak.

Why didn't I listen?

❧

At the bottom of the stairwell, I pushed through the heavy steel door into the glass-enclosed lobby below Meredith's office. The area was empty, except for a tiny woman, slightly hunched, her crippled fingers struggling to close her dripping umbrella. The beautiful spring day had given way to a dark and vicious storm. I didn't have anything to keep me dry. Worse, through the pounding rain, illuminated by flashes of lightning, I saw Jack's car. It was still in the lot.

I glanced at the elevator door. He would emerge at any moment. Rather than risk running into him, where I would say something I shouldn't or, worse, burst into tears in front of him, I dropped my head and pushed into the windy torrent.

As I made my way to the far side of the lot, dodging puddles, getting battered by the unseasonably icy sheet, I accepted the sad twist of fate. Jack left Joan for me. He was leaving me for Victor. If ever there was punishment, which the strict Catholic school of steel-edged rulers had more than confirmed, I was getting mine. If ever there was revenge, Joan was about to get every ounce she deserved.

Surely, the rest of Jack's family would also feel vindicated to learn they were rid of me. I didn't know Jack when he left Joan the first four times, but to each member of his family I was more than the fifth reason he strayed; I was the reason he never returned. I filled with an odd combination of sadness and relief at the loss of a family I tried so hard to know, to love, to become a part of.

No matter how hard I tried, I never felt accepted by any of them, except Charlotte.

Married to Jack's only nephew, Charlotte and I were as different as the blacktop that stretched long between us. Infused with a deep Georgia drawl and Lilly Pulitzer gingham, Charlotte was private and, at times, inflexible, at least around Jack's family. She didn't care much for sports, which his family centered on, and she didn't pretend. Raised with strict southern etiquette including tea parties served on fine china, Charlotte learned what to wear, how to sit, and when to smile. She worked hard to please her own mother and father but cared less what Jack or any member of Jack's family thought.

Not me. I craved the acceptance of Jack's family over my own. Underneath my desire lay a willful, steel-town, blue-collar little girl who grew up in hand-me-downs and chaos, with little social training and a hefty dose of defiance and determination. I had been known to yell, throw, and stomp when I didn't get my way. And when Mom and I were at odds, which happened frequently, especially during my teens, I'd take the forbidden walk or drive Mom's off-limits car to the garage where my dad worked. Once there I'd stretch my head under the raised hood of whatever vehicle Daddy was repairing or rebuilding.

"Can you teach me?" I tried to mask my need for his attention as a desire to learn his trade.

My father knew better. He'd step back from under that hood, wipe his large, blackened hands on some stained, orange towel, and say, "Go home. A grease-stained four-bay with dirty tools and filthy jokes is no place for my little girl—no matter how old you are." Then he'd add, "Whatever it is, we'll talk about it later."

Although Charlotte and I were women of distinct differences, what kept us both outside the Dunigan family circle was something we had in common—our positions in the hierarchy. She was the only other second wife. Even though she had married Jack's nephew, Matt, after his wife left him—a divorce he did not want and struggled to survive—she, too, had always been on the fringes. Both of us had been banished to perpetual purgatory—not quite a member, not quite an outcast—of this too-close clan with their happy unions, high incomes, trendy appearances, and designer day-care kids. A life they made look far too easy, yet totally out of reach.

❧

As I approached my car the downpour paused. I pulled my white Oxford shirt from my wet skin and glanced back at the lobby. Jack was watching. Inside, perfectly dry, he fixed on my every move. Not unlike the way he once used to stare at me, his desk next to mine. Then, he couldn't wait to touch my skin, smell my hair, possess every inch of me. Now, with that same intensity, he could not wait to set me free.

Anxious to get out of the rain and out of his line of sight, I dug through my clutch, removed my wallet, lip gloss, nail file, pen. Jack bought me this used Jaguar XJ Vanden Plas after our last separation, begging my forgiveness, promising he'd never leave again. His offering, designed to satisfy his guilt or illustrate the seductive benefits of his wealth, or both, didn't come with a remote. It didn't come with any real guarantees either.

Fumbling to unlock the car, tears formed—as much from the mascara in my eyes as from embarrassment. First in Meredith's office, again in the parking lot, and each and every time I had to tell family and friends he'd left again. This time would surely be the worst. How could I ever tell my staunch Catholic mother, mortified by the sins of her beloved church, that my husband was moving in with a pedophile?

I was barely settled into the tan leather seat when my cell rang. It was Shari. The bony-legged, braces-wearing little sister I used to threaten and bribe when, at our mother's insistence, she trailed me to places I wasn't allowed to go, had grown to be a beautiful woman with a life of her own. A life based less on things, more on love and children and family—not perfect, but far more stable and content than I could ever hope mine to be.

"I only have a minute," she said. "Wanted to see how you're doing."

"He wants a divorce. Said he needs to get away from my sexual abuse issues."

"He said that?"

"Yep!" I pushed the mousy-brown strands out of my eyes and wiped the greasy steaks from my face. "He's moving in with Victor."

"What?"

Deep in my gut I believed Jack would never hurt a child. I also believed that once he moved in with Victor, others would not share my conviction.

"I'm so sorry. Is there anything I can do?"

"Tell me what in the hell he's thinking?" I thrust my car into traffic, cutting off a Silver BMW indiscernible in the gray foggy downpour that, like me, had begun to pick up fury.

"These past few months have been tough on both of you."

"Damn right they've been tough, but I stood by him."

"Yes, you did."

"And I took him back how many times?"

"Maybe too many." Her voice trailed off and I knew what she was thinking. Each time Jack left she'd counsel, "You'd never put up with that with anyone else. What happened to my strong, confident sister?"

"No more," I said. "I'm going to make him regret this decision."

"Well, don't do anything you'll regret," she said.
"Like slashing his tires or setting his SUV on fire?"
"Or buying a gun," she responded, and we both laughed.

72

MEDIATION

Joan and Jack chose mediation when they divorced. After paying lawyers thousands of dollars, Tony and I met at a restaurant, drew a line down the middle of a yellow tablet and divided our assets. Despite what I had done, Tony kept our divorce amicable and fair. In the dissolution of the marriage to Jack, despite what had happened, I intended to do the same. So, although I didn't see the purpose of mediation, if Jack wanted to do it that way, I trusted Meredith to guide us through it.

"You'll never guess who I ran into," Jack said as he entered Meredith's waiting room and took a seat across from me.

"No clue," I replied.

"Mitch was at the Gandy Dancer the other night."

"Is he still as crazy as he used to be?"

"Absolutely." Jack laughed.

"Did he ever marry that pretty blonde? She was so sweet." I shook my head, trying to recall. "Was her name Ellen?"

Just then Meredith's office door opened and without interrupting our conversation, she waved us in.

"She was with him, but you know me, I couldn't remember her name." Jack followed Meredith and I followed him.

"*Not you.*" I exaggerated the words and we both laughed.

"They never married, but they seem really happy," he added.

"Maybe that's the secret." I snickered, shaking my head.

"Maybe it is." He laughed. "Oh, and by the way, I have a few things for you." He laid a brown manila envelope on the end table beside him.

"I have something for you, too." I pointed to a bag on the floor next to my leg. "Maybe we can exchange in the lobby later?"

Jack agreed.

"You two seem to be getting along nicely." Meredith glanced between us.

"No sense making this harder than it has to be," I said.

With that Jack handed Meredith a check and mediation began.

"Jack, do you still want to go through with this?"

He said yes, but shook his head no.

"Are you sure?" she asked.

"In fact, I'd like things to move quickly." He looked at me. "I filed, Linnie. I'm sorry. Your attorney will be getting some paperwork."

"Things can't move as quickly as you'd like," I said.

"Why not?"

"We need to be married at least ten years."

Even though we worked equally hard and owned the business equally, Jack collected a much larger check. We set it up that way. He would retire earlier. He told me it was essential we max out his Social Security first. It would benefit me in the long run. When he was gone, he said I could collect the larger of the two checks. So long as I didn't remarry, that right continued after divorce. But

Jack and I had to be married at least ten years. With our ninth anniversary a few months away, one more year didn't seem unreasonable—at least not to me. Since Jack was the plaintiff—the one who filed—and I was the defendant—the party filed against—he controlled the action, I controlled the timeline. At least that's what I understood.

After a brief silence Jack said, "Well, I guess there's nothing we can do about that."

"Nope," I confirmed.

Changing the subject, Meredith asked if Jack was settled in and how things were going with Victor. Then we talked about a few final repairs that still needed to be completed at the house, how I was holding up, and how we were going to handle bills and mail. With all of that out of the way, Meredith got down to rules of mediation.

"Once we start the process, I will no longer be a therapist to either one of you. I can meet with you separately, relative to the marriage, so long as the other person gives permission." She looked to each of us for acknowledgement. We nodded. Then she set another appointment in two weeks stating, "The next time we meet we will begin asset distribution. Is that acceptable to both of you?"

He nodded and even though I had no intention of returning to mediation, at least not anytime soon, I agreed.

"Before we wrap things up today, do either of you have any questions?"

"I do." Jack turned toward me. "I hate to ask, but do you think I could have my mother's ring back?"

"I'll think about it."

After our session, I followed Jack to a small bench in the glass-enclosed lobby. He handed me a manila envelope with copies of bills he'd paid and a few pieces of my mail that had gone to his post office box.

I reached into the bag on the floor beside me and pulled out a small gold gift bag, stuffed with glittery white tissue paper. A long bow of curling ribbon hung from the handle.

He looked at me a long second before he reached between the tissue paper and pulled out a tiny black velvet box. He snapped it open. I had taken his mother's engagement ring to the jeweler, gotten it cleaned, and purchased a new box for it. His eyes welled up.

"I never would have kept it." With manila folder in hand, I stood and looked at Jack. "Good luck with Victor, Jack. I really hope things work out for both of you."

73

CHARLOTTE'S DIAGNOSIS

A MONTH LATER, while in the throes of the separation and the trial and the unfinished punch list at the house, Jack received bad news. "Charlotte has breast cancer." He told me in an email.

He went on to explain that his brother's family had gone to dinner to celebrate a birthday or an anniversary. While passing the bread, Charlotte mentioned the oddest thing. Her tongue had been numb. At the urging of her mother, a breast cancer survivor, and Jack's sister-in-law Judy, a nurse, Charlotte agreed to call her family doctor.

Charlotte's PCP sent her straight to her gynecologist, calling ahead to say she was en route. By the time Charlotte's mammogram had been read, an oncologist was standing by. He wanted to perform additional tests without delay. But Charlotte decided to postpone further diagnostics until she returned from vacation. As they had done every year, Charlotte, Matt, their two small children, Charlotte's brother, and her parents all took a one-week trip to the shores of Orange Beach.

The minute they returned, tests were performed, and a diagnosis confirmed. At thirty-four, the stay-at-home mother of two preschoolers had stage 4 breast cancer already metastasized to her spine, brain, liver, and lungs.

74

THE STORY EMERGES

Francie sat across from me in our regular booth. "I got an email from Jack yesterday," she said. "A group notice about Victor's arraignment on Friday. Wasn't sure you knew."

"I wasn't part of the group, but he did message me. He wants everyone to be there to support Victor. Just doesn't want anyone to know he wants me there, too."

"You going?"

"I want the truth."

"I don't blame you. There have been so many stories." She took a forkful of grilled chicken salad and dipped it into her side of ranch dressing. "When Jack first said a Trojan horse had taken control of Victor's computer and attached kiddie porn to those raunchy jokes these guys were emailing back and forth, I wasn't sure I believed it."

"Seemed farfetched, but Jack did race his computer off to have it purged."

"He did?"

I nodded.

"Must have scared him to death," Francie added. "Maybe one of these days we'll know what really happened."

"Last night on the news they said this started over a year ago when state and local police, the FBI, and the Postal Inspector raided Victor's home."

"All those guns and badges." She clicked her tongue. "A year is a long time to keep that quiet."

"He didn't even tell Jack, which shook my husband to the core."

"Do you think Jack knows what really happened?"

"Jack told me six CDs were found in the suspended ceiling of Victor's basement."

"How on earth were they discovered?"

"Some cable guy running new FIOS lines came across them. Slid one into the computer in the basement."

"Dear Lord. Doesn't that violate some search and seizure law?"

"I guess not. Police descended. Sounds like there were hundreds of images. Supposedly sixty or so were pictures of prepubescent children. The family maintains it was adult porn with a few child images accidentally mixed in."

"I suppose if someone's willing to make child porn, he'd go to any length to distribute it," Francie said.

"And of course now someone is alleging chat room activity, which I don't believe for a second."

"Piling on." Francie shook her head. "True or not, this is going to get worse before it gets better."

"On Friday at this hearing or arraignment or whatever it is, the prosecutor will read aloud each of the charges in full detail. Then I guess Victor has to plead guilty or innocent to each one." I sipped a spoonful of soup. "I can't believe Jack wants any of us there."

"Tim thinks he's in denial. I wonder how he'll handle the truth?"

"Maybe he'll realize these aren't videos of two seven-year-olds playing doctor." I shifted in my seat.

"My fear is what the gruesome details will resurrect for you. You shouldn't go alone."

"You're probably right."

"I'd go, but Tim has another doctor appointment." She sighed. "That's my life right now. Kidney disease, cardiovascular disease, diabetes, and wounds that won't heal. Oh well." She hesitated while pouring the last of the dressing over her remaining salad. "Nothing I can do about that. I'll just focus on getting us moved into the next phase of our lives."

She was referring to her future home at a state-of-the-art progressive lifestyle community where residents transition from private luxury carriage homes to assisted living to nursing care as needed.

"You'll feel better after you and Tim are finally in there." I dipped a cracker into my broth and took a bite.

"And you'll be better off once you and Jack are finally divorced."

I couldn't help but laugh. I wanted her to be right, but I didn't believe her on that day any more than I believed her when she had said it to me the three previous times.

She added, "It'll be hard to make the standard of living adjustment, but you'll be fine."

"A girl's gotta do—"

"Well, don't *do* anything until you see your attorney." Her voice was firm.

"Why? Is he hiding money or something?" I tried to joke, but couldn't cover my concern.

She peered at me over her readers. "If Tim gave me any inkling that he might, I'd tell you." Then she sipped her coffee and continued. "What I mean is, don't go accepting some settlement without first discussing it with your attorney. He's tried that before."

"I see Joel in a few days. I think I'm going to see a financial advisor, too."

"Good."

The waitress refilled Francie's coffee and laid separate checks on the table. "No hurry, ladies."

"By the way, I almost forgot." She dug for her wallet. "If you're not busy Saturday, Tim and I would like to have you over for dinner."

"Thanks, but I already promised Nora. We're going to this place called The Back Door."

"Never been."

"Good food, good band." I imagined the bar surrounded by older men, mostly retired. All of them balding and with aches and pains they wanted to conceal. It was a discouraging thought, but trendy downtown clubs were for the young. Two weeks shy of fifty, I no longer fit into that category.

"I'm free Friday night, if you are." I was hoping she'd save me from an evening alone.

"Jack's coming," Francie said half-smiling. She knew it was hard for me to hear that, harder if she hadn't told me. "Next weekend then?" She blotted her lips and removed her readers.

"Next weekend."

I was grateful for my dear friend's wisdom and support. She had my best interest at heart. But for the first time, I didn't know how to stay close to Francie while she and Tim maintained a friendship with Jack.

75

FIRST TIME IN FIVE WEEKS

EACH OF THE charges would be read in detail and Victor would plead guilty. His family asked that no one attend the arraignment.

Shortly thereafter another critical email circulated. Again, I was privately invited.

> *Sentencing is scheduled for July 25th. Please attend. Please show your support for Victor. We want the judge to see how many lives this man has touched, how much support he has in the community.*

This was the moment Victor's legal team had been working toward.

Unable to sleep as a blend of nervousness about the hearing combined with anxiety over seeing Jack for the first time in five weeks, I got up, dressed, and left home early. After a thirty-five-minute commute, I pulled into a spot on the second floor of the parking garage. It was 7:15. I locked the car, took the elevator to the first floor, and walked up Fifth Avenue. I turned left onto Grant Street and stepped through the revolving door of the U.S. Post Office building. Two men guarding the entrance smiled. I was dressed in a suit, so perhaps they thought me a lawyer or maybe they could see how nervous I was. I don't know; I smiled back.

"Can I help you?" one asked.

I fumbled to open the email I held in my hand. "I'm here for the trial in Judge…"

"Judge Carr," one of the men interrupted.

"Yes," I said, relieved.

"No cell phones," he instructed. I knew that. The letter attached to Jack's email had said so. I told the security guard I had locked my cell in the glove compartment of my car. He nodded, then instructed me to put my heels and handbag into a small plastic bin. As directed, I padded in stocking feet through the metal detector.

"You're good to go." The man on the other end held out the container that held my belongings. He whispered, "Doesn't start till 9:30."

I blushed.

"Cafeteria is up one floor. Have a cup of coffee while you wait." He pointed toward the elevator.

I poured myself a coffee, paid the cashier, took a seat in a far corner of the room. Over and over that morning I asked myself, "Why are you doing this?" I asked as I dressed, as I pulled out of the driveway, as I merged onto the highway. I asked as I drove into the parking spot. If you had asked me, I would have said, "To see for myself." That was true. But the reason I could not admit, not to myself or anyone else, was that I was also doing this for Jack.

My estranged husband loved his friends and expected me to love them, too. This wasn't just *any* friend. It was the man who had been there for Jack when no one else was. If I didn't show up, Jack would not only take my absence as a judgment and rejection of Victor, he would take it as a judgment and rejection of him.

Close to 9:00, I made my way to the eighth floor. It was cold and dark and empty. I had once been in a hot, noisy, over-crowded county courtroom. Children ran the halls, and everywhere I looked furniture needed to be repaired or replaced. I had never been inside a federal courthouse, much less a federal courtroom. I don't know if it was the gleaming floors, so polished I could almost see myself, the oversized doors that stood locked before me, or the power of this federal judge who held in his hand the fate of a man that none of us would ever really know was guilty or innocent.

Off to the side of the large, vacant vestibule, I stepped into the restroom and switched on the light. After washing my hands, I lingered at the sink. Staring into the metal-framed mirror, I considered each line that had, in the past year, appeared on my thinning face. Aging amplified by stress. I fussed with my hair and reapplied my lipstick before returning to the waiting area, where people had begun to gather in small whispering groups. Jack was in the center of one such cluster when he caught a glimpse of me. I expected he would nod from a distance, but he made his way across the room.

"Thanks for coming," Jack said softly.

I looked at him. It was a sad day for Victor's family and friends, for the man accused, for the judge who would cast the sentence. Most of all it was a sad day for Jack and me, torn apart by this tragedy. There was nothing to say. I turned from Jack and headed back into the bathroom.

76

THE TRIAL BEGINS

The carved wooden doors opened and, as though entering a church sanctuary for a funeral, the mass of supporters and colleagues and reporters followed the defendant's daughter and two sons down the carpeted center aisle.

Situated in the rear half of the procession, I stepped into the majestic two-story courtroom. Dressed in rich, raised crimson paneling, the walls matched every desk and every chair. The exquisite ceiling, trimmed in what appeared to be sculptured plaster crown molding, featured at its center an expansive medallion around which eagles soared. Up a few steps, the judge's bench towered in size and presence. On the wall behind the bench, a seventeen-foot fresco mural known as *Steel Industry*, by Howard Norton Cook, had been installed in 1936. A testament to the importance of protecting all, especially the working class. The attention to detail in that courtroom was as meticulous and critical as the cases that were heard there.

One by one, each person slid across one of the five double-wide wooden pews on either side of the aisle. Three rows back, on the left-hand side, behind what I would later learn was the defendant's table, I sidled in next to Helen. On her other side sat her husband Marcus.

Marcus had drafted wills and deeds, corporations and agreements for Jack from the moment he opened his real estate business. He had done the same for Victor before that, and for me after Jack and I married. Most of all, Marcus resolved the occasional dispute with a tenant or a buyer, with a homeowner association or a contractor, in a mature, calm, and compromising way. "Better not to fight," he always said.

Not the typical motto of any attorney I had ever known, not that I knew many. I trusted Marcus so much that on more than one occasion, I sought his advice about my relationship with Jack. I saw him as a father figure. That day, I found comfort sitting next to him and Helen. A comfort I needed more than I realized at that time.

The room grew still when, escorted by the marshal, Victor entered, his head low, his walk stuttered by shackled ankles. My heart sank for his family. What could his children be thinking—feeling—seeing their father like that? If there was any bright side, his children had to be relieved to see their father in his own conservative blue suit, white shirt, striped tie, rather than the damning orange jumpsuit we were warned he might be forced to wear.

As soon as Victor took his place at the defendant's table, the law clerk stepped to the center and announced, "Please rise." We did. The judge entered from a door off to the right of his bench. He sat and the law clerk said, "Please be seated." As though rehearsed, in unison, we sat.

There must have been an army of people on both sides working behind the scenes to prepare. But that day, Victor was represented by two attorneys, Mr. Berry, a nondescript man, and Ms. Allen, a tall blonde woman. One man, Mr. Harlan, stood for the prosecution.

This wasn't some Perry Mason television show where lawyers faced the gallery or the jury and spoke loud enough for all to hear. There was no jury. This was not a trial. It was a sentencing hearing. Everyone spoke directly to the judge.

Court convened at 9:30 a.m., and any prior discussion of the evidence or how it had been discovered, or any lingering conjecture over guilt or innocence, no longer mattered.

The judge began. "On June 18 of 2007, the defendant, Victor Martin Tolbert, pled guilty to Count 1 of the information in this case. The record should show that the court has received 131 letters concerning the defendant, which we'll mark as court exhibits and make part of the record of this hearing. If counsel and defendant come forward, the clerk will place the defendant under oath."

Victor shuffled forward with his attorney and stood before the judge. Victor raised his right hand, exposing cuffed wrists. It gave me pause to see a man I had held in such esteem bound and chained.

After Victor was sworn in, the judge asked, "Mr. Tolbert, have you read the presentence report?"

"Yes, I have," he responded. Then, as instructed, he returned to his place and listened while his attorney reiterated what we already knew.

Victor pled guilty to avoid a costly grand jury indictment or a trial. He saw a psychologist. This offense came at a time when he was experiencing extraordinary mental and emotional distress associated with his wife's severe, unrelenting, and ultimately fatal disease. Fred Berlin, Director of the Institute at Johns Hopkins for

Sexual Disorders, concluded that Mr. Tolbert was not a pedophile and represented no danger to children. And of the pornography he possessed, only a small fraction, 15 percent, was child pornography. This offense occurred over a short period of time.

"In addition," his attorney continued, "The presence of so many friends and relatives in this courtroom today is their indication, their belief in Victor Tolbert, notwithstanding what he did, which was wrong and illegal. But there's something about this man they must think a lot of, and I thank each of them for writing letters and for being here today."

Mr. Berry spoke at length about the due diligence he had personally conducted on the character and reputation of the defendant, with stellar results. He cited something about adequate deterrence to criminal conduct, which I didn't understand, and protecting the public from further crimes of the defendant. Then he went on to recite several similar cases that received reduced sentences.

"Your Honor, I've handled a lot of cases on both sides of the table, so to speak, and handled a number of them in front of you. This has been one of the hardest cases I've ever had to handle because I've gotten to know Mr. Tolbert. He's a humble and good man, a giving and caring man, a man who was under tremendous emotional stress that many of us probably can't imagine when he committed this offense. He's been charged; he's pled guilty. He's disgraced. He will be required to register as a sex offender. He has been in jail for five weeks. The first time I saw him was about a week ago, and he was wearing striped prison garb. I've never seen that in the jails that I've been in. He has been through so much over these past years. Under the circumstances I am suggesting to this court a substantial variance and I would submit that it would not be unreasonable."

His substantial variance—home detention. Then with permission the attorney handed the court what was referred to as "sentencing exhibits."

"They are admitted," the judge replied, and the hearing moved to the next phase.

"The court has been informed that you have two witnesses to present."

"Yes, Miss Allen will conduct their direct," Mr. Berry answered.

"We're ready to hear them."

As Mr. Berry sat, Miss Allen pointed out to the court that in most sentencing hearings one would expect that those who come to watch and those who come to testify are, for the most part, standing against the defendant. Not this time. This arms-length, non-touching crime has no tangible victims who could be called upon to tell their side of the story. She emphasized that both witnesses and everybody filling the gallery, save the few who were there to report and inform, had come in defense of the defendant.

"Your Honor, the first witness we would call is Jack Dunigan."

Jack stood, adjusted his tie, buttoned the middle button on his navy suit coat. He looked as he always did in formal attire: striking, handsome, confident. He stepped into the wooden box and raised his right hand. After being sworn in, he sat in the green leather swivel armchair, the witness chair. All eyes were on him.

"Good morning," Miss Allen began.

"Morning." Jack cleared his throat.

"Where do you reside?" she asked.

"Franklin Park."

"How long have you been a resident?"

"I grew up there…graduated from North Allegheny High School."

The attorney continued, "That would be more than a few years or so. Would I be correct?

"Yes," he answered.

True, but not the whole truth. Jack hadn't lived in the community since 1994 when he left Joan, except of course for the past five weeks when he left me and moved in with Victor.

"Where were you educated, sir?" she asked.

"I was educated in college in VMI, received a Bachelor of Science degree." He tripped over his words. Something I hadn't seen him do before.

"Did you have any military service?"

Jack explained that upon graduation he was commissioned as a second lieutenant, an executive officer of the military police in charge of the stockade at Fort Lewis, Washington.

"My mission, or our mission, at Fort Lewis was to apprehend the AWOLs that had gone—deserted the Army and were heading to Canada."

"Could you explain to the court the nature of your occupation?"

"I'm a real estate developer, ma'am."

"Would you tell the court how you met Mr. Tolbert?"

"I met Mr. Tolbert at a function in North Park when our wives belonged to the Junior Women's Club...Mr. Tolbert and I were assigned to, asked, to take the harp off the stage...That's when I first met him."

"You've been friends ever since?"

After answering yes, Jack talked of family trips they had shared, real estate both men had developed, built, and sold, and a lengthy list of notable volunteer projects they had been involved in together.

"Over how many years has this activity spanned?"

"Over thirty-five years."

"And we're not just talking about stroking a chick; are we, sir?"

"No. We're not. We're talking about on the field."

"Roll your sleeves up and work for the organization?"

"Dig in. Yes, ma'am."

"Now, did there come a time, after you had learned that Victor Tolbert had gotten into the trouble that brought him here today, that you and Mr. Tolbert discussed devising a community service project, with one of the objects, frankly, being if he were sentenced to home detention, he could work on, in an effort to give back to the community?"

"We became aware of a project in Boston, Massachusetts."

"Tell us about that please."

He explained how Homes for Troops takes the most seriously wounded veterans returning from the Iraqi War and builds for them handicap-accessible homes.

"And did you bring a project to their attention that you wanted to do with Mr. Tolbert?"

"Mr. Josh Palmieri flew in, at the expense of the Tolbert Organization. We explained what our intentions were. And we also disclosed at that time the gross misjudgment that Mr. Tolbert had in committing the crime, and his pleading."

"And they approved your proposed project, knowing the circumstance?"

"The indication was, we were going to work together to build these homes."

"Was this project abandoned?"

"On July 16, we received a call from Homes for Troops, along with a letter, that they were withdrawing because of the situation that involved Mr. Tolbert and his charges, and the fact that he had pled guilty to them."

"So, what did you and Mr. Tolbert and your other partners do about that?"

Jack told the court how they formed their own 501(c)(3) non-profit; they would build one-level handicap-accessible homes, free and clear of any financial obligations to the veteran and his family. They even had a local veteran selected.

"What role is planned for Victor Tolbert in this charitable work?"

"Mr. Tolbert is going to be the project manager."

"Now, would you be supervising this work?"

"Yes. He'll report to me and the Board of Directors."

"Is this project close to your heart?" the attorney asked.

"My stepson is on the Harry S. Truman nuclear aircraft carrier. He's on his way to the Persian Gulf. That's why I wear a pin of the U.S. flag and the Navy flag." With two fingers Jack tapped his lapel.

My son was not on his way to the Persian Gulf. He was in the Mediterranean, headed to Roda, Spain. Although annoying, that didn't bother me as much as what came next.

"Mr. Dunigan, can you tell the court where you are presently residing?"

"I'm residing in Mr. Tolbert's home. When Mr. Tolbert heard of my present situation of the separation of my marriage, he said, 'I have a four-bedroom home. Why don't you come and live here until things settle out and you understand what you're going to be doing?'"

"If Judge Carr were to sentence Mr. Tolbert to home detention, would you be willing to remain in that home with Mr. Tolbert during that period of time?"

"Yes."

There it was.

❧

The only other witness, the defendant's son, Jay, took the stand. After being sworn in, he shared details of their very close family, all who would check in on their father; then he emphasized the stress his father had been under during his mother's illness and death.

"Is there anything you would like to say to the court before your father is sentenced today?" Ms. Allen asked.

"Yes." He looked at the judge. "Your Honor, when I first learned of the charges he was facing, I was devastated. It was impossible for me to believe that the man I've known my whole life could be involved in this activity. However, I love my dad....We have—he has seven grandchildren...and there is an eighth due in December...These kids absolutely love and adore their grandfather. A little over a year ago, when my mom passed away, my kids lost their grandma, and now, more than ever, they need their grandfather and his loving influence. And I know you have a very difficult decision to make. However, I implore you, I beg of you, to show leniency in your decision and please return him home to us as soon as possible."

Miss Allen turned to the court. "I have nothing else, Your Honor."

"Mr. Harlan."

"No questions, Your Honor."

❧

As the last witness, Victor's son, made his way to his seat, the judge enumerated the three sentencing guidelines necessary to issue his final ruling.

The judge continued, "The defendant requests the court depart based on his alleged diminished capacity and mental and emotional condition...the defendant here can establish neither. The defendant next argues that the court should depart because of his extraordinary charitable acts and good works...While the charitable acts in which he engaged are admirable, none are exceptional for an individual of his socioeconomic status. The defendant next argued that his extraordinary acceptance of responsibility and post-offense rehabilitation warranted departure...His efforts to cooperate and to admit his offense after his arrest are simply not substantially different from the conduct in which many defendants engage after being arrested. Finally the defendant argues that 2G.2(b)(6) unfairly punishes those who use a computer for obtaining child pornography more severely than those who use other means.

"The advent of the Internet has made it easier to produce and distribute child pornography. The National Center for Missing and Exploited Children estimates that the number of child pornography images online has increased by 1,500 percent since 1997. Accordingly, the court finds that…Section2G2.2(b)9(6) enhancement is therefore essential in properly sentencing defendants in these sort of cases.

"Although the defendant argues that he has not attempted to have any inappropriate contact with a minor and that he did not attempt to solicit any child…defendant has helped perpetuate and sustain the system which injures children…the creation of pornography. As the United Nations report on child pornography noted, sexually exploited children are put at great risk for sexually transmitted diseases and injuries...Further, many mental and psychological health problems result from this abuse, including serious depression, devastated self-esteem, distorted perceptions of sex, impaired learning ability, and impaired attention and memory span, and an ability to trust, to name just a few.

"During congressional hearings on online child pornography in 2006, Dr. Sharon Cooper described studies find that…children were twenty-eight times more likely to be arrested for prostitution over their lifetime. When the photos or videos are posted on the internet, those images live on forever, potentially haunting victims for the rest of their lives.

"These children are not only victims of child pornography. Law enforcement officers, psychologists, and other experts have attested to the fact that child pornography is used by child molesters and pornographers to trick children into engaging in depicted activity…Even if an individual is not out and molesting children, the mere possession of pornography helps create and fuel a market where children are being raped, abused, and victimized…In sum, because of the seriousness and magnitude of the defendant's offense, a sentence that does not include a significant term of incarceration would not satisfy the purposes set forth in Section 3553(a).

"The court will, however, take the defendant's circumstances into consideration…With that in mind, if there are any additional comments on what the sentence ought to be, you have an opportunity to do that now, Mr. Berry."

Mr. Berry stood. "I would like the record to reflect that we take exception to Your Honor's ruling in not applying any of the variables...And with that, I'll sit down."

"Mr. Harlan."

"Your Honor, we had much more to say, but in light of the court's eloquent and thorough exposition of the dangers of child pornography, the harm to society, the need for deterrence, and the specific and terrible harm to the victims of child pornography, we simply concur with the court's stated intention to sentence the defendant within the guideline range."

"Will the defendant and counsel come forward?"

Victor and his attorneys stepped in front of the judge.

"Mr. Tolbert, if you wish to make a statement on your own behalf, or present any information in mitigating your sentence, now is your opportunity to do so."

"I have already apologized to my family, my friends, and to God for the wrongful deeds that have brought me here today. Today

I apologize to you and to the court, and most of all, I apologize to the young people who were victimized by the possession of child pornography. I am very ashamed of myself for ever looking at pictures of those children, and I hope what has happened to me will be a warning to others…I never bought, sold, produced or distributed child pornography. I now realize that my actions helped to create a market for those who take advantage of these young victims. I am certain I would not have done what I did under normal circumstances, and I am most certain I will never do it again. I've never had any inappropriate interaction of any kind with any child or adult, and I never will. Your Honor, I humbly ask for your leniency in judging me. My children, who are here today, and especially my grandchildren, who live nearby, need a grandfather in their lives and I need them. Thank you."

"Pursuant to the Sentencing Reform Act of 1984, it's the judgment of the court that the defendant, Victor Martin Tolbert, is hereby committed to the custody of the Bureau of Prisons for a term of forty-six months."

A gasp rose up from the gallery.

"Upon release the defendant shall be placed on supervised release for a term of life. The defendant shall report to a probation officer...participate in a mental health…and/or sex offender treatment program…And further, the defendant shall register as a convicted sex offender in any state where he resides…The defendant shall pay a fine of $25,000…within fifteen days." The judge then said, "The record should show the defendant is already in custody."

"Your Honor," Miss Allen spoke. "Would you recommend Morgantown for his incarceration?"

"I'd be glad to."

Mr. Berry added, "And I would also make an unusual request.

In light of the sentence imposed, I would request that the court permit him to visit his grandchildren and self-report, all in the same day."

"No, I won't do that. If his family, including his grandchildren, want to visit with him, we'll make an arrangement for them to do so in the marshals' quarters. We'll adjourn."

77

MILITARY MANNER

I BURIED MYSELF in the middle of the crowd as we slowly departed the courtroom. Head down, I was careful not to look in Jack's direction. I had no idea Jack was going to testify, much less promise God and country that he would live with Victor for as long as the court deemed necessary. For God's sake, he couldn't live with his wife for more than two years. I have to admit I wasn't surprised. Going all out for a friend was the kind of thing my husband's military training had taught him to do. And, if I'm being truthful, the discipline and focus of his military manner was one of the things I first fell in love with.

I could listen for hours to his stories about the all-male Virginia Military Institute. The silent honor code and wide-eyed nobs (freshmen) who believed so long as they had each other, they could survive anything: hazing, gutter walks, SMIs (Saturday morning inspections), even war.

Jack graduated as the Vietnam offensive was launching. He

never saw combat, but he felt the pain of that war. As an officer at Ft. Lewis, two of his primary responsibilities were to apprehend AWOLs and to accompany the chaplain when delivering news of fallen soldiers to young wives and surviving families. Conflicting duties required he stare down hardship, stay strong, and suppress his emotions.

With the loss of good friends and respected comrades, he understood, firsthand, why no man is left behind. For Jack that oath became the truest example of patriotism, loyalty, and undying friendship.

In an intimate moment, early on, while holding me so tight against his chest I couldn't see his face or the tears he would later wipe away, he told me how lucky he felt to have avoided those front lines; how guilty for not having gone. Then he told me about the loss of his friend Gage Harrison, only eighteen months out of VMI. While rescuing members of his armored platoon on the Michelin Rubber Plantation, Gage was killed by a buried five-hundred-pound bomb. It was December 7, 1966, the anniversary of Pearl Harbor. The events of that day were memorialized in a 1992 book *We Were Soldiers Once…and Young* and then in the 2002 movie with Mel Gibson. Long before there was a book or a movie, Jack vowed to find a way to repay Gage and all those who had sacrificed so much. It was a promise he could never fulfill—one he would never forget.

Jack's military experience taught him discipline, something his alcoholic father never modeled and his hard-working mother clung to. He learned never to accept defeat. He learned that so long as one remained unemotional, organized and focused, with planning and hard work, anything was possible. For Jack, *anything* went beyond the military. Doing whatever it took carried into his whole life, whether establishing a successful real estate company or rescuing a good friend—even at the expense of his marriage.

78

UNRAVELING

From the courthouse I went straight to my vehicle. I put the key in the ignition. Rather than starting the car, I leaned my head against the steering wheel. I don't know how long I stayed that way, but it was at least a few minutes before I opened the glovebox and withdrew my phone to see a message from Francie. "Tim's been admitted."

At the hospital I found my friend in an armchair in the far corner of the room holding vigil while her husband took a needed nap. She would have gone with me to the hearing, if she could have—for me, not herself. Francie had a way of accepting life as it came. "It is what it is," she would say. "Not much we can do about that." But like most people in small-town Pittsburgh, she knew how the hearing had ended.

"At sixty-nine he's about to spend the next four years in a federal penitentiary?" She shook her head. "He might not get out of there alive."

"Speaking of getting out, how's Tim?"

"Better than you," she said. "You're white as a ghost."

"Talk about blindsided! I knew nothing about these people from Boston, this Hope Project, or some board of directors. I surely had no idea Jack was going to testify, much less promise to live with Victor for the rest of his life."

I benefited from Francie's relationship with Jack. I hurt from it, too. When he and I were apart, she told me how miserable Jack was. She provided work updates because she knew my name was on every credit line, every loan. And she told me when Jack took the woman who purchased our home out to lunch, a lunch date. If she knew Jack was planning to stay with Victor, surely, she would have told me that, too. Wouldn't she? I needed to change the subject. "What happened with Tim?"

"His potassium level was unsafe. This is the second time."

"That's serious. Hope they figure it out quickly..." My voice trailed off as I caught a glimpse of the newspaper lying on the windowsill. I picked it up and scanned the front-page article: "Child Porn Sends Real Estate Developer to Prison."

I flooded with more hurt, more anger. My friend had enough on her plate with her husband. The last thing she needed was me, there, falling apart.

"Are you okay?" Francie asked.

"I have to go." I put down the paper. "Now." I hurried out of the room.

In my car tears flowed. I told myself I'd feel better if I let it out. The more I cried, the worse I felt. My husband couldn't stay with me for more than two years at a time, but he could promise God and country to stay forever with his friend, a convicted pedophile.

If I had my first breakdown when my childhood memories returned, I had my second one that day, while driving home. I dialed Sue, Francie, Anna. Each had maintained a friendship with both of us.

"I want him out of my life."

"What happened?

None of them had been at the hearing. As far as I was aware, only Francie knew what Jack had done. I didn't care. Rather than explain, through tears, I just started yelling. "I can't be friends with you if you're going to be friends with him."

"What are you talking about?"

"You have to choose."

Sue was angry. Francie was crushed. Anna, the therapist, arrived at my house, twenty minutes after I did. She found me on my knees in the middle of the family room floor, sobbing. She got down next to me, wrapped her arms around me, and said, "When I saw the dead flowers on your front porch, I knew exactly what I would find inside."

79

A NEW JOB AND A NEW START

THE SENTENCING HEARING was over, Victor was in prison, and Jack and I were done. It was time for me to get a job. I cleaned my house, tossed the dead plants, and updated my resume. The only thing left was a desperately needed haircut.

One of my neighbors had recommended Lance way back in 1991. After that first cut, he was the only person I would let touch my hair. He and I became close friends. We went through divorces at the same time; and yes, I told my hairdresser things I told no one else.

"This is the last time I'm going through this with him," I insisted as Lance snipped away.

"I understand why." He spun me around to face him and told me to stand.

"It's time to look for a job," I said.

"Really?"

"I'm ready."

Lance leaned in and whispered, "My manager just gave notice. Might work for both of us."

"Just might," I whispered back with a smile.

"Can't talk here." He slipped me his card. "Call my cell if you're serious."

I slept on it.

The next day, I talked with several people, including Francie and my sister, Shari.

"I don't know if I should work for a friend. Isn't that just as bad as working for a spouse?"

"Take the job," Francie insisted.

"Take it," my sister agreed.

The following Tuesday, the day Lance worked from home, I called. "I've given it a lot of thought and I'm interested."

"Great," he said. "Let me find out when Gary is available to interview you."

An interview? I didn't know anything about Gary, except that he was somehow related to the owner of the group of salons with which Lance's salon was now associated. And the thought of an interview left me a wreck. I had formally interviewed for a job only a few times in my entire life; even though every meeting with every client was, in a way, an interview, I didn't consider myself skilled.

I got to work. I updated my resume detailing my experience and success in ways that were relevant to the salon. Both companies were small and required I wear multiple hats. Both focused on sales, motivating employees (or subcontractors), solving problems, ordering supplies, managing expenses, and, most importantly, increasing profits.

In a new chocolate-brown pantsuit with coordinating copper pumps, I twirled left and right in front of my favorite store's dressing room mirror. Feeling confident, I said out loud, "I can do this."

❧

On the afternoon of the job interview, I loaded my matching chocolate-brown bag with a manila folder that contained three copies of my resume. I threw in my keys, purse-size tissues, and my wallet. I didn't want it to be bulky and I didn't want my bag to be seen as a purse. Don't ask me why. It was a purse. I was just trying hard to look professional. Trying too hard.

I arrived early and took a seat in the waiting area in the front of the salon. Lance stood behind his chair, styling someone's hair. When Gary walked through the front door, he told the girl at the front desk, "When he's done, send Lance to the back."

After Lance and Gary spoke, the receptionist escorted me to an area in the back, where the men were sitting at a small, round table. I answered standard questions like, tell me about yourself, how do you think you can benefit the salon, and why are you interested in this position, all asked by Gary. As the meeting came to a close, Gary added something else: "Oh, by the way, our colors are black and white."

I knew that. I had been going to that salon for, well, forever, and the staff always wore black and white. But somehow that thought completely escaped me the day I purchased my new brown pantsuit.

"Not a problem," I assured him through a warm face.

"Lance will be in touch in a few days," Gary said.

"Thank you." I stood, shook Gary's hand, and made my way out the door.

Two days later Lance called. "You'll train at our McMurray location.

"I'll be there," I said. "And I promise to wear black and white."

80

MAKING A DIFFERENCE

Designers spun their seats and pulled waiting room chairs to form an oddly shaped circle in the center of the workspace, where hair was normally cut and color applied. The anxious group sat.

"Good morning, everyone," Lance called out as staff trickled in. "Thank you all for making the effort to come in so early on this chilly morning. Before we get started, Linda bought some fresh baked goods from the shop across the street. They're in the kitchen. If you haven't already done so, please help yourself."

After everyone settled in with hot coffee and a sugary treat, Lance discussed an upcoming training session and introduced a few new products. Then he said, "Enough about that. Linda has been doing a great job. Let's turn this over to her."

As Lance sat, I began. "Good morning, ladies." Then I looked at the only man in the room and added, "and Lance." We all chuckled. "I'd like to thank each of you, again, for trusting me to help you expand your business."

A discussion launched over the marketing campaign I had put into place for the previous month and the new ideas I hoped to help them implement for November.

"When your business grows, we all grow. And your business is growing!"

Gina, a more experienced stylist, said, "Your ideas are great. I don't think I have ever seen a Thursday that busy."

"Last Thursday was our most profitable day to date." I beamed. "And with the holidays coming, we are going to get even busier! Who isn't ready for that?" Everyone nodded. "To that end, as you know, I've put together a little contest."

I looked at Gina. "Since some of you have been in the business a long time while others are just getting started," I glanced at our newest member, Tiffany, "to keep it fair, the award, a Visa gift card, will not be based on overall income, but rather on the percentage of increase from one month to the next." I peeked at the spreadsheet in my hand. "This month the stylist who increased her business by the greatest percentage is…" After Lance gave us his signature drumroll, I called out, "Crystal!"

Everyone clapped as I handed the young stylist the prize.

"Again, thank you all for coming. Have a great day and remember, if you need *anything*, anytime, I'm here."

As chairs were pushed back into place, Rosa approached. "Thank you for those heat wraps. My back is feeling so much better."

"Nothing worse than an aching back, especially when you're on your feet all day. I'm glad you're on the mend."

"Me, too!"

When Rosa made her way to her station, I noticed one of our younger stylists. Sierra had been quiet throughout the meeting, distracted. She was beautiful and talented, but for some reason she lacked self-confidence. Add to that, she was in a turbulent relationship and had arrived at work more than once in tears. As styling stations were being set up for the day, I motioned Sierra to follow me.

"Everything okay?" I whispered as we walked toward the front of the salon.

"Another big fight. I don't know. It might be over." She fought tears. "What am I going to do?"

"Let's go outside." I wrapped my sweater around her shoulders and we sat on the iron bench in front of the salon. "Look, I don't know if it's over between the two of you or not, but I do know that you are a bright, beautiful, kind, and talented young lady. You have so much to give. The last thing you need is a man, any man, especially one who doesn't treat you right."

She shrugged.

"Well, you don't." I took her hands in mine. "Focus on *you*. Build your career. Get strong and independent. Then, when you're ready to let a man into your life, you'll be ready to walk away if he doesn't treat you the way you deserve to be treated. Make sense?"

She nodded.

"If you need anything..."

"I know," she said as she gave me a hug.

"Come on." I stood. "You're shivering. Let's get you in there where you can get warm and make some money."

❧

That evening I was on the phone with my friend Jennifer, planning our weekend.

"Sonia is coming into town," she said. "I was thinking maybe we could go to Shadyside, walk, shop, and grab a bite to eat.

"Sounds great. I'll see if Nora is available."

Jennifer and I were buttoning down the details when another call beeped in. I ignored it. He called again—and again.

"Is that him?" Jennifer asked.

"How did you know?"

"What in the hell does he want?"

"I have no idea. I haven't heard from him in months, not since the hearing."

"I don't care how long it's been. I know his act. He's not going to leave you alone until you answer. Call me later." With that she hung up.

Jack continued calling that night until I powered off the phone and went to bed. The next evening was no different. By the third night I couldn't stand it one more moment. I grabbed my cell. "What do you want?"

"I need you."

"Of course you need me *now*—your friend is gone."

"No. I mean…I had to go to the ER." He sounded scared.

"Why?" I remained skeptical.

"My heart was racing. I was sweating. I couldn't breathe."

"What was it?" I tried to sound compassionate, even though this whole act could have been nothing more than a ploy.

"An allergic reaction. A panic attack. I don't know. They don't know. I need to get my life together."

"That's an understatement."

"It wasn't supposed to be like this, Linnie."

"I'm sorry things didn't work out with Victor. I really am—"

"Not with Victor. With you. I never intended to be away from you."

"What are you talking about? You left me."

"It wasn't supposed to be forever."

"You filed for divorce."

"I thought you would move in here with me…with Victor."

"Have you lost your mind? Three of our children hold teaching licenses. Did you honestly think they could be anywhere near us if we were living with a convicted sex offender?"

"I wasn't thinking."

"No kidding." I took a breath and softened my voice. "Look, I'm sorry you're not feeling well. I really am, and I don't want to fight with you. That isn't good for either of—"

"I'm better when I'm with you," he interrupted.

"But you don't stay."

"I'm going to fix that."

"Uh huh."

"I mean it. I have an appointment to see a psychiatrist."

"I'll believe that when I see it."

"Come with me."

"Oh no. You need to do this on your own."

"Will you at least meet with me…to talk…before I go?"

"Talk about what...?"

"About us. About me. About why I do this."

"Isn't that what your doctor is for?"

"Come on. I keep screwing things up."

"You're right about that."

"So, you'll help me?"

"No."

"Just one cup of coffee."

"I don't think so."

"Friday at Farmhouse. Please? You like it there and I know that's your day off."

"How do you know when I'm off?"

"Come on, I'm trying."

"I know you are…it's just that…"

"Please?"

"I'll think about it."

"Please?" he pressed softly. "I need your help."

I sighed, then said, "I suppose."

As I hung up the phone, I whispered to myself, "I hope I'm not making another mistake."

81

CHARLOTTE'S GONE

On Thursdays we opened at 7:30 a.m., often with a client waiting outside the door. Most of the time, after counting the drawer and sweeping the floor, we didn't finish until 10:30 at night. Since it was our most profitable day, I worked open to close, bringing in backup for the rush.

Seven months after Victor's sentencing hearing, that Thursday was busier than usual. There were gift certificates to fill out, products to sell, massages and facials under way. The salon was bustling with hair and nail appointments. It was Valentine's Day.

Around 10:00 a.m., Jack walked through the front door with a platter of heart-shaped cookies. He placed the tray on the check-in counter.

"How sweet." I pulled back the cellophane and offered one to a client who was just checking in.

"Thank you," she said.

"Can I get you some coffee to go with that?"

"No, no." She tipped her head toward Jack and whispered to me, "You're busy."

After that first cup of coffee at Farmhouse three months earlier, Jack and I met for lunch, and then for dinner. Things developed slowly. I went with him to see that doctor a few times. When the time was right, we flew to our condo in Clearwater for a long weekend, mostly to talk, and there was much to talk about. He even spent the night with me at my place now and then. But no matter how good things seemed to be, my protective instincts remained on high alert, especially after the psychiatrist told us that Jack did not need medication.

As salon clients brushed passed us, Jack asked, "Can you talk for a minute?"

I motioned for Lexie to take over the desk, then followed Jack into the empty waiting area of the spa.

"What's going on?" I whispered.

"It's Charlotte." He cleared his throat. "She passed this morning."

Her health had deteriorated significantly in the few months from her diagnosis through her birthday in November. After that things seemed to hold steady, at least that's what I understood. This seemed fast—unexpected.

"I'm so sorry." I touched his shoulder as I spoke.

"Matt never got a chance to say goodbye." Jack's eyes began to well with tears.

"Oh, no…"

"When he got the call, he hurried. But by the time he dropped the kids and made his way through Atlanta's rush hour traffic, it was too late."

"She wasn't alone, was she?"

"Her mother was with her." A tear slipped down Jack's cheek.

"I don't need to ask how Matt is doing. How is your brother?"

"A mess."

"Judy?"

"Same."

"You?" I asked.

He shrugged.

"Any word on the arrangements?"

"Not yet. But I need you to go with me."

"Yes. Yes. Of course."

"Can I come by tonight?" Jack asked.

"I'm not sure what time I'll get out of here."

"I don't care. I'll have dinner ready for you."

I don't know if it was the pain in my husband's face, the loss I personally felt, or knowing that Matt would have given anything to have his wife back, but my resistance gave way.

"That would be nice," I whispered as a client stepped into the spa waiting room.

"I'll sit over here." She pointed to a seat on the far side of the room.

"You probably need to get back." Jack tipped his head toward the salon.

I nodded. "One of the busiest days of the year."

"See you tonight, then?"

"See you tonight."

Before he turned to leave, he said, "Linnie, I really want to get this right."

"Me, too."

As he made his way to the door, I repeated to myself, *me, too.*

82

QUITTING THE SALON

IT WAS A beautiful spring day, a few months after Charlotte's funeral, when Jack popped by the salon. I had a job I enjoyed and things between Jack and me had been better than ever. I was happy.

"I didn't know you'd be in this neck of the woods today." I smiled when my handsome husband poked his head inside the front door.

"Got a minute?" he asked without entering the salon.

"Sure." It had been a quiet Tuesday morning, as Tuesdays usually were, so it wasn't hard for me to leave the desk.

I joined my husband on the iron bench that sat in front of the salon. "Is everything okay?"

After giving me a quick peck on the cheek, he said, "A couple of the guys and their wives are heading to Florida on Friday. I want us to go."

"That's short notice."

"Come on, I'm paying for that beautiful condo every month and we never get to enjoy it."

"I know, but I only get one week of vaca…"

"They don't pay you enough not to go whenever you want to go."

"It doesn't work that way. You know that."

"I'm going." He stood. "And I'm not going alone."

"What?" *Did he just threaten to take someone else?* I suppose I shouldn't have been surprised at anything he might do, but I was shocked. In the hopes that I had, perhaps, gotten it wrong, or that maybe, despite the serious look on his face, he was kidding, I repeated, "What's that supposed to mean?"

"You don't want me to take someone else, do you?"

I rose to confront my husband. "Are you threatening or are you kidding?"

"What do you think?" With that he turned and walked away. Without looking back at me, he said, "Let me know what you decide."

Stunned, I stood there watching as he climbed into his SUV, then drove down the street and out of sight.

My boss, who didn't work at the salon on Tuesdays, had stopped by to pick up timecards. He saw the whole thing from the front window. The moment I stepped back inside, he said, "You're leaving us, aren't you?"

The people at the salon were like family to me. But that didn't matter, I had to choose. Without the courtesy of notice, I grabbed my purse and left a job I loved to be with the man I needed.

83

DAKSHA'S DIAGNOSIS

"**Anybody home?" Francie** called when she came through the front door with her pesto recipe card held high in her hand.

"Back here." I waved from the kitchen.

"I'm looking forward to this." She laid her recipe on the island, next to the ingredients I had laid out, ready for prep and measure.

"I was, too." I smashed another clove of garlic under the side of my knife. "But after last night...well...I'm just glad you and Tim will be dining with us this evening."

Francie put down the pine nuts she had just poured into the measuring cup. "Don't tell me that husband of yours is acting up, again."

"Nothing like that. I'm sorry. I thought Jack would have told Tim and Tim would have told you." I laid down my knife and wiped my hands on the dish towel that, as my mother always did, I always kept across my left shoulder while I was cooking. "Daksha was rushed to the ER. I don't know all of the details, but, apparently, they raced her down the hall and straight into surgery." I picked up the knife again, turned it on its side, and continued crushing cloves of garlic. "We just found out. She's been in there since Christmas Eve."

"Since Christmas Eve?" Francie grabbed a handful of fresh basil from the bowl in the middle of the island and began pulling leaves from the stems. "Must be big stuff."

"Stage 4 cervical." I carried a large pot of water to the stove and turned the heat up high.

"I thought she had breast cancer."

"She did. Stage 2 about four or five years ago. Discovered it when they were planning to have a second child."

"So, breast cancer metastasized to the cervix?"

"No." I stopped what I was doing and looked at my friend. "Daksha has two *primary* cancers."

"I didn't know that was possible."

I shook my head. "Me neither."

"How is Kush going to raise that little girl by himself?" My friend asked as she added the garlic, olive oil, pine nuts, and parmesan to the food processor.

"I have no idea. He's a mess."

"I'm sure." She secured the lid and pressed the start button.

The grating of the machine matched the grinding in my stomach. It was all so unfair, so wrong. Despite our cultural differences, Kush and Daksha were not only good neighbors and good people, they had become our good friends. I agreed with their belief that you continue to be reborn—or at least should be—until you get this life *right*. I didn't understand the coconut placed at their front door; was it to ward off evil or welcome guests? And, of course, there was the issue of arranged marriages. Daksha made me laugh when she told me, with rolling eyes, that for them it was not at all love at first sight. But it didn't take long before the handsome pair grew to trust and deeply love one another. "Divorce isn't even a word in our culture," she once told me. I suppose that could be awful for some, but for them it was wonderful and beautiful. I have to admit, I envied their commitment. They made it seem effortless, unlike my issues with Jack and our on-again-off-again marriage.

"When Kush called last night, Jack went straight over. He was there a long time. He's good in emergency situations, good at calming people in crisis." I opened the cabernet.

"You're good at it, too."

"I don't know about that. Another young woman with cancer leaves me weak in the knees." I took a deep breath and exhaled loudly. "But I'm going to have to get good at it. When she's strong enough, I'll be the one taking her to her chemo treatments."

"She's lucky to have a friend like you."

"If she was lucky, she wouldn't need a friend like me." I swallowed back the sickening feeling bubbling in my stomach. "Where are those men?" I added pasta to the rolling boil. "Dinner will be ready soon."

PART THREE

2010

84

THE SECOND CALL

Right after college and shortly before her wedding, Cheryl and her fiancé had moved to Indiana. The minute she laid eyes on the town of Woodruff Place with its stately Victorian homes on oak-lined streets named East, West, Middle, and a cross street not surprisingly named Cross Drive, she fell in love.

Many years later, the birth of their third child left the growing family bursting at the seams of their tiny starter home. Cheryl couldn't bear to leave her neighborhood. With nothing for sale, she and her husband agreed to a smaller version of a two-story addition. Nine months later, with dirty work complete, it was time to decorate.

On a Wednesday, following short workdays, Jack and I made the five-hour drive to visit his daughter. This trip wasn't just about grandchildren, it was about installing new curtain rods and drapery panels. Not only had Cheryl requested my assistance in designing the addition to her home, she sought my input when choosing the colors and fabrics she would use to decorate it. Then she ordered her custom treatments from the same small shop in Pittsburgh that Jack and I had used. It was more than a compliment; our relationship had evolved. What started as resentful became cautious, then respectful. Now it was more. Through a few tests we both passed along the way—and maybe in some small way because I, like her mother, always took her father back—Cheryl began to trust me. I did not want to disappoint.

The day before Jack and I left, I retrieved the five sets of drapery panels that had taken almost two months to make. Two employees followed me to my car, each holding thick padded hangers over which the pressed dotted fabric hung. The team guided the plastic-covered textiles through the hatch and across the folded-down rear seats of our newly purchased, four-year-old SUV. Jack loaded our suitcases on either side of the fabric in an attempt to keep the expensive cargo from shifting around. Off we went.

As soon as we arrived, led by excited grandchildren, we hung the panels in the hall closet. Then we located the rods that had been shipped directly to Cheryl's house. With her husband already off on his three-day business meeting in one city, Cheryl was packed and ready for her overnight work trip to another. After transferring car seats from her minivan to our vehicle, she was gone. Jack and I were left to enjoy an evening of macaroni and cheese and cartoons, a bit of homework for the oldest, then a bedtime story and lights out for all, including the exhausted two of us.

The next morning, I packed a lunch, which I hadn't done in a decade, and was grateful for the help of a nine-year-old. After getting my little helper off to school, while Jack gathered tools, I dressed the two little ones. Then Jack and I set about the task of hanging the first rod, which went up quickly and without an issue.

Our drapes had been professionally installed, so getting that second one in line with the first introduced a new challenge. Do we measure from the floor up or the ceiling down?

"Floor up," five-year-old Logan decided as he stretched out the cloth measuring tape we had given him.

After discussing several options, and letting the children cast the deciding vote, we agreed a template might make the process faster and more precise. We cut a long piece of cardboard from the side of the empty rod box. Using our guide, we installed the second set of brackets, then coaxed the second set of panels onto the second pole.

Stepping back to admire our success, Jack said, "Perfect."

Logan gazed up as he tugged at Jack's shirt. "I'm hungry, Pap."

"Me, too." Jack ruffled the hair of the preschooler. "It's time for a break. Let's go get something to eat."

We grabbed our coats and made our way to the car. With kids securely fastened, Jack put the key in the ignition and turned. Other than a sick *rrrearring* sound, there was nothing. He rotated the key again and this time the car gave off less of a sound, even less of an attempt to start. He looked at me. I knew what to do. The AAA membership was in my name. I dialed.

"We'll be there within the hour, ma'am. Stay by the car and keep your phone handy. We'll call when we're close."

"Great," I said, handing my phone to Jack. I took his cell and he popped the hood. While he grumbled about corroded battery terminals, and the reasons he hated to buy a used car, I unbuckled the kids and took them inside.

"I'm hungry," Logan repeated as I peeled off his jacket.

"Let's get you a snack." I handed each of the children a yogurt squeeze and a tangerine I had pulled into a blooming flower shape. "As soon as Pappy gets the car started, we'll go. I promise."

I had barely settled the kids in front of the television when Jack's phone rang. I hurried to see if my husband was calling to tell me the car had started. It was Jack's dearest, oldest friend.

"Hey Reed," I said. "Jack's outside waiting for AAA. We're in Indiana. New *used* car won't start. Just the way that goes, right? How are you?"

Reed hadn't been feeling well. He had been too tired to keep up with his grandchildren on a recent trip to Disney. Even more concerning was the pain that radiated from his back around to his abdomen. He even had a root canal when his dentist suggested an infection from a bad tooth might be the culprit. When that didn't do the trick, Reed's diagnostics continued.

"I'm lying on a gurney at the hospital," Reed blurted out.

"What? What's going on?"

"Did a test. Didn't like what they saw. Sent me to Presby for an MRI—on my *pancreas*."

"I'm sure it's just precautionary." I tried to dismiss the fear in his voice even though Presbyterian University was one of the best hospitals for hard-to-diagnose, difficult-to-treat, and, well, the worst of the worst. More than that, Reed sat on the board at a small outlying health center; if the doctors he knew there had sent him to Presby, it had to be bad.

"Not precautionary," his voice quivered. "Cancer. I have pancreatic cancer."

"Oh my God. Let me get Jack." I ran through the mudroom door and out onto the driveway, the phone extended from my outstretched hand, "Jack, Jack, it's Reed," I called. "It's important. He's at Presby."

Color drained from Jack's face as he rushed toward me, reaching for his cell. Even though I wanted to stay with my husband to hear what was happening, the children needed me back inside.

❧

Cheryl arrived home that evening after I had taken the kids upstairs for a bath, a story, and bed. When I returned to the first floor, I saw Jack sitting on the edge of the family room sofa across from his daughter. Having recently lost her mother-in-law to a horrific battle with cancer, she understood what her father was about to face. I was glad she was there. Not wanting to interrupt, I stayed in the hallway on the far side of the kitchen and I watched. With head down, Jack told his daughter that he was about to lose another best friend. The man with whom he had survived hazing and gutter walks and physics at VMI. Two men who, not all that long ago, almost died together during one whitewater rafting trip neither should have taken. Best friends for almost forty-nine years.

Jack and I had been back together for three good years—maybe our three *best* years. Could my husband survive another loss? Could we?

85

INOPERABLE

Back in Pittsburgh, Jack did not empty his suitcase or check the mail. He went straight to the kitchen. He opened drawers and doors as though he couldn't remember where something was kept or what he was looking for. Empty-handed, he moved to the sink. He turned on the water and bent over the full stream as the warm spray beat against the empty stainless steel basin. "Inoperable," he said. "Inoperable."

Without another word, he reached for a towel, dried his face, grabbed his keys. He disappeared into the garage. I didn't need to ask; he would not be back anytime soon. I turned off the water, wiped the counter, said a prayer for my husband, for his friend, for us.

❧

In the weeks following the diagnosis, Reed was consumed with medical visits, blood work, and a round of chemo that left him writhing on the bathroom floor.

"If I only have twelve weeks, I want to live as many of them as I can. No more chemo," Reed declared.

"You've gotta fight," Jack said.

Reed wasn't having any of it.

Jack showed up at Reed's house with flowers. The fragrance made Reed vomit even more. They were moved outside. The next day he brought food that no one ate. Then he offered to take his friend to medical visits—give the family a break. But the family needed to attend those visits, for their own reasons, on their own. Hanging on to what was slipping away, Jack called everyone he could think of and visited his friend every day. I wondered when the family had their time with Reed. But true to the promise I made to myself the day we got the news, I shut my mouth and supported my husband.

A few weeks later Jack took me to see the ailing patient. Although pale, Reed walked freely, albeit slowly, from the kitchen to greet us. He talked with us, even joked about a miracle cure. The next time I saw Reed, a little more than a week later, he leaned on a cane. The following visit he hunched over a walker and after that he was wheelchair bound. The last time I saw Reed, he was gaunt and gray. His lips were chapped. His hair tussled in the back and on the sides made me wonder if the family had gotten him out of bed for our visit. He barely spoke, didn't make eye contact, didn't smile. It was almost impossible not to burst into tears. I could only imagine how my husband must have felt.

It didn't take long for the cancer to progress to Reed's brain, and as doctors expected, put him into a coma. Also as predicted, almost three months to the day he was diagnosed, Reed passed away, at home, his wife at his side.

Jack invited everyone to the funeral home to celebrate Reed's life and say goodbye. He arranged an extra room dedicated to the Pittsburgh VMI Group, co-founded by Reed. The space was adorned in VMI paraphernalia, including a mannequin bearing Jack's full-dress coat and red sash. Jack's shako sat proudly atop. Each man sported his class ring. They hugged, shared stories, and honored the man who was no longer with them. The more Jack talked about and memorialized Reed, the more the color drained from my husband's face.

As afternoon visitation came to a close, Reed's oldest son whispered that the family was sneaking off to grab a bite in a private room at one of Reed's favorite restaurants.

"You ready?" my husband took my hand.

"I don't think we should." Taking a half step back, I tugged at his grip.

He didn't care. Off he went, pulling me behind him. We parked our car, made our way inside, pulled up chairs in the middle of the long table. The family needed a private moment to remember the husband and father and grandfather they lost. They did not need us there. With head down and hands on my lap, I spoke not a word. If I was quiet, maybe no one would notice me there.

At the packed funeral service, one of Reed's dear friends gave a touching four-minute eulogy. Then Jack stood, buttoned his black suitcoat, and stepped to the podium. The only other non-family member to speak, Jack gave a forty-two-minute oration. He made people laugh. He made people cry.

In the weeks that followed, Jack sat in the stands of Reed's grandson's wrestling match and hung out with Reed's kids. Was he trying to stay connected to his friend or trying to replace the man who could not be replaced? When several couples decided to take Reed's wife, Clara, to her favorite Italian restaurant, Jack never mentioned a word to me. He picked her up, sat next to her, probably paid for her meal (or tried to). Rumor had it that a short time later my husband invited Reed's wife to dinner—alone. A date? She graciously declined.

"Death is a gripping loss," Clara later told me. "It's permanent, but it's not abandonment."

86

ANOTHER BIRTHDAY

My fifty-third birthday loomed.

I was tired. Jack was exhausted. I had little confidence about how my husband's fixation with Reed's family and Reed's wife would go. I was thrilled when he asked me how I wanted to celebrate.

"You've been so loving and supportive," he said most sincerely. "I want to make your birthday special."

"You do?" I couldn't contain my smile.

"Anything you want."

"We've barely seen each other these past months." I wrapped my arms around his neck. "Do you think we could go to our place in Florida for a week or two—just the two of us?"

"You got it, Smiley." He set our departure for two weeks to the day. We laid out clothes, rotated the tires on the car, and planned an overnight stop at his brother's in Atlanta. This was really going to happen.

A few days later we received an invitation to dinner at Anna and Ted's house. Ted and Anna had been a comforting presence during every one of our separations, an invaluable support with Victor, a guiding light through Reed's illness and death. We clung to them.

When we arrived, I handed Anna the bottle of wine we brought and gave Ted a personal letter I had written to him. In it I thanked him for his friendship and pastoral guidance over the previous three months. I told him his involvement was the reason Jack and I made it through. I told him how grateful I was that he had not been the one who was ill.

After silently reading, Ted folded the letter onto his lap. "I have something to tell you."

Anna bowed her head.

"I have prostate cancer."

My stomach dropped.

"Early stages," he added.

It didn't matter how early or how manageable. I couldn't handle one more thing. Could Jack?

Ted told us that Roy and Meghan had invited us to join them for a long weekend at their cottage at the lake in Jamestown. "Maybe we could drive together," Ted added.

For the past few years, Ted and Anna and Jack and I had received that invitation. The six of us boated across the lake to lunch or dine. It was charming and great fun. But each year the invitation was always extended for the weekend of my birthday. I wanted to go, just not on my birthday—not *that* year. I grew warm all over. I felt myself shake.

Anna must have seen it. She intervened, "That's Linda's birthday."

Jack turned to me, "Can't we can celebrate your birthday when we get back?"

It was a reasonable request. I should have said yes. I should have done it for my husband. After all, he had just lost one close friend and just learned that another friend, Ted, was ill. I should have done it for Ted. Ted had always been there for us. But I couldn't. I rationalized that prostate cancer wasn't going to take Ted's life in three months as it had taken Reed's. Even if it had been an aggressive cancer, I wouldn't have been able to do it. I needed to get away from all the death and despair. I needed to recover. I needed to reconnect with my husband.

"You go." I looked at Jack. "I'll drive to Florida, ready the condo, and pick you up at the airport after." I had done it before. It was no big deal.

❧

It didn't matter that Jack went with me rather than his friends; he barely spoke to me from that day forward, including on my birthday. I didn't fight with him. I didn't have any fight left. I felt horrible for putting my needs first. I was so glad he chose me that I was willing to take whatever I could get.

As our trip progressed, he softened. We visited friends, enjoyed sunsets, ate lobster, and watched over the cordoned-off turtle nests. We even joined the Clearwater Turtle Club, for which we received bright red T-shirts that we proudly wore.

As we drove home to Pittsburgh, we got a call. "Do you still want to sell it?" the Realtor asked about our beachfront condo that had been listed for almost a year.

"Yes. Yes!" Jack said.

"I have an offer."

Even though it was for much less than we had paid, we took solace that the crippling expense would soon be behind us.

❧

As September came to an end and the closing on the condo drew near, Jack reviewed the final numbers and asked me to sign the closing documents in advance. Then he made arrangements to meet his brother in Atlanta. The two would drive to Florida and empty the condo of any personal effects that did not transfer with the turnkey sale. I didn't care if his brother was coming, I wanted to go. One last time to splash in the warm water, watch a sunset, say goodbye to the place I loved and the friends we'd made.

Jack said, "No."

87

CHEMO DAY

Shortly after we returned from Florida, Jack found me in the kitchen. "Heading out?"

"Daksha has chemo today." I laid my sweater and book on the table. "I thought I told you yesterday."

He set his cup under the brewer. "Isn't there someone else who can take her?"

"Not really. Why?" I dug through my tote—the chemo bag—to be sure I had the all-important mints, a travel pack of tissues, and a collapsible puke bag.

"Because you need a job."

"What do you mean? I have a job." I gathered a few bottles of water, packages of saltines, and apple juice drink boxes. I placed them on the table. "I work anytime we have a client who wants a custom build—like the woman I'm working with now."

"One client in six months doesn't make a full-time job." He put a pod in the brewer and pressed the start button.

"Managing rental properties doesn't count?"

"We only have eight units since I sold my twenty-four-unit apartment building, and those eight units don't generate income."

"I didn't hear you talk about income when your friend was sick." I continued packing the bag.

"I'm talking about it now," he said.

I stopped what I was doing and faced my husband. "Your friend just died. He had loads of money. My friend has suffered for more than nine years—two years longer than anyone thought possible. She has lots of money, too. I'm sure each of them would gladly have given every nickel they had if it meant beating this thing. It doesn't work like that, Jack. Money can't fix cancer."

"All I'm saying is maybe one of those other women can get her to chemo once in a while." He was referring to Daksha's friends, the women I coordinated to take turns delivering her lunch (not that she ate) and sitting with her every afternoon.

"I have no idea how long she's going to live—surely not long." I added my sweater and a book to the bag, then took a loud breath. "You were there for your friend. I intend to be there for my friend, too." I pulled the tote to my shoulder and grabbed my keys. "When she's gone, I'll get another job."

With that I left.

❧

Daksha and I made the one-hour commute through rush hour traffic, chatting about neighbors and kids, houses and husbands—anything but cancer and chemo. A few minutes before 8:00 a.m., we pulled into the garage of the Hillman Cancer Center. I parked the car and together we made our way inside.

"Good morning, Daksha," the woman behind the check-in desk called out when she saw us. "How are you feeling today?"

"I'm good," Daksha said as she signed in.

When my friend returned from bloodwork with a thumbs up, an indication that her numbers were sufficient for another round of chemotherapy, we made our way up the elevator and down the corridor to the infusion center. A nurse led us past a bank of reclining chairs, to a private room at the end of a long hall. Daksha lay back on the table. The minute the nurse readied the syringe, my friend's face went white. I gave Daksha the miniature metal box.

"Thank you." She popped a mint in her mouth.

Each session began with a saline flush. Daksha knew the saline didn't make her puke for days on end, but the distinctive smell, coupled with the anticipation, sent her heaving. In those first few chemo sessions, not only was it awful to see my friend hugging a trash can or whatever vessel we could quickly grab, my heart broke each time she apologized for her reaction. Early on, a seasoned oncology nurse handed my friend some mints. "These will help," she said. She was right. The strong scent masked the smell of the saline and the tiny miracle had been a staple in my bag ever since—right along with the collapsible puke bag that same nurse had given me. For every treatment thereafter, Daksha kept a mint in her mouth until the Benadryl drip calmed her nausea and put her to sleep.

With the Benadryl almost done, as the nurse readied the first of two IV chemo cocktails, my friend grew sleepy and shivery.

"Is it okay if I grab her a warm blanket?" I asked the nurse.

The kind woman smiled. "Do you remember where they're kept?"

I nodded.

When I returned, the nurse was gone. I covered my friend, grabbed my book, and settled into a chair for the first half of the long day.

❧

Daksha was asleep when the lunch cart clanked down the linoleum hall. Before the volunteer could knock, I cracked the door and whispered, "Nothing today, thank you, sir. She's asleep."

"What about you?" the white-haired man whispered then raised a brow. "You've gotta eat, too, you know."

"She might wake up." I shrugged. "Food isn't always a friend."

Shortly after he disappeared, the first three-hour chemo drip neared its bottom. Not wanting the incessant IV beeping to wake my friend, I found her nurse.

The nurse switched out the bag, then helped me cover my friend with a fresh warm blanket. When she left, I settled back into my chair and waited out the remainder of the afternoon reading, answering emails, and quietly nibbling the saltines that silenced my gurgling stomach. As the second three-hour cocktail approached its end, my friend began to stir. Right on time.

"Almost done?" I whispered my question when the nurse entered the room.

"That's it for today," she replied softly. "Whenever you're ready, you can get the car. I'll bring her down shortly."

My dear friend, who had had the strength to walk herself into The Hillman Cancer Center, could not walk herself out. Too weak and wobbly to manage on her own, Daksha required the assistance of her nurse to get from the wheelchair into the car.

When we were almost home, I alerted Daksha's daughter. Then I dialed the pharmacist. "Hey Ted, I'll have Daksha home in fifteen and be straight over to pick up her meds."

"They'll be ready," he confirmed.

Everyone had a job; everything on cue.

As I pulled into the driveway of Daksha's house, her daughter, Avni, stepped outside.

"Dad home?" I asked as I came around the back of the car.

"He's working tonight so he can be with Mom tomorrow morning."

Avni took one arm, I took the other, and together we guided Daksha into the house and up the steps to her bedroom. We sat her on the side of her bed. Avni would get her mother into pajamas as soon as I left.

"I'll be right back with your mom's prescriptions." Before heading down the stairs I looked back at the pair. "Need anything else?"

"No. Thank you." The teenager, always sweet, at least in front of me, was just like her mother, grateful and polite.

After delivering Daksha's prescriptions, I headed for home. Approaching 7:00 p.m., I was tired, hungry, and unsure of my husband's mood. But I didn't care. Jack and I had what Daksha and Kush did not have—or would not have for long. We had each other and we had our health. As far as I was concerned, we had it all.

88

MOVING UPSTAIRS

THE DAY BEFORE Jack was to head to Florida—without me—to close on the condo we both dearly loved, I spent an exhausting ten hours with what had transformed from an easygoing buyer to an extremely demanding client. After working weeks with our architect on endless changes to her custom-designed floor plan, she and I set out to make selections and estimate final costs. Jack made it clear to me that he and I needed the business and I was doing everything to earn it. While my client and I traveled from store to store, choosing flooring and cabinetry, lighting and paint, she told me about her daughter's music-mogul husband, jailed for murdering a woman. "He's been wrongly convicted."

I comforted her as tears flowed.

I don't know if she was overly needy or I was overly tired, but she sucked from me whatever I had left. With a pounding head and burning feet, I arrived home that evening to a miserable husband. Or maybe I was the one who was miserable.

"Why are you so damn tired?" Jack snapped. "You don't do anything."

"What are you talking about?"

"You worked one day."

We both knew that wasn't true. I should have let it go, but I didn't. I don't recall what he said next or what attacking words I said back, but as was always the case, after we both said things we shouldn't, he grew quiet, I got loud. That's all it took.

Jack left the next day. He never called to tell me he had arrived safely at his brother's. He never called to say he and his brother had made it to Florida. For nine days the two of them swam in the warm waters of the Gulf of Mexico, ate at wonderful seaside restaurants, and worked hard to pack the SUV and the trailer they would tow. The sale of the condo was another loss for both of us, but for my husband it was also the loss of a dream.

"Have you heard from him?" my sister asked.

"Not a word."

"Uh oh."

"You got it. As soon as he gets home, he's going to tell me he wants to take ninety days to decide about divorce."

❧

Ten days later, as I fixed my first morning cup of coffee, Jack padded down the stairs from the second-floor bedroom. "Morning," he said flatly.

"Morning," I replied without looking at him.

Before I finished stirring cream into my brew, without any reference to his brother, the closing, or the car and trailer sitting in the driveway, he said, "I'm going to take ninety days to decide if I want a divorce."

With spoon in hand, I spun toward him. "No."

"What?"

"If you want a divorce, get a divorce. There will be *no* ninety days. I'm not doing that again."

"Okay," he said, taking a half step back. "Divorce it is."

He made his way into our first-floor master, gathered his belongings, and moved himself upstairs to the guest bedroom where he had slept the previous night.

❧

My sister was on her way to work a few days later when she called. She could tell from the sound of my voice that I was upset.

"What happened?" she asked.

"I was right."

"Not a*gain*?"

"Fifth time."

She could have said any of the things people said when I told them he was, again, leaving. *When will it be enough*, and *why do you let him do this to you*, and *you deserve better*. She did not. She only asked, "What did your therapist say?"

"I saw her yesterday." I stopped speaking.

"And?" my sister probed.

"She said she can't help me as long as I want him back."

89

THE REVELATION

In the days since we had separated, in early October, six months before, I had been busy building my real estate business. I moved my license to the local agency at the invitation of my new partner, Penny. She was grateful to have someone with a similar work ethic to cover for her when she traveled, which was occurring more frequently since her husband's recent retirement. I was grateful for the business she would share with me while she was away. During the day I became acquainted with the new forms and procedures, while many of my evenings were occupied with listing homes and showing houses.

Jack wasn't home much either. When he was, occasionally he would order General Tso's or a pizza and offer me some. Otherwise, we barely saw one another. Beyond a polite hello or goodbye, we lived separate lives in the same house. So separate he'd been driving back and forth to D.C. to visit an old high school flame—a woman with whom he'd rekindled a romantic relationship.

I had no idea what he had on his mind that rainy evening in late April when he entered my room, his CPAP tucked under his arm. I was sitting up in bed reading. I laid down my book and watched him as he made his way around my bed. Without a word he climbed between the sheets, rolled on his side, wrapped his arm around me. After a few minutes I clicked off the light. It was comforting to have the warmth of someone next to me after so many chilly nights alone. It was disconcerting.

I woke around 7:00 a.m. to the sound of Jack rattling in the kitchen. After I had gotten dressed, he rapped on the closed bedroom door.

"Come in," I softly called.

He entered, offering me a steaming mug of freshly brewed coffee. As I accepted the cup, I acknowledged the small pink envelope that was under the saucer. "What's this?"

"For you," Jack said.

I set down the coffee and opened the card. It wasn't a gushy, romantic card. It was thoughtful and sweet, the kind of card a middle school boy might give his middle school sweetheart.

"I miss you, Linnie," he began. "I've been thinking about you. About us. About a way we could make this work."

I waited.

"Maybe we could get divorced but stay together?"

"And date?"

"And live together," he clarified.

For a long second, I considered his offer. *Why not? I'm never going to get married again. I wouldn't have to move. Wouldn't have to change my life. Wouldn't have to break up the family or hurt my kids.* Then like a bomb with delayed detonation, I lost it. "How dare you? You just want me here when your D.C. girlfriend isn't around."

"No. No…"

"You'd be free to do whatever you want with whomever you choose. An open marriage with no financial strings *and* my permission. Is that what you want?"

"That's not…"

"I've never been so insulted." I grabbed a stack of books and threw them at him. He jumped out of the way as I screeched, "Who do you think you are?" I flung my little jewelry box. Trinkets went everywhere. "How stupid do you think I am?" And then I did the thing I should not have done. I took his CPAP off the nightstand and with full force flung it against the wall. It hit with a crack and a thud and a splash.

"What's wrong with you?" He picked up the device and rubbed his hand around the machine to see if it had been broken. "I need this." Then he shook his head and stormed out of the room, slamming the door behind him.

What was it about Jack that left me so raw, so over-emotional, always on the verge of coming apart? As I looked around at all of the things I had thrown, I remembered another day I felt as much hurt and betrayal as I felt that day. A day from my childhood.

I had been sitting by myself on the concrete sidewalk, building a house from a deck of playing cards. My father taught me how so I'd have something to do when I didn't want to play with the other kids. It was a thick August evening and third grade was about to begin. I had just turned nine.

My father's younger and only brother pulled up in a car my dad had rebuilt for him. My uncle walked over to where I was playing and crouched down. The cigarette clenched between his fingers sent a ribbon of white smoke curling above his head.

"I won't be coming around anymore," he said.

"Why not?"

"I'm getting married." He smiled like he expected I would smile back.

"You said you were going to marry me."

"I can't marry a nine-year-old," he sneered. "Come on. You know that."

"But you said."

"Don't you get it?" He stood and brushed at his slacks. "I just needed to practice."

Without words to express how I felt, I took one long-armed swing at my five-story paper house, sending my brand-new deck of clean, white, glossy playing cards all over the sidewalk and out into the gritty street.

"I'm sorry," he said. "But Dot is going to be my wife. Okay?"

It wasn't okay. He didn't care. I might have been a kid, but I was old enough to know that.

Then he pointed at me with the two fingers that clutched the burning Marlboro. "You can never tell anyone. Ever!" He flicked the butt into the gutter and snuffed it out with the pointy toe of his brown leather shoe. "Do you understand?" Without waiting for me to answer, he stepped into my yard, down the concrete walkway, and through my kitchen door. "Guess what?" he called to my parents as he disappeared inside. "I'm getting married."

The relationship with my uncle had turned on urges and needs a child isn't equipped to handle. Feelings that could not be turned off. He stole my innocence and left me dirty, damaged, and different. But, as an adult, I confronted those demons. I went to PAAR, wrote the letters, cried the tears. I accepted what had happened and forgave everyone—even *him*. Why was all of this coming back now?

Then I thought about an early session with my therapist at PAAR—a conversation I had, until that very moment, dismissed.

"When you were good, he rewarded you?" she asked.

"Yes."

"And when you were bad, he withheld love?"

"Yes."

"In the end he left you?"

"Yes."

"Jack sounds a lot like your uncle."

"I was talking about my uncle."

I could no longer deny her words. My relationship with Jack had been like my relationship with my uncle. Jack had been my pathway to remember and confront. I needed to walk that path—no matter how rocky or painful. I will always be grateful to him for that. That day, it became clear that my trauma was not *just* the abuse. The part of my relationship with my uncle that had affected me just as much was the *abandonment*.

Jack left every two years. He did it to his first wife; he did it to me. Whether he was tortured by some cyclical form of bipolar disorder, boredom, or an inability to commit, it no longer mattered. I needed him to stay. He needed to leave. The reality was undeniable. Staying with a man who left repeatedly would keep me forever entrenched in the very thing I needed to move beyond.

It was time to formulate a plan and call my attorney.

90

IT'S JUST A DANCE

Reconnecting with old friends had become one of the best side effects of being single. Although I first hesitated when invited, it wasn't long before I warmed up to the idea of a relaxing night with safe and fun friends. We'd see a movie, go to dinner, or enjoy an evening at one house or another. So, when Jennifer called to say the gals were getting together on Friday night, I looked forward to going.

"Nora is taking these ballroom dance lessons and they're all going to be there."

"Instructors, too?"

"Instructors, too," she giggled. "It's going to be fun."

"I can't wait."

⁂

The music was loud and the dance floor was packed when we arrived around 9:30. It didn't take us long to find the large, round table that one of the gals from the ballroom dancing group had reserved for us. Jennifer and I ordered beverages and joined our friends on the dance floor.

Halfway through the evening, I returned from a quick trip to the bathroom to find my friends still going strong. I could have jumped back in, but with feet aching, I decided to sit this one out. As I took a sip of my Cosmopolitan, I noticed a well-toned, well-dressed man with salt-and-pepper hair. With one hand tucked in his pocket, he strolled toward me. As his other arm swung, his diamond cuff link caught the lights.

"May I have the honor of this dance?" He extended his hand.

A few years ago, I would have jumped at his offer and the possibility of an older man to rescue me. But as I looked up at him, I realized, for the first time in my life, I had no visceral reaction, no emotional response. Nothing. I had no interest in this handsome, older man or in having him, or for that matter, having anyone, rescue me. I was content being unattached, and, to my surprise, I was doing a pretty good job of providing financially for myself. More than that, I truly had no interest in anyone older.

As the man walked away alone, my friend, who had just come off the dance floor, plopped into her seat, the straps of her shoes dangling together in one of her hands, her drink in the other. "Why didn't you dance with him?"

I shrugged.

"It's just a dance." She took a sip of her cocktail.

It should have been just a dance. But in the past, my interest in older men had always been so much more. Those days were over. It had taken my entire adult life, the return of two devastating childhood memories, and the fifth separation from my second husband, but I was finally over my childhood, my uncle, and Jack. I also knew that whenever I was ready to let someone in, I could move on without the risk of repeating the same old destructive mistakes.

I raised my glass to my friend. "It's just a dance."

91

RANDY

TEN YEARS YOUNGER than my dad, Sonny was a friend of my father. I ran into him one evening when Nora and I went to The Back Door for a drink and a little dancing. Rumors said the lounge had been named for a door that led to a private room in the back of the place where bookies worked night and day taking bets. I have no idea if that was true. But after Sonny lost his wife to cancer, he could be found sitting on the second stool on the right-hand side of the U-shaped bar, in perfect view of the front door, the back room door, and the dance floor. His friend owned the place, and Sonny had become the self-appointed watchdog.

"Aren't you Joe's daughter?" Sonny studied my face as I stepped up beside him, my hand in the air, hoping to catch the attention of the bartender.

"I am, and you're Sonny, right?"

He nodded, then called to the man behind the bar, "Luigi. Take care of this pretty little lady for me, would ya?" Wiping his hands on a clean white towel, the bartender nodded as he approached.

"A Cosmopolitan and a cabernet, please." I turned my attention back to my father's friend. "How are you?"

"Vecchio burbero," he said, which I knew from my Italian grandmother meant grumpy old man.

I laughed.

"How's your dad?" he asked.

"Passed away a couple of years ago."

"Sorry to hear that. Can't say I'm surprised. When I saw him last, he didn't look too good."

I nodded.

"How you doin'?" he asked.

When I told him Jack and I had separated, he said, "Man has a reputation."

Just then the bartender returned with my drinks. "I got this." Sonny peeled a twenty dollar bill from a thick wad he held in his hand, then took a business card from his wallet and gave it to me. "If there's anything I can do, just call."

Thinking I'd never need him, I thanked my father's friend, grabbed our drinks, and headed back to Nora.

Turns out I would need Sonny's help.

My attorney retired. Joel recommended a bright new addition to his firm. Younger than my daughters, this wunderkind couldn't possibly have that much experience. I didn't expect my divorce to be an ugly battle, but fight or no fight, she would be responsible for protecting my financial and legal well-being. Although my gut told me to find someone else, given Joel's resounding commendation, I handed over a retainer.

Shortly after my check cleared, I left a message asking her to give me a call. She never replied, but my next retainer statement showed a deduction in the amount of $62.50 for a fifteen-minute phone call that never happened. Enough of that.

Not only did Sonny find me a new lawyer, anytime I asked him some stupid question like "Why is Jack doing this?" or "How should I respond?" Sonny told me what to do. When he mentioned he didn't have anyone to accompany him to the fundraiser his best friend held every year in honor of his deceased son, I told Sonny I would be honored to be his plus one.

❧

The fundraiser took place nine months after Jack moved out of our master bedroom, three months after he filed for divorce, and four days before my birthday.

I never saw myself as country club material. Even when Jack took me to the Chairman's Club, I felt more comfortable chatting with the staff than the club members. Of all the country clubs, I especially did not want to go to this one—where so many of Jack's friends were members. This annual fundraiser, I would later learn, was always held on the last Monday in July, a day the club was closed. I had never attended, and honestly, didn't want to go. But I had promised.

Sonny told me he bought a new suit, so I selected from my closet a short, black, strapless dress that I'd purchased one crisp fall evening about eight years prior. Shortly after Jack left me that time—whichever time *that* was—a few caring friends dragged me to the Waterfront. My friends and I drank, ate, and laughed. Then we shopped. I wondered if I had lost my mind as I zipped myself into the dress priced beyond the budget I had yet to figure out how to live within. As I turned side to side in front of the dressing room mirror, I realized that this dress had been made for me. I hesitated before stepping out of the dressing room to present myself to my friends. I knew they'd insist I buy this flattering cocktail dress. They did.

I can't tell you how many times I'd worn that little black dress, except to say that it had more than paid for itself. That night, in spiked strappy heels that only pinched a bit at the pointy toe, diamond-studded earrings, and a heart-shaped pendant necklace, I found myself ready and, as always, early. I planted myself on the loveseat, behind the always-closed master bedroom door, in the room that had become my small sanctuary in the big house. I dialed the phone.

"I don't want to go."

"It'll be fun," Francie said.

"What if I run into one of Jack's friends?"

"Slim chance but if you do, just smile and nod."

I felt my stomach tighten. "What if Sonny wants to be more than friends? He's a sweetheart, but I don't feel that way about him. I don't feel that way about anyone.

"That's normal."

"It's not normal for me. I don't know. Maybe I'm supposed to be alone."

"Well, enjoy the company. You're a pretty awesome person to be with."

After we hung up, I climbed into my car and drove to my office parking lot, where Sonny sat waiting, fingers drumming on the steering wheel of his running vehicle. I settled into the passenger seat of his new black Cadillac. *Why did I agree to this?*

When we arrived at the country club, Sonny opened my car door and I stepped out. I lowered my head, slipped my arm through his, and stepped through the wooden front door. Inside I found a small, private gathering, a few familiar names but no one with whom I had ever known Jack to socialize. I eased into a deep breath and a long sip of the cabernet that Sonny handed to me.

"Hey, babe," Sonny spoke softly in his Italian street-inflection, like you might hear on *The Sopranos.* "Go see if you can find something you want over there." He tipped his head toward the auction tables. "I need to talk to a few people." He motioned toward a small group of dark-headed men huddled together in a tight, serious circle.

I wondered what Sonny did in his many private meetings, but I knew better than to ask. I strolled to the far side of the room. In front of floor-to-ceiling windows with a gorgeous view of the lush greens and gently rolling slopes sat a U-shape of tables. The tables displayed beautifully packaged gift baskets, gift cards, and other generous donations normally found at these affairs. To my right, out of the corner of my eye, on one of the tables, I noticed the top half of a mannequin dressed in a man's suitcoat. I moved toward it. The prize read "custom-made suit." Thinking I was alone, I said out loud, "Wow. That's quite the labor of love."

"You're not gonna bid on that now, are ya, ma'am?" A warm blend of Texas drawl and country twang flowed from behind me.

I spun toward him. "Why? Do you want it?"

"As a matter of fact, I do." He stretched the word do-o-o extra long.

I giggled at the almost neckless man, about my age, with broad shoulders and muscular arms. Dressed in a golf shirt, shorts, and sweaty brow, he seemed to have just come in from the links.

"But you probably want that for your man," he added.

Flooded with a self-confidence I hadn't felt in longer than I could remember, I let my eyes lock on his. Holding back a smile, I said, "I don't have a man."

"Well, do ya want one?" he asked in a soft, somewhat bashful tone.

For the first time since Jack and I had separated, I thought I just might be ready to give love another chance. "As a matter of fact, I think...I do."

❧

Three weeks later, after Randy and I spoke several times on the phone, and after he asked me out not once, but twice, we began dating.

92

DAKSHA'S GONE

THE MINUTE I pulled to the curb in front of the last home I would show to my first-time home buyers that warm August day, my phone rang. It was Avni, Daksha's fifteen-year-old daughter.

"Mrs. Dunigan?" Her voice shook and my stomach tightened. "Mommy passed…a few minutes ago."

We all knew it was a matter of days—hours—but somehow it seemed sudden, even unexpected.

"Can you call everyone for me?"

She was referring to the list of Daksha's friends that I had coordinated these past months to bring food and sit with her mother each afternoon.

"Of course, Avni."

"Can you come to the hospital?"

"I'll be there as quickly as I can."

With the young couple waiting, I took a deep breath and then made my way to the front porch colonial. As I put the key in the lock, I forced a smile. "Let's see if this is a better fit than the others we saw today."

My clients, a newly married young couple, followed me inside. After touring the four-bedroom two story, they decided that although it was the perfect layout, the house was too small and in need of too many updates.

"We don't have the time or money for so many fixes. Are we being too picky?" the young man asked.

"Absolutely not," I said. "Remember renting is a courtship, buying is a marriage. It costs money to get in and it costs money to get out."

They laughed.

"We can adjust your price point or widen your geographic parameters if you'd like—but you didn't compromise on each other and you shouldn't compromise on this."

"How will we know when it's the right one?" the young woman asked.

"You won't have to ask. You'll know. I'll know, too." I double checked the knob to be sure the front door was locked, then turned to look at them. "For now, we keep looking."

"Next weekend, then," he said as we made our way down the walkway and to our cars.

⚜

As soon as I was fastened into the driver's seat, I dialed Randy.

"Hiya beautiful," he said. "You writing a contract this afternoon?"

"No contract, but…" I cleared my throat and tried to steady my shaky voice.

"Uh oh."

"Yep." I took a breath. "This afternoon."

"You okay?"

"I don't know. I think. Everyone is at the hospital."

"Go. Do what you need to do."

"But I don't know when I'll be home..."

"Don't give it another thought. I'll cancel our reservations. You need to take care of your friend's daughter. You need to take care of *you*."

"You're amazing."

"Nah, but I'll have a snack waiting when you get home. You might be hungry. Text when you're on the way."

When I arrived at his apartment that evening, Randy had drawn me a bath and poured me a glass of wine. I slipped into the hot water and laid back. He sat on the floor next to me holding a plate of cheese and crackers. Occasionally I nibbled. I was exhausted. Having someone take care of me was exactly what I needed.

The next day I entered the funeral home to find my dear friend not in a coffin, but laying on a silk-covered table in the middle of the viewing room. Her jet-black hair and creamy white skin were striking against the rich red and vibrant golds of her clothing. Rose petals were scattered on her, on the table, and on the floor around her. I had never seen anything so beautiful. She didn't look like someone who had fought two different cancers for the past ten years. She didn't look like someone whose insides had been so consumed with tumors that in the end she wasn't able to eat or even sit in a chair. She looked radiant and, more importantly, she looked like she was finally at peace.

Francie came up beside me. "How are you holding up?"

"No more suffering."

"No more suffering," she repeated, nodding her head.

After we gave hugs to Daksha's husband and Avni, Francie followed me across the room to pay respects to Daksha's mother-in-law, who lived with them. The frail woman spoke little English, and although she would nod at me, she never once said a word when I picked up Daksha, dropped her off, or delivered her meds. I often wondered if she saw me as an invader in their private lives. But that day at the funeral home, she held me, and she rocked me, and together we sobbed.

When I finished sharing my condolences with all of the women who had, alongside me, taken turns caring for Daksha, Francie followed me to a far, quiet corner of the room, out of the way. I hoped for a moment to gather myself. No such luck.

Jack noticed us and made his way across the crowded room. "You were a good friend, Linnie," he said, extending his arms as he grew close.

Before he could give me a hug, I whispered through gritted teeth, "Don't you dare." Then I turned from him and walked toward a couple from the old neighborhood who had just arrived.

93

MOVING ON

WE'D BEEN LIVING separate lives for over a year, but we hadn't once discussed separating the assets. The divorce action that Jack had filed five months prior couldn't proceed without it. It was time.

Jack drew a line down the center of a page. He had sold the apartment building a few years back when the residential market was still soft but the commercial market was viable, and he closed on our Florida condo one year earlier; that simplified things. Of the remaining assets, he got 60 percent, including one rental property and our house. Both were owned free and clear. He also got the business: assets, income, and debt. I got seven of our eight rental properties, all with mortgages. Although my net value was far less, the future value would be plenty for me. Jack also offered me whatever personal items I wanted from the house. I took only what was mine.

"If you'd like you can stay here 'til spring when one of your rentals becomes available," he said.

"That would help."

As soon as we finished the distribution of assets, Jack laid down the pen and added, "My brother and Judy are coming next month for a long weekend visit."

"Would it be easier if I stayed at Jennifer's?"

He nodded. "Thank you."

"I'd like to say hello…if you don't mind?"

"That would be fine," Jack said.

❧

The night before Dave and Judy arrived, I packed my bag and off I went to spend the night at Jennifer's. Jack never told me when I could say hello. I didn't press the issue. That's how divorce goes. Families are split, friends are divided. You don't get rid of the issues—you just lose control of them.

Tuesday morning following their visit, I pulled in front of the house and noticed Jack's brother's car still in the driveway. I sent Jack a text. "I'm on my way to a closing. Can I run in and grab my file?"

"That wouldn't be comfortable," he replied.

I knew what that meant. It had nothing to do with his brother and sister-in-law. Jack's girlfriend was inside.

What goes around comes around. I cheated on Tony with Jack. Jack cheated on me with her. I slept with Jack in his marital bed. He slept with her in mine. The universe had evened the score. It was time for me to go.

On November 20, less than a month later, Russ, our friendly moving expert, carried my belongings out of the house. Whenever Jack came across something I'd missed, he'd send a one-word text like "box" or "mail" and I'd swing by and fetch whatever it was from the front porch. Other than a few miscellaneous personal items, the deal was done. The divorce didn't take months, as

I expected. Ten days after I moved out, Jack insisted his attorney hand carry the divorce order to the judge. The judge signed, the decree was issued, and our divorce was final.

❧

Settled in my new life, I continued to work on myself, build my business, date Randy. Randy continued to be warm and kind, generous and intriguing. He didn't chase me. He waited until I was ready. One day I was.

Randy pulled up to the curb in front of the house he had just purchased (from me). I parked behind him. After helping me out of my car, he took my hand. As we approached the front door, he stopped, spun toward me, and dropped to one knee.

"Will you marry me?" He looked up at me with his penetrating blue eyes.

Even though I thought I'd never again marry, I said, "As a matter of fact, I will."

He scooped me into his arms and carried me across the threshold.

Thirteen months from the day we met, we flew to Las Vegas. In an intimate ceremony at sunset, we married at the Chapel of the Flowers. It was the day before my birthday.

94

COMING HOME

Two years after we had returned from our honeymoon, Randy's employer had transferred us to St. Louis. Since then, I had been traveling back and forth to Pittsburgh, every other week, a ten-hour commute each way, to work, visit my children, and occasionally see my therapist.

One day, when Randy arrived home from work, he called out to me. "Where you be, beautiful?"

It was a little past six. I had arrived home from one of my many trips to Pittsburgh about an hour before and was unpacking in the second-floor master bedroom. "Up here."

"You up for a walk?" he asked as I scurried down the steps to greet my husband with a hug and a kiss.

"I have something to tell you," I replied.

He smiled and pointed outside. "Tell me in the rain."

Randy and I enjoy quiet evenings with good movies, bumping elbows while cooking in the kitchen, and walking in the rain.

The latter started during one of our first dates. We were strolling along the riverwalk from the restaurant to his apartment in the Waterfront, when the sky let loose with an unexpected downpour. Soaked to the bone, we giggled and held on to one another. We considered it good luck and ever since, anytime we get the chance, we walk in the rain.

That day, the minute we stepped outside into the soft drizzle, I told my husband my good news. "I saw my therapist yesterday. She doesn't think I need to see her anymore."

"That's amazing." He squeezed my hand. "Getting to this point was no small feat."

"It was more like sifting through the rubble of an earthquake. Some things were easy to uncover, others were unrecognizable for a long time. But I have learned that our past formulates our self-worth, how we attach to others, and how we believe we deserve to be treated. Some people try to recreate the past in order to gain control over what they couldn't control as a child. I was trying to get the outcome I did not get as a child." I shook my head as I considered the complex ways in which trauma can affect us. "Either way, as my therapist reminded me, if I hadn't done the hard work of healing, I would have just landed with another unhealthy partner."

"Well, I'm glad you landed with me."

"Wait. It gets better," I continued. "She's retiring. And she said she hopes we can still meet for coffee once in a while. She considers me her friend."

"That's quite the compliment."

"I thought so, too." I beamed at him.

"I have something to discuss with you, also," he said.

I felt my stomach tighten. Those were the exact words he used when he told me we were moving to the Midwest. Could his job be taking us even further away from my family and my work in Pittsburgh?

"How would you feel about going back home?"

I stopped and spun turned toward my husband. "What? Are you serious?"

"I've been researching a couple of jobs and one of them has materialized."

I hugged him. "I miss my kids so much. I wasn't there for them when they were growing up, like I wanted to be. I'd love the chance to be there now that they are having children of their own."

He chuckled. "How fast can you pack?" Each of us had moved about seventeen times, so we were masters at it—and he knew I could have us ready in just a few days.

"Is tomorrow too soon?" I teased.

"Tomorrow is perfect," he said and then we kissed.

Two months later, after a quick sale of our St. Louis home, we headed east. When we arrived in the northern suburbs of Pittsburgh, most of our belongings went into storage. The minimum we needed fit in the tiny, one-bedroom apartment we had rented sight unseen—our temporary residence. Each weekend we drove through our favorite neighborhoods looking for a home. One day something caught my eye.

"There's a foreclosure coming." I pointed to a house as we rounded a cul-de-sac.

"You sure?" Randy asked.

"See that piece of paper taped to the front door?"

He nodded, then rolled to the curb and parked the car. "Let's check it out."

After peeking through the front windows at the junk piled high in each room, we made our way down the driveway to the large, level, fenced-in rear yard.

I pulled on the fence latch. "We can't get in. The gate is locked." I grimaced.

"Come here." Randy hoisted me over the four-foot fence, then jumped over it himself. We made our way up the rickety stairs and onto the back deck where we could partially see into the kitchen, family room, and what appeared to be a first-floor master bedroom – exactly the layout we wanted. Each room was in disrepair and filled with trash. We didn't care.

From that day forward, I checked the multiple listing service daily, and the minute the house was officially for sale, we wrote an offer. A few counteroffers later, our bid was accepted.

Since that day, we have updated both second-floor bathrooms. We gutted the entire first floor, moved walls, added an office and a fireplace. We installed hardwood flooring, a new kitchen and powder room, and reconfigured the master bedroom and master bath. Sometimes we employed the help of a contractor. Sometimes, side-by-side, we did the work ourselves. Two independent thinkers who don't always agree, sometimes we had to negotiate which of us made the decision. But we always worked it out.

To this day, four years later, when Randy and I are not overloaded at work or busy with our top priority—our children and our grandchildren—we can still be found side by side, sawing trim, painting a room, landscaping the yard—turning the house into our forever home. Right now we are converting a walk-in attic into a rustic, wood-paneled library. We never plan to move, but we are always moving forward, together.

ACKNOWLEDGMENTS

I owe so much gratitude to so many—family, friends, colleagues, and therapists. I cannot name everyone, but I would like to mention a few.

To my dearest husband, Randy, thank you for all of the evenings you sat up in bed debating a word or a phrase or the placement of a chapter, when you really needed to sleep. Thank you for encouraging me when I had lost faith in myself. And thank you for not allowing me to quit any of the hundred times I said I was quitting. Without you this book never would have been finished.

To my children who endured this painful journey with me and because of me. From the bottom of my heart, I can never express the depth of my gratitude that you have loved me and forgiven me despite my broken self. And I can never fully express how proud I am of the successful adults and caring parents you have become.

To my first husband, a man who deserved so much better. I cannot thank you enough for your understanding and support, for forgiving me, and for being a kind and compassionate man with whom I am lucky to co-parent our beautiful children.

To my mother, for teaching me how to hang on, survive, and rise above the pain and heartbreak life has thrown in my path. You are an amazing woman and the best mother in the world. After I got married, I thought I had nothing more to learn from you—what a juvenile idea and so untrue. The older I get, the more you teach me.

To my sister, thank you for listening, understanding, encouraging, and, at times, biting your tongue.

To my friend, whose real name is not Francie, thank you for your friendship, your love, and all of your support throughout this turbulent time in my life and the long journey of writing this manuscript. I have no idea how I would have gotten through this without you.

To my therapist whose real name is not Meredith, thank you for telling me you could not help me. That must have been as hard for you as it was for me. But it was exactly what I needed to hear, at the exact moment I needed it hear it.

To all my writing friends—especially Caren and Judy—thank you for being in my circle, for listening to everything I wrote, and for your always kind, yet always honest criticism.

To Lilly Kauffman, thank you for your friendship and support, for your thoughtful edits and good advice, and for your never-ending inspiration and motivation. I will always be indebted to you.

To Stewart Williams, thank you for your outstanding creative design and for knowing what I needed even when I did not.

To Laura Stember, Chief Editor at Leonella Press, thank you for your insight, your intelligence, and your unfaltering faith in this project and in me. I could not have done this without you.

RESOURCES

- Rape Abuse & Incest National Network (National Sexual Assault Hotline) / www.rainn.org 800-656-4673
- National Center for Victims of Crime
www.victimsofcrime.org 202-467-8700
- Victim Connect Resource Center
www.victimconnect.org 855-484-2846
- National Sexual Violence Resource Center
www.nsvrc.org/organizations 800-394-2255
- National Domestic Violence Hotline
www.thehotline.org 800-799-7233
- National Center for Missing & Exploited Children
www.missingkids.org/gethelpnow/cybertipline
800-843-5678
- Women's Law.org—Advocates & Shelters
www.womenslaw.org/find-help/advocates-and-shelters
- National Suicide Prevention Lifeline
www.suicidepreventionlifeline.org 800-273-8255

- Veterans Crisis Line
  www.veteranscrisisline.net 800-273-8255 Press 1

- National Institute of Justice www.nij.ojp.gov/topics/articles/overview-rape-and-sexual-violence 202-307-2942

- The United States Department of Justice
  www.justice.gov/ovw/sexual-assault

- Office on Violence Against Women
  www.justice.gov/ovw

- Office on Women's Health
  www.womenshealth.gov/relationships-and-safety/sexual-assault-and-rape

- National Institute of Health
  www.nimh.nih.gov/health/topics/suicide-prevention/

- National Child Traumatic Stress Network
  www.nctsn.org/what-is-child-trauma/trauma-types/sexual-abuse

- How to Report Sexual Misconduct by Law Enforcement
  www.justice.gov/file/1312756/download

- Centers for Disease Control and Prevention
  www.cdc.gov/violenceprevention/sexualviolence/index.html

- National Association of Adult Survivors of Child Sexual Abuse www.naasca.org

READING GROUP GUIDE

1. Why do you think the author was willing to share such an intimate story?

2. Linda's mother shared with her daughter things that are beyond the scope of what a child should know. How does this mother-daughter dynamic hurt or serve Linda as a child? As an adult? What impact did her mother's abuse have on Linda?

3. We learn that Linda's father required little of his oldest daughter but was always there for whatever she needed, even when she did not ask. Yet, Linda chose to keep quiet a very painful secret, despite its enormous weight. Did Linda do the right thing by keeping the details from her father? Would any good have come from telling him?

4. In Chapter 6 the author described the night a car full of older boys invited her to go for a ride. Without regard for her mother's unwavering orders that she was never to get into any car with any boy—ever, or her own common sense, Linda stepped off the curb toward the revving sedan. What drew Linda to that car? How would her life have been changed had her classmate not stopped her?

5. Given that Linda grew up believing that "mental illness and sexual assault were both disgraceful sins to be hidden," how did her friendships with other women help her make decisions? What advice might you give to a friend in a similar situation?

6. The author was one of the countless women to have been seduced by the power and control of an older, married boss. What drew her to this man? What kept her holding on, needing him, even after she knew he was not going to leave his wife? What do you think this example says of the cycle of abuse?

7. It is easy to understand why a child might not tell, but statistics show us that three out of five adult intimate sexual assaults are not reported. Why do you think Linda did not report the assault by her boyfriend/boss? What, if anything, do you think can be done to make women more likely to report?

8. The author desperately wanted to confront her childhood abuser, so much so that although she never mailed her letter, she stuffed it into an envelope and found herself standing at a curbside mailbox. Why do you think Linda doesn't say much about her reaction to his suicide? What long-term impact do you think she may have felt?

9. Only after her engagement to the man who would become her second husband did Linda's repressed memories return. What was it about that man that brought forth these memories? Was there anything else Linda could have

done to confront her childhood trauma earlier or in a more controlled way?

10. Each separation from Linda's second husband, Jack, lasted longer. How did the author evolve through those separations?

11. What aspect of this story do you most relate to? What did you already know regarding the complex and intertwined subjects covered—what did you learn? If you encountered a friend who was in an unhealthy relationship, would reading this book change any advice you would share?

12. If you had the opportunity to ask the author one question, what would it be? How would you sum up this book in 140 characters?

ABOUT THE AUTHOR

Linda is an author, speaker, and an advocate. In addition to writing two books, articles by Linda and about her first book have appeared in national magazines including *America's Family Resource*, *Seventeen*, and *Teen Voices*. Her books have been endorsed by professionals across the country, and Linda has appeared on local, national, and international radio and television—including the *Montel Williams Show*. Additionally, Linda has traveled the country advocating for children. With her second book, *Entrenched: A Memoir of Holding On and Letting Go*, Linda will advocate for and educate women everywhere.

If you would like to invite Linda to speak at your next event, please contact her through her website: LindaLeeBlakemore.com or through her publisher: LeonellaPress.com.

CPSIA information can be obtained
at www.ICGtesting.com
Printed in the USA
BVHW030603100122
625813BV00001B/1